A KISS BETWEEN THE RAINDROPS

Bella tipped her head back. Spiky wet lashes framed his fathomless brown eyes. A raindrop slid down his cheek and she reached up to catch it with a fingertip. His skin was cool, yet at the same time warm to the touch. Mesmerized, she traced the strong line of his jaw, the hint of his day's beard a mere gentle scrape. She let her hand drop past his shoulder to his upper arm.

Honey gold skin backed the wet, white lawn shirt, which molded to the contours of his biceps. There was absolutely no give to the solid muscles beneath her hand. Over the years she had come to associate strength in a man with unpleasantness, but Mr. Rosedale's well-honed body roused only passion and a pressing desire to see more.

He stood perfectly still, and she knew he was letting her do as she pleased. That he was giving his body up for her pleasure. She looked up into the face tilted down to hers and found patience and delight from her exploration. And a bit of arrogance as well, judging from the faintly smug curve of his mouth. The man had to know he was put together perfectly.

Unable to resist the lure a moment longer, she placed her hands on his broad shoulders and lifted up onto her toes. She could taste the cool, spring rain on his lips . . .

Turn the page for rave reviews for
Her Ladyship's Companion . . .

"An enjoyable romantic romp . . . Some explicit sex scenes turn the heat up in this book and keep the reader turning the pages, one after another." —*Sacramento Book Review*

"What a pleasure it is to read a debut romance from a promising author!" —*All About Romance*

"A very tender and passionate love story that really tugs at your heartstrings . . . Exciting, thrilling, sensual, and pure reading bliss." —*Fresh Fiction*

"An exhilarating heated Regency romance . . . Fans will relish the relationship between the lady and her companion as a refreshing historical with a torrid seductive edge." —*Midwest Book Review*

"Intensely passionate, sexually charged, and deeply touching." —*Romantic Times*

"Ms. Collins takes the reader on an emotional roller-coaster ride like no other. *Her Ladyship's Companion* is a riveting love story I could not put down." —*Fallen Angel Reviews*

"Ms. Collins builds this story step-by-step in a way that will leave the reader unable to put the book down . . . This is definitely an author I want to watch for in the future." —*The Romance Studio*

Berkley Sensation titles by Evangeline Collins

HER LADYSHIP'S COMPANION
SEVEN NIGHTS TO FOREVER

Her Ladyship's Companion

EVANGELINE COLLINS

BERKLEY SENSATION, NEW YORK

THE BERKLEY PUBLISHING GROUP
Published by the Penguin Group
Penguin Group (USA) Inc.
375 Hudson Street, New York, New York 10014, USA
Penguin Group (Canada), 90 Eglinton Avenue East, Suite 700, Toronto, Ontario M4P 2Y3, Canada
(a division of Pearson Penguin Canada Inc.)
Penguin Books Ltd., 80 Strand, London WC2R 0RL, England
Penguin Group Ireland, 25 St. Stephen's Green, Dublin 2, Ireland (a division of Penguin Books Ltd.)
Penguin Group (Australia), 250 Camberwell Road, Camberwell, Victoria 3124, Australia
(a division of Pearson Australia Group Pty. Ltd.)
Penguin Books India Pvt. Ltd., 11 Community Centre, Panchsheel Park, New Delhi—110 017, India
Penguin Group (NZ), 67 Apollo Drive, Rosedale, North Shore 0632, New Zealand
(a division of Pearson New Zealand Ltd.)
Penguin Books (South Africa) (Pty.) Ltd., 24 Sturdee Avenue, Rosebank, Johannesburg 2196,
South Africa

Penguin Books Ltd., Registered Offices: 80 Strand, London WC2R 0RL, England

This is a work of fiction. Names, characters, places, and incidents either are the product of the author's
imagination or are used fictitiously, and any resemblance to actual persons, living or dead, business
establishments, events, or locales is entirely coincidental. The publisher does not have any control over
and does not assume any responsibility for author or third-party websites or their content.

HER LADYSHIP'S COMPANION

A Berkley Sensation Book / published by arrangement with the author

PRINTING HISTORY
Berkley Sensation trade paperback edition / May 2009
Berkley Sensation mass-market edition / February 2011

Copyright © 2009 by Evangeline Collins.
Cover design by George Long.
Cover illustration by Jim Griffin.
Interior text design by Kristin del Rosario.

ISBN: 978-0-425-23983-4

BERKLEY® SENSATION
Berkley Sensation Books are published by The Berkley Publishing Group,
a division of Penguin Group (USA) Inc.,
375 Hudson Street, New York, New York 10014.
BERKLEY® SENSATION and the "B" design are trademarks of Penguin Group (USA) Inc.

PRINTED IN THE UNITED STATES OF AMERICA

10 9 8 7 6 5 4 3 2 1

To Chris,
my wonderful and very supportive husband,
for always believing in me.

MIDNIGHT. The appointed time was so close Bella could almost taste the kiss waiting for her. Even the cool night air floating in through the open carriage window seemed to carry the scents of horses, hay, and leather. The scents she so closely linked to him.

"And her grandson returned from the war with a bride in tow. Can you believe it, Lady Isabella? Some chit from Italy, and he . . ."

Lips curved in a small smile and features schooled in polite attention, Bella found it was nothing at all to feign mild interest as her chaperone relayed the latest bit of gossip. It was the same expression she had worn all evening. The one she had spent the majority of her last eighteen years perfecting. And it effectively masked the very unladylike thoughts occupying her mind.

Midnight. The stables. The memory of Conor's voice drifted over her. The potent desire in the whispered words shivered down her spine. She hadn't been anticipating them, but the second before he lifted her onto her horse for her five o'clock ride through Hyde Park with today's bland lord, he whispered them in her ear. And those words stayed with her all evening. "Midnight," he said. Never before had seven hours passed so slowly.

Her perpetually straight shoulder brushed the wall of the carriage as the driver made the final left turn onto Grosvenor Street. The anticipation that had been tickling and teasing roared through her veins. Wicked and heady, it lit up every nerve in her body.

The edges of her lips twitched. Almost home.

After what felt like an eternity, the carriage stopped outside of Mayburn House, the London residence of her brother, the new Earl of Mayburn. Through sheer force of will Bella remained seated on the black leather bench, her hands folded demurely on her lap, waiting for the footman to open the door.

"I do so hope you feel better on the morrow." The light from a nearby street lamp illuminated her chaperone's wrinkled face, etched with genuine concern. "Lady Knolwood is hosting a musicale tomorrow evening and everyone will be there."

The pang of guilt at deceiving her indulgent chaperone could not compete with the prospect of Conor. A passing comment about a headache brought on by the overheated ballroom was all it had taken to ensure their prompt departure at the necessary time.

"I am sure a bit of rest is all I need. Good evening, your ladyship." With a tip of her head, Bella exited the carriage. The front door of the stately townhome swung open as she approached. The house was empty save for the servants. Still, she did her best to walk serenely up the stairs, the almost unstoppable impulse to bolt straight to him, to run into his arms, winding tighter and tighter with each measured step.

When she reached the landing, she glanced over her shoulder. Her brother's butler had his back to her as he locked the door. Seizing the opportunity, she lifted her skirts with one hand and raced along the hall and down the narrow servants' stairs.

Her pulse pounding, her breaths light and fast, she threw open the door to the stables and stopped just inside. Her hand fluttered to her chest, her heart beating high and hard against her ribs. The golden glow from a small lantern along the aisle barely penetrated the darkness. Except for the sounds of the horses moving about in their stalls, the stable appeared empty.

"Conor?" she whispered, hoping she was not too late yet at the same time suddenly tentative. A cool breeze blew in through the open door, wrapping her silk skirt about her calves and rustling the leaves on the tree in the courtyard. She glanced over her shoulder, toward the white stucco walls of Mayburn House. Perhaps she should turn back and—

"Lady Isabella." Low and rich, and with a deliciously lyrical Irish accent, his voice drifted from the darkness, vanquishing the apprehension that had begun to settle in her belly. "I am here."

A sob of relief shook her chest. She darted forward, the soles of her slippers tapping swiftly on the bricks, the sound of his voice pulling her into an open stall and straight to him.

The moonlight seeping in from a window at the back of the stall outlined the broad line of his shoulders and gave his black hair a bluish tint. Tall and rugged, he had the build of a laborer, of a man who spent his days putting his muscles to good use.

"What brings the lady to the stables at such a late hour?" Head tilted down slightly and with his dark blue gaze locked with hers, he advanced. Straw crunched beneath his dusty boots with each slow, predatory step.

She didn't take issue with his teasing question. If not for his arrogance, for that cocky self-assurance, she'd still be fantasizing about what it would be like to kiss a man rather than having experienced it. And more than anything, she wanted to experience it again tonight.

"You," she said, lifting her chin while she backed up, keeping the distance between them and stopping only when her back encountered the wall.

He continued to advance, coming closer than any gentleman had ever dared. He braced a hand against the wall, about level with her shoulder. With his other hand, he trailed his fingertips up her bare arm, leaving a trail of gooseflesh in his wake. A tremble wracked her body.

His lips curved in a devilish smirk. "I am honored," he said, pressing so close her breasts brushed his shirt with each rapid rise and fall of her chest.

Then he claimed her mouth as only he could, as only he had. Bold and aggressive, he took what he wanted, and she eagerly gave it to him. Every bit of restraint left her as she threw her arms around Conor's neck, reveling in the urgent demand of his kiss. His tongue tangling with hers, his mouth slanting harshly over hers, the hard bulk of his body surrounding her as an incredible, intoxicating rush of passion overtook her.

Growling low in his throat, he tugged at the low neckline of her bodice. Cool air hit her breasts, drawing the tips into hard buds. She closed her eyes as a pinch of modesty threatened to infiltrate the luscious haze of sensations. Then he dragged his lips from hers, his breath scorching her neck, his teeth nipping her skin, sending desire clamoring full force once again through her veins.

He dropped his head to her chest, his day's growth of beard an unexpected tickle on the soft underside of her breasts. She gasped for breath, threaded her fingers into his thick black hair, and shifted beneath him, wanting more. The next instant she felt him gathering her skirt, reaching beneath, work-roughened fingertips trailing up her thigh. He captured a nipple between his lips and suckled, pulling the hard tip into his hot mouth.

At the sharp lance of pleasure, her eyes fluttered open and her gaze fell on a figure standing just outside the open stall door. The black greatcoat broadened his already impressive frame, making him appear that much more imposing. A leather saddlebag was clutched tightly in one fist, the ends of his horse's reins in the other.

The light from the sole lantern three stalls down pro-

vided enough illumination for Bella to make out her elder
brother's face, slack jawed with horror. Then the horror
abruptly faded, replaced with such outrage it doused every
trace of desire coursing through her body, leaving her
once heated and flushed skin icy cold.

For a moment, she could do nothing but stare in pure
disbelief into Phillip's narrowed eyes. *What was he doing
here? He had said he would be gone for a week and he left
but a handful of days prior.*

"Get off of her."

The low, vengeful rumble snapped her to her senses,
and Conor apparently as well. With a curse, her groom
untangled himself from her. Hands shaking with a near-
paralyzing mixture of humiliation and panic, she tugged
up her bodice to cover her breasts and straightened her
skirts.

Conor hastily turned to face Phillip. "Your lordship . . .
I-I—"

"You. In my study. Isabella, go to your room." The
words were a growl.

Horrid, heavy guilt descended. Unable to think of anything to say to him, for no words could excuse her conduct,
she darted past Conor and Phillip, past the burly black
hunter standing patiently in the aisle, out of the stables,
and into the house.

LADY Isabella Riley paused before the oak door. Phillip
had not said a word to her for two long days. Bella had
not even laid eyes on him. She had stayed ensconced in
her room, alone save for the servants who delivered her
trays and returned to take away the untouched dishes. She
had already missed one musicale and an afternoon tea,
but had not received a note from her chaperone inquiring
about her absence. Which meant Phillip had spoken to
the old dowager or somehow word had gotten out about
her indiscretion. And if that happened, she was absolutely
ruined, no use to Phillip at all.

All the years she spent perfecting the ladylike veneer, polishing that image of what everyone wanted and expected her to be, were for naught. She had always known that wickedness was inside of her, and she had done everything to fight it, stifle it, deny it the light of day. But when the test came, when it truly counted, she failed. Failed Phillip. Failed her younger sisters, Kitty and Liv. Failed her mischievous little brother, Jules. She had failed.

If word had truly gotten out, there was no way she could repair the damage. Gossip and rumor ruled a lady's reputation. The virginity she had managed to keep intact had lost all value. No respectable gentleman would ever wed her. Phillip had been fully confident she'd succeed in bringing the needed husband to heel by the end of her first Season. Together, they would right the earldom and secure their younger siblings' futures. But the massive debts their father left behind would now continue to go unpaid. They could lose everything, all because she hadn't been strong enough to resist.

Conor was the first man who had not been fooled by the icy façade, by the defenses she raised against herself. The first man bold enough to test it, to steal a kiss. And that kiss, on that fateful morning when she ventured innocently into the stables, had been her downfall. With him, she had been able to be, for the first time in her life, simply herself. And her mind had not been able to focus on anything else but him—not even the consequences of getting caught with one of her brother's grooms.

Heart clenching in despair, Bella pushed aside the threat of tears pricking the corners of her eyes. Phillip expected her—his terse note requested her presence. Her arm felt like it weighed ten stone as she slowly raised it to rap her knuckles on the solid oak.

"Enter."

She opened the door and walked serenely across her late father's study. The fact that Phillip did not look at her cut to the quick. Inwardly shaking, she paused before the large oak desk, clasped her hands in front of her, lifted her chin, and waited.

When he finished the letter he was writing, he slipped his pen into the silver penholder. His short brown hair looked as though he had recently run his fingers through it in frustration. Frustration brought on by her reckless actions. He was only twenty years old, yet since he inherited a few short months ago, the heavy weight of the earldom had aged him beyond his years. Instead of being able to bring him a reprieve, she'd brought him yet another defeat against the constant battle to keep them afloat.

The thick silence pressed in on her, a physical force compressing her lungs. "Phillip, I—"

"You will wed Lord Stirling." There was absolutely no inflection, not a trace of his usual brotherly warmth in those cold, flat words.

Bella swallowed past the lump in her throat. "Yes, Phillip."

When his blue green eyes met hers, she truly wished he would go back to staring at his letter. Anger she could take, but his disappointment she could not. It was too much for the practiced calm to hold up against. Before she crumpled to the floor, before she wept for his forgiveness, she fled the room.

The coldness in his eyes said she could never make it up to him—the bond they once shared had been irrevocably shattered, never to be repaired. The only hope she had was to wed a stranger, this Lord Stirling, this husband Phillip had found for her, and somehow through it, perhaps, someday, become worthy of being Phillip's sister again.

One

APRIL 1816
BOWHILL PARK, SELKIRK,
SCOTLAND

LIPS pursed, Bella cocked her head and debated the stretched white linen on her lap. *Not another red one.* She had too many of those already. Over the last five years almost every towel, napkin, and pillowcase at Bowhill Park had been gifted with a red rose. Her fingers hovered over the tin box next to her hip on the settee before selecting the yellow silk thread and slipping the end through the eye of a needle.

The logs in the hearth crackled. The fire chased the spring evening chill from the small parlor. The soft flick of a page of a book being turned barely penetrated her concentration as she focused on her embroidery. Drawing the needle through the linen, stretching the thread taut, carefully placing the next stitch. Slow and meticulous, with absolutely no reason to hurry.

It was a ritual she knew well, one she repeated most every evening, but at least she wasn't alone tonight. Her cousin's presence, infrequent though it may be, was a treasured respite from the usually long, lonely days.

"You need a man."

"Pardon?" Her hands stilled. She glanced to her cousin, Madame Esmé Marceau, who sat across from her.

Reclined elegantly in a floral chintz armchair, Esmé closed the small leather-bound book of poetry—*The Works of Anacreon and Sappho*—and placed it on the end table next to her half-filled glass of wine. "You need a man, Isabella."

Amusement tickled Bella's chest. Esmé definitely did not fit the mold of demure English propriety. Widowed at nineteen and long accustomed to arranging her life as she pleased, the Frenchwoman thought nothing of speaking her mind. Clothed in the latest fashions and backed by her husband's wealth, the striking brunette found few who dared to match wits with her. Bella just happened to be one of the few.

"Do I, now?" Actually, Bella did need a man, but she wasn't about to admit it, let alone the reason why.

"You're in need of a flirtation. You have become much too maudlin. It's just the thing to raise your spirits."

Her violet eyes, an exact match to Bella's own, were devoid of their usual impish spark—that look that made others feel as though Esmé knew their most scandalous secrets. The amusement seeped out of Bella, leaving behind a very faint tremble in her hands as she tucked the needle into the linen. Esmé was not teasing her. She was not being her usual bold, playful self. She was deadly serious, and that fact alone concerned Bella far more than her perceptive suggestion.

"Esmé." She forced a firm note into her voice to cover the alarm tightening the straight line of her spine. "I do not need a flirtation and I am not maudlin."

"You are significantly more subdued than when last I visited. I have only been able to coax but a handful of smiles out of you this past fortnight."

Unwilling to risk revealing the source of her malaise, Bella dropped her gaze and studied the partially embroidered yellow rose. "The weather has been so dreary of late. I do not believe the sun has shown itself for days. And it did nothing but rain yesterday."

"The weather?" Esmé gave her a look of patent disappointment. "Do you truly believe that will work on me? My dear Isabella, surely you can conjure a better excuse than that."

She should have known her attempt at nonchalance would not fool her cousin.

Esmé let out a soft sigh and reached for the glass of Bordeaux. "I have extended the invitation countless times, yet you refuse to come to France to see me." The hint of her native French accent gave her voice a sophisticated lilt. "If it's the long journey that has put you off, why not go to London instead? Though you have yet to use it, I can attest to the quality of your traveling carriage."

"I am more than content to accept your word on the quality of my carriage." Shipping a traveling carriage across the Channel was a cumbersome affair. Not that Bella had ever endured the process, but that was what Esmé gave as the reason she hired a carriage at the docks to take her to Scotland and borrowed Bella's when her visit was over. But the long journey was not the cause of Bella's reluctance to leave Bowhill.

"I heard Julien's in Town. Your brother would be happy to see you."

Jules probably had the entire female population of London at his feet. At the thought of her mischievous little brother, a smile teased Bella's lips, and then vanished. "But Phillip would not be happy to see me."

A scowl marred Esmé's brow, but thankfully she did not argue the point. "Then don't stay at Mayburn House. Rent a suite at the Pulteney and go to the theatre. While you're there, select one of the many gentlemen who will undoubtedly be vying for your attention and spend a few days with him."

"I have no desire to go to Town. I prefer to stay at Bowhill." It was so much easier to be good, to resist temptation, if she stayed where her husband had put her.

"But you're much too isolated up here. All you have are your servants to keep you company."

"I have callers," Bella said, doing her best to sound indignant.

Esmé's amethyst silk dress rustled as she pulled herself up from her elegant slouch to lean slightly forward. "Who?"

"The neighbors, Mr. and Mrs. Tavisham, come to dine on occasion."

"They're an old married couple." Esmé dismissed them with a wave of her hand. "You need someone your own age. Someone other than those roses to entertain you."

"I enjoy the gardens. Tending the roses is very peaceful and rewarding," Bella said, repeating the words she told herself on too many occasions to count, when the isolation and loneliness threatened to overwhelm her. "I do not need a man. In any case, I am married. I have a husband." She lifted her chin.

Esmé took up the challenge, just as she always did. "When was the last time you saw him?"

Fighting to keep her shoulders from rounding against the jagged shudder skipping down her spine, Bella paused for the space of two heartbeats. "Before Christmas."

"And how long did this husband of yours stay?"

"A day," Bella confessed, dropping her chin. It had been a day much too long.

Esmé's expression hardened, her full lips thinning into a straight line. "He is not a husband to you. We both know your marriage is not a love match. And before you even say it, any man who abandons his wife in the country for years cannot expect fidelity. Lord knows he certainly has not been a monk."

Unnerved by her words, Bella did not contradict her. "Even if I wanted to indulge in a flirtation, I could not. I cannot very well enlist any man from around here. Men talk, they brag about their exploits, and word could get back to Stirling."

Esmé's eyes twinkled with mischievous intent. "Since

you won't leave Bowhill, if you agree, I will hire you a man and have him sent to you."

Bella sucked in a swift, startled breath.

Esmé let out a soft tsk of annoyance. "Don't presume to be scandalized. You're not some innocent young miss."

She caught the correction before it could leave her lips. "But Esmé, how could you possibly suggest—"

Esmé cut off her protests. "Most of the married gentlemen of the *ton* visit brothels and a few of the married ladies do as well. You are a woman and you are my cousin, Isabella. We share the same blood. And I am telling you, you need a man." She spoke the last words very clearly and deliberately.

Esmé did know her. She knew Bella better than her siblings, even better than Phillip. Knew her well enough to know what lay beneath the well-schooled façade. As such, her cousin was the only person who had not been shocked and appalled at the reason behind her exile from London. Her only comment on the whole affair had been—*Maybe the stables weren't the best choice of venue. I myself have always been partial to the comfort of the indoors, though the feel of sun-warmed grass beneath bare skin does hold a certain appeal.*

Bella should be brimming with outrage. She should look Esmé in the eye and tell her she had gone too far this time. Yet she could not deny how Esmé's wicked suggestion simmered and sparked, igniting that part of her she had kept firmly locked away for so very long.

"But I cannot have a man come up here. The servants will talk and then . . ." Her mouth tightened with worry. She was married, as she had recently reminded Esmé.

Esmé shook her head, dismissing her concerns. "The servants adore you. They wouldn't say a word to Stirling. But if it concerns you, I will simply mention to your housekeeper that I will soon lose the distinction of being your sole family relation to call upon you at Bowhill. That I have finally managed to convince another of your cousins to pay you a visit."

"But the whole notion of having some strange man come to my home, and pay him?"

"Therein lies the beauty of it, my dear. Why do you think so many men pay women? It's neat, simple, no ulterior motives, no expectations beyond the obvious. Trust me. I will find you one who will suit. And he doesn't have to stay here. You can install him at Garden House. If you don't like him, send him back to London. But if he does appeal . . ." She let her voice trail off, one fine dark eyebrow raised, her lips quirking. "You don't even have to take him to your bed. You just need a man. A deliciously handsome man. Someone to give you a bit of attention, to remind you that you are a beautiful woman. And you needn't worry the man would not be attracted to you."

Bella's mouth twisted in a grimace. "Of course he'd act as if he were attracted to me. That's what you'd be paying him for."

"It wouldn't matter. With you, he'd have to be made of stone not to be."

Closing her eyes, Bella shook her head. She should not agree. She really shouldn't. But it had been so very, *very* long since a man had looked at her. Looked beyond the lady and seen the woman within. It had been too long since she felt the brush of warm lips against her own, the admiring caress of a strong hand and the answering fire that could burn so quickly through her veins. Burn so hot and so bright it consumed her.

Her pulse quickened, her breaths turned shallow, as the vintage memories seized hold. For a brief moment she savored the flush of arousal. The way her head went light, the way her thighs begged to clamp together to deliver some hint of pressure to the region between her legs that needed, more than anything—

"Isabella."

Her eyes snapped open. The lady instantly masked the wanton.

"You needn't give your answer tonight. I don't leave until tomorrow." Esmé set her now empty wineglass on the pedestal tea table beside her chair, picked up her slim volume of poetry, and stood. "But don't think on it too long or you will convince yourself not to go through with it. And you should. You need to do something for yourself, just because it is what you want. There's no need to keep punishing yourself, Isabella. Five years have been quite long enough."

She did not immediately rise after Esmé left the room, but remained still as a statue on the settee, her mind locked with indecision. After many long moments, she carefully set down her embroidery and entered her bedchamber, which adjoined the sitting room. The deep rose coverlet on her four-poster bed was folded back, revealing the white sheet. A fully stoked fire burned in the marble fireplace. Her young ginger-haired lady's maid, Maisie, stood by the vanity and bobbed a short curtsey.

At the plain white nightgown folded over the girl's arm, Bella said, "Not that one. The ivory." She sat on the vanity stool as Maisie crossed to the nearby dresser and selected the requested garment.

One by one, Maisie removed the many pins until the heavy weight of Bella's pale blonde hair tumbled down her back. She closed her eyes as the long, mesmerizing strokes of the brush and the gentle scrape of the stiff bristles against her scalp coaxed her spine to relax. Not enough to be noticeable, but just enough to ease the constant tension. At the light click of the silver-backed brush being placed on the vanity, she reluctantly opened her eyes and stood so Maisie could help her undress. Then she donned the ivory nightgown.

Within an instant the heat of her body warmed the cool silk. Narrow ribbons tied at her shoulders held up the plunging bodice. The intricate lace-edged hem skimmed her bare ankles. The thin silk revealed the outline of her body. It was the type of garment designed with a man's tastes in mind. Provocative, tantalizing, and easy to remove. But no man's hands had ever touched this nightgown, and no man's eyes had ever seen it. Still, she did so adore it.

And there were certain nights, like this one, when she could not resist the urge to wear it.

With a tip of her head, she dismissed her maid and slipped under the blankets of her solitary bed.

Sun poured through the tall arched windows, bathing the breakfast room in rich golden light. Small spirals of steam rose from the ivory cup beside her plate. With a start, Bella blinked, pulling herself from the mesmerizing sight, her eyelids heavy from a sleepless night that had been for naught.

Morning had come and she still had not reached a decision. For endless hours she had lain awake in bed, alternating between chastising herself and fantasizing about the type of man Esmé would send her. Would he be a fair-haired Adonis or a dark-eyed devil? Every man her eye had ever paused on flashed before her mind. Would he be like him? Or him? Or him?

Just when she would linger over one, when her nerve endings would awaken, she'd wipe the tempting image from her mind with a firm and painful reminder of what happened the last time she let that wicked part of her rule. She was a lady, and ladies did not contemplate paying a man to do things to them, be they wonderful things, decadent things, wicked things. Things that fed that part of her she tried so hard to deny.

She shook the thought aside. The last five years had been hard enough. But if word reached Phillip's ears, or if her husband found out she had an unrelated gentleman at Bowhill . . . she did not know how she would endure if the next five proved worse than the last.

But it was *oh*, so tempting. She had been so good, done her best to be so perfect. Had not said a word of complaint about Stirling to anyone, not even to Esmé. Surely she had earned a bit of a reward. Just one glimpse. A few days out of her life to be herself. To indulge, to luxuriate, to fully experience passion, and then, then no more.

Scowling slightly, Bella moved the fluffy yellow bits of egg around her breakfast plate with the silver tines of her fork. The decision should not be so hard as it was something she very much wanted. No, needed. The prospect of spending the rest of her life a virgin had at first been more painful than the results of Stirling's rage. To never again be kissed, be touched by a man—her soul had screamed in agony. Time had dulled the pain to an ignorable ache, one she had long reconciled herself to. Yet Esmé's scandalous offer . . .

If she hadn't mentioned it, Bella would never have known the possibility existed. Now that she did know, she could not ignore it. Could not blithely dismiss it as ridiculous, unheard of, outside the realm of any conceivable, plausible notion.

"I prefer to stop in Langholm for the night, Porter." Bella heard Esmé's voice a second before the woman appeared. "The inn there is far more suitable." Dressed in a smart blue carriage dress trimmed in pale yellow, Esmé walked into the room, her manservant beside her.

"Yes, madame," Porter replied in the calm, neutral tone of a proper servant. Tall, broad of shoulder, and a man of few words, he had accompanied Esmé on every one of her visits to Bowhill Park, seeing to the travel arrangements and ensuring her safety. Yet there was something about the way the Englishman moved when he was near Esmé that made Bella wonder if there was more to their relationship than met the eye.

"*Bon matin*, Isabella," Esmé said with a smile as she approached the dining table.

Bella set her fork beside her plate. "Good morning."

Porter pulled out the adjacent chair and Esmé sat down. "I will inform the driver of your wishes, madame," he murmured, bowing over her shoulder, his neatly trimmed chestnut hair falling over one eye as he spoke close to her ear. With a sharp tug on the end of his plain brown coat, he left the room, his long strides hindered by the slightest of limps.

The footman who had been stationed along the wall poured Esmé a cup of coffee and added a splash of cream, just enough to turn the black liquid to a rich chocolate. With an absent flick of her fingers, Esmé dismissed the servant, leaving the two of them alone. She had done it on purpose to ask for her answer, and Bella still did not know. Anxiety and trepidation coiled low in her belly as Esmé brought the ivory cup to her lips, her gaze on Bella.

"I must be going. The carriage is ready. I wish I could stay longer, but . . ." She lifted one slim shoulder.

Esmé never stayed longer than a handful of weeks, but the fact that she made the long journey to see Bella meant the world. Her infrequent visits were the only thing Bella ever looked forward to, and the only physical link she had left to her family.

"Do I have a reason to stop over in London?"

With one hand, Bella worried the corner of the linen napkin on her lap. "Esmé, I . . ."

"Say yes. Trust me. Don't deny it—you know I'm right. You need a man, Isabella," she said with a teasing glint in her violet eyes, her lips twisting in a knowing smirk.

"How long would he stay?" Bella asked, stalling.

"A fortnight."

She raised her eyebrows. "So long?"

"It will take you a few days just to get comfortable with him, and he will be traveling all the way from London. Should keep him long enough to cover the time there and back." Esmé spoke so casually, as if hiring a man for one's pleasure was a simple, easy decision. For her, it probably would be. Bella could well imagine her cousin perusing a line of handsome men and making a selection like one would choose a pair of new slippers. *The blond. And have him delivered today.*

"Oh, I—"

"Say yes," Esmé said softly, tempting her. She laid a hand on Bella's resting on the white linen tablecloth and gave it a squeeze. "Let me do this for you. Let me give you a reason to smile. No one will know besides you and me and your guest. I will take care of all the arrangements. You just have to be here, at Bowhill, where you always are."

Bella closed her eyes against the battle raging within. She pressed her lips tight together to keep the word inside. It was right there on the tip of her tongue, demanding voice. Esmé had countered every one of her arguments, leaving the path clear, offering her this one chance. The chance she never thought would present itself.

But she couldn't take it. It went against the very person she worked so hard to be. It mocked all the promises she made to herself to never give in to temptation again. To never be reckless again. Above all, it could mean the end of any hope she had left of ever earning Phillip's forgiveness.

So she swallowed the word she desperately wanted to utter and spoke another that caused her starved soul to cry out in agony.

"No."

❦

THE tall clock in the corner of the room struck three. The echo of the last chime lingered before fading to nothingness. Stretching out his long legs, Gideon Rosedale settled in the leather armchair. He lifted the newspaper to catch the daylight from the window behind him.

Manor house, land with income of £4,000, 5 miles east of Reading . . .

"Too close to London," he muttered.

Manor house, land with income of £1,000, north of Brighton . . .

Scowling, he shook his head. Definitely not near Brighton. Too many ladies went there on holiday. In any case, the property would not bring in enough income. He skimmed down the front page of the *Times* and paused on the last advertisement.

House with 6 best bedrooms and 70 acres, Derbyshire, South of Hartington. Lease hold—

He was not even aware he had held his breath until the last two words caused him to release it in a dejected *whoosh*.

No. Not that one either. He would have a hell of a time convincing anyone to lease a property to him. An outright purchase was his only option, one that would cost significantly more than a mere lease, and one he should not contemplate at this point in time. There was no use taunting himself with something that could not be, at least not yet.

He picked up a heavy, cut-crystal glass from the end table and took a large swallow. The fine aged whisky burned a pleasing trail down his throat and effectively aided his effort to turn his mind to other, less disheartening matters. He set the glass down and opened the newspaper.

A sharp double knock reverberated in the quiet parlor, pulling his attention from the latest parliamentary debates. He folded the newspaper, stood, and laid it on the brown leather armchair. A note was thrust at him the second he opened the front door.

Rosedale—your immediate presence is required at my office to greet a potential new client.

The note wasn't signed but the scarlet and black liveried servant standing in the doorway identified the sender well enough.

Suppressing a resigned sigh, he set the note on the console table next to the door. When had the prospect of a new client become a chore? No, that wasn't entirely correct. It was only a chore when he had to see *her*. "I'll be but a moment."

"Better hurry," the manservant said with a surly twist of his mouth.

Ignoring the comment, Gideon crossed his comfortable and well-appointed front parlor, went through the small formal dining room and into his bedchamber. He took but a minute to pull on the navy coat his Bond Street tailor delivered yesterday. It fit perfectly to his specification, with simple, clean lines and was cut just loose enough so he could don it himself. He didn't stop to glance in the oval mirror above the dresser, but simply picked up the silver pocket watch and affixed it to his iron gray waistcoat.

He locked the door to his apartment, slipped the brass key in a pocket, and followed the servant down the stairs leading from the top floor suite. A weak afternoon sun greeted him as he walked out the front door of the exclusive bachelor residence.

She had not used the word *immediate* lightly. A black town coach with scarlet trim stood at the ready. The coal black coats of the four horses in the traces held the same shine as the heavily lacquered coach. He could not remember the last time she put herself out to the extent of sending her carriage for him. This new client must be someone worth impressing and someone in a hurry if she was unwilling to wait the extra ten minutes it would take him to travel the distance on foot.

The arrogant manservant did not bother opening the door for him, nor had Gideon expected it. The interior of the carriage was lush opulence, just like its owner. The soft cushioned benches were upholstered in scarlet velvet. Rich satinwood lined the walls, and all the fittings were crafted of highly polished brass. He pulled down the shade, cloaking the interior in cool semidarkness, and within minutes the carriage stopped in a small back courtyard.

He took the usual route to the private office, up the back stairs and down the servants' corridor, but stopped when he rounded the corner. A man stood in front of the office door, shoulders squared, hands clasped behind his back, and legs slightly spread. The brown coat and tan breeches signified he was not one of the brothel's employees. Nor was he a client. The coat was too plain, his expression too detached, his entire bearing too . . .

An ex-soldier. Gideon had seen enough about Town since the war ended. This one must be in the employ of Gideon's potential new client.

Wonderful. A client with an overprotective servant.

The man caught his gaze and held it. Unflinching and steady gray eyes bored into his.

The hairs on Gideon's nape pricked. He squared his shoulders and was just about to demand the man move aside—not ask, that stare did not warrant the courtesy—when the man opened the door.

Without a word, Gideon strode into the room, the door closing behind him. A woman with dark brown hair pulled back in an elaborate knot sat in one of the scarlet leather chairs facing the teakwood desk, her back to Gideon. He stopped a few paces behind her and slightly to her left.

She didn't turn to look at him but merely lifted one small pale hand and flicked her fingers. "Come around so I can see you."

A Frenchwoman. Interesting. Though in his experience, they tended to be rather haughty. He rounded the chair and stopped next to the side of the desk.

His potential new client lounged casually in the chair with an ease that indicated she was comfortable in her own skin and confident of her appeal. Telling this woman she was beautiful would simply be repeating the obvious and the aloof, slightly bored expression on her face said she would not welcome gratuitous flattery.

Her gaze traced the length of Gideon's body. He had no doubt her violet eyes took in every detail of his person.

He looked to the other woman seated behind the desk, silently asking for the required introduction.

Clad in one of her standard figure-hugging scarlet silk gowns, Madam Rubicon merely arched one eyebrow. The yellow blonde hair piled high on her head fully exposed the jewels draped around her neck, which he knew to be paste. The few errant strands pulled from their pins had been purposefully arranged to draw the eye to the ample, barely covered bosom. She was the very picture of a purveyor of costly flesh, and unfortunately, she was also his employer.

Rubicon brought a plain, short glass to her lips and finished off the remaining gin in one swallow. "This is Mr. Gideon Rosedale. As you can see, he is simply perfect."

Christ, how he hated it when she made those gloating

comments. He did his best not to visibly bristle, but knew he failed by the sharpening of the Frenchwoman's violet eyes.

"Madame has some very specific requirements and I, of course, thought immediately of you, Gideon."

Her rouged mouth smiled but her kohl-rimmed eyes did not. He heeded her warning and waited to hear what the woman had to say.

"Before we go any further, are you available for the next few weeks?" the Frenchwoman asked.

A few weeks? Gideon hesitated. "Yes."

"What is your opinion of ladies?"

The question took him aback but still he replied truthfully. "I hold women in the utmost regard. They deserve nothing less than my full respect."

His answer got him an interested raise of a fine dark eyebrow. "And what is your opinion of gentlemen?"

Why would she ask him that? He furrowed his brow, his mind jumping to the ex-soldier outside the door, the man's protective stance, the hard stare. A ménage? How did one say no without saying no? "I do not have one." It was the most neutral response he could think to give.

The violet eyes flared. The woman had not expected that answer, yet Gideon could understand her ill-concealed surprise. Gideon was a rarity in a world where those of his kind earned the bulk of their income from servicing men. And his exclusivity had earned him a fair share of animosity from Rubicon's other employees. Jealousy and spite had long ago severed the old friendships of his youth, but he didn't mind. Not much, at least.

She quickly recovered and continued with her inquisition. "What do you do with your clients when you pay them a visit?"

"Whatever they wish. Within reason. I'd never hurt a woman, even if she asked me to."

This time Gideon got a single tip of the perfectly coifed dark head. "And what measures do you employ to avoid conception?"

"French letters," Gideon replied matter-of-factly. That question, at least, was one he was accustomed to answering.

"Always?"

"Always and without fail."

Eyes narrowed and full lips slightly pursed, the woman studied him. Hands clasped behind him, Gideon waited for her to render judgment. He never yet had one refuse him; still, these moments always proved most uncomfortable.

"Before you make your decision, I must tell you," Rubicon said into the silence, "he does have one eccentricity. He requires his own accommodations. She should not expect him to play the besotted husband, but the traditional one."

Must she speak of me as though I'm not in the room?

The woman waved a hand. "There is a guest cottage on the estate which should prove suitable. Private but within walking distance of the manor house." She paused, her gaze sweeping up and down Gideon's body. "How much?"

Even though the woman was looking at him, Gideon knew the blunt question was not directed at him. Rubicon pulled a neat square of white paper from her desk drawer, scrawled out a figure, and pushed the note across her desk. "You will find the price for perfection to be . . . within reason."

The woman picked up the paper and took in the figure. Then she flicked the note back to Rubicon. The white paper slid across the highly polished surface of the desk. Gideon caught the scowl that pulled Rubicon's mouth at the dismissive gesture.

"When can you be ready to depart?" the woman asked.

"Within the half hour." Gideon kept his trunk packed, just for such an occasion.

"He will do," she said to Rubicon as she dropped a hefty stack of pound notes pulled from her reticule onto Rubicon's desk. "Porter." She didn't speak any louder than she had during their rather odd exchange, yet the door opened as soon as the name left her lips.

"Yes, madame."

"Take Mr. Rosedale to the carriage and give him his instructions."

His instructions?

"Yes, madame." Without so much as a glance to Gideon, he turned on his heel and left the room.

Feeling distinctly wary, Gideon took up pursuit. The man didn't turn left toward the back stairs Gideon always used, but continued straight ahead and down the main stairs leading into the receiving room. The sound of low grunts and feminine moans hit his ears before his feet touched the plush carpet. Two beauties flanked a young buck sprawled on a red velvet settee. The diaphanous, jewel-toned silk wraps did nothing to hide the girls' charms. The man groped the honey blonde's quim as he kissed the raven-haired girl who had her hand down the front of his unbuttoned breeches. Another young man, obviously the other's acquaintance judging by the similarity in afternoon merriment, occupied the opposite settee.

Gideon's lip curled. Impatient whelps. Rubicon had plenty of rooms. There was no need to indulge here.

One other beauty lounged on a nearby divan waiting for her next customer. At the sight of the ex-soldier entering the receiving room, her languid pose took on a provocative cant. She flicked her auburn locks over her slim shoulder, exposing rouged nipples straining against a sheer ivory wrap.

"Sir." She rose and intercepted the man.

Gideon suppressed a groan and stopped one pace behind him.

She placed a pale hand on the man's forearm and batted her eyelashes. "Surely you are not leaving so soon?" Her purred words grated down Gideon's spine. Her gaze flickered to Gideon and the lustful gleam took on a mocking edge. "I can offer you any pleasure *he* can, and more."

Gideon kept his chin up and did his best to ignore her, and the spectacles on either side of him. The distinctive scent of male arousal hung heavy in the air. An unmistakable suckling noise was added to the low grunts. His cock twitched with envy. He hadn't been sucked off in ages.

The man removed the girl's hand from his arm. "No, thank you, miss."

With an affronted pout, the girl stepped aside. The man continued out of the receiving room. The pout turned nasty as Gideon passed the girl.

"Do let me know how his cock tastes."

Gideon gritted his teeth. The spoiled creature's softly hissed barb was the perfect accent to what was turning into an entirely unpleasant day. Within minutes, word of who she believed to be his new client would spread throughout the house. If the next few weeks were anything like the last twenty minutes, then they would prove to be very long.

He received a quick double take from the two massive ex-pugilists guarding the entrance to the decadent West End brothel and continued out to a traveling coach stationed just down from the scarlet front double doors. A burly man with a shock of untidy red hair jumped down from his perch on the driver's bench to open the carriage door. Gideon followed the ex-soldier into the carriage and sat on the opposite bench.

"This carriage will take you to Selkirk, Scotland, where you will meet Isabella, Lady Stirling. You will stay at Bowhill Park for a fortnight unless the countess chooses to send you back to London earlier. Lady Stirling's household is preparing for a visit from her cousin. The driver is in her employ, but his silence has already been assured. He will see to any expenses incurred on the way to Scotland and back to London." The tone was brisk and no-nonsense, as if they were discussing the details of a mundane business transaction. "Any questions?"

It took a full second for the man's words to solidify in Gideon's mind. The woman in Rubicon's office wasn't his client. She was acting in another's stead, sending Gideon to another. A Lady Stirling. Goddamn Rubicon! That bitch knew all along. She had only wanted to watch him squirm.

"No," Gideon replied, a tad sourly.

Though the man moved not a muscle, the air in the closed carriage shifted subtly, causing the hairs on the nape of Gideon's neck to prick with unease, just as they had done when the man had stared him down earlier.

"If word should reach my ears that you displeased Lady Stirling in any fashion, you will be most sorry. You have one half hour. Alert the driver when you are ready to depart."

After a hard, piercing stare, the man alighted from the carriage.

The slam of the door unleashed a wave of bristling indignation, twisting Gideon's mouth into a hard sneer. He didn't need the man's damn warning and it would not change the way he behaved with Lady Stirling one bit. But instead of shouting a rash reply, the prospect of receiving half of the large stack of pound notes on Rubicon's desk kept him silent. He could not deny he could do with a new client, for it would put him one small step closer to leaving all of this behind.

Two

SOMEHOW Bella kept the shocked screech from making its way past her lips.

No. She couldn't have. No, no, she couldn't.

Bella sent her mind frantically back over their last two conversations, searching for anything she might have said that could have been misinterpreted as approval. But found nothing.

Nothing.

She must have read it wrong. There was no way Esmé could have. She couldn't. She didn't.

Isabella—

If my timing proves correct, then Bowhill Park will receive a guest on the afternoon of your receipt of this letter. Mr. Gideon Rosedale will be situated at Garden House. He is prepared to remain at Bowhill for the fortnight. Please be so kind as to inform your housekeeper of the imminent arrival of your dear cousin. I promised

*to find you one who would suit, and I do believe
this one will suit.*

    *Regardless of how displeased you may be with
me, I do hope you at least invite your guest to
dinner before dispensing with him. If not for
yourself, then do it for me, because I love you and
only wish for your happiness. S'il vous plaît, take a
holiday from your penance.*

—*Esmé*

She did.

The note fluttered from Bella's limp fingers to the neat surface of her writing desk. For the past week she had fought with herself, in the way one only could with regret. She had bemoaned her decision and convinced herself she should have said yes. It was so much easier to say yes in hindsight, when she did not have to live with the consequences. The complications were lessened, the risks easily ignored. Bella had even indulged in a daydream yesterday afternoon when she had been in the hothouse cutting a few new blooms, and her musings had been most pleasant indeed.

But it had been just an idle daydream. A fantasy.

It was not supposed to actually happen.

But now it *was* going to happen. Esmé had found her a man. A man who was currently en route to Bowhill. The timing of Esmé's note was not lost on her. She could have easily sent the note via express post and it would have arrived before today.

"Damn her," Bella muttered.

Esmé had succeeded in flustering her to the point of cursing and she wasn't even here to witness the event. If Bella knew where to reach her, she would pen her a scathing reply. But Esmé never stayed long in one place. She could be anywhere in England or on the continent. Esmé could send her letters, but she did not have the luxury of doing the same. Bella wrote her notes, but they were never sent, nor placed in her hand. There were moments when she simply found solace in the act of writing words, which were never to be read by another.

She allowed herself a brief slump in her desk chair and let out a deep, unladylike sigh. Well, there was nothing to be done for it. Cursing her high-handed cousin would not remedy the situation, and Bella could not take her ire out on Mr. Gideon Rosedale. It would be the height of rudeness to turn the man away without at least inviting him to dinner, especially after such a long journey from London.

Her glance fell onto the small porcelain clock on the corner of her desk. She abruptly straightened in her chair. It was ten o'clock. As the roads to Selkirk from London had proved, a few hours could easily be gained or lost. Her guest could arrive momentarily or late tonight or even tomorrow. And Bowhill was not prepared in the least.

She rang for a servant and requested her housekeeper. As she waited for the woman to arrive, she folded Esmé's note and slipped it into the top desk drawer, pushing it to the far right corner. As she was sliding the drawer closed, the door opened and Mrs. Cooley walked into the sitting room.

With her black hair streaked with silver and her tall, sturdy frame, the woman brought to mind the image of a headmistress of an orphanage. *Stern* was an understatement. When Bella first came to Bowhill, she had not known what to make of the woman. Over the years she came to realize the ironlike countenance was just the woman's way. The two women had never been close, but Bella had caught the usually hard gray eyes soften with what could have been compassion, or even pity, on more than one occasion.

"Yes, your ladyship?"

"I have received word from Madame Marceau that she has convinced another of my cousins to pay me a visit. Mr. Rosedale is traveling from London and is due to arrive this afternoon. Please see that Garden House is aired out and made ready." Esmé's explanation flowed smoothly off her tongue.

Bella received a questioning look from Mrs. Cooley at the mention of Garden House. Esmé always stayed at the manor house, in the yellow bedchamber, and as she was Bella's only guest, she never had a use for the cottage.

Her chin remained up and her composure in place. The small staff at Bowhill saw to her comfort, but was paid by Stirling. Even if she only allowed Mr. Rosedale to stay one night, it was critical they never know he was not what she led them to believe.

"Yes, your ladyship. I will see to it immediately."

"Alert the kitchen we will have a guest for dinner." Bella picked up the previously approved menu from her desk. She kept a scowl from marring her brow. The simple, light fare would not do. She picked up her pen, dipped it into the silver inkwell, and paused, the black tip an inch from the paper.

What would he prefer? She had not the faintest notion. All she knew about him was his name and that he was traveling from London. Keeping her attention on the menu, she spoke with a dismissive casualness that belied the butterflies in her stomach. "Dinner will be at six this evening. Please see to Garden House. I will have the menu sent down to the kitchen."

"Yes, your ladyship."

The moment Mrs. Cooley left the room she dropped her pen and pressed a sweat-dampened palm to her forehead. Bella still could not believe she had done it.

Esmé had sent her a man.

Gideon contemplated the manor house at Bowhill Park as he walked up the front steps. The home was modest by country terms. Not a sprawling many-winged structure built upon over the decades designed as a showplace to impress callers. Rather, it was a square Georgian mansion with two sets of Ionic columns carved in relief into the stone walls flanking the arched portico. The sort of house he imagined himself owning many years from now. Neat and understated, he doubted it was the Stirling family seat. Earls preferred much grander homes to tout their status over lowly viscounts and barons. If that were the case, then what kind of woman would he find waiting for him if her husband found her unworthy of the Stirling estate?

With that question lingering in his mind, the front door swung open a second after he knocked. The dour-faced butler didn't ask his name, but simply gave Gideon one long look down his hooked nose and motioned for him to enter. The man led him to a drawing room and, with a barely audible yet purposeful little huff of displeasure, closed the door with a smart snap.

Long accustomed to dealing with a client's servants, the butler's slight didn't even prick Gideon's pride. But clearly that one already doubted the ruse. Experience taught Gideon that as long as he kept up the oft-employed guise of a visiting relative any suspicious servants would hold their tongues. The veil of propriety was what mattered to them, not the truth hidden behind it.

He paused in the center of the room and glanced about. A home could reveal a lot about a woman, and this one spoke volumes. An ivory silk brocade settee, two chairs, and a low table formed a sitting arrangement between a pair of tall windows. A fire burned invitingly in the white marble-mantled fireplace. Gilt-framed paintings featuring lush gardens and flowers in full bloom dotted the walls covered in chinoiserie paper.

Not a single object was out of place. The formal drawing room was clean, without a speck of dust. The housekeeper he spotted on the way to this room, lurking midway along a long corridor leading to the back of the house, certainly had the capable, efficient look of one who did not tolerate lazy maids.

But it was more than that. This room spoke of sophistication, refinement, and attention to detail. The Ming vase on the sideboard told of wealth, the red roses arranged within told of an appreciation of things beautiful. He doubted Lady Stirling was past her prime. The furniture was not gently aged, but less than a decade old. The English ambience, the absence of anything remotely Scottish, said she was not a native but imported by her husband.

The woman who decorated this room would not flout convention. She would be constrained, the typical English lady. And she would want him to be . . . Gideon glanced about the room again. A gentleman. One of her kind.

He strode to a window, clasped his hands behind his back, and took in the view of the grounds surrounding the side of the house. The sun hung low on the horizon, streaking magenta across a sky that faded to deepest midnight. One could see nothing but open acres framed in the distance by thick woods. It was pleasing to the eye but felt secluded from the world. Now he knew why he was here.

Lady Stirling was lonely.

Well, at least we have something in common, he thought sardonically. But he had long ago realized physical acts could not fill the void where a family should reside. If anything, it made the emptiness reverberate with a painful echo that drove home just how alone he was in the world.

Gideon shook his head, dismissing the thought. He was here for Lady Stirling. And she wanted a gentleman, not a maudlin fool. Taking a deep breath, he righted himself to his current task.

The sound of a door opening reached his ears. With a welcoming smile, he turned from the window.

He blinked. Then remembered to take a breath.

Refined and sophisticated, without a button or hair out of place. She was everything this room had foretold. But he had not been prepared to find this.

Lady Stirling was . . . *exquisite.* An ethereal beauty with alabaster skin and white blonde hair pulled up in an expert chignon. The gown draping her graceful willowy body told him something else about her. The rich cranberry silk said she did as she dared. She was not as conventional as she would like one to believe.

He quickly recovered his wits and walked forward

to greet her. "Good evening, Lady Stirling. Mr. Gideon Rosedale."

"Good evening." She offered her hand.

He executed a smooth bow, bringing her hand up to his lips but not quite brushing the back. "It is a pleasure to make your acquaintance."

"Would you care for a glass of wine before dinner, Mr. Rosedale?"

"Yes, thank you." He held up a hand when she took a step toward a table laden with a bottle of wine and two goblets on a silver tray. "Allow me, and would you like a glass as well?" Though she appeared outwardly calm, he had been conscious of a faint tremor during the brief moment when she had laid her hand in his.

She tipped her splendid head a fraction to indicate acceptance.

Gideon poured two glasses of Madeira and delivered one to her. She sat on the settee, her delicate hand curved just so around the fragile goblet, and took a long sip, downing half the glass's contents. With her other hand, she motioned to the green and ivory striped chair angled toward the settee. He dropped into the chair. After tasting the sweet wine, he set his glass on a nearby table. He needed to keep his wits about him. It would require a fair share of charm to soothe the nerves she attempted to conceal.

She turned her straight shoulders to him, the sleek indent of her waist evident by the curve of her upper body. "I hope the journey from London found you well?" Her voice carried smoothly on the air. Soft, melodic, and definitively feminine.

"Yes. It only rained a bit through Carlisle. The roads were in as good a shape as can be expected in the spring. All in all, a pleasant ride."

She brought the wineglass to her lips for another long sip. "And how do you find Garden House?"

"Charming." When the driver had deposited him at the quaint cottage this afternoon, his initial assumption had

been that she would visit him there in an effort to keep
their liaison as discreet as possible. He had been pleas-
antly surprised to find a note on the small dining table
written in flowing feminine script requesting the pleasure
of his company for dinner. "The roses"—he gestured to
the bouquet—"were grown in the hothouse?" He had
passed the stone and glass walled structure on the walk to
the manor, its many windows misted against the crisp evening air.

"Yes." The smile of an angel spread across her face,
softening the almost unapproachably elegant features. He
barely kept his jaw from dropping in awe. *Christ*, she was
beautiful. "It is a small hobby of mine. The hothouse al-
lows the less hearty varieties to thrive even through the
frigid Scottish winters."

"I would be honored if you would show it to me."
There was no teasing lilt to his voice. He employed no
suave charm. It was simply a request, infused with enough
honest interest to take it past the purely polite.

Her long lashes swept down, hiding her exotic violet
eyes, as she tipped her head. Then she set her empty glass
on an end table and gracefully rose to her feet. Instinctively, he stood as well. The silence was broken only by
the soft *swoosh* of her silk skirts as she glided across the
room. One lean arm reached out to lightly, lovingly brush
a red bloom with the tips of her fingers as she passed the
sideboard before stopping in front of the same window he
had gazed out of earlier.

Twilight was full upon them. The sun's rich amber rays
no longer made their way into the room. The light from a
nearby lamp flickered across her aristocratic profile. The
smile was gone. She was a study in elegance.

He clasped his hands behind his back and waited patiently for her to speak.

"Mr. Rosedale, your presence is only required for dinner this evening. After that you are here by choice, free to
take your leave anytime you choose. You needn't provide
a reason. Just as I am free to request your departure from

this estate. I wish our time together to be a consensual flirtation."

THE rapid beat of her heart filled her ears. Bella kept her gaze straight ahead, fighting the impulse to glance to Mr. Rosedale, his presence a physical force that demanded her complete attention.

But Mr. Rosedale's reason for being in this room was a double-edged sword. It pricked her interest, but also pricked at her conscience. The thought of him kissing her, touching her, all for the lure of money . . . it struck a chord deep within her. A chord that did not sit well at all. She knew before even meeting Mr. Rosedale that she could not match Esmé's blasé attitude about such financial arrangements, and therefore, she had devised her terms. A flirtation was something she could possibly engage in. A paid servant was not.

But how would he react to her terms? She still could not believe she had laid them out like that. Cool. Impersonal. Her voice had not wavered the slightest bit. Remarkable, given her nerves were drawn tighter than an archer's bow.

"Your ladyship, dinner is served."

She whirled from the window at McGreevy's words. The butler had opened the double doors leading to the dining room. Mr. Rosedale walked to her side and offered his arm. Bella laid her hand on the fine black wool, and the second before he took a step he caught her eye and gave her a small smile. If it was meant to put her at her ease, it worked. The tension slipped away and in its place settled a definitive, undeniable spark of attraction.

He led her into the dining hall and to the far end of the long mahogany table where two places were set. The light from the silver candelabras stationed at regular intervals along the table danced on the gold bands encircling the crystal goblets. The table was set with her finest Limoges china, stark white linens, and heavy silver flatware. Velvety darkness backed the three tall, arched windows on one wall, acting as a curtain closing out the rest of the world.

Lowering into the chair Mr. Rosedale pulled out at the head of the table, Bella watched as he settled himself with complete ease into the adjacent chair, as if his presence at such a formal dinner was a natural and frequent occurrence.

The footman poured the wine and placed a bowl of leek soup before each of them. Though she had tried not to stray from her usual routine with Esmé, she had taken great care in the selection of the dishes for this evening's meal. As she waited for Mr. Rosedale's approval, she reached for her glass. The full-bodied Bordeaux did little to calm the butterflies infiltrating her stomach.

His silver spoon skimmed the surface of the sage green liquid then he brought it to his lips. The man had the most beautiful mouth. Firm. Sensual. Made to bestow kisses.

"My compliments to your cook."

She let out a small sigh of relief and picked up her spoon. "I'm pleased you approve."

His whisky brown eyes locked with hers. The edges of his lips quirked. "Most assuredly."

His deep voice wrapped around her like a gentle caress, leaving her with the impression he wasn't just referring to the soup.

"You have a beautiful home, your ladyship. Yet it pales in comparison to you."

The heat of his gaze seared her skin. A flush rose from her chest, pricking her neck, her cheeks. She smiled and tipped her chin, her shoulders rounding before she caught herself and straightened her spine. "Thank you." She licked her lips, struggling to find a topic to discuss. "Do you travel often?"

"On occasion."

He brought his spoon to his lips again. She silently cursed the stark white cravat for hiding his throat. How she would love to watch the strong lines of his neck work as he swallowed. "Have your travels taken you to Scotland before?"

"No. This is a first. I rarely stray beyond a couple of days' ride from London." He leaned back as the footman removed the first course and laid out the second. Mr. Rosedale's shoulders were so broad the wooden back of the chair was completely hidden. "And what of you? Do you stay close to Bowhill, or do you dare to venture beyond?"

Her fingers tightened around her fork. "I haven't traveled to England in years."

His smile soothed the knot forming in her belly. "How fortunate for Scotland to be given such a gift. London is prized for its diversions, but most grow bland after a short time. There is one, however, that never loses its appeal."

"And what would that be?"

"The British Museum. Just when I think I've explored every one of its treasures, I discover a new find."

Fortunately, he kept the conversation flowing, for she knew she was failing miserably in her role as hostess. It took considerable effort to simply refrain from studying him too closely. Time and again her naughty mind attempted to wander down paths that included such musings as if the body beneath his strict black evening attire matched the classic angles and planes of his face.

His features were those of the marble statues she had once glimpsed on a long-ago visit to the very museum of which he spoke. But even the Italian masters would have been hard-pressed to achieve such flowing symmetrical precision in their works. He was not overly masculine— there was nothing rugged or blunt about him. Nor was any angle too sharp, or plane too flat. He was the ideal brought to life—a timeless image of man in his prime. His freshly shaven, chiseled jaw held not a hint of his dark brown hair, the color of deepest sable, which was just a snip from being too short. And those eyes . . . she could definitely lose herself in the rich golden-flecked depths.

I believe this one will suit, Esmé wrote. And Mr. Rosedale did suit. Bella could feel her spirits rising with each admiring glance and each word from his lips. She had forgotten what it felt like to be the object of a man's attentions. It was infinitely pleasing and gave the evening a rosy glow. Whether she would be brave enough to seize the opportunity and take him to her bed in the coming days . . . of that she wasn't yet certain.

So when dinner was completed, she instructed the footmen to clear the table. As her guest partook of a glass of port and she of a cup of tea, she allowed herself a few more minutes to bask in his attention. Then she set her empty cup on the barren white linen and moved to stand. He drew out her chair before the footman stationed along the wall could move a muscle, and led her out of the dining room to the foot of the staircase leading to the second floor.

Her hand drifted off his arm as she turned to stand before him. Then she let her gaze travel down his body once more. He was tall, even taller than she. A rarity, given the number of gentlemen she had met who were on eye level or less. And he carried the height very well. Not lanky or bullish, but broad shouldered and with a fitness that spoke of frequent exercise. Yet his imposing presence did not intimidate her. Maybe it was the overwhelming totality of his perfection that prevented, until now, her noticing the magnitude of his height.

"Thank you for dinner, Lady Stirling. I had a very enjoyable evening."

She swallowed to moisten her suddenly dry mouth. "As did I. Would you care for a carriage to be brought round to see you back to Garden House?"

"Thank you, but it's a pleasant evening and the walk will do me good."

His mouth curved in the most divine little smile. Heady warmth washed over her, lulling her senses. Breeching the line of polite distance, he took one small step toward her and slowly reached out to rest his hand on her waist. The heat of his palm penetrated her silk gown, sending a bolt of lush sensation through her.

"Dinner is over. Our flirtation begins," he said, his voice a deep, suggestive rumble.

In his fathomless half-lidded gaze, she glimpsed carnal pleasures beyond her most scandalous dreams. A flush of arousal swept up from her belly. Her breaths turned short and heavy. The air crackled between them.

The moment stretched on, growing taut, pulling tighter . . .

He lowered his head then paused, his mouth an inch from hers. Unable to resist the offer, she swayed into him, her eyes fluttering closed.

Warm lips brushed hers. Once. Twice. The lightest of touches.

Blindly seeking more, she lifted up onto her toes and flicked her tongue against the seam of his lips. Large hands grabbed her backside, jerking her tight against his muscular body. He slanted his mouth harshly over hers. An intense wave of desire saturated her senses. She opened her mouth eagerly, her kiss strong and full of unleashed, unbridled passion. Passion that had been locked away for too long. Passion that reveled in this small gift of freedom.

A moan of pure, unadulterated longing shook her throat. She clutched his broad shoulders, the muscles hard beneath her hands. The rich, masculine scent of him filled her every breath. The hot brush of his tongue against hers fed the flames burning white-hot inside her, until they threatened to consume her.

And then he was gone, so abruptly a light breeze brushed across her parted lips. Her senses reeling, she blinked open her eyes to find him staring at her.

His dark eyebrows pinched together. The next instant, he took a quick step back, reached for her hand hanging limp at her side, and executed a smart bow. "Good night, Lady Stirling."

He turned on his heel.

Why is he walking away? Closing her eyes tight, Bella struggled to calm her racing pulse. She could still taste his port-sweetened tongue.

The click of the door closing reverberated in the

marble-floored entrance hall, hitting her like a splash of cold water.

Breath catching, her eyes flared. Her heart stumbled.

She had let him kiss her in the entrance hall. Anyone could have walked by and seen with one glance that Mr. Rosedale was not at all what she led them to believe. The narrowly avoided ramifications passed through her, quick and familiar, and did nothing to aid the effort to slow her pulse.

A sudden weakness gripped her. Her legs trembled. Bella locked her knees, resisting the urge to crumble onto the step and hold her head in her shaking hands. She was so very close to sending Mr. Rosedale packing, to calling for her butler and letting the request for the traveling coach tumble out of her mouth. With one kiss he had pulled such an extreme reaction from her—if he had but given the word, she would have let him take her virginity right there on the steps.

The lithe grace of his every movement, the inherent power in his impressive frame, the easy confidence of his smile . . . everything about him spoke to her on a deep, sensual level. Never before had a man's mere presence roused passion on this scale. She wanted what Mr. Rosedale could offer. God help her, she wanted it desperately to the point where she did not trust herself.

Turning, she placed a hand on the smooth wooden banister and walked up the stairs on still-weak legs. She placed her other hand on the bare expanse of chest below her collarbone. Her heart beat mouse-quick beneath her palm. By the time she arrived at her bedchamber the lingering traces of heady arousal had dissipated, her pulse had slowed, and her breathing had returned to something approaching normal, so when her lady's maid asked which nightgown she would prefer, she was able to answer in her usual calm tones.

As Maisie unbuttoned her gown and unlaced her stays, Bella couldn't help but question if this flirtation had been a wise choice. This afternoon as her household had prepared for Mr. Rosedale's visit, she had convinced herself the best course of action was to leave the fortnight open, to let it unfold as it may. It was too unique, too unprecedented an opportunity to blithely push aside. In any case, it would have been rude to dismiss Esmé's offering so succinctly.

Rude? She suppressed a sardonic snort and pulled her nightgown over her head. The cool silk flowed over her bare curves until the lace-edged hem settled at her ankles. That had been one of her reasons—a fear of being rude to her cousin. A cousin who thought it perfectly acceptable to hire her a man. What a poor excuse, and a blatant show of how desperate she had become. Grasping for anything to give her a reason to allow her guest to stay longer than one evening.

Her mind too wrapped in itself to do anything but react on routine, she sat on the cushioned stool before the vanity and closed her eyes as Maisie pulled the pins from her hair. If she had sent him home the moment he had arrived, as she should have done, as a proper lady would have done, then she would not be in this predicament, this war with herself. Fighting temptation, yet at the same time wanting more than anything to give in.

But she hadn't been able to resist the lure of him. And not merely the obvious lure, but of a companion. Someone to spend a day with. Someone to talk to other than her roses.

"Is there anything else I can do for you this evening?"

With a start, Bella glanced to the oval mirror above the vanity, barely registering the concern on her maid's face. "No. That will be all."

The girl curtseyed and left the bedchamber. Bella doused the candle on the vanity. The newly stoked fire in the hearth created a pool of golden light that touched the black legs of the nearby Egyptian armchair, the rest of the room cloaked in darkness. On bare feet, she strode to the window next to her bed and held aside the heavy damask curtain.

The stars provided enough light to make out the curved

gravel paths cutting through the dark mounds of the rose-bushes. She strained her eyes, trying to see past the grass clearing beyond the garden, and could just make out the jut of a chimney and the straight lines of a roof among the surrounding trees. Garden House. And Mr. Rosedale.

She worried her bottom lip between her teeth. She knew the sincerity of every word from his beautiful mouth should be doubted—the man was a prostitute and surely an expert at making a woman feel cherished, desired, wanted. Yet . . . he had made her smile when she had almost forgotten how.

Bella learned long ago the days passed by a bit quicker and did not blend together to form a monotonous, single entity if she seized the simple pleasures in life. Treasured them, cherished them, siphoned what joy could be had from them. An evening spent with Mr. Rosedale was indeed a pleasure. A pleasure she could quickly grow accustomed to.

Therein lay another worry. Even if their flirtation never went beyond a pleasant evening's meal, she already knew watching him leave Bowhill would be difficult. And more time spent with him would simply make it harder to return to her isolated existence.

On a long shaky sigh, she released the curtain, covering the window and blocking out the view of Garden House. She pressed her palms to her closed eyes.

"One day." The pleading tone in her whisper echoed in the quiet room. "I'll let him stay one more day, and then . . ."

She shook her head, unable to give voice to the words she did not want to speak. Slipping beneath the blankets, she did her best to push aside the worries and allow sleep to overtake her.

Three

A knock at the door pulled Gideon from his morning routine. With the long length of his cravat loose around his neck and his newly shaven jaw still damp, he left the back bedchamber, went down the short hall to the parlor, and opened the front door, revealing a young maid with a wicker basket in hand.

Her freckled face blanked with the sort of awe natural wonders usually inspired. He gave her five seconds to gather her wits and then raised both eyebrows in expectation.

She bobbed an abbreviated curtsey and lifted the basket, offering the purpose for her visit. "Good morning, Mr. Rosedale." The brogue could not disguise the hoarseness of her voice.

He opened the door fully and allowed her inside. She set the basket on the small dining table in the adjacent kitchen as he finished tying his cravat.

"Is there anything you require, sir?"

"Does Bowhill receive the *Times*?"

"No, I don't think so. But I can check down at the vil-

lage if ye'd like," she said with a mixture of nervousness
and an obvious desire to please.

"Thank you." He might be in a different country but he
did still need to keep current on the comings and goings
of London.

She lingered by the table, fiddling with the end of the
embroidered towel covering the basket's contents. Before
she could work up the courage to ask if he "required" anything else, he sent her politely on her way. Nestled inside
the basket with the warm bread, sausages, and fresh fruit
was a note requesting his company for an afternoon stroll.
It wasn't signed but the flowing feminine script could only
belong to her.

Contemplating her note, he picked up a piece of bread
and took a bite. Lady Stirling had not changed her mind
come morning. That was always a risk, but one he had yet
to have the misfortune of experiencing. Those terms of
hers though . . . was she serious, or were they just a means
to ease her conscience? Being free to leave was an unac-
customed-to concept, and one he was not planning to fa-
miliarize himself with. Unless she requested otherwise, his
next thirteen days and twelve nights would be spent at
Bowhill Park catering to the beautiful lady's every whim
and desire.

Those little smiles she cast him during dinner . . . each
one had made a bolt prod his nerve endings. He had not
felt that in, well he didn't know how long, but the sensation was almost as pleasurable as the short time spent in
her presence. And that kiss. The first kiss revealed a woman's true nature.

And that kiss . . .

One glimpse. All it had taken was one glimpse of the
passion hidden beneath the cool, contained exterior, and
he had momentarily forgotten where he was and whom he
was with.

Very uncharacteristic.

He furrowed his brow, still not pleased with how abruptly
he had left her last night. Should he have accepted the invi-

tation in her kiss? *No, no.* She had made it quite clear she wanted him to return to the cottage alone. Yet . . .

With a quick shake of his head, he dismissed the question forming in the back of his mind. Grabbing another piece of bread, he went back to the bedchamber. After he finished dressing, he cleared the contents of the wicker basket and passed the solitary morning hours in the comfortable front parlor rereading the *Times* he had brought with him. When afternoon approached, he donned his navy coat, pulled on his kidskin gloves, and set out for the manor house.

The butler didn't show him to the drawing room but left Gideon to cool his heels in the entrance hall.

The wait was not long. She emerged from down the long hall. The Kashmir shawl about her shoulders exactly matched her brilliant Prussian blue walking dress. The housekeeper, trailing two steps behind her, was a somber figure in black.

"Good afternoon, Lady Stirling," he said with a tip of the head.

"Good afternoon, Mr. Rosedale."

She was all polite distance, her posture strict and her tone impersonal. He did not take it to heart—their audience required a performance.

He ignored the hard stare from the housekeeper. "Shall we be on our way, cousin?"

"By all means." She laid her gloved hand on his proffered arm.

The butler shut the front door behind them with a smart click. She paused at the foot of the stone steps, outside the shadow of the portico, and tilted her face up to the sun to catch the golden rays under the brim of her bonnet. Long satiny lashes caressed her high cheekbones. A hint of yesterday's angelic smile pulled on the edges of her mouth.

With her icy cool beauty, Gideon had taken her as a winter queen. But in that moment Lady Stirling was a sun goddess, soaking up its rays, feeding off the warmth, infusing it into the deep recesses of her being as if she needed it to draw breath. Yet her skin was a flawless alabaster. There was not one freckle on the bridge of her straight nose, not even a brush of pink on her cheeks. He held silent and still, aware he was witnessing a rare event.

"It is so kind of the sun to come out again today. I feared it would go back into hiding after yesterday's brief appearance."

"I take it Scotland's springs are like London's?" He spoke quietly, not wanting to break the spell.

"Yes," she said on a regretful sigh, her eyes still closed against the sun. Her lashes swept up and she looked at him. "But colder." The polite distance returned, the winter queen regaining her dominance.

Gideon discovered a newfound interest in the weather. It had always been a bland topic of conversation, something to discuss to fill a void. Yet now he was rather hoping the coming days would be devoid of the usual gray clouds and rain showers. Not for himself, but simply because it would give her pleasure. Because it was something she needed.

"If you are not averse, we can begin with a short tour of the garden," she said.

"If it would please you, Lady Stirling, then it pleases me." Her wishes, her desires, were his command.

Side by side, with him matching his stride to hers, they made their way around to the back of the house. He had passed the rose garden a total of three times since he had come to Bowhill, but on each instance he had not breached the garden's boundary. It was not lack of interest but rather fear of intruding. The large rectangular space, though outdoors and not formally enclosed by stone walls, had an air of sanctuary. Before he even had the pleasure of meeting Lady Stirling, he'd known this was not merely a bit of landscaping to complement the manor house. It was a part of her.

They passed between a break in the bushes bordering the garden and traveled along a path wide enough for two. With each matched stride, the sounds of the gravel crunch-

ing beneath the heels of his black boots drowned out her
lighter steps. He knew it to be a rose garden by the foliage
but could spot not a single bloom. It was a vast sea of
green.

She must have sensed his thoughts for she broke her
silence. "The garden is at its best in the summer. None of
the roses here bloom as early as April. The Cerisette la
Jolies are the earliest and should begin to form buds by
the end of the month." She waved a hand, indicating the
roses on either side. "By May a few blooms will show
themselves and by June everything will be in bloom. The
Great Maiden's Blush will grow tall, forming a six-foot-
high border of double blush pink blooms. Inside, crimson
pink from the Jolies will give way to a thick line of red
from the Duchess of Portlands, which will flow to the pink
of the Celsianas at the center and end with the pink-kissed
white of the Shailers White Moss. And the scent . . . strong
and sweet upon first entering the garden, then you will be
enveloped by an exquisite, deep, potent fragrance."

He closed his eyes, picturing her words, then opened
his eyes again and saw the garden in a new light. There
were no physical boundaries between the bushes, but the
shifts in the green tones of the foliage marked the different varieties. It would be a truly spectacular sight come
summer and he felt a twinge of regret knowing he would
not be here to witness it. "Do you care for the garden
yourself?"

"I do what I can. The majority of the initial planting
was done by the small staff of gardeners who come up
from the village to see to the grounds. Since there are so
many plants they also manage cutting them back. Now
that the roses have matured they do not require constant
care. Just a watchful eye."

"You do yourself a disservice. The garden is breathtaking and it is clear it thrives under a woman's touch."

The small gloved hand on his arm tightened. She tilted
her head, hiding her face under the brim of her bonnet. If
he didn't have the hamper in his free hand, he would have

captured her chin to view the blush he was certain warmed her cheeks.

When they reached a fork in the path, he followed her lead and headed to the right. The gravel gave way to a grass clearing. A large stone statue marked the center of the garden. A single ring of short green bushes encircled the statue's marble pedestal. Three weathered wooden benches were stationed at intervals around the clearing.

Lady Stirling walked a few steps from him to inspect one of the roses bordering the outer center of the garden. He almost snatched her hand back when her hand left his arm. He had grown accustomed to the light, warm weight and now the spring breeze cooled the space where her hand had rested.

Cocking his head to one side, he studied the statue. If he wasn't mistaken, he knew whom she had chosen as the centerpiece for her garden. Oddly, he wasn't surprised by her choice but rather intrigued. "Why is the goddess of love presiding over your rose garden?"

She glanced over her shoulder. An amazed smile curved her lips. "You recognize her?"

He tipped his head. "The museum has a similar statue of the goddess Aphrodite."

"Are you a student of Greek Mythology?" she asked with patent interest.

"No. Never studied it. I read a book on mythology once, but that was years ago."

Lady Stirling walked to the statue, her gaze on the lush, nude female form of the goddess, whose pose was a bit more than slightly provocative. "It was actually Chloris, the goddess of flowers, who created the rose. Though it was Aphrodite who gave the rose its beauty and its name."

"Who made the rose smell so sweet?"

A little chuckle, light and airy, and so short it would have been missed if his attention were not fully focused on her, bubbled from her lips. "Dionysus."

"Ah. The god of wine. Capital chap, Dionysus."

"And do you worship at his altar?"

Was she teasing him or questioning him? Gideon wasn't certain. "No. No worshipping." He decided to go with the former and gave his head a playful shake, his lips quirking. "Merely appreciate his gifts."

Violet eyes searched his face. She turned on her heel and headed back toward the path. "Come. I have something else you may appreciate."

His naturally longer stride brought him to her side before she reached the fork in the path. She turned right instead of going back the way they had come. His gaze followed the winding path and a jolt of pleasure bounced off his chest when he realized where she was taking him.

The door swung silently open on well-oiled hinges and he was greeted with a profusion of red. The contrast with the green of the outdoors was shocking. Before his eyes had a chance to adjust, a strong scent hit his nose. *Lemons?*

"They don't smell like roses," he said, speaking the thought passing through his head.

She hung her shawl on a hook beside the door and donned a plain white apron. "No. They are unique in many ways. These are the Chinas, Slater's Crimson Chinas to be specific, the first China brought to Britain, and they bloom almost year-round. They are from the East and would not survive one year in Scotland if not for the shelter of the hothouse. Come, have a closer look," she said, pulling on a pair of leather work gloves.

He followed her down the straight dirt path. The dark green bushes weren't the typical thick and full, but spindly and sparse, yet covered in red flowers. A true rich, brilliant red. The same red that graced the Ming vase in the drawing room. The majority of the hothouse was given over to the Chinas, as she proudly called them, but not the entire space. The dense, pure green of the bushes along the walls marked them as a different variety. He felt like he had just walked into a summer day. Sunlight streamed from the tall windows along the stone walls and from lean windows in the steep roof. The air was noticeably warmer and more humid than the outdoors, and held that lemony scent in addition to the scent one associated with newly turned fields. "And you called this a small hobby?"

"It passes the time," she said with a little lift of one slim shoulder.

The time she must have to herself to be able to produce this result . . . It was a staggering view of how truly lonely she was up here in Scotland. But he didn't need the hothouse to tell him that. The simple fact that a woman as beautiful as Lady Stirling had called on the services of one such as him was testament enough.

She paused next to a wooden bench stationed along the path and leaned down to gently cup a fully open red blossom with her palm. "What do you do to pass the time, Mr. Rosedale? Do you have any hobbies, any subjects that interest you?"

"Nothing as grand as yours."

A smile tugged her mouth. "It is not grand."

She did not speak the words with a coy bat of the eyes, begging to be contradicted. She spoke with the self-consciousness of a woman unaccustomed to receiving compliments. But Lady Stirling was too lovely to have never been told so by a man. She had that rare combination of beauty and bearing that turned most men into fools. Could it be she had never had a man compliment her on something other than her appearance? If that were so, then he would gladly be the first. "You are a rose breeder."

"Oh no," she denied, straightening. "I would never bestow such a lofty title on myself, nor should others. I enjoy my roses, that is all."

He gave her a smile, one that said he knew otherwise, but was indulging her refusal. She held his gaze for a moment then continued down the path. This time he was able to view the blush rising over her high aristocratic cheekbones before she turned her back to him, hiding the proof of her modesty.

The path ended at what must be her work area. A large stone hearth, made of the same gray stone as the hothouse, dominated the far wall. To the left were a white wicker settee and a small round table. To the right, three long, aged wooden tables stood in parallel, laden with young plants, mature plants, and others covered with glass domes.

Stepping into a sunbeam streaming from a window in the roof, she stopped before the closest table to check on her charges. The golden light gently caressed every inch of her willowy body, giving her an angelic radiance that caused his stride to falter. It felt as though time slowed down. He could see the tiny dust particles shimmering in the bright rectangle of light surrounding her. The sound of distant birdsong reached his ears.

An irresistible urge seized hold. To feel her sun-warmed skin beneath his hands, his lips. To touch her, kiss her, to take her here in the hothouse amidst the roses with the scent of fragrant blooms heavy in the air.

Before he was aware of it, he had pulled off his gloves, baring his hands. With both leather gloves clutched in one fist, he strode to her. Slow and predatory, his steps made nary a sound in the compact dirt beneath his feet.

He was within three strides of her when he stopped in his tracks.

Too soon. He was certain of it. The questioning glances, the rigidity of her posture, the physical distance she kept between them—her reticence was a tangible force. She wasn't ready to go the next step, let alone skip ahead to the final one. The last thing he wanted to do was rush her. Women moved at their own pace, each unique unto themselves. He needed to continue to follow. To keep things light, flirtatious, while fanning her desire for more.

Patience, he reminded himself, as he shoved his gloves into his coat pocket. After all, thirteen days remained, and ladies did not invite a man such as himself to their home without an agenda in mind.

Not wanting to crowd her, he took up a spot a few paces from where she stood. Orange brown clay pots were arranged in two neat lines on the table. Small and dense, the young plants looked like miniature bushes. Except for one. "That one doesn't look like it's doing very well."

"No." She pulled off a glove to check the soil. "Not too wet. Not too dry. Perfect, yet she is most unhappy. I've tried everything, even changed her soil and moved her from the other side of the hothouse."

He moved a step closer. Her skirt brushed his leg. The skin beneath his breeches tingled. He flexed his hand by his side, resisting the impulse to reach up and trace the delicate curve of her cheek. "Perhaps she just needs to be out in the sun."

"But there's plenty of sun in here and this table will soon have full sunlight."

"You misunderstand. Out in the sun, experiencing the elements. Perhaps it's too sheltered in here. The little rose may yearn for the full force of the sun, not merely that which comes through the windows." *Like you*, he was tempted to add.

She wiped her hand on her apron and replaced her glove. "She *is* a Celsiana and can take the Scottish weather," she murmured, brow furrowed, clearly contemplating his suggestion. With a gentle touch, Lady Stirling examined a thin, spindly branch covered with few leaves. "Perhaps that is the answer, but the gardeners aren't due until tomorrow. She'll have to wait another day. Hopefully it won't rain. It's been so lovely of late that we are past overdue for a few days of clouds and showers."

At the disappointment on her beautiful face, he said, "I can do it for you."

His offer was greeted with three seconds of silence.

"Do you have experience with gardening?" she asked, her tone a combination of doubt and expectation.

"No, but I'm fairly confident I can dig a hole and I can follow instructions, so just tell me what to do. I am at your service, Lady Stirling." He took a step back and gave her a bow.

Her chuckle filled the hothouse. "All right then. Since

I am loath to wait another day, I accept your kind offer. Thank you."

When she moved to pick up the plant, he stopped her. "Allow me. And do you have a shovel?"

"Thank you, and yes. In the cabinet by the door."

With the clay pot cradled in one arm, he followed her to the door. He waited for her to place the shawl about her shoulders then he picked up the shovel on his way out of the hothouse.

Gideon had grown accustomed to the warmth of the hothouse and the breeze that ruffled his hair seemed cooler than it had been before he had gone inside. She adjusted the shawl, pulling it tighter around her. The bottom edge ended above the neat bow at the small of her back. The gentle sway of her hips as she walked along the path leading to the break in the rosebushes made the white ties of her apron brush ever so faintly against her backside.

"She needs to go in the middle, with the others of her kind." Lady Stirling's voice drifted back to him.

His attention fixed elsewhere, he merely stopped when she did and only looked up when she turned to face him.

Standing in the grass clearing, framed by springtime green bushes and with the contrast of the nude statue of Aphrodite behind her, she was the very picture of innocence. The shawl softened the straight line of her shoulders. The wide brim of her hat cast a shadow on her face, masking the elegant features, but could not hide the pure delight in her eyes. She quite simply took his breath away and for a split second he questioned the real purpose behind his stay at Bowhill. Then he wiped away the nudge of uncertainty. She was a married woman, one whose kiss contained raw passion the likes of which he had never before encountered. No, she couldn't truly be *that* innocent.

BELLA indicated one of the weathered wooden benches lining the perimeter of the center of the garden. "You can set her down. It will take me a moment to find a home for her."

With a nod, Mr. Rosedale complied. She turned, her gaze sweeping the surrounding area. If she recalled correctly, there was a large enough space beyond the statue where the gardeners had removed a diseased rose last fall. She walked to the spot in question. The bushes on both sides and the one behind had not yet encroached to fill the vacancy. Crouching, she carefully poked in the soil, checking to see if the neighboring plants had grown offshoots. All was clear. The space would do nicely. "Over here. And bring the shovel."

She picked up a few dead leaves from the ground and slipped them into her apron pocket. At the sound of Mr. Rosedale's approaching footsteps, she straightened and turned. Her breath caught on a little gasp. She glanced past him, craning her neck to see around the statue. A neatly folded dark blue coat graced the back of the bench.

He stopped, the shovel in one bare hand. A hint of a smug, devilish smile pulled one corner of his mouth. "You want me to work, don't you?"

The man had to know he was throwing her senses into a riot. Standing casually before her in a state of semi-undress, he appeared somehow more virile, more masculine. Not one button on his white shirt or pin-striped waistcoat was undone, and his cravat remained tied in a simple knot. Yet the removal of his coat made her insides quiver.

"My lady, I await your instructions."

Take something else off. "I need you to dig a hole. Here." She pointed to the patch of dirt with a finger that shook only slightly.

"How deep?"

"Not quite two feet, but almost. And be careful of the surrounding bushes."

"I will," he said with deliberate patience.

Her shoulders tightened, dousing the arousal coiling inside her. "My apologies."

"There's no need to go that far," he replied in a wry tone. "So how wide do you want it?"

"About the same."

Bella stepped aside to linger by the statue. Mr. Rosedale took up her previous place and started digging. Her lips parted as she soaked up the view he presented. He had quite a nice backside, the buff breeches stretching taut each time he placed a booted foot on the flat edge of the blade. The soft sheen of his silk waistcoat seemed to attract the sunlight, yet it did nothing to hide the bunch and play of his muscled back as he lifted the shovel to deposit the dirt in a neat little mound.

Her pulse picked up. Burgeoning arousal sparked anew. She wondered how he would look without the shirt and waistcoat. His upper body bared, the sun kissing his honey gold skin. Liquid warmth pooled between her thighs and she fought to keep from shifting against the sensation.

"Done." He turned to her.

"Oh. Ah . . ." She struggled to recall exactly why they were out in the garden. "You need to plant her next."

"Of course." He smiled. "The purpose for my labor."

He crossed to the bench, returning with the Celsiana. Dropping to one knee before the newly dug hole, he had the clay pot in one hand, the other reaching for the base of the rose, when she scurried forward, then stopped. Her mouth worked soundlessly.

How did one say "be careful" without actually saying it? She was loath to deliver an insult, especially given his willingness to help her, yet he did mention he had never gardened.

He glanced over his shoulder, his whisky brown eyes alight with expectation. "Yes? Am I doing something wrong to cause that look of concern?"

"No." *Not yet.* "Just give the pot a couple of taps to loosen the soil. She should come out easily. And put some of the loose soil in the bottom of the hole first."

He set the pot down and moved to grab a handful of dirt.

"Wait."

His bare hands stilled over the mound of dark earth.

"You're not wearing gloves. You'll get your hands dirty. Why don't I transplant her? I still have my work gloves on, and she is delicate." Bella shifted her weight, suddenly conscious of how ridiculous it was to get this anxious over something as mundane as putting a plant into the ground. If the remainder of the fortnight unfolded as it possibly could then she would be trusting him with something more important than the young rose.

"My lady. Dirt washes off."

He seemed to have infinite patience, even when she was certain she was trying it. And she found it to be . . . settling. Soothing, offering a sense of steadiness. Something she could depend upon. Mr. Rosedale would not raise his voice at her if she pushed him too far. Her ears would not ring from the force of his screams. And he wasn't holding back. He wasn't masking his true nature.

"Yes, dirt has been known to wash off."

Her flippant statement got her a quizzical look. He shook his head, a rueful grin on his lips. "Am I allowed to proceed?"

She gave a dramatic sigh but spoke the word *yes* with a wide smile. Not wanting him to think she was watching him over his shoulder, she wandered off to check the surrounding plants—though she did sneak a few peeks from the corner of her eye. His large hands were infinitely gentle as he coaxed the young rose from her pot and set her into the ground.

"I believe I'm finished here, that is if my work passes your inspection."

At his confident words, Bella turned from the other roses. Suppressing a grin, she slanted him a "we'll see" look and flicked her fingers. He stepped aside. Already the little Celsiana appeared stronger in her new home. He had done an expert job. Not one leaf lay lost on the fresh, dark soil under her branches.

"Well done, Mr. Rosedale. You make an admirable gardener."

He tipped his head. "I try, ma'am."

Bella chuckled at his failed attempt at humility. She turned on her heel. "Come along. We're done here."

"Yes, ma'am," he replied, the grin clear in his voice.

He stepped ahead of her when they reached the hothouse. The shovel and empty pot held in one arm and his coat slung over one shoulder, he opened the door.

"Thank you," she murmured as she walked past him, untying the ribbons of her bonnet.

He replaced the shovel inside the cabinet. "Where does the pot go?"

"You can set it next to the worktables by the other empty pots. There's a bucket of water by the hearth if you wish to wash up." She pulled off her bonnet and ran a hand over her head, smoothing any stray hairs.

The grin just wouldn't leave her lips. If all days could be like this one . . .

Water splashed as Mr. Rosedale washed off the dirt from the garden. He wiped his hands on an old embroidered towel. Bella walked to the left and set her bonnet on the settee, removed her gloves, dropping them atop her discarded shawl, and reached around to untie her apron.

"Allow me."

His deep male voice washed over her, so close it tickled her ear. Slightly damp, cool hands stilled hers. Gooseflesh rose up her arms. She took a quick breath against the sensation and dropped her arms to her sides.

Slowly, lazily, he pulled one apron tie. It was so quiet she could hear the fabric unravel. She felt the instant the bow released. His fingers brushed the small of her back as he pulled the tie loose. He reached around to take hold of the top center of the apron. Instead of removing it, he pressed his palm to her waist, holding it in place. He leaned closer. Heat scorched her back. Her derrière tingled where the top of his thighs brushed the sensitive flesh. She was still fully clothed, but felt exposed. As if she stood bare before him.

The scandalous image formed in her mind. He exactly as he was—in buff breeches, black boots, white lawn shirt, and a proper pin-striped waistcoat. And she . . . naked, the warm air in the hothouse caressing every inch of her skin. A quiver seized her body.

Held within his light embrace, she could do nothing but close her eyes against the heavy flush of raw need. She knew all it would take was one movement, one word and he would release her. But she stayed still as a statue, fighting the impulse to rock back against him, to feel the long length of his body pressed fully to hers.

His other hand coasted up her side, grazing the sensitive outer swell of her breast to settle on her shoulder. A gasp expanded her lungs as his warm lips met her neck. Shamelessly, she arched, granting him access. He caressed the point of her racing pulse with the tip of his hot, wet tongue before laying openmouthed kisses on her neck. The brush of teeth grazing her skin incited her passion. Her hand clutched over his at her waist. Unable to resist a moment longer, she thrust her hips back and encountered the unmistakable evidence of his arousal. A low groan shook her throat.

"Dinner tonight?"

The soft, husky words shot to her core, his deep voice a potent source of lust. She shifted, needing to ease the ache. "Pardon?"

He nuzzled the small cove behind her ear. "Dinner. Tonight. Am I to be your guest?"

"Oh," she gasped, trying to right her mind and focus on his question. "Yes." *Always. Forever.*

He laid a light kiss on her neck then stepped back, his hand sliding out from under hers. "What time?"

She blinked her eyes open and turned, her mouth jealous of the attention her neck had received. "Ah . . ." Time didn't matter. She wanted him to kiss her, to feel his lips upon hers, to taste the hot recesses of his mouth. "Six," she heard herself say.

He stepped around her to drop the apron on the settee. "Six it is."

Discomposed, Bella smoothed her hands down the front of her dress, her senses still in a riot. Yet he spoke so casually. Mild irritation clashed with thwarted desire. She looked through the windows until she found the sun. "I should go."

"Why?"

"It's getting late and I need to dress for dinner."

"You needn't stand on formality with me."

"But it's dinner." She rarely had guests and going through the feminine ritual of dressing for dinner was one she was loath to skip.

"Surely you can stay a bit longer," he cajoled. "You've only shown me a few of your young roses."

He sounded earnest, as if he truly wanted her to stay and wasn't just being polite. "Another time," she said with a smile.

"All right then. Six." He sketched a short bow. "I shall count the hours, my lady."

Four

BELLA scanned the menu on her desk and made a few necessary adjustments for tonight's dinner. The light scratch of her pen was quick and deliberate. Then she slipped her pen into its holder and lifted an ivory cup to her lips. The crisp, tart Earl Grey tea exactly matched her mood. She had awoken this morning with a new sense of purpose, of confidence in the coming days. It was as if her sleeping mind had worked over all her worries, casting aside the frivolous and leaving the remaining neat and organized.

She was glad she had not sent Mr. Rosedale packing after their first dinner together—that would have been foolish, beyond impetuous. She was a grown woman, fully in control of herself, and if she wanted to indulge in a harmless flirtation then she would. Her eyes were open. The situation understood. The ramifications known.

Mr. Rosedale earned his living pleasuring women. Many men employed the services of whores and thought nothing of it. Surely she could do the same, or at least something similar. She would simply look at the situation as Esmé suggested—see it as a practical arrangement, with very nice benefits. As Esmé had pointed out, she was under no obligation to him. She did not have to take him to her bed. In fact, the way he turned from her last night indicated he was the gentleman he appeared to be.

Last night's dinner had been a thoroughly enjoyable affair, yet it had not ended with a kiss. *Oh*, she had wanted one, especially after being teased to distraction in the hothouse. But he had been more aware of her butler's hovering presence by the front door than she. Mr. Rosedale ended the evening with only a sincere "Good night, Lady Stirling."

Tonight she would again be denied the opportunity for a kiss. She had extended a dinner invitation to her neighbors weeks ago. While she would prefer to cry off and spend the evening with him, it would be most impolite. In any case, she had no excuse at the ready, at least none that wouldn't rouse suspicions or get back to the wrong ears. But today . . .

Dragging a fingertip over her impatient lips, she glanced out the window of her sitting room. The curtains were drawn back, exposing the tops of trees in the distance and a clear sky. A grin curved her lips as the answer came to her—a carriage ride. They wouldn't be alone, but the driver's attention would be on the horses. Surely there'd be an opportunity or two, or more, for Mr. Rosedale to steal a kiss as they toured the estate.

A quick word with a servant was all that was needed to have the landau readied and sent to Garden House to pick up her guest. She left the last of the household matters completed on her desk and entered her bedchamber. After donning a short amber spencer over her cornflower blue walking dress and tying the ribbons of her bonnet in a neat bow, she went down to await the landau in the entrance hall. The crunch of gravel under horses' hooves and carriage wheels made its way to her ears as she descended the staircase. McGreevy opened the front door, his expression more sour than usual. Ignoring him, Bella stepped out of the house and into the sun.

A smile tugged Mr. Rosedale's mouth. He stood beside the carriage dressed in buff breeches and a dark brown coat that was the exact same shade as the hair currently hidden beneath a proper black top hat. He was the very image of an afternoon gentleman, arrived to take his lady on a drive through Hyde Park.

"Good morning, Lady Stirling."

"Good morning, Mr. Rosedale." The smile at the prospect of spending another day with him could not be suppressed. A short gust of wind ruffled her bonnet ribbons, the bow tickling her cheek as she descended the stone steps.

Setting her hand in his, she stepped into the open carriage. He settled beside her on the black leather bench. The driver snapped the lines and the carriage lurched forward.

He leaned close, his broad shoulder grazing hers. "Where are you taking me this morning?" His conspiratorial whisper tickled her ear.

She kept her gaze straight ahead and on the driver's back, resisting the urge to turn and brush her lips against his which were *oh* so close. It wouldn't do to behave like a tart while within easy view of the manor. "You had mentioned you'd never been to Scotland before. As your hostess, it is my duty to show you the beautiful countryside."

"How thoughtful of you. Thank you." He gently tugged on the amber ribbon of her bonnet, releasing the neat bow. "The sun is shining today. You should enjoy it before it goes back into hiding."

She didn't dare think to protest when he removed her bonnet, and simply passed a quick hand over her head to smooth her hair. Setting the bonnet on the opposite bench, he picked up the folded blanket.

"Though it is still April," he said. "Wouldn't wish for you to catch a chill. The wind is rather brisk." With a snap of his wrists, the navy tartan billowed before them as he settled it over their legs.

"Thank you," she murmured, a blush warming her cheeks at the thoughtful gesture.

"My pleasure," he replied, his voice a shade lower than normal.

Bella took a deep breath against the new intimacy of being under a blanket with a man and a scent hit her nostrils. It wasn't thick or sweet like cologne, rather a light fragrance that rode over the brisk outdoor air, hinting of cloves, lemons, and clean male skin.

She continued to take deep, even breaths, taking in the scent of him as the driver guided the team of four along the lane. The horses' chestnut coats gleamed like newly hammered copper. Their hooves beat the ground in steady cadence. The blanket effectively trapped the heat rolling off the male body next to her, and it warmed more than her legs.

The trees blocked the sun as they traveled under the thick canopy arching over the path; it reappeared once they reached the north entrance to the estate. The driver turned the team to the right, onto the dirt road that bordered Bowhill.

"That's Moorehead, the Tavisham estate." Bella indicated the Tudor-style, modest mansion that could be seen in the distance to her left. Mr. Rosedale leaned forward to view the house around her. His thigh pressed against hers. The hard long muscles were evident through the layers of clothing. Her deep breaths stuttered. "They're a delightful, if eccentric old couple. Mrs. Tavisham shares my affinity for roses and recently imported a new variety from the continent. I have not seen them as yet, but once the plants have acclimated to her conservatory she's promised to make a gift of a cutting. In fact, she is to bring news of her new additions this evening."

"You will have guests this evening?" he asked, his attention on Moorehead.

"Yes," she said with a trace of unease, hoping he would not see it as a slight against him.

He tilted his head to look at her from the corner of his eye. "Well then, I insist you extract all the details of your forthcoming gift and relay them to me on the morrow."

His tone was casual, as if he understood and accepted the delicacy of the situation.

Seemingly satisfied with the view of Moorehead, Mr. Rosedale righted himself, resting against the bench, but his thigh stayed pressed against hers: one long continual line from her hip to her knee. She turned to him and expected to meet whisky brown eyes, for he always seemed to be looking at her, but his gaze was downcast. The sunlight just made its way past the short brim of his top hat to bathe the ends of his dark lashes.

"Is the plaid doing its duty, or shall we head back to the manor house?" he asked.

"The blanket is sufficient, thank you. We needn't turn back on my account."

"A lady's account is the only one that matters."

She tipped her head. "Ever the gentleman."

"Of course," he said with a teasing smirk. "Would you care to fill our carriage ride with a parlor game?"

His question gained her full attention. "What sort of game?"

"It's more of an old gypsy's trick than a game. Shall I show you?"

Her curiosity piqued, she nodded.

He removed his black leather gloves and set them on the bench. Turning his broad shoulders toward her, he held out a hand, palm up. "If you please," he murmured.

She eagerly placed her right hand in his. He rubbed his thumb over the back of her gloved hand. Once, twice, three times. The caress slow and decadent, as if he were touching a different part of her body. He turned her hand over. The small mother-of-pearl button holding the glove closed posed no difficulty. With a deft flick of his fingertips the button was undone, exposing her wrist. She swore she could see her pulse beat lightning-quick though the lattice of thin blue veins. One finger at a time, he pulled on the leather, loosening the cream kidskin, until with a final tug the glove slipped off her hand.

The spring breeze cooled her skin, but did nothing to

cool the blood drumming through her veins. Caught on
the hook of suspense, she could only stare at their hands.
His dwarfed hers, her skin palest ivory against his honey
gold.

With the back of her hand cradled in his left palm, he
passed his right hand over hers, the simple weight of his
hand drawing her cupped fingers flat. In that brief moment
her hand was pressed between both of his, surrounded by
strong warmth and the unique feel of his skin. Velvety
soft, yet her suddenly highly sensitized nerves could feel
the ridges on his fingertips. Heat radiated up her arm and
across her chest until she was so warm she welcomed the
chill wind brushing across her flushed cheeks.

"It is said the hands reveal the most about a person."
Slow and light, he traced the creases in her palm with the
tip of his index finger. A tremble seized her body. "Every
feature is significant. The length of the fingers. The shape
of the palm. The strength and intersection of the lines."

"Palmistry," she said with wonder, guessing his game.
Her gaze left the infinitely appealing sight of their joined
hands to meet his eyes.

"Yes. But I am only a novice."

"Where did you learn it?"

"From a woman whose grandmother was a gypsy. I
simply learned palmistry because . . ." He gave a little huff
of self-directed amusement. His voice lowered, as if he
were divulging a scandalous confidence. "I was thirteen
and had a certain fondness for my instructor. The lessons
gave me an excuse to spend time with her. The naivety of
youth. She was more than double my age."

She smiled at the thought of him as a boy. Lanky, eager,
and without the smooth polish of charm and experience.

The broad line of his shoulders tightened. His composure
vanished for a brief moment, a blink of an eye. The way he
startled himself with the admission of a youthful infatuation
gave him a vulnerability she had not sensed in him before.

He regained his composure in the next instant, once
again the charming suitor. "And I haven't tested those par-

ticular skills in years, so I beg your forgiveness in advance if I am a bit out of practice."

"There's no reason to beg, Mr. Rosedale. A simple request will suffice."

"Yes, ma'am," he replied, with a tip of his head. The same one he had given her yesterday. And as before, the confidence of his posture destroyed any attempt at humility. "May I proceed?"

She squared her shoulders. "Please," she said, using her haughtiest tone.

A faint chuckle rumbled his chest as he bowed his head and focused on her hand. "These are the heart and head lines." He traced the two lines crossing the upper portion of her palm. "This is the life line," he said, indicating the faint creases curving around the pad at the base of her thumb. "And this one is the fate line."

Her breaths stuttered as he drew his fingertip down the center of her palm. The sway of the carriage made his broad shoulder brush against hers. The continual press of his thigh branded her skin. The intoxicating scent of him filled her every breath. It was all she could do to sit still and not launch herself at him, wrap her arms around his neck, and demand he kiss her.

"We shall start at the top and work our way down." A toying lilt entered his voice, adding one more layer to the arousing sensations threatening to overpower her. "The heart line reveals responses of an emotional nature." He lifted one dark eyebrow. "Ah, a curved heart line, and steeply curved at that. Passion, in abundance."

She slanted him a sly, questioning glance. "Abundance? Are you certain?"

Those beautiful, kissable lips quirked. "Most assuredly." The soft tease of his fingertip moved down to trace another line. "And here is your head line. This one is forked, indicating creative talents. Your hothouse and garden are certainly stunning examples of your creative talents, Lady Stirling."

"Thank you," she demurred.

"My pleasure," he said softly before continuing. "Your fate line starts at the life line. Ever the proper Englishwoman, you have a strong sense of duty toward your family." He indicated three creases on the lower left side of her palm. "These little lines here . . ." His fingertip lingered on the highest line, which was longer and stronger than the other two and ended on her fate line. He leaned back just enough to fully hold her gaze under the brim of his hat. "Which do you think I am?"

The heavy tone in the question gave her pause. She glanced at her palm, looking for the answer, though she didn't understand his question. She replayed everything he told her in her mind, everything he divined, which had been surprisingly accurate. She shook her head and posed her own question. "What do the lines signify?"

Serious and searching brown eyes swept her face. Just when she did not think he would answer, he spoke, the word almost too low to hear. "Affairs."

Her entire body went rigid. *Three.* The number reverberated in her head. *One, two . . . where was the third?* Would there be a third in her future? Anxiety coiled low in her belly. "Does a marriage count?"

His gaze took on a concerned aspect, his dark eyebrows lowering. "Yes."

Three. Him, him—she fought the cringe—and *him.* The tight beats of her heart slackened. The tension left her limbs. Mr. Rosedale was rubbing his thumb over her palm. Large, slow circles that had nothing to do with any intention of arousal and everything to do with comfort. His expression was so intent she wasn't sure he was aware of the way he soothed her.

Then everything shifted. It was subtle, for neither of them moved, but she felt it down to her bones. His brown eyes darkened, the amber flecks glowing gold bright. Her breaths turned heavy and short. His eyes never leaving her rapt gaze, he removed his top hat and set it on the bench beside him. The horses moved at a brisk canter, their harnesses jangling with each rhythmic stride. The wind tickled the ends of his hair. The short locks shone a rich, deep sable under the sun.

He slowly leaned toward her, his head tilting to one side. She felt herself sway, an involuntary feminine reaction. He reached up his free hand to gently cup her cheek. His long fingers curved around her neck, tickling the fine hairs at her nape. The warmth of his hand seared her skin. Lust crashed over her, flooding her senses. A thick, potent, undiluted wave. Her head went light, her eyelids fluttering against the sheer overwhelming force.

"Kiss me," she whispered hoarsely, needing more than anything to feel his lips against hers.

"My pleasure," he murmured.

He closed the last remaining distance, his sinfully dark eyes locked with hers. Her lashes swept down the instant before the soft brush of his warm lips.

THE intensity of her response caught Gideon off guard. Given their first kiss, he should have been expecting it. But nothing could have prepared him for the full force of Lady Stirling's honest and uninhibited kiss. It bowled him over, momentarily stealing his wits and leaving him feeling like a green lad, struggling to keep up as she took each sweep of his tongue and gave back threefold.

She arched into him, her perpetually rigid spine supple as a blade of tall grass in the wind. One breast pressed against his chest and he swore he could feel the hard tip of her nipple even through the many layers of clothing. Heat lanced to his groin and he shifted to accommodate his rapidly hardening cock.

She kissed him with complete abandon. A mixture of untutored eagerness and raw need that demanded he respond in kind.

A primitive need to mate, to possess, one he thought long ago forever tamped down, surged from deep within. His kiss turned fierce as he plundered the hot depths of her delectable mouth. He grabbed her waist, the sleek indent made for his hand. He was but a moment from wrapping his arm around her, hauling her to him and settling her astride his lap, when the snap of leather lines broke through the haze of lust.

They were in an open carriage. The driver's black-coated back not five feet from them.

He suppressed a groan. *Not here.* When she came to her senses, she would be mortified. In any case, gentlemen did not make love to proper ladies in open carriages traveling on Scottish country roads.

Through conditioned force of will, he ignored the demands of his own body, ignored the hard cock crammed in his breeches, dismissed the ballocks drawn up tight begging for release, and took control, reining the kiss in to gently nip her full lower lip.

On a breathless mewl of protest, she pressed closer to him, seeking his lips. In less than a second, his mind raced through his vast catalog of sensual experience and quickly selected an acceptable compromise. At least that was how he rationalized it—a compromise for *her.* Inwardly, he could not deny the impulse to take this elegant creature over the edge, to watch the passion shatter the poise.

He trailed openmouthed kisses down the column of her long swan's neck. Her skin was fire hot and rose petal smooth, and the scent of her . . . Not a hint of perfume. Inhaling deeply, he flared his nostrils. Clean, fresh as a spring morning, the distinct note of feminine arousal, and something else, something indefinable that made him want to taste every inch of her skin.

The image slammed into his mind—her lithe nude body offered up on white sheets, his face buried between her lean thighs, as he tasted the most enticing part of her.

Focus!

On that harsh reminder he mentally shook off the image. Righted to his current task, he delved a hand beneath the woolen blanket. Caressing the point of her hammering pulse with the tip of his tongue, he slowly gathered her skirt, bringing the hem up past her stocking-covered knee, his senses attuned for any sign of refusal, no matter how small, that she was not an eager participant. With her skirt bunched over his forearm, he reached up, fingertips whispering over the line of her garter to the soft warm skin of her inner thigh. Then he paused, hand splayed, his index finger curving over the taut tendon at the very top of her thigh.

Back bowing, a tremor shook her entire body. "*Please.*"

The word was so low, so soft, a mere tremble of sound, yet it was as clear to him as if she shouted.

Permission granted.

He smiled against her neck. "Shh, Isabella."

He brushed his fingertips over her thatch of curls. Gossamer soft, and he knew without looking it was as pale as the hair on her head. Supplicant and eager, her legs parted at his gentle request, bathing his hand in scalding heat. He thought the appeal of such a benign act had been blunted long ago, no longer the titillating play of his youth. Yet his heart pounded in anticipation, as though he was on the verge of opening a great treasure. He knew he would not find relief this afternoon, but the prospect of touching her added another inch to his already painful arousal. On a deep breath of self-restraint, he slipped one finger between the silken folds of her sex. He swallowed hard, finding her drenched.

Her breath hitched on a whimper.

"Quiet now. Quiet, Isabella, and I'll give you what you need." He looked into her face, intent on watching every minute, committing every sigh, every gasp, her every reaction to memory.

Long satiny lashes rested on her high cheekbones. Her lips, still damp from their kisses, parted on short, quick breaths. Her chest heaved, luscious breasts straining against the expertly tailored spencer. One small hand clutched his free hand so tightly her nails bit into his skin. With her other hand, she grabbed the blanket, fingers clenched tight in the tartan. She tilted her head down and to the side, hiding her flushed cheeks from view of all but Gideon.

In an effort to keep her from coming too quickly, he

worked her carefully. Not too swift, not too hard, with just enough teasing pressure to keep her at the point of maximum pleasure. Playing at the soaked entrance of her body, giving her just the merest hint of penetration before sweeping up to graze her clit. He wanted her to savor, to take from this a taste of the pleasures he could offer, to prompt the invitation he needed her to extend.

But it was no use. Once it was tapped even *he* could not check her passion. Within a very small handful of minutes she came violently. Back arching, thighs clamping tight around his hand, shudders wracking her body. Exquisite bliss reflected on her beautiful face.

Gideon silenced her eminent cries with a kiss as he petted her, calmed her, gently easing her back to the present. He pulled his lips from hers and trailed light kisses across her silken cheek to nuzzle at the fragile shell of her ear. He slipped his hand from between her now lax thighs and out from under the blanket.

He gazed into her eyes and found them heavy-lidded and glazed with desire, glittering like precious gems. Her lips were plumped from their kisses. Her cheeks flushed rose pink. The winter queen looked utterly debauched and more beautiful than ever. The vision prompted a surge of triumph, victory, and pure male pride.

She gave a start. Her supple body went rigid. Her breath hitched sharply. She released his hand so quickly one would have thought his touch burned.

Damn. The smug grin vanished from his lips. Had he taken her too far, too soon? He was certain she had been ready, but now . . .

Her eyes darted left and right then fixed directly over his shoulder.

"It's all right," he murmured, relieved, at what he hoped was the true source of her distress.

"But—?"

He shook his head, cutting off her words. "It's all right. Your driver picked me up in London. His silence has been assured."

Needing to erase the concern pulling her fine eyebrows, he cupped her cheek again. His thumb caressed the corner of her mouth, drawn in a straight line. Her body relaxed under his touch but the worry still invaded her eyes. The same worry his impetuous question had produced.

What had made him even entertain the notion that the long, sweeping line on her palm could have anything to do with him? His time with her so short, so insignificant, it would not even manifest itself. It had been meant to be a game. A light, flirtatious game. And all it had done was make her anxious as his amateur fortune-telling had inadvertently hit a very raw nerve.

He would have to carefully choose what games he played with her. She wasn't merely a lonely woman who had been left too long without the pleasures of a man. The worry, the concern, that damn flash of true fear that had flickered across her face . . . it made him want to wrap his arms around her, hold her close, and—

A sharp lance of longing pierced his chest, stopping the unprecedented thought before it could go any further.

This was the third time she had managed to slip under his skin. He really did need to be careful with her. And right now what *she* needed was to forget their last game.

"Truly. It's all right," he said, leaning closer to whisper the words against her lips.

He stole one quick kiss. Soft and light, but with enough intent to distract her from her worries.

When next he pulled back to gaze at her beautiful face, he found a delightful little sparkle in her violet eyes.

He smiled as he pulled on his gloves and replaced his hat on his head. "It's a beautiful day for a drive, is it not?"

"Yes," she replied on a bashful chuckle.

Rose du Roi."

Bella forced her mind to her current dinner guests and processed Mrs. Tavisham's words. "All the way from France?"

"Yes, from Dupont's own garden. Of the three plants, two are doing very well but one is struggling. Most distressing. I talk to her for endless hours, but maybe she simply misses the sound of a French voice," said Mrs. Tavisham in all seriousness.

Bella could empathize with the little Rose du Roi, but the voice she missed at the moment was an English one. *Quiet, Isabella, and I'll give you what you need.* The memory of Mr. Rosedale's soft croon flowed over her, bringing to mind his tantalizing caress. Oh, he had most definitely given her what she needed. The residual hum from the orgasm he'd given her had yet to leave her senses. Conscious of Mrs. Tavisham's rapt gaze, she took a deep breath and was quite pleased with the way the exhale flowed smoothly and without even one telltale hitch. "Being uprooted from one's home is never pleasant but at least there are two others of her kind to keep her company."

Mrs. Tavisham replied with a solemn nod. "I moved one of the young Cuisse de Nymphs next to her pot and this morning she seemed a bit more cheerful. Perhaps I will have a new variety come fall." Her hazel eyes twinkled at the thought of playing matchmaker. "While we are on the subject of love matches, I must tell ye, the butcher's youngest daughter is to marry, and she'll be wed before the eldest."

"That gel's a tart," Mr. Tavisham declared in his harsh brogue. He speared a green bean onto his fork and popped it into his mouth.

"Walter!" His wife shot him a remonstrating glare from across the table.

Bella kept the startled chuckle from making its way past her lips. The Tavishams were an odd pair, yet Bella adored them. They were truly the only two people in Scotland she enjoyed socializing with.

Well, there was a third—her own new addition to Scotland. What was he doing at this very moment? Her wicked mind jumped significantly past the mundane. To Mr. Rosedale, his large hand wrapped around his cock, pursu-

ing the orgasm he had denied himself earlier. Her pulse
quickened. She squeezed her legs tight together in an effort to ease the ache building between her thighs.

"And what of you, Lady Stirling? Do you have any
news?" Mrs. Tavisham asked.

*Yes, an impossibly gorgeous man ravished me in my
carriage. Quite a most delightful afternoon.* Bella resisted
the urge to lick her lips and instead smiled politely. "No,
nothing of interest."

"You aren't planning a visit to London?"

"No. Why do you ask?"

"I thought that was why you have developed a taste for
the news. I myself prefer the scandal sheets. Though Tavisham is in accord with you and takes the *Times* on occasion."

Bella furrowed her brow. The *Times*? Then her heart
stumbled.

Mr. Rosedale.

Feeling the color leech from her face, she picked up
her knife and fork and cut the squares of tenderloin on her
plate into smaller pieces. She cast her mind desperately
for some excuse, some plausible explanation to divert
Mrs. Tavisham from discovering she had a man staying at
Garden House who apparently had a preference for the
Times.

And why did it not surprise her to find out Mr. Rosedale read the daily paper?

She looked to Mrs. Tavisham. "No, I'm not planning to
visit London. I am most content here at Bowhill. I merely
asked for the *Times* to be delivered in the event it would
please Lord Stirling."

"Is Lord Stirling due to arrive soon?" Mrs. Tavisham's
look of innocent inquiry couldn't cover the eagerness at
the possibility of a new piece of gossip to share with the
village.

Bella dropped her gaze to her plate. Why had she mentioned Stirling? She hated to admit her husband did not
keep her abreast of his comings and goings. It made her

feel so unimportant, so trivial, as if her continual presence at Bowhill was not even worthy of an afterthought. She swallowed to ease the tightness in her throat, and unable to lie about everything to the one woman she called friend, said, "I do not know the exact date of his lordship's arrival, but I arranged for the paper so it would be here when he does arrive."

"You have family in London, do you not?"

"Yes, Mrs. Tavisham. My elder brother divides his time between Mayfair and Norfolk, the family seat." Her appetite completely gone, Bella unclenched her fingers from her knife and fork and set them with deliberate purpose on either side of her plate. When had the thought of Phillip become worse than Stirling? Probably when she had given up that last drop of hope of receiving even a note from him, let alone a visit.

"That's right. Your brother is the Earl of Mayburn. I often forget, as you rarely speak of him. A shame his responsibilities keep him from visiting Bowhill, but it would not do for a peer to be away from Town when Parliament is in session."

Phillip did not need the excuse of Parliament to keep him from Scotland. Her presence kept him away well enough. "Yes, he is a most busy man who takes his many responsibilities very seriously."

"Good to hear," declared Mr. Tavisham with a gruff nod. "Nothing worse than a lord who doesn't take his seat. Some of those young lords should be ashamed of themselves. Gambling away their fortunes, bleeding their estates dry, leaving their families with nothing. Appalling!"

No, Phillip would never be so irresponsible as to forget his duty. She alone bore that distinction.

"Walter." A mulish frown creased Mrs. Tavisham's pudgy face. She selected another slice of tenderloin from the large silver platter stationed conveniently close to her place at the dining table. Then she let out a gasp that caused her large bosom to quiver. "I almost neglected to tell you. Our old mare had a filly on Saturday. All long, spindly legs and with the softest little nose. Such a curious thing. You must stop by to see her."

Bella nodded and did her best to hide her sigh of relief. It had simply been a matter of time before the older woman tired of the subject of Bella's family.

They retired to the drawing room, where Mr. Tavisham indulged in a glass of port and she and Mrs. Tavisham partook of tea. As the evening wore on, as the conversation returned to the comings and goings of the inhabitants of the village, Bella found it increasingly difficult to keep her mind on the present company. Her thoughts skittered past the distressing topics of Stirling and Phillip to settle eagerly on Mr. Rosedale. To all the wonderful things he had done to her that afternoon, and to all the decadent things he had not yet done.

But when at last the Tavishams took their leave, Bella tamped down the impulse to run straight to Mr. Rosedale, and instead forced her legs to take her up to her bedchamber.

Passion did not rule her—she ruled it.

Five

GIDEON absently reached out a hand. The edges of the leaves gently scraped his bare fingertips as he walked along the line of bushes bordering the rose garden.

He had received no note from Lady Stirling last night, nor this morning. Left to his own devices, he had used the *Times* and a few games of patience to pass the morning hours. Lady Stirling's servants were as attentive to detail as she. All it took was one request for the London newspaper to become a standard part of the breakfast basket delivered to the cottage every morning.

But as the morning had turned to afternoon, he found himself growing oddly restless. The only sounds in the cottage were the rapid tap of his boot heel against the floorboards and the flick of cards as he sat at the dining table and uncharacteristically lost one game of patience after another. Frustrated, he laid the blame on being unaccustomed to having so many hours to himself when at a lady's home. Visits to the country were typically only a handful of days and therefore his clients rarely allowed too many hours to pass without calling on his services, be they sociable or other more pleasurable activities. Proximity was also a factor. His accommodations usually consisted of a guest room, one conveniently close to theirs, in the main house. Evenings, as well as every meal, were spent with them. A simple walk down a hall could bring him face-to-face with the lady of the manor.

Having the use of a guest cottage was therefore a luxury. Or Gideon had considered it a luxury before the solitary hours got the better of him.

It wasn't that he needed the constant companionship of another. When his schedule was open, he enjoyed spending a day or two alone at his apartment before stopping in at his tailor or testing his luck at a West End gentlemen's gambling hell. But it was different here. He felt like a racehorse confined in its stall too long. He knew his purpose for being at Bowhill and the suspense of when he would be called to the track kept him from being able to relax.

Outright worry had not set in yet—there were still many days ahead of him. The outcome of yesterday's carriage ride kept away any concern he was losing his vaunted touch with the fairer sex. She would come around. It was simply taking longer than usual for her to get comfortable with him. Still, the "when" had begun to nudge at the back of his mind. So instead of being reduced to pacing the front parlor, he had set out for a walk.

"Mr. Rosedale."

Glancing up from his study of the lush grass, he saw a maid walking toward him. He stopped. "Yes?"

"For you, sir."

He took the proffered note. "Thank you."

He waited until she took her leave before opening the note. An invitation to an afternoon tea. A smile curved his mouth. He pulled out his pocket watch and scowled at the small black hands. Three hours until he could present himself at her front door.

He let out an impatient huff, turned on his heel, and strode back to the cottage.

Gɪᴅᴇᴏɴ set his empty teacup in the saucer on the nearby end table. "Would you care for more tea?"

"No, thank you."

"How about a tart? They're delicious."

He made the attempt, but somehow knew what Lady Stirling's answer would be. She had taken precisely three bites of the scone on her plate, and they had been small bites. Very ladylike. Given her lean figure, she wasn't holding back on his account. Her hunger for food apparently was not an indication of her hunger for other things.

"No, thank you," she said.

"You're in need of nothing?" He leaned forward in the chair to rest his elbows on his knees. "Nothing?"

Her lashes swept down and a slow smile spread across her mouth.

That was a new smile. He hadn't seen that one yet. He'd give just about anything to know what was going through that beautiful head of hers. Perched on the edge of the ivory settee, her emerald skirts arranged just so over her long legs, her shoulders and spine perfectly straight, she appeared so regal, so unapproachable, almost cold. But he knew better.

Lady Stirling glanced up. "A walk. I've been in the house all day and could use a walk."

That had not been what had caused the wicked curve of her lips. Oh well, it wasn't as if she would tell him yet. At least not while they were having tea in the formal drawing room, the door open, revealing occasional glimpses of servants going about their day. Too many glimpses. Her housekeeper must have walked by at least five times in the past twenty minutes. "Well then, if you're finished, we can depart."

She declined his offer to have her bonnet or shawl fetched, insisting the long sleeves of her cambric day dress would be sufficient. Side by side they stepped out of the house. She glanced up to the gray sky as they walked across the gravel drive, which curved in front of the manor.

"If I could, I would summon the sun for you."

Her step faltered and she looked slowly over to him with a smile full of unexpected joy. "Thank you, but I don't need the sun today."

"And why is that?"

"You're here," she said simply, as if that were answer enough.

It was the finest compliment anyone had ever given him. Tongue-tied and feeling strangely exposed, Gideon swiftly averted his eyes to the expanse of lawn before them and studied the trees in the distance. He had only given her one orgasm in the four days he'd been at Bowhill, so there was no reason for her to believe he rivaled the sun. With a mental shake of admonishment, he threw off the discomposure. He was looking for a meaning that wasn't there. Her words had been playful lover's banter and nothing more.

Reassured, he glanced to her, his confidence back in place. "Where shall we walk today?"

"The gardeners are around back, so why don't I show you the grounds in the front of the house?"

"We shouldn't wander far. The clouds look like they're holding some rain."

She passed a dismissive eye over the iron gray clouds on the horizon. "No. It will hold off. We have hours before those clouds move in."

Gideon tipped his head. "I concede to your greater knowledge. I am but a recent guest to your country."

"We are only four hundred miles from London, Mr. Rosedale," she said dryly. "It's not as if we are in Egypt. That cloud will make its way to England by nightfall."

"My, my. Aren't we a tad cheeky today?"

"Does my cheek offend your gentleman's sensibilities?"

"Oh no, not at all. I quite like your cheek." His roguish wink cracked her purposefully haughty face and got him a chuckle.

"Good. I'm glad." The laugh lingering in her voice rippled down his spine.

How he liked her smiles. Not the polite ones—the real ones. The rare ones. But they were becoming less rare as their days together wore on. "You never did tell me about your morning."

She smoothed a hand down the front of her dress. "Nothing of any real interest."

"I beg to differ. You are infinitely interesting."

She gave him a disbelieving shake of the head. "You exaggerate. I am nothing of the sort. But if you must know, I met with my secretary."

"And what did you discuss, if you don't mind me asking?"

"The estate, which isn't very large, so Mr. Leighton doesn't need to come up to the house often. Today he wanted to give me an update and needed to check an old account ledger. He's technically an estate manager, but he's more comfortable with the term *secretary* as that was his position before he agreed to postpone his retirement and work for Bowhill."

She spoke as if the secretary reported to her and not her husband. Gideon looked down to her ungloved hands folded casually before her. No ring. Though it was a rare occurrence when one of them wore a wedding ring during a visit from him. He had her features memorized and therefore didn't need to look at her beautiful face to confirm she was in her midtwenties. Too young to be a widow. No—she was married, else there would be no reason for him to play the visiting relative.

So what sort of man installed such an exquisite creature in the country?

A foolish one. Most likely an old, foolish one. A man who couldn't recognize the treasure he had been gifted with. An uncomfortable sensation tightened Gideon's gut, recalling him to his present surrounds and vanquishing any more unwanted thoughts of the man who had come before, and would come after him, from his mind.

"Do you have tenants?" he asked, in an effort to pick up the conversation where he had let it drop.

Lady Stirling looked up from her study of the grass, which brushed the bottom edge of her emerald green skirt. "Yes. Bowhill is comprised of three separate properties. There's this," she gestured to the surrounding grounds, "and two other, more productive properties closer to the village. One's a farm and the other is a large pasture for the sheep."

"You have sheep," he said, amused by the notion. "How very . . . Scottish of you."

She slanted him an arch glance. "They were not my choice, Mr. Rosedale. They were there when I arrived."

"Did Mr. Leighton's update include the incumbent beasts? Did they make it through the winter to see the spring?"

"Yes. They all made it through the winter. There are even a few new lambs, with more due later this spring."

"Congratulations on the additions to your flock. You must be most proud." His comment got him a condescending raise of her eyebrows, one worthy of a queen. "What? You don't take interest in your sheep? Think of how they would thrive if they received the same attention as your roses."

"And what sort of interest should I take in them?"

"Oh well, why not do it properly? You'd make a wonderful lady shepherdess standing amidst the flock with your long staff and a large white bonnet. A vision of loveliness," he said grandly.

She shook her head as though the idea was beyond ridiculous. "No, thank you, Mr. Rosedale."

"No? And why not?"

"They smell," she replied pertly.

"And how can you be certain?"

"How can you not?"

Gideon laughed as she threw his question right back at him. "I can't. The closest I've been to a live sheep has been while in a carriage, passing the wee beasts in a distant field."

"Since I am more knowledgeable about said beasts, being that they are on the property and all, I say they smell." She lifted her chin, daring him to challenge her. Her lips quirked from the grin she suppressed.

"Who am I to contradict a lady? I again concede to your greater knowledge," he said with an exaggerated tip of the head. At the divot in the lush grass ahead of them, he reached behind her to lay a hand on her trim waist and pull her close. "Rabbit hole," he murmured.

She tipped her face up to him. "Thank you." Her soft words barely reached his ears.

"My pleasure. Wouldn't want you to turn your ankle. Then you'd be stuck in the house for much longer than a mere morning." His fingertips skimmed the curve of her derriere as he reluctantly released her.

A short gust of wind loosened a few of her long, white blonde hairs from their pins. With a slight scowl, Lady Stirling tucked them back in place. "And what of you? How did you spend your morning?"

"Nothing of any real interest."

"Since that answer did not work for me, it will not work for you." She gave him a superior little tilt of her head, clearly pleased with herself.

Dull. His morning had been extremely dull. Gideon passed a hand across the back of his neck. "Truly, it was very uninteresting. I read the paper."

"That was all? You spent the entire morning with the *Times*?"

How did she know which paper he read? Then he dismissed the question. A servant, obviously. "I also played a few hands of cards."

"Oh, and do you gamble, Mr. Rosedale?" she asked with sharpened interest.

Conscious of the hours he did spend at the gaming tables, he evaded her question. "It is rather difficult to gamble with one's self. A win is a loss."

"Not this morning. In general."

"What English gentleman doesn't gamble from time to time?" He glanced over his shoulder. They had traveled farther than he realized. "We should head back."

"Not yet. A little bit farther," Bella pleaded.

A frown worried Mr. Rosedale's brow as he assessed the sky. "We really should head back. The wind is picking up and you didn't bring your shawl."

His concern would have touched her if she wasn't so focused on remaining outdoors with him. Alone. Away from prying eyes and ears. "I'm not cold in the slightest." His stride slowed. Impulsively she reached for his hand and gripped it tightly, keeping him with her. "Honestly. I'm fine."

"All right," he said, as if against his better judgment. "A little farther."

She smiled in thanks. It felt nice to have a man indulge her whims. Then she chanced a glance over her shoulder. The house was too far in the distance for anyone to be able to make out their joined hands. So she didn't release her hold on him, and instead moved closer so her shoulder grazed his bicep with each step.

A pressing need to know more about him prompted her to ask, "So you like to gamble and read the paper. What else interests you, Mr. Rosedale?"

At length, he simply looked at her. His mouth quirked, as if he found something unexpected. "You."

A warm blush crept up her cheeks but she didn't divert her gaze from his. The honesty in his whisky brown eyes tempted her to believe him. The large hand wrapped around hers loosened, and for a moment she feared he meant to let go, branding her a fool for daring to believe he could be truly interested in her. Not the body or the face that had drawn men's interest in the past, nor the money Esmé paid him to come to Scotland, but simply her.

Then his palm shifted, turned, until her fingers slid between his. Long fingers wrapped over her knuckles, resting lightly on the delicate bones and veins on the back of her hand. Bella had never held hands with a man like this before. It was simple, quiet, almost common, yet brought such a feeling of reassurance, of togetherness, that she felt closer to him now than when they had kissed in her carriage.

A drop of cold water hit her forehead, pulling her attention from their interlocked hands. Wiping it from her brow with her free hand, she glanced up. The dark clouds that had been on the horizon were moving closer, aided by a quickening wind that held the distinct scent of an imminent storm.

No. No. Not yet! "So we can add women to your short list of interests." The words rushed out of her mouth, falling over each other in her need to keep him from noticing the threatening sky.

"No. That's not correct. I didn't say *women*. I said *you*." He punctuated the last word with a tightening of his grip.

"Oh." She opened her mouth, though she didn't have a clue as to what she should say. A part of her warned he spoke words she wanted to hear, and yet the words didn't feel false. The tingle spreading through her body gave them the weight of truth.

She didn't notice he slowed his steps, or that she slowed hers with his, until they were stopped. He turned to stand before her, blocking the direct force of the wind, but those stubborn hairs whipped across her cheek. Before she could tuck them back in their pin, he reached up. His fingertips were a mere whisper as he tucked the strands behind her ear.

The intimate gesture struck her as nothing else ever had.

And that empty part of her heart, the one that echoed with loneliness, that needed to be wanted again, that needed to feel loved, began to beat anew. Bella wasn't so far gone as to mistake his kindness for genuine love, but the mere brush of it, the echo of it, was more than she had felt in ages. She hadn't realized how much she missed it, until the glance of it made tears prick the corners of her eyes.

The tumult of emotion must have shown itself on her face, for Mr. Rosedale spoke her name with true concern. "Isabella? Are you—" Three raindrops hit his face in quick succession. His head snapped up. "Bloody hell." He winced. "Pardon, Lady Stirling."

"It's quite all right," she said, taken aback by the swiftness of his apology.

He looked past her, his mouth opening then closing on what she was certain was a suppressed curse. The intermittent raindrops swiftly shifted to a steady downfall. Cold water soaked through the bodice and sleeves of her dress, chilling her skin and turning the once bright emerald cambric dark.

His gaze swept the grounds. He growled low in frustration. "Here." He unbuttoned his coat, shrugged it off, and held it out to her. "Put this on."

Bella stared at his offer. No man had ever done anything so chivalrous as to give her the coat off his back. Then she snapped to her senses and turned to slip her arms into the silk-lined sleeves. He settled the coat on her shoulders, turned her around, and slipped two of the buttons through their holes. The ends of the sleeves hung to her fingertips and the coattails grazed the backs of her knees, but to her it fit perfectly. She felt surrounded by him. The black wool retained the warmth of his body and his unique masculine scent.

Before she could luxuriate in the scent of cloves, lemons, and Mr. Rosedale, he held out a hand. "Are you up for a run?"

Smiling eagerly, she nodded and placed her hand in his wet palm.

With that, they were off. It wasn't a true sprint, more of a jog, one she was certain he kept slow enough to accommodate her. Their footsteps squished in the wet grass.

The giggle bubbling in her chest could not be contained. Squinting against the driving rain smacking her face, she saw he was taking her toward the group of trees farther up along the drive. The wind gusted so fiercely it exposed the sage green backs of the leaves.

He passed the closest tree and stopped at the one behind it whose branches were high enough for them to stand underneath. The spring canopy wasn't thick enough to completely block out the rain, but it was enough to shelter them against the full force of it. Fat drops fell from the branches, but for the most part it was comparatively dry. The dirt surrounding the thick tree trunk had yet to get wet.

Releasing her hand, he turned to stand before her. He ran both hands through his dark hair, pushing the wet strands off his forehead. "We should be all right under here. As long as it doesn't lightning, that is."

He wasn't the least out of breath, whereas she panted lightly from their short run. "No, I don't think it will. It's just a usual rain shower."

"More of a deluge." His face tightened with remorse. "I'm sorry. We should have stayed closer to the house."

"It's not your fault. I'm the one who insisted on going out and staying out. You were merely obliging me, as I am finding you are apt to do."

He gave a short huff. "That doesn't excuse my lack of common sense."

She wanted to kiss the self-reprimanding wince off his mouth. He shouldn't be the one to feel guilty. It should be her, for getting them caught in the rain, for even being with him today. For where she wanted her fortnight with Mr. Rosedale to go. But oddly, she did not feel even a brush of guilt.

Shifting her weight, Bella pulled his coat tighter around her trying to find the last bit of warmth from his body that had not seeped out of the fine wool. The damp, chill air penetrated to her bones. Her hair was soaked, as if she had just washed it. Her skin pricked with gooseflesh as a gust of wind wrapped her cold, wet skirts around her legs.

"You're cold," he stated.

"No, I'm—"

"Yes, you are. Your teeth are starting to chatter."

She fought to keep the tremble from her limbs. "No."

"Isabella," he admonished.

"Bella," she corrected. No one had called her Bella for years, yet for some unknown reason it was now important Mr. Rosedale did.

He looked taken aback for an instant then shook his head, as if dismissing a thought. "You're going to catch your death," he muttered gruffly. "Come here, Bella."

Without a glimmer of hesitation she stepped into his open arms. Wrapping her arms around his waist she leaned into him, the copper silk waistcoat slick and wet against her cheek. The strong steady beats of his heart drowned out the hum of the driving rain. She could stay here, in the twilight darkness under the tree, in the comfort of his embrace, forever. Taking in the scent of him with each breath. Soaking up the heat from his powerful male body. Feeling her heart slip ever faster to his.

"Better?" His warm breath tickled her ear.

"A bit." She snuggled closer, loath to say anything to cause him to release her.

"Just a bit? That's all?" he asked, with teasing twist.

Bella tipped her head back. Spiky wet lashes framed his fathomless brown eyes. A raindrop slid down his cheek, and she reached up to catch it with a fingertip. His skin was cool, yet at the same time warm to the touch. Mesmerized, she traced the strong line of his jaw, the hint of his day's beard a mere gentle scrape. She let her hand drop past his shoulder to his upper arm.

Honey gold skin backed the wet, white lawn shirt, which molded to the contours of his biceps. There was absolutely no give to the solid muscles beneath her hand.

Over the years she had come to associate strength in a man with unpleasantness, but Mr. Rosedale's well-honed body roused only passion and a pressing desire to see more.

He stood perfectly still, and she knew he was letting her do as she pleased. That he was giving his body up for her pleasure. She looked up into the face tilted down to hers and found patience, and delight at her exploration. And a bit of arrogance as well, judging from the faintly smug curve of his mouth. The man had to know he was put together perfectly.

Unable to resist the lure a moment longer, she placed her hands on his broad shoulders and lifted up onto her toes. She could taste the cool spring rain on his lips. Unsatisfied by the simple chaste kiss, she slanted her mouth over his and moaned as his tongue twined with hers. Outside was cold driving rain, but inside a tropical summer blazed. It heated her up from within and pushed her closer to him, seeking more. Unwilling to stop for even a second, she continued to kiss him as she pulled at his cravat. But her cold fingers struggled against it. The simple knot seemed to have seized from the rain.

The possessive weight of his large hands left the small of her back. His fingers settled over hers, stilling her anxious movements. He lifted his head just enough to break the kiss. "Allow me," he whispered.

Panting lightly, she nodded. Too impatient to stand idle, she slipped her hands from under his and kneaded his rock hard upper arms. Muscles flexed as he deftly managed the knot, unwound the cravat, and unbuttoned the top button of his shirt. Biting the edge of her lip, she watched his Adam's apple bob under the taunt skin as he swallowed. Then she kissed his throat, her tongue slipping out to taste the heat of his skin between quick little nips of her teeth.

Wrapping her arms around his neck, she dragged her mouth back to his lips and kissed him with complete abandon, reveling in the pure decadence of his mouth. It must surely be a sin for a man to taste this good. It was like kissing the summer sun, hot and luxurious, with a very faint hint of tart Earl Grey tea.

His hands roved up and down her sides and she wished she wasn't wearing his coat, or her dress. That his hands were gliding over her bare skin. As one large hand coasted up from her hip, it diverged from its path, curving in between their bodies. Bella trembled in anticipation. He cupped her breast, molding the weight in his palm. She sighed into his mouth as he brushed the pad of his thumb across the tip. Her nipple tightened into a hard bud, sending shivers down her spine. But his whisper-light touch didn't satisfy in the slightest. It served only to torment her, increasing the urgency drumming through her body.

He shifted his stance, putting one leg between both of hers. Instinctively she arched into him and rubbed along the long muscle of his thigh, trying to ease the ache centered between her legs. Sensation sparked through her, but it wasn't enough. Not even close.

Beyond desperate, beyond any thoughts of proper, ladylike behavior, she reached down. The length and breadth and sheer magnitude of his arousal made her breath catch sharply. But the moan that followed had nothing to do with any reservations. Her insides fluttered and her head went so light she swayed on her feet.

Leaning closer, she tightened her grip, trying to convey her need without words. A short grunt issued from his throat. The iron-hard length twitched, and somehow, unbelievably, swelled even further. The silken sweep of his tongue faltered. His hand settled over hers, pulling her fingers away from the object of her desire. He slipped his hand under hers to clasp it.

His kiss shifted, slowed, softened. *No, no, no!* With her other hand, she threaded her fingers in the short, wet hair at the nape of his neck, and gripped tightly, refusing to allow him to stop. The moment she thrust her hips against his thigh, he moved his leg to bracket hers. A groan of pure frustration rattled her throat.

He lifted his head, effortlessly breaking the kiss against her wishes. "*Shh*, Bella-Bella. *Shh*."

His soft croon only served to further her agitation. "No. I-I . . ." She closed her eyes, dropped her arm to her side, and ducked her chin, suddenly mortified by her overwrought passion. The desire that beat so swiftly and fiercely through her veins withered and died, and in its place dropped the cold, crippling weight of abject humiliation. It never occurred to her that he would not want her. *Oh*, but it should have. If she had learned nothing else from her marriage, it was that not all men jumped at the chance to bed every woman who crossed their path. With a jagged roll of her shoulder, she tried to take a step back, but Mr. Rosedale held tight to her hand.

"Bella, don't." He cupped her cheek, lifting her face to his. His dark eyebrows were lowered, his mouth set. Tension gripped the strong lines of his body. "It's not—"

She gazed desperately into his eyes, willing—no—needing him to finish the sentence. But he took a deep breath and rested his forehead against hers. His hand coasted down her arm to take hold of hers. With both of her hands now held in his, he gave them a squeeze. He let out a long sigh, his warm breath tickling her lips.

For a moment, neither of them moved. The rain tapped a steady beat against the sodden ground beyond the shelter of the tree. Eyes closed tight, Bella simply stood there, battling to make sense of what had happened this afternoon. She had felt the bond between them, she had been sure of it. Then his refusal had evaporated even the tiniest trace of confidence she had in her own judgment. And now she didn't know what to think. She needed something from him, some sign, something more than a couple of words. Words so open to interpretation. Words her mind rapidly completed. "It's not . . ." *you*. "It's not . . ." *what I want*. "It's not . . ."

His head snapped up. "Your carriage."

She blinked her eyes open. "Pardon?"

He let go of her hands. The efficient way he did up the buttons on her, well his, coat was so familiar. Then she remembered—he had already buttoned the coat once. When had it become unbuttoned? His cravat was managed just as quickly. At the sound of wheels on gravel, she looked to the right to see her carriage pulling to a stop not twenty paces away.

"Lady Stirling!" Her driver sat hunched within his black greatcoat, the leather lines held tight in his hands. Water dripped off the brim of his hat, pulled low over his eyes. One of the horses stamped an impatient hoof, splashing in a puddle on the gravel drive. With a jangle of harness, the other of the pair tossed its head.

Mr. Rosedale held out his arm with the distant air of a proper gentleman. Instinctively, she pulled her spine straight, lifted her chin, and placed her hand on his arm. The wet lawn shirt was surprisingly warm, as if he had donned it right after it had been washed in hot water.

Without a word, he led her to the carriage and opened the door. The storm had abated, the gusting winds gone, but the rain still fell in a steady, unyielding pattern that marked the Scottish spring. Eager to be out of the rain, she stepped quickly inside and sat on the black leather bench. With tight motions, she arranged her sodden skirt about her legs. A large hand settled over hers, stilling them for the second time this day.

One hand on the door, he leaned into the carriage. "Come to me."

His hoarse words swirled around her. His gaze stayed locked with hers, intent, serious, and almost, almost uncertain.

He shut the door and rapped once on the carriage. "Order a hot bath drawn for Lady Stirling the moment she arrives at the house," he called to the driver, his voice crisp and sure.

"Don't you want a ride back to Garden House?" the driver asked.

"Thank you, but no. The walk will do me good."

Bella reached for the small brass lever, intent on opening the door and demanding he ride back with her, when the carriage lurched forward. She was left to merely stare out the window and watch his retreating back as he walked across the lawn.

Six

"MAY I take . . . your coat, m'lady?"

"No, McGreevy," Bella said using her coldest tone. She sailed across the entrance hall without a glance back to the butler at the open front door.

"McGreevy, tell Cooley to have a bath drawn for her ladyship. Mr. Rosedale ordered it."

Her driver's raised voice easily reached her ears as she ascended the main staircase, as did McGreevy's answering condescending huff. She stiffened her spine. The man would have been dismissed long ago if she did not fear Stirling's reaction, and the smug butler knew it.

Upon entering her bedchamber, she found the large claw-foot tub positioned in front of the fireplace. Efficient as ever, her housekeeper had anticipated the need before the request could be made. The warmth from the fully stoked fire filled the room and was a welcome change from the chill damp of the outdoors.

"Oh, m'lady, you're soaked through," exclaimed Maisie, a worried expression on her young face. "Come. We'll get you out of those wet clothes in a thrice."

Bella allowed her maid, the lone household servant she had personally hired, to do her job. Fairly vibrating with eagerness to help, Maisie reached for the buttons on Mr. Rosedale's coat. Bella tamped down the impulse to swat the girl's hands away and instead forced her arms to remain at her sides. *It's simply a coat*, she reminded herself. She wasn't truly giving him up.

The maid folded the coat over the back of the nearby Egyptian armchair and ran a hand over the black wool. "'Tis very fine. Hope the rain hasn't ruined it. 'Twas thoughtful of him to lend it to you."

Afraid one wrong word would give away her wanton conduct with Mr. Rosedale, Bella kept her expression blank and merely tipped her head. Maisie quickly removed Bella's wet clothes then held out a quilted alabaster dressing gown. Bella tied the cloth belt at her waist and sat on the vanity stool. Maisie set to the task of removing the pins from her hair. The maid was combing the wet length when the bedroom door opened. Bella glanced into the oval mirror above the vanity.

Mrs. Cooley strode into the room, followed by two servants. "Into the tub," her housekeeper commanded. "Then run down and get the rest."

Water splashed as the servants emptied the buckets then scurried to do Mrs. Cooley's bidding. At her housekeeper's soft *tsk*, Bella turned her head.

Mrs. Cooley stood at the Egyptian armchair. "Is this *his* coat?"

"Yes," Bella said, a surge of possessiveness turning the word into a challenge.

Mrs. Cooley's thin mouth pursed in distaste as she examined the garment. "A mess."

It was nothing compared to the mess Bella had made of this afternoon. Marshalling her rank, she lifted her chin. "Have it cleaned and pressed then returned to me."

Assessing hard gray eyes held Bella's for a long moment. Only her maid broke the silence as she dropped the comb onto the vanity and picked up a silver-backed brush.

The usually long, relaxing strokes of the brush were short and tight.

Bella felt as though Mrs. Cooley could see every place where Mr. Rosedale's hands had branded her skin. Her cheek. Her waist. The small of her back. Her breast. Her skin pricked with awareness, with the memory of those strong hands, but she managed to keep her composure in place and not avert her gaze.

Mrs. Cooley nodded. "Yes, your ladyship."

"Alert the kitchen I will be dining in my room. Have a tray sent up at six, and another sent to Garden House."

The housekeeper's eyes flared slightly upon word there would be no dinner for two this evening. But Bella needed time. Time away from him. Time to think. To ensure the mistake from years ago was not repeated. She could not allow passion to rule her completely, for when that happened, in its wake came regret. And regret was the last emotion she wanted to associate with Mr. Rosedale.

"Yes, your ladyship." Her housekeeper turned on her heel and left the room.

Maisie set the brush on the vanity and collected the wet clothes from where she had dropped them on the floor in her haste to remove them. Bella stood and walked to the window beside the four-poster bed. She didn't glance about the garden or to the gray sky. Her gaze went immediately to him, as if some part of her had known exactly where he would be.

The sounds of the servants coming and going from her room, filling the white porcelain tub with bucket after bucket of water, faded away. Mr. Rosedale walked across the back lawn, his head bowed and shoulders hunched against the light rain. A wince pulled her brow. Poor man. It looked as though he just took a bath but neglected to remove his clothes. He must be freezing. Even with the luxury of being indoors and out of her sodden dress, she had yet to warm up.

She curled her toes against the cold floorboards and crossed her arms, wrapping the dressing gown tighter around her body. Why hadn't he ridden back to the house with her? Why had he insisted on walking to Garden House, alone? On the short ride in the carriage, she had ceased the endless questions on why he refused her only to contradict himself and ask for her to come to him. She would never be able to determine the true answer herself, nor would she ever have the courage to ask him. Some questions were better left without answers—of that she knew well.

He walked between the break in the bushes bordering the garden. His long strides slowed to a stop. He looked so very alone standing amidst the roses, their many green leaves glistening from the rain. Mr. Rosedale ran both hands through his hair, disheveling the short, dark locks plastered to his head. The gesture reminded her acutely of her brother. It was one Phillip had employed frequently in the few short days before her wedding.

She let out a soft sigh that only hinted at the fierce war waging within. It was so terribly bittersweet to know the man standing in her rose garden, the man who had the power to make her feel so much more than blind passion, was in direct opposition to the hope she had held for so long. Phillip would never look on her as a sister again if he found out she had had a male prostitute at Bowhill. And one who had been there explicitly for her pleasure.

She had convinced herself if only she was really good, then her elder brother would forgive her. If only she could show him she wasn't the trollop he believed her to be. That she did care about duty and responsibility. Cared enough to do her best to be a good wife, even to a man like Stirling, though it would not gain Phillip one extra guinea to pay off the debts their father left behind. Debts which could have been gone, if only she had not turned her back on her family and acted recklessly so many years ago.

Yet how would Phillip know if she was good when she hadn't seen him in five years, nor even received a note from him? He wouldn't. He had passed judgment, rendered his verdict, and did not care to be swayed. She should let it go, this need to get back into Phillip's good graces, but she could not release it completely.

She lifted one eyebrow. Though maybe she could for the next ten days.

Phillip would never know, she reasoned. And Stirling . . . She let out a contemptuous breath, one she would never dare indulge in while in her husband's presence. No man who treated his wife the way he did deserved even the appearance of fidelity.

Her life stretched out before her, bleak and lonely. Unchanged from the last five years. Her gaze fixed again on Mr. Rosedale. Did she have the courage to seize the opportunity? To trust in herself? To do what her newly awakened heart begged?

Come to me.

"M'lady, your bath is ready," Maisie called from behind her.

A smile curved Bella's lips. She turned from the window, no longer the slightest bit cold.

GIDEON kicked a small stone, sending it skidding down the gravel path. Had his actions been that of a selfish man? He gave a sardonic snort. *No.* If he had been truly selfish, then he would not have needed a long walk in the cold rain to cool down. Christ, there was no way her driver would believe he and Bella were having a polite conversation under the tree, just innocently waiting for the rain to let up. Hopefully the silence the ex-soldier had secured would continue to hold up. But at least he had been able to get himself somewhat under control before the carriage arrived. In that, his perplexing behavior was well timed.

But what the long walk had not done was reveal the cause of the inherent distaste that had sprung out of nowhere overtaking her there under the tree. On the cold, damp grass, or up against the rough tree trunk. He had done it many times without a second thought, and in more challenging situations. It would have been nothing at all to wrap her long legs around his waist, brace one hand against the tree trunk, hold her tight with his other arm, and give the lady exactly what she wanted.

But for some reason he had not been able to do it. For the first time in his life, his body had been willing but his mind had not. Labeling the experience *unpleasant* would be a severe understatement.

Gideon thought himself so adept at keeping them out, at guarding the boundaries where true emotion crossed with physical pleasure. For it would be the height of folly to be swept up in the very fantasy he carefully constructed for them. Yet somehow she kept slipping beneath his defenses. There was something about her—

No! He gave his head a hard shake. It was simple arrogance to believe he would never meet a woman who truly intrigued him. He should be thankful he had been able to go ten years before this happened, and very thankful he recognized it before it turned into something more.

Something that could not be.

Gideon raked both hands through his wet hair. He should leave. She had given him permission to do so and he needn't provide a reason. But he couldn't. He had extended the invitation and could not back out now.

There was "leave the lady wanting more" and there was crossing the line into displeasure, annoyance, irritation. He very much feared he had crossed that line. But Lady Stirling hadn't been displeased. He upset her. She had the look of a woman stripped of all self-confidence. Exposed and raw. Afraid she was not desired. And that he could not tolerate. No woman should ever be made to feel that way, and especially not by him.

Therein lay the reason for extending the invitation. To erase the hurt in her beautiful violet eyes. It had nothing to do with any desire on his part to spend more time with her.

For nothing should ever have anything to do with his desires, his wishes, his needs. Only theirs.

If she did not come to him though . . .

He pinched the bridge of his nose, trying to distract from the incredible pressure inside his head. "She must," he muttered through clenched teeth. It was exactly what needed to happen. It would put him back on steady ground. Allow their time together to proceed, as it should have many days before. Then he would be in familiar territory and no longer feel this . . . He grunted in frustration. Whatever it was, it left him completely unsettled.

Gideon took a deep breath and continued on his way to Garden House. Lingering in her rose garden would not solve his problems. She had until tomorrow evening and if she did not come to him by then, he would need to leave.

THE next morning, a light, rapid tap broke through Bella's thoughts. With a start, she stilled her hand. She hadn't realized she was tapping the end of her pen against the silver inkwell. Glancing to the folded letter on her desk, it took her a moment to remember what she had been doing. *Oh, yes.* She received a letter from Liv, her baby sister, the prior week. What with Mr. Rosedale's appearance at Bowhill, the reply had completely slipped her mind until this morning when she had been looking for something to fill the hours.

After writing out the address of Liv's finishing school, she set down her pen and looked over to the porcelain clock on the corner of the desk. It was almost time for luncheon. An odd mixture of nerves and anticipation kept away any trace of hunger, but perhaps *he* did not suffer from the same affliction. Bella nibbled at the edge of her bottom lip. It wouldn't be at all well-done of her to make her guest eat alone for three meals in a row. A proper hostess would join her guest for luncheon, and, well, he may have need of his coat. Since he was kind enough to lend it to her, she should return it to him personally.

It wasn't that she needed to see him, and she certainly was not running to him. *No, no,* she told herself as she called for a servant and requested a light luncheon for two to be packed. It would simply be the right thing to do.

She walked quickly into her bedchamber to check her reflection in the oval mirror above the vanity. Pursing her lips, she tugged on her bodice and smoothed her hair. Then she looked out the window beside the bed. Yesterday's thick gray clouds had yet to dissipate. The tops of trees in the distance swayed under the breeze. On the way out of the bedchamber, she grabbed her navy woolen cloak and settled it about her shoulders.

With a wicker basket loaded with food and drink in one hand and his black coat folded over her arm, Bella set out for Garden House. This afternoon she did not linger over even one of the older, heartier rose bushes growing in abundance in the garden or pause to inspect the health of a green leaf. She traveled purposefully along the gravel path, her attention not straying to the hothouse to the left of the garden. She passed the statue of the goddess Aphrodite, passed through the yew bushes marking the perimeter of the garden, crossed the expanse of lush lawn dotted with large maples, opened the gate of the white picket fence surrounding the stone cottage, and stopped at the brown wooden door.

With the sound of her double knock ringing in her ears, it occurred to her—she could be intruding. *Should I have sent a note first?* Eyes flaring, she was a heartbeat from turning and walking briskly back to the manor house when the door opened.

"Lady Stirling," he said with a welcoming smile.

He stepped aside on a short bow and she entered the cottage. Mr. Rosedale was dressed casually. No coat or cravat, only dark brown loose trousers and a powder blue waistcoat. The top of his white linen shirt was undone, exposing a hint of the hollow of his masculine throat. She captured her bottom lip between her teeth, as she recalled the feel of the smooth, taut skin beneath her lips.

"I have come with luncheon and to return your coat," she said, forcing an even note into her voice.

His mouth pulled in a half smile as he took the proffered garment and hung it on one of the pegs lining the wall by the door. "Thank you."

"No. Thank you."

She stood perfectly still as he reached for the metal clasp on her cloak. A little surge of satisfaction shot through her at the way his gaze dropped to the expanse of bare skin above her bodice.

"It was nothing." His whispered words were soft and light, like a reverent caress. He unfastened the clasp. Her breath stuttered as his warm fingertips brushed her collarbone. He pulled the cloak off her shoulders, draping it neatly over his arm before relieving her of the burden of the wicker basket.

She smoothed a hand over the front of her dress. Nervousness kept her from recalling anything on the topic of polite conversation. Just seeing him again, being in his presence . . . Her pulse raced with a mix of anticipation, arousal, and anxiety. She was here, at his request. He knew the true purpose of her afternoon call. Yet he seemed so casual, so at his ease, whereas she did not know what to do with herself.

With an awkward roll of her shoulders, she glanced about the parlor in an effort to find some subject to discuss.

A fire in the stone hearth warmed the room. A thick-cushioned brown couch took up one wall with two armchairs opposite. A series of three landscapes hung above the couch. A leather-bound volume, most likely selected from the squat bookcase beneath the large front window, was on the square table between the armchairs.

The cottage had been designed as a guest retreat. A comfortable place to escape the formality of the manor house. But at the moment, she was anything but comfortable.

GIDEON hung up her cloak and set the basket on the dining table. Lady Stirling had finally fallen in line, done the expected. He was again in familiar territory. He could still taste the relief that washed over him at the sight of her on his doorstep. Hell, he had been a wreck since yesterday afternoon. But she had come to him, and now he could slip into the role he had perfected over so many years. Ignore the disconcerting foreign emotions she sparked within him and react purely on a physical level.

After removing the cork from the bottle, he selected one of the glasses from the basket and filled it with a generous amount of Bordeaux, all the while studying her from the corner of his eye. The pale blonde hair was pulled back in the usual tight knot at the nape of her neck. An empire-waist lilac day dress, the exact shade of her eyes, obscured the sleek curve of her waist and the long length of her legs, yet received his wholehearted approval, the bodice so wonderfully low her luscious breasts were a deep breath from spilling free. But she was visibly nervous and it clashed with the cool elegance.

Only the very bold and seasoned could take a paid lover to their bed without a bat of an eye. But he knew exactly what to do to ease Lady Stirling, to calm her. This past week had been nothing but a lead-up to this moment. He would take all he had learned of her and use it to strip away the edge behind her uncharacteristic fidgeting and replace it with a sharp hunger that would have her begging for more. The charming gentleman had done his job. It was time for the calculated seducer to take over.

Gideon picked up the wineglass then loosened his grip. This *was* the reason why he had been hired, proving her no different than all the rest. No matter the hours spent in pleasant conversation or playful flirtation, it always came down to this. That was all they truly wanted of him, and all he needed from them. Nothing more.

Definitely nothing more.

A woman like Lady Stirling would never want more from a man like him than a blissfully mind-numbing orgasm. And he was quite looking forward to receiving one himself. By the way she responded to his kisses, he knew she would be a very enjoyable bed partner.

Focusing on that goal, he closed his eyes for a brief moment and blocked out everything, leaving a calming sense of single-minded purpose. Then he turned from the table.

Seven

"FOR the lady," Mr. Rosedale said with a charming smile.

"Thank you." Bella took the proffered glass and drained half the contents in a few unladylike swallows.

"Come." He strode past her with a flick of his head and settled on the couch, casually resting his elbow on the tufted arm. "Tell me about your morning. And I warn you now, 'nothing of any real interest' is not a satisfactory answer."

She chuckled. He was impossible to resist, his teasing mood infectious. She took another long sip of wine. "If you must know," she said, sighing dramatically as she sat down beside him, "I caught up on my correspondences."

"Are you a diligent correspondent?"

"Of course," she said with mock affront. "What proper English lady doesn't write from time to time?"

"Such an admirable trait."

She lifted one shoulder. "I try."

"So, you spent the morning with a pen in hand. That was all?"

"I also met with my housekeeper."

"Ah, the woman in black."

He made Mrs. Cooley sound so sinister. Bella threw him a playful, reprimanding scowl as she brought the glass to her lips. "Yes, she does wear black often. In fact, I don't believe I've seen her in anything but."

He took her empty glass and set it on the floor by his feet. "She doesn't put your castoffs to use then?"

"No." Bella grinned at the absurd thought of stern Mrs. Cooley in one of her own vibrant silk gowns.

"A shame." He shook his head. "Would liven up the house. Myself, I've always been partial to a spot of color. Very nice, by the way," he added in a silken tone, his gaze raking the length of her body.

"I'm pleased you approve," she whispered, hoarsened by a sudden infusion of lust.

"Very much so."

He turned his broad shoulders to her, the long length of his thigh pressing against hers, and slowly ran a fingertip along the ribbon trim of her bodice. A shiver gripped her spine at the faint brush of his skin against the swells of her breasts. Her gaze locked with his, she licked her lips.

The edges of his mouth quirked with a hint of a smile. Everything seemed infinitely right, as if it was always meant to be, when he leaned in for a kiss. A corner of her mind marveled at this man's ability to make her so comfortable. She had not noticed when it happened or how he had done it, but the stifling nervousness and awkwardness were blessedly gone. *Because he's done it so many times before.* She quickly shoved the unpleasant reminder of his profession aside and focused only on Mr. Rosedale and his wonderful kisses.

Just when she became fully immersed in his kiss, in the sublime delicacy of his mouth, he broke it to whisper in her ear. "Come with me."

He nipped at her earlobe and stood, extending a hand, palm up. The amber flecks in his eyes mesmerized her. They glowed golden bright, making the surrounding brown appear as black as a starless midnight. But beneath the lust she sensed a never-ending well of patience. His words were not a demand. She did not feel even a glance of pressure.

Gazing up at him through the veil of her lashes, she smiled softly and placed her hand in his.

Hand in hers and ahead of her by one step, he led her out of the parlor, down the narrow hall, and into the bedchamber. She immediately identified the scent in the air. Cloves, lemons, and the man who would make her complete.

He released her hand to close the door. Glancing about, she stepped further into the room. Like the rest of the cottage, the room was small, yet had a distinctly cozy atmosphere. Hazy daylight seeped through the gauzy white curtain covering the window. Flanked by spindly legged side tables, a bed, the one he slept in, dominated the room. A fire burned in the small hearth. A silver-banded wooden trunk stood on the floor next to a mahogany dresser. The various male accoutrements on the washstand caught her eye. An ivory comb. A wood-handled brush. A leather shaving kit. Each object personal. Each one his.

At the click of the lock turning, she started, whirling around to face the door. She clasped her hands before her.

Hand on the brass key, he lowered his head a fraction. "No?"

"It's all right."

"Are you sure?"

She had a feeling he wasn't referring to the locked door. "Yes." *I want you to be my first, my only.* Yet she kept the words inside, hoping he would not be able to discern the full truth. The last thing she wanted was to answer any questions regarding her marriage.

"Good." His heart-stopping smile melted away the last lingering bit of nervousness.

He stepped from the door and cupped her cheek. She closed her eyes and tipped her face up, lips parted and eager for him to pick up the kiss exactly where he left it in the parlor. Instead he pressed his lips to her temple, the arch of one eyebrow, her closed lashes, the crest of one cheekbone. Slowly worked his way down her features, blessing each one with a soft, playful kiss. All the while, he teased the corner of her mouth with the pad of his thumb.

Frustrated by his languid pace, she nipped at his thumb. The trail of kisses on her face ceased. She sneaked a peek at him from beneath her lashes. He gazed down at her with a most satisfied expression, as if it had been his intent all along to goad a response from her.

"Kiss me," she whispered, not caring in the slightest if he thought her bold.

The corners of his mouth curved in a devilish smirk. "It would be my pleasure."

She sagged against him in gratitude when his mouth met hers. The kiss was more than the one in the parlor. The strong, possessive sweep of his tongue infused a shot of desire into her already thrumming veins, quickening her pulse.

Large hands moved up and down her back, deftly working the buttons of her dress and the laces of her stays. She shifted her weight, impatient to be free of the confines of her clothes. Then he brought his hands up to her shoulders and dragged them down her arms. Nipping at his lower lip, she quickly shook her wrists free of the sleeves and reached for him again. Fabric *whooshed* to her feet. Cool air hit her heated skin. Tangling her fingers in his hair, she slanted her mouth full over his and writhed against him.

The sensation of bare skin against his fully clothed body intoxicated her. The tantalizing slip of smooth silk against her bare breasts. The press of small fabric-covered buttons along her chest. The brush of soft wool trousers against her stocking-covered legs. Her head swam as if she had drank three glasses of wine instead of one.

She was vaguely aware he was pulling the pins from her hair. The heavy weight of it tumbled down, the ends grazing her lower back. Lifting up onto her toes, she hitched a leg about his hip and encountered the hard arch of his arousal.

Large hands grasped her backside, jerking her closer,

pressing them intimately together. On a low grunt, he thrust, grinding his trouser-covered cock against her sex in a seductive rhythm. The deliciously rough caress made lust blaze, fierce and hot. Clutching his broad shoulders, she moaned into his mouth, wanting more.

Then she felt herself being lifted. Urgently kissing him, she held on tight, more than eager to move to the bed. To have the solid weight of his male body cover her. To have him inside her.

Her derriere pressed against cool, smooth wood. His lips left hers. Panting heavily, she blinked open her eyes. She was perched on the edge of the mahogany dresser. He stood between her legs that were still wrapped loosely about his waist.

"This isn't the bed."

A low chuckle vibrated his chest. "No, it's not," he said with a smirk, as he toyed with the violet ribbons on her garters. "On or off?"

For a moment she couldn't decide. The question was one she never before contemplated, even in her most scandalous fantasy. And the thought of wrapping silk-covered legs around his bare waist was tempting indeed. The height of decadence. Yet—

"Off." Her answer came out on a shaky whisper.

"Excellent choice," he said, giving her a smile steeped in sin.

Kneading her hips, he bowed low, his tousled dark hair brushing her lower belly. The powder blue waistcoat stretched taut across his broad back. Warm breath fanned the pale blonde triangle of hair between her legs, teasing her sensitive flesh. A tremor shook her body, her pulse clamoring through her veins. Turning his head, he nuzzled her inner thigh then dragged his lips down to the garter above her knee. Holding the ribbon in his teeth, he pulled, releasing the bow. Straightening, he lifted her leg to slowly peel off the silk stocking. The position opened her, fully exposing her sex. His dark lashes swept down. His even breaths hitched. The heat of his regard sent a burning jolt of sensation through her.

"So pretty," he said in a husky murmur that flowed like rich velvet over her skin.

Perched naked on the dresser and with one leg lifted to his shoulder, she arched one eyebrow. "Thank you."

That got her a chuckle. He tipped his head. "You're very welcome, my lady."

Lips curved in a confident smile, she trailed her fingertips along his jaw, marveling at her boldness. This was the side of herself she had tried to deny for so long—the tart. Wicked and shameless. Bold and demanding. Ruled solely by lust.

That impulse to tamp it all down, to lock the lust away, to hide it from prying, judging eyes, was absent. Completely nonexistent. For the first time in her life she felt truly free, and it was all due to him.

He removed her other stocking in a thrice. Flicking it to the floor, he stepped closer, coasting his hands up from her knees to cup her breasts. "And these are very pretty as well."

Holding the weight of each, he pinched her nipples and drew out the tips. She groaned as a sharp lance of pleasure shot from his clever fingers to her core. The apex of her pleasure throbbed with an undeniable need for his touch.

He dropped his head to her chest and suckled on one breast and then the other. Throwing her head back, she lifted her chest, offering herself up to him. He delivered a sharp teasing nip then blew lightly over the tip. Her nipple hardened, tightened. Shivers gripped her spine. Lashes fluttering, she let out a shaky moan and clutched his broad shoulder.

Her hand slipped on smooth silk, reminding her he was still fully clothed. She tugged on his waistcoat. "Take this off," she said, more demand than request.

He dragged his lips up her chest. "As my lady wishes," he murmured against her neck.

She arched, granting him access. He alternated between openmouthed kisses and short little nips as he removed his waistcoat. Impatient, she pulled his shirt from his trousers and slipped her hands underneath. Muscles rippled beneath her questing fingers. He pulled back to whisk the white shirt over his head, revealing a torso that perfectly matched the classical lines of his face.

Leaning close, she ran her fingers through the light sprinkling of dark hair on his chest and down the defined ridges of his abdomen that she had so recently explored. She pulled eagerly on the waistband of his trousers. "These, too."

With a flick of his wrist, the buttons on his falls were undone. Dark brown trousers whispered down his long legs.

Bella sucked in a short breath. Didn't men wear drawers? Obviously not *all* men. His manhood freed, it jutted proudly from his body. Long and thick and beautifully formed. The sight both impressed and intimidated her. God, the man was perfection.

Squaring his shoulders, he lifted his chin. "Do I meet with your satisfaction?"

The piercing look he gave her indicated he had absolutely no doubt what her answer would be, but she gave it nonetheless. "Oh, *yes*."

"I'm pleased you approve."

He did not give her another moment to soak up the image of his gloriously nude male body, or allow the implications of his magnificent, splendid arousal to settle in her mind. For his arms wrapped around her, his lips found hers, and her passion careened out of control.

Writhing against him, she reveled in the unique feel of bare skin against bare skin. The velvety smoothness of his hips as she wrapped her legs around him. The hot press of the hard arch of his arousal against her inner thigh. The soft chest hair lightly abrading her nipples. One hand clutching the nape of his neck, she held him close, frantically kissing him, unable to get enough.

One of his roving hands paused to pull her leg from his waist. Hooking her knee over his elbow, he braced his arm on the dresser. His other hand followed her thigh up to brush the thatch of hair between her legs. A long finger slipped over the slick folds of her sex, teasing lightly, tormenting her, before finding that point of amazing sensitivity. Her entire body jerked against the sharp lance of pleasure. "*Yes*."

He grunted, the sound pure masculine satisfaction. "So wet, my lady. So ready for me."

Needing more than the light pressure, she ground her hips against his hand. Imminent bliss coiled tighter and tighter. The release she needed more than anything in the world was right there, almost within reach, almost, almost—

"Oh, so impatient." His drawling voice both reprimand and encouragement. Lowering his head to her shoulder, he removed his hand.

"No!" she cried, frustrated close to the point of tears at being left in this tortured state. Agitation rode over every nerve in her body.

"Ah-ah. Not yet." She could feel him smile against her neck as he spoke. "I want to be inside of you when you come. Now hold on." Grabbing hold of her backside, he effortlessly lifted her and carried her the short distance to the bed.

And she was on her back, the mattress soft beneath her; he crouched over her. His mouth left hers to trail kisses down her chest. Strung tight to the point of desperation, Bella wrapped a leg around the back of his hair-dusted thigh and pulled his head up before his lips could reach her nipples.

When his whisky brown eyes met hers, she gasped, "No, I need—" With a thrust of her hips she attempted to fill in the unspoken words.

He shifted off to the side, reaching toward the small bedside table.

Panting heavily, she was a hair's breath from pushing him onto his back and straddling him. She needed him.

Now. To fill the aching emptiness inside of her. "What are you—?"

His mouth was at her ear. "*Shh*, Bella-Bella, just a moment and I'll give you what you need." His hands moved between their bodies.

Perplexed, she glanced down. He was tying a ribbon at the base of his cock to secure a thin sheath. "What is—?"

One dark eyebrow lifted. "To protect against any unwanted guests."

His lips were on hers before she could process his words. Bracing his weight on one arm, he settled full between her spread thighs. Using his other hand, he teased her sex with the blunt head of his cock, kept her teetering precariously on the brink. She wiggled her hips, trying to get him where she needed him.

His heavy-lidded eyes locked with hers. "Yes?" he queried.

"*Please!*"

The smug arrogance in his grin should have earned him a slap, but her overwhelming need masked all dignity. Instead, a sob of undiluted gratitude shook her chest as he paused at the entrance of her body.

Finally, he eased inside the tiniest bit. Torn between intense pleasure and stretching pain, she shifted beneath him, struggling to take all of him. She wanted all of him. Needed all of him. But that flicker of fear settled in her mind. He was *much* too large.

Closing her eyes, she gripped his shoulders, fingernails biting into the smooth skin.

"Relax. I won't hurt you," he murmured, nuzzling her cheek.

She opened her eyes to find him nose to nose with her. Her tight breaths mingled with his steady ones. No, this man would never physically harm her.

"Here. Allow me."

He stole a quick kiss then began to move, but *oh* so slowly, easing a short distance in and almost completely out, giving her just the head of his cock, just a taste of his full penetration. In no time at all her body turned liquid. Every sense heightened. The intense pleasure wiped away any trace of discomfort.

Until she craved more.

Until the hard bite of impatience made her thrust up sharply into his next short downward glide, fully impaling herself on his cock.

The discomfort returned. A quick stab, like a prick of a needle. There and then gone. On a surprised "Oh," every muscle in her body tightened.

And so did his.

His once half-lidded eyes flared wide, shock written all over his handsome face and in every line of the powerful body crouched over hers.

Oh no.

Before he could take issue with her virginity, she grabbed his head and slanted her mouth over his.

Her delicate flesh stretched taut by his thick length, she quivered on the knife-edge of bliss. He felt so amazing, so incredible, beyond anything she could have ever imagined, that with the first hesitant sweep of his tongue against hers, an orgasm rushed upon her, sending her senses reeling. She gasped into his mouth, the heavy tide of sensation rushing from her core out to her fingers and toes.

He started to thrust. Short, slow strokes through her climax. But she didn't want slow. She didn't want consideration. That release had been so quick, so hard, it only served to heighten her appetite for more. Bella rocked her hips, bumping against him, lengthening the strokes, increasing the pace.

Bracing his forearms on either side of her shoulders, he drove into her. Throwing back her head, she arched beneath him, a slave to the voluptuous sensation of his possession. Each controlled slam of his hips brought her closer, closer, and in no time at all she came again.

With the thick, heady pleasure still washing her nerves, he slipped a hand under the small of her back. He gathered himself, as if to change positions.

But she wanted none of that. No disruption in the rapturous rhythm. She grabbed his buttocks, the hard muscles flexing in time to his thrusts, and wrapped her legs around his. "No. Don't stop. *More*."

Her breaths turned labored. Hard, heavy pants through parted lips. Her skin heated with sweat. Her strength dwindled, but she simply could not get enough of him.

He dropped his head to her shoulder. His thrusts quickened, hard and demanding, pushing the all-encompassing pleasure swamping her nerves to new heights. She was right there, on the verge of another orgasm.

A tremor wracked his body as he let out a low groan she feared could only mean one thing.

"Not yet!" Though she knew her protest came too late. He had just found his release.

"Yes, Bella," he whispered, only slightly out of breath. He kissed her gently. Soft, light comfort kisses. When he made to pull back, she tightened her legs wrapped around his in an effort to keep him inside. "Bella-Bella," he crooned, brushing the tip of his nose against hers. "We have days ahead of us and I don't want to make you sore."

She didn't protest further when he moved off to lay on his side. With his head propped up on a bent arm, he trailed his fingertips up and down from the center of her chest to her navel. Rather than tickling, his light touch lulled her overwrought senses.

Bella smoothed his tousled hair. The short dark locks were warm silk between her fingers. A sense of utter relaxation stole over her. She let out a soft sigh of contentment. Not a whisper of regret passed through her. Not even a brush of guilt settled on her shoulders. She was infinitely thankful it had been him, for no other could have been able to take his place.

He grinned down at her.

Was it her imagination, or did his grin seem tight, taut, almost forced?

"Hungry?" he asked.

She meant to say no, but the word *yes* came out of her

mouth. A soft rumble echoed in the quiet room. Bella clamped a hand over her stomach and tucked her chin to her chest. "Sorry."

"Don't be." He dropped a kiss on her forehead, swung his legs over the side of the bed, and walked to the wash-stand.

Bella levered up onto her elbows to leisurely soak up the sight her impatience had denied her earlier. He was, quite simply, perfect. Sublime. A feast for her greedy eyes. His broad shoulders tapered to a hard waist. The sight of his back completely captivated her. All rippling male mus-cle and solid, strong bone beneath honey gold skin that looked as soft and smooth as the finest kidskin. She could still feel the memory of those lean hips between her thighs. She shifted, rubbing the arch of her foot up her calf. And his firmly muscled backside . . . She sighed. How was it that after he had given her so much, she could still want more?

After donning his trousers, he returned to the side of the bed. "Need assistance?"

Her gaze darted to his inquiring face and then to the damp towel in his hand. Oh, *that* had been what he washed up. A rush of modesty heated her cheeks. She snatched the towel. "No. I can manage."

He tipped his head. "I'll be right back."

A tight knot of trepidation infiltrated her stomach. What with the way he was practically racing to the door, she wasn't at all sure he spoke the truth.

Eight

Gideon pulled the bedroom door shut and pinched the bridge of his nose so hard his arm shook.

Holy Mother . . . bloody fucking hell!

He had not been expecting that. He had not been prepared for that.

She was not supposed to have been a virgin.

And she had been a virgin. If nothing else, the faint crimson smear on the sheath proved it well enough.

Why had she given her innocence to him of all people? He was the last man who deserved it. Gently bred ladies did not choose him. Gideon had half a mind to turn around and demand to know why. Why him? Why the hell had she been a virgin? She was supposed to be married!

And how dare she not say anything, or at least give him a hint? Here he had toyed with her, taunted her, tormented her, taken perverse satisfaction in the sight of her laid out before him, her lithe body writhing in unfulfilled ecstasy. But that moment when everything clicked sharply into place, when his stomach dropped to the floor—quite frankly, he was amazed he hadn't gone limp from the shock. And he probably would have, if not for the fact he had been buried hilt-deep, her tight heat gripping his cock like a fist. Hell, he was lucky he hadn't come right then and there, before he gave her one orgasm.

He shook his head, short, hard, and utterly frustrated, and then removed his other hand from the doorknob lest he give into temptation. Forcing his feet to move, he walked down the short hall to the dining room. He should have known. Five days was an unprecedented length of time before they took him to bed. This appointment had been different from the start. The fortnight should have been the first clue. For country visits, a few days were standard. A week within the realm of the usual. Fourteen days were unheard of.

And what had driven her to procure the services of a man to relieve her of her virginity? Lady Stirling was beauty personified, body and soul. Men would sell all they owned for a chance to be with her. She needn't stoop so low as to pay one. It was pure chance Rubicon had thrown her to him. That heartless bitch could have easily chosen any one of the other three men in her employ. A cold shudder gripped him at the thought of Bella at the mercy of one of those three. Whores, the lot of them. Utterly without discrimination, willing to do anything for money, anything Rubicon commanded of them. None of them had the patience this appointment demanded. Focused solely on their own pleasure, they would have pressed their attentions on Bella, forced her hand before she was ready. And she would have gifted her innocence to a man who cared nothing for her and cared only for the gold in his pockets.

Gideon's stomach turned. A wave of imminent bile filled his throat. He grabbed the bottle of wine and brought it to his lips, took two long swallows, then slammed it on the table with a derisive snort. Bordeaux should be savored, not poured down one's throat.

He needed a real drink but there was no liquor in this damn cottage. He knew, for he'd already scoured the place last night after the servant delivered his solitary dinner. He should have given into his frayed nerves, gone up to the house, and requested a bottle of scotch. Then at least he'd have something stronger than wine to throw back. Christ, gin would be acceptable at this point.

But he had not left the cottage for fear of word reaching her ears that her "cousin" was a drunkard. In any case, he never presented himself at their doors, be it bedchamber or front, without an express invitation.

Cringing, he glanced swiftly down the hall. He never lingered overlong in bed with a woman, but he had never bolted like that. That look in her eyes, the one that bespoke a bone-deep trust, had scared the daylights out of him. The control he had fought so hard to keep in place was dangerously close to shattering. It was not the height of tact, but leaving, and quickly, had been his only option.

Resting his hands on the table, he hung his head, suddenly weary and defeated, as if facing a battle he could not come out of unscathed. One deep breath. And another. Focusing on the air filling his lungs and whooshing out his nose.

He righted himself, pushing the heels of his palms to his closed eyes. "Pull it together," he muttered.

She had been a virgin. He accepted the fact. He was bound to come across one sooner or later, so it was his own fault for not letting the possibility enter his head. Walking out the door and returning to London today was not an acceptable option. His shock behind him, his frustrations vented, he could face her again. He knew what he was dealing with now, and he was confident he could handle it like he handled all his other appointments. Their long walks, their conversations, that indefinable "something" he had sensed from her had nothing to do with him. It had all been the product of her untried state.

As for why him? He pushed the question from his mind. The answer did not matter. He would be leaving in ten days, so it was best if he kept it all in perspective.

Gideon chuckled, the sound cutting self-mockery.

Well, he had been wrong—Bella was not *exactly* like all the rest.

A clock sounded in his head, ticking off the time remaining before her curiosity seized hold and she came out of the bedchamber. She deserved an extra measure of consideration given what she had lost today, and to whom. So he should get back in there and play the charming gentleman.

Grabbing the wicker basket, he returned to the bedchamber and found her standing before the dresser tucking a pin into her hair. *Damn.* He wished she had left it unbound a bit longer.

Arms bent up to her head, Bella glanced over her shoulder. Her white zephyr silk chemise was so thin it revealed the long, slim lines and graceful curves of her body. Why was it he felt like a thief, as if he had stolen something that did not belong to him?

Her lips curved in a failed attempt at a smile. "Hello."

"Need help?" he asked, doing his best with an open, friendly tone, while inwardly hoping she wasn't already regretting their afternoon.

"No, I can manage."

He smoothed the rumpled coverlet and set the basket on the bed. "Shall we have our picnic in bed?"

She hesitated. "All right."

He was unpacking the food when she bent to pick up her dress from the floor.

"Don't bother with that, or you'll make me feel woefully underdressed." Gideon climbed onto the bed, laying on his side and stretching out his legs. "Come on. Into bed with you."

His mock-gruff command got the response he was hoping for. She shook her head ruefully, a genuine smile curving her lips. Dropping the dress to the floor, she joined him on the bed. Bella smoothed her chemise to cover the long legs folded elegantly beside her and selected the smallest chicken leg from the silver bowl.

They sat in silence for a few short moments; he focused solely on her, while her attention never strayed from her plate.

"I thought you were married?" His careful tone begged to be confided in, even when it was the last thing she should do.

"I am," she said quietly, not meeting his gaze.

"How long have you been married?"

"Five years."

"But then, how could you have been . . . ?"

Ducking her chin, a wince flittered across her brow. "H-he can't. He's incapable."

How could such a beautiful, passionate young woman be married to an impotent old man? Fate could not have been crueler. He reached out, intent on lifting her chin, on not letting her hide, but stopped at the tension gripping her posture. Rigid to the point of brittleness. He should not feel this compassion, but he couldn't help himself.

Glancing down, he furrowed his brow. "Bella. The knife and fork are not necessary."

Her hands stilled over her plate.

"It's a chicken leg, designed to be picked up with your bare hand."

With a self-conscious lift of her shoulders, she set down the knife and fork and hesitantly reached for the leg on her plate, as if fearing a reprimand.

"Now take a bite. Your stomach will thank you." He took a generous bite of his own chicken leg and winked.

Her chuckle eased the rigidity of her body. She mimicked him, right down to the roguish wink. If she could laugh, then everything would be just fine between them, he assured himself.

After their picnic, he helped her to dress, deftly doing up the row of neat buttons down her back. He pulled on his shirt and waistcoat before seeing her to the door. Gideon draped the cloak about her shoulders, fastened the clasp, and pulled up the hood.

Bella smiled in thanks. "Mr. Rosedale, I would greatly enjoy your company for dinner this evening."

"It would be my pleasure."

She turned to leave.

"And Bella . . ."

She looked over her shoulder. The navy hood framed her features. Her fine eyebrows were raised in question. The crests of her high cheekbones were still flushed a faint pink from the orgasms he had given her.

"It's Gideon, if it pleases you."

She gave him a small nod and he caught a glimpse of an abashed grin before she headed out the door.

HE and Bella repeated their dinner ritual that evening, but things were more intimate than they had been on previous occasions. There was a certain softness about her, a languid ease to her movements, a look in her eyes. It was obvious to him now that next to him sat a woman secure in her sensuality, a woman without regrets, whereas two days ago he dined with an innocent.

When dinner was completed he was there to walk her to the staircase. Bella made to ascend the stairs but he stayed at the foot. She turned on the first step and looked at him askance. She was tall for a woman, about five foot eight, and the height of the step put her a hair above his six one.

"Would you care to retire to the sitting room for a glass of whisky or a cup of tea?"

The intention behind her invitation was crystal clear. But Gideon had never been with a virgin before and had decided it would be best to take the conservative approach. The last thing he wanted to do was hurt her. "Thank you, but I believe I shall retire early this evening."

She gave her head a tiny shake.

"Tomorrow," he whispered, holding her gaze. At the uncertainty flickering across her face, he added, "It's not that I don't want to. It's not that I'm unable"—he couldn't keep the smug smirk from his lips—"but you need to rest."

"No. Tonight," she replied, so softly he more read the words on her lips than heard them.

"Yes. Trust me. Tomorrow."

Mindful of the maid he spied entering the nearby drawing room, Gideon only bowed, bringing her hand up to his lips. A shiver wracked her body as he traced the lattice of light blue veins on her exposed wrist with the tip of his tongue. Then he left her on the stairs and returned to Garden House.

The next evening he accepted the invitation and ascended the stairs with her. He did not pause in the sitting room, but confidently went straight through to her bedchamber, shutting the doors and turning the locks behind him. And this time, there were no jarring surprises.

Bella was urgent, demanding, impatient, ever-greedy in her passion. Like an addict who had been denied for far too long, she couldn't seem to get enough. How she managed to go so long without a lover, to keep all of this contained beneath the usual cool exterior, was beyond his comprehension. She was a completely different woman in bed than out. And he found he liked this side of her, liked the dichotomy, and was *almost* too fond of the fact he was the only one to see her throw off the chains of propriety.

She was amazingly responsive—arching and writhing beneath him. It took hardly any effort on his part to make her come. Her orgasms were quick, many, and hard. But while Bella had enthusiasm in abundance, she was definitely lacking in patience. There was more to the act than her lying on her back, and the prospect of introducing her to the full spectrum of sensual delights was very, very appealing indeed.

The first night in her bed he acceded to her wishes for a while. Well, a long while. Then he gave her a taste of what she was missing.

When he shifted to pull out, he refused to heed her command to stay put, refused to heed the hands on his back, the long legs wrapping around his hips, and made his way down her body. He didn't stop to pay tribute to her luscious breasts, but went straight for his target. He settled his shoulders between her lean thighs and the moment his tongue touched her clit, she whimpered in comprehension.

Since he had a fair idea of how Bella's mind worked, at least in bed, the moment her little gasping moans began to crescendo, he crawled swiftly up her body and slid back into her tight heat, thrusting hard through her climax.

He gave her one more orgasm, then another, because well, she was Bella. And this time after Gideon allowed his release he did not practically jump from the bed, but remained beside her for many long moments, holding her close, before giving her one last kiss and returning to Garden House. Alone.

Nine

THE next few days passed by in a blur for Bella. The afternoons were spent taking long walks with Gideon, stopping here and there to steal kisses, and evenings . . . those were her favorite. Behind closed doors, in the sanctuary of her bedchamber, where clothes were not a requirement. Where bare skin was the preferred attire. And where Gideon took her to new heights of passion.

Instead of another walk, this afternoon she had suggested a drive. Just she and Gideon, no driver to accompany them. A quick stop in the stables was all it had taken to have a horse harnessed and put in the traces. After helping her into the carriage, Gideon had taken up the lines, driving the horse at an easy trot down the dirt lane bordered by neat lines of fences on either side.

She twisted around on the bench to look behind her. The two-wheeled gig left a small cloud of dust in its wake. She saw one of the grooms leading a black horse toward the open door of the stables, but could not make out which groom it was. Deeming them far enough down the road, she turned around and tugged on the end of the ribbon tickling her cheek, undoing the bow. After removing her bonnet, she tied the amber ribbons in a loose knot and slipped it over her arm.

She tipped up her face, savoring the sun's warmth. The Scottish spring weather was being remarkably cooperative. In fact, it had rained only once since Gideon came to Bowhill. Two days of gray clouds in the last ten. All it had taken to chase away those clouds was the loss of her innocence. The beginnings of a laugh teased her belly. If she had known that was the way to appease the sun, then perhaps she would have . . . *No*. She chuckled for being foolish enough to let the thought begin to form in her head. It could only have been him.

"Does my driving amuse?"

"No. I was just thinking." She turned slightly to Gideon. One could never find fault with his skill. He drove with the expertise of a gentleman, the leather lines held with an easy confidence in his strong hands.

He clucked and the horse obediently lengthened its stride to a smart trot. "About what, may I ask?"

She did not want to tell him the truth. Her husband, and why he had not consummated their marriage, was the last topic she wanted to discuss with Gideon. Instead, she told him what had been on her mind a few minutes ago. "I was thinking about yesterday. And the day prior. And the day before that."

"What about them prompted the chuckle?"

"You."

He slanted her a look. The sun bathed the classic angles and planes of his face. The wind ruffled his short dark hair. The teasing twist of his mouth could not hide the genuine male affront. "Me? Should I be relieved you didn't burst out in full-blown laughter?"

Bella rolled her eyes skyward. Silly man. "I wasn't laughing *at* you. It was more . . ." She shook her head, struggling for the words to describe how perfect the last few days had been. She could not remember ever being so happy, and so at peace with herself. It was as if by giving herself to him something inside had shifted, settled, finally slipping into balance. And it was not just their evenings, or instances like yesterday's stopover in the hothouse when she had not been able to wait until later. It was Gideon. "They were wonderful days, as today is sure to be."

"Such confidence. I shall have to do my best to ensure today lives up to your expectations."

"You needn't sound so grave. I'm not hard to please."

His gaze raked the length of her body. He smiled, slow and sinful. She pressed her thighs together to fight the tide of lust rising within, heating her skin. Her body half-primed, poised for arousal, whenever he was near.

He looked ahead and guided the horse around a bend in the road. "No. You are not at all hard to please."

Slow and smooth like warmed honey, his deep voice flowed down her spine. She took a quick breath and swallowed to moisten her suddenly dry mouth.

"Is my lady impatient?" His attention was on the road, yet somehow he knew without looking which direction her thoughts had turned.

"A bit," she confessed, trying to match his casual tone, but the hitch in her breath gave her away.

"Well then, I'll have to see what I can do about that. Which way? Left or right?"

Bella pulled her gaze from his handsome profile. The road forked up ahead. Open fields to either side dotted with the occasional tree. They must be well beyond the stables, for the wooden fences marking the pastures were behind them. "Left. Stay on the property. The road will take us through a small forest."

He nodded. "Good choice. Do we need to hurry?"

"Yes." The word rushed out of her mouth, the thought of having him now foremost in her mind.

"Your wish is my command." He snapped the lines and the chestnut mare broke from a trot to a ground-covering canter. "Hold on."

She grabbed the side of the carriage. She was glad she had slipped her bonnet ribbons over her arm, for at the

pace they were traveling it would have flown out of the
carriage if she had merely set it beside her. The gig clattered along the dirt road. Wind whistled past her ears. Ex-
hilaration and lust sang through her veins. She tipped her
head back and laughed, full and straight from her belly.

They hit a particularly hard bump and she grabbed his
thigh, but did not release him once she regained her balance. His legs were slightly spread, booted feet braced
against the floorboards. The muscles of his thigh were
hard beneath her hand. She adored touching him, running
her hands over the hard contours of his body, and what she
adored most of all was just a little bit higher.

A mischievous smirk curved her lips as her hand crept
up until she encountered a prominent bump under the
fawn breeches. He twitched, his already hard cock lengthening, swelling. She had taken him in her hands and into
her body many times in the last few days, yet his dimensions never ceased to amaze. And he was always so *ready*,
whenever she wanted him. The experience was novel—
having a man so willing, and able, to accede to her every
whim. She shifted closer, pressing her thigh against his,
her shoulder against his biceps, and swirled her fingertips
over the head of his cock.

"Are you trying to distract me?"

"No, I wouldn't want to do that," she said coyly, rubbing her cheek against the soft wool of his coat sleeve,
breathing in the enticing scent of him. Cloves and lemons
and fresh outdoor air. And *him*. Gasping, she closed her
eyes against a heavy flush of raw need. She rotated her
hips, seeking the friction of the cushioned bench. Her silk
shift rubbed maddeningly against her sex, teasing her innermost flesh.

"Faster?" he asked.

"Yes!"

He snapped the lines over the horse's back. The gig
lurched forward. She closed her hand around his manhood
as much as the breeches would allow, and squeezed. He
pulsed beneath her hand, solid as iron. Leaning into him,

she reached farther up his thigh, lightly grazing her nails along the thick length. She gently cupped the heavy weight of his ballocks. On a throat-scraping grunt, he flexed his hips, his long legs falling open, granting her greater access to touch, to play. A low moan escaped her lips. Just touching him, the anticipation of what was to come, had her on the brink of orgasm.

He slowed the horse's pace as the road narrowed, leading them into the forest. Tall trees blocked out the sun, cloaking them in cool dark shadows, but it did nothing to cool the blood pounding though her veins. He pulled the brake and looped the lines around the rail. "Now then, what was on your mind?"

She pulled urgently at the buttons on his falls.

"Oh. That." All casual nonchalance, he lifted one arrogant eyebrow while fevered desire rode over every inch of her skin.

"Stop teasing me, and . . . and . . ." *Fuck me.* She clenched her jaw to keep the coarse words from being uttered. Abandoning the half-opened placket of his breeches, she shook her bonnet ribbons free from her wrist and leaned full over him, grabbing his head, seeking his lips. His tongue tangled with hers, his mouth hot and delicious. She levered up onto her knees, slanted her mouth full over his and threaded her fingers into his hair, his scalp warm, the silken strands cool from the wind.

He leaned back against the bench and she moved with him, unwilling to give him up. A draught of air hit her stocking-covered legs as he gathered her skirt, bringing it up to her thighs. She quickly straddled his lap, her knees on either side of his lean hips. He had showed her this position in the hothouse yesterday afternoon. She would have never guessed her wicker settee could be put to such a scandalous use, or that the removal of clothes was not an integral component of making love. Now she knew better.

He twisted his head, breaking the contact of their lips. "Sit back," he urged, low and hoarse.

Nodding, she complied, resting her bottom on his knees.

Lifting his hips, he undid the remaining buttons on his breeches. A grimace tightened his lips as he reached inside to pull out his cock. It sprang up at attention, pointing straight to the canopy of leaves and branches overhead. A drop of fluid seeped from the small slit in the head. Her innermost muscles clenched, liquid warmth pooling between her thighs. She could almost feel him buried deep within her, stretching, filling, invading her. Her breaths coming hard and fast, she licked her lips and reached toward the object of her desire.

"Just a moment," he said, intercepting her hand and placing it on back onto her thigh.

She scowled, wanting to feel the hot silken skin, to trace the prominent vein running up to the head and marvel anew at the ironlike rigidity. But it did no good as his attention was trained on his coat as he pulled a waxed paper envelope from an inside pocket. The next instant his magnificent arousal was sheathed, a rather untidy bow tied at the substantial base.

With one hand he gathered her skirt at her waist, baring her upper thighs and her sex, and took himself in hand. She could not explain it, but the sight of his large hand on his cock was infinitely arousing, wickedly so. Long fingers wrapped fully around it, his grip sure. Eager to feel him inside of her, she braced her hands on his shoulders and lifted up onto her knees. The blunt head brushed the apex of her pleasure. Sharp sensation jolted through her body. Wincing, she flinched. Nerves coiled so tight, the light contact was almost painful.

"Sorry," he said quickly.

She shook her head. She did not want an apology, she wanted—

"*Yes.*" The word came out on a shaky moan, her insides fluttering, as he positioned himself at her core.

Biting the edge of her lip against the onslaught of undiluted pleasure, she sank slowly down. She was drenched with desire, yet still, she had to wiggle her hips and spread her thighs wider to accommodate his cock. He stretched her perfectly to her limits. Rapture flooded her brain.

A climax crashed over her, assaulting her senses, before she even took all of him. Her cry echoed off the surrounding trees.

Head thrown back, eyes closed tight, hands gripping his shoulders, she rode his cock, ravenous for more. The soft wool of his breeches gently abraded her inner thighs. Her silk-covered knees slipped a bit on the leather bench with each downward slam of her hips. It was wicked, it was scandalous, making love like this in a carriage. And it was spectacular, adding a tantalizing forbidden layer to the passion drenching her senses. No one would stumble upon them—they were on Bowhill property, and there was no reason for any of the servants to wander out here. Yet still, urgency nipped at her heels. She wanted to bare her breasts, feel his mouth, his teeth scoring her hard nipples, but there wasn't time.

Another orgasm. Then another. Hard. Fast. Sapping her strength. Hands spanning her waist, he aided her efforts when her muscles began to tire from her frenzied movements. But she did not stop.

One more. Just one more was all she needed. Head bowed, she gasped for breath. Sweat pricked between her shoulder blades.

"Bella. Come for me. *Now*," he urged.

Her head snapped up. Intent and heated, his dark eyes blazed, searing a path to her soul, sparking the orgasm hovering just out of reach. As the ecstasy claimed her, stealing the last of her strength, he thrust up on a groan, his cock pulsing within her, climaxing with her.

Bella slumped against him. Drained and satiated. Reveling in the languor relaxing every muscle in her body. Her pulse pounded thickly through her veins. Her fingers and toes tingled delightfully. She was suddenly aware of the sounds of the forest, as if a door had just opened, letting in the outdoors. A bird chirped overhead. Leaves rustled in the breeze. The harness jangled softly as the horse shifted in the traces.

"Where to now?" he asked, his breath tickling the hair on her head.

"Ummm." She smiled against his chest that rose and fell beneath her cheek. She wanted to stay here like this with him. Her arms slung around his neck. Her skirt bunched at her waist. His hands skimming up and down her back. Content and drowsy, she arched like a cat. "The lake," she mumbled. "See the swans. They're beautiful."

Levering up, she cupped his jaw and pressed a light kiss to his lips. Then she ran her fingers through his hair, carefully smoothing the sable locks that had been disheveled by her hands. She smiled, feeling like an infatuated young girl, wanting only to be with him, to savor this moment in all its perfection.

He gave her bottom a playful smack. "Up with you. The swans are waiting."

"All right," she conceded on a sigh, knowing they truly could not stay here all day.

He lifted her and settled her gently on the bench. As she straightened her skirt, he removed the French letter, tucking it back into the envelope and into his pocket. So considerate, she thought, not to toss it to the ground. Then he buttoned his breeches. Her dress was wrinkled beyond all hope from their hasty coupling, yet there was not one crease in his dark brown coat. He looked, as always, like a privileged London gentleman, the same variety she had encountered many years ago. Her lips pursed then she shrugged, practicality descending, soothing the feminine vanity that threatened to object. Her rumpled appearance would not rouse any suspicions from her servants when they arrived back at the house, at least not when paired with his.

Gideon gathered the lines and drove out of the small forest, through a wide field and stopped before the lake where three snow-white swans glided peacefully along the surface, their long necks bowed in a graceful arch, occasionally dipping their heads underwater in search of a meal. After a long walk, she and Gideon returned to the carriage and set off for the stables at a leisurely pace.

Her lust briefly appeased, she simply sat beside him and soaked up just being with him. The way his arm brushed hers as he guided the horse. The way he glanced at her every now and then, his gaze warm and filled with masculine appreciation. Living alone for so many years, she was accustomed to quiet. So one would have thought she'd have been eager to talk with another person, to fill every possible moment with words. Yet she stayed silent, lost in him.

When she had initially received Esmé's note, she had never imagined a man like Gideon would appear at her home. Well, she had never met a man of his kind before, so she honestly hadn't known what to expect. Regardless, she would have never allowed herself to hope for someone like him—a man who gave her the confidence, the courage, to simply be herself. A man who made her feel truly alive for the first time in her life. He was the ideal companion, so much so it was easy to forget Esmé had hired him.

She closed her eyes and pushed the unwelcome thought away, as she did every time the reminder tried to intrude on her happiness.

There were little pokes and nudges, of course, ever since she had muffled her conscience with her terms. Gideon never stayed the entire night in her bed, always leaving well before midnight and before any servants could wonder too long or hard over why it took so long for their mistress and her "cousin" to partake of a nightcap. But she and Esmé often talked for hours before retiring for the evening, so she did not put much worry into her servants' musings and did her best to ignore the creeping desire for Gideon to remain with her.

And they of course could not engage in any open flirtation when in view of the servants. There were no passionate kisses when he arrived at the manor house for tea or to escort her on a walk. But even though her lips tingled with the need for his whenever he was near, one could not so easily push aside a lifetime of proper English decorum. So it didn't feel out of place to have to wait until they were alone. If anything, the anticipation made his kisses sweeter.

After dinner that evening they retired to her bedchamber. Gideon had quite opened her eyes over the last few days. Quick trysts in carriages were one thing, but when they were in bed . . . *Oh*, the things he did to her. He maneuvered her, flipping and turning and arranging limbs as though she weighed nothing. The rhythm never lost, each change in position finding some new sublime spot.

But as he moved on top of her, under her, and behind her that night, the passion-soaked haze lifted just enough, like dense fog rising under the force of the morning sun, for her to realize that while she was always mindless and fully absorbed in him, he never seemed to lose control. And once she became aware of it, it stayed with her, keeping her from dropping back into the sensual fog.

The first tingle of ache pinched her wrists from the strain of holding her upper body up on all fours. The next moment, before the tingle in her wrists could turn into the slightest bite, the large hands grasping her hips shifted. One hand coasted up to splay across her chest, the other glided down to her lower belly. The thick length of his cock left her on the next stroke as he leaned full over her to nip at her shoulder, teeth grazing her skin in a playful lover's bite. Cradling her in his arms, he turned her onto her back. Her arms and legs wrapped around him in welcome when he settled between her spread thighs and braced his weight on his forearms, but her eyelids did not even flutter when he glided back into her.

It had not been quite calculated or orchestrated, but the effortless ease with which he moved, the way he always seemed to know a second before she did what she wanted, began to disturb her. It was a practiced ease, born of countless repetition, speaking much louder than words that this was his profession. While she knew men his age were rarely without experience—her own long-ago groom probably had scores of lovers before and after her—it was the knowledge Gideon got paid for this which kept her from losing herself in him. It tugged on the back of her mind, harder and harder. A mild irritant that rubbed until it became a full-blown wound, demanding the undivided force of her attention.

Closing her eyes, she tried to push it away, to ignore it. But the knot forming in her stomach refused to unravel. They were as close as a man and woman could be, yet he felt so very far away. She was strangely conscious of his every move, as if she were a mere spectator.

He must have sensed her distraction for his rhythm changed. He gave deep long thrusts, pausing at the end of each downstroke to grind his hips, rubbing his groin against her clit. It should have sparked an immediate orgasm on her part, but it did not spark anything pleasurable at all.

"Come for me." His words were a plea, whispered hotly in her ear.

He dropped his head and grazed his teeth across the hard tip of her nipple. Instead of arching beneath him, moaning her approval, coming for him, all she could think was—*Does he do that with all of them? Is he thinking about me, or is he thinking about the hundreds of pounds Esmé surely paid him?*

Her stomach dropped, like a lead weight thrown into the sea, plummeting to her feet. She needed him to stop. *Now.* Each decadent thrust drove home the fact she was just one of many, one more job, one more set of wages.

Before Gideon could claim her lips again, she pushed hard on his shoulders. Perspiration slicked the hollows behind her knees, but the velvety skin beneath her hands was warm and dry.

The word building in her throat pushed with such incredible pressure, finally working itself free. "Stop."

Lifting his head, he went still. Whisky brown eyes met hers, his lips wet from their kisses, his gaze questioning.

She swiftly broke eye contact. Without a word, he shifted off to lie on his side.

She wanted to pound on his chest, demand to know if he felt anything at all. But she could not bring herself to speak. Thick tension filled the room, constricting her throat. Her heart beat a tight, rapid rhythm against her ribs. Her gaze was fixed unseeing on the dark canopy above. She could not even look at him.

Regardless of her terms, she was nothing but a fold of pound notes in his pocket. She had been a fool. A fool to try to turn their fortnight into something it could never be. A consensual flirtation? No, he had simply been working all along. She was just another woman in a long line of many. One month from now, he likely would not be able to distinguish her from all the rest.

Her heart felt like it was trapped in a vise—crushing, twisting, wrenching in agony. Tears pricked the corners of her eyes. She swallowed hard, fighting them down.

She meant nothing to him.

The past had repeated itself.

No, it was worse than that. For this time she had given her virginity to a prostitute, and had naively fallen in love with the man.

Ten

HAD he done something wrong? Gideon wracked his brain, quickly replaying the prior few minutes. No—he had done nothing new, nothing out of the ordinary to warrant *this*.

"Bella?"

He laid a hand on her hip, a silent request for an answer. But the instant he touched her silken skin, she flinched. Startled, he removed his hand.

"Bella. What's—?"

Cutting off his words, she rolled onto her side, showing him the lean lines of her back and the rigid set of her shoulder blades. The sweet musky scent of her recently aroused body filled his every breath, a primitive mating signal his body refused to ignore. He clenched his jaw, his ballocks aching with the need to come. Starting and not finishing was never a pleasant experience, but tonight . . .

Mentally floundering, he groped for anything to explain her odd behavior.

"Do you feel anything for me at all?" Bella asked, in the barest of whispers.

Fuck.

The breath whooshed out of him. His erection withered to embarrassing proportions.

He knew exactly why she had told him to stop. He opened his mouth, knowing she needed him to reply now and not hesitate. Yet the reassuring words refused to flow smoothly off his tongue. "Of-of course, I-I—"

"Stop. Please." The tremble in her quiet voice cut right through him.

He wanted to take her in his arms, to kiss her lush mouth until she went lax with passion, to tell her . . . Hell, he didn't know what to tell her to make it better.

Women were so very different than men. He had seen countless men walk into Rubicon's, selecting a different beauty on each visit. The only differences in their appearances when they left were slightly rumpled clothes and a sated, smug expression. But women . . . he had lived with enough as a boy to know how easily the inexperienced could confuse physical acts with true intimacy.

No matter his client, they were still women and he never wanted to cause them pain, in any form. As such, he long ago learned how to keep his appointments on a strictly physical level. Any conversations were kept on the surface. Any time he felt one of them begin to soften, he took a step back, creating the necessary distance.

He had done his best over the last few days. Kept his guard up and tried to keep her focused on the pleasures he offered. But it had obviously all been in vain, and well, one could not get more inexperienced than a virgin. Christ, she had even chosen to give her innocence to him. At the time, it had been a question he did not want answered. Yet now, the answer lay right next to him. Still, quiet once again, and clearly in pain.

Oh, Bella. Gideon took a deep breath, expanding his chest that felt unnaturally constricted.

There truly was nothing to be done for it, and he could not stay in her bed when she no longer wanted him.

He let out a shoulder-slumping sigh and swung his feet

over the edge of the bed. After quickly gathering his clothes and boots from the floor, he made to leave the room. Hand on the brass knob, he glanced over his shoulder.

Please, please look at me.

The moonlight caressed the gently rounded curves of her backside and the graceful length of her legs. Her long tresses were fanned behind her and shone silvery white against the tousled sheets.

But he did not stay. He could not, should not stay.

He went into the sitting room and closed the door to Bella's bedchamber behind him. The soft click reverberated with a heavy finality. As he pulled on his clothes in the near-dark room, he told himself it was better this way. Better she remembered their respective roles. Better she remember now who and what he was before the lines that needed to remain clear and unmarred became too tangled to separate. She was still new to this concept. She needed to harden her heart. Remember he was not a man she should lose herself to.

Gideon sat in a chair by the window to pull on his boots, then buttoned his coat and left the room. He walked down the empty hall, down the stairs, out the front door and back to Garden House. Alone. Not bothering to light a candle, he went to the back bedchamber, stripped off his just-donned clothes, and laid on the bed.

When the first rays of dawn lit the white curtain on the bedroom widow, he gave up sleep as a lost cause. After a quick shave, he dressed, packed his trunk, and sat in an armchair in the front parlor. And waited.

He had a strong feeling a carriage would show up at the door to take him back to London. But he did not want that carriage to appear. They still had four more days left. He wanted Bella to knock on the door, but he knew she would not.

She had never been comfortable with his reason for being here. If nothing else, her terms screamed loud and clear she was not the type of woman who indulged herself with someone of his ilk. There were those who could and those who could not, and Bella was in the latter group. She had not even written to Rubicon herself but sent another in her stead.

As Gideon waited, as the rising sun filled the small parlor with bright golden light, he told himself firmly it should not matter if she sent him home now. He shouldn't worry about it, or dwell on it, or even let it pass through his head. The only thing that should matter was he would still get paid in full, and therefore Rubicon would not get pissed if word reached her ears he returned early. And, he reasoned, he would have a few more days to relax before his next appointment.

The thought of "that" did not sit well, so he very quickly pushed it from his mind. Resting his elbows on his knees, he hung his head in his hands and instead did his best to not think of anything, especially not the long-limbed ethereal beauty who was most likely, at this very moment, requesting a carriage to be readied for London.

THE blue or the rose, m'lady?"

Bella was aware of her maid speaking behind her, but Maisie's words were not significant enough to stand out amongst the clutter already filling her mind.

"Or perhaps the emerald cambric?"

What must he think of me? She closed her eyes, blocking out the view beyond her bedchamber window, but could not block out the crisp clear light of the morning sun. It bathed her closed eyelids in a warm deep orange glow, mocking her, taunting her, reminding her anew she could not escape her actions. It was morning, and with it had come the crushing weight of humiliation. She could not believe she had done *that* last night. On a wince, she rolled one shoulder. The pop and creak of her joints seemed unnaturally loud.

"No? Perhaps the amber muslin? Though it may be a

bit light for spring. Are you planning a walk with Mr.
Rosedale today? You'll need a shawl. The light blue cashmere would do nicely."

What must he think of me? Those words kept bouncing off her skull, refusing to leave. The very concept of
Gideon negated a faithful relationship, or a relationship of
any kind. And he was free to leave whenever he chose. He
did not have to be intimate with her. He could have left
after their first dinner. Yes, he got paid for this. Yes, she
knew this, had known it all along. Had convinced herself
a week ago she understood the terms of their flirtation.
That she could treat it as a practical arrangement. Yet she
had acted the part of a novice last night. A foolish young
girl, shocked out of her wits when she had finally seen her
starry-eyed fantasy for what it was.

"M'lady? Lady Stirling?"

"What do you want, Maisie?" Sharp and quick, the
words rebounded off the window before her.

"I-I . . . Which day dress do you prefer, m'lady?"

Bella took a deep breath and forced her fingers to unclench from the drapes, the damask wrinkled and dampened
from her anxious hand. She should not take her frustration
out on her maid. The girl sounded downright cowed, her
voice a tiny little squeak. Maisie was an ally of sorts, and
Bella did not want to turn the maid against her. Ever since
she began bringing Gideon to her room, Maisie had conveniently stopped tending to her in the evenings. The fire
lit, the drapes drawn, the coverlet pulled back, but Maisie
absent by the time they reached the bedchamber.

She took another deep breath, pulled her dressing
gown tighter around her body, and turned from the window, the calm façade back in place. "The Prussian blue
will do fine."

Standing beside the open door to Bella's dressing
room, Maisie wrung her hands, her blue green eyes huge
in her pale face. "Would you care for some tea? I can ring
for a tray."

"No, and alert the kitchen that I will not be down for breakfast." There was no way her stomach could tolerate food this morning.

Maisie nodded, disappeared into the dressing room, and reappeared a moment later with the chosen dress in her arms. Chemise, stays, and stockings were already folded over the back of the Egyptian armchair.

Neither said a word as the girl helped her to dress and pin back her hair. Bella simply went through the motions, standing, turning, and sitting as required.

"Is there anything else I can do for you?"

She looked into the oval mirror above the vanity. The maid's ginger eyebrows were lowered with obvious concern. Bella opened her mouth then closed it, shying away from the request. It would be horribly awkward to have one of the servants report back that Mr. Rosedale was no longer at Garden House. She would have to determine that information for herself. "No. There is nothing else."

Maisie nodded. Her mouth thinned into a determined line. "Shall I order the kitchen to burn his breakfast?"

It took Bella a moment to realize what the girl was asking. "No," she replied with a poor attempt at a chuckle. "If there are any sausages to be burned, they should be my own." She tipped her head, excusing her maid before the girl could ask the imminent question twisting her young face.

As soon as the door closed, Bella went back to the window. The sun shined brightly, her roses soaking up its nourishing rays. The overabundance of pleasant days would coax buds to form earlier than usual. Her gaze strayed to the view she could not ignore. The leaves on the trees surrounding Garden House swayed in the breeze. The small stone cottage looked so very idyllic, as if it had been taken straight out of a fairy tale.

If that was not ironic, she did not know what was.

Closing her eyes, she pressed her fingertips to her temples. Their fortnight could not end so soon, could not end this way. Fully aware she had fallen in love with him regardless of his profession, she decided it could not get much worse. When he left she would be alone again, and she would rather have him for a few more days than not at all. The prospect of going this one day without seeing him, of allowing the sun to set without feeling the brush of his lips against hers, was unbearable. And almost frightening.

Turning from the window, she left her bedchamber and set out to walk in the garden with the express purpose of wandering upon Garden House. After stalling in the rose garden for a good half hour, she finally worked up the courage to knock on the door.

The first thing she noticed when Gideon opened the door was that he was fully dressed in a dark blue coat and cream silk waistcoat, complete with leather gloves and a black top hat held loosely in one hand. The next thing she noticed was that he looked tired, as if he had not slept well last night.

"Good morning, Mr. Rosedale. Would you care to take a turn about the garden?"

His tight nod left her with the impression he had been expecting someone else, or some other question.

He hung the hat on one of the pegs lining the wall by the door and stepped from the house. She laid her hand lightly on his proffered arm. Ever the gentleman, he swung open the gate of the white picket fence surrounding the cottage and gave her a slight bow as she passed. They walked side by side along the path winding through the garden. The air was thick with the scent of spring. Their usual companionable silence stretched tight. There was a tangible distance between them. She no longer felt free to reach for his hand or lift onto her toes and capture his lips with hers.

The need to say something, anything to breech the distance, pressed in on her. She wanted, *needed* everything to go back to the way it had been before she had gone and acted the novice.

She chanced a glance at his profile. *Oh,* he was so

handsome it almost hurt her eyes. His dark hair was much shorter than fashion dictated, just a tad from being so short it was cropped, with just enough left on the ends to give it some movement in the late morning breeze. If his hair were longer it would have distracted from his features. As it was the shortness drew her eye to the perfect symmetry of his face—the defined jaw, the straight nose, the smooth contours of his cheekbones, and the dark eyebrows which were currently the tiniest bit pinched. She doubted he spent much time under the sun, so the warm honey tone of his skin must be natural. Plus, she had the distinct pleasure of seeing him completely bare and knew every muscular inch of him bore the same smooth, honey-kissed skin.

He must have felt her regard for he glanced to her. She should say it now before she lost the nerve.

"My apologies."

He slowed to a stop. "For what?"

She stopped and shrugged uncomfortably, feeling like a child who didn't want to confess to her crime. "For last night."

The slight pinch between his dark eyebrows strengthened. "You don't need to apologize, Bella."

"Yes, I do. It was not well done of me." Clasping her hands in front of her, she twisted and untwisted her fingers together. "I behaved like a . . . a . . ." *Fool. An inexperienced fool.* "I don't know what came over me." That wasn't quite the truth. She knew exactly what came over her, but there was no way she could admit she had fallen in love with him.

He covered her hands with his, stilling her nervous motions. "It's quite all right. There's no reason to fret. Don't think on it a moment longer."

His words were calm and reassuring, yet his eyes held such uncertainty. She glanced to their hands, his covered in soft black leather. He had answered the door with his gloves on and hat in hand. Had he intended to leave? Did he still intend to leave? Did he believe she wanted him to leave?

Oh, Lord, no. If he believed that, then she needed to rectify his misconception straight away.

She took a deep breath, gathering the words. "I would very much enjoy your company for dinner this evening, Mr. Rosedale."

The pinch between his eyebrows immediately disappeared and a charming, almost relieved smile stole across his mouth. "It would be my pleasure. But . . ."

Bracing herself for the worst, she looked at him askance.

"Only if you call me Gideon."

A surge of giddy happiness tingled through her body. Chin tipping down on a nod, Bella gave him an abashed grin, fully relieved she had not done something irreparable last night. "Dinner will be at six, Gideon. If you will excuse me, I must see to the arrangements."

She turned to leave but he held her back with a hand on her wrist. A gentle tug brought her around. Before she knew it, his lips were on hers, his silken tongue sweeping into her mouth, tangling boldly with hers.

For the first time the kiss was completely unexpected and she sensed in it a quality she had never felt from him before. But before she could identify it he took a step back, leaving her dazed. Her hand fluttered up to her mouth, fingertips brushing her lips, as if touching could somehow reveal the answer.

"I shall be counting the hours, my lady." He executed a short bow and strode back to Garden House.

Dinner that evening was a pleasant affair. The distance from the morning was gone, but neither was the comfortable ease they once had shared present. She felt as though Gideon was watching her more closely than usual, gauging her, assessing her. He did not seem quite as sure of himself as he had been in the past.

So when dinner was completed and he led her to the foot of the stairs, she took his hand in hers and led him up to her bedchamber.

And like that, everything went back to the way it once had been.

W HY did it have to rain today, of all days? A steady hum tapped against the tall arched windows of the formal drawing room. Scowling, Gideon glanced out a window. Rain blurred the view of the grounds on the side of the house. "A walk is out of the question, unless you'd like to get wet."

"No. I don't have a pressing desire to get drenched today. Perhaps tomorrow." Her expression one of patent aristocratic hauteur, Bella brought her teacup to her lips.

He chuckled, amused as always by her dry wit. "We could take a closed carriage and tour the countryside."

"No. Then the driver would get drenched."

"Such consideration."

"I try." Seated on the settee, she leaned forward to place her teacup on the short table before them. He took the opportunity to admire the low neckline of her bodice.

"*Hmm*," he mulled, forcing his mind from her luscious breasts and back to the topic at hand. How to fill the remainder of their last afternoon together? He did not want to waste it, as he'd be leaving on the morrow. He scratched his jaw. There was the obvious answer, but—

"What would you like to do, Gideon?"

He went utterly still. Had he ever heard that question before? *No.* None of them had cared to ask. But Bella had.

"Gideon?"

He gave his head a short shake and met her inquiring gaze.

"What would you like to do?" she repeated slowly, as if speaking to a young child.

"*Ahh . . .*" The prospect of so many options was intimidating, to the point where he did not know how to choose. Maybe he could get her to help by narrowing them down. "Do you have a particular preference I should be aware of?"

"No." She clasped her hands on her lap and raised her eyebrows, expectant and willing to accede to *his* every whim.

He shifted in the chair, completely tongue-tied, and he had done nothing today to tire that particular muscle, at least not yet. Desperate, he searched her face for some hint of a leading question or of an ulterior motive for putting him so bluntly on the spot, but found only a small smile curving her lips.

She was the most beautiful woman he had ever met.

"I want to sketch you."

The way the words popped out of his mouth startled him. They rang in his ears as if not his own. And once out, he could not take them back.

"You're an artist?"

"No, no. Not at all."

She cocked her head, furrowing her brow.

"We don't have to if you don't want to. We can do anything you want. Anything." Was she disappointed because he had suggested something so benign? Had she expected him to suggest an afternoon tryst? Women always liked to hear that they were wanted.

"No. I want to be your model. I'm interested to see how you'd draw me."

"Well, don't expect a masterpiece. I'm not very good," he mumbled. He leaned forward to caress her knee through her skirt and lowered his voice, needing to test the sincerity of her response. "There are other things I'm much better at."

Her breath hitched, just as he knew it would. He ignored the rising disappointment, the sinking sense of misplaced hope, and gave her a slow sinful smile.

She swatted off his hand creeping up her thigh. "You aren't getting out of it that easily. Come along." She rose to her feet. "We'll need to go to my sitting room."

In a *swish* of turquoise silk, she turned and walked from the room.

BENT over at the waist, Bella searched her desk drawer. Was he coming or not? At the sound of approaching footsteps in the hall, she smiled. She knew the moment he entered the room. The air changed, charged with his presence.

"I see you remembered where my sitting room is located." She did not wait for Gideon to respond. "Pencil or pen? Sorry, I don't have any charcoals. Watercolors are the preferred medium for ladies, but you said sketch, not paint."

"Never used charcoals. Never had 'em."

She glanced over her shoulder. Hands clasped behind his back, face absolutely without expression, he stood just inside the room, the door still open. It had been his idea, so why did he look like he was waiting for a dressing-down from his father? Well, as she had told him already, he was not getting out of it. She had grabbed hold the moment he offered up the suggestion and was not about to let go.

"Pencil or pen?" she asked again.

"A pencil will do."

With a nod she glanced back down and found a pencil mixed in with her letters at the back of the drawer. Shutting the drawer, she placed the pencil on the desk atop two sheets of white paper. "Here, or would you prefer to go back to the drawing room?"

He glanced about the room, as if just realizing where he was. "Here is fine."

"Where do you want me?"

He glanced about the room again. "The settee."

"Shall I sit? What do you want me to do?" This was getting ridiculous. Almost comical. But she was not as adept as him at making one feel comfortable. If they went on like this much longer, then she would be placing the pencil in his hand and asking him if he wanted to draw a line or a circle.

"What would you normally do if you were just sitting here?"

Asking a question was a start in the right direction. "Usually I embroider."

The edges of his lips quirked. "The roses are yours. The pillowcase on my bed, the towel on the washstand, and the one in the basket that carries my breakfast. They are all adorned with embroidered roses."

She smiled self-consciously. "One must pass the evening hours."

"I like the ones on the pillowcase in particular. They look like the roses in your hothouse. Chinas." He shut the door and stepped further into the room, his strides comfortable and easy. "Gather your things and have a seat on the settee."

"All right." She went into her bedchamber and collected her embroidery hoop and tin of thread. When she returned she found him settled on the chintz chair opposite the lime green settee, pencil in hand, one leg crossed, booted ankle resting on his knee to prop up a thick volume upon which laid a sheet of paper.

Bella sat and arranged her skirts to drape neatly over her legs. She folded her hands over the hoop on her lap. "How should I sit?"

Mouth pursed, Gideon contemplated her. She resisted the urge to fidget under his intense scrutiny.

He stood and set down the book and pencil. He pulled a few blonde hairs from their pins, his fingers brushing her ear. Gooseflesh rose on her arms. "You were too perfect."

His low words made her breath catch. She fought back the lust that threatened to spark just minutes ago in the drawing room. He was doing it on purpose again, she was certain of it. "Is there such a thing as too perfect?" she asked, raising one eyebrow in defiance.

He held her gaze. He seemed even taller, standing while she sat with her head tipped slightly back. Yet, as always with him, she did not feel even a brush of intimidation.

"Yes. But in art, you do not want perfect." With that very artistlike response, he settled back in the chair.

"What should I do?"

"Embroider."

"But how can you sketch if I'm moving?"

"Don't worry. I have the image in my head. Just do what you normally would. Pretend I'm not here."

That was impossible. There was no way she could block him from her mind. His broad shoulders overpowered the feminine armchair, just as his presence overpowered her. But doing her best to heed his request, she picked up the hoop, removed the needle that had been tucked into the stretched linen, and resumed work on the partially embroidered pink rose.

The soft scratch of pencil on paper lulled her senses. Her fingers worked, pushing the needle through the linen and drawing the thread taut before placing the next stitch, while her mind wandered.

When she had awoken this morning, she had initially cursed the rain, wanting to spend their last afternoon together walking through the rose garden. She wanted to absorb every minute with him, not let any moment go wasted, and feared he would return to Garden House after their tea. Thus, she jumped at his request to sketch her. A request she had not expected from him. She should have, though. He certainly possessed the hands of an artist—long-fingered, strong yet elegant, nimble and wonderfully deft.

Their fortnight had slipped by too quickly, passing in a whirl of blazing passion and comfortable companionship. Why couldn't those days have been like all the others in the last five years? Stretching infinitely long. Seconds feeling like minutes. Minutes like hours. She should have stopped and savored them. But they were gone, and now all she could do was soak up their remaining hours, commit them to memory, and never let them fade.

She glanced up to find him studying her. His legs were stretched out before him, the book on his lap, elbows resting casually on the arms of the chair, the pencil held loosely in his long fingers. "Are you done?"

He flashed her a grin. "That's not a question a man likes to hear from a woman's lips. But yes, I'm done."

"So soon?" Five minutes could not have passed. She was sure of it.

He chuckled, a low rumble she felt in her bones. "Again, not a question a man wants to ever hear. But in my defense, I took at least twenty minutes. And yes, I'm done."

Suddenly impatient, she dropped the hoop on the settee. "I want to see it."

When she stood, he tipped the book up, shielding his work.

"Please. Show me."

"I warned you once. I'm not very good. Haven't sketched in ages. It was more of a childhood hobby than anything."

Poor man, he looked so very uncertain. She wanted to reassure him, to tell him she was certain it was wonderful. But she sensed in the tight line of his broad shoulders that such a straightforward approach would not be welcome. Instead she feathered her fingertips over his lips trying to erase the mulish frown. "Please."

His gaze testing, he glared up at her. Bella waited, hoping she had earned at least a bit of his trust at some point over the last thirteen days. At that moment, it was more important to her than anything that he trust her enough to show her the picture, to share something more of himself than his body and his conversation skills.

His broad chest rose and fell on a deep breath. He let the book fall onto his lap.

She did not know what she had expected, but the sketch took her breath away, his raw talent evident by the sweeping, purposeful lines. He had drawn her not seated in the sitting room, but in the garden on one of the weathered benches that lined the center. The bushes behind her were dotted with roses in full bloom. Her expression serene, yet the look in her eyes was one of burgeoning passion. She could imagine herself there in his picture. It was exactly how she would look if he was walking toward her.

"It's . . . it's . . . remarkable."

A faint blush stained the crests of his cheekbones. Her heart swelled, seeming to fill her entire being. She blinked, trying to keep the tears pricking her eyes from falling.

"Dinner tonight?" he asked.

"Pardon?"

"Am I to be your guest?" He looked up at her inquiringly. Every trace of discomposure, of self-consciousness, gone.

"Oh, yes." Bella shook her head, rattled more by his abrupt change in demeanor than by the change of topic. "Six. As usual."

"Well then, I shall leave you to dress." He stood, tipped his head, and strode from the room.

She bent to pick up the book, intending to place it back on the bookshelf beside her desk. She frowned. The sketch was gone. He must have taken it with him.

Even though she had wanted to keep it, she smiled, very willing to relinquish her claim on it to the artist himself.

THE fire in the hearth had burned down to embers. A single candle on the bedside table was all that lit the room. Deep shadows obscured everything beyond her fourposter bed, cloaking her and Gideon in a world she did not want to leave.

Impatient lust sated, Bella could simply luxuriate in being with him, spooned together, her back pressed against the hard wall of his chest. One arm draped over her waist, he held her close. Her hand rested over his, their fingers lightly intertwined. The tips of her toes grazed his calves. Wrapped in velvety warm comfort, she let out a small sigh, wanting to remain in his embrace forever.

He slipped his hand out from under hers to slowly caress her thigh. The strong body behind her shifted to move in for the final kiss he would lay on her exposed neck.

Trepidation shortened her breaths. She stiffened. The moment had arrived. The moment when he left her bed. Maybe it was because he would be leaving on the morrow, but tonight, more than any night, she wanted him to stay. And tonight, she found the courage to say the word.

"Stay."

Gideon pressed his lips to her neck, his answer in the infinitesimal shake of his head.

She persisted. "Stay."

"No." The word was the faintest of whispers, more breath than sound.

Reaching out a hand, she turned to face him. "Yes. Stay."

He pulled back. Not enough to be out of reach, but enough for her hand to drop to the rumpled sheet. "I cannot."

His response gave her pause. She pushed up onto a straight arm and tilted her head. "Cannot or will not?" There was a critical difference. "Cannot" implied forces beyond his control. "Will not" meant he was choosing to leave her.

He levered up onto an elbow. "Bella. Don't."

"Yes. Stay."

"You don't know what you're asking."

The frustrated edge tightening his words doused the last lingering bit of postorgasmic languor infusing her limbs. "Yes, I do. I want you to stay. Don't leave."

Regret flashed briefly across his face before hardening with conviction. "I must."

"Why? I want you to stay, Gideon," she pleaded, sounding like the most desperate of women to her own ears. The need for him to remain with her wiped away every worry she ever had about his profession and his visit. Stirling and Phillip no longer mattered. They no longer occupied even a tiny space in her mind. All that mattered was to convince Gideon to stay.

His brow furrowed. Whisky brown eyes sharpened. "For how long, Bella?"

She swallowed hard. "You don't need to leave. Remain

with me." *I love you. Don't leave.* Somehow she kept the
full truth from tumbling from her lips.

"What do you plan to do when your husband returns?
Shall I hide in Garden House and sneak up to your bedchamber at night? Will you keep me like one of your
horses, just waiting to be trotted out of the stables whenever you deign to take me for a ride?"

"No!" she said, shocked he would think such a thing.

"Then what are you asking?"

"I want you to stay with me. You don't need to leave."
She didn't want to think about the consequences. She just
needed him to stay.

"I. Must."

She sensed she was within a word's space of discovering the limit of his patience. His unyielding stance hit like
a mighty hammer to her fragile heart. "Don't you want to
stay?" She gasped, left breathless from voicing the question.

The look he gave her clearly said she did not understand. The patronizing edge unleashed her anger. Hot and
swift, it rushed unchecked through her veins, mixing violently with the desolation, turning her into someone she
did not recognize. "You're leaving me for someone else,
aren't you? You can't stay because you have some other
woman's bed to crawl into."

A muscle ticked along his clenched jaw. "Bella, don't."

"That's it, isn't it?"

"Bella." His tone was low, a warning to stop.

But she couldn't. She knew she was getting hysterical,
but she could not stop herself. Shaking with uncontrolla-
ble jealousy, she sat up and glared at him. "Who is she?"

Sitting up, he swung his legs over the edge of the bed.

"What will it take, Gideon? What will it take for you to
choose me over her? Name your price," she demanded
to the tight lines of his sculpted back.

There was a short, tense, thick pause, filled only by the
soft thump of one of the burnt logs shifting in the fireplace.

He bowed his head, exposing the taut tendons of his

neck. His fists clenched into the rumpled sheet. "Goddamn you, Bella."

The tone of the softly spoken curse startled her. The anger was easily detected, but beneath it she sensed genuine hurt. "Gideon?"

She reached out to the hard bulk of his bicep. The tips of her fingers grazed silken skin.

He strode swiftly across the room, his clothes and boots in hand.

Oh, dear Lord, what have I done? She scrambled to the edge of the bed. "Gideon, wait!"

He did not pause, but continued out.

The sharp slam of the door shattered what was left of her heart.

Eleven

DONNING his clothes quickly was a skill Gideon had mastered long ago, but tonight he did it in an exceptionally short amount of time.

She should count herself fortunate I even dressed. He pulled the door shut. The slam echoed in the empty corridor. It was tempting indeed to stalk out of the house naked as the day he was born. There was an unholy need burning in the pit of his stomach to flaunt the truth behind his stay at Bowhill. Yet through sheer ingrained habit, he had found himself tugging on his trousers. From there, it had been only a matter of seconds to throw on the remainder of his clothes.

His strides harsh, he descended the stairs. His hands shook with barely suppressed anger as he tied his cravat in a poor excuse for a knot.

Didn't she understand? Even if they did not have a husband, even if they were widows, he never spent the entire night in their bed and *never* slept beside them. It would be too much intimacy. They would be too easily confused.

He gave a snort of derision. Like sleeping beside Bella

would have made matters any worse. That she had asked him to stay screamed loud and clear she did not understand the basic rules of their liaison. No sleeping together, no personal conversations, French letters were not an option but a requirement, and the length of the appointment was decided in advance. They were the rules, damn it, and they had to be preserved. Could not be broken, not for anyone.

And he could not believe she had stooped that low. To throw money at him, as if it alone could buy his complete submission. *Damn her!*

At the distant sound of footfalls mingling with his own on the marble floor of the entrance hall, Gideon glanced over his shoulder. A tall, sturdy woman clad entirely in black walked down the hall leading to the back of the house. He turned on his heel. "Mrs. Cooley."

Bella's housekeeper stopped and turned. Her eyes flared, obviously shocked at his state of undress. He had made it down the stairs before he could attack the buttons on his waistcoat and coat. Her mouth thinned.

Servants never failed to pass up an opportunity to let him know, no matter how subtle or obvious, what they truly thought of him when their mistress was out of sight. He believed himself long immune. Yet the condescension on her face, the sneer of distaste twisting her mouth, cut sharper and deeper than a decade ago when a butler had shown him into a lady's home for his first appointment outside of Rubicon's brothel.

She could not know for certain he was a prostitute, and likely only assumed he was a gentleman, an acquaintance of some sort of her ladyship's. The "cousin" ruse was now totally up. Yet it was enough that *he* knew the truth. He wished he had taken the time to put himself together before leaving the sitting room. He was acutely aware that his hair was likely standing on end, disheveled by Bella's greedy fingers.

Gideon shoved aside the impulse to offer up an excuse

for his hasty appearance and called upon the anger still pounding hard and fast through his veins, directing it at this haughty servant. "Have a carriage readied for London and sent to Garden House. Immediately."

She glared at him. Then she nodded once, curt and short.

He yanked open the door. But instead of walking out, he paused to glance over his shoulder, up the stairs, toward Bella's bedchamber. And the anger vanished. Gone. Leaving only . . .

He winced against the unidentifiable force gnawing at his chest.

It was over. This appointment was done. And his parting words assured she would never seek him out again.

His shoulders slumped as he let out a heavy exhale. Closing the front door carefully, he left Bella's house.

THE news her traveling carriage had returned from London jolted Bella from the painful indecision that gripped her for the past week. After turning the lock on her sitting room door, she sat at her writing desk, pulled out two sheets of crisp white paper, dipped her pen in the inkwell, and began writing. The first letter was easy—it contained a thank-you to Esmé.

The second letter was more difficult.

With the black tip of her pen poised half an inch from the unmarred white paper, she sat still as a statue for half an hour before writing out the three-line missive. Then she folded Esmé's note and tucked it away at the back of a drawer. The second letter was folded as well, but left just inside the drawer, for it was not ready to be sent yet.

Focusing on her goal, she went down to the first floor. She wrinkled her nose at the musky scent as she entered the study. The room was rarely used, and when inhabited, it was usually by Bowhill's secretary, Mr. Leighton. As she locked the door, she shook her head at the papers and account ledgers littering the surface of the large walnut desk. Mr. Leighton's previous piques of temper over any attempts at organization had prompted the servants to leave this room off their regular cleaning schedule. Bella had witnessed the man's last fit and had had to fight back the laughter that had threatened at the sight of the short, rotund older man, gesturing wildly, huffing in indignation, and mumbling under his breath about how he would never find what he needed in the recently tidied stacks of paper.

Stepping through the narrow beams of sunlight streaming through the breaks in the closed curtains, Bella crossed the room and rounded the desk. Purposefully averting her gaze from the portrait, she tugged on the corner of the heavy gilt frame. The portrait swung on its concealed hinges, revealing a small steel door. After unlocking the door, she opened it. Various documents, some rolled up and others in neat stacks, filled the majority of the space. Careful not to disturb the loaded dueling pistol at the back of the safe, she pushed aside the documents and after many long minutes of debate, counted out a large stack of pound notes.

Her quarry in hand, she shut the door and swung the portrait back against the wall, hiding the safe. She grabbed a blank sheet of paper from the disorder on the desk and wrapped it around the pound notes. She made to leave the study, but a prickle on the back of her neck turned her around when she was only halfway to the door.

A middle-aged man with dark blue eyes stared back at her from the portrait. His auburn hair was combed back, revealing features that could shift from passably handsome to downright ugly in a heartbeat. He was seated in a leather armchair, yet the sheer breadth of his shoulders told one he possessed the substantial frame of a pugilist.

Her pulse quickened, short beats filling her ears. Her breaths turned shallow, little pulls that did not quite reach her lungs. He was not even here, and she was infinitely thankful for that, yet just looking at him had the most disturbing effect on her. She swore he had the portrait hung over the wall safe deliberately—a constant reminder of whose money lay beyond the steel door. He had never specifically forbid her anything. Setting rules, expectations, was a kindness he did not bestow upon her. But she knew. Knew without a glimmer of uncertainty if he ever learned of what she planned to do, never mind what she had already done, his reaction would be most unpleasant indeed.

Paper crinkled as she tightened her grip on the stack of pound notes, drawing strength from the proof of her defiance. She met the dark blue stare, her gaze now hard and steady.

"I hate you," she whispered, her mouth twisting with the need to shout, to scream, to unleash all the pent-up hate she had forced herself not to acknowledge for so long.

She turned on her heel, dismissing her husband in a way she would never dare to do in his presence, and marched out of the study. She passed her housekeeper in the entrance hall.

"Mrs. Cooley, send Seamus to my sitting room," Bella said as she ascended the stairs.

A burly young man with a forever-untidy shock of red hair appeared in her sitting room minutes later.

"Yes, your ladyship?"

"I need you to take the traveling coach and return to London, to where Madame Marceau located Mr. Rosedale." She held out her carefully written letter made thick by the pound notes enclosed within. "Give this to the proprietor, await a response, and return with Mr. Rosedale posthaste."

"Yes, your ladyship."

To Bella's great relief, Seamus did not question her, nor did he hesitate to take the letter. The rebellion that had seized hold in the study, gifting her with the strength she needed to see this task through, started to wane, and it took considerable effort to keep her composure in place.

Seamus tipped his head and left the room.

Then she waited two very long weeks.

Iᴛ was midafternoon when Gideon entered his employer's office, his mood already soured from having been
summoned by one of her minions.

"Do come in and have a seat, Mr. Rosedale," Rubicon
purred. She waved a hand to one of the scarlet leather
chairs facing her desk.

His senses sharpened. She never called him Mr. Rosedale. It was usually *Rosedale* or *Gideon*, depending on her
mood, and *Mr. Gideon Rosedale* when she was flaunting
him in front of clients. His only greeting was a tip of his
head before settling in the chair.

She appraised him for a long moment, the look shrewd
and cunning. A look that made his skin crawl. "You have
quite the admirer, Mr. Rosedale."

His face purposefully blank, he said nothing.

"Pack your trunk."

"Excuse me?"

"You have an appointment and, judging by the driver
who delivered the *request*, you are headed back to Scotland."

She waved a sheet of folded white paper. He leaned forward and snatched it from her. The sight of the flowing
feminine script made his heart leap. Then he read the words.

> *Mr. Rosedale's company is requested for the space
> of a fortnight. Inform the driver when Mr. Rosedale
> will be available to depart. If the enclosed is not
> sufficient, send word back with the driver.*

He swore he felt something inside of him rip in two.
"How much?" he asked, hating the hollow tone.

A slow, satisfied smile spread across Rubicon's rouged
lips. "I do so love how you leave them wanting more. But
really, Mr. Rosedale, you haven't even been gone three
weeks."

"How much?" He balled his hand into a fist, the crisp edges of the paper scoring his palm.

"It makes me wonder if I should raise your price. I hope I haven't been giving you away all these years."

His tolerance of her constant games was running extremely thin. "How much?" he said through clenched teeth.

She tossed a thick envelope across the desk. "That's for you."

Gideon quickly looked inside. Rubicon took half off the top, but what was in that envelope . . .

He tossed it back with a sharp snap of the wrist. "Send someone else. I already have arrangements and they can't be broken."

"Not to worry. I've already broken them for you. Markus is, at this moment, traveling to Devon to give her ladyship your regrets."

"What?" The word snapped out of his mouth on an affronted bark. How dare she rearrange his schedule without his consent? And how the hell had she known where he was headed?

"You can see her some other time as you will be in Scotland until the end of the month."

"No."

Her eyes narrowed to thin slits. Her face hardened, revealing the lines around her mouth and on her forehead she tried so hard to conceal with artfully applied makeup. "Yes. Go pack. You are leaving today. The carriage is waiting to depart posthaste." The teasing, toying lilt was gone. The words held an edge sharpened with unyielding command.

The game had ended and he had not come out the victor. A low, defensive growl shook his throat. He snatched the envelope off Rubicon's desk and stalked from the room.

"Oh, and Mr. Rosedale, do be so kind as to leave her wanting more again," she called to his retreating back, a noticeable chuckle of triumph in her voice.

THE light scratch of a knife and the soft click of a fork against porcelain were the only sounds that broke the silence. *Is he still upset with me?* Bella brought the glass of wine to her lips. Should she have waited longer to have Gideon return?

No. She had needed to see him, needed to be with him again. The prior four weeks had passed by slower than the previous five years. The stark contrast of her life without him had physically hurt. And the way he had left, the things she had said. Mrs. Cooley reported he had left that night, not even waiting until morning. He had not been able to get away from her fast enough.

But he had come back, so he could not be too displeased with her. Still, he was much more distant than he had been at previous dinners. His eyes had only met hers a handful of times and his conversation was so stilted and impersonal she had given up any attempts before they walked into the dining room. He gave the distinct impression of a man going through the motions. The warmth that had once radiated from him was frighteningly gone.

She needed to talk with him, apologize, assure him she would never make such demands again. That she understood she should not make such demands. But even though silence reigned, his impassive face did not give her the opening she so desperately needed.

The neat slices of roasted pheasant on her plate looked divine, but the tension knotting her stomach made it impossible for her to bring a small square to her lips. Gideon's appetite was not much better. The little mound of peas on his plate had yet to be disturbed and only one of the three slices of pheasant had been cut into.

The footman picked up the silent cue and cleared the last course. With a tight flick of his fingers and a sharp glance, Gideon dismissed the servant. The dining room door clicked shut, and before the sound could fade into nothingness, he spoke. "Is dinner over?"

"Yes," she responded, perplexed by the obvious.

He nodded once. "Have the carriage readied. I wish to depart for London tonight."

She went utterly still. Her pulse pounded swiftly in her ears. "Pardon?"

"Your terms still hold, do they not?" The nasty edge in the challenge chilled the surrounding air.

A shiver gripped her shoulders. Eyes wide, she nodded.

"Dinner is over. My obligation has been fulfilled. I wish to leave."

"But-but why did you come all the way up here if you had no intention of staying?"

"Why? There was no choice involved. Your *request* was a very thinly veiled command that I drop everything and hop in your waiting carriage."

"But—?"

"For Christ's sake, Bella, five hundred pounds? What were you thinking?"

Oh no. It had not been enough. The bottom dropped out of her stomach. "But Seamus never said a word," she said, leaning forward in the chair. "I wrote to have the driver notified if it wasn't sufficient."

"Not sufficient? It was too much," he said, incredulous and indignant, as though she had delivered the highest insult.

"What?" The word was an exhale that slumped her spine. The blood drained from her face.

"And I can't believe you wrote directly to Rubicon." Disappointment layered with sharp disdain pulled his beautiful mouth into an ugly sneer.

"But, who—?" Her mouth worked soundlessly, her mind seized with shock. She dropped her gaze to the barren white linen tablecloth. Forcing each breath, she struggled to project a calm façade, to erect a safe wall behind which she could hide.

She had gone and done it again. But this time it had not been in a fit of anger and jealousy. Somehow she had deeply offended him. And the way he looked at her . . .

The pain of being separated from him was nothing compared to this agony lancing her chest. She tried to swallow
down the threat of tears, but it felt as if there were thorns
lodged in her throat. Nothing had ever hurt like this before. She would take Stirling over this any day. Those
were wounds that healed, but this one . . .

It hurt too much, too much to bear.

With as much poise as she could manage, she stood
and left the dining room while she still had the strength to
do it.

GIDEON stewed in a noxious mixture of indignation,
anger, and wounded male pride. He heard the light tap of
footsteps quicken and fade as Bella walked down the
hall. The sound muffled once she reached the stairs. The
faint sound of a door clicking shut snapped him to his
senses.

"Holy Mother . . . Bloody hell!" Had he absolutely no
tact? He could not believe he had just yelled at her—
Bella. The woman who never raised her voice above polite levels unless she was demanding more or pleading
with him to stay in her bed. And that parting glance she
had given him—he had pierced her very soul.

Gideon pushed back from the table and darted after
her. Senses focused on her, he did not give a glance to the
maid in the hall or the butler standing guard at the front
door. The stairs were devoured in seconds and he was
skidding to a halt outside her sitting room. He turned the
knob but the door would not open.

He jangled the knob in frustration. "Bella? Bella?"

A quick press of his ear to the door revealed nothing.
She must be in her bedchamber, most likely behind another locked door. He quickly appraised the brass knob
but he had never learned to pick a lock and did not think
it best to attempt his first try tonight.

He looked to the right and left, and glanced over his
shoulder. Then he surveyed the corridor again, studying

the doors, the distance between each and their relative positions. If Bowhill was anything like every other country house he had been in, then there was another way into her bedchamber. Gideon crossed to the door directly opposite Bella's and found it unlocked. Focused only on the doors he needed to pass through to get to Bella, he did not glance about but walked quickly through first one door then another.

After opening a third narrower door, he went straight forward through a dark room. One hand out to the side to guide his way. Silk, cashmere, and fine wool folded on shelves tickled his fingertips. The other hand stretched out in front until it encountered cool wood and a smooth round knob. He turned the knob and pushed open the unlocked door.

Compared to the pitch darkness of the dressing room, the moonlit bedchamber was quite bright. He spotted her crumpled on the floor a few paces from the ornate four-poster bed with its tapestry hangings. Her amethyst skirt looked like black silk pooled around her. Her bowed pale blonde head glowed silvery blue in the moonlight streaming in from the tall windows. Her quiet sobs struck him straight in the heart.

The thick rugs silenced his footsteps as he slowly approached. Dropping to his knees, he crooned, "Oh, Bella, please, Bella, don't cry."

She gave a start when his hand settled on her back. "Gideon, I'm sorry. I didn't mean . . . I didn't know." The soft words caught on her sobs.

"Please don't be upset," he begged, rubbing her back in large soothing circles.

"I just needed . . . I'm so sorry, Gideon."

"No, don't be. You needn't be. Oh, Bella, I shouldn't have railed at you. It's not your fault."

She pushed up onto her knees and turned to face him. Her violet eyes were thick with tears. Her beautiful face a canvas of sorrow. "I just needed—"

"*Shh.*" An unexpected, indefinable burst shot through

his body the moment he wrapped his arms around her thin frame. She leaned into him, pressing her cheek against his waistcoat, hiding her face. "I know. I understand. Please, please don't cry. I should have told you how to contact me, where to write. I shouldn't have been angry with you," he whispered into her ear.

Gideon had been in such a state when he had left her that he had forgotten to leave a note with the address. He never had them go through Rubicon. He had earned the right, the privilege, many years ago to manage his own affairs. There would always be a discreet envelope awaiting him in his separate room when he arrived at a client's home. And when the appointment was over, he would take half to Rubicon. Well, more often, send her half. The less he saw of her the better. The less he walked into that establishment the better.

But Bella had been unique. She hadn't originally written to Rubicon or visited. A close friend had not referred her to him either. And the French woman who'd secured his services had paid Rubicon. Bella had been left out of the specifics. Everything had been arranged for her. She would have had no idea how to contact him directly, or how much was insultingly too much, what all the niceties were, the etiquette as it may, for hiring a male prostitute.

Heavy guilt pulled at his chest. None of it had been her fault. He had directed his anger at the wrong source, and hurt her, Bella, in the process.

He leaned back to wipe the tears from her pale cheeks with the pads of his thumbs. Christ, she was beautiful even when she cried. With tears usually came red, runny noses and puffy, swollen eyes. But not Bella. He lowered his lips to hers and begged for her forgiveness the only way he knew how.

She instantly deepened the light kiss and brought her arms around his neck to hold him tight. Gideon felt the instant when her passion ignited. The deep kisses turned greedy, her movements became tight, jerky, and demanding as she nestled closer to him, straddling his hips.

He gave her a moment. A moment for her to kiss him as she wanted. To do with him as she pleased. A moment for him not to be the one in control. To simply experience the full force of Bella's ardent kiss.

Then with his lips never leaving hers, he gathered her in his arms, stood, set her down on the edge of the bed, and dropped to his knees. This was Bella—there was no gentleness as he shoved her skirt up to her waist, pushed her thighs wider, and settled his mouth on her pink, wet flesh. He plied her with light flicks of his tongue, soft presses of his lips, and teasing grazes of his teeth, as he slipped first one finger inside her, and then another. Her body gripped his fingers tightly and he grunted against her clit, his cock swelling to painful proportions.

Within no time at all she came on a rapturous moan. Her back arching, fingers tangling in his hair, legs spreading wider. But he did not crawl up her body. He stayed right where he was, pleasuring her until he threw her over the edge again.

Those fingers in his hair turned rough, pulling almost to the point of yanking. "Gideon, please. I need—"

She groaned, then sucked in a swift breath as he eased yet another finger into her, alternating between thrusting and wiggling, hitting those perfect spots deep inside her. She rocked her hips in counterpoint, an urgent rhythm his cock knew only too well.

"Gideon." The word was ripped from her throat on another climax. She pulled his hair again, hard. Her silk-clad legs wrapped around his back, heels pressing upward on his shoulder blades. "Please."

But he ignored the demand, refused the request—determined to make her come again and again and again, until she could take no more. To give to her the one thing that was in his power to offer her.

"Gideon. Please. *Fuck me.*"

This time it was he who shuddered, he who groaned. That crude command from her lips—it almost, almost, *almost* made him break the unbreakable rule. He tore at the falls of his trousers, one button undone, before he regained his senses.

He cursed himself, cursed the spite that had made him bring not even one French letter with him. He had absolutely no intention of bedding her when he went to the manor house, had every intention of leaving immediately after dinner. His trunk hadn't even been unpacked, but still stood inside the door of Garden House. That spite was now keeping him from the one thing he wanted, from the one thing he needed.

He knew the raw desire consuming him had nothing to do with the past four weeks of celibacy. It had everything to do with *her*. He needed to feel her lithe body writhe against his own, her nails score his back, her long legs wrap around his hips. But, damn it!

He wanted to howl at the injustice of it all, but also could not allow her to suffer for his misplaced spite. So he intensified his efforts, using all the skills he had acquired over the past thirteen years, since he had lost his virginity at age fourteen, to wring every last orgasm from her body.

Bella did not want to be denied. She persisted, repeating those two words again and again, until it was all he could hear, even above the pounding rhythm of his heart and his labored breaths, pushing him to a point he did not know he had, until he could take no more. Until he had to silence her lest the next "fuck me" drove him beyond rational thought and beyond control.

He lifted his head. "No." The refusal was harsh, guttural, abrupt.

She went still. Startled violet eyes met his.

"I can't," he added at the injured look finding its way onto her face.

"Why not? I need you, Gideon."

Her heavy pants filled the room. He was so close every breath he took was filled with the sweet scent of her body. The taste of her fresh on his tongue, his lips wet from her.

"I can't. Not tonight, Bella. Just let me pleasure you."

He could tell she did not understand, could tell she was starting to see this as some sort of punishment, retribution, revenge for her summons. The lean muscles of her thighs went rigid under his splayed hands. On a wince, she averted her gaze.

"I didn't bring . . . I don't have with me . . ." He took a deep breath, struggling to gather his thoughts, to gather the words. "I left them at Garden House."

She looked back at him. "Left what?"

"Sheaths. French letters. I won't take you without one."

"I don't care, Gideon. I need you." With one arm braced behind her, she reached out to cup his jaw.

He soaked up her caress. Her small, warm hand. Her fingers resting gently on his pounding pulse. Then denied her again. "No, Bella."

This was what he had tried to avoid. He had wanted to wring so many orgasms out of her she would be too lax and sated to do anything but fall asleep in her bed. Bella was inherently spoiled. A beautiful woman was not accustomed to refusal. And he almost gave in again. But not for his own needs, but to stem the fight, the test of wills, he knew would ensue.

"Please, Gideon. It doesn't matter. I want you. I want to feel you, skin against skin, just once. Please." Even in the darkness he could read the plea in her stark and honest gaze.

Sex without protection was unthinkable—the risks were too high. There were other methods to prevent conception, but the lust and need drumming though his veins warned now was not the time to attempt his first try at a well-timed withdrawal. And he knew at that moment he could not risk it just to avoid the possibility of getting her with child, but because he could not risk the intimacy. And not just the risk of her confusing their respective roles, but of him as well.

"No, Bella," he repeated before she could tempt him anew. There was a definite note of regret in his low tone, and he did not try to disguise it. "Please don't insist. I can't. I won't. Tonight let me give you pleasure, and tomorrow you can have it all."

On his knees and completely at her mercy, he held his breath, fearful she would persist. Or worse yet, take his refusal the wrong way. Or even worse, dismiss him.

Holding his wary gaze, she nodded. "Tomorrow," she whispered.

A relieved smile spread across his face. "Tomorrow."

Then he made good on his promise.

Twelve

"LEAN over."

Gideon's words tickled her ear. The heat of him warmed her back. Gooseflesh rose up her arms. Her insides quivered. Keeping her face purposefully blank, Bella complied.

"More." When she did not immediately heed his command, he added, "It was your suggestion to fill the afternoon. If you don't want to play . . ."

Resting her forearms on the green felt, she bent over at the waist. "Like this?" She glanced over her shoulder, eyebrows raised in mock hauteur.

His sinfully dark gaze lingered on her derrière. His lips curved in an appreciative half smile. "Perfect."

She wanted to arch her back, rotate her hips, invite him to play a different game. Instead she looked ahead before her impulses got the better of her.

He leaned over her, resting a hand beside her elbow. She closed her eyes and took a slow breath. Just the scent of him made her pulse race, but to have him behind her like this . . . Bella swallowed.

"Now then, take this." Wrapping an arm around her, he held out a long wooden stick.

She shifted her weight, pushing up onto one hand and pushing back into his broad chest, to take the cue stick. The highly polished wood was cool to the touch.

"Not like that. Like this." He reached full around her, his arms bracketing hers. His hair brushed her ear. She let her hands go slack, allowing him to reposition them. "One at the end to provide the thrust. The other at the middle to guide. No, no. Don't grab it. Curl your index finger and thumb around the stick, but loosely. You need to be able to freely slide it between your fingers. See."

Placing his hands over hers, he moved the stick back and forth a few times. The smooth wood slid between her fingers, bringing to mind the way *he* slid between her fingers, though she would never be able to hold him between two fingers like this. Gideon put the thin cue stick to shame. The image of his magnificent cock sprang into her head. She suppressed a moan as a wave of lust washed over her. Her innermost muscles tightened, recalling how perfect it felt to be impaled upon his cock. The impressive length. The substantial width. The hard, heavy thrusts that sparked orgasm after orgasm. Yesterday evening he had made good on his promise of two nights ago, and then some. She had been so exhausted she could not even remember his last kiss before he slipped out of her bed.

But she had awoken this morning invigorated and wanting more. The masculine billiard room with its heavy velvet curtains drawn closed to keep in the warmth of the fire blazing in the hearth provided an ideal indoor location for an afternoon tryst. But first, she really did want to learn how to play the game.

With that thought in mind, she did her best to ignore the way the hard muscles of Gideon's body surrounded her. The buttons of his navy coat grazed her lower back. His long legs bracketed hers.

"I think I've got it now," she said, trying to project the manner of a proper student.

Air cooled the backs of her hands as he released them. Bracing his weight on a straight arm, he positioned the ivory ball a hand's space in front of her stick. "All right then. Next step. Slide the cue stick back and forth a few times as you aim for one of the red balls at the end of the table. Then, with a good snap of your elbow, strike the ball."

He rested his other hand on her hip. Sensation rippled through her body. She wanted him to grab her hips with both hands, to hold her steady for his powerful thrusts. To slam into her with all the force of his lower body. On a short indrawn breath, she squeezed her eyes shut to regain her composure. But as she focused again on the path between the two balls, a draught of air hit her lower legs, pulling her mind from the game and to Gideon as he slowly gathered her skirt.

"Remember, don't grab the stick so tightly. You need it to slide easily toward its target."

She forced her fingers to unclench then gripped the cue stick anew as his fingertips brushed her outer thigh and curved in to tickle the sensitive skin of her inner thigh. An anticipatory jolt shook her body, lust spiking her senses.

"Relax," he said softly.

The way he was nuzzling her neck was not helping her efforts. A mix of chills and desire chased over her skin and rushed down to settle at her core. With the lightest of touches, he brushed the damp hair covering her mound. Reflexively, she went up onto her toes then sank slowly down. His finger parted the folds of her sex. She let out a low moan.

"Are you going to hit the ball or not?" he asked, as casual as could be, as if he did not have his hand up her skirt, teasing her drenched core.

Forcing deep, even breaths, she lined up the shot and drew the stick back. As soon as the smack of the felt-covered tip against the ivory ball rent the air, she planted her palms on the billiard table and hung her head.

"Damn, you're wet. How long have you been like this?"

His blunt words added to the decadent sensations coiling tight in her belly. "Since you walked in the front door," she managed to get out between short panting breaths. "And you know it."

He chuckled, full of smug male pride. He might sound unaffected, but from the corner of her eye she could see his biceps bulge beneath his coat sleeve. The tendons on the back of the large hand splayed on the green felt were taut. He nipped at her exposed neck, his heavy breaths scorching her skin.

Rounding her shoulders, she rocked into his caress, increasing the pressure on her clit to a maddening level. An orgasm tickled the edge of her mind. She rotated her hips, rubbing against his groin, pressing the hard arch of his manhood erotically between the two halves of her bottom. The sensations gathered. Her nerves tightened to an unbearable level.

He removed his hand. Her skirt whooshed down her legs.

"Don't stop!" she gasped, glancing over her shoulder.

"Oh, I'm just getting started." He winked.

Paper crinkled. Fabric rustled. He gathered her skirt at her waist, baring her to his view. She arched like an eager tart, lifting her bottom, widening her stance. *God*, it felt so wicked to be bent over the billiard table.

He grasped her hip. Her breaths stuttered in anticipation as his cock nudged the entrance to her body. As soon as the broad head made the breech, she pushed back, eager for more. Eager for his hard thrusts. Eager to come on his cock.

He held her steady. "Wait. Until I'm all the way in."

"But—?"

"You're so tight, I don't want to hurt you," he murmured, eyebrows lowered with concern.

Frustrated, she shook her head, but held still. He rocked, pushing slowly, easing in, stretching her delicate flesh. She trembled, impatient and needy, wanting it all. *Now.* Her eyelids fluttered. Her swollen clit throbbed, sending heavy pulses throughout her body. Her climax so close . . .

A knock sounded on the door.

Gideon snapped his head up. He froze, buried almost hilt deep inside of Bella, her innermost muscles gripping his cock like a fist.

"Lady Stirling?" came her butler's voice, muffled by the thick door.

"Fuck," he cursed under his breath. The interruption could not possibly have come at a worse time.

"Oh no!" Dread soaked her whispered exclamation.

He stepped back, flipped her skirts down over her delectable bottom and turned her around. "Bella?" he whispered urgently as he whipped off the French letter. Suppressing a wince, he shoved his hard cock into his breeches. Her face was pale, her eyes wide, her breaths coming in shallow, quick pants. "You have to open the door. Now."

She closed her eyes. The long column of her neck worked as she swallowed. Then she nodded. Her lashes swept up, the cool composure in place. Smoothing a hand over her hair, she walked serenely to the door.

His hands shook as he buttoned his breeches. He grabbed Bella's discarded cue stick and the ivory ball, leaned over the table and set up a shot.

She opened the door revealing her haughty butler. "Yes, McGreevy?" she asked, her shoulders ramrod straight and her tone all bored condescension.

"You have a caller. Mrs. Tavisham."

"See her to the drawing room."

"Yes, your ladyship." McGreevy's gaze flittered to Gideon. His thin nostrils flared.

Gideon lifted one eyebrow then took aim. The ivory cue ball whizzed across the green felt, connecting sharply with the red ball and sending it into the corner pocket.

The butler turned on his heel. His footsteps echoed and faded as he walked down the hall.

Bella closed the door, turned, and sagged against it. Eyes closed, she pressed a hand over her mouth.

He dropped the stick and rushed to her. "Are you all right?" He made to rub her shoulders, but with a harsh jerk, she shrugged him off.

"Don't touch me. You'll make it worse."

"Oh, Bella. I'm sorry. I-I promise, I'll make it up to you." His hands hovered over her thin shoulders. He wanted to touch her, to take her in his arms, to feather light kisses over her tightened brow, to soothe away her distress.

"I'll hold you to it." Her mouth twisted in a grimace. "I need to come so bad it hurts."

I know how you feel.

She glanced down his body, her gaze settling on his groin. His cock strained against the placket of his breeches. He had tried to will it down, but the effort had not yet produced the desired result. The scent of sex hung heavy in the air, a signal his body refused to ignore. There was no way her butler could have mistaken the scent for anything but.

"How did you get that in there?"

He gave a self-deprecating chuckle. "It was not pleasant. If it's any consolation, it aches something terrible."

She *harrumphed*. "Good."

"I had no idea you had such an evil side. Should I be worried?" he teased, needing to lighten her mood.

Her lips twitched with a hint of a smile. "No. Never." She took a deep breath and stepped from the door. "I shouldn't be long."

He tipped his head and reached around her to open the door, careful not to even brush her skirt with his forearm. Admiring the smooth sway of her hips, he watched her glide down the hall. He had seen her do it so many times, yet it still amazed him how quickly she could don the cool aristocratic mask. Just looking at her one would never know that minutes ago she had been writhing on his cock, her lush derrière lifted high, begging for more.

Gideon closed the door, blocking out the view. Closing his eyes, he clenched his jaw, willing away his erection. He had not been exaggerating—it ached something terrible. His ballocks were drawn up so tight it was beyond painful. And damn it, he had forgotten to lock the door when they entered the billiard room. Luckily, Bella had well-trained servants.

Frowning, he glanced about the room. He did not want to wait here, that was for sure. Without Bella by his side, he felt distinctly uncomfortable in the manor house, like an unwelcome guest who refused to leave.

He opened the door. Bella and her neighbor were in the drawing room, and judging by the way her soft melodic voice drifted down the hall, he guessed the door was open. He would have to slip out the back. The drawing room windows faced the side of the house, so they would not spot him walking through the back garden.

He stepped from the billiard room and was about to turn toward the kitchen when Bella's words caught his attention.

"You are too kind. Won't you stay for tea?"

He and Bella were supposed to have tea together and now she was offering his place to another. *I shouldn't be long*, he mouthed silently, suddenly sullen and grumpy. How quickly they forget. His shoulders slumped. He should be used to it by now, and he shouldn't be so disappointed—it was only tea. But . . .

He let out a dejected sigh. There was nothing he could do about it. When it was convenient, when she wanted him again, she'd seek him out.

He returned to the cottage and grabbed the *Times* off the dining table. After sprawling on the couch, he snapped open the paper. But the news did not hold his interest. With a weary sigh, he set the paper aside, located his deck of cards, sat at the dining table, and tried to focus on a game of patience.

Three games lost and zero won turned his mood even darker. He was about to swipe the cards from the table, let them scatter about the floor, announce defeat, when a knock sounded at the door. He pushed back from the table and went to see what the servant wanted.

"Bella."

She stood on his doorstep, smiling brightly. "Hello, Gideon. Aren't you going to invite me in?"

"Oh. Yes. Sorry," he mumbled. He stepped aside, allowing her to pass. Her appearance should have chased away the dark cloud hanging over his head, but strangely it did not. "To what do I owe the pleasure of this visit?"

She lingered by the armchair, trailing her fingers over the high back. He remained at the door. "I came to see you."

No. You want me to make you come. He tipped his head. "Thank you."

She studied him. "Gideon, are you all right?"

"Did your neighbor return home already?"

"Yes. She came by to deliver the Rose du Roi."

"Ah. Your delayed gift. Has it recovered from its journey from France?"

"Yes. I had one of the servants take the rose to the hothouse." She furrowed her brow. "Gideon, are you all right?"

"Why wouldn't I be? You're here." He pushed from the door and sauntered to her. "I seem to recall I made you a promise recently," he said, lowering his voice to a level he knew she liked.

"Well, yes, you did." She tipped her chin down. A blush colored her high cheekbones. "But I'll call it in later. I stopped by to ask if you wanted to come see my new rose."

He blinked.

She cocked her head, her beautiful face twisted in puzzlement. "Why do you look so surprised?"

He gathered his wits before she could stumble over the answer. "I'm merely pleased." And he was pleased, ridiculously so. He was certain he was grinning like an idiot. "Does your rose have any blooms yet? Or is it too young?"

She gazed up at him, eyes soft and shining with an emotion he could not place. But whatever it was, it made his stomach do an odd little flip. Then she surprised him further by lifting up onto her toes and pressing a light kiss to his lips, scrambling his wits anew.

"Come along. You can see for yourself," she said as she grabbed his hand, hanging limp at his side.

Still dazed, he allowed her to lead him from the cottage, no longer caring in the slightest that she had given his tea to another.

Thirteen

THE late May afternoon sun was high in the sky, bringing a strong hint of summer. It was so warm outside many of the hothouse windows had been opened to allow a fresh breeze to pass through. With scissors in one hand and a wicker basket at her feet, Bella carefully set to pruning another bush. Chinas did not require or want much in the form of pruning, but the bushes still needed some attention to keep them at their healthiest. With a snip of her scissors a spindly, weak offshoot was removed and dropped into the basket at her feet.

There were servants to see to the task, but she had found long ago that she enjoyed doing it herself. It was peaceful in the hothouse and it gave her something to do to while away the usually long, lonely days.

But today she was not alone. Nor had she been for the past ten days. With a glance to her left, her gaze fell on Gideon. As had become his habit when she was working in the hothouse, he was sprawled on the wooden bench situated along the dirt path, perusing the latest copy of the

Times. One booted foot was on the ground, the other bent up on the bench, an elbow resting on his knee.

She had the distinct impression he enjoyed their lazy afternoons just as much as she did. It was so very easy to be with him. There were no inhibitions—she could just be herself. There was no fear he would think less of her if she behaved like an ill-bred tart. In fact, he encouraged her wicked side. But it was more than that. With Gideon came not only searing passion, but also a sense of comfort the likes of which she had not felt in years, like a warm, sun-filled blanket.

A soft sigh escaped her lips. He must have heard her for he looked up. A smile curved his lips. She gave him one in return, and then turned back to her roses.

She had wondered since she first laid eyes on him how he had come to be in his current profession. And as she had gotten to know him, as she had been fortunate enough to spend time with him, that curiosity had grown. In addition to being a perfect gentleman and a highly skilled and attentive lover, he was also an intelligent man. Surely someone of his caliber could have easily found a more respectable form of employment. And he did not strike her as inherently lazy. Gideon could have been a man of Quality—a lesser son. But somehow she thought he must be of common birth. Still, there were other avenues available to him, other means of employment, even if he did not wish to be a servant. Gideon as a footman? No—she could not imagine that.

It had not escaped her notice that he had a tendency to be closed-lipped about himself. Any time she had begun to ask him anything personal he steered the conversation so deftly elsewhere it would be several minutes later before she realized what he avoided.

But they were better acquainted now—she could feel the bond between them. Hoping it was strong enough, hoping he felt comfortable enough with her, she asked as casually as she could, her attention trained on the red bloom before her, "Gideon, how did you come to be a . . . companion? Why this?"

The only sound was the faint buzz of bees flittering from one bloom to the next.

Her shoulders tightened. She swallowed hard. "Pardon. You needn't answer if you don't wish. It's not at all well-done of me to pry," she said, fearful she had just committed a grave mistake and wishing she had not allowed her curiosity to get the better of her.

There was a rustle of paper as he set the *Times* down. After a long pause, he spoke, his voice casual with a shrug behind it. "I entered the family business. Seemed the thing to do."

She glanced over her shoulder at him, doubly shocked he answered and by his response. "Your parents know what you do? They condone it?"

"I assume my mother's aware," he said. "She left to live with a paramour years before, but she kept in contact with some of the other women. My father . . . his opinion matters not as I've never met the man."

"You don't know who your father is?"

"No. One of Christina's paramours, no doubt."

"Christina?"

"My mother," he clarified. "Though I seldom think of her as such. She's more the woman who happened to give birth to me. Christina was not made for children. Too high-strung, too pampered, to give much thought to anyone but herself. But I don't hold it against her. It's just who she is."

He was a bastard—the result of one of his mother's gentlemen. Bella had never met a by-blow before, but somehow Gideon was not what she would have expected. Since he had answered her first question, she decided to try a second one. "How does one become a . . ."

"A companion to ladies?" he finished for her.

She nodded.

"I grew up in a brothel," he said. "Well, I lived with an old aunt until I was seven, but I was not a calm seven and she was getting on in years. So after that I went to live with

Christina, which was kind of her. She could have simply abandoned me, and fortunately, the owner of the brothel allowed me to stay. I kept out of the way and worked to earn my keep. Odd jobs, fetching things for the other women, tending the fires, and helping in the kitchen. And when I was old enough, I changed jobs. Couldn't fetch sweets for the women my whole life."

He made it sound so ordinary, as if his upbringing had been commonplace. "When?"

"When what?"

"Did you change positions?"

"Oh." His eyebrows pulled together as he thought for a moment. "About seventeen."

He had been but a boy. Outrage pounded through her veins. How could his mother have allowed that? He should have been in the schoolroom or at boarding school, not earning his living pleasuring women. He should have been chasing after girls his own age, not being hired by adult females. And what sort of person would employ a boy for work such as that?

Gideon must have read the indignation on her face, for he shook his head indulgently. The corners of his mouth pulled with a bemused smile. "It wasn't as horrible as you may think. Given my other options, my current line of work is much preferred."

"But surely there were other avenues available. A man such as yourself? You could do anything you put your mind to."

He gave her an odd look, one she could not define. "You don't approve?"

"Well, it's just . . ." Had she insulted him again? Discomposed, she looked down to the basket at her feet, then back up to him, gathering her courage. "I am very fortunate to have the pleasure of your company. I am infinitely glad to have met you and very grateful to Madame Marceau to have had her send you to me. It's not that I don't want you to be here, rather that there is more to you than this. Don't you wish for something more?"

His eyes widened. He dropped his foot from the bench
to the gravel path and tugged at his coat sleeve. "Of course
I do. I-I want . . ."

Not meeting her eyes, he shook his head, his voice tail-
ing off. But she was desperate to learn what it was this
man wanted out of life. What was important to *him*. The
rigid set of his shoulders warned she had reached a point
where he did not want to venture further. Yet she needed
to know. "What do you want, Gideon?" she asked gently.

He looked to the paper lying beside his hip and toyed
with a crisp corner. Just when she had given up on the answer, he spoke. "A wife. A family. But first, I need money.
A whole lot of it."

"Whatever for?"

"What woman in her right mind would have me without it?"

I would. Her heart clenched at the defeat in his gruff
tone.

"When I have enough, I'll buy a property in the country.
One with a respectable income. And hopefully, it and my
bank account will garner me a wife." He crossed one booted
ankle over his knee and met her gaze. Every trace of discomposure was gone, as if it had never been there. "Who is
Madame Marceau?"

It took a moment for her mind to adjust to the abrupt
change in topic, but she recognized it for what it was—he
did not want to discuss his future any longer. "My cousin.
The lady who made the initial arrangements."

He nodded sagely. "Wondered who she was. Why would
a lady's cousin arrange for a man such as myself?"

"She . . ." Bella's cheeks burned but she resisted the
urge to glance away. "She believed I was in need of a flirtation. She is French; therefore, a flirtation cures all."

Gideon raised one dark eyebrow. "What was I to cure?"

"Madame Marceau believed I was getting much too
maudlin."

"And are you cured?" The teasing lilt was gone. He
asked as though he truly cared about the answer.

Bella tipped her chin, hiding under the wide brim of her straw hat. "When I'm with you, I am," she admitted.

Another spindly branch was quickly selected and clipped from the bush then dropped to the basket at her feet. She waited for him to ask why she had been maudlin. Waited for him to ask about Stirling. But the question she did not want to answer never came. Whether it was because he did not care or because he sensed her reluctance, she did not know. She only knew she was grateful for the silence, whatever the cause.

At length, she heard the rustle of paper as he picked up the *Times* and went back to perusing the news. It was many minutes later when her pulse finally slowed, when the tremble disappeared from her hands, when the tightness left her throat and she was again able to relax and enjoy just being with him. But it was not the same feeling she had but a half hour ago.

The questions she asked and the answers she received reminded her anew he would leave soon and go to another. Bless another with his presence, with his charm, with exquisite pleasure. She did not want him to go, but she knew better than to ask him to stay. As he had once pointed out, there was no place for him with her. He wanted a wife someday, and that woman could never be her.

The last lonely five years had not been her penance at all for failing her older brother. This was. This knowing she could never have more of Gideon than this—these short visits, these glimpses of what she had thrown away years ago.

But it had been worth it. If not Stirling, then some other like him. She would have never found with a husband selected by Phillip what she found with Gideon. This was unique. This was different. This was what she was never destined to have.

She would not ask Gideon to stay, and she did not know if she could even write to him again.

⚜

A parting fuck or one last tumble. It didn't matter to
Gideon what it was called. He was simply grateful Bella
had found a way to arrange it this morning.

Crouched over her, he paused at the end of a downstroke. He needed to give her one last orgasm. With a
hand braced on the bed, he wrapped his other arm around
her. "Hold on," he whispered in her ear. The slim arms
wrapped around his neck tightened. Her lean thighs cradling his hips, he pushed up onto his knees, bringing her
with him, the contact of their bodies unbroken. Capturing
her lips, he settled back on his heels and grasped the neat
indent of her waist. Tongue twining with hers, he flexed
his hips.

Bella twisted her head, breaking the kiss. "Gideon,"
she moaned.

She tried to rock against him, increase the pace. With
a light yet firm hold, he held her steady and pushed in
deeper into the tight depths of her body. Her eyes drifted
closed and she relaxed into his slow, steady thrusts. The
three orgasms he'd already given her this morning must
have taken the edge off her impatience. Fingers tangled in
his hair, she allowed him to set the pace, to bring the climax to her.

He slid one hand up her back. Hand splayed between her
shoulder blades, he nuzzled her neck. Arching, she threw
back her head, offering herself up to him. He pressed a light
kiss to the delicate hollow of her throat and dragged his lips
down her flushed chest. Her skin was so smooth, like the
finest silk. He flicked his tongue over her nipple then
opened his mouth and suckled on the hard bud.

The fingers tangled in his hair tightened. Her little
breathy moans began to crescendo. "Gideon," she gasped,
arching her hips, writhing against him in a seductive rhythm.

Her clit rubbed maddeningly against his groin. He tried
to keep the pace slow, to draw out the moment. To keep
her suspended on the brink of orgasm, desperate and needing him.

But it was no use. The climax he had managed to keep at bay teased the base of his spine, quickening his thrusts. Sweat beaded his brow. His heart hammered in his chest.

Her body tightened around his cock. He grunted, deep and low from his gut. "Come for me, Bella. Now," he said, beyond desperate not to come before she did.

Her spine went taut. Eyes closed and lips parted, she gasped.

Abruptly, he pulled her close and slanted his mouth over hers, capturing her screams of ecstasy.

The orgasm raced up his cock. He kissed her fiercely as he came, his groan lost in the hot recesses of her mouth.

Bella sagged against him, pliant and sated in his arms. Forehead resting on his shoulder, her labored breaths brushed across his chest. He combed his fingers through her hair, gently smoothing the tousled locks. She had the most beautiful hair. So long it covered her back, the ends grazing the firm swell of her backside.

A light knock sounded on the dressing room door. "Lady Stirling?" came a muffled voice.

Bella sighed. "Yes, Maisie?"

"The carriage is ready."

Gideon winced.

"Thank you, Maisie." Bella leaned back.

He forced an easy smile the moment before her gaze met his. "I should be going."

Her lashes swept down. She nodded.

Reluctantly, he lifted her off him and set her on the bed. He swung his legs over the side of the bed. His joints ached from having his legs folded under him. Christ, he was getting old. He resisted the urge to rub his thighs and instead removed the sheath. Bending, he picked up the wax paper wrapper from the floor, folded it over the used sheath, and tossed it into the nearby waste bin.

He grabbed his trousers from the floor and stepped into them. Standing, he pulled them up and buttoned the placket. A small hand grabbed his arse.

Startled, he glanced over his shoulder.

"Couldn't resist," she said, smirking. Lounged on her side, pale blonde hair tumbled over her slim shoulder and alabaster skin flushed from four orgasms, she was the picture of temptation.

Turning, he leaned down, cupped her cheek, and kissed her. Hot and quick, pulling back before temptation got the better of him.

"Your carriage awaits," he murmured, needing to remind himself it was time to leave.

The smile on her lips faded. "Yes, it does," she said, with a little lift of her shoulder. Rolling onto her back, she arched and stretched her arms overhead.

Gideon turned from the tantalizing image and walked about the room, locating his clothes and getting dressed.

"We never finished breakfast," she said.

He pulled his shirt over his head and tucked the tails into his trousers. Last night she had invited him to breakfast before he left for London. Their very first breakfast together. But when he'd arrived at the manor house and her lady's maid had shown him to the informal sitting room adjoining the bedchamber, he had known Bella had had plans for the morning that did not include food. Plans he wholeheartedly approved. "Correction. We didn't start breakfast. If I recall correctly, the silver covers were not even removed from the dishes. If you're hungry I can bring the tray in for you. The food is likely still warm. Or I can order up another tray."

"No, thank you. I'm not particularly hungry at the moment." Bella sat up and flicked her hair behind her shoulders. She glanced about the room. The late morning sun streamed through the windows. The crisp golden light caressed her bare skin. "Do you see my chemise on the floor?"

"Yes. Why?" He tied his cravat in a simple knot and pulled on his gray pin-striped waistcoat.

She rolled her eyes. "I need to get dressed. See you to the carriage."

He shook his head. "Stay in bed. Laze the morning away. I can see myself out."

Her lush lips pulled into a straight line, her gaze testing. Then she flopped back down on the bed. "All right. I must admit, I am a bit tired."

He chuckled as he buttoned his navy coat. "I wonder why?"

She rolled onto her side and rested her cheek in her palm. "Smug man. You know exactly why."

He tipped his head and tugged on the end of his coat to straighten it. He was dressed. He should leave now, but there was one last thing he needed to see to.

Taking a deep breath, he reached into his coat pocket. He walked to the side of the bed. "Here."

Her brow furrowed as she looked at the proffered note. She held out her hand and he pressed the folded note into her palm.

"My address." He swallowed past the lump in his throat. "If you wish to contact me, simply send a note to that address."

She held his gaze. There was something in the violet depths which caused his chest to tighten.

"Do you understand, Bella?" Hell, it wasn't all that difficult, and Bella certainly was not a simpleton. Why did he need her reassurance?

Ducking her chin to her chest, she nodded. "Yes," she whispered.

He lifted his hand from hers. Her fingers closed over the note. "Thank you, my lady. I had a very enjoyable fortnight."

The corners of her mouth curved in a soft smile. She peered up at him from under her lashes. "As did I."

Gideon sketched a short bow, turned on his heel, and walked out of the room. He closed the bedchamber door, leaned against it, and tipped back his head.

He had practically begged her to hire him again. What was wrong with him? It was always left in their hands

with no expectations either way. But with Bella, with
Bella . . .

Frustrated, he dragged his hands through his hair, not
able to explain it to himself. He pushed from the door, left
the sitting room, and went down to the front door.

He found the traveling carriage waiting for him at the
foot of the stone steps. The four chestnut horses in the
traces shifted impatiently, their harness jangling. One tossed
his head. Another stamped a hoof. The silver banding on his
trunk glinted in the sunlight. One of Bella's servants had
collected it from Garden House and strapped it to the back
of the carriage.

All was ready.

A footman leapt down from the driver's bench and
opened the door as Gideon approached.

Awfully eager to get me back to London, aren't they?

Never one to be rude to a client's servants, he tipped
his head to the footman and sat on the black leather bench.

The door closed. The carriage shifted as the footman got
back onto the driver's bench. There was a snap of leather
and the carriage lurched forward.

Paper swooshed to the floor. He looked to his feet. The
Times? He let out a *harrumph*. It meant nothing. Efficient
servants, nothing more.

He refolded the paper and set it beside him. He crossed
one ankle over his knee then shifting, stretched out both
legs as much as he could in the confines of the carriage.
Bella had not asked him to stay. He should be relieved, so
why wasn't he? And why had it been so hard to leave that
house?

After being at a woman's beck and call for more than
a handful of days, he usually looked forward to returning
to his comfortable bachelor apartment, where he could
relax and do as he pleased without thought to what they
wanted to do. Yet today, he found London was not where
he wanted to be.

He glanced to the sky. Large white clouds were scattered among the blue. A fresh breeze blew into the carriage, ruffling his hair. It was a perfect afternoon for a stroll about the gardens, or for lounging on a bench reading the *Times* and watching Bella tend to her flowers.

And it struck him. It wasn't her body he would miss, but simply her. Bella.

Lady Stirling. He squeezed his eyes shut and did his best to ignore the pain in his chest.

Her ladyship.

Not his. Never his.

She was a lady and he only played the part of a gentleman. No, it was more than playing, and he was well aware of it. He could vividly remember the moment when that need had seized hold. Eight years old and watching from around the corner of the receiving room, he wanted to be like those men who came to Rubicon's. With his cast-off clothes and hands dirtied from piling coals onto the grates, he envied the polished gentlemen as they moved among the beauties. Status and wealth radiated from their perfectly tailored clothes and their confident bearing. Their well-bred blood gave them a security he had never known.

As he had grown older, he recognized the folly of his boyhood dream. Those nameless lords did not live perfect lives. He knew there were some who did not know their true father, but unlike him, they at least had a man who claimed the title.

Yet still, he had made himself into the image of a gentleman. Spent hours upon hours teaching himself everything a tutor had never taught him. He frequented their tailors, lived in one of their apartments, and lost his money at their gaming tables. The veneer was perfect but it could not change what he was inside. A bastard son of a whore. A prostitute. Only wanted by Lady Stirling for the pleasures he could offer and for nothing more.

Gideon pinched the bridge of his nose in an effort to regain his composure. The fortnight had ended. The appointment was over. Nothing would come from dwelling on it. He needed to let it go, push Lady Stirling from his mind. Push the memories of her, that indefinable feeling of simply being with her aside and focus on returning to London, whether that was where he wanted to be or not.

His own wishes were, as always, irrelevant.

Fourteen

ONE month later Gideon was still struggling to push Lady Stirling from his mind. Seated in a comfortable leather armchair, elbow resting on the edge of the chess table, he absently turned a black pawn over and over between his fingers.

With a soft click, the black queen fell to the board in defeat.

"You made it much too easy that time. You needn't let me win. I promise not to pout."

Gideon looked up and focused on the voice's owner. "You shouldn't make promises you can't keep." The smooth words flowed off his tongue without conscious thought.

A light chuckle tickled Helen's lips as she nodded, conceding the point. She did pout, just a bit, whenever he beat her at chess. But he had not let her win this time. In fact, he could not even recall the game.

He glanced back down to the black-and-white checkered board. There were black pieces scattered about, so he must have participated. Not very well though. He had left her with a clear opening, his queen completely undefended.

"Your mind is elsewhere, is it not?"

There was no censure in her query, yet he felt exposed to have been so obvious. "No. Never. I am with you."

"You needn't lie to me, Gideon. You should know that by now. There is no need to flatter me."

He did know that. Still, it was pride that pushed him to reassure her. But he held back.

They had a standing appointment, he and Helen. She was one of the few he visited at regular intervals. Since Helen, Lady Knolwood, the widowed marchioness, was currently in Town, it had been but a quick drive to her stately townhome versus the three-hour carriage ride to her Hertfordshire country estate.

Gideon liked Helen. He had known her for years. Theirs was an easy friendship, though how he could define it as "easy" when he had no others to compare it to he was not quite certain. Maybe it was because she sought his companionship more than anything these days. It had long ago stopped being about sex. More often than not, they simply talked, played chess or a hand of cards, or had a pleasant meal. Every now and then she would make her wishes known. Some subtle hint she wanted more from him than his conversation skills. But that had become few and far between.

Not that it had ever been a bother. Though well into her forties, Helen retained a youthful beauty and her figure was what it had been a decade ago. The gray scattered in with her strawberry blonde hair was only noticeable when the light hit it at just the right angle, and her heart-shaped face held only a few faint lines from the ready smiles that brightened her sky blue eyes.

Even if she hadn't been a beauty that would not have put him off. He had found long ago he had a certain knack for looking beyond the surface and seeing the beauty within. He liked women—there was no way he couldn't in his line of work. But it was more than a passing appreciation of what made them different than him, a man. He *truly* liked women—their little quirks, those unexpected eccentricities that made them who they were.

But tonight he was rather hoping it would not end in her bedchamber. Strangely, he found himself without any will to bed her, or to even press his lips to hers. Maybe that was why he had been such a monk of late. On some level, perhaps he had known—

"Does she know how lucky she is?"

Gideon pulled his thoughts back to the woman seated across the chess table. "Pardon?"

"She who has your heart. Does she know how fortunate she is to have secured that which, I am certain, many a lady would commit murder for?"

Every muscle in his body tensed. He held his breath, fearing the next words out of her mouth, but helpless to stop them.

"I do so hope she is worthy."

"Helen, I assure you, I do not know what you're speaking of," he said, unable to mask the defensive note in his voice.

She gave him a little look, one that said he was fooling no one, least of all her. "It's all right, Gideon. I'm happy for you, truly I am. I was the one who started you off in this life and I feared, for a while there, that because of it you had hardened your heart and would refuse to give it up. I am quite relieved to find you have entrusted it to another."

Helen had been his first, though at the time she had not known it. It had been years later when they were teasing each other one night that he let it slip. She had been taken aback, and even more shocked when he revealed his age.

If I'd have known, I would have never asked for you. I thought you worked there.

I did, just in a different capacity.

I would have never guessed it had been your first time.

My first lady, but not my first time.

The three years before his first appointment had been

spent in various beds at Rubicon's. An adolescent male in a whorehouse? It would have been unthinkable for him to reach the age of seventeen a virgin. He'd have never turned any of them down at that age. He had been in heaven—countless beauties willing to show him all sorts of interesting things. They had been quite the adventure-packed formative years.

"Who is she?" Helen asked, dragging his thoughts back to the present.

Gideon turned his head. One lady was never mentioned to another. But more than that, he could not bring himself to answer, for Helen had it spot-on. And it shook him, rattling at the core of how he defined himself as a man. Unreachable, in control, and one who knew better than to form an attachment to any client, no matter how intriguing the lady. He had seen enough of Rubicon's girls reduced to tears when a favorite client chose another, and had long ago vowed to never make that mistake himself. Never let them in.

He had not recognized that feeling in the pit of his stomach for what it was until Helen pointed out the truth.

He had let one in.

Now faced with it, he did not want to examine it for there was no hope.

"Oh, Gideon. I'm sorry. She's one of your clients, married to another, is she not?"

The genuine compassion in her tone was not comforting in the slightest. Gripping the black pawn tightly in one fist, he stared blindly into the fire burning down to embers in the nearby fireplace.

"Is he elderly, her husband?"

"I don't know," he replied stiffly. Bella's husband was the last person he wanted to think about.

"Does she know?"

"Know what?" He glanced uneasily at Helen from the corner of his eye.

"What you've given her?" she asked gently.

How could Bella, when he hadn't known himself until

mere moments ago? Still as a statue, he again averted his gaze and focused on keeping his breaths slow and even, forcing the ragged note away.

"When will you see her again?"

"I don't know. I don't know if she plans to hire me again." Every morning he awoke with a glimmer of hope of receiving a letter from Bella, and every afternoon he was disappointed. It had been a month. A very long month of disappointing afternoons.

Helen let out an exasperated sigh. "Gideon. If you care for her, you should go see her. Or at least write to her."

Eyes flaring at the absurdity of her request, he glared at Helen. "No. I can't."

"Why not?"

"It's not done. I can't . . . show up at her front door without an invitation." He would not do it. Would not arrive on her doorstep like a lovelorn fool. Would not dare to step that far above his place. Could not survive the distinct possibility of rejection.

"Yes, you can. It's not uncommon for married ladies to have male callers, or to indulge in discreet affairs. If nothing else, find out if her husband is elderly or in poor health. Perhaps she'll be as fortunate as I, and her husband will pass away, leaving her free and with his fortune."

Ever the practical Helen. He looked back to the fire, unwilling to even tease himself with the hope Bella could someday be his. Even if she were not married, a woman like her would never choose a man like him.

"Gideon, you have to stop thinking of her as a client and start thinking of her as the woman you love. Fight for her, or at least do something. Don't continue down this path you're on. If ever there was a man deserving of happiness, it is you. Give yourself a chance, for you will regret it forever if you do not."

Biting the inside of his cheek, he squeezed his eyes shut, determined not to completely lose his composure in front of Helen. He wanted to press the heels of his palms to his eyes, to scream against the force tearing at his chest.

But he could do nothing but endure it, and hope that with time it would fade.

There was a rustle of fabric as she got to her feet. "Thank you, my friend. This is where we part and where I wish you luck, for you will need it," she said sagely.

He stood and dropped a kiss on the back of her proffered hand. "Thank you, Helen," he said, hoarse from the tide of emotion crashing inside of him.

"If ever you should feel the need, I would welcome a letter from you. And you must drop me a note if you win your lady."

THAT evening Bella lingered in the hothouse for as long as she dared before the darkness of night pushed her toward the bright manor house, toward the safety of her rooms. She walked through the garden and opened the back door just enough to peek her head around it. The kitchen was empty. She let out a relieved breath and, careful not to make a sound, stepped into the house and closed the door behind her.

She crept through the kitchen. *Why had he returned today?* The loneliness and isolation were much preferred to this feeling of being on edge. She never felt comfortable around him, even when he was being amicable. This waiting, this constant suspense, it was tiring, yet she never slept well when he was at Bowhill. It wouldn't be for days after he left until her guard would finally fully drop.

And why had he brought "them" with him? Stirling was bad enough, but to have his latest band of followers in her house? Those disreputable souls, soaked in vice, did not inhabit the edges of polite society but some place far beyond. They were loud, crude, and forever inebriated. And they were not merry drunks either.

The loud riot, the squeals of the local tavern wenches, and the bellows of laughter signaled they had taken up in her drawing room. It would be safer to take the back servants' stairs to her rooms. She pivoted on her heel and strode back down the hall. With a quick glance over her shoulder, she turned a corner and bumped into a solid object. Instinctively she reached out to regain her balance, but snatched her hands back at the feel of slick silk and cool metal buttons.

"What have we here?"

A large hand grasped her waist, halting her attempt at a hasty retreat. His dark, half-lidded eyes sparkled with malicious intent.

"Release me," she said in her haughtiest voice, icicles stuck to the words.

"You aren't one of the locals, that's for sure. So you must be the wife. Stirling said you were a prime piece, and he wasn't exaggerating."

Her pulse raced in her ears. She lifted her hands and made to push him away, but could not bring herself to touch him. "Release me."

The man leaned close. A chunk of his black forelock fell over one eye. A lecherous smile curved his lips. "I think not. Now that I've caught you, I'll be keeping you."

She averted her face. "You will do no such thing. Release me this instant!"

"Where is the hospitality? Don't you want to properly welcome one of your guests?"

That hand on her waist glided upward and curved inward, the large fingers spreading, reaching toward her breast. Her skin crawled in revulsion. "You are no guest of mine and you are *not* welcome."

His dark eyes narrowed into hard slits. The teasing hint was gone. Before she could brace herself, he pushed her roughly against the wall, knocking the breath from her chest.

"Isabella."

The harsh whip of her name quickened the pulse racing in her veins. Stifling dread descended, a thick heavy blanket that almost brought her to her knees. She had managed to avoid him all day and now—

"You will give Lord Ripon your apologies," Stirling said as he advanced on her. The swiftness of his stride

blew his tousled auburn hair away from his face. His passably handsome features were contoured with fury. He
wasn't but a decade older than her twenty-four, but years
of vice and dissipation had aged him. The buttons on his
scarlet waistcoat strained under the force of his well-fed
belly. Every time she saw him she swore he was taller and
broader than the last. Her husband was not a man many
men provoked and for good reason.

Gathering her teetering courage, she squared her
shoulders. She had done nothing wrong, save try to stop a
man from mauling her. "I will do no such thing."

Her head snapped sharply to the right, connecting hard
with the wall behind her. Sparks danced before her eyes.
Pain shot from her left eye and radiated through her entire
skull.

"Apologize," Stirling growled.

Lord Ripon's cruel chuckle barely made it through the
pistol fire-like buzz filling her ears. She moved to shake
her head but it made the blinding pain worse.

"Apologize."

She hated the words, but the pain would only intensify
if she did not heed his command. He would not allow her
to disobey him, especially not in front of one of his fel-
lows. She could feel her eye swelling shut, skin stretching
under the agonizing throb. Clasping her hands, she dug
her fingernails into the delicate bones and veins on the
backs to resist the urge to press her palm to her eye. Her
arms shook under the strain. The pain was incredible and
having to stand before Stirling and Lord Ripon, Stirling's
features harsh with the threat of more and Ripon's satisfied and gloating, intensified it to unbearable levels.

Swallowing the tears clogging her throat, she tipped
her chin in submission. "Lord Ripon, you have my apologies. You are ever welcome in Lord Stirling's home." The
words were stilted and slow with the effort required to
give them voice.

She caught Ripon's answering smug nod from the corner of her right eye. Her humiliation was complete.

"Ripon!" A drunken male voice shouted from the drawing room.

"Pleasant wife you got there, Stirling." Lord Ripon turned and strode down the hall, leaving her alone with her husband.

Hot, whisky-soaked breath fanned her face as he leaned close. He loomed over her, more than thrice her size, as broad as a barn, and seemed to take up the entire hall. She shrank back against the wall. Every muscle instinctively drew tighter in preparation, her chest struggling under the force of her panic-laden pants.

"Remember your place. If you should ever speak to one of my acquaintances like that again, you will deeply regret it."

Then he was gone, his heavy footfalls fading down the hall. The instant his broad back disappeared into the drawing room, her spine collapsed on a great silent sob. Crouched on the floor, she buried her face in her hands. Her tears were like fire, searing her bruised eye. But she could not make the tears stop. They just kept coming, as if from a bottomless well.

Why does he hate me so much? After five years, she should be used to this. It was not the first time he had blackened her eye or humiliated her in front of others. Yet . . .

The image of a handsome face with a kind smile and fathomless whisky brown eyes materialized behind the lids of her closed eyes. *Oh, God, I miss you.* She clenched her jaw to keep the words inside, trembling against the onslaught of pure longing, pure need to be with him. Every day she missed him, and every day she cherished the memories of him. Yet today, right now, she needed him more than ever.

The sound of footsteps in the marble-floored entrance hall reached her ears. On a hitched breath, she bolted upright, darted around the corner, and slipped through a small door. She closed the door behind her, cloaking the narrow servants' stairs in darkness. With one hand on the wall to guide her way, she rushed up the steps, head bowed and left hand still pressed to her eye.

She collided with an unexpected object and stumbled back. A hand grabbed her wrist, righting her. Instinctively, she ducked her head from the flare of candlelight.

"Lady Stirling?"

Bella took a moment to steady her breaths before speaking. "Pardon, Mrs. Cooley."

She waited for her housekeeper to release her wrist, but the older woman's grip merely shifted until it resembled a comforting hold.

"Are you all right, your ladyship?"

"Yes."

Mrs. Cooley sighed. "No. You are the furthest thing from all right."

It was one thing to have Stirling hit her in front of his friends, but quite another to have her housekeeper, a woman Bella had to face every day, see her like this—shaking with fear, tears streaming down her cheeks. She tugged. Mrs. Cooley let go of her wrist, turned, and went up the stairs.

Bella stood still for a moment. But down the stairs led back to Stirling, so she reluctantly followed her house-keeper. The golden light from Mrs. Cooley's candle threw shadows on the walls. When they reached the second floor, Mrs. Cooley uncharacteristically poked her head around the door before opening it fully.

She motioned to Bella. "Come along. Shall I have Maisie sent to you?" she asked, once again the efficient house-keeper.

"No." Bella quickly stepped into the empty hall. She slipped into her bedchamber, her knees buckling the instant she turned the lock on the door.

ONE month later, Gideon stared out a carriage window at a tall black door. The half moon window above it was dark, as were the windows flanking the door and those on the second and third floors. But he knew the townhouse was not empty. There was one person inside. A woman to be exact, and she was likely growing very impatient by now.

He prided himself on punctuality, on arriving at the specified time. Yet ten o'clock had come and gone before he had left his apartment. Thus the reason why he sat in this carriage. It would have taken thirty minutes to walk to Lady Devlin's and, no matter how much he was avoiding it, it really would not do to arrive after eleven.

Pulling out his pocket watch, he held the face up to the window to catch the light from a nearby streetlamp. Ten minutes to eleven. He sighed. He could not put it off any longer. In any case, if he stalled much longer, his coat would pick up the smell of this old rented carriage, and dust and mold were two scents a lady would not welcome into her bedchamber.

"Ye gettin' out or not?"

"Yes," Gideon said defensively. He exited the carriage and paid the impatient driver. With a snap of leather lines, the driver left Gideon standing next to a streetlamp. Once the carriage was out of sight, he walked up the front stone steps, turned the knob, and opened the black door. After locking the door, he gave himself a moment to get oriented to the dark house.

"Third floor," he said, recalling his notes from his appointment book.

When he reached the second floor landing, he paused to let out a contemptuous snort. One would think he was climbing the steps to the hangman's noose. It would be midnight when he reached Lady Devlin's bedchamber if he kept up this pace.

More to prove a point to himself than anything, he bounded up the next flight of stairs. Yet he paused at the door at the end of the short hall and stared at the shiny brass knob.

"Enough," he muttered, completely disgusted with

himself. This inner resistance would disappear if he could just get this one appointment behind him. Then he could go on, as he always had. For this was what he did. This was what he was. And he needed to work if he had any hope in hell of ever leaving all of this behind some day.

He closed his eyes and righted himself to his current task.

Lady Devlin. Five foot one. Lush, petite brunette. *Not so bad, could be worse*, he thought with an apathetic shrug.

He knocked once and opened the door.

Damn.

His stomach sank. So much for any hope of easing into it. The many lit candles stationed about the room illuminated Lady Devlin in all her nude glory sprawled on the large four-poster bed.

"Gideon," she exclaimed as she hopped off the bed. She rushed across the room. "Naughty man. You kept me waiting."

She did not wait for a response but threw her arms around him. Avoiding her parted lips, he pressed his mouth to her neck. He tried to close his mind, shut it down and react purely on male instinct, but everything was wrong. The scent of lilacs filled his nostrils. Full breasts pressed too low against his chest. Breathy mewling noises filled his ears. The skin under his tongue tasted of salt and scent.

Small hands reached eagerly for the falls on his trousers. Somehow he resisted the impulse to jerk away and instead adroitly, smoothly, took her hands in his. He absently tickled her palms with the tips of his fingers as he debated where to place her hands. He did not even want her to touch him. Pulling her arms behind her back, he held them there as he nuzzled the small cove behind her ear.

Seemingly excited by the hint of bondage, she pressed those mountainous breasts against him again. "Yes," she sighed.

Maybe he should tie her to the bed. But then what would he do with her? His mind refused to cooperate. All he could think about was getting away from her. And his body—he'd had a strong inkling the moment he stepped into this bedchamber that *it* was not going to cooperate.

She took a step back, moving toward the large bed that dominated the room, but he kept his feet firmly rooted to the floor. There was no way in hell he was getting in that bed. He should not have come to this house tonight. He should have stayed on his self-imposed celibate path.

The many notes he had received these past weeks had been ignored, left to pile on his dining table. None of them bore the distinctive flowing feminine script he had been waiting for. But even if his clients did not complain about his silence, Rubicon would soon. He hadn't paid her in months. And in order to fill his long, lonely days, to divert his mind from the reason why he did not want to work, he had been frequenting the gaming tables.

The memory of last night's loss washed over him, and it did not help his current predicament. He could not believe he had sunk so low as to play roulette. It was common knowledge the odds were heavily stacked in favor of the house. Yet still, he had thrown those chips onto the green baize and numbly watched as the croupier snatched them up.

He had absolutely no will to bed this woman, and it wasn't just her. He had been as limp as an impotent old man since he returned to London, without even a trace of a morning erection.

Gideon felt her squirm to take another step back and he tried, truly he did, to summon up something, some hint of desire. Anything. The lurid images swam before his mind's eye.

A woman on her knees, her rouged mouth on his cock, her raven tresses skimming her derrière. Two beauties on a bed, their lithe limbs twined together, hands playing at each other's quims, an open invitation in their half-lidded eyes for him to join them. A lush harem houri on her hands and knees, her perfectly rounded backside lifted high, begging to be rammed to the hilt.

But there was nothing. Not even a twitch. He had never been so flaccid in all his life.

His cock had never let him down before. It was the most reliable part of him. He did not even have to think on it— he just got hard whenever he needed to. It never occurred to him before this night that his most trusted of body parts would let him down. He felt like a musician who suddenly could not play a note. A soloist standing before the orchestra without his violin. It shook him to the core, rattling loose every bit of confidence he had in himself. His entire adult life had been built around that one body part, and now—

"Oh, Gideon." She lifted up onto her toes and tried to capture his mouth with hers.

Tightening his grip slightly on her wrists, he bent her upper body back, keeping those questing lips away from his own. She threw back her head and he sprinkled a necklace of light, nipping kisses on her exposed neck, moving his attentions to her other ear.

Sweat pricked between his shoulder blades. His cravat felt like a damn noose. He needed to get out of this room. She would only allow him to nuzzle her neck for so long before she started voicing demands.

The seconds ticked down in his head. Urgency pressed in on him. For the life of him he could not figure out how to leave without delivering the deepest of insults. He did not want to hurt her feelings, but there was no way he could go through with it tonight. No matter how hard he tried to will it, his body simply would not cooperate.

And it felt so wrong to be here, the taste of betrayal thick in his throat. How was he to get out of this room, this house? He wracked his seized brain. Pretending as though he had another engagement was not an option. Lady Devlin had been on his calendar for months. Lord Devlin had planned an excursion to the country after Parliament closed for the summer and Lady Devlin had decided to indulge in her husband's absence. She had even managed to get all the servants out of the house.

Maybe he could plead a headache, or feign sickness? He certainly felt ill. Each mewl from her lips made his stomach churn as though it was filled with live eels.

Yes, that was it. Dinner was not sitting well. And the thought of him ensconced in the washroom puking his guts out should douse her passions, if nothing else.

Fifteen

THE next day Gideon paced the length of Rubicon's office as he waited for his employer to make an appearance. Ignoring the well-stocked liquor cabinet, he kept his strides determined and his thoughts focused on his errand. He could no longer avoid the inevitable. But strangely, it was not an errand that brought dread, rather something that resembled relief.

After a very long ten minutes, the door hidden in the paneled wall swung open. Rubicon glided into the room and took her place behind the teakwood desk. Her blonde hair was pulled up in its usual deliberately tousled coif and her face was painted in the standard madam's mask. He must have interrupted her at her toilette, for the figure-hugging scarlet gown had been replaced with a laced-edged pink silk wrapper.

"Good afternoon, Rosedale. How convenient you came to call. I haven't heard from you in so long I was beginning to grow a bit concerned."

He ignored her not-so-subtle reminder that he had not paid her in months and walked to the desk, dropping a slim black leather book onto it. "I have come to give you my resignation. You may contact my clients and if they are amenable, send someone else in my place."

Her expression did not change as she picked up his appointment book, which contained the names and addresses of every woman he had visited in the last decade, less Bella. There was a little *swoosh* of paper as she flipped the pages. At length, she closed it. "Have a seat."

"No, thank you. I prefer to stand."

"Sit."

He opened his mouth to argue then closed it and sat down. It was the last command of hers he would ever obey.

The edges of her lips curved in satisfaction. Her gaze dropped to the leather volume. "I never knew you were so organized, Rosedale. It is a rare trait in this business." She tapped her finger against her chin. He could almost hear her mind whirling. Her kohl-rimmed eyes met his, and the hard gleam put him immediately on his guard. "I do not accept your resignation."

He blinked. "Pardon?"

"You are much too valuable to me. You will go to Hampshire tomorrow and leave her ladyship with a very big smile on her face."

"Rubicon, you do not understand. I will not work for you ever again."

"No, Gideon, it is you who does not understand," she said. "I will not release you. I will not allow you to pimp yourself out on your own, or to go to some other establishment and deny me my rightful profits. You will remain in my employ."

Stupid, greedy woman. She thought he was trying to make a go on his own. "I quit. Completely. I have no intention of ever bedding a woman for monetary gain again."

"Oh, so you've developed a conscience, have you?" she asked archly.

"I have developed a severe dislike for my line of work."

"You'll just have to learn to like it again."

Frustrated at her insistence, he shook his head. "I will never like it again as I will never do it again."

"Whether you like it or not is of little concern to me. You will adhere to my wishes."

"I can't," he said coldly, taking perverse satisfaction in his response. She could push him at women all she liked. It would not bring her even one shilling.

Rubicon cocked her head, as if his words caught at something in her greedy brain. She was silent for a moment. "Can't or won't?"

"Both. I am of no use to you anymore. Ask Lady Devlin if you doubt."

She picked up the appointment book, flipped a few pages, and studied it. The slow, knowing smile that spread across her face made him distinctly uncomfortable. "Couldn't get it up? I assume you displayed the appropriate level of tact and didn't blame it on the lady."

"It had absolutely nothing to do with Lady Devlin. It could have been anyone." Well, not anyone. There was one, but he would likely never get to see her again. Two months had passed and she had not written to him.

"Not to worry, Rosedale." Rubicon waved a hand, casually dismissing his life-altering problems. "This happens to all my men at least once. Overuse. Overstimulation. A rest is all you need. I shall send Albert to handle your appointments for the next month and you shall stay in Town and recover. After a month of no women, of not touching your cock for anything but the necessary, you'll be so hard up even a three-hundred-pound matron won't put you off."

His lip curled in distaste. "Rubicon, it has nothing to do with a need for rest. I simply *cannot* anymore. Nothing will work. I've tried. Believe me. I am completely useless to you." And he had tried. Done everything he could think of, even taken himself in hand. But it had all been in vain. He could not deny it. He was ruined, broken, no longer "simply perfect." And would never be again.

Her eyes narrowed to hard slits. Flattening her palms on the desk, she half rose out of the chair. Her breasts threatened to spill from the deep V-neck of the thin wrapper. "It's that Scottish bitch, isn't it? The one who requested your company for the space of a fortnight. She's gotten to you, hasn't she?"

Rage surged, hot and thick. Gideon bit the inside of his cheek in an effort to hold back the unwise retort and gripped the arms of the chair to keep his hands from flying out to strangle Rubicon. How dare she refer to Bella like that?

"You fool," she spat. "Did she profess her undying love for you? Did you actually believe her? You are a prostitute, Rosedale. Nothing to her, or to any of them, but a servant. In fact, you're less than a servant. You're merely a means to an orgasm."

Somehow he kept from flinching at the hard truth in her cruelly slung words. He knew it already. He did *not* need Rubicon to remind him of the reason why he couldn't even bring himself to write to Bella. At length, he felt calm enough to respond. "I will no longer work for you," he said flatly. "Nothing you say will change that fact."

"You owe me," she said, any vestige of composure now long gone. "If it wasn't for me, you would be nothing." Her gaze raked the length of him. Her rouged mouth thinned in disgust. "I've clearly spoiled you. I let you move out of this house. I indulged your pride and allowed you to refuse paying clients simply because they were men. And this is how you repay me? I was the one who convinced Christina to bring you here. Your mother didn't want anything to do with you, but I saw your potential. I let you live here, clothed you, fed you, and never once had you whipped even when you left your sooty little handprints on the walls. If it weren't for me, your mother would have left you to rot in the street. And this is how you repay me?"

Gideon bristled at the reminder. "I am well aware of that. But any debt I owed you is long since paid. I've been working for you in one form or another since I was seven."

"No, it is not paid until I deem it so," she said. "Do you

know how many offers I turned down for you when you were a boy? I kept the lechers away from you, saved you until you were older. Gave you the luxury of learning in my girls' beds for years before I hired you out. You haven't come close to paying me back yet."

"What?" he asked, with a confused shake of his head.

Her cold, mocking laughter grated down his spine. "Did you actually believe they swived you because they wanted to? None of my girls spread their legs without my consent. Your education was my doing, Rosedale. I ordered them all to fuck you, to teach you how to please a woman. I molded you into the perfect instrument of pleasure. I made you, and you *will* work for me until such time as I release you."

He dragged a shaky hand through his hair. "But I am of no use to you anymore."

She raised one blonde eyebrow, her lips quirking at the desperation in his tone. "I can find a use for you. Even a eunuch has his uses in a whorehouse."

His gut tightened in trepidation, but he squared his shoulders, held his ground. "No, Rubicon. I refuse."

She ignored him, as if he hadn't spoken. "In fact, I have the ideal use for you. And if you even think of refusing me, you will find yourself on the prison hulk *Justitia*, arrested for sodomy."

"What? I-I have never—" he sputtered, too outraged to finish the sentence.

"You are a prostitute, Rosedale, and the purpose of male prostitutes is to be used by other men. No one will believe you've worked this long without bending over at least once. You may try to deny it. You may even try to cast me in the role of vindictive madam. But it will do you no good. No one will believe you. I have many friends, and the captain is a special favorite. Very useful man to have on one's side. He has a particular pleasure and I am one of the few who can provide it. If you try to refuse me, you will find yourself in the bowels of his ship where even the guards rarely go. A man such as yourself? Ah, they will fight over you, Rosedale. So handsome, so pretty. They'll never leave you alone. And I won't let them kill you. You will waste away down there, until disease takes you. You will beg to go ashore to the Warren for hard labor, but you will never again see the light of day. So the choice is yours. Either work for me, or work on the *Justitia*. You can't escape me, Rosedale. Wherever you go, I will find you."

He had known she was a ruthless woman, one not to be crossed, but had never expected this. She had a network of informants. Her reach was far. As for her threat . . . it was neither idle nor empty. He had no doubt she would see it through.

No one could live in London without knowing of the converted old ships of the line anchored on the Thames at Woolwich. They were worse than Newgate, than any prison on land. He had heard the tales often enough and knew what would await him. Gideon was certainly no coward, but even the hardest of criminals blanched at the prospect of serving time on a prison hulk. The lowest level, prisoners kept in irons, the overcrowed conditions, the hatches screwed down tight each night—chaos and darkness would reign. And she would ensure he never set foot on land again.

He had no choice. None at all. His kind rarely did.

His shoulders slumped in resignation. He hung his head. His will, his pride, gone.

"What will you have me do?" he asked hollowly.

A gloating smile spread across her face. "You will take Timothy's place tonight. He is currently . . . recovering. But don't worry. I will have someone watching the room lest matters get out of hand again. I wouldn't want anything to happen to you. I charged quite a pretty price for Timothy. For you I can charge even more. And your little problem won't be a hindrance. Timothy rarely got to fuck them. His clients' interests lay elsewhere."

THE heels of her slippers clicked on the stone floor as the woman walked slowly around him admiring the result of her handiwork. Careful not to make eye contact, Gideon kept his face blank and stared straight ahead at the gray stone wall.

He had never been in this room before. He knew it existed, but even when he had worked here as a boy, he never had cause to enter it. It was tucked below, away from the other rooms in the house. The wooden door was thick to muffle the sounds from within. There were no windows, only sconces placed at regular intervals along the bare walls. A bed stood against one wall. The leather lines tied to the wrought iron frame lay stretched on the sheet waiting for their next victim. A massive cabinet dominated another wall and was filled with everything the room's occupants might need. A straight-back wooden chair stood by the door. That was it. The room was very spartan and definitely not a pleasant place to find oneself.

The slow clicks stopped as she paused before him. A very pleased smile curved her lips, her eyes alight with sat-isfaction. Dark, almost black hair hung in a straight sheet down her back. The creamy swells of her breasts spilled from the black lace corset tied so tightly it pulled her body into a severe hourglass. The triangle of hair between her thighs was just as dark as that on her head, and framed by black ribbons tied from the bottom of the corset to the tops of black silk stockings.

The end result should have produced at least a nudge of desire. But he was as unaffected by her as he had been by every other woman since he had left Scotland. It was a rather good thing, for the black leather breeches she had him don were so tight they were almost cutting off his circulation. A hard cock in these breeches would have been most uncomfortable.

He had always done his best to avoid the likes of her. His tastes did not run toward bondage or sadism. Pain was never needed to incite his passions, and he refused to inflict it on others. His gift was in giving pleasure.

But this had nothing to do with pleasure. It was about control and domination. Her desire to inflict her will upon him, to vent her frustrations.

She would leave here tonight and go back to her townhouse, slip back into the rigid rules of society, bow to her husband's wishes and to the dictates of propriety. None of her vaunted acquaintances would ever guess that beneath the ladylike demeanor was this.

Without a word she resumed her circuit, her gaze sweeping possessively up and down his body, which was bare except for those damn breeches. A small hand grabbed his arse. He flinched, powerless to do anything to stop her as she groped him at will. She squeezed hard, almost pinching, and then smoothed her palm in slow circles.

"Very nice," she purred, warm breath fanning his bare shoulder.

He winced. The chains locked around his wrists stringing his arms out and up to the ceiling rattled harshly at the startled jerk of his body as she brought a riding crop down smartly on his backside.

Bloody hell. She knew how to wield that thing. She had quite the snap in her wrist and the leather breeches did nothing to dampen the blow. He could feel the line across his arse stinging and smarting.

Tapping the end of her crop against her palm, she came around to stand before him again. A very smug smile curved her rouged mouth. The unholy gleam in her pale blue eyes did not bode well for him. "Did you like that?"

His gaze snapped to hers.

"I did not give you permission to look at me," she admonished.

Gideon obediently averted his gaze to the stone floor.

"Answer me. Did you like that?"

This was it. This was all he was good for anymore—to serve as a pampered lady's whipping boy.

He knew his role. He knew the answer she wanted to hear. And he wiped his mind clean of every thought, every wish, every need and of all emotion. Until there was nothing left inside.

Bowing his head, he closed his eyes and said in a toneless voice, "Yes, mistress."

Sixteen

THE door clicked shut as she left the room. Gideon stood there, completely numb, for what felt like an eternity. Head bowed and eyes closed, he waited.

His ears registered a door opening, the shuffle of footsteps, and the scrape of a chair being dragged across the stone floor. Thick, callused fingers brushed his wrist. With a click, the lock opened and his arm dropped like a dead weight to his side. A moment later the other arm was freed. Fiery pain snapped along his muscles as he rotated his shoulders. His fingers started to tingle, like needles pricking the skin, as blood flowed anew.

"Do you need anything?" a male voice asked gruffly.

Gideon did not look at the voice's owner. He couldn't. He just shook his bowed head.

And the footsteps retreated, the door closed, leaving him alone.

He would not do that again, could not go through that again. She had toyed with him for well over an hour, alternating between whipping his arse and taunting him, like a cat torturing a mouse. Every one of her questions had been answered with the same two words—*yes, mistress*. After she'd grown bored of him, she had pressed her back against the wall and pleasured herself, the whole while asking him if he wanted her.

He had stood there, chained, his backside stinging and burning, as she came. The flush of arousal that had tinged the creamy swells of her breasts and the soft pants from between her parted lips had no effect on him. He had just waited until she was done.

The pulse that had stayed strangely even the past hour started to pound through his veins. His breaths turned short and ragged. His muscles trembled.

God, he felt so wrong. He could not even stand himself. He wasn't a man, but something much less.

There is more to you than this.

On a low, pained groan, he clenched his jaw and squeezed his eyes shut tight. He took a great gulp of air and clung tightly to her words. The words Bella had spoken with such conviction, with such certainty. They fortified him, giving him the strength to peel off those breeches, put on his clothes, and leave that room.

Regardless of what Rubicon believed, he wasn't completely without acceptable options. There was one left. One he had previously refused to even consider.

After slipping unnoticed out the back door of Rubicon's, he traveled the short distance to his apartment on foot and quickly stuffed a few things into a leather saddlebag. He opened the top drawer of his dresser, pushed aside the neatly folded cravats, and pulled out a plain wooden box. He lifted the lid, set aside the bundle on top, and stared at the box's contents.

The small fortune's worth of gold sovereigns and pound notes had never felt like enough. Not when it needed to blind a woman to what he was and where he had come from. For the past decade women had been paying him, and he had been saving their money to buy himself a wife. He chuckled, oddly amused at the irony.

But when he looked into that wooden box, it now felt like too much. At the moment, he did not feel like he was worth more than a farthing. He felt like the cheapest of whores—those poor souls who let themselves be used for a bottle of gin. But Rubicon believed him to be worth quite a bit. He could only hope he had enough to placate her greed.

He stuffed the box in his saddlebag and grabbed the bundle on the dresser, but before pocketing it he unwrapped it. It wasn't the fold of pound notes inside that made his heart clench, but the paper wrapper itself.

With a shaky fingertip he traced the aristocratic curve of her cheekbone, the lush lips pulled in the faintest of smiles and the graceful length of her lean arm. His throat tightened, his body trembling with longing. He was a hack of an artist and had not done her beauty justice, but his soul remembered the look in her eyes he had tried to capture. That look had made him feel like a king among men. Only Bella had ever looked at him like that.

He loved her. *Christ*, he loved her and he could not possibly go on without at least seeing her. And the only way to see her was to give up on his boyhood dream, to give up all he had. There would be no house in the country, no family to call his own in his future. He'd be left with nothing save his love for Bella, and that was all that mattered anymore.

After carefully refolding the sketch over the pound notes, he slipped it into his coat pocket. He left, not pausing to give a last glance to his cherished apartment before closing the front door.

Fifteen minutes later he was opening the door to Rubicon's office.

Slamming her glass of gin onto her desk, she stood from her chair. "Where have you been? I have another client who has been waiting for half an hour. Get your arse back down to the dungeon." She pointed a hard finger at the closed door behind him.

Unfazed by Rubicon's anger, he stopped in front of her

desk. "She'll be waiting an awfully long time if she wants me. I quit."

"We have been through this once already, Rosedale. Have you developed a preference for men? Do you wish to be raped? If not, then I suggest you take off that fine coat of yours and get your pretty arse back down to the dungeon."

Ignoring her, he pulled the wooden box from his saddlebag. The distinctive clink of coins as he dropped the box onto her desk caught her attention.

"You claim I owe you. So, I'm paying you back. The choice is yours," he said coldly, relishing the opportunity to throw her words back at her. "You can either accept this or nothing, for I shall never work for you again. Go ahead, throw me in the *Justitia*. No one will pay for me down there."

Shaking with fury, she glared at him and he stared right back, daring her to doubt his conviction. Her eyes widened as she opened the lid of the box, but she quickly masked her shock. "I'm not sure if this is enough," she said, sounding like a peeved adolescent.

Standing tall, he clasped his hands behind his back and lifted his chin. "It's enough. The deed to my apartment, along with the key, is in there as well."

She poked a finger into the box, investigating his offer. "I suspected you were tucking some money away, but . . . This is everything?" she said, her tone both a question and an awed statement.

"Everything," he lied. "If you accept it there will be no going back. No claim I still owe you even one penny." There was honor, even among thieves and whores. Rubicon may be a vindictive greedy bitch, but he had never known her to go back on a deal.

For a long moment, she was silent. She must have sensed this was his best and final offer, her last opportunity to ever receive a shilling from him for she nodded curtly. Her greed won out, just as he hoped.

"Good-bye, Rosedale."

Without even the courtesy of a parting nod to the woman who had kept him off the street, he left and headed for the nearest livery. He rented the swiftest horse, threw himself into the saddle, and tore down the lamplit streets of London. His horse's hooves thundered on the dirt roads.

There was no relief at finally being free of Rubicon. Only an all-consuming need to reach Bella. She was the only thought in his head. She would welcome him, he reassured himself over and over again, as he kept his heels pressed to the mare's sides. He could not go back to what he had been and could not go on without her. She would cleanse his soul, fill his heart, make him feel like a man again. Make him whole.

He traveled relentlessly, stopping only to change horses. Not stopping to rest and only stopping to eat when his body felt as though it was going to shut down. His backside was past numb—he severely doubted he'd ever have feeling in it again. But he refused to hire a carriage. It wasn't fast enough. He could not reach Bella fast enough.

What he would say to her, what he hoped to accomplish . . . that he did not know. He only knew that he needed to see her again—a few hours, a few moments, anything.

BELLA squinted against the afternoon sun as she looked out her bedroom window. Her roses were in full bloom, the back garden a wash of pink, red, and white. The roses needed her and she needed them. The only time she approached calm these days was when she was with them. Yet she hadn't been to the hothouse or the garden in over a week. The hot August days had been luring her guests outdoors for lawn games and various other drunken revelries, and she did not dare leave her rooms for fear of crossing one of their paths again.

Why hadn't they left yet? Moreover, why hadn't *he* left

yet? Stirling had never stayed this long before. Usually it was just a brief stopover on his way to another of his estates in Scotland, or on his way back to England or Edinburgh. A few days, a week at best. A month was unprecedented. Hopefully he had not decided to take up residence. If he had . . .

A scowl marred her brow. Irritation seeped into her near-constant anxiety. He didn't even care for this property. Bowhill meant so little to him he had conceded to Phillip and included it in the marriage settlement. Yet her husband had decided to torment her and spend this particular summer here, at what could someday become her house, that is, if he went to his grave before she went to hers.

A knock sounded on her dressing room door. She tensed.

"Lady Stirling?" came her maid's voice through the narrow door.

Bella unlocked the door and opened it. "Yes, Maisie?"

"Lord Stirling wishes to see you in his study," she said, ginger eyebrows lowered and shoulders hunched, clearly reluctant to be the bearer of bad news.

A tight knot twisted Bella's stomach. Keeping her spine straight, she nodded. The maid left. Bella checked her reflection in the mirror above her vanity. The old bruise now long gone, her face was pale, her cheeks slightly more hollow than usual. Her simple morning dress would have to do as she did not dare take the time to change.

After unlocking the doors to her bedchamber and sitting room, she crept down the steps, her senses attuned for any sign of his guests.

The study door loomed at the end of the hall. As she neared it, she told herself perhaps he simply wanted to inform her of his imminent departure. It was wishful thinking, as he never kept her abreast of his plans, but she clung tightly to the thread of hope.

Her arm shook as she lifted it to knock on the door.

"Enter."

Willing the anxiety in check, she took a deep breath and entered the room.

Stirling sat behind the walnut desk, his attention on an account ledger. A full glass of amber whisky was on one of the untidy piles of paper at his elbow. Mr. Leighton's filing system, or lack thereof, never seemed to upset Stirling. Her husband granted Bowhill's aging secretary limitless largess while she received none.

She stopped two paces from the desk. As she waited for him to acknowledge her presence, her glance slid over his broad shoulder. Her heart skipped a beat.

His portrait was swung against the wall exposing the open safe.

She felt the color leech from her face.

Stirling looked up from the account ledger. "Ah, wife. You are my wife, aren't you? I've been at Bowhill for a month and only recall seeing my wife once."

His reproachful gaze swept up and down her body. She lifted her chin and tried to hide the way her knees trembled.

He sneered. "Haughty cold bitch. That's you." He leaned back in his chair and threw back half the contents of his glass. The man consumed whisky as if it were water. "I've had enough of your temper tantrums. You have been quite negligent in your duties as hostess. You will be at dinner tonight. I expect you to be polite and gracious, and not at all your usual self. You will charm our guests, leave them panting in your wake. Leave them believing I am the luckiest of men to have you for a wife."

She wanted to say no. Presiding over his table, pretending as if he were not a monster . . . She could not do it. The effort required to hold back the word pulled her brow and tightened her mouth.

"Yes, my dear? You have something you wish to say?"

He gave her the opening to at least voice the word, but she did not take it. Yet she couldn't remain silent either.

"Where are your guests this afternoon?" The house was quiet—too quiet. And she had not seen them from her window.

"They went out for a ride."

Foxed men on horseback. She could only hope a few of them lost their way, or cracked a skull taking a jump. It would be particularly pleasing if Lord Ripon was one of the unfortunates. Then she wouldn't have to see his gloating, leering face across the dining table.

Stirling picked up his pen and went back to studying the account ledger. Through sheer force of will, she kept her gaze from straying to the open wall safe and waited. Waited with baited breath, nerves strung tight with suspense. And just when relief began to wash over her, just when she was about to turn and leave the room, his deep voice broke the taut silence.

"You're an expensive one to keep. That pathetic dowry I got off your brother doesn't even begin to cover you. Over five hundred pounds gone since I last visited. Your modiste should be kissing my boots. Since you now have ample gowns to choose from, I expect you to dazzle my guests." He didn't look at her as he flicked his fingers in her direction. "Something revealing. Ripon liked your tits."

The way he spoke, as if she were an object, a pet to parade in front of his friends. She had endured *his* temper tantrums, his tirades, his neglect and abuse for years! And had never once complained, but this . . . this . . .

The hate welled up. Hot and thick. Every trace of fear vanished. Her hands balled into fists and she asked the question that had plagued her for five years. "Why did you marry me?"

Startled, he glanced up.

"Why? You clearly hate me. You've never shown the slightest interest. As you so eloquently pointed out, there wasn't a fortune attached to my name. You never even danced with me when I had my coming-out. So why did you marry me?"

Lip curling, he averted his gaze. "Because everyone wanted you, at least until you proved yourself a whore. But that, dear wife, was the ultimate appeal. A woman who looked like you yet would fuck a stable boy? You were a guaranteed good ride. You were supposed to fix—" He clenched his jaw, cutting off the words.

Bella gaped at him as it dawned on her. She was supposed to have been his cure. He hated her because she had not cured his impotency. It made perfect sense. She hadn't felt hate from him on the day of their wedding. It had made its first appearance that night.

"But you're a haughty, cold bitch, both in bed and out. And yes, I hate you."

Any trace of compassion she started to feel for him disappeared. "I didn't buy any gowns," she said calmly.

He looked taken aback at the abrupt change in topic. She reveled in the confusion on his ugly face. A little triumphant grin pulled her lips.

"The five hundred pounds," she said. "I didn't buy any gowns with it. I hired a man, one who could do what you cannot. I freely gave him what you could not take. He was amazing, both in bed and out, and I love him. And yes, I hate you."

As soon as the words left her lips she went utterly still. Her voice echoed strangely in her ears. The courage slid out of her body, leaving her weak. Did she actually say that?

Stirling did not move. For a seemingly endless moment, neither of them moved. She knew she had made a grave mistake, a mistake she would pay dearly for, yet her feet were locked to the floor.

A flush rose up his neck. His eyes narrowed. A low rumbling growl filled the study.

On a strangled cry, she turned and ran. Out of the study, down the hall. Holding her skirt high to free her legs, she used her other hand on the banister to pull her upward as she sprinted up the stairs. The heavy footsteps behind her sent her pulse racing to panicked levels. She wrenched open her sitting room door and slammed it shut. Gasping for breath, she fumbled desperately in her pocket for the key, but her hands shook too hard to cooperate.

The brass key was finally in hand when the door flew open, knocking her to the ground. The back of her head smacked the hard wooden floor, sending her senses reeling.

"You whore!"

A large hand grabbed her upper arm, wrenching it almost out of the socket. He yanked her roughly to her feet. She caught a glimpse of eyes wild with fury before being thrown against the wall. Her shoulder blade connected painfully with the sharp corner of a picture frame. Instinctively, her arms flew up to cover her face.

She tried not to cry, not to plead for mercy, as he rained blow after vicious blow on her. Her ears rang from the deafening force of his screams.

"You fucking whore!"

The moment before the pain overwhelmed her, one strangely coherent thought flickered in her mind. Either his fists were a lot harder than she remembered, or he must be hitting her with something. It felt like a candlestick. Probably the silver one that had been on the small console table right inside the door.

Pity that, she had been rather fond of it.

THE sight of the manor house pulled a great sigh of relief from Gideon's chest. Praying Bella's husband was not in residence, he pulled the sweating horse to a stop and landed on his feet. He grunted, knees buckling for an instant before he willed them to work. After looping the reins over the wrought iron rail, he marched up the stone steps and knocked on the front door.

It was late but hopefully not too late for Bella to be in bed. He hastily buttoned his coat and swatted at his sleeves, sending up little puffs of dust from the road. Christ, he must look a sight. He hadn't shaved or bathed since he left London. Perhaps he should have stopped and cleaned himself up before—

The door swung open, revealing Bella's dour-faced butler. After a quick look at Gideon the man flared his thin nostrils.

Gideon squared his shoulders. "I am here to call on Lady Stirling."

"Lady Stirling is not at home."

His eyes flared. Panic seeped into his voice as he asked, "Where is she?"

"Lady Stirling is not at home to callers," the man clarified, looking down his hooked nose at Gideon.

He shook his head. Why hadn't he caught on? The butler had not meant she was not physically at home but that she wasn't receiving. "Tell her Mr. Rosedale is here to see her."

"Lady Stirling is not at home." The butler moved to shut the door.

Gideon put his foot in the jamb and placed a hand on the door to keep it open. "Tell her," he demanded desperately.

Half hidden by the partially closed door, the butler turned his head. Gideon heard a low female voice, not Bella's. A grimace pulled the butler's thin mouth. Then he nodded once and opened the door, fully revealing Bella's housekeeper. The capable, efficient air was gone. Her face was taut with unease. The tension pouring out of the open door pricked the hairs on the nape of Gideon's neck.

"You are here." There was a hint of astonishment in her statement.

"Where is she?"

Gideon's forceful demand pushed the woman back a step. But the butler held firm, the unflappable guardian of Bowhill.

"Is Lord Stirling here?" Gideon asked, fearing the possible answer.

"No," she said with a short shake of her head.

Alarm tightened his gut. "Has he been here?"

The gray eyes heavy with regret, with sadness, answered his question.

Gideon pushed the butler roughly aside, clearing a path for him to sprint into the house and up the stairs.

"Mr. Rosedale?" Mrs. Cooley's voice echoed in the hall, her quick footsteps behind him.

"Bella," he called as he approached her door. The knob turned but the door wouldn't open. He threw his shoulder into the door but it held. Bella must have blocked it. Dread skittered lightning quick through his veins. He rattled the knob in frustration. "Bella!"

"Mr. Rosedale. Do stop." The censure in the house-keeper's slightly out of breath voice turned him from Bella's door. "It won't do any good. I've already unlocked the doors but she won't answer."

"Did you tell him?" Every muscle drew tight in trepidation. If he had brought the earl's wrath down on Bella . . . He swallowed hard.

Affronted, she lifted her chin. A sneer twisted her mouth. "That Lady Stirling has had a male caller at Bowhill who is not her cousin? No."

There was a brief, very brief moment of relief before the possible true cause of the blocked door set in.

Why had he never asked Bella about her husband? She had told him she had been maudlin, had given him the opening, but he hadn't taken it. It had been too ingrained in him not to take it.

Forcing aside the question of what had pushed Bella to employ a chair in addition to a lock, he studied the door. It was big, imposing, and thick. Too thick. But not all the doors in this house were constructed like this one.

"Mr. Rosedale?"

Gideon ignored the housekeeper and disappeared inside the earl's unlocked sitting room. Beneath the scent of lemons and wax, of newly polished floorboards, was the distinct odor of a man. The room had been recently inhabited. Instinctively he held his breath as he passed through the bedchamber and into the dressing room. He turned the knob on the door but to no avail.

But this door was narrower and felt to be constructed of thinner wood. He knocked on the door first and called softly, giving Bella time to realize it was he. To open the door.

He received no response.

His muscles vibrating with panic, he took a step back and threw his shoulder into the door. The wood creaked but held. He took another step back and kicked under the knob with all the strength in his body.

The door flew open under the onslaught. Under the sound of wood splintering was the clank of metal. The room was dark, the curtains drawn tight.

"Bella, it's Gideon. Don't be frightened." Breaths sawing in and out, he lit the candle on her vanity. The flare of golden candlelight illuminated a figure curled on the massive bed. He rushed to her side, put one knee on the mattress, and brushed the tangled pale blonde hair from her face. "Bella-Bella," he whispered, the tone heavy with anguish.

Violet eyes snapped open. "Gideon?" She spoke his name as if she feared he was a ghost.

"Yes, Bella. I'm here." He made to take her in his arms, but she recoiled like an injured animal. "*Shh*," he crooned.

"It hurts," she confessed in a childlike whisper.

"What hurts?"

"Everything. Everywhere."

"Can you stand?"

"I don't want to."

"Please, Bella. Let me help you. I need to see you."

At length, she nodded and allowed him to help her off the bed. Careful and slow, he unbuttoned her dress. It slipped from her arms, fluttering in a violet wave to the floor, revealing a familiar white zephyr silk chemise. The lace-edged hem skimmed her calves.

When he made to undo the tiny buttons on the bodice of her chemise, she started again. He crooned lightly, begging her to trust him. His fingers brushed the smooth warm skin of her chest as he undid the row of buttons. She mutely lifted her arms and he pulled the garment over her head, dropping it to the floor.

She stood bare before him, trembling like a blade of grass in the breeze. The single lit candle did not provide an extraordinary amount of light, but the rays that reached the bedside were plenty enough. Dark bruises on her torso and outer thighs stood out in stark contrast from the patches of pale ivory skin. She was much thinner than he remembered. The firm breasts had lost some of their fullness. The jut of her collarbone was more pronounced and her lean hips had lost their gentle curve.

"You have not been eating well," he commented, his voice detached.

She tipped her chin down in a gesture of patent submission. "He makes me nervous."

The dark smudges under the worried violet eyes probably matched his own. But there wasn't a single mark on her beautiful face. He glanced to her forearms and found the answer. The backs of them were heavily bruised from taking the intended blows.

He reached out to turn her around but stopped, hands hovering an inch from her thin shoulders, afraid to touch her for fear of hurting her. "Turn around," he said softly.

She gave a little nod and obeyed.

He swept the heavy sheet of pale blonde hair over her shoulder and the sight of her back made him suck in a swift breath. "What did he hit you with?"

"A candlestick." She rolled one shoulder uncomfortably, the sharp plane of her shoulder blade working with the motion.

"Why? Why would he do this to you?"

"I told him about you. I shouldn't have said it, but I couldn't stop the words."

She confirmed his worse fear. This was his fault. He struggled to catch his breath. "When did he do this to you?" he asked, thankful she could not see his face.

"Yesterday afternoon. I heard them leave shortly after."

"Them?"

"Stirling and his acquaintances."

"Will he return?"

Bella shook her head. "He probably won't be back for many months. I don't know why he stayed as long as he did. He's usually only in residence for a day or two, a week at most."

Two strides brought him around before her and he embraced her as gently as he could, as though she were made of the thinnest, most fragile porcelain. She burrowed into him, hiding her face. Shivers wracked her body.

"Where are your nightgowns?"

"In the dresser," she mumbled into his chest.

He reluctantly released her and strode across the room, but a glint of metal stopped him short. Stooping down, he picked up a silver letter opener from the floor near the vanity. He stared at it a moment, then his gaze moved slowly, hesitantly up to the dressing room doorframe. Straightening, he leaned in closer.

There was a small gouge in the molding, flush with where the door would be when it was closed. He glanced back to the letter opener in his hand. The tip was blunted. With a shaky breath, he set the letter opener on the vanity and closed the dressing room door the best he could. But his kick had misaligned the hinges, leaving the door ajar.

Mindful of the naked woman standing a few paces behind him, he went to the dresser. He selected the softest nightgown from the neat stack in the middle drawer. Then he helped her to put it on and climb into bed. But he didn't join her.

"Where are you going?" she called to his retreating back.

"I'll be gone for only a moment. I need to speak to your housekeeper."

"Why do you need to speak to Mrs. Cooley?" There was a fearful suspicion in her tone.

He paused at the door to her sitting room and looked

over his shoulder. "The whole household is worried about you. I'll be right back; I promise."

After seeing Bella, he had a clear understanding of the terror that had driven her to lock and block every entrance leading to her rooms. But that gouge in the doorframe . . . it wasn't fresh. That letter opener had been put into service many times. It was an easy trick, one he had used as an adolescent when he had need of uninterrupted privacy. Jam the end of an object, in his case a knife, in the frame of a closed door. The length of the knife prevented the door from swinging open. Required little strength yet highly effective.

As he removed the straight-back chair from under the sitting room doorknob and made to put it back in front of her desk, he noticed another object out of place. A candlestick lay on the floor a few paces from the desk. It was sleek and long, clearly more an object of art than practicality. He picked it up, the weight of it heavy in his palm.

The candlestick clutched tight in one hand, he opened the door. He found Mrs. Cooley waiting in the hall, an odd mixture of censure and anxiety on her face.

"Is she—?"

Gideon nodded curtly. "Fetch a doctor. I want him here now."

Mrs. Cooley's eyes flared at the sharp, commanding tone laced with fraying fury, but she did not nod in agreement. "How is Lady Stirling?"

"Black-and-blue. Fetch a doctor. *Now.*"

"Is anything broken?"

Amazed at the woman's line of questions, he gave his head a half shake. "I do not believe so, but that does not mean she is not injured. Fetch the damn doctor."

She shook her head again.

"Why not?"

"The local doctor and his lordship are acquainted."

"And? If my presence is a worry, I will make myself scarce."

"No, it's not that. If his lordship had wanted the doctor fetched, he'd have done it himself."

"Do you honestly think a man would call for a doctor after he has beaten his wife?" Gideon asked, incredulous.

"This is not London. The doctor is well-known in the village. Her ladyship would be humiliated if word got out. And the doctor may mention it to his lordship, and that would only incite his fury anew."

Gideon willed away the outraged anger. He was powerless in this household, his place undefined, but certainly below that of the vaunted housekeeper. Unless Bella requested the doctor herself, and he highly doubted she would, the man would not be making an appearance. "Do you have anything medicinal in the house? Laudanum, anything to ease her pain?"

"Only spirits. Her ladyship refuses to keep laudanum in the house. His lordship has a fondness for it."

Brilliant. In addition to being an abuser of women, Bella's husband was also an addict. No wonder she had been maudlin. "Warm some brandy and have it delivered to Lady Stirling's room immediately. And take this." He thrust out the candlestick.

"Whyever for?"

"Just take it. I don't care what you do with it. Lady Stirling is never to lay eyes on it again."

With something that resembled a nod, Mrs. Cooley snatched the candlestick and left to do his bidding.

Gideon stood alone in the hall for a long moment, battling with the need to take Bella away from here, to keep her safe with him always. But he had nothing to his name, no means to support her. And he was a whore, even if a retired one at that.

A sense of utter powerlessness threatened to overwhelm him. Squeezing his eyes shut, he fought the prick of tears.

When he felt he had regained some semblance of composure, he returned to Bella.

❧

FOR the first time in many weeks, Bella awoke with a feeling of peace and tranquility. A dull ache rode every inch of her body, but she felt safe. She opened her eyes to find a very handsome gentleman lying beside her. Gideon was sprawled on his stomach, one arm bent under his head, the other slung across her waist.

Awakening next to a man was a singularly wonderful and unique experience. The heat radiating from his body warmed the surrounding sheets. The mattress shifted the tiniest bit with each of his deep, rhythmic breaths.

She did not remember asking him to stay. In fact, she didn't recall much after she had finished the glass of brandy he'd insisted she drink. Had he intended to stay the night? He must not have, for he was still mostly dressed. The only concession to comfort he had given himself was the removal of his cravat and coat. She slowly stretched out a leg and located his calf. Her bare toe skimmed over soft wool. He had also removed his boots. How thoughtful.

Sleep relaxed his face, giving the classic angles and planes a younger, more vulnerable smoothness. She lightly trailed her fingertips along his jaw, the few days' worth of dark beard bristly beneath her fingers. She had never seen him anything but clean-shaven, and the effect made him less the polished gentleman and more the rugged man. But it could not distract from his beauty. If anything, it added to it.

Her fingertips whispered up to brush the silken curve of his eyelashes, the thin skin beneath darkened with fatigue. He had been quite the sight last night when he'd burst through her dressing room door. The lamplight illuminating a man who had looked as though he had just traveled to the ends of the earth.

Dark lashes fluttered and swept up to reveal soft, drowsy eyes. "Good morning." His voice was raspy from sleep.

"Good morning," she said with a smile.

"How are you feeling?"

"Much better, now that you're here."

Dark lashes swept closed. A deep breath, with an ever so faint hitch, expanded his chest.

"How did you know to come?"

"I didn't. I needed to see you," he replied hoarsely, eyes still closed, eyebrows pulling together.

She snuggled closer to him. "And what a sight I am."

He rolled onto his side and fit her gently next to his body. The press of bruised flesh against his hard long body should have been painful, but it wasn't. It was immensely comforting, his presence a balm that cured all her ills.

She brushed her cheek against the soft silk of his waist-coat, soaking up the masculine scent of him. "I missed you."

"As I did you." Soft lips nuzzled her neck, his bearded jaw a bristly scrape against the sensitive skin. A strong gentle hand coasted up and down her side then paused on her hip. His body drew tight. "Did he hurt you?"

Bella tipped her head back to meet his gaze, her eyes questioning.

"Did he force himself on you?"

"No."

Dark eyebrows lowered and whisky brown eyes sharpened, testing her answer.

"No. I thought you understood. He . . . can't. He's, oh, I don't recall the term." Discomforted, she dropped her gaze and traced one of the fabric-covered buttons on his light gray waistcoat. "He used to try when we were first married but it never ended well." A jagged shudder skipped down her spine. "He hates me. Absolutely loathes me because of it. He can be polite and charming when the situation demands it, but he is a cruel man at heart."

Seemingly satisfied, Gideon went back to nuzzling her neck. His lips whispered across her cheek to find her mouth. How she loved his kisses—they made everything rosy. He kissed her softly, his lips brushing lightly. A comfort kiss. And suddenly the kiss shifted, his mouth slanting over hers, his tongue possessing the hot cavern of her mouth.

He had kissed her like this once before, and then she hadn't been able to identify the element that had made it different. But now she could, for it took up the entire kiss, hiding under nothing else, layered with no other intention.

This kiss was Gideon, honest and pure. Just him.

Just when she lost herself in that kiss, forgot everything but the feel of his body pressed against her, the urgent tremor in his limbs that matched hers, he broke the kiss. She moaned at the loss. Determined to get him back, she gripped his skull and rocked against the hard arch of his arousal straining beneath the placket of his breeches.

"Bella-Bella," he whispered.

She reluctantly opened her eyes.

"Good morning," he said with a wide smile, lips wet from their kisses. The crests of his cheekbones were flushed lightly. His eyes sparkled with happiness.

Before she could form a reply, he asked, "Are you hungry?"

"Famished," she sighed, sagging into him.

"Good. I'll see to breakfast." He got off the bed.

Breakfast? She hadn't been referring to food. Bella put out an arm and made to sit up. An ache seized her entire body. Suppressing a grunt of pain, she dropped back down onto the pillows. As she waited for him to return, she realized maybe she was a bit hungry.

Seventeen

SPANNING from floor to ceiling, the shelves filled the length of one wall. Rows upon rows of books, all lined up like neat little soldiers. Yet not one of the books had ever been the slightest bit of help. The Earls of Mayburn before him had chosen to fill their London study with books on history, literature, art, poetry, and philosophy. Phillip had come across a few on the erotic arts. He had read them, of course. What man wouldn't? Yet he had rather hoped at the time his father had not been the earl who added those particular books to the library.

But what the impressive library did not hold was one single book on how to pull the earldom out from beneath the crippling pile of debt he had inherited at the age of twenty. Apparently all the other Earls of Mayburn had not deemed such a book fitting for their library. At the moment though, Phillip could use a bit of advice for he was fresh out of ideas.

Staring down at the account ledger, he rested his elbows on his desk and held his head in his hands. No matter how hard he willed it, the numbers did not change. He was still in dun territory. At least he had been able to make some progress over the last five and a half years, though most of it had come courtesy of his resourceful little brother.

When Julien had won a frigate in a card game four years ago, Phillip had pressed him to promptly sell the ship. Instead, Julien named himself captain, pulled together a crew, which happened to include a stowaway in the form of their sister Kitty, and sailed out of the London Docks, insisting he would return with far more than the ship was worth. That first voyage had not been as profitable as either of them had hoped, but Phillip couldn't deny that Julien had been right. And he also couldn't deny that it rankled a bit that Julien's ship was the only decent investment in the Mayburn earldom.

He dragged his hands through his hair. Julien better get back soon, and he best not return empty-handed like he had the last time he'd stopped over in London. Though Julien hadn't left empty-handed, at least that was what Phillip assumed given Kitty and her new husband had vanished the same night Julien departed. Phillip let out an exasperated sigh. He had more pressing matters on his mind than errant siblings, like an account ledger which refused to cooperate.

Olivia's finishing school would demand payment by the end of the month and it would not do to be late again. Phillip could only hope the expense was worth it and by this time next year his littlest sister would have succeeded where the other two had failed. It was cruel of him to expect so much of her, but there wasn't much to be done about it. The earldom needed an obscenely large influx of money, the size of which could only be had by an extremely advantageous marriage.

Phillip picked up an ivory cup and took a long sip. The coffee was hot and rich, exactly the way he liked it, but it did little to revive his exhausted brain. The morning rains had turned the roads from Norfolk into a muddy mess. It had taken him all day to travel from Mayburn Hall to London. He should have gone straight to bed, but the bills and correspondences that had piled on his desk in his absence would not take care of themselves. At least it was August and the House of Lords had recessed for the summer, giving him one less thing to worry about.

Trying to ease the tight knot at the base of his neck, he rolled his shoulders. Then he turned his attention back to the ledger. A moment later a light scratch on the door pulled him from the family's finances.

"Enter," Phillip said.

The door opened, revealing his elderly butler, Denton. "You have a caller, milord."

Phillip picked up his pocket watch from the desk. Past midnight. Debt collectors rarely came at this hour. Well, the unsavory ones did. But unless a debt had changed hands without his knowledge, there would be no cause for their kind to be calling at the door of Mayburn House.

He looked to Denton and raised his eyebrows in expectation.

"A young man, and judging by the brogue, he hails from Scotland," Denton said.

"I will see him." Suppressing a weary sigh, he closed the ledger and pushed it to the corner of the desk. He had just unrolled his shirtsleeves when the door opened again.

A sturdy young man with a wild shock of untamed red hair entered the study. The man looked more exhausted than Phillip felt. Mud flecked his boots and tan trousers. The lightweight coat over the equally mud-flecked shirt was dusty and travel worn. The young man stopped inside the door and, wringing his hat in his hands, gave Phillip a nervous nod. "Good evening, milord."

"Come. Sit." Phillip motioned to the two maroon leather armchairs facing his desk.

The young man hesitated before crossing the room and dropping into the chair not already occupied by Phillip's discarded coat. "Thank you, milord."

"What can I do for you?"

"I've been sent to give ye this." The man wrestled with

a pocket of his coat and eventually produced what looked to have once been a folded note.

Phillip took the proffered missive. *The Earl of Mayburn, Mayburn House, London* was scrawled neatly across the paper in unfamiliar script. He pulled a letter opener from the top drawer of his desk and used it to break the seal. His eyes swept quickly over the written words. The knot in his neck tightened. "Who sent you?"

"Mrs. Cooley, Lady Stirling's housekeeper."

"Your name?"

"Seamus MacKenzie, milord," the man said with a deferential nod.

Reaching behind him, Phillip grabbed the bell pull. Within a moment his butler was at the door again. "Take Mr. MacKenzie to the kitchen and see he has a decent meal. If he so desires, he is welcome to stay the night in the servants' quarters. Then have my bag packed. I depart for Scotland tonight."

Denton gave a short nod.

"Thank you for your haste, Mr. MacKenzie. If you have need of anything, Denton can see to it."

"Thank you, milord," Seamus mumbled. He nodded again and took his leave.

His mind fixed on Isabella's housekeeper's note, Phillip stood and rounded his desk. He stopped short beside the armchair the young man had occupied. He bent down to retrieve a crumpled sheet of paper. "Mr. MacKenzie."

The man turned at the open door. His eyes widened at the sight of the paper in Phillip's outstretched hand. "Oh, sorry, milord." He scurried across the room.

The instant before Seamus's dirt-smudged fingertips touched the note, Phillip snatched it back. "Who is Mr. Rosedale?"

Hand outstretched, Seamus froze. He gave his head a short, nervous shake.

"How can you not know? Were you not to deliver this note?"

"Don't need to no more."

It did not escape Phillip's notice that the young man had ignored his first question. "Why not?"

"I was only to deliver that one if you were not here."

He glanced back at the note. There wasn't an address. Just the name, *Mr. Rosedale*, scrawled in the same script as his own letter. "Who is Mr. Rosedale?" he asked again.

Seamus's uncomfortable wince was answer enough for Phillip.

Damn Isabella. Would the girl never change her ways? "Where were you to deliver this?"

Seamus backed up a few quick steps at the flush of anger making its way up to Phillip's forehead.

"Where?" he demanded.

"Don't recall the exact address," Seamus mumbled, cowering before him.

He glared at Seamus, using his height, his broad frame, and the weight of his title to his full advantage.

The intimidation tactic worked. The young man swallowed uncomfortably and dropped his gaze to his mud-flecked boots. "To the house with the two red doors on Curzon Street."

Phillip kept his expression from changing as the bottom dropped out of his stomach. After a short pause, he spoke, his voice once again calm. "Denton will see you to the kitchen."

Clearly relieved, the man nodded and quickly left the study. Phillip ripped open the seal and read the note. It was similar to his own—a request that he was needed immediately at Bowhill Park.

As Phillip pondered the note, he heard the slam of a door then footfalls in the marble-floored entrance hall. He looked up to see Julien striding toward him.

"Evening, old man," his younger brother said with a wry grin. "No need to look so grave. Kitty and that husband of hers are back in London, disembarked this afternoon, and the two of them are disgustingly besotted with each other. Positively nauseating. You can thank me properly over a glass of French brandy. I have an entire case of the wonderful spirit being unloaded from my carriage as I speak. A gift for the earl," Julien added with a grand bow.

"I am relieved to hear you have returned with our sister and Lord Templeton," Phillip said. "The dowager viscountess was most distressed at the unexpected disappearance of her son and her new daughter-in-law. I had to placate her with a tale of a wedding holiday I had given the newlyweds as a gift."

"Wedding holiday? That's a unique way of looking at it. I will have to inform Templeton when I call on Kitty. He's sure to find it most amusing."

Phillip shook his head, not in the mood to ask his brother what he meant. For to ask would mean answers, and he had long ago found it was better to be kept in the dark where it concerned Julien and his precious frigate, the *Mistress Mine*.

Julien dropped down onto the brown leather couch and crossed a booted ankle over his knee. Passing a lazy hand through his sandy blond hair, he tipped back his head. A very satisfied smile curved his lips. "God, I love London."

Phillip rolled his eyes. "Is that the first thing you do once you get off that ship of yours?"

"Of course," Julien scoffed. "I was gone for almost two months."

Two months—an inconceivable amount of time for his brother to go without a woman. But to Phillip, two months were the same as a day, and were the same as a year. The passage of time did not matter when one's mind was forever fixed on the family's never-dwindling debts. "I thought you had one in every port?"

"I do, but there wasn't time. Busy," Julien replied with a casual shrug. He took a deep breath and bellowed, "Denton!" He shot Phillip an annoyed frown when the man did not immediately materialize at the open door to the study. "Where's that butler of yours? The man is always sulking about but disappears when you need him most. That brandy will turn rancid by the time he gets around to having it unloaded."

"Julien, it's good to see you, too. But I haven't time for a drink and neither do you. I need your help."

Julien's blue green eyes sharpened at Phillip's serious tone. The latent after-sex haze vanished as if it had never been there. "With what?"

Those in London might take Julien as a wastrel, an indolent second son who fluttered in and out of Town on a whim, and spent his evenings at the card tables and his nights with the Season's most coveted ladybirds. They could not see past the ruse, or more so, past Julien laughing at them all as he had a jolly good time filling his pockets with their coins and winning their ladies. But Phillip knew him better. At the core of Julien was rock solid, unswayable loyalty. He knew that no matter what, Julien would always be there when he needed him, and the boy had proved it time and time again. Brothers did not turn their backs on each other.

"We need to find out who Mr. Rosedale is, and how he's associated with Isabella. And we haven't much time. We leave for Scotland tonight." He handed Mr. Rosedale's letter to his brother, who quickly read it.

Julien shot to his feet, stance strong and expression determined. Even in black evening attire and a brilliant pink silk waistcoat, Phillip could well imagine him on the deck of the *Mistress Mine* shouting orders to his crew.

"We'll go to the docks. I need to stop at the ship and inform the crew I will be unavailable. In the meantime, Fodder, my first mate, can pull up some information on Mr. Rosedale. The man's mighty quick. Within an hour he'll be able to tell us the name of Mr. Rosedale's wet nurse. Do you know where this was to be delivered?"

"Curzon Street. The house with the twin red doors."

"I know that house."

Phillip could not help but take satisfaction at the shock on his brother's face as he said gravely, "So do I."

⚜

BELLA'S days with Gideon were a stark and very welcome contrast to those of the last two months. He was infinitely careful with her, infinitely patient. He refused to allow her to leave her bedchamber for the first few days and very rarely allowed her to leave the bed. But she wasn't bored. The loneliness and anxiety were gone. Gideon was always by her side. Bella forgot about Stirling, forgot she was a married woman, forgot she had an older brother who would not at all approve of her houseguest, and lost herself in being with Gideon.

The only thing she found vexing was he kept pushing food on her. Two light meals a day and an afternoon tea were quite enough for her. But he was continually calling down to the kitchen for something or other to tempt her. The small table by the dressing room door held a silver tray heaped with dishes and bowls that were perpetually filled. And the door—it had yet to be repaired since Gideon refused to have a carpenter hammering and creating a racket.

She did her best to be patient with him, to politely refuse when he insisted, though she came close to snapping at him when he wouldn't put that bowl of fruit down.

"Just one bite, Bella. The strawberries are perfectly in season. Fresh and ripe and sweet."

"Gideon, I'm not hungry. We had breakfast less than an hour ago."

But he would not stop and the pleading look in his eyes, as if her refusal was hurting his feelings, made her snatch the berry and pop it into her mouth. The kiss he gave her—the taste of Gideon mixed with sweet, succulent strawberry—now that was delicious.

Finally judging her strong enough to venture beyond the sitting room door, the next day he decided she could leave her bedchamber, though the outdoors was strictly prohibited and he even carried her down the stairs cradled in his strong arms like a small child.

They had dinner in the dining room, just as they used to. The only difference being she was clad in an alabaster dressing gown over her white nightgown, versus the appropriate attire for an evening meal. She hadn't even bound her hair because Gideon seemed to have developed a fondness for running his fingers through it.

After an early dinner they retired to the drawing room, he seated on the settee, she curled up beside him. There were very few words between them for none were needed. His arm was slung protectively around her shoulder, absently toying with a lock of her hair. She rested her cheek against his chest. The strong steady beat of his heart lulled her into a sort of semiwakefulness.

The sun slowly set. Its warm amber rays gently receded until all that lit the room was the faint glow of a single candle. A cool summer night's breeze floated in from an open window.

"Are you tired?"

"No." She could lay here with him for hours, but was not the least bit tired since she'd done nothing all day save walk a few steps and lift her fork to her mouth.

"What would you like to do?"

At his open question, she grinned mischievously.

He covered her hand with his, halting the upward glide along his thigh. "Not that. Not yet," he said, indulgent but firm.

Pouting, she pursed her lips. "Anything that doesn't involve going back to my bedchamber."

He chuckled softly, his chest vibrating against her cheek. "How about a game of chess?"

"That would be lovely. But you shall have to teach me, as I've never learned how to play."

"*Umm*, my lady Bella. The things I will teach you."

His sinfully rich voice pulled a purr from deep in her throat. She clung tightly to him as he gathered her in his arms and carried her the short distance to the chess table.

He settled her in a chair, and as he set up the pieces, he explained the game. It didn't sound all that difficult, but her assumption was quickly proved wrong.

"Bella, sweet, a rook doesn't move that way. Over and up," Gideon said, his warm fingertips on hers as he corrected her play.

"But I wanted it to be there."

"That's the intriguing part of chess. Each piece conforms to its own set of rules. The challenge is getting them where you want them, constraints and all." Leaning one elbow on the table, chin in his palm, Gideon pondered the board. The candlelight played happily on the perfect angles and planes of his face.

"You are taking an awfully long time to decide."

He chuckled lightly. "Ever my impatient Bella."

The way he said *my*—how she would love to be his. Those endearments had been popping out of his mouth of late. He had referred to her as "Bella-Bella" for quite some time; a name owned by him. But since he had broken through her dressing room door, his vocabulary had broadened to include *sweet, angel, my dear, my Bella*. She liked the *my* ones best.

In fact, his words were not the only things that were different. Gideon was different. The veneer of the skillful lover was gone, leaving just the man, Gideon as he truly was. It was a side to him she had longed to see. That feeling of pretense, of manipulation, but not of her, of him manipulating himself to please her, was gone. When his gaze fell on her, it was not because he was gauging her reaction and calculating his response, but because he simply wanted to look at her.

At length, he lifted his free hand from the table, fingertips hovering over a rook before settling on a black knight. A notched *V* pulled between his dark eyebrows.

"Are you trying to figure out how to let me win?"

Startled whisky brown eyes snapped to hers.

Daring him to try and deny it, she arched her eyebrows.

"You may capture my queen. I promise not to hold it against you."

"But where's the challenge in that? The game would be over in a matter of minutes."

Bella huffed in mock offense. "Are you telling me I'm easy, Mr. Rosedale?"

His lips quirked. "You, easy? Never." He moved the knight. "Let's see what you do with that. The door is open. Can you find it to walk through it?"

He was setting up a play for her again in an effort to teach her the game. She studied the board, struggling to remember how all the pieces moved and searching for that open door, when she heard the sound of horses' hooves on gravel.

She froze, her chest excruciatingly tight. It was suddenly very difficult to draw breath.

The slam of a door interrupted Gideon's concerned "Bella?"

His head snapped to his right, attention on the drawing room door, at the sound of strong, agitated male voices.

She hadn't heard it in years, but she knew the owner of one of those voices. The door to the drawing room burst open and Bella received no pleasure at learning she had guessed correctly. *Oh, dear Lord.* Why had he come, and now, of all times?

Gideon got to his feet and positioned himself in front of her, his stance defensive.

Her brother, the Earl of Mayburn, strode across the room, another gentleman on his heels. Phillip's short, medium brown hair was wind-tousled, his face flushed with anger. "Mr. Rosedale, I presume," he bit out through clenched teeth.

Gideon nodded once.

"Step away from Lady Stirling."

"Phillip," Bella protested. She stood beside Gideon and took his warm hand in hers. She felt him try to pull his arm away, but she held tight, needing his strength. "How dare you come into my home and behave so rudely toward my guest."

The man on Phillip's heels stopped next to her older brother. She peered into the man's face. The years had matured his features and broadened his frame, but even with the days-old dark blond beard and tanned face, she recognized him. "Jules?"

"Good evening, dearest sister. I must say, you sure know how to pick them."

The cutting tone pushed her a step closer to Gideon. Where Phillip was projecting severe irritation and displeasure, Jules, her mischievous, hotheaded little brother, was radiating venom the likes of which she had never seen before. Stirling's wrath was blunt and primitive compared to Jules's razor-sharp tongue and pinpoint precise malice.

Shoulder to shoulder, her two brothers loomed before her, an intimidating duo in long dark greatcoats with matching narrowed blue green eyes. Too dissimilar in personality, she had never known them to work as a pair. The fact they were seeing eye to eye tonight did not bode well.

"I assume Stirling is not in residence," Phillip said.

"As a matter of fact, you just missed him. He retired early tonight." Phillip's face blanked at her sarcastic comment. Good. He deserved a bit of shock. "Of course he's not here, Phillip."

"I should be pleased to find you're displaying a bit more discretion this time. But I'm not pleased. Not in the slightest. I wonder why?"

Did Phillip expect some sort of answer? The muscle ticking along his strong jaw was a resounding no. That horrible sense of guilt washed over her. It felt so familiar, settling easily on her shoulders as though it had never left. But an apology would not be attempted this time. She would not repent for what she had found with Gideon, for what Phillip had tried to deny her.

"Take her to her room. Mr. Rosedale and I need to have a discussion," Phillip said in a coldly ominous tone.

Jules nodded once and walked toward her.

"No. You have no right to order me about." Holding her ground, she glared at Phillip. But Gideon shifted, pulling his arm forward, pushing her at Jules. Gideon's hand went lax and her gaze shot desperately to his, but he would not look at her. His impassive eyes were fixed on Phillip.

He was a stranger to her at that moment. It shook her enough so that when Jules took her free hand and pulled her away from Gideon, she did not resist.

You have the advantage over me, sir."

"You will address me as 'your lordship.' I am the Earl of Mayburn, Lady Stirling's brother, and you are not welcome in this house. Do not come here again. Do not attempt to contact Lady Stirling. Your services"—he spat the word—"are no longer needed."

His face blank, Gideon nodded. Mayburn knew. There was no point in trying to hide it. Protesting would only bring more shame onto Bella.

The last few days had been heaven. A tranquil paradise. A glimpse of true happiness. He had known it couldn't last, but he hadn't expected to be torn from Bella so soon. With great effort, he resisted the urge to howl with misery. "You will take care of her?"

He didn't think it was possible, but somehow it was. The man's response was to glower harder at him. It hadn't been wise to ask anything of the earl, but he had to be certain the man would take care of Bella. He didn't want to leave her alone. It was too soon. She was still too weak, too bruised, too frail.

Gideon reached into a pocket of his navy coat, pulled out a paper-wrapped bundle, and held it out to Mayburn. "If you could return this to Lady Stirling. It belongs to her. I had meant to return it to her . . ." He trailed off, averting his eyes. The way the man was looking at him, as if he were gutter trash.

He felt the bundle leave his hand.

It was done.

Those pound notes had been ever in his pocket, with
him, since he left London. Many a time he had been on
the verge of pulling them out and returning them to Bella.
But he had resisted, not willing to risk upsetting her in any
way. Not wanting to remind her of what he had once been
to her. No—what he *was* to her.

There was no place for him here. There never had
been. Bella's brothers had arrived. They would take care
of her now, and they could protect her far better than he.

He should at least be thankful that he'd been left with
this brother to deal with. For they were definitely brothers.
They possessed the same cold blue green eyes and the
same commanding presence—that innate indicator of
good breeding, of Quality, of superiority. The other one,
the younger one, the one who'd taken Bella from him, had
a dangerous lethal edge. One that bespoke death, of having inflicted it without remorse. If Gideon had been left
with that brother to deal with, he would have highly
doubted his ability to walk out of this room.

As it was, walking away from Bella was almost worse
than death. In fact, at this moment, he rather thought he
would prefer death, even welcome it.

There was a light rap on the door.

"Enter." The earl's command cut through the taut
silence.

"Your lordship, the mount is ready."

Mayburn didn't turn to the servant. "Good day, Mr.
Rosedale."

Gideon walked solemnly past Mayburn and out of the
drawing room he had once shared with Bella, the earl on
his heels, intent on ensuring he left the house, no doubt.
The butler stood at his usual spot guarding the entrance to
Bowhill. The older man's dour face held a satisfying, superior smirk.

By sheer force of will he resisted the urge to glance
over his shoulder, up the stairs, and instead, without pausing, walked out the front door and to the waiting horse.

He took the reins from the groom, flipped them over the

horse's head, threw himself into the saddle, and left Bowhill. Left Bella's brother standing on the top stone stair, the
fold of pound notes, his wages from Bella, clutched in one
large fist.

✤

A prostitute, Bella? What were you thinking? To dally
with the servants is one thing, but to actually hire a man?
I can't believe you paid him. Does Stirling know where
your pin money is going?"

Bella flinched. Not because of the cruelly muttered
words, but because Jules's long strides were devouring the
hallway and with each stride she received a tug on her
arm, the one that felt as though it hadn't fully settled back
in its socket. She struggled to keep up with him as he
pulled her to her rooms, growing weaker with each step,
hurting more with each step.

As the distance from Gideon grew, that cloak of comfort, the one that gave her the strength to stand up to her
brothers, lifted. She ached in places she had not ached for
days. The impact of each step reverberated up her spine,
smacking each half-healed bruise on her back.

By the time Jules reached her sitting room, every inch
of her hurt. He slammed the door shut, released her hand,
and swung around to face her. She shrank back against the
door from the disdain pulling his mouth.

"Do you have any idea the trouble Phillip went through
to find Stirling for you?" he said. "But an earl's not good
enough for you. No—they're *too* good for you, aren't they,
Bella? You like to pull them from the gutters, the lower the
better. Phillip could have saved himself the expense of
your dowry and just let that groom have you. As if he
doesn't have enough problems to deal with that he's got to
drop everything and hightail it to Scotland. Is this how you
repay Phillip for all he's done for you?"

She shook her head as he battered her with his words.
The impacts hit harder than Stirling's fists ever had.

Jules stood over her, hands clenched at his sides. "We

traveled straight here, not stopping except to change horses, worried out of our minds. And we find you having a quiet evening with your whore. Christ, you're barely dressed. You look like you just crawled out of bed. Was he worth it, Bella? Did you get your money's worth?" he sneered.

She pulled her dressing gown tight around her stomach, acutely aware of her state of undress. "No, Jules. I didn't . . . didn't pay him to come to Bowhill," she sputtered, finally finding her voice.

"Oh, that's rich," he said, all mocking condescension. "Try your lies on someone else. I know what he is."

"No, it's not like that. I didn't even send for him this time. You don't understand. He cares for me."

"All he cares about is your money. He doesn't care about you, and if you believed him, then you're a fool."

"No." She glared up at him. Jules had gone too far. She would not allow her *little* brother to speak of Gideon that way. "He needed to see me. You don't understand. I love him. Gideon cares for me. He needs me like I need—"

The words stopped in her throat. Bella started, her eyes going wide. The sound of gravel under horses' hooves grated on every inch of her skin, as though those hooves were traveling over her. Breath held, she strained to hear. That was the distant sound of one horse galloping.

Only one.

"No! He can't. Phillip can't!" She whirled around and threw open the sitting room door with such force it banged against the wall. She heard Jules protest behind her. A hand pulled at the back of her dressing gown. Twisting her shoulders, she let her arms fall behind her as she escaped the garment, eluding her brother. Halfway down the stairs, she felt that hand again, but her pace was no match for the comfortable well-worn cotton. With a loud rip of fabric, she broke free of Jules again, her gaze fixed on the lone broad silhouette of Phillip framed by the open front door.

Beyond desperate, she flew through the entrance hall,

through the open door, but was caught by strong arms. "Gideon!"

"Isabella, stop it," Phillip commanded.

"No. No. You can't. Phillip, I need . . . Gideon!" she cried, struggling against her bonds.

"Isabella, he's gone. He will never come back."

The panic at the threat of losing Gideon had numbed her to everything but reaching him. But at Phillip's implacable words, the whole-body ache returned with such startling force it overwhelmed her nerves, swamped her senses. Using her last reserve of strength, she wrestled free of the iron-band arms encircling her sore back and crumpled to her knees.

"No, no, no," she wailed, over and over again.

Phillip had sent him away, just as he had sent everyone away from her. The physical pain was nothing, a mere pinprick, compared to the knowledge she would never see Gideon again.

DAMN it, Phillip. Don't just stand there. Do something," Julien said, with a faint pant in his voice.

"Me? You were to keep her in her room."

"I tried. She's quicker than Kitty. It's those long legs of hers." Julien scowled, clearly indignant at being bested by a female.

The two men glared at each other, daring each other. But Phillip was locked to the spot. A part of him refused to aid her. She deserved this anguish. She had brought it on herself. He had merely been cleaning up after her, yet again. But Isabella was a woman. His sister. And the sound of her wails, soaked in misery, pulled heavily at his chest.

He was still amazed he had the presence of mind to grab hold of her. The sight of her running toward him, her white nightgown and pale blonde hair streaming behind her—for a moment he had feared she was a ghost.

Julien cursed under his breath. Then he dropped to his knees. "Bella," he whispered. Her long hair covered her bowed head and back like a silvery blanket. He gathered the heavy mass in one hand, pulling the ends up from the stone landing and uncovering her face. He sucked in a swift breath. "What the bloody hell?"

Both men stared, aghast, at her prone form. A large tear in her nightgown exposed the frail lines of her back. The light from the lanterns on either side of the door illuminated a grotesque assortment of long, thick bruises mixed with fat impacts.

"Rosedale's a dead man," Julien seethed.

"No. It wasn't him," Phillip said, quick to keep his brother's wrath from landing on the wrong target. He curled his hand into a fist, gripping the fold of wrapped pound notes tightly. He had only glanced at the image sketched on the paper before Bella had come down the stairs, yet he knew the artist would have never hurt his sister.

A mighty torrent of rage roiled up from his belly, but knowing he needed to keep a clear head, he fought it down. He dropped to his haunches on the other side of her. "Isabella? Who did this to you?" He was succeeding in keeping the rage contained for he was able to suppress the urge to rip someone, anyone, limb from limb. But he had failed at his attempt at a gentle, nonthreatening question.

She shook her bowed head. Her wails had died down, the intensity gone, but still she whimpered over and over again, "No, no, no."

"The note."

At Julien's words, his attention snapped from their sister.

"This was why the housekeeper sent for you."

Annoyed by the obvious, Phillip nodded once. "Get Rosedale."

"Pardon?"

"Bring him back. Now. I don't care how you do it. Just get him here."

"Why?"

"We'll get nothing from her, but Rosedale knows what happened." The man's request had seemed odd, out of place at the time. But this was what he had been referring to. This was why Rosedale had needed to ensure someone would take care of Isabella in his stead. "Go, Julien. Now. Before he gets too far. I'll see to Isabella."

His brother's response was to get to his feet and sprint in the direction of the stables.

Eighteen

AFTER about a mile, Gideon judged himself a satisfactory distance from the earl and pulled the mare to a walk. His right pocket now empty, he had less than five pounds left to see him wherever he was headed. He needed to conserve the mare's strength, for he hadn't the coin to exchange her for a fresh horse if he wore her out.

In fact, those notes and spare coins in his pocket were all he had left to his name. He had nothing.

Impotent frustration welled up inside of him. An angry force that made him want to scream, shout, bellow at the injustice of it all. His jaw locked, he clenched the reins tight. *Goddamn Rubicon!* If that bitch would have just accepted his resignation, he'd have a small fortune at his disposal. Something, anything, to show for himself. Not that it would have helped. He was still a son of a whore. If he had been anything but a bastard retired prostitute, he would have stayed at Bella's side and stood up to her brothers. Given them a piece of his mind for allowing her to wed a monster like Stirling. Cold-blooded, greedy aristocrats. Willingly sold their kin for a title without thought to the consequences.

But what had he done? Given her over to her brothers and walked out the door. There had been no other option available to him. Nothing, because he was nothing.

The mare picked up her head, ears swiveling back toward the sound of an approaching horse. With a nudge of his leg, the mare moved off to the side of the dark road. The approaching horse skidded to a halt next to him, kicking up dust and dirt.

"Rosedale."

Just his luck. It was the other brother. The one Bella had called Jules.

Gideon's response was a mute turn of his head.

The man's narrowed eyes caught the moonlight, making them stand out in the shadows of his face. "Come with me."

Not trusting himself to speak, he turned from the man and nudged the mare forward, but pulled up at the unmistakable sound of a pistol being cocked. Judging by the volume, it was aimed right at his head.

"I am in no mood to argue with you. Turn around and return to the manor house," the man said in a chillingly flat voice. After a brief pause he continued, whatever patience he had been displaying coming to an abrupt halt. "Now," he snarled. "Do not tempt me. I *will* shoot you. I'd rather Bella blame me for your death than return empty-handed, proving you are not the man she believes you to be."

It was not the promise of a bullet, but the prospect of Bella that brought Gideon's hand to his hip, quickly turning the mare. With a kick of his heels, he prodded the horse into a ground-covering gallop.

Bella's brother surprisingly said not a word on the short ride back to Bowhill. But that could have something to do with the fact that Gideon had yet to say one word to the man. Maybe "Jules" had finally picked up the hint. Or it could simply be that they were traveling too fast for conversation to be practical.

Gideon pulled the horse to a halt at the foot of the front steps, leapt off, and tossed the reins to a waiting groom. He stopped one pace inside the house, eyes sweeping, ears straining, heart beating rapidly—and spotted Mrs. Cooley hovering in the hall by the drawing room. He pinned her with a hard questioning stare.

Her gaze flickered over his shoulder before landing once more on him. "Lord Mayburn took her ladyship to her rooms to rest."

With a short nod of thanks, Gideon headed for Bella. The sound of her voice flittered down the second floor hall. Though he could not make out the words, the heartache and desolation in the weak protests pulled him, picking up his pace.

He passed through the sitting room and stopped inside her bedchamber. Closing his eyes, he soaked up just being in the same room with her again. He took a slow deep breath, her presence filling the emptiness inside of him. Then he opened his eyes and opened his ears again.

"No, Phillip. No!"

Mayburn stood over her, clearly trying to keep her on the bed. "Calm yourself. It will be all right."

Half sprawled on the bed, she struggled against her brother's caging arms. "No, it won't. It never will be again. Please. I need him back. I need . . . *Gideon*!" The last word was ripped from her soul as her wide violet eyes met his over Mayburn's broad shoulder.

Gideon was before her in an instant. Bella rose up onto her knees and flung herself at him, face pressed against his chest. He wrapped his arms gingerly around her frail body. His gaze left Bella long enough to flicker to the earl standing beside him. He took in the grave face and nodded.

Mayburn turned from the bed.

All of Gideon's attention, every nerve in his body, focused on Bella. "Shh, Bella-Bella. Don't cry," he crooned over and over again, until her soft sobs eased and her body went lax in his arms.

He laid her gently on the bed and dropped to his knees so he could be on eye level with her. Crooning to her all the while, he gently combed the silken strands away from her face, revealing the long spiky-wet sweep of her down-cast lashes and tearstained cheeks. At length her breathing turned deep and even, and thinking sleep had overtaken her, he moved to get to his feet but was stopped by an urgent hand on his wrist.

Wet lashes framed large, pleading eyes. "Why did you leave me?"

"Bella, I—" He swallowed, tried to speak again, stopped, then forced the words. "Your brothers are here. They can take better care of you than I."

She gave a short, callous huff. "I haven't seen either of them in five years. Haven't heard from either of them in just as long. That's how much I mean to them. How much they care about me."

"They're your family, Bella." The admonishment was gentle and soft, yet held a hint of intense longing. To have a chance to see Bella, he had freely given up any hope of having a family to call his own. Yet still, that longing had not gone away.

She gave that sardonic huff again, the one steeped in pain. "They are a poor substitute for you."

His breaths turned shaky at her words. He bowed his head. *I love you.* He wanted to tell her so badly it hurt, but the words would not leave his throat. Instead he pressed a chaste kiss on her forehead and got to his feet.

"Gideon, don't leave me. Not again." Tears pooled anew in her eyes.

"No. No. I'm not leaving the house. I just need to have a word with your brothers."

Desperation weighed heavily on her face. "Don't let them send you from me. Don't. No matter what they say.

No matter what they do." At his silence, she pushed up onto an elbow and gripped his wrist harshly. "Don't. Don't let them. Promise, Gideon. Return to me."

"I promise," he said solemnly, hoping beyond hope he wasn't making a vow he would not be able to keep.

Her whole body relaxed and she slumped back onto the pillows. He covered her with a light blanket from the foot of the bed, doused the candle on the bedside table, and left the room.

He found Mrs. Cooley at the bottom of the stairs.

"Lord Mayburn is in his lordship's study," she informed him.

Her face was implacable, yet her gray eyes saw right through him. She may have suspected before but the scene Bella's brothers had put on this evening confirmed the truth. In less than a day the entire household would know he was not Lady Stirling's relation, nor that he was merely her ladyship's gentleman caller. Experience had taught him what to expect from this point forward from the Bowhill servants. They would be subtle, but the message would be clear.

Squaring his shoulders, he went to Stirling's study. Without bothering to knock, he opened the thick oak door for the first time. Over the past few days, he had purposely not entered this room. A study was a man's sanctuary, and this one was Bella's husband's. The room wasn't as large as he had imagined, but rather the size of Bella's sitting room. Judging from the many shelves of books lining the walls, it appeared to serve as both an office and a library. And it was surprisingly disorganized. The books weren't in neat tidy rows on the shelves and papers were heaped on the desk.

Mayburn and his brother looked out of place in this room that had the air of a dotty old man. They stood behind the desk at the rear of the room. By the agitated stance of the younger, Gideon had clearly interrupted an argument.

The earl shot his brother a warning glance, and then

looked to Gideon. "Have a seat," Mayburn said calmly, indicating a chair in front of the desk with a flick of his hand.

Gideon did as instructed, settling in for the interrogation he knew was forthcoming. It was not a comfortable situation to find one's self in, but he wasn't worried. After all, he had been called back to the house and not left for dead on the side of the road.

The other brother moved to stand at the side of the desk, the better to pierce Gideon with that cold mutinous stare.

Arms crossed over his chest, Mayburn contemplated Gideon. "I know my brother well enough to know that the niceties often elude him at times like these. Therefore, an introduction is in order. This is Mr. Julien Riley, Lady Stirling's younger brother. You will be relieved to hear there are only two of us brothers, so you needn't worry about a third making an appearance."

"Two are more than enough, thank you."

Mayburn raised an eyebrow at Gideon's glib comment and sat in the chair behind the desk. Gideon had not noticed it before, for Mayburn had been standing in front of it, but the portrait on the wall now had his undivided attention. He was vaguely aware his breathing became harsh and uneven as he stared at the portrait of a man in his prime with auburn hair and dark blue eyes.

If that was who Gideon thought it was—

"Mr. Rosedale?"

Gideon's gaze snapped to Mayburn. "Who is that man?"

The earl looked taken aback at the abrupt question then glanced over his shoulder. "Lord Stirling. I take it you have never met?"

Gideon shook his head. "When was that portrait commissioned?"

"I haven't the faintest notion, but it looks to have been commissioned within the last few years."

Clenching his jaw, Gideon closed his eyes. A part of

him had hoped Bella's husband was elderly. A frail old man on death's doorstep. The bruises that covered her back had proved the frail part quite wrong. But old? He had clung to that hope. An old man would have used a weapon against a woman. But the man in the portrait was powerful enough to never need the aid of a heavy silver candlestick to inflict pain on another. Yet he had done so.

Rage the likes of which Gideon had never known pounded swift and fierce through his veins. His muscles shook with the force of it.

"Rosedale."

Gideon's eyes snapped open. "What?"

Mayburn's polite contained demeanor teetered on the brink of collapsing. The muscles in his arms bulged beneath the well-tailored black coat. The blue green eyes were not cold like Riley's but burning with malicious intent. "Who hurt my sister?"

"Him," Gideon snarled.

Mayburn glanced quickly over his shoulder again. His dark eyebrows met. "Lord Stirling?" he asked, as if fearing the answer.

"Yes."

A look of pure horror spread across Mayburn's strong face, speaking louder than words—the man knew nothing of Stirling's abuse of Bella. His shoulders sagged with the weight of his shock. "When?"

"Five days ago."

"Why?"

Gideon shook his head. "You need to pose your questions to Lady Stirling."

The shock vanished in a blink of an eye. Mayburn's face darkened with rage. He placed his hands flat on the desk and leaned forward in a clear effort to intimidate Gideon. "I will get nothing from her and you know it. You will tell me everything or you will not walk out of this room. I want to know why my sister looks like she's been run over by a carriage."

Gideon debated how much to reveal. "Lord Stirling took exception to something Bella said."

A muscle along Mayburn's jaw ticked at Gideon's use of his sister's given name. "What did she say to him?"

Gideon swallowed hard before admitting the truth. "Bella told him about me."

"Why would she do that?" Mayburn's demand reflected Gideon's own disbelief.

"I don't know." He cursed himself for not asking her what had possessed her to tell her husband she had a paid lover. She had to have known Stirling's reaction would be severe.

"Has he hurt her before?"

"Yes."

Mayburn passed a shaky hand over his jaw. "How often? How many times?"

"Only once that I know for certain, but I suspect many more. According to Bella, he hates her."

Riley advanced a menacing step. "You knew, and you allowed him to hurt her?"

"I did not know, not until a few days ago," Gideon shot back. "However, I am not the one who ignored her for five years."

Both men flinched, as if Gideon had struck them.

Riley was the first to recover. His entire body vibrated with barely suppressed rage. "You know nothing—!"

Mayburn held up a quick hand to stay him. Riley glared at his brother. Riley looked as though he was going to argue, but instead broke eye contact on a low, short growl. Then he pierced Gideon with that hard stare, as if the silent argument and his defeat had been Gideon's fault.

The earl turned his attention back to Gideon. "Has she had other lovers?"

"No."

"How can you be certain?"

"Oh, I'm certain," Gideon replied darkly.

Mayburn scoffed in disbelief. "*If* that is true, then why in God's name did he hate her?"

"Because he cannot bed his wife."

The earl's jaw dropped. His face was wiped clean of all emotion. "He is impotent?"

"Great choice, Phillip," muttered Riley in scalding derision, his arms crossed over his chest.

Mayburn ignored his brother. "How can you be certain?"

"For the same reason why I am certain she did not have any other lovers."

The earl's brow furrowed, then his eyes flared as he caught what Gideon did not explicitly state. "That cannot be. She was not an innocent when she married Stirling."

"Yes, she was. I have experienced the proof," he said with grave conviction. Mayburn stared at him, refusing to believe the truth. But Gideon wasn't done yet. "Stirling's impotency is not a recent phenomenon. According to Bella, past attempts not only didn't meet with success, but also did not end well."

He knew exactly the moment when Mayburn believed him. It was probably the instant when the image clarified in his mind of a virginal Bella in bed with her brute of a husband, as the man vainly forced himself on her then vented his frustrations. It was the same image that had tormented Gideon when Bella had confessed the truth of her marriage. The same image that still tormented him.

"Phillip—?" Riley's voice broke through the silence.

With his eyes closed, Mayburn shook his head, a clear dismissal of any question his brother wanted to pose. He raked both hands through his hair, and when next he opened his eyes, he had regained some semblance of composure. "How long have you been associated with Lady Stirling?"

"Since April of this year."

"And how did you make her acquaintance?"

"A woman came to London and"—Gideon lifted his chin—"hired me for her ladyship."

"What woman?" At Gideon's silence, Mayburn said, "Who?"

At his continued silence, Mayburn demanded through clenched teeth, "Who? Who hired you to fuck my sister?"

Somehow Gideon kept from flinching. "Madame Marceau."

"Esmé?" Riley said in incredulous disbelief. "Why the hell would she have hired a man for Bella?"

Gideon directed his answer to the earl. "She believed Bella was getting too maudlin. That she was in need of a flirtation."

"Esmé's answer for everything," Riley muttered in disgust.

Mayburn raised a weary eyebrow at the comment.

Riley's gaze slanted to meet his brother's. "I'll have a word with her." His words were barely audible, but the conviction was crystal clear.

Mayburn nodded once. "Is Madame Marceau aware Stirling beat her?"

Gideon thought for a moment. "No. I don't believe so. Her solution would not have been fitting. In fact, when Lord Stirling was informed about me, Bella's situation only got worse."

"Is Madame Marceau aware Stirling is impotent?"

"I don't know."

Mayburn was silent for a long moment. A very long moment. The silence stretched thin. Then his eyebrows pulled. "Mrs. Cooley sent two notes to London. One addressed to myself and one addressed to you. I know you did not receive yours as it is in my possession. Therefore, how did you know to come to Scotland? Did Lady Stirling send for you?"

That housekeeper had sent him a note? The woman must have been near panic to have been that desperate for someone to help Bella. "No. Lord Stirling was in residence and had been for quite some time. Bella would not have sent for me as she didn't know when he would choose to depart. I came on my own."

"Why?"

Gideon certainly wasn't going to answer that question, least of all to Bella's brother.

At length, Mayburn shrugged, as if realizing the question had been foolish to ask. "You have told me what I needed to know. You may take your leave."

Gideon did not heed the earl's command. He remained seated, uncertain if the man was trying to get him to break his word to Bella and leave not only the study, but the house.

Mayburn gave a short exasperated sigh. "You are welcome to stay, if it pleases Lady Stirling." The earl winced at the innuendo in his own words, while his brother snorted on a roll of his eyes.

Gideon got to his feet and left the study but stopped at the top of the stairs. As he debated his destination, a maid approached.

"The blue room has been readied for you."

The destination settled for him, he nodded and followed the girl down the hall in the opposite direction of Bella.

She gave him a cool assessing glance from the corner of her eye as she opened the door. Word had gotten out, and quickly. Any deference she had once paid him as a guest of the lady of the manor was now gone.

Gideon shut the door and doused the candle beside the bed. In the darkness, he pulled off his clothes and slipped under the cool sheets. He should be used to sleeping alone—he'd done it all his life and deliberately at that. But the last few nights with Bella had erased the familiarity. He had grown very fond of falling asleep with her slender body pressed gently against his, and now he felt like a child denied his favorite toy to snuggle up with.

He rolled over, punched the fluffy goose-down pillow, then settled in and tried to get to sleep.

BELLA rapped lightly on the door and turned the knob. She had already checked all the other guest rooms. This

one was her last hope. "Gideon?" she called softly into
the dark room.

*Please, let him be here. Please, Phillip could not have
sent him away again.* Mrs. Cooley had reported no loud
arguments. But with Phillip, volume was not always
needed to inflict his will on others.

"Bella?"

The anxiety vanished, leaving behind a distinct note of
indignation. She closed the door and flew to the bedside.
A dark figure sat up and turned to her.

"You promised," she admonished.

The moonlight seeping between the partially closed
curtains was enough for her to see the sigh that slumped
his broad bare shoulders. "I didn't leave the house."

"You promised to return to me."

"Bella, I can't share your bed when your brothers are
here."

"Nonsense. This is not their house. You promised," she
said, sounding hurt to her own ears.

He sighed again and lifted the sheet. "Come here."

She hesitated half a second, but it was long enough for
him to speak again.

"Please, Bella."

The soft plea had her dressing gown and nightgown on
the floor in an instant, and then she was crawling into the
bed, into Gideon's waiting arms. The lingering ache disappeared the moment his arms wrapped around her.

With her hands on his jaw, she pulled his lips down to
meet hers. Pleasure, desire, rapture instantly saturated
every nerve in her being. Bare skin rubbed deliciously
against bare skin as she moved against him. She felt him
trying to contain the kiss, but she would not be denied.
She wrapped her limbs around his body. Clinging desperately to him, she trailed eager kisses down the line of his
jaw and mouthed his neck, her tongue caressing his rapidly beating pulse.

"Make love to me," she whispered against the smooth
taut skin.

"No. Not yet. I don't want to hurt you."

"Yes."

"Bella—"

She hitched up her hips and slid down until the hard arch of his manhood met the soft folds of her sex. "Yes."

Every trace of resistance, every trace of refusal, left him. His kiss was harsh, demanding, unyielding, and she loved it, drank it up, met him hot stroke for hot stroke of his tongue.

A large hand skimmed lightly down her back, over the swell of her bottom, and between her thighs to play at the apex of her pleasure. Seeking more, she writhed against him as his long fingers dipped into the wet, aching cove of her body.

And then she was on her back; he crouched over her, his strong arms bracketing her shoulders. The hard satiny length of his cock pressed against her inner thigh. She hooked a leg over his hip, pulling him closer. "Now," she said into his mouth.

But instead of complying, he reached over the side of the bed.

Realizing at once what he was after, she grabbed his upper arm. "No."

"Yes, Bella."

"No. I just want you. Just us." She heard the soft shift of fabric and the crackle of paper. His hard bicep flexed with his movements.

"Bella, I won't take you without it."

She brought her hands up to cup his face. "Just once." She had never needed him like this before. It was more than lust, more than a wish for shared pleasure. She had almost lost him forever.

He gave a short shake of his head. "I can't. Don't ask it of me. Not tonight," he said intently, his breaths coming hard and harsh, his body drawn tight above her.

"Gideon—"

"Either agree or nothing. Your choice."

"But—"

"I don't want to argue with you. Please, not now. Not this night. Don't push me. Don't ask—" His throat worked under her fingertips. Even in the darkness she could make out his strained features.

The last time they had had this clash of wills he had been prepared to walk away from her. She could not risk that happening. Yet she sensed in the rapid beat of his heart and in the faint quiver seizing his muscles that he was almost at the point of giving in. Just a few more words from her would take him past that point, giving her what she wanted.

But he did not want it. He would be acting against his conscious will. She trailed her fingertips past the taut cords of his neck to settle on his hard shoulders. The skin wasn't its usual velvety warm but hot with the threat of sweat.

"All right," she conceded on a nod.

He tipped his chin. His deep exhale tickled her nipples. He shifted enough to reach between their bodies and tie the sheath on securely. Then his lips met hers, the thank-you clear in the kiss for a fleeting moment before passion took hold.

The hard muscles surrounding her gathered, as if to change positions. She clung tightly to him, her nails scoring his back. "No. Here."

"Bella," he said harshly in her ear. "I don't want to hurt you. You shouldn't be on your back."

"But—"

With her leg still hooked over his hip, he rolled them onto their sides, cutting off her protests. He reached down, positioned himself at her core, and with a thrust of his hips, slowly glided into her. A groan rumbled the back of his throat. She threw back her head, reveling in that first stroke. The tightness of her body, the inherent resistance to the intrusion, the way every inch of him felt like ten.

When he was only halfway in, he pulled out and began a rhythm of short, compact, slow nudges. She could tell he was holding back, could tell he was determined to be careful. And it frustrated her. She'd waited days for him to agree to make love to her and she did not want careful. She did not want slow. She wanted hard and fast. Wanted to feel him slam against her. Needed every inch of him, body and soul.

Determined, persistent, demanding, she rocked her entire body in counterpoint to those careful thrusts. A warm hand settled on her hip, trying to force her to accede to his pace. She shook her head. "More."

"Bella—"

"More."

"Angel, please. Don't." The request was torn from his throat.

"More," she gasped, thrusting her hips into his with all the strength in her body.

Beyond impatient, beyond frustrated, she brought a hand to his shoulder and pushed him onto his back, the contact of their bodies unbroken. She planted both palms on his sweat-slicked chest and sat up on a low, drunken moan as she sank completely down onto him, fully to the hilt. Exquisite pleasure swamped her senses and for a moment, she could do nothing more but sit there impaled on his cock, her body trembling against the onslaught of sensation.

With a hard abrupt thrust, he flexed his hips, pushing somehow incredibly deeper. Her eyes flared then rolled back on a rapturous groan as an orgasm crashed over her. Swaying slightly, she struggled to catch her breath. It was almost too much.

"Is that what you wanted?" he asked with a distinctly feral edge.

"Yes," she moaned. Rocking her hips, she chased the next orgasm teasing her senses. Her clit rubbed maddeningly against his groin. "More." She could feel it getting closer, each thrust pulling it faster toward her.

He levered his upper body up and the second his hot mouth captured one hard nipple, she came. Fingers gripping his skull, she clutched his head to her chest and ground her hips hard against him, seeking even more.

He pulled free of her grasp. "Enough, Bella," he gasped, hot breath chilling her wet nipple, drawing it tighter.

"No. More." She never wanted this to end. Never wanted to be parted from him again.

"Bella, I can't hold back . . . . Oh, *God*."

All pretense of gentleness vanished. He grasped her hips, quickening the pace. Each thrust was punctuated by a raspy masculine grunt. He tipped his chin up, seeking her lips. She wrapped her arms around him, the muscles of his back rippling beneath her hands, and kissed him passionately as the orgasmic shudders gripped his body.

He dropped his forehead to her chest. His lungs heaved like bellows. "Oh, Bella," he sighed, amazement heavy in the low tone.

She couldn't help but smile. She had actually made him, Gideon, lose control.

Nineteen

I'LL start in the stables." Julien pushed from the dining room table. His expression determined, he stood and gave his black coat a sharp tug to straighten it.

Perhaps it hadn't been the wisest decision to unleash his brother on Isabella's household, but there was nothing to be done for it. Phillip was pressed for time and he still had a couple of errands to see to this morning. Errands he shouldn't put off any longer, no matter how much he dreaded one in particular. "If you could, please try not to upset the servants."

Julien rolled his eyes. "I'm not going to threaten them with bodily harm. Just ask a few questions."

"Try to be civilized. That's all I ask. We're Isabella's guests and it would not be well-done of us to terrorize her servants."

"Shall I follow your example from last night?"

Phillip clenched his jaw. He didn't need to be reminded of his sins. He had all of last night to recount the ways he'd failed Isabella. Behaving like a domineering ass was just one of the many. "Just go to the stables, Julien."

With what was undeniably a condescending bow, Julien turned on his heel and left the room.

Arrogant whelp. Phillip shook his head, then took a large swallow of coffee and set his empty cup on the white linen tablecloth. A footman approached, a silver pot held at the ready. With a flick of his fingers, he waved the footman away. The last three cups hadn't helped in the slightest, so another would do no good.

Resting his elbows on the table, he rubbed his eyes. Christ, he hadn't gotten a wink of sleep in well over twenty-four hours. Exhaustion pulled heavily on his mind but it couldn't silence the words that resounded in his head.

She is your responsibility. And you failed her.

He was the eldest. It was his responsibility to take care of his brothers and sisters. And he could not have done worse by Isabella if he had tried.

Yet she hadn't once complained or protested. Even when he'd stormed into her home and assumed the worst, she had not railed at him for marrying her to a man who beat her. Her only concern had been for Rosedale. For the man she obviously loved, who loved her in return.

Sometime during the long, sleepless predawn hours, he had come to a decision. It went against all he had been taught and against the rules of polite society, but he didn't much care. All that mattered was that he find a way, however small, to make it up to her.

He pushed from the table. He could delay his errands no longer. Since he needed an answer from one before seeing to the other, he set off for the guest bedchamber down the hall from his own.

⚓

SHAFTS of morning sunlight pierced the gaps in the heavy curtains. Completely content, Gideon sighed as he absently rubbed a lock of pale blonde hair between his fingers. Through heavy-lidded eyes, he gazed at the beautiful woman who shared his bed. Her back rose and fell in the rhythmic pattern of one in a deep sleep. Even sprawled half on top of him, the innate elegance of her long limbs could not be denied.

Nor could he deny the strength in those long limbs as they had been wrapped tight around him last night.

He should have been gentler. Hell, he should not have even given in to her. He should have waited longer, until she fully healed. But the combination of two months of abstinence and a demanding, impatient Bella . . .

He let out a low grunt. He had never come like that before—the orgasm rushing upon him, too swift, too fierce to be denied. His cock swelled, pressing against the smooth skin of Bella's upper thigh. The idea of waking her was tempting indeed, but he resisted. After last night, she needed her rest. So he closed his eyes, content to fall back asleep with her warm body draped over his.

There was only a very brief knock in prelude to the sound of Mayburn's strong voice. "Get up, man. I need—Oh!"

Jolted awake, Gideon yanked the blankets up to cover Bella's naked body. Apparently the light knock and the sound of her brother's voice weren't enough to wake her, but Gideon's movement was enough.

She lifted her head from his shoulder, her eyes half-lidded. "Good morning," she said drowsily.

She must have read something on his face, for she twisted around and sucked in a startled breath. On a little squeak, she dove under the blanket, huddling close to him.

Gideon draped one arm protectively over Bella's back and stared at Mayburn, daring him to take issue with Bella's presence in his bed. He was not about to apologize for making love to Bella. In any case, she had come to him.

"Is he still there?" a meek little voice asked from beneath the blue blanket.

Gideon couldn't help it. He chuckled. "Yes, Bella. Though it looks like you scared him more than he scared you."

Mayburn snorted, the jest bringing him to his senses.

"Sorry, Isabella. I didn't know . . ." He shook his head. Then his voice returned to its normal strong tone. "Rosedale, I need to speak with you."

Gideon lifted one eyebrow.

"Alone. I will await you in the hall. And put some clothes on." Mayburn stalked out of the room and shut the door.

It took a bit of doing to disengage from Bella, and three promises on his part to return promptly before she would consent to let him out of the bed. He pulled on the trousers he had left in a heap on the floor and quickly buttoned them. Pulling his wrinkled shirt over his head, he walked to the door.

Hand on the knob, he looked over his shoulder. Clutching the blanket tight to her chest, she sat on the bed. Her pale blonde hair was loose and disheveled around her shoulders, her eyes wide with uncertainty. And he gave her one more "I promise" before slipping out the door.

The hall was empty save for Mayburn, who stood a few steps to the left of the room. Gideon stopped before him and waited for the earl to speak.

Mayburn dragged a hand through his hair. "We shall pretend that did not happen," he muttered.

"Define *that*," Gideon said hesitantly.

"I did not just see my sister naked. That makes two of them. Here's hoping the third doesn't follow in the others' footsteps."

Gideon shrugged. He didn't know what to say. He had not known Bella had sisters.

The discomfort disappeared from Mayburn's face, leaving a stern frown in its wake. "There is something I need to ask you and I expect an honest answer."

Gideon bristled at the condescending tone. He squared his shoulders. "You may ask all you like. Whether I chose to answer is another matter."

The earl did not react to Gideon's snide comment. "Are you still in the employ of Madam Rubicon?" he asked, voice pitched low.

Gideon tried, truly he did, not to get rattled by Mayburn's question. The man clearly had had him investigated. No wonder Mayburn had been so livid when he had come to the house. Gideon could understand the man's need to verify his employment status. He was still amazed Mayburn had allowed a known prostitute to remain at his sister's home last night. Yet he could not help but feel exposed by the blunt reminder of his past.

"No." At Mayburn's hard glare, Gideon clarified, "It is true I had been employed by Madam Rubicon for a number of years. However, I have since resigned."

Mayburn crossed his arms over his chest. The way the earl studied him reminded Gideon vividly of the way Madame Marceau had appraised him many months ago in Rubicon's office. As in that instance, he had to fight to keep his chin up and not to shift his weight.

After a long moment, Mayburn nodded. "Riley and I are leaving for London this morning."

"So soon?" The man was an earl. Still, to be so busy he could not spend even twenty-four hours with a sister he had not seen in years? A sister who had recently been severely beaten by her husband?

"Yes. I was unexpectedly called away," Mayburn said. "There are business matters that require my attention and Riley has his own business to attend to. I am leaving Isabella in your care. Bring her to London immediately if Stirling returns. She knows the way to Mayburn House. If I am not there when you arrive, inquire with the butler. He'll know my whereabouts."

"But—"

Mayburn continued as if Gideon had not spoken. "I have already informed the household that Lady Stirling has been placed in your care. You have my authority to act as you see fit. You are to keep her safe, at all costs."

"But Stirling is still her husband," he pointed out.

Mayburn tipped his head. "And I expect Isabella to remain safe while in your care. No harm is to come to her. I don't care what you have to do. She is to be protected.

Do you understand?" His blue green eyes bored into Gideon's.

"Yes," he replied, stunned. It sounded as if the Earl of Mayburn trusted him.

"According to Mrs. Cooley, Stirling rarely visits. He shouldn't be due back until after the new year."

Gideon nodded again.

"Until then, you are to focus all your efforts into Isabella's recovery. What did the doctor advise? Shouldn't she limit her physical activity?"

He resisted the urge to roll his eyes at the underlying meaning in Mayburn's words, and instead admitted, "The doctor has not seen her."

"What?"

"I tried, but Mrs. Cooley advised heavily against it. Nothing was broken. Bella was just very badly bruised." The excuse sounded pathetic even to his own ears.

"What possible reason could that housekeeper have?"

"Many and varied," Gideon said. "The doctor and Stirling are acquainted. Bella would have been humiliated if word got out. If Stirling had wanted a doctor, he would have called for the man himself—"

"That's absurd."

His shoulders slumped. "Yes, I know. But short of going into the village and knocking on every door in an attempt to locate the man, he would not be making a call."

Mayburn glowered, bringing to mind the image of an extremely displeased feudal lord. "If you feel a doctor should see Isabella, call for him. I will have a word with Mrs. Cooley. She will get the man here, if need be."

Gideon nodded. He was relieved, but a bit emasculated to have his station in this household so thoroughly revealed.

"Good. I expect a note if any problem should arise."

"Yes," Gideon droned. He felt as if he were being put in charge of a group of young children for the day and getting his orders on how to care for them properly.

"I need to speak with Isabella before I leave."

"Alone?"

"Alone."

"Tell her I went down to the kitchen to get her some breakfast." At the odd look on Mayburn's face, he added, "I promised her about four times that I'd return. Immediately."

Mayburn snorted. One corner of his mouth pulled in a rueful grin.

He left the earl knocking on the door and went to fetch some food for Bella. She was still much too thin. He had tried everything he could think of and everything the kitchen staff suggested, but she didn't seem to have a preference for much.

As he went down the stairs on bare feet, he debated the merits of various dishes to tempt her. Definitely some eggs. Sausages? Maybe. Kippers? No. But yes on the fruit. She seemed to like that.

He came upon Riley in the entrance hall by the front door. Hands on his hips and stance wide, it was obvious Riley was not having a pleasant chat with the unfortunate young footman.

"Are you certain?" Riley questioned.

"Yes, sir."

Riley scowled at the footman. The piercing gaze quickly left the servant, took in Gideon's disheveled appearance, then snapped up to meet his eyes. Gideon tipped his head in greeting but said not a word. As he made his way down the hall, he could feel those blue green eyes scorching a hole through the back of his neck.

Yes, it was a good thing the brothers were leaving today. He did not much care for that one.

❧

THERE was a soft knock on the door followed by a low, hesitant, "Isabella?"

"Yes, Phillip."

"Are you dressed?"

Sitting in the center of the bed and huddled in the blue blanket that retained the scent of Gideon's warm body, she couldn't bring herself to admit the truth.

Phillip must have suspected though. "Can you, please?"

Bella reluctantly discarded the blanket, scooted off the bed, and pulled on her nightgown and dressing gown. She kicked Gideon's boots, waistcoat, and coat under the bed; shook out the blanket to cover the rumpled sheets; and, running her fingers through her hair, tamed the tousled locks as best she could.

She sat in the armchair by the window. "Phillip, you can come in."

The door slowly opened. Eyes shut, he took one step into the room then opened one eye. At finding her dressed, he opened the other eye.

With effort, she straightened her spine and tipped her head to the chair next to hers.

He sat down. "Julien and I are leaving shortly. I have notified the household that you are in Mr. Rosedale's care. You are to follow his instructions."

Bella nodded. With his medium brown hair, strong features, and powerful build, the sight of him alone was a heavy reminder of their father. But when he spoke to her in that paternalistic tone, she could have sworn he was the man himself.

"If Stirling returns, you are to let Mr. Rosedale deal with him. He has been instructed to bring you to London immediately. If anything should happen or if Mr. Rosedale is removed from you, I want you to come straight to London, to Mayburn House."

She maintained her serene expression and nodded again, effectively hiding the apprehension his dire words sparked.

Phillip's mouth tightened. His brow furrowed. Somehow she managed to sit perfectly still, to not even reclasp the hands folded demurely on her lap.

"Why did you never write?" His tone was soft, probing, almost injured. "Why did you never say anything? If you didn't want to tell me, you could at least have told Esmé."

"What good would it have done?"

He leaned toward her. "Isabella, he was hurting you."

"He is my husband," she stated calmly, careful to keep any censure or accusation out of her tone.

Still, Phillip looked as if she had slapped him across the face. His throat worked soundlessly. But when next he spoke, she had the distinct impression the words were not those that had lodged in his throat. "Kitty has married."

"She has? Liv didn't mention it in her last letter." Bella was a bit piqued at the omission. While Kitty's letters were infrequent due to her travels with Jules, Liv was a diligent correspondent and Bella counted on her to keep her apprised of events related to their family.

"It was a rather hasty informal affair much like your own. There wasn't time to fetch Olivia from school so she could attend. Likely her next letter will include the news."

Kitty, the unconventional girl who grew up in Jules's shadow, had needed a quick wedding? Hopefully Liv would relay the details. "And who is the chosen gentleman?"

A wince pulled his mouth. "Lord Templeton."

Bella tipped her head in approval. She remembered the rugged, imposing gentleman from years ago. She'd have never thought to match the two up, but Lord Templeton was a viscount, and though not fabulously wealthy, a well-respected one at least.

"From what Julien reports, they are quite happy together."

She was relieved to hear that—Jules would know if Kitty was truly happy. "I shall write to them and extend my congratulations."

They sat in silence, strangers who had run out of polite topics to discuss. A cool morning breeze ruffled the curtains. The distinct scent of roses wafted into the room.

She stared at her clasped hands. Once they had been quite close. Kitty had Jules and she'd had Phillip. They had understood each other, understood their roles, and had a similar desire to be the people their parents had wanted them to be. But the bond they once shared had been crushed by her own hand. Every shred of trust he had in her was long shattered. Phillip had become the man he had wanted to be. He was the very image of their father, a living replica of the man they lost six years ago. Whereas she . . . she had let him down. He had to come up to Scotland and have the full extent of her continued fall into disgrace revealed to him.

"How are you faring?" Phillip asked, breaking the silence. "If you need anything, tell Mr. Rosedale."

She glanced up. "I am quite well, thank you, and I will notify Mr. Rosedale if I require anything."

It was Phillip's turn to nod. He reached into an inside pocket of his dark green coat and held out a poorly wrapped bundle. A thick fold of pound notes was visible beneath the paper wrapping.

Bella looked blankly at the offering. Why was he giving her this? Did he believe Stirling denied her pin money?

"Mr. Rosedale asked that I return this to you."

She froze. The quick beats of her heart filled her ears. How had Phillip gotten ahold of it? "No. I don't want it. It belongs to Mr. Rosedale."

He thrust the bundle at her. "Isabella, take it."

"No." She leaned back, keeping her distance. It was one thing to have Jules accuse her. Quite another to have the proof so harshly and plainly before her, and to have it come from Phillip.

"What would you have me do with it?"

"Return it to him. I do not want it," she said, her voice strengthening in intensity.

"Isabella," he admonished. "I will do no such thing."

"Why not?"

"Because he does not want it." Incredulous, Phillip stared at her. "I thought you cared for him. Do you have any idea the insult you would be delivering if I were to return this at your request? I will not do it."

Frustrated at his insistence, she snatched the bundle from his hand. The weight of it felt wrong. Brow furrowing, she thumbed through the stack.

Phillip frowned. "He didn't spend it, if that's what you think. I suspect his employer has the other half. You will never see it."

"Half?"

"Yes. That's how it usually works," he said wearily.

"But there's more than two hundred and fifty pounds here, unless . . ."

"Unless what?"

She shook her head. "Nothing. I miscounted." Quickly, she refolded the paper over the pound notes. She was not certain if Phillip was aware Gideon had been hired twice to come to Bowhill. If he wasn't, then she did not want to inform him Gideon had returned his wages from both occasions.

And he had returned them. Without even knowing the sum Esmé had parted with, she was certain she held exactly half of what she and Esmé had paid for Gideon. The significance of the paper wrapping did not escape her notice. It was worn and wrinkled, the pencil marks slightly smudged, but even half covered by the pound notes she recognized the artist's hand.

Bella wasn't sure which meant more to her—the fact he returned the money, or that he had kept the sketch for so long.

Phillip shifted, dropping his gaze then resolutely meeting hers again. "Isabella, you're my sister. I never meant to see you harmed."

"I know, Phillip," she said softly. While he had been upset with her at the time, and rightly so, she had never been so foolish as to believe Phillip had married her to Stirling with full knowledge of his true character.

He slumped heavily in the chair and ran a hand through his hair. "I never should have had you wed Stirling. You didn't even know the man. I'm sorry. I had no idea he would . . ."

The obvious pain on his face tore at her chest. Stirling was not Phillip's fault. She had inflicted him on herself. She would not apologize for Gideon. That she would never do. But she did still owe Phillip an apology of her own.

"I'm sorry, Phillip. I-I'm sorry I let you down all those years ago. I shouldn't have been so reckless. I should have tried harder. I should have expended an effort to bring a gentleman to heel. If I would have then . . ." Closing her eyes, she shook her head, trying to find the words. "Kitty and Liv write to me. They are never so blunt, but it's obvious you're still struggling. I can't help but feel if I wouldn't have failed you when you needed me most then—"

"Isabella."

She looked up and took a swift breath at the mingled horror and disbelief on his face.

"No," he said harshly. "The state of my finances is not your fault. Nor is it your responsibility. Don't think it. Ever." He leaned forward and grasped her hand firmly. His gaze bored into hers. "It is I who failed you. I should have been more understanding. I shouldn't have tossed you out onto the marriage mart mere months after we lost Mother and Father. Hell, the least I could have done was send you a note within the last five years. Let you know that I . . . that I still—"

Eyes clamping shut, his face contorted on a wince. He released her hand and pressed his palms to his temples. Dragging his hands down his face, he took a deep breath. The tension slipped out of his broad shoulders. He met her gaze: his steady, hers wary. "I want you to be happy, Isabella. Don't worry about me. You do what will make you happy. And whatever that is, I will always be your brother."

She bit the inside of her cheek to keep the calm façade in place and nodded. There had been a time when she had been certain he would never call himself her brother again.

He stood on a weary sigh and tugged on the end of his coat to straighten it. "Take care of yourself."

"I will."

He turned and left the room on heavy footsteps.

"I still love you, too, Phillip," she whispered as he closed the door quietly behind him.

Do you know where you're going?" Phillip asked of his brother, who sat sprawled in the maroon leather armchair facing his desk. After an arduous journey back to London, the two men had cleaned up, and then met in the study to start in on the French brandy.

"A maid overheard Stirling mention he was headed to Rome," Julien said. "One of his cronies has a villa outside the city where they plan to spend the winter. Christ, he had a whole group of them up at Bella's house. Judging by what the servants reported, they were a raucous, unpleasant bunch. Emptied the wine cellar and all. Bella's housekeeper said she was still working on righting the house."

If Julien thought Stirling's friends raucous and unpleasant, then that was saying a lot. "Will you take the ship or go overland?"

Julien passed a hand over his jaw. How could he stand to go so many days without shaving? The sight of the scruffy, dark blond beard made Phillip's neck itch.

"It'd be best to go via sea," Julien said. "Couldn't discover anything as to their travel route, but by the time I reach Rome they should be well settled in."

"When are you leaving?"

"As soon as I can get the crew back on the *Mistress Mine*. Rounding them up will be a chore. May require a day or two. The crew hasn't even had a week of shore leave yet and most of them scatter the instant I give the word. And I'll stop over in France, see if I can locate Esmé. I still can't believe she hired a man for Bella. What was she thinking? If she thought Bella unwell, she should have mentioned it to you or me. I saw her over the winter and she said not a word."

"I don't know why she didn't mention it," Phillip said. "But you know her better than I. Just don't be too hard on her. She was trying to help Isabella, in her own way."

Julien snorted his disgust, clearly at odds with their cousin's methods. Phillip didn't condone them either. But ever conscious of how quickly Julien's temper could escalate when he believed one of his own had been wronged, Phillip felt the need to add a few calming words of wisdom. They might fall on deaf ears, but at least he made the effort.

He swirled the remains of his brandy, watching the amber liquid catch the nearby candlelight. At length he posed the question that had been weighing heavy on his mind for the past few days. "Julien, is Kitty truly happy with Templeton?"

"Of course she's happy. I already told you. It's nauseating to be in her presence. A more lovesick pair I have yet to encounter."

"He would never hurt her, would he?" Phillip asked carefully.

"No. Never laid a hand on her, and she's given him ample reason to do so. She ran that man ragged. Even made me feel sorry for him at times—but not too sorry. He rather deserved it for daring to trifle with our sister. He is a good man though, has her best interests at heart. And he positively adores her. Got to, to put up with Kitty. She can be quite a handful."

"Good to hear," Phillip said, immensely relieved. At least he had managed to get it right once.

With a thud, Julien dropped the foot that had been crossed over his knee onto the floor. His eyes narrowed. "I'm assuming you did not know what sort of man Stirling was when you tied Bella to him?"

"No, I didn't," Phillip said with forced calm. "Though I'll admit, I didn't know the man very well. He was simply the only peer I could find who was willing to take her."

Julien *harrumphed*. "Could have expended some effort to have him investigated."

To be scolded by his younger brother was not a pleasant experience. Resisting the urge to drop his gaze, he squared his shoulders and glared at Julien. "Yes, I could have. And I normally would have, but at the time the possibility never entered my head that he could be an impotent abuser of women." He purposefully left out the "he had seemed like a nice enough chap" comment. "And I had to act quickly. For Christ's sake, after finding her with that damn groom I feared she could have been with child."

"Well, we now know *that* wasn't a possibility." Sarcasm dripped off Julien's words. "And you couldn't have chosen more poorly if you tried. An impotent husband for a woman like Bella? That's a punishment if I ever heard of one."

The barb hit sharply home. "Enough, Julien. I feel bad enough as it is. I don't need you to make it worse."

"Good. You should feel bad. She's our *sister*."

The fierce protectiveness radiating from Julien's hard words rankled far more than it should have. "Yes, she is. *Our* sister. Convenient how that fact slipped your mind for five years."

"I've been occupied earning the money that pays for your damn servants."

"'Earning' money, that's an interesting way to put it. I thought the correct term was *smuggling*."

"At least it's something. What the hell have you done? Besides ignore our sister."

"Everything!" Phillip shot back. Though they felt like trivial, inconsequential matters compared to Isabella's well-being. "You have no concept of what it takes to manage an earldom, and you never bothered to learn. You were too occupied swiving anything in a skirt."

Julien flinched, as if Phillip had actually hit a raw nerve. But in the blink of an eye, he recovered. "Bugger you, Phillip. You're the earl. You chose Stirling. I trusted your decision." His sandy blond forelock fell over eyes blazing with anger. Gripping the arms of the leather chair, he looked ready to launch himself at Phillip. To take out all his pent-up rage on a brother whose decision had ultimately caused harm to their sister.

Phillip made not a move. Merely stared blankly at Julien. There was no defense to be had against the truth. Frankly, he was surprised it hadn't come to this point sooner. "Go ahead. Hit me. I certainly deserve it."

For a moment, Phillip thought Julien *would* hit him. But after a few tense seconds of silence, he leaned back and loosened his grip on the chair. Apparently he had a better leash on his temper than Phillip gave him credit for.

"What are you planning to do about Rosedale?" Julien's tone held only a shadow of its previous animosity.

"Nothing."

"Nothing?" His brother gaped at him. "You're going to allow a prostitute to live with our sister?"

"Former prostitute," Phillip clarified. "Rosedale is no longer employed by Madam Rubicon. He resigned."

Julien snorted. Clearly his brother thought that detail to be of little significance.

"He cares for her. And more importantly, she cares for him. She deserves a spot of happiness in her life after all she's been though. I will not stand in the way. Neither will you," Phillip said firmly.

Julien looked as if he was going to argue, then he tipped his head, submitting to Phillip's will.

In an effort to ease the guilt gnawing viciously at his gut, Phillip took a long swallow of brandy. Gripping the crystal glass tightly, he stared at the sliver of amber liquid coating the bottom. "I never before realized how much power a man has over his wife." His voice was low as he spoke the thoughts plaguing his mind. "It's disturbing and completely unnecessary." He glanced up to Julien. "Do you realize Stirling practically owns her? I'm an earl, her brother, and still there's not much I can do for her. If I thought it would help, I'd try to get her a divorce. But I doubt Stirling would be agreeable. He'd fight it. What man would want his marriage nullified due to impotence?

And if he wanted to be rid of her, he'd have done so himself by now. Instead, he keeps her up at that house, rarely visits, and when he does, he beats her."

Phillip dragged a hand through his hair in frustration. He had hated leaving her, but he had too many responsibilities in London and at Mayburn Hall to let either place go unattended for any length of time. He felt like he was being drawn on the rack, pulled in opposing directions. But at least he had not left her alone. He was confident he had gotten through to Rosedale. Isabella would be kept safe under her devoted beau's watchful eye in Scotland.

"Well, that problem will soon be solved." Julien got to his feet and set his empty glass on the desk. "I better start rounding up the crew."

"Be careful in Rome." Phillip refilled his own glass of brandy.

The remark got him a smug, devilish smirk. "Of course. When have you known me to be anything but?"

Twenty

GIDEON glanced out the dining room window. It was early October. Autumn had arrived in full force. The Scottish winds held a definite bite of winter and often kept Bella and him indoors. The last rays of the setting sun picked up the deep ambers and golden yellows of the leaves on the trees in the distance. Scotland was beautiful in the autumn, but it could not compete with the woman seated on his left who was currently moving neatly cut squares of lamb around her plate with the tines of her fork.

Relocating her food was a sure sign she was not going to eat another bite. He had stopped arguing with her. It was a battle he rarely won, and in any case, she had regained some weight. Her figure was back to being lean and willowy, no longer on the verge of being labeled *gaunt* or *frail*. The last of her bruises had faded to nothingness weeks ago. He should know, as he had ample opportunities to examine every inch of her soft alabaster skin.

His cock began to swell, as thoughts of Bella's lithe

naked body slammed into his mind. Closing his eyes, he willed the erection down. An hour or two wasn't an unreasonable amount of time to wait to indulge his desires.

Reaching for the glass of wine, he downed the remaining Bordeaux in one swallow. It certainly couldn't hurt to speed the evening along.

"Are you finished with dinner?" He knew the answer, but it was always best not to assume where a woman was concerned.

Her hand stilled in the process of pushing a square of lamb toward the barely touched mound of peas. She looked up from her plate. "Yes."

He flicked his fingers. The footman stationed along the wall jumped into action, clearing the table of plates and silverware. "Do you have a preference for our afterdinner activity tonight?"

Bella's lashes swept down. Slow and sensual, a thoroughly wicked grin curved her mouth. "Yes, I do. But I'm almost finished with the embroidery on the pillowcase I plan to send Liv. I should take care of that first or it won't get done tonight."

Quickly revising his earlier timetable, he pushed back from the table. That grin said Bella would have her embroidery completed in significantly less than an hour. He stood and glanced to the footman. "Have tea and a glass of scotch delivered to her ladyship's sitting room."

Loaded down with the remnants of their dinner, the footman tipped his head and left the dining room.

Gideon pulled out Bella's chair and held out a hand, helping her to her feet. She looked as regal as a queen in the deep amethyst silk gown. The vibrant color was the perfect complement to her fair complexion. His glance fell to her chest and his fingers itched with the need to tug on the low neckline. It wouldn't take much to free her luscious breasts, and then he could take the weight of them in his hands and lift them high to suck on the hard tips.

"Have I told you yet how beautiful you look tonight?" Gideon asked, as they walked out of the dining room.

"Yes, you have. Twice in fact, if I recall correctly." She lifted her skirt with her free hand as they ascended the stairs. "Thank you, and you look rather handsome yourself this evening."

He stopped at the top of the stairs and gave her his best indignant expression. "Rather?"

She turned to face him, stepping so close her breasts brushed his stark white waistcoat. Placing a hand on his shoulder, she lifted up onto her toes. "Very handsome," she whispered and pressed her lips lightly to his.

Her fingers drifted down his chest to brush the placket of his trousers before taking hold of his hand. The light contact made his cock twitch with impatience. He resisted the urge to pull her against him and kiss her soundly. The servants knew he and Bella shared a bed, but it would not be well-done to engage in a tryst in the hallway.

Hand in hand, he followed her into the sitting room. Her naughty fingertips caressed his palm as she released his hand. She disappeared into her bedchamber to gather her embroidery hoop and thread. He stopped before the tall narrow bookcase next to her writing desk. *What to read this evening?* He needed something to take his mind off Bella's luscious breasts for the next half hour or so.

A maid entered the room carrying a silver tray laden with an ivory tea service and a crystal glass half filled with pale amber liquid. The teacup rattled on its saucer as she set the tray on the table beside the settee.

"For you, sir," the maid said.

He glanced to his right to find the maid beside him. "Thank you." He took the proffered glass.

Smiling slightly, she gave Gideon an abbreviated curtsey. The maid busied herself lighting the fire in the small hearth then left the room, closing the door behind her.

With the glass in one hand, he skimmed a fingertip over the leather spines of the books. Ever since Mayburn had left the servants had treated him, well, not quite like a lord, but definitely not like someone below their ranks and with distinctly more deference than a mere guest. It had taken him a few weeks to stop bracing for the usual resentment and grow accustomed to his new status in the household. And it was a rather nice feeling to be looked upon as a man and not as an object worthy of scorn.

After making a selection, he settled in the floral chintz armchair, crossed one leg, resting his ankle on his knee, and opened the thick leather-bound book.

Bella gave him a soft smile as she walked back into the sitting room. She poured a cup of tea and sat on the settee. The crisp scent of Earl Grey made its way to his nose. With a flick of her wrist, she arranged her skirt about her legs and then set to work. Her long swan's neck was bowed in concentration, her fine eyebrows pinched together the tiniest bit.

The logs in the hearth crackled. It was so quiet in the room he could hear the sound of the needle and thread pushing through the taut linen as Bella embroidered. He took a sip of scotch and savored the pleasing burn down his throat. With a soft click, he set the glass on the end table and flipped a page in the book.

The minutes slipped peacefully by, one seamlessly into another. Every now and then there would be a little snip as Bella used her small scissors to cut a thread.

"Finished. I do hope she likes it."

Gideon looked up. "I'm sure she will. It's a gift from her sister, and a beautiful gift at that."

She brought the ivory cup to her lips. "How can you say that when you haven't even seen it?" she said, setting the cup on its saucer.

He shrugged. "I just know, but you could show me if you like." He let the book fall to his lap and beckoned her with one finger.

Her little chuckle was music to his ears and never failed to make him smile. She removed the pillowcase from the embroidery hoop and crossed the short distance to stand before him.

He ran a finger over one of the expertly embroidered

red roses. "Chinas. My favorite, and beautifully done. As I said, I am certain Liv will like it."

She tipped her chin. A faint blush colored her high cheekbones. "Thank you. But even if it were atrocious, I believe you'd still tell me it was beautiful."

"Of course," he said with a wink.

She rolled her eyes and snatched back the pillowcase. "I'm going to retire for the evening. Are you coming?"

"In a minute. Just want to finish this section."

Peering down at the book, she titled her head to read the words upside down. "Rose propagation? Why would you read that? You don't grow roses."

"No. But you do."

The smile she bestowed on him made his heart thump against his ribs. It was the same smile she had given him after he sketched her many months ago. But this time, the need to pull back, to retreat from what he saw reflected in her eyes was absent. If anything, he now longed for more.

She cupped his jaw. Her warm fingertips rested lightly on his neck. "You are the dearest of men," she whispered. She brushed her thumb across his lips. He flicked out his tongue, tasting her skin.

She took a swift breath then turned in a *swoosh* of silk. "One minute." Her back straight and her head held high, she disappeared into the bedchamber.

He laughed as he turned his attention back to the book. *One minute.* He better read quickly.

After he finished the chapter on grafting techniques, he replaced the book on the shelf. He went into Bella's bedchamber, closed the door quietly behind him, and turned the lock. Leaning back against the door, he absently worked the knot on his cravat.

She was seated at the vanity, bare ankles crossed and tucked to one side under the stool. The thin straps of her chemise framed the delicate planes of her ivory shoulder blades. The amethyst gown, crossed with a pair of white silk stockings, draped the back of a nearby chair. Her young lady's maid, Maisie, moved around her pulling the pins from Bella's hair and releasing the glorious length from the confines of its tight knot.

He loved to watch Bella undress in the evening. He knew the ritual by heart. The maid and her lady working in harmony. The mirror above the vanity reflected Bella's beautiful face. Her eyes closed, her expression relaxed, yet her back was still ramrod straight.

These were the moments he treasured above all. When he could believe, truly believe, she was his. That she was not another man's wife. That he belonged here, in this room, watching her undress night after night. That this was his life, their life. The life they should have together.

He squeezed his eyes shut, his heart pleading, his soul begging. He knew it could not be forever, but for one night, just one night, he wanted the fantasy to be true. He wanted Bella to be his.

A sense of rightness washed over him. *He* loved her. Loved her with all of his heart, all of his soul. He would do anything for her. Had given up everything for her. She should be his. She was *meant* to be his.

A shiver of anticipation raced up his spine. The blood surging through his veins felt different. It was lighter, yet mixed with excitement. With the prospect of what was to come. A grin curved his lips. He began unbuttoning his coat. As his gaze fixed once again on Bella, his grin turned positively sinful.

Maisie finished brushing Bella's hair. Long pale blonde tresses hung straight down her back, tickling the top of her white chemise-clad derrière. He flexed his hands then shrugged off his coat.

"Good evening, Mr. Rosedale." The maid gathered the amethyst gown in her arms. She turned toward him, took a step, and halted in her tracks. Her eyes flared. A crimson blush stained her round cheeks. She yanked her attention from his groin, her gaze darting about the room as if uncertain where to look.

He chuckled, a low, amused rumble. The girl was accustomed to his presence in Bella's bedchamber, but on previous occasions he hadn't been fully hard, his cock straining beneath black wool trousers. Apparently he had embarrassed her. Too bad. He was not up to the task of hiding his desires until she left the room tonight.

"Shall I take your coat, sir?" the maid said in a tiny voice, refusing to look at him.

He pushed from the door and held out his black coat. "Yes. Thank you."

She darted forward and grabbed his coat. Her gaze flickered again to his groin before she turned on her heel and scurried out the dressing room door.

"Hello, Gideon." Still seated on the stool, her back to him, Bella tapped her fingernail on the porcelain clock on the corner of her vanity. "You took longer than a minute."

He smirked. *Cheeky little thing.* Strides long and predatory, he crossed the room. He said not a word as he stopped behind her. Sweeping her silken hair over one shoulder, he pressed his lips to her exposed neck. On an indrawn breath, she tilted her head, granting him access.

He alternated between nipping and kissing the long column of her neck. The plunging bodice of her chemise revealed the valley between her breasts. He let out a short grunt. The need to slide his cock in that valley, to feel the firm mounds cushion his hard length, to come on her nipples, coat them with his seed, gripped hold. Quick and ruthless. An unbidden urge he could almost not suppress. But he fought it back, fought it down. Not that way. And not yet.

Bella squirmed, her breaths coming short and quick. One hand skimmed down her side to the sleek indent of her trim waist, while the other glided over her shoulder to lift a firm breast and test the weight of it in his palm. Locating her nipple beneath the chemise, he rolled the hardened tip and delivered a sharp pinch.

She moaned his name. "Gideon."

"Come to bed," he whispered in her ear, lust drumming thick and hot through his veins.

"Yes, yes," she breathed.

He leaned fully over her and gathered her in his arms. He tossed her gently onto the four-poster bed they had shared for the past two months. She landed with a small gasp, her hair fanning the pillow. She levered up onto her elbows and gazed at him with hungry violet eyes. The lace-edged hem of her chemise rode high about her hips, exposing the long length of her legs. Hard nipples strained against the thin white fabric.

He stood beside the bed, struck motionless. In awe of her. "God, you're beautiful." So beautiful she took his breath away.

She arched, rubbing a bare foot along her calf, clearly reveling in her sensuality, tempting him to join her.

It was a siren's call he had no will, no desire, to resist. He attacked the buttons on his waistcoat, yanked it off, and whipped his shirt over his head. With a hard tug on the placket, his trousers were undone. They fell to his feet.

Her gaze fixed on his erection. A wicked smile curved her lips. He was acutely aware of the heavy weight bobbing between his thighs as he crawled to her on all fours.

Crouched over her, he met her hotly passionate gaze. He stayed still as a statue, letting the attraction between them coil tighter and tighter. A tangible force. It swirled over his skin like a teasing brush of silk. He could feel it licking his ballocks. His cock so hard it arched up to brush his stomach.

He abruptly rocked back onto his knees and grabbed hold of the plunging bodice with both hands. Tore it down the center, exposing her breasts, her stomach, the pale blonde triangle between her thighs. Her eyes flared then fluttered closed on a moan of approval as he dropped down to feast on her breasts.

He kneaded one while plying the other with his mouth. Sucking on the hard tip, delivering teasing little nips, lapping with his tongue. She arched beneath him, fingers tangling in his hair, holding him tight. Demanding more.

He gave it to her. Dragged his mouth down her chest,

down her stomach. Paused only long enough to swirl his tongue around the crease of her navel. A quick spasm wracked her limbs, her stomach muscles twitching. A breathless chuckle broke the rhythm of her short pants.

Lips pressed against her lower belly, he grinned. *God*, he loved the sound of her high, tinkling laugh. Then he spread her thighs wide. Wide enough to accommodate his shoulders. Crouched on his knees and bowed over her body, he looked up. She was spread out decadently before him. Her hands fisted in the rose coverlet. Tendrils of pale blonde hair graced her shoulders. Her eyes were heavy-lidded, glazed with desire. The violet depths glittered with passion, for him.

Using his thumbs, he parted her sex, baring her to his view. Pink folds glistened with the proof of her desire. The sweet musky scent of her arousal was almost his undoing. Lust clawed at his gut. His cock hardened even further, the skin stretched so taut it added a heady tease of pain to the lust spiking every nerve in his body. But he didn't give in to the demands of his desire.

He dropped his head and allowed his breath to fan her clit.

Her entire body tensed in anticipation. "Please," she whimpered.

He licked a slow path on either side of her clit, savoring the taste of her. Sweeter than honey and with a spicy hint, like that of a well-aged brandy. Raw need swamped his brain as he drank of her body. Lapped at her soaked entrance. Slipped his tongue into her wet depths. Paid tribute to every delicate fold of her sex, while deftly avoiding her clit.

Feet planted on the bed, she thrust her hips, alternately pushing on his head and pulling on his hair. "Please, please, please," she chanted, over and over again.

He splayed one hand on her lower belly, holding her hips still, and captured her wrists with the other. He continued his sensual onslaught, his senses fully attuned to her body. Waiting.

Her little breathy mewls began to crescendo. Her thighs gripped his shoulders with surprising force. One light flick of his tongue over her clit and she would come. *Perfect.* He lifted his mouth from her sex, left her dripping wet and poised for climax, and crawled swiftly up her body, spreading her legs with his knees.

Her arms wrapped about his neck. Her calves hooked around to rest against the backs of his thighs. Her lips parted and wanting his kiss. Her hips lifted, eager for him.

Braced above her, he paused. His cock aimed right at her core. Scalding heat bathed the head, sent flames roaring through him. Instinct screamed to lunge into her, to pound his cock relentlessly into her welcoming body. But he held back. He needed to be certain she wanted him, bare, without the protection of a sheath. He needed her permission.

"Do you want me?" His voice was so hoarse he almost didn't recognize it as his own.

Her brow furrowed. She glanced down between their bodies. She gasped. Met his intent gaze. "Yes. Please, Gideon. I want you." Her words were a beg, a plea, a vow all in one.

Closing his eyes, he hung his head against the rush of raw gratitude. Unexpected tears pricked his eyes. His muscles shook as he struggled to draw air into his lungs.

Soft hands skimmed the length of his heaving sides. Her touch patient, calming, accepting. Then a small hand grabbed his arse, fingers digging into the crease. She levered up and nipped at his lower lip.

"Take me," she said, thick with passion.

Lust slashed through him. Seized him. For the first time in his life, he willingly turned himself over to it. Let it have him completely. He let out a feral growl and claimed her lips, his mouth slanting harshly over hers, the kiss hot and demanding.

He broke the kiss, grabbed her luscious bottom in both hands and slid into her on one long stroke, settling to the hilt.

Holy Mother of God. His jaw dropped. Heat, pure liquid heat surrounded his cock, gripping him tight. Bella remained still beneath him, as if she understood one move from her, one little lift of her hips, would shatter his control. Breathing heavily, he gave himself a moment to absorb the decadent sensation, allowing his body time to accustom itself to the unprecedented event.

When he regained a thread of control, he slowly pulled out, savoring the slick glide, the way her body tugged on his cock as if never wanting him to leave. Holding her awed half-lidded gaze, he slammed sharply home.

Body arched like a bow and head thrown back, she let out a high screech of delight. He swooped down and kissed her fiercely, passionately, possessively, laying claim to her as he began an unyielding rhythm.

Her first orgasm almost pulled his own out of him. It was right there, gripping his ballocks, demanding to be released. Somehow he managed to hold back, to hold off, determined to wring ever more out of her, unwilling to allow this night to come to an end so soon.

With a hand at the small of her back, he pulled them up onto their knees. Hands spanning her waist, he held her tight against him as he flexed his hips, thrusting deeper, harder. She writhed against him, hard nipples scorching his chest, nails scoring his back, her kisses devouring him. Pushing him onward. Driving him forward. Past the point of any semblance of control or rational thought, until his passion matched hers.

It was sex like Gideon had never experienced before. The lines separating them blurred. He felt each tremor, every quake that shook her body as if it were his own. Every mewl, every rapturous moan from her lips pulled an answering growl from his throat. He turned her, flipped her, rolled her this way and that. Moving over her, under her, behind her, like a man possessed, unable to get enough. Until the blankets were twisted and hung off the bed, until the pillows were thrown to the floor, until his skin and hers was slicked with sweat, until he could barely catch his breath, until he couldn't hold back anymore, until he didn't want to hold back anymore.

Until her next orgasm sparked his own.

His climax surged through him. A white-hot wave, thick and fierce, more powerful than anything he had ever experienced. He threw back his head and roared as he came, buried deep inside her.

With the orgasmic shudders wracking his body, she wrapped her arms around his neck, pulled his lips down to meet hers, and kissed him with such intensity, such stark blinding bare emotion that he could feel her love in that kiss.

And his kiss matched hers.

Eyes half-lidded and mind fogged with sleep, Gideon rolled onto his side and propped his head up on a bent arm. In the darkness, he could just make out Bella sprawled on her stomach. The sheets tangled around her legs, her hair half covering her back.

Dawn had yet to break. After last night he would have thought himself so drained and sated he'd have slept well into the morning. Yet he had awoken a few minutes ago with a pressing need to look at her, be with her, verify last night had not been a dream. He wanted to wake up beside her for the rest of his days. Never wake up alone again. This was why he had staunchly avoided sleeping beside any other woman. The intimacy of this moment could not fail to soften even the most hardened of hearts.

He had had the pleasure of waking beside Bella every morning for the past two months. Yet this morning it was different. As if it was their first morning together.

An urge to capture this, capture her, seized hold. Her face softened with sleep. Lush lips slightly parted. The long sweep of her downcast lashes. The graceful lines of her back.

Careful not to disturb her, he got out of bed, donned the

trousers he left on the floor last night, and padded over to the hearth on bare feet. The fire had burned down to faintly glowing embers, but he needed a bit more light. He crouched to grab a log from the metal rack. It crackled and popped as he tossed it onto the fire.

After unlocking the bedroom door, he went into the dark sitting room. He passed the desk to throw open the curtain. The sky outside the window was deepest midnight. The crescent-shaped moon provided little light but it was enough—his eyes having adjusted to the darkness.

He went back to the desk. In the first drawer he opened he found a neat stack of stationery. With a couple of sheets of paper held in one hand, he opened the top drawer. A pencil rolled into view. He pulled it out and scowled at the dull tip.

His fingertips encountered folded paper edges as he reached into the drawer. Searching, he pushed them out of the way. Realizing he'd never find a small penknife in the dark drawer, he lit the candle on the desk. Blinking against the flare of light, he looked back to the open drawer. His brow furrowed at the name "Esmé" written in flowing feminine script across a folded piece of paper.

Esmé—her cousin, Madame Marceau. Fingertips hovering over the note, Gideon glanced guiltily to the open bedchamber door. He shouldn't read it. He'd be invading her privacy. If she found out, oh, she would not be pleased. But . . .

Curiosity made his fingers close over the note. Bella had only mentioned her cousin once and Gideon had only met her one time. He was curious what the letter would reveal about a woman who would hire a prostitute for a cousin.

Just one peek, he promised himself.

The sound of crinkling paper echoed in the room, a remonstration Gideon ignored as he opened the letter.

Why does he hate me so much?

The hastily scrawled words jumped from the page.

Gideon blinked, his eyes going wide. Cold dread invaded his gut. His hands started to shake as he forced himself to read from the beginning.

> *August 10, 1814*
> *Esmé—*
>   *When will you come to visit again? You haven't been to see me in ages. I miss our conversations. I miss our walks. Though I know you've no real interest in my roses, you are so kind to listen to me prattle on. I miss being with someone who does not hate me. Why does he hate me so? He returned today. I try to avoid him, but he seems to take perverse pleasure in seeking me out, in finding fault with me. He accuses me of being cold, frigid, and many other things I cannot put on paper. All the while his eyes blaze with loathing. I hate the way I tremble in his presence. I believe he likes to watch me cower before him. Why would he do that? I almost wish he would get it over with so he can leave. Please, Esmé, please come to see me. I don't like it when he is here. I detest this waiting. I know he will not leave without leaving his marks on me and it's summer. I don't want to have to ask Maisie to pull my long sleeved dresses from the attic.*
>
>   *—Isabella*

Gideon stared at the letter. His heart pounded deafeningly in his ears. Then he dropped the note and wrenched the drawer fully open. There were more—he'd felt them. Frantic, he pulled out over a dozen neatly folded notes. All bore the name "Esmé"—no address, just the name, indicating she had never sent them.

No longer trusting his knees not to buckle, he sat in Bella's straight-back desk chair and began reading. One was so blurred by watermarks, the handwriting almost illegible, he could only make out some of the words.

Esmé—

I'm scared. He's still here and he hasn't left.
Yet, what more could he wish to do to me? . . . It
hurts to breathe and . . . Why does he hate me? I
don't . . .

By sheer force of will, he resisted the urge to crumple
the note in his fist. He set it with great purpose on the desk
and picked up another. They were all the same. Pleas for
help. Pleas to know why Stirling hated her so very much.

He felt her terror in each quickly scrawled word. Felt
her fear in each disjointed sentence. Resting his elbows on
the desk, he dropped his head in his hands. His entire
body trembled. He never felt so helpless in all his life.
Five years she had lived in fear. He had seen the results of
Stirling's rage. Seen the broken woman the man left in his
wake after every visit.

He wanted to protect her forever. To never have her
feel pain again. Yet he had not a shilling to his name. No
home to call his own. No means of employment. He had
nothing but himself, and that wasn't much.

Pressing the heels of his palms to his eyes, he shook his
head. Mayburn had instructed him to take Bella to London
if Stirling returned. *What the hell am I waiting for?* For
Stirling to return? And the man would return eventually,
Mayburn had told him as much. Stirling rarely visited
Bowhill, but he did visit. Gideon should have taken Bella
to London weeks ago. Kept her far out of harm's way. But
he hadn't. He had selfishly ignored the whispered warn-
ings, those little nudges on the back of his mind. For he
could not live with her at her brother's house. These days
they had shared, their wonderful autumn, it would be no
more. To keep her safe, he would have to turn her over
into another's care. Her brother was an earl—far more
able to fend off any claims by Stirling that the man could
do as he pleased with his own wife.

A harsh wince pulled his mouth. *Damn it.* She was still

that man's wife. No matter how much he did not want it
to be true, he could not dispute that fact.

She belonged to another. A vicious pain tore at his
chest. He squeezed his eyes shut against the urge to howl
with misery. *No, no, no!* She should be his. *He* loved her.
He would never harm her. A wretched groan, one of purest
agony, erupted from his soul.

He sagged back in the chair on a shaky sigh and stared
unseeing at the notes for many long minutes. One by one,
he carefully folded them along their creases, gathered
them up, and put them back in their hiding place. Tucked
in the very far corner of the drawer, its white corner just
visible, was another note. It wasn't addressed to Esmé, but
to Lady Stirling at Bowhill Park.

Fearing what he would find, he opened it.

Isabella—

*If my timing proves correct, then Bowhill Park
will receive a guest on the afternoon of your
receipt of this letter. Mr. Gideon Rosedale will be
situated at Garden House. He is prepared to
remain at Bowhill for the fortnight. Please be so
kind as to inform your housekeeper of the
imminent arrival of your dear cousin. I promised
to find you one who would suit, and I do believe
this one will suit.*

*Regardless of how displeased you may be with
me, I do hope you at least invite your guest to
dinner before dispensing with him. If not for
yourself, then do it for me, because I love you and
only wish for your happiness. S'il vous plaît, take
a holiday from your penance.*

—Esmé

It took two passes before the meaning sank in.

"Oh." The exclamation came out on an awed exhale as
he saw their first fortnight in a whole new light. Every
glance, every word from her lips, it all had a new mean-

ing. And those terms of hers . . . his lips quirked. The fact a virgin had hired him always stood out as odd. But Bella had not hired him. Well, not the first time. Madame Marceau had acted on her own. It had been the Frenchwoman's idea to send Gideon as a gift.

It should rankle, it should abrade his pride, to have been given as a gift. To be chosen like one would choose a necklace or a bauble. A shiny trinket to brighten a lady's day. But it didn't. He cocked his head, searching for any hint of wounded male pride. Nothing. In fact, he was pleased.

He chuckled, the sound low and tired, as he tucked the note back in its hiding place. He picked up the pencil and tapped the end against the desk. His hand stilled and he nodded slowly. Two more days. He'd give himself two more days, then he would take Bella to London.

Twenty-One

THE soft scratch of pencil on paper roused Bella from sleep. Eyes closed, she rolled onto her back and stretched. A smile pulled her lips. She felt decadent. Divine. Last night had been amazing.

He was amazing.

Gideon had taken her, possessed her, claimed her as he had never done before. By giving himself so completely, by trusting her enough to let go of every bit of control, he had made her his own. He had imprinted himself on her heart and on her soul. She didn't think it possible to love him more, but she did.

A soft sigh escaped her lips. She reached out and encountered cool sheets. Rolling onto her side, she opened her eyes. Gideon had moved the Egyptian armchair near the bed. Clad only in black trousers, he was sprawled in the chair. The drapes on the windows flanking the bed were pulled back, letting in the morning sun. A large leather-bound volume was propped on his thighs. The quick, deft movements of his hand indicated he was sketching.

She levered up onto an elbow and tucked her hair behind her ear. "Good morning."

His hand stilled and he glanced up. The corners of his mouth lifted, but didn't quite form a smile. "Good morning."

She rubbed the sleep from her eyes and studied him. He had turned his attention back to the sketch. A crease notched the space between his dark eyebrows. Lines bracketed his mouth. Even the set of his shoulders seemed tight.

She pursed her lips. He looked entirely too serious. It was too early in the morning for him to be working so hard.

The impatient side of her loved their nights. Frenzied, hard, and fast. Orgasm after orgasm until she couldn't take anymore. But over the past few weeks Gideon had showed her the beauty of mornings. Languid and lazy, her impatience dulled by sleep, when she could fully appreciate the erotic sensation of skin rubbing against skin.

A slow wave of lust washed over her. Pressing her thighs together, she bit her lip on a low moan. Her hungry gaze wandered over his body. His sable hair was tousled, his jaw darkened with his morning beard. The golden light of dawn bathed his broad chest and well-muscled arms, giving the honey-kissed tone of his skin a rich inviting glow. Loose black trousers, the hems of which grazed the tops of his bare feet, concealed the power of his long legs.

Passion ignited, a flame that burst from her belly, wrapping her in sensual heat. Her body begged to feel the velvety warmth of his skin pressed full against hers. But she did not beckon him, did not lure him to her, did not demand he take her. A need to please him seized hold. To repay him for all the pleasure, for everything he had given her.

She sat up and threw her legs over the side of the bed.

At the sound of the mattress shifting, he lifted his head. A scowl marred his brow. "No, don't get out of bed."

She walked the short distance to stand before him. "The last time you said I could move, that you had the image in your head."

Her hair fell over her shoulder as she bent at the waist. He made to tilt the book up, shield his work. With a shake of her head, she placed a hand on the sketch, holding it down.

The extent of his talent once again took her breath away. "It's beautiful."

"It's not done," he grumped.

"You'll have time to finish it later." She pulled the book and sketch from him and, letting her hips sway, walked to the bedside table to set the items down. When she turned from the table, the mulish frown had vanished from his lips. Her skin tingled from the force of his passion-soaked gaze. Except for the long hair covering her breasts, she was bared to his view.

The pencil fell from his grip, clattering to the wooden floor. Bracing his hands on the arms of the chair, he moved to rise. Soft wool brushed her outer thighs as she stepped to stand between his legs. The light smattering of dark hair tickled her fingers as she placed a hand on his chest, the muscles hard, the skin hot from more than the heat of autumn's morning sun. A jolt shot up her arm.

He gazed up at her in question then relaxed back into the chair.

Cupping his bristly jaw, she pressed her lips to his. His mouth opened and she swept her tongue inside, delighting in the taste of him. He kneaded her hips. She shifted her weight, loving the feel of his hands on her bare skin.

But before she lost herself in his kiss, she pulled back.

His hands shifted. Long fingers rested just under the swells of her buttocks. He tugged. "Come here." His voice was a low rumbling command.

Bella gave him a coy shake of her head and swirled one fingertip over a flat copper nipple. It hardened beneath her touch. She marveled anew as she ran her hand over the defined ridges of his abdomen. The man was put together perfectly. He didn't spend long hours in the saddle or swimming in one of the many ponds on the property. His body was a gift from God.

Well, their nights could have something to do with keeping him in such sublime shape.

She glanced to his lap and licked her lips. "I believe one of us is overdressed."

He chuckled. He captured a lock of her pale blonde hair and moved it aside, revealing her breast. Her nipple hardened under his gaze. "Perhaps," he said, his lips quirking.

Lifting his hips, he started to unbutton his trousers.

She laid a hand over his. "Allow me," she said, using one of his phrases.

His brow furrowed then he tipped his head. He removed his hands, resting his elbows on the arms of the chair.

One by one, she undid the metal buttons. The last one proved difficult, but with a determined tug, it released. His stomach muscles contracted as she reached inside to gently pull out his erection. She had at first thought to remove his trousers, but the sight of him sprawled decadently in the chair, legs spread, the placket open and draping his upper thigh, magnificent cock standing at attention . . . No, the trousers would stay exactly where they were.

Dropping to her knees, she took hold of his thick length and bent toward the broad head.

His hand settled on her shoulder, effortlessly holding her in place. "No. You don't have to do that."

Startled at the quick reprimand, she looked up. She was under the assumption men liked this particular sensual act, but the tension gripping every line of his body, from the tight line of his mouth to the rigid set of his shoulders, made doubt settle in her mind. "But I want to give you pleasure."

He stared back at her, his gaze heavy with what was almost guilt. His chest rose and fell on a shuddering breath. "You do. More than any man should be allowed."

"Oh, Gideon." Heart clenching, she scrambled up onto

the chair and straddled his hips. His arousal bumped her inner thigh. She threw her arms around his neck and kissed him, telling him what was in her heart. But now was not the time to voice the words. Now was the time to show him.

She nipped at his ear. "Then allow me to give you more."

Dragging openmouthed kisses down his chest, she moved back to her previous position. Her knees protested against the hard wooden floor, but she didn't give any heed to her own needs. For once, she focused solely on him, intent on bringing a smile to his lips.

Taking hold of him again, she feathered her fingertips over the impressive length. Without the French letter, she had been able to intimately feel every detail of his cock last night. Her insides fluttered at the memory.

She swept her hair behind her shoulder, bowed her head and paused, lips poised over the crown. A drop of fluid leaked from the small slit.

"May I?"

His cock twitched. "Please," he said, hoarse with need.

She allowed instinct to guide her. Pressing her hand flat against his groin and holding him steady with her forefinger and thumb, she started at the base. With the tip of her tongue, she followed the path of the prominent vein. When she reached the top, she opened her mouth wide and took him inside.

On a deep groan, he tipped his head back, exposing the taut cords of his strong neck. Eyes closed and lips parted, his expression was one of sensual agony. He never looked so handsome, so starkly masculine.

"Oh, God, Bella. *Yes.*"

His low grunts urged her on, telling her what pleased him. She bobbed up and down, taking as much as she was able. Pausing every now and then to lavish the head with attention. She reveled in the hot glide of his cock in and out of her mouth. The thin skin felt like wet silk on her suddenly highly sensitized lips.

She could tell he was trying to remain still, yet his hips thrust up and down, tiny uncontrolled movements in rhythm with her attentions. Determined to shatter his control, she suckled on the head of his cock while pumping the iron-like length with a tight fist. Biceps bulging, he held tight to the chair arms and let out a growl.

She purred in response. The heady masculine scent of him filled her every breath. The salty tang of pre-come teased her tongue. Desire spiraled low in her belly, sending tendrils of fire to lick every nerve in her body.

Was this how he felt when he plied her sex with his clever, agile mouth? Submitting oneself wholly to another's pleasure. Devoted to another's needs. There was such pleasure to be found in giving. Her clit throbbed, making her head light. The folds of her sex felt slick with arousal. An orgasm was one touch away. She resisted the urge to reach between her legs and instead channeled all of the lust saturating her senses into pleasing him.

His short thrusts lengthened. His cock bumped the back of her throat and she instinctively relaxed into his strokes, letting him fuck her mouth at will. Hand wrapped tight around the rigid length, she continued to stroke him. The scent of male sweat pushed her lust even higher. With her other hand, she reached down to cup his ballocks.

Abruptly, he pushed her away. "No more. I'm going to—" He clenched his jaw, cutting off the words.

She glanced down to the head slick and flushed with need. "Allow me," she said, leaning forward, but the large hand on her shoulder kept her in place.

"No. I want . . ." The sound of his heavy breaths filled the room. "I want . . . I—" His gaze met hers. His eyes narrowed into thin slits. His lips twisted into a feral grin. "I want to come on your tits," he growled.

She arched her back, his wicked demand calling to her inner tart. "Yes," she said on a throat-scraping purr.

He loosened his hold on her shoulder but didn't let go. With both hands, she pumped his cock, long firm strokes from the base to the tip. Her hands slid easily over his skin slicked from her mouth. He swelled, hardening even further, until there was absolutely no give to the thick length. His entire body drew tight. She leaned forward, aiming his cock at her breasts.

He tipped back his head. "Oh fuck," he roared, shooting hot seed onto her chest, hips thrusting in rhythm to the heavy pulses seizing his cock.

He let out a heavy shoulder-slumping sigh and sagged, chin dropping to his chest. His eyes were heavy-lidded, his expression one of utter exhaustion. Then he sucked in a swift breath, his body jerking, as she swirled the blunt head over one hard nipple coated in his seed.

"No, no, no." He pushed her back. "Too much, too sensitive," he gasped.

She curled her toes and arched, pleased to her bones she had reduced him to such a state. Arousal still rode over every inch of her skin, but the pressing need for satisfaction had shifted, enveloping her in a heavy veil of sublime decadence.

Releasing his cock, she leaned back and grabbed his shirt from the floor. After wiping away the proof of his explosive climax, she tossed the shirt aside and crawled up onto the chair.

Snuggling close to him, Bella curled up like an elegant kitten on his lap. Arms draped loosely about his shoulders, silken cheek pressed to his sweat-slicked chest. Her warm breath tickled the smattering of dark hair.

Gideon's chest rose and fell with each labored breath. Surely she could hear his heart pounding against his ribs. His limbs felt too heavy to move. With effort, he wrapped his arms around her.

She had, quite simply, blown him away. His mind reeled from the force of his orgasm. A thick haze of sated lust seized his wits. He hadn't been sucked off in ages. It was a luxury rarely bestowed on him and one he never contemplated asking for. Well, *never* was no longer entirely correct. The chains he placed on his desires had been shattered. He could well see himself asking a thing or two of Bella in the future.

Christ, she'd not only sucked his cock but he had come all over her luscious tits. He lolled his head back and let out a low tired chuckle. *What has become of me?* His lips twisted in a wry grin.

Love. He was in love.

He sighed and pressed a kiss on the top of her head. He wanted to lay her on the bed, make love to her all day and into the night. Gorge himself on her, while savoring every moment until he had to tell her he was taking her to London. He had a feeling she wouldn't be pleased, but he would find a way to make her understand. He couldn't keep her here just to appease his own selfish needs. She was much too precious to him.

Bella shifted closer and nuzzled his chest. The soft drag of her lips made his spent cock twitch with life. Her fingers played lazily in the short, sweat-damp hair at the nape of his neck. Arousal curled slowly down his spine.

"I love you." She spoke so quietly, the words holding the barest hint of sound, yet it was as if she spoke directly to his heart.

He held his breath, and for a moment he could do nothing but listen to the echo of her soft melodic voice ringing in his head. He thought he had felt it last night, but he didn't dare tease himself with the hope of someday hearing the words from her lips. Yet she had said them.

Clutching her tightly, he bowed his head over hers and struggled to draw air into his lungs. "Bella—" Completely overcome with emotion, he squeezed his eyes shut and gritted his teeth. His entire body trembled. He never believed he would find someone who could truly love him. "Bella, I—" The word lodged in his throat, refusing to leave.

Her hand skimmed down to rest on his chest, directly over his heart. "It's all right, Gideon." Her quiet voice held a lifetime's worth of patience.

Frustrated, he shook his head and opened his mouth again.

The distant sound of a door slamming broke his concentration. He lifted his head. The rumble of a deep male voice reached his ears.

Bella went utterly still. "S-S-Stir—"

Dread slammed into him. "Oh shit. Get up, get up, Bella." He didn't wait for her to move but lifted her off him and set her on her feet.

Within a second, his trousers were buttoned. He leaned down to reach for his shirt then stopped. Not that one. He'd have to find another. Grabbing the hand hanging limp at her side, he pulled Bella toward the dresser and pulled open a drawer. *Fuck!* Why the hell hadn't he taken her to London already?

He snatched a chemise from the drawer. "Bella, put this on. We need to leave."

She made not a move, but stood still as a statue next to him. All the color had leeched out of her face. Trembles wracked her body. Her teeth began to chatter. She looked as though she had just emerged from the icy cold Thames in January.

Her terror struck at his heart, knifed through him. "Angel, put this on," he said with a calm he did not feel in the slightest.

She blinked then gave him a jerky nod.

"But Lord Stirling—" came a young female voice from out in the hall.

"Maisie," Bella whispered, identifying her maid's voice. With shaking hands, she pulled the chemise over her head, tugged it down, and flipped her hair out from under it.

"Get out of my way, gel," answered an agitated male voice, which held a hint of a Scottish accent.

Bella's gaze met his, her violet eyes wide with a panic that made dread knot and tangle in his stomach. Disheveled pale blonde hair draped her narrow shoulders. The thin white chemise did little to hide her lithe, fragile frame. "Gideon?" she said in a weak little whisper.

"Don't worry. I won't let him hurt you," he vowed, tucking a strand of her hair behind her ear.

He would do everything he was physically capable of to keep Stirling away from her, but that didn't mean it would be enough. Bella had told Stirling about him. When Stirling found him with Bella, it was a distinct possibility the man would summon the magistrate, have Gideon arrested for prostitution. He wouldn't be able to protect her in a prison cell, and the law could easily forgive Stirling for killing his wife, a woman who had hired a prostitute, in a fit of rage.

Grabbing her waist, he pulled her to him. He clutched her tightly and slanted his mouth over hers, needing to experience her kiss, to feel her love. She clung to him, her tongue tangling desperately with his, as if she too knew this might be their last chance.

At the sound of the sitting room door slamming against a wall, he tore his lips from hers. His head snapped around to stare at the bedchamber doorknob. *Damn.* He'd forgotten to lock it.

Thump. Thump. Thump. Coming ever nearer, the sound of heavy footfalls reverberated through the closed door.

He glanced frantically behind him. He should have shoved Bella into the dressing room, not paused to cover her naked body. For Christ's sake, there were plenty of dresses in the dressing room. But it was too late.

Forcing his arms to release their hold around her waist, he turned, positioning himself in front of her. "I won't let him hurt you," he repeated, muscles drawing tight in preparation.

Soft lips brushed his bare shoulder blade. "I know."

The bedchamber door banged harshly against the wall.

"Isabella, are you hiding from me again?" Bella's husband stopped one step into the room. His eyes flared, his mouth curving in what could only be described as gloating satisfaction. "How did I know this was what I would find? My dear wife has called for her whore."

Taking hold of Gideon's hand, Bella moved to stand beside him. "He is not a—"

Gideon tightened his grip, cutting off her words. Startled, she glanced up to him. He gave his head a tiny shake. Now was not the time to debate such an insignificant point. They had a much larger problem to deal with.

Stirling's cruel chuckle raised the hairs on Gideon's nape. "The slut accedes to her whore's wishes. How pleasant. Does she do everything you ask, I wonder?"

Gideon clenched his jaw against the unwise retort and met Stirling's hard, deep blue gaze. The man was huge. Taller and more powerful than Mayburn. Built like a pugilist who had gone slightly to seed. The sight should have instilled a bit of intimidation into Gideon. But it did not.

This man had hurt Bella. Frightened her. Scared her. Terrified her. Gideon squared his shoulders, widened his stance. *Never again.*

With a smirk, Stirling sauntered into the room. "You have spoiled my winter in Rome, Isabella. I made it all the way down to Florence before I had to turn around. Couldn't abide the thought of my dear wife fornicating under my roof."

As Stirling spoke, Gideon splayed his hand, but Bella held tight. Her shoulder grazed his biceps as she shrank closer to him.

"Let go," Gideon muttered, tracking her husband as the man slowly advanced on them.

For a split second, he feared she'd refuse his command. Then the small hand released, delicate fingertips caressing his palm. He flexed and clenched his hands at his sides, testing his fists.

Stirling's arrogant gaze swept the room, taking in Gideon's discarded clothes and Bella's torn chemise clinging to the edge of the disheveled bed, before settling on Gideon. "How much did this one set me back? He looks mighty expensive. Did you call for him the moment I left, or did you wait until your pretty bruises healed?"

A bolt of fury shot through Gideon. The muscles in his right arm vibrated with the need to give Stirling a few pretty bruises of his own.

The earl stopped a couple of paces in front of Gideon and wrinkled his nose. "Bloody hell, it smells like sex in here."

"How would you know?" a surprisingly strong voice asked from the vicinity of Gideon's shoulder.

He resisted the urge to close his eyes on a groan. Why the hell did she have to goad him?

Stirling's gaze snapped to Bella. A deep scarlet flush rose quickly up his neck. His eyes narrowed into hard slits, his face contorting with fury. The arrogant, mocking earl vanished to be replaced with a monster.

Gideon shoved Bella behind him at the same instant Stirling screamed, "You fucking bitch!"

Teeth bared, Stirling lunged for Bella. Gideon jabbed his left arm, fist connecting with flesh and bone. With a deafening roar, Stirling's boulder-sized fist redirected in midswing.

"Gideon!" Bella shrieked.

His head snapped back. The impact of Stirling's blow reverberated across his skull. Right fist at the ready, he swung blindly at the spot where Stirling's chin had been.

His knuckles grazed a bristly jaw, the miss throwing him slightly off balance. Stirling swung again. Gideon managed to knock the thick arm aside and threw another punch. Stirling met him blow for blow, and then some.

He hadn't fought since he'd been a boy, scrapping in the back alleys with the pickpockets. Rage surged through his veins, but his reflexes were rusty. Hitting Stirling was like hitting a goddamn brick wall, and the man's massive size did not slow him down in the slightest.

The air was knocked from his lungs by a well-placed punch to the gut. Staggering back, Gideon doubled over, gasping for breath.

"No!" Bella latched onto Stirling's arm, which was poised to deliver another punch.

Pure horror gripped him. "Bella. No. Get out of here." Gideon lunged for Stirling.

Swinging his other arm, the earl turned. A pained cry rent the air.

Deep savage crimson clouded Gideon's vision. Fury erupted, overflowed at the sight of Bella sprawled on the floor.

"You bastard!" Grabbing a fistful of auburn hair, he jerked Stirling's head back and slammed his other fist into the side of the man's head.

Stirling let out a roar and twisted violently, breaking free of Gideon's hold. Stirling's arm shot out, fist connecting with Gideon's jaw, knocking him against the wall. Rage, thick and hot, the likes of which he had never known before pervaded every inch of his being, blinding him to the pain. With a feral growl, Gideon dropped his head and rushed Stirling, wrapping his arms around the thick waist, pushing the man out of the bedchamber and away from Bella.

Twenty-Two

BELLA pushed up onto her hands and knees. Her head swam. She shook her head to clear it then groaned as a heavy ache seized the back of her skull. Pushing her hair from her face, she looked up. Her vision blurred then focused. The open sitting room door framed Gideon as he grabbed her straight-back desk chair and swung it in a determined arc.

There was a loud crack of wood followed by an angry bellow, like that of an irate bear.

Fists at the ready, Gideon darted out of her view.

"Oh, my dear Lord, they are going to kill each other," she said in a horrified whisper. Bella scrambled to her feet. A wave of dizziness threatened to send her back to her knees. She clutched one of the bedposts. Gritting her teeth, she forced her mind to clear.

The prospect of Stirling's death meant nothing to her. But Gideon's . . . She refused to think about it. Couldn't think about it.

Heart in her throat, she ran from her room then skidded to a halt. Her eyes flared at the wreckage the men had left in their wake. The remnants of her chair littered the sitting room floor. The tall, narrow bookcase had been pulled down, books and papers scattered everywhere. The gilt-framed painting of roses in full bloom hung at a sharp angle on the wall.

The unmistakable thumps of fists impacting with bone and flesh drew her attention to the hall. The two men were locked in combat. Fighting like rabid animals, enraged beyond rational thought. Gideon's fists flew almost too fast for her to make them out. A constant stream of obscenities poured from his mouth, uninterrupted by Stirling's answering blows.

"Bloody cocksucker!"

Barefooted and bare chested, Gideon took every one of Stirling's hits as though he couldn't feel them. The muscles in Gideon's back bunched and flexed with each swing. His biceps bulged. A fine sheen of sweat coated his skin.

"Fucking bastard." Gideon punctuated his curse with a jab to Stirling's jaw.

She had never seen Stirling take a punch. Blood smeared his nose and his once neatly tied cravat was completely askew, but her husband appeared to be faring just fine. Alarmingly fine.

Panic and dizziness threatened to overwhelm her. Knees shaking, Bella gripped the sitting room doorframe, determined to stay on her feet.

She gasped as Stirling's fist connected with Gideon's abdomen. Gideon grabbed Stirling by the ears, jerked forward, and smacked his forehead against her husband's. Bella's hand flew to her mouth to stifle a shocked scream. As Stirling staggered back a step, Gideon locked his hands and swung both fists together aiming for Stirling's neck.

Stirling crashed against the wall. Arm raised and fist clenched, Gideon lunged forward. "Useless prick!"

With an almighty bellow, Stirling grabbed Gideon, using Gideon's momentum to hurl him into the closed door opposite her sitting room.

She jumped at the deafening crack of wood followed by a hard thump. Dodging the mess on the floor, she raced into the hall. The door to Stirling's rooms was open, the wooden frame cracked.

Gideon got to his feet just in time to block Stirling's blow. But he wasn't fast enough to block the second. He let out a grunt and gave his head a sharp shake, backing up. Relentless, Stirling advanced. His olive green coat stretched taut over his broad back as he rained blow after blow on Gideon, driving him against the wall. Gideon valiantly tried to fight back but his once lightning-fast punches weren't as quick. Before her eyes, his reactions slowed. His face was still a mask of undeniable rage but beneath it she saw desperation.

It was clear he could sense his impending defeat.

She knew in her bones Stirling wouldn't stop until Gideon's broken body fell to the floor, never to rise again.

Her breaths sharp and fast, she glanced frantically about the room. An empty crystal vase on the fireplace mantle. A neat row of thick leather-bound books on a shelf. A brass lamp on an end table beside the maroon leather armchair. Nothing here would be enough to stop Stirling. But—

Turning on her heel, she darted from the room. Her feet barely kept up with her as she ran down the stairs. Grabbing hold of the banister, she turned right at the bottom of the staircase, ignoring the cluster of worried servants in the entrance hall. The door to Stirling's study was slammed against the wall. She rushed across the darkened room and rounded the desk. Praying Stirling hadn't decided to lock it when last he visited, she swung the portrait and turned the handle. The square steel door opened.

Thuds sounded overhead, vibrating through the floorboards in Stirling's room. Hastily pushing aside documents and stacks of pound notes, she froze as her fingers encountered cool metal.

I left it loaded, Isabella. Though I doubt you'd even know which end the bullet comes out of.

Stirling's words from years ago echoed in her head. He had showed her the dueling pistol when he had first deposited her at Bowhill—his only thought to her safety while he left her at the remote estate for months on end.

"It's the end I'm going to point at you," she muttered, grabbing the pistol. She had grown up with Jules and Kitty, after all. She had even partaken in one of their little competitions, though her shots had gone far wide while her siblings had argued over which of theirs was closest to the mark.

But her current target was significantly larger than the scrap of paper Jules had tacked to the trunk of the old oak tree.

Leaving the safe open, she ran from the study. Conscious of the lingering servants and the pistol in her hand, she took the narrow servants' stairs and skidded to a halt at Stirling's sitting room.

Her heart caught in her chest. Gideon was sprawled in a heap on the floor amidst the splintered remains of a broken end table. Bruises and scrapes marred the perfection of his sweat-slicked back.

"Get up, whore," Stirling snarled, standing over him.

Struggling, Gideon pushed up to his feet, his muscles shaking with the effort, his head bowed in fatigue. Before he could straighten, Stirling punched him in the jaw. Gideon crashed against the wall and crumbled to the floor.

"You dare touch my wife? Dare touch something of mine?" Stirling drew back a leg, as if to kick Gideon in the stomach.

Holding the pistol with both hands, she brought her arms up. "Stop."

Stirling stilled. He looked over his shoulder. Tension gripped his broad shoulders for the briefest moment, then a sardonic grin tipped his lips. "Ah, my dear wife comes to the aid of her fallen whore. Quite admirable of you, but also very unwise."

Swiping his forearm across his bloodied mouth, he turned. Completely at his ease, he sauntered toward her.

"Do you think to shoot me? Your husband?" He shook his head, all mocking condescension. "No. You won't."

"Yes. I will." The urge to flee, to run, pressed heavily on her. It took all of her willpower to keep her feet rooted to the floor, to stand her ground, as he slowly advanced.

"You can't."

"Yes, I can. I will," she said, desperate to convince herself.

When the barrel of the pistol pressed against his waistcoat, he stopped. "Prove it."

She swallowed hard and locked her elbows. All she needed to do was pull the trigger and all of this would end. All she needed to do was kill her husband. A living, breathing man. Gritting her teeth, she closed her eyes. Her finger trembled against the smooth curve of the metal trigger.

Stirling let out a sigh, like that of an annoyed parent. "Whatever am I going to do with you, Isabella? Clearly you have not learned your lesson."

The pistol was wrenched from her hands. Instinctively, she flung her arms up to cover her face, eyes still closed tight.

A feral roar filled the room. She opened her eyes, peeking between her forearms, to see Stirling turn.

"Don't touch her!" Gideon screamed, swinging a leg from the broken end table at Stirling's head.

Ducking, Bella scurried aside. Stirling crashed into the wall, exactly in the spot where she had been standing.

Eyes narrowed and mouth twisted in a furious grimace, Gideon attacked Stirling as if he hadn't just been beaten within an inch of his life. Avoiding a blow, Stirling dropped down and grabbed Gideon's leg, pulling him to the ground. Rolling, twisting and kicking, the two men wrestled for dominance. They knocked into furniture, sending objects crashing to the floor, until Stirling straddled Gideon, both large hands wrapped around his neck. With one hand, Gideon aimed punch after punch at Stirling's elbows, attempting to break the man's hold, while with his other, he tried to pry Stirling's fingers from his throat.

"No!" Beyond desperate for him to stop, she launched herself at Stirling's back. Pulled his hair, scratched his face.

"Get off, bitch." Stirling grabbed her arm and flung her as though she weighed nothing.

Landing hard on her shoulder, she scrambled to her feet. The pistol. Where had it gone? It was the only way to stop Stirling, for he would never let Gideon up alive. She cursed herself for not having done it earlier. This time, she would not hesitate. Wreckage covered the floor. The pistol could be anywhere. Panting heavily, she tried to calm her pulse, force the panic aside and focus.

A deafening blast smacked her eardrums.

For a split second, everything stopped.

Then Stirling slumped over Gideon.

She stared blankly at her husband's prone form. The broad back was eerily still, the olive green coat marred by a singed hole between his shoulder blades.

"*Bon matin*, Isabella."

Whirling around, she nearly jumped out of her skin at the sound of a familiar voice.

Her cousin walked casually into the sitting room. A few strands of her dark hair had escaped their pins but other than that, and the dueling pistol held lightly in one gloved hand, she looked as if she were merely paying an afternoon call. She arched one elegant eyebrow. "Though it doesn't appear as if you've had a very pleasant morning. Are you all right, my dear?"

"Yes, I'm—Esmé? What—?" Bella's mind seized with shock. What was she doing here?

Bella heard the *thumps* of rapid, slightly off-rhythm footsteps in the hall. "Madame?" Porter said, concern heavy in his tone, as he appeared in the open doorway, his stance strong, ready to do battle. His astute gray gaze swept over the room, the straight line of his shoulders sagging the tiniest bit when it stopped on Esmé. He quickly shut the door. "Madame," he said, his hand outstretched, his tone once again that of a proper servant.

With a tip of her head, Esmé gave him the pistol and he slipped it into his coat pocket.

A low groan came from the vicinity of Stirling. Bella tensed, fearing Esmé's shot hadn't been enough. With another groan, Gideon shoved Stirling's body off of him.

"Damn, he's heavy," Gideon muttered as he got to his feet.

"Oh, Gideon." The most profound relief washed over her. Bella rushed to him and threw her arms around his waist, burying her face against his sweat-slicked chest. The strong beats of his heart made tears prick at her eyes. "I thought I was going to lose you."

He held her tight. "Never. You will never lose me," he whispered hoarsely, pressing his lips to the top of her head.

She leaned back to look up into his face. "You're bleeding." She pulled her arms from around his waist and feathered her fingertips over the cut on his temple.

"It's nothing." Yet he stood still, arms wrapped around her and head bowed, allowing her to fuss over him.

"Your poor jaw, and your nose, and your brow." She graced each bruised feature with the lightest of touches. "And he cut your lip," she admonished, running her fingertip over his bottom lip.

"Doesn't hurt," he said with a shrug of one shoulder. His gaze slid over the top of her head then he stiffened.

"Good morning, Mr. Rosedale," Esmé said.

Esmé. Bella had momentarily forgotten about her. Taking hold of Gideon's hand, she turned to her cousin, suddenly quite conscious of the fact she wore only a plain white chemise.

"Good morning," Gideon said, in a measured tone. "You are Bella's cousin, Madame Marceau, are you not? Thank you for your most timely arrival."

Esmé's lips curved in a knowing smirk, her violet eyes glinting with a hint of the usual impish gleam. "My timing is always impeccable. Though Julien won't be pleased, that's for certain. He planned to do it himself."

She gaped at Esmé. "Jules?"

"Yes. He stopped by to pay me a call on his way to Rome. Didn't say too much. Porter didn't give him much of a chance. He didn't care for Julien's tone," Esmé added, though the explanation was unnecessary as Porter's heavy scowl spoke for itself. "Those brothers of yours . . ." Letting out a little sigh, she shook her head. "After Julien and his broken nose left, I came straight up to Scotland to see you. Given that, I'm a bit taken aback to find Stirling here. Julien had been certain Stirling was planning to winter in Rome." She paused. "I wish you had seen fit to confide in me. I would have had Stirling taken care of for you long ago."

Bella took a breath, a mixture of apology and explanation on her tongue, but Esmé held up a hand.

"I understand what drove you to stay silent. I just wish you hadn't. You needn't have suffered so." Then her attention shifted to Gideon and the heavy note left her voice. "What month is it, Mr. Rosedale?"

"October," Gideon said, clearly confused by the question.

Esmé tapped a fingertip to her lips. "Last I checked there was considerably more than a fortnight between April and October. Yet, here you are."

Bella tensed at the steel behind Esmé's casually spoken words. She sensed Gideon stiffen as well, his grip on her hand tightening.

"Did you have a nice holiday, Isabella?"

Her face twisted in confusion before Esmé's meaning struck home. *S'il vous plaît, take a holiday from your penance.* It seemed ages ago when she had received her letter. A smile flittered on her lips. "Yes, very much so."

"Good to hear." Esmé winked. Then the teasing glint left her eyes. "Now, about Stirling, we'll need to—"

A knock on the door interrupted her.

"Mr. Porter?" came her housekeeper's worried voice. "Did you find Lady Stirling and Madame Marceau? Are they all right? That noise, was it a gunshot?"

"Yes, yes, and no, Mrs. Cooley," Porter replied. "Please have Lady Stirling's traveling coach readied."

There was a short pause. "Yes, Mr. Porter."

"You're leaving?" Bella asked Esmé the moment Mrs. Cooley's footsteps faded down the hall.

"Oh no, my dear. I just arrived," Esmé said.

"He's leaving." Porter tipped his head toward the large body on the floor.

"Where is he going?"

"You needn't concern yourself, Isabella." At her look of obvious confusion, Esmé rolled her eyes. "Do you want the authorities to investigate his death? They will ask questions you won't want to answer. Stirling had clearly been in a rather serious fight prior to his death. You don't have a bruise on you and neither do I or Porter, yet Mr. Rosedale does."

"Only because he took Stirling's punches in my place," she said in staunch defense of the man she loved. "Stirling was going to kill him."

Esmé waved a dismissive hand. "It doesn't matter. Stirling was a peer and your husband. The local magistrate may not accept your word that Stirling beat you, and even then, well, they may not care. The only other witnesses to the events of this morning are myself, who happens to be a woman, and Mr. Rosedale, who happens to be a male prostitute. While I—"

"Not anymore," Gideon interrupted. "I resigned months ago."

Esmé lifted her eyebrows and tipped her head. "I am pleased to hear that, but it won't matter. It doesn't change the fact Isabella has a lover living with her at Bowhill. As I was saying, I am more than willing to tell the magistrate that I shot Stirling. But I'm not English or Scottish. I'm French, and the war hasn't been over for that long. The situation could become dreadfully messy. Therefore it's best Stirling disappear for a bit, and you, too, as well, Mr. Rosedale."

"No," Bella and Gideon said in unison.

"I'm not leaving her," Gideon said resolutely. Then he closed his eyes on a heavy sigh. "But I will continue to make myself scarce when callers come to Bowhill. Except for the servants, no one will know I am here."

The resignation in his tone, the pain on his face . . . it tore at her heart. How he must have felt every time a caller had come to the door. He had not said a word though, had simply made himself scarce. And it struck her—he had done it so easily, so effortlessly, because he had been doing it all his life, since he had been a child in that brothel. Staying out of sight every time his mother had callers.

Esmé nodded. "Isabella, you will receive word within a month or so that Stirling's body has been found. And when you do, please be sufficiently shocked at the dreadful news of your husband's untimely death."

"What about the servants? They may talk," Gideon said.

Esmé's face hardened with conviction. "Their silence will be secured. Stirling was never here."

"McGreevy won't stay silent," Bella pointed out. "He's worked for Stirling's family for too long, and he has never cared for me."

"Well, I have never cared for him," Esmé said, a scowl marring her features. "That butler won't say a word. In fact, I believe it's time to pension him off." She looked to Porter, who still stood guarding the door. "If you would."

"Yes, madame." He crossed the room and dropped to his haunches beside Stirling. He laid a hand on the man's chest and another on his thick neck. "He's dead."

"Of course he's dead. I shot the unpleasant man, and I never miss." Esmé flicked her fingers in Gideon's direction. "Mr. Rosedale, give Porter a hand. We need to get him down to the carriage."

Gideon began to move toward Stirling then stopped. He glanced down at their joined hands. "Bella." His gaze met hers. "You can let go."

"No." Ducking her chin, she bit her bottom lip. She couldn't explain it and she knew it was irrational, but she did not want to let go of his hand. She didn't want to lose the warmth of his palm, the strength of his grip.

With a light touch, he lifted her chin. "It will be all right. I'll be right back. I promise," he said softly.

She gazed into his eyes. She loved him so much it hurt. "I'm sorry," she said, whisper-soft, only loud enough to reach his ears. "I didn't mean to make you feel as though I was ashamed of you. As though you were something I needed to hide. I was just so afraid Stir—"

He cupped her cheek. His thumb settled over her lips, cutting off her words. "Bella, it's all right. I understand." He pressed a kiss to her forehead. "Why don't you get dressed and I'll meet you in your bedchamber in a few moments."

Trying to keep the tears at bay, she took a deep breath. He was so patient it made her want to weep. "All right."

"I promise," he said again when she released his hand.

She left him crouched beside Stirling. She found her maid sweeping the litter from the sitting room floor. Mrs. Cooley had been efficient as ever. The gilt-framed painting on the wall had already been straightened, the bookshelf righted, and another chair placed before her desk.

"Maisie, you can leave that for now."

The broom clattered to the floor as Maisie looked up in shock. "Lady Stirling, you're all right. Oh, I was so afraid he had hurt you again."

Bella shook her head. "Mr. Rosedale took the brunt of it for me."

"He is a wonderful man, Mr. Rosedale." A dreamy little smile played across the maid's lips. Then Maisie regained herself, bending to pick up the broom and lean the wooden handle against the desk. "Shall I help you dress?"

"No, that won't be necessary."

With a short curtsey, Maisie left the room. Bella entered her bedchamber but she didn't go into her dressing room. Instead, she sat on the edge of her newly tidied bed and waited for Gideon to return to her.

She was free of her husband. Free of the man who hated her. And she felt not a drop of grief over his death. Esmé though . . . She shook her head, unable to reconcile her old image of her with the determined woman she'd left Gideon with. Years ago, before Stirling and before her ill-fated Season in London, when she lived at Mayburn Hall with her siblings, Jules had once whispered to her— *It wasn't an accident. Esmé's husband didn't shoot himself while cleaning his pistol.* Had Jules been right? Bella didn't much care if he was. Esmé had arrived at Bowhill at a most opportune time. She had killed Bella's husband, thus saving Gideon's life. Bella owed her cousin a great deal.

It seemed wrong she would have to pretend to be married to Stirling for a bit longer, but in her heart she hadn't been his wife for quite some time.

Her heart belonged to another.

She glanced to the clock on her vanity and let out a frustrated breath. Another who was taking an awfully long time to return to her.

Bella was smoothing her chemise over her knees when Gideon entered the room, closing the door behind him.

"Madame Marceau is settling into the yellow bed-chamber, and Porter said he'd be back by nightfall," Gideon said as he walked across the room.

She sucked in a horrified breath. She had been so focused on his handsome face earlier that she failed to notice what Stirling had done to the rest of him. Her body ached in sympathy, yet he seemed completely unaffected. Deep purple bruises marred his honey gold skin. On his ribs, his shoulders, his chest. Around his neck she could make out the distinct imprint of Stirling's thick fingers. A shudder gripped her at the reminder of how close she had come to losing him.

She hopped off the bed and took hold of his forearm. "Gideon, you need to rest." She glanced up to his face. Fresh blood smeared his temple. "And you're still bleeding." She tugged on his arm. "Lie down. I'll clean it for you."

He resisted her efforts to get him onto the bed. "Bella, I'm fine." He gently removed her hand from his forearm. "Sit. Please. I need to talk with you."

His serious expression gave her pause. With a nod, she complied.

He turned from the bed. The muscles in his back flexed, strong shoulder blades working under bruised and freshly scraped skin, as he dragged both hands through his hair. On a heavy sigh, he turned back to her, his eyes downcast. He shoved his hands in his trouser pockets then pulled them out. A wince flickered across his brow. He opened his mouth then closed it, pursing his lips in annoyance. His gaze shifted up to meet hers before dropping to the floor. "Will you marry me?"

She blinked in shock. Of all the things he could have been working up to say, she would have never guessed a marriage proposal.

Gideon shook his head, his shoulders hunching. "My apologies. Forget I asked. I shouldn't have presumed—"

She jumped off the bed and pressed her fingertips to his lips, silencing him. "Yes, yes," she said quickly, needing to erase the doubt and pain clouding his whisky brown eyes. "I will marry you."

"Really?"

"I would be honored to be your wife, Gideon." She chuckled, unable to contain the all-encompassing joy washing her senses.

But no echo of her radiant smile graced his lips. Mouth drawn in a firm line, he nodded curtly. "Sit. Please." His hands were infinitely gentle as he guided her back onto the bed. "I need you to understand the implications. And if you change your mind, I will understand."

Taking a step back, he clasped his hands behind his back. "If you marry me we cannot live in London. We cannot mix in Society. No matter where we live, there is always the possibility we may run into someone who recognizes me. You must be prepared for that. Society will look on you differently if they learn what you married. I can offer you very little, Bella. Only my name, and you will be a mere Mrs. and no longer Lady Stirling."

"I thought you wanted to marry me? Yet it sounds as if you are trying to persuade me otherwise."

The serious façade began to crack, letting her glimpse the vulnerable man within. "I do want to marry you, Bella. I want to be able to call you my own, more than you could possibly imagine. But you must understand what you are agreeing to. I don't want you to regret a decision made in haste."

She nodded. He was concerned for her, but he need not be. She had never been more certain of herself in her life. Phillip had told her to do what would make her happy, and becoming Gideon's wife would make her beyond happy. Yet she remained silent, letting Gideon continue, allowing him to reassure himself she understood.

"I-I don't yet know where we will live." His gaze shifted to a spot over her shoulder. A barely perceptible flush colored his cheeks. "I-I honestly have nothing, Bella. Not even a halfpence to my name. But I will find a way to support you. I'm not good for much, but somehow I will find a respectable means of employment, one that will not reflect poorly on you."

"Gideon," she said, tilting her head, "how can you be penniless?" She winced as soon as the words left her mouth. She shouldn't ask, but the question came out before she could stop it. The state of his bank account didn't matter, not in the slightest, yet he had worked for a decade. Where had it gone?

"I'm not irresponsible, if that's what you think," he grumbled. "I had saved a small fortune over the years, but I-I traded it all. Everything. Even my apartment."

"Why?"

"For you. For a chance to see you again. My employer was not pleased to learn of my resignation. It was the only way to convince her to accept it."

Her jaw dropped at the significance of what he had done. *A wife. A family. But first, I need money. A whole lot of it.* That was what he had told her months ago when she'd asked him what he wanted out of life. And he had given it all up. For her. For simply a *chance* to see her.

"Oh, Gideon." Stifling the sob welling up in her throat, she bit her lower lip and tried to rein in her emotions. "You needn't worry about where we will live. This house is mine. Phillip arranged it in the marriage settlement. The property isn't part of the earldom, but came to Stirling through his mother. Upon Stirling's death, it reverts to me. And it will become yours once we are married. You will have a property in the country, one that generates a decent income, just as you wanted."

He gave her a weary lift of his lips. "That's all well and good, but it doesn't make up for the fact I come to you with nothing."

She stood and took his hands in hers, squeezing them tight. "All I want is you. You feed every part of my soul, with comfort and kindness and searing passion. You give me everything that is important in life. Everything I need. Titles and wealth mean very little to me. I would gladly trade it all to become Mrs. Rosedale."

Abruptly, he pulled their joined hands behind her back, jerking her toward him. He slanted his mouth over hers, silencing her gasp of surprise. The kiss began fierce and desperate, his tongue twining with hers, as if he couldn't get enough. Then it shifted, softened. He dragged his lips across her cheek. Gooseflesh pricked her skin as he nuzzled her ear.

"I love you, Bella."

His whispered words unleashed the tears she had tried to keep at bay. And they were not quiet ladylike tears, but big, loud, sobbing ones. She ducked her chin, embarrassed by her overwrought emotions.

"Oh, Bella. Don't cry. Please, don't." There was a chuckle in his soft croon.

"I'm sorry," she said between great pulling sobs. "It is just that it has been so long since I've heard those words."

His arms tightened around her, pressing her closer to

the warm expanse of his chest. "Bella-Bella," he whispered in her ear. "You shall never again have to go another day without hearing them. I promise you."

She didn't think it was humanly possible, but somehow she cried even harder. She hadn't realized how much she had missed them. They were three small words, but hearing them from Gideon had the power to erase the long years of famine.

With tears of joy streaming down her cheeks, she cupped his jaw and pulled him down for a kiss. And she started the kiss with those three treasured words whispered hoarsely against his lips. "I love you."

Epilogue

COINS clinked as Gideon grabbed the black bag from the vault then closed the square steel door. March had come, which meant it was time to pay the household servants their quarterly wages. With a flick of his wrist, he swung the picture frame to cover the vault. He had lost the battle over what would replace Stirling's old portrait, a portrait Bella had taken great delight in burning in the fireplace. In his opinion, his simple pencil sketch looked entirely out of place in the heavy gilt frame, not to mention hanging in a position of prominence in the masculine study. But his wife had insisted something from his hand should grace the space. And who was he to deny her what she wanted?

His lips twisted in a rueful grin. He settled in the leather chair behind the desk, set down the bag of coins, and opened the account ledger. In an effort to make himself useful, he had taken over management of the estate and Bella's ancient part-time secretary had been more than willing to be pensioned off. The man was a disorganized nightmare with almost illegible handwriting, which fully explained why this room had been the only room in the house that hadn't been as neat as a pin.

Bella strode into the study. The door snapped shut behind her. "Gideon."

He set down his pencil. "Good afternoon, Mrs. Rosedale," he said with a wide smile. God, how he loved to call her that. He had wanted to marry her the moment she agreed to be his wife. The moment she agreed to be his forever. But he had to wait until after the government official had notified Bella of Stirling's death, and then had to wait an additional four long months to avoid throwing any suspicion onto her first husband's "unfortunate" death at the hands of unknown highwaymen on an infrequently traveled road outside of Carlisle.

Lips thinned, she stopped in front of the desk and flicked an envelope at him. It bounced off his chest then landed on the account ledger. "Who is Lady Knolwood?" Her violet eyes flashed with a strain of jealousy only women were capable of producing.

"She is an old acquaintance," he said calmly.

"What sort of acquaintance?"

Gideon leaned back in the chair, pushed away from the desk, and beckoned her. "Bella, sweet, come here."

She did not move an inch. "Was she one of your—"

He let out a low sigh at the pain, the heartache that kept her from voicing that last word. Gideon had thought nothing of it when he had tossed the note to Helen onto the silver tray with the rest of the day's outgoing post. He had no intention of hiding the letter from Bella, but he should have known she would see it and question it. She had been in her sitting room for the past hour corresponding with her sisters. She was a woman—there was no way she would set her letters on the tray and not notice her husband was corresponding with another lady. And especially when he was that husband.

"You have no cause to get so worked up. Come here."

Her fine eyebrows met in uncertainty. "Was she—?"

"Bella, my love. Please, don't. Come here."

Her hands clenched into fists at her sides. She stared hard at him, needing the answer.

So he gave it to her. "Yes, she was. But it's not what you think. Open it, read it, if you will. I've known Lady Knolwood for years. She's the only friend I have and she simply asked that I drop her a note if I ever won my lady. And so I did. I couldn't resist the urge to tell her you married me." He had no one else with whom to share the most important news of his life. There was no one else who cared to know.

Her eyes flared. "You spoke to her about me? Did you—?" Her ragged, uneven breaths caught in her throat.

"Oh, Bella." He got to his feet and rounded the desk. "No. No. I played chess with her. That was it. I was so caught up in you I lost quite horribly. Pathetic," he added with a disgusted shake of his head. "I've known Lady Knolwood for a decade. It stopped being about 'that' years ago. She knew though, even before I did, that you had captured my heart. She wished me luck and asked me to let her know if I won you. That's all, Bella."

He wrapped his arms around her and held her tense, lithe body close. But she did not hug him back. "Bella, love, my lips have not touched another woman's since I first laid eyes on you. I can't be with anyone else. I don't want to be with anyone but you. Honestly, Bella. You have no idea how much it shook me when I realized . . ." He gave a short, sardonic snort. "I was a male prostitute who couldn't get it up. Nothing. Not even a twitch. Why do you think I came to see you? I needed to be with you. Only you. I couldn't stomach the thought of another woman. I didn't even want them to get close to me, let alone touch me. All my body, my heart, my soul wanted was you."

She tipped her face up to gaze into his eyes.

He nurtured the flicker of hope in the violet depths. "You never have cause to be jealous. Never have reason to even let the notion pass through your beautiful head. You have ruined me, Bella. Completely. But being ruined is a good thing. It's wonderful. I much prefer it to all else because it means I love you. Only you."

Her lower lip trembled.

"I haven't said them yet today, have I?" He had never spoken those words to anyone but Bella. They were hers. In the morning he awoke and told a sleepy Bella he loved her. In the afternoon over tea he told her he loved her. In the evening, with her in his arms, he told her he loved her. It was as if there was a glut that had built deep inside of him over the years and needed to get out.

She shook her head, looking as though she would burst into tears at any moment. She was right there, at the precipice.

"I love you, Mrs. Rosedale," he said softly. "And you are the only woman who has ever heard those words from my lips."

A pleased little amazed smile curved her mouth. "I love you," she whispered.

Countless women had said those words to him in the heat of the moment. But they had not truly loved him, simply what he could do to them. But Bella, she did love him.

Her long lashes swept down on a soft sigh of contentment. "There is something else you haven't done yet today."

She peered up at him and his body reacted instantly to the hunger, the passion, burning in her eyes. His hands coasted down to cup her firm backside. He pressed her close, hard, so she could feel what she did to him, even through the layers of muslin skirts and wool trousers.

Bella's eyelids fluttered as she arched into him, kneading his shoulders. "Yes. Now," she breathed.

He could not hold back the grin—his impatient Bella. With her, all it took was the knowledge he was ready to rut and her senses would focus on nothing else.

He nuzzled the small space behind her ear. "Come upstairs with me."

"No. Here. Now."

"But—?" His attention flickered to the unlocked study door.

"You're my husband. You're allowed to ravish me in the study." She pulled at the waistband of his trousers as she stepped back, bringing him with her. With a little hop, she perched on the edge of the desk. Her long legs wrapped around the backs of his thighs, pulling him in as she freed his swollen cock. "*Now*," she said, desire thick in her voice.

"Of course, Mrs. Rosedale," he drawled as his hands drifted up from her knees, gathering her skirt. "Don't I always give you what you need?"

Don't miss the *New York Times* bestseller from
MADELINE HUNTER

*Provocative
in Pearls*

Their marriage was arranged, but their desire was not . . .

After two years, the Earl of Hawkeswell has located his
missing bride, heiress Verity Thompson. Coerced into
marrying Hawkeswell by her duplicitous cousin, Verity
fled London for the countryside. Now, the couple must
make the most of an arranged marriage—even if it
means surrendering to their shared desire.

M702T0510

THE NEW VICTORIAN HISTORICAL
ROMANCE NOVEL FROM
USA TODAY BESTSELLING AUTHOR

JENNIFER ASHLEY

Lady Isabella's Scandalous Marriage

Lady Isabella Scranton scandalized London by leaving her husband, notorious artist Lord Mac Mackenzie, after only three turbulent years of marriage. But Mac has a few tricks to get the lady back in his life, and more importantly, back into his bed.

"I adore this novel."

—Eloisa James, *New York Times* bestselling author

M713T0510

Enter the rich world of
historical romance
with Berkley Books . . .

Madeline Hunter

Jennifer Ashley

Joanna Bourne

Lynn Kurland

Jodi Thomas

Anne Gracie

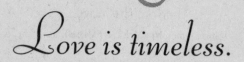

Love is timeless.

"How does it feel to be the Queen of Sex Advice?" he asked, smiling slightly.

"Silly," I told him, and it really did.

At least the centerfold of the month can justify her title by her body. What did being the Queen of Sex Advice mean in measurable job terms? That I could look up the answers in Kinsey, Masters and Johnson, et al., to any sex question faster than the next writer? That I didn't mind saying "penis" or "cock," for that matter, in print or aloud?

"You must intimidate a lot of men," he said, pressing his lips against my hairline.

"Do I intimidate you?"

I straightened out my legs and leaned back against the pillows and closer to him. I was still wearing the buttery soft lavender leather suit I'd selected for the press conference that morning. Women back home have belts wider than this skirt was long. My panty hose, the only underwear I had on, were a deeper shade of lavender. I had, of course, kicked off my lavender heels.

"Do I look intimidated?" he asked, grinning.

He put his hand on my thigh, and the fingers curved possessively around my flesh. My breath came faster. Before climbing onto the bed, he'd removed his socks and shoes; his feet, I suddenly noticed, were as long and slender as his hands. He was tall, thin, elegant, and graceful. His penis, I imagined, was average length. . . . If he'd kept his hand on my thigh much longer, I might have written an epic poem to it, sight unseen.

"No. You don't look intimidated. That's what I like best about you."

I knew as Charles caressed my thigh with his long sensitive fingers that we were going to have sex that night. . . . I would be in love with him by morning.

FEMALE SUPERIOR POSITION

SUSAN CRAIN BAKOS

ZEBRA BOOKS
KENSINGTON PUBLISHING CORP.

This book is for Tamm above all, and also for Rich, Mike and Dan, Barb and Gary, JDK and CK, and Kim.

Part One

TALKING SEX

Chapter One

●━━━━━━━━━━━━━━━━━●

L ooking back, I wish I could say that an anticipatory shiver passed through my soul as the makeup brushes drifted across my face, but I was aware of nothing more cosmic than a vague tickling in my nose. I was being made-up in preparation for an appearance on the Olive Whitney show. Olive was number one in the ratings, but to me it was just another talk show, a routine event in the life of a frequent guest. I had no clue that my life was about to change.

As a makeup artist was stroking brown shadow across the outer third of my left eyelid, I was obsessing on eyelids, not life. My left lid is larger than the right and thus requires more shadow so it won't appear to droop on screen. It's surprising how much the camera sees that the eye misses. I was thinking about cameras and eyelids, not about the first threat on my life received only hours before the show in an express mail envelope delivered directly to my apartment.

It never even occurred to me to wonder if any other members of WIP had received, or would receive, death threats. At that point, I wasn't what you would describe as "close" with any of the members of my support group, Women In Porn—or the WIPs, pronounced "whips" by Tim Price, one of the three men with whom I was more or less involved at the moment. The other

WIPs called me "The PTA Mother of Porn." While nobody ever said it to my face, I think they thought I was *"cute,"* just a degree or two to the not-so-respectable left of Kathie Lee Gifford. The WIPs tend to divide women into two groups: Those who have fucked in front of a camera; those who haven't. And I haven't—which is all it takes in their set to type you as a distributor of tea and cookies, not that I haven't been on the serving end of tea and cookie trays in the typical life of a suburban wife I led before becoming a sex journalist.

"You know, honey, you should never wear any other color lipstick," Olive's makeup artist, José, said as he filled in my lips with "peachy-pink, the color of Georgia clay" or so he claimed it was. I've never seen Georgia clay. Joan Rivers's makeup person said I should never wear any other color than rose-pink. Who to trust? "It's perfect for blondes," José cooed. "And you're sooooo blond. It's natural, isn't it?" he asked, peering suspiciously into the roots.

I said "Yes" through my lips scrunched into the semirelaxed open "O" makeup artists prefer for lip work. It is natural—naturally blond, fine, thin, and limp. WASP hair. Have you ever seen a real blonde who didn't have a bathroom full of hair-thickening products?

"You're lucky, you know. Women would kill for hair this shade of blond. And the blue, blue eyes, too, lucky you. Sooooo perfect!"

In addition to making you look as good as possible for the camera, makeup artists psych you up for the ordeal ahead. A really good one, like José, can make you believe you're beautiful, exactly the way a really good lover can. A really bad one can leave you convinced he'll be laughing backstage about several of your least attractive facial features even as you're being introduced to a probably hostile audience.

"Just a teeny touch of blue eyeliner on the lower lid.

Now, don't look at me that way." He put his hands on his narrow hips, affecting a queen's posture. *"Everybody* knows nothing is more outré than blue eyeshadow. I said liner, not shadow. Don't you be thinking José is that down-home!"

I wasn't thinking down-home. No. I come from down-home, southern Illinois; nobody like José ever grew in the cornfields back there. I was wondering if he is gay, bi, or merely an effeminate straight guy playing into the prevailing stereotype about the sexual preferences of makeup artists and hairdressers by sending off gay vibes.

My mind wandered while he worked. When I shut my eyes briefly, I could see the letter I'd pulled out of the express mail envelope. On cheap white typing paper, letters apparently cut from magazines spelled out: "Superlady, You must pay for your life with what you have done." Nothing more. The letters, with capital and small letters randomly mixed running first up, then down the page, were innocent in themselves, like a child's plastic letters tossed out of the container onto a flat surface. What kind of nut would choose to arrange them in that way?

When José was finished, he rested his hands lovingly on my shoulders and smiled with genuine joy into the mirror above my head. Our eyes met. Gay. I can always tell in the eye clinches. I nodded in the affirmative, sharing his happiness. He'd given me peaches and cream skin to go with the peachy-pink lipstick. My eyes looked huge, alluring, yet intelligent. All in all, it was the best TV makeup job I'd ever had, even though he couldn't really hide the fact that I was forty years old. What do you do with those major grooves running from nose to corners of mouth? Some artists fill them in with gunk, which only runs by the first commercial break, making it look like you're losing your face which must be following the mind you'd already lost when you agreed to be there in the first place. Rather than trying to fill in the craters, José put the blush high on the cheekbone and shaded it upward to direct the observer's eye away from the fact that everything from my nose down was going south. It worked fairly well. Thirty-seven or -eight. I could pass for that.

In the "green room," which was not painted green, I joined the other "guests"—a talk show industry code word for the human offerings presented five days a week to audiences composed largely of fat, frigid, and frumpy wives defending the state of dependency with their carefully applied polyurethane claws. Each time I euphemistically agree to be a "guest" on a talk show, I assume the experience will be better than the ones before. I don't know why I assume this. It never is, *I* never am. In countless appearances representing the "pro" side of sex issues, I have failed to distinguish myself in "talk"—industry code word for the stilted monologues exchanged by opposing forces each armed with well-barbed rhetoric—but somehow I don't remember that until I am seated in a preshow waiting room, the "green room," *never* painted green, facing the opposition over a tray of donuts and Danish no one dares eat for fear of messing up our lipstick or getting greasy crumbs on ties.

"Hello," I said, smiling at the younger blonde across the table. She barely acknowledged me with a slight inclination of her head in my direction. Obviously this was not the other Easily Orgasmic Woman or if she was, her ease of bodily response didn't extend to smiling. "Elizabeth Thatcher, I presume?" Another slight inclination of the head.

"Oh!" squeaked a trim and prim little brunette in her late twenties, obviously one of the show's many producers, as she came through the door. Why do the women behind the scenes in talk TV look like they've never been laid? "You two shouldn't be in here alone to-gether!"

The producers believe opposing sides lose their edge if they're allowed to fraternize without supervision over coffee. What, Goddess forbid, if we should discover we go to the same hairdresser in civilian life? Or, that we both buy garlic bread twists from Balducci's in Green-wich Village? Could we still glare effectively at each other on camera if we shared such intimate details of the other's life?

"Where's our expert?" she asked. "Where's our other Easily Orgasmic Woman?"

"Makeup," said the young and beautiful gay man, clearly the PA, or producer's assistant, prancing two steps behind her and carrying a clipboard. "José is doing everyone today, so he's backed up."

"I'm Amy McHenry," she said, extending her hand first to me and then to Elizabeth Thatcher, public rela-tions officer of Women Worried About Wantonness Among Women, the WWAWAWs, a right-wing con-servative group recently formed as an offshoot of Women Concerned For America—the group who backed that Wisconsin husband after he had his wife charged with adultery as a criminal offense under an old law still on the books. Women Concerned For America are loosely allied with Women Against Pornography—the group started by Susan Brownmiller back in the late seventies when feminism and porn were both briefly "in" at the same time, shortly after Jackie O was report-edly seen leaving the theater showing *I Am Curious Yellow*.

The WWAWAWs are more blatantly antipleasure than the other two organizations. Concerned Women imply they don't mind your husband having an orgasm. WAPs imply they don't mind lesbians having an or-gasm. WWAWAWs come right out and admit they would prefer that nobody ever had one, the exception being men when impregnating women to whom they are wed in the eyes of God and under the law; if anyone could figure out a way for men to ejaculate without enjoying it, these girls would be for it. They have elevated the traditional woman's statement of sexual piety—"I don't really need an orgasm to enjoy lovemaking"—to a credo. If my threatening letter writer—or is "letter assembler" a better term?—belonged to an antiporn group, I would have bet on the WWAWAWs. The WAPs could never have said it in so few words.

One of the new breed of post-Schlafly conservative women who are young—this one might have been late thirties, probably younger—pretty, articulate, and invariably clad in a bright red or floral print silk dress, Thatcher got the attention of talk show producers everywhere when she answered Joan Lunden's question, "Why another antiporn group?" on "Good Morning, America," by saying, "We can't be comfortable as members of WAP because it's infiltrated with lesbians. We have no objection to lesbians as long as they aren't sexually active. If they are fighting their lusts, we support them in their struggle against their sex demons. But, we have reason to believe many of these lesbian WAP members are indeed having active sexual relations, which breaks God's laws." She was a gift from talk show heaven: A natural and definite "anti" for any sex story.

Somewhat reluctantly, Elizabeth Thatcher shook McHenry's limp hand as the gay PA nervously brushed a sweep of hair so black it had to be dyed back off his forehead. The door opened again, admitting our expert, Dr. Adrian Prescott, author of *Any Woman Can Be Easily Orgasmic: How To Get More Pleasure With Or Without A Man,* his arm protectively around the shoulder of the other Easily Orgasmic Woman, Lisa X, who was keeping her last name secret so her husband wouldn't be embarrassed by her appearance on national TV. At the eleventh hour, she'd been talked out of enforcing her initial proviso—that she appear in silhouette only behind a screen with a muted voice like a member of the Federal Witness Protection Program, who had recently testified in a Mafia trial. But, she was still adamantly insisting on the X behind her first name.

"Carolyn, you look wonderful!" Adrian said, taking my hand and raising it to his lips. Every talk show segment has an expert on the panel, usually the author of a book and preferably a therapist. Adrian is both. Though I am not a therapist, I am, as a columnist, often billed as an expert, too, but today I am a combination expert and regular person confessing something about my life. Absolute bona fide experts, the PhD types, don't ever confess. They explain the confessions of others.

"It's been too long, darling, I've missed you," he said.

Gratefully, I leaned toward his soothing presence. Though Adrian looks the part of the stereotypical TV expert—major hair, pancake tan marred only by crinkly smile lines at the eyes, blue-tinted contacts, pearly white smile, quiet tie—he is a likable guy. We met as guests of ex-porn star/erotic video producer/ erotic photographer/performance artist Tiffany Titters (Tiffany has many "careers" because nothing she does is sufficiently financially lucrative for her to do that one thing alone) at the Carnival of Sleaze, a performance art evening at The Kitchen, a dark and dank space in the Village where the audience either stands or sits on the floor. Whenever I go to The Kitchen, I put a roach trap in my handbag to be sure the ones who will inevitably accompany me home are dead or dying, not alive. For the uninitiated, a performance art happening is where a collection of people who have little recognizable talent, but don't mind exposing themselves in some way most observers find discomforting, do just that for minimal fees. Karen Finley, the most famous performance artist, got her start at The Kitchen by shoving yams up her asshole, but that night she accepted her check on stage and left without performing, labeling it "the sleaziest thing I could possibly do."

As the only two people backstage who were even slightly embarrassed by Tiffany's large and naked breasts bobbing around all over the place, Adrian and I had something in common. She had unleashed them for the Booby Ballet, a dance of the mammaries punctuated by much swishing of tasseled pasties, and never put them back in harness. When Adrian told me about his research for a book on easily orgasmic women, I told him about my multiple orgasms; that's how I became part of his book.

"I don't know," Lisa whimpered, and Adrian drew her closer to his side. "Oh, God, I don't know." He rubbed her arm up and down. She probably hadn't had this much attention since the last time she'd given birth. "If Owen knew I was doing this, he'd kill me."

"But, who'll ever tell him?" McHenry asked, all innocence, accentuated by a hint of blusher, pink lip gloss, and mascara.

Talk show producers wear minimal makeup, the better for projecting sincerity among the overly made-up guests. Yeah, right. Who would possibly tell her husband she was on "Olive" talking about her orgasms? My guess was someone would have it on the TV at his office, even if there was no TV normally kept in the office, ten minutes into the show, max.

"Believe me, even people who know you don't pay the slightest attention to who you really are on TV," McHenry said. "They're caught up in the dialogue, in the topic of the moment. I was once a guest on a talk show panel, and my own mother watched without realizing it was me."

"Are you sure?" Lisa said, lisping slightly.

Another blonde, though definitely bottle, she was in

her early thirties, maybe as young as twenty-nine, presenting the possibility of the three of us looking like the aging of the blondes if they seated us in chronological order. Her skin under the thick makeup wasn't great, but the camera would smooth it out thanks to José's skill with the brush. Maybe her husband wouldn't recognize her without the visible pimples. McHenry nodded vigorously and patted her arm.

"Okay, okay, I said I would so I guess I should. What do you think?" Lisa asked, turning to me.

"Uh . . ." I was aware of Adrian's other hand pressing gently into my arm. He was capable of playing coach simultaneously to two women with differing emotional support requirements, a more impressive feat really than fucking us both simultaneously would have been.

"Well, I'm not worried about it, personally," I said.

What makes these ordinary people spill their guts— or, "share," as the process is more popularly labeled— on Oprah, Geraldo, Phil, Sally, and Joan? The free make-overs? The airfare and hotel rooms for out-of-town guests? Did they really believe Andy Warhol when he said we all are going to be famous for fifteen minutes?

"I'm sure it will all be fine," I said. "You're doing good, really. Think of all the women out there who rarely if ever reach orgasm. You can help them."

She nodded thoughtfully, a modern Joan of Arc headed toward her martyrdom.

"Really, it will be fun," I finished in that relentlessly cheery voice of the aging Valley Girl, a voice I hate but too often use as a hiding place. I should have put my arm around her from the other side and said: Does fifteen minutes of fame really compensate for the ignominy of having your home video shown at family reunions for life? No? Then, we're out of here.

"Okay," she said, "if you're not worried, I'm not."

I thought she was incredibly naive. Of course, *I* wasn't worried about appearing on national TV discussing *my* orgasms. For me it was all part of the job. And, *I* didn't have a husband at home who might consider the discussion an invasion of his privacy, too. No, at the moment I had three men in my life who were never in the same room with me when I was having an orgasm. What would they care?

Looking back, *I* was incredibly naive. So, what is the fleeting wrath of a husband who, after all, has just been identified by his adoring wife as a gonzo orgasm giver, compared to what I was going to face? The "Olive" show changed my life. It merely gave her something to talk about for the rest of hers.

"Carolyn," McHenry said, beaming at me. I looked at the heading on the paper in her hand. Today's show was titled: "Women Who Enjoy Sex Too Much." She caught my eye and hastily covered the title line. Conned again. She'd told me the show was "Why Some Women Like Sex More Than Others Do." She smiled winningly. "How do you want us to introduce you?"

"Our first guest is the Superlady of Sex, Carolyn Steele!" Olive said; the audience tittered. "Carolyn's sex advice column has appeared in *Playhouse* magazine every month for the past five years; she's an ex-pert"— she drew out the word and ended it on an up note—"on *sex*," she finished on the downbeat. The audience tittered more loudly. "Yeah!" Olive squealed. "Okay, Carolyn, what makes you an expert on sex?"

"Well," I said solemnly, as if I'd just been asked to explain the meaning of life, "I have a master's degree in math, which makes me a good research person. I keep up with all the latest studies, and interview sexologists and therapists from around the country, the world even, to answer readers' questions." I continued, sounding sillier and sillier.

"O-kay," Olive said. "Audience, what about that? A math major who knows about sex!"

Once on a local show in Seattle, I answered the What Makes You An Expert? question, "I like sex; I'm comfortable with sex. I'm good at it." I liked that answer. I felt good about it. Three hours later, while wandering through Pike's Market looking for Market Tea, Seattle's own blend of orange spice tea, which turned out to be too sweet, I walked into a tiny shop selling herbs and spices. The aging hippie owner, long hair nearly reaching his waist, single earring in left ear, sandals, tie-dyed shirt—yes, the entire nine-yard cliché—said, "I saw you on television this morning. I thought, 'Oh, Christ another expert. What makes this one an expert.' But, I liked what you said. It was honest." I wish I'd felt more comfortable about his endorsement.

". . . but what she's got to tell us about herself probably isn't what you ever expected to hear from your math teacher . . ." Olive was saying. Math teacher? "Tell us, Carolyn, how many *orgasms,*" she lowered her voice deliciously on the "O" word, "can you have at one time?"

"Well," I began. I caught my reflection in the monitor. My nose was already greasy, and the camera had given me chipmunk cheeks, the fate of those who have no bones. The tag line at the bottom of the screen under my inflated face read: "Easily Orgasmic Woman." I looked back at Olive. Her face was even fatter than mine. What were we doing in a place like this? Why not radio for us? "I don't count them."

"Then how do you know you're really multiply orgasmic?"

"Well, I *have* counted."

"You *have* counted," Olive said, coming in for the

kill. "When you *have* counted, how high did you count?"

"A couple dozen, but then I stopped counting."

The audience gasped. A few women groaned. I heard one hiss something that included the word "disgusting." Olive's mouth opened wide. She was certainly putting the weight back on, but she's still surprisingly beautiful.

"Good-ness!" she said, and the music came up, signaling an imminent commercial break. "We'll be back in a minute with another Easily Orgasmic Woman and the man who knows more about these women than any man in America, Dr. Adrian Prescott, author of *Any Woman Can Be Easily Orgasmic: How To Get More Pleasure With Or Without A Man.*" She held the book up. "And, maybe Carolyn will tell us if she had those couple dozen orgasms with or without a man!"

The commercial rode in on a gale of audience laughter.

". . . and, it was almost a religious experience for me, having my first orgasm finally, with my husband, after all those years," Lisa said softly. Adrian, who had just finished explaining how easily orgasmic women get that way in part by thinking about sex before they do it (a concept he calls Pre-Sex Mental Foreplay), had one arm around her shoulders. He was beaming proudly at her. The camera caught the glint of tears in her luminous green eyes. The pimples didn't show, and, since she had prominent cheekbones, her face didn't even look fat. The audience loved her, because she had *worked* to become easily orgasmic. I was just born that way, which made them angry. They kept getting hung up on the word "easy" which they translated as "promiscuous." Nothing gets an American TV audience more outraged than sexual pleasure. "Adrian's book changed my life," Lisa lisped. "It saved our marriage."

"And, you really believe *any* woman can learn to have orgasms as easily as you do simply by reading this book?" Olive asked—again, waving the book.

"Oh, yes," she said, the lisp quite pronounced. In the front row, a woman was dabbing the corner of her eyes with a tissue. "And, I really believe every woman owes it to her husband to become multiply orgasmic."

"All right, audience," Olive said, squelching their applause. She spotted the woman with the tissue, ran over to her, and put an arm around her shoulders. "Sister," she said to her. "It's okay. Almost every woman in America has had trouble having orgasms at least once in a while." The audience laughed and clapped delightedly; she had to silence them again by waving her mike. "Now, you've heard from two Easily Orgasmic Women. For Carolyn, having an orgasm is as easy as falling off a log, but Lisa had to learn to have them easily and in fact had her first *just . . . last . . . year* at what age, Lisa? No, girl, I'm kidding. You don't have to tell your age! Now, audience, I get the feeling you're a little uncomfortable with Carolyn. Why is that?"

Olive stuck the mike in front of a white woman with a bad perm, who said, "She doesn't say anything about love! What about love? I don't think it's right to be having all those orgasms with someone you don't love. She's a slut." Accepting the applause, she grinned for the folks back home. "Besides, she writes for *that* magazine."

"Okay," Olive said. "Okay. That magazine bothers you, does it?" The bad perm bobbed vigorously up and down. "Why is that, girlfriend?"

"It exploits women. I think. . . ."

But, Olive had turned away from her. "Okay, audience, is that what you think? Does Carolyn's magazine exploit women?" Resounding applause. "Well, Caro-lyn—"

"Olive," Adrian interjected. "I don't think that's our point here. Our point here is orgasms and how every woman can have them easily and often. Our bigger point here is how orgasms can improve a woman's relationships with men."

"Even if she has them without men as your book promises she can whenever she wants?" Olive asked.

"Yes, of course, even having them without men improves her relationship with men. In my book I teach women how to become orgasmic through self-pleasuring, which is, as you may know, the most reliable learning path to orgasm." In private, among friends, Adrian calls female masturbation "woman's own whanking." On air, he says "self-pleasuring" in tones so civilized, he should be holding a teacup in the digits often used for such activity. "Self-pleasuring is good for relieving tension as well as teaching women how to have orgasms. Can you honestly tell me you don't think a relationship is improved when a woman is relaxed?"

"Well . . ." Olive said, lowering her voice, playing into the titters. "I don't know what to say about that. But, stay tuned! When we come back, our next guest, Elizabeth Thatcher, spokesperson for Women Worried About Wantonness Among Women is going to tell us what *she* thinks of all this pleasuring going on!"

I looked over at Thatcher, her face set in an accusatory mask. I knew she was going to crack, but I didn't know how wide the fissure would be . . . or how deranged the woman was behind the mask.

". . . thank you, caller," Olive said firmly, and the woman with the nasal Jersey accent was sent to oblivion after congratulating Elizabeth Thatcher on the "fine work" she's doing to save America from female wantonness, which, of course, is responsible for everything from teen pregnancy to AIDS. Olive was standing in the audience, her arm tightly around a sobbing woman who had just confessed she'd never had an orgasm. "Okay, Elizabeth, you and the caller and a lot of our audience agree that you don't need an orgasm to enjoy sex." She hugged the sobber. "And, that's fine! That's great! But, are you saying you think there's something wrong with a woman who *does* need an orgasm to enjoy sex?"

"Olive, if I may interject," Adrian said. "It isn't okay to say you don't need an orgasm to enjoy sex if in saying that you really mean you don't believe you deserve an orgasm."

"Thank you, Adrian. I hear what you're saying. You don't want women to feel guilty about desiring sexual pleasure. Elizabeth, how do you feel about that?"

"I am not opposed to sexual pleasure for married women," she said, carefully choosing her words, "as long as it doesn't become a separate goal in itself. Orgasm," her lips seemed to go numb around the word, "should be a by-product of the loving communion between husband and wife. It shouldn't be a goal. Too many orgasms can cause a couple to focus on their carnal feelings, not their higher love for one another. Before you know it, a woman is trying to have more and more orgasms to the exclusion of showing her love and tenderness for her husband. Making sexual pleasure a goal denigrates the marital relationship."

"Now, how does it do that?" Olive asked.

"Marriage, Olive, is a union blessed by God. Its purpose is higher than our navels." An outburst of laughter and applause greeted that obviously well rehearsed bon mot. "When you strive for sexual pleasure in marriage, you lose sight of its higher purpose."

"So, you're saying orgasm is okay if it happens, but don't try to make it happen?" Olive asked. Elizabeth

Thatcher smiled and nodded enthusiastically. "Then you think Lisa's marriage didn't need an orgasm to save it?"

"I think Lisa is misguided and misinformed. If she had come to me, I would have sent her to the scriptures for solace, not his book. But, I don't condemn her for what she's done," Thatcher insisted, smiling beatifically on the sinner to her left. Adrian appeared to be winking at the audience. "She's been brainwashed by a sex-mad media. *Her,*" she said, indicating me, "I most certainly and soundly do condemn."

"Well, I guess by your definition, Carolyn is part of the sex-mad media, isn't she?" Olive asked.

"Most assuredly," Thatcher replied. She turned in her chair, leaned across Adrian to face me. The hairs in my nose stood on end.

We were in the last segment of the hour, the place where I lull myself with the thought, *It's almost over, and I'll never do this again.* I start making bargains with the Goddess to whom I rarely otherwise converse. *Get me out of here, Goddess, and I swear I'll never say yes to a producer again.* During the preceding commercial break, José had whispered into my ear when he powdered down the grease around my nose, "Madame X's husband is on the phone, and he is not amused." Adrian was making the connection between early masturbation and women who are easily orgasmic without the help of his book.

Olive asked Lisa X if masturbating had helped her, and she blushingly said, "That's too personal."

Adrian said apropos of nothing, "Some women in my study have orgasms with extragenital stimulation." Olive nodded, but I don't think she got his point. "For instance," he continued, "they can achieve orgasm by having their breasts or other nongenital body parts stimulated."

"I once had an orgasm in the subway when my lover

nuzzled my ear," I said, and I saw Elizabeth Thatcher quickly cover her left ear with her right hand.

"Your ear?" Olive shrieked. "Girl, you're putting me on!"

"She's not," Adrian said.

"I'm not."

A significant percentage of the audience was glaring at me. It was true, but why did I choose that fact to share? If I had said to these women, "Look, I haven't had partner sex since my lover left me for a twenty-year-old seven months ago," they would have taken me into their collective heart with its arteries clogged by cholesterol and sentimentality. I would have been one of them, a female victim. But, no. I had to tell them about the time I orgasmed on the 1 train. I had to set myself apart from them, didn't I? My fierce and misguided sense of pride which wouldn't let me admit I shared many of their same fears and sorrows was standing in my way again. I couldn't see past it. Why, I'd never admitted childbirth had been painful, so great was my need not to be like other women.

"I was already aroused from thinking about the sex we were going to have when we got back to his apartment," I said, attempting to soften the blow.

"That's Pre-Sex Mental Foreplay in action," Adrian said.

"Wow!" Olive said. "That's some action! How old were you when you had your first orgasm anyway?"

"Eleven. I was shimmying down a tree. I didn't know what it was, only that it felt good. I asked my older sister, and she said I'd had an orgasm, and I didn't need the tree to do it again." The audience laughed and hooted, except for the sobber who started crying again. I saw Elizabeth Thatcher's face go red with fury, but, perversely, I continued. "Think of the splinters I could have gotten if she hadn't told me."

"That's disgusting!" Thatcher snapped.

"Olive, if I may interject . . ." Adrian began.

"Now, just a minute!" Olive said to Thatcher, ignoring him. "She's describing a perfectly normal and natural physical response . . ."

But, Thatcher couldn't take her eyes off me. I wiggled my middle finger at her, the one I use to masturbate. Before any of us knew what was happening, she had leaped from her chair and had her hands around my throat. She made me famous.

Chapter Two

●━━━━━━━━●

Dear Superlady of Sex,

I am a forty-year-old white woman having an af-
fair with a twenty-five-year-old black man, my first
adventure into the heart of darkness. Frankly, his
penis is a disappointment. It isn't any bigger than a
white man's—and it's NAVY BLUE! Is he an excep-
tion or is that stuff about big black cock not really
true? I haven't told him I'm let down, but maybe he
can guess.

Also, on the subject of stuffing, he doesn't get very
hard. No matter what I do, he seems semi-hard to
me, so I get tired of trying and just stuff him in as
best I can. Is this normal for a man so young? I've
had to stuff old guys, but never someone so young.

was going through the mail in bed, which is where I
normally read, eat, sleep, watch TV, talk on the
phone, and do any work not performed on the computer. Modern urban life does that to people. When not
on the streets engaged in the combat of daily life, dodging the homeless with their hands out, avoiding eye
contact with the crazies while being careful not to step
in dog shit, and schlepping each day's necessary pur-
chases because we have no cars with trunks to fill on a
weekly basis, we retreat to our beds surrounded by

Chinese take-out cartons, newspapers, magazines, and the assorted chaos of our own "stuff," by which we imprint our style on our surroundings. My stuff is largely books, novels from Trollope to Atwood, and mysteries, especially with female detectives, and the occasional volume of feminist literary criticism. Piles of books leaned into the bed on either side.

How I envied the letter writer her navy blue penis. I knew I could make it hard. How much longer would I be able to stand this job without getting laid? It was like being a food writer on an eight hundred calorie a day diet.

> *Dear Disappointed, You Bitch,*
>
> *Over forty years after Kinsey told us the average black penis measures approximately two-tenths of a centimeter more than the average white penis— hardly enough to get excited about—the myth of the BIG Black Penis still lives. And, most men at twenty-five rarely need to be "stuffed." But, a woman who regards your navy blue penis as something short of spectacular could have that effect on a man.*

Okay, this answer would need a little more work, but I was only playing. It didn't surprise me to see the Georgia postmark on the letter writer's envelope. Nobody buys into the big black penis myth like a southern white woman—unless it's a black man. The average black man does seem to have more sexual confidence than the average white guy. Could it be all the positive PR his penis has gotten?

Paying minimal attention to the telephone conversation I was having with Tim, I put the letter aside and picked up another.

"And, how does that make you feel?" Tim asked. It was his favorite question of me. My favorite question of me was rapidly becoming: Why do I put up with him and The Question? Listlessly, I put down a letter requesting advice on the etiquette of asking a woman who's had a mastectomy to leave her blouse on during sex. *(Make wild passionate love to her on the sofa, removing only the necessary items of clothing. But, make sure she's convinced you couldn't stop long enough to get to the bedroom.)* I sighed and let my thoughts stray to my clit, the source of my greatest pleasures in life. I was lying on my back, knees up, legs open, accessible. I have strong, taut thighs from riding the exercycle in the corner of my bedroom. I love my thighs. Somebody has to love them.

"This has to be arousing some powerful feelings in you," he prompted. "I know it would in me. Jeez, this is big stuff. Big stuff."

"It doesn't make me feel that great, okay?" I said crossly. I was losing patience with him. During the first two months I'd dated Tim, I took pains to answer The Question as carefully and honestly as if he'd been a real shrink and not the editor of *The Journal of New Age Psychology,* an obscure quarterly published in the basement of a sagging brownstone in the East Village.

The first two months of dating Tim were like the first two months of dating any man in my post-35 dating history: I invested him with qualities he didn't have to justify my interest in him. When it started to become painfully obvious that he, like the ones before him, was simply the product of my overactive romantic imagination, I grew irritated with him. After irritation, comes embarrassment and the horrible question: *What did I ever see in him?*

I'll tell you what I saw in them: They weren't engaged, married, or living with another woman. Availability was the deciding factor which explained why my recent past was littered with geeks, losers, wimps, nerds, lying womanizing sleazebuckets, and just plain jerks.

Dating at forty is like shopping for a good wool dress at a department store clearance sale the last day of January. It's okay if you have a closet filled with dresses at home. But, imagine how you'd feel if everything you'd owned had just been lost in a fire?

I was tired of The Question and the condescending yet pseudo-therapeutic tone of voice in which Tim asked it. He has a bachelor's degree in psychology and, at forty, was still trying to decide if he wanted to go back to school and become a psychologist. Really, he wants to be paid for earnestly asking, "How does that make you feel?"

"That's good," he said enthusiastically. "That's valid. It doesn't make you feel great. Sometimes, we know what we do feel by eliminating what we don't feel first."

I sighed again. He spends all his discretionary income, what little there is of it, on therapy himself. For the past four years he'd been seeing a Jungian who treated him at a discount in exchange for Tim rewriting his papers which were then published in the journal. And, for two years he'd also been in a therapy group run by an MSW who combined Freud and "body work," something involving exercises of the nonaerobic variety. During the first session each member stripped to underwear or a bathing suit to have his body "read." In a typical session, talk alternated with bizarre mat activities, in which someone ended up on the mattress in the middle of the floor with the "expert" helping him or her let go of blocked emotions. According to Tim, the mat interludes could get so "intense" that barf bags were kept handy for participants who let go of lunch as well as old emotions.

"I know how I'd feel if my picture were on the front page of the *New York Post* with the headline, 'Sexpert Nearly Expires of Pleasure!!'," he said smugly—smugly because, of course, nothing so tacky would ever happen to him.

"Tim, please." I groaned, shoving the *Post* under the down comforter with my left foot. Why had I called him anyway? What kind of woman would find emotional solace in a nutcase like Tim? "I can't stand it."

"That's good, that's good. Let it out. Let your feelings out on this one."

Now *he* sighed; more deeply than I could ever sigh, of course, thanks to his body work breathing exercises which, with daily practice, had taught him to sigh from his gut. Too bad he doesn't practice other things with his gut, like regular sit-ups. Tim is medium height and build, except for the soft, expansive middle. With his thinning brown hair and sparse facial and body hair, he is far from a sex object. I only wanted him because he was hard to get. If he'd tried to seduce me on the first date, I would have hastily declined, bolted the door behind me, turned on the answering machine, and never returned his phone calls.

Instead, he'd announced, "We aren't going to have sex right away," over the first cappuccino we'd shared, and I was hooked temporarily. As my best friend Morgy says, I only want what I think I can't have. Why didn't it occur to me that his sexual position was probably fear of being with a woman of my assumed experience?

It didn't occur to me because I was in the midst of a midlife crisis which had temporarily left me unsure of myself and seeking validation, and masochistically accepting the refusal of it, from the geeks of the world.

"You must be feeling really out there right now, really alone," he said. "Yes, that's it, out there and alone, a visible target for women's anger. I know how you feel."

"You should know how I feel. You've been a visible target for the anger of every woman you ever dated."

The last woman left him when he failed to renew his driver's license so he could share the driving on a trip they'd planned to take upstate. It was, she said, the "last straw," the last of many times he'd let her down in many ways ranging from the insignificant, like forgetting to buy her a corn muffin one Saturday morning when he went out to get *The Times,* to the incredibly important, like wearing a shirt that reeked of stale sweat and smoke when she introduced him to her kids. It was, he said, only an excuse she'd used. The real truth: They were playing out their scripts. She was a leaver; he, who feared abandonment, always chose leavers. Oh, get real, Tim, what woman worth having wouldn't eventually leave you?

"My ex-lovers adore me," I continued, my turn to be smug. "They send flowers on my birthday. My ex-husband still calls on our wedding anniversary." True, but why is this so important to me? Tim was right about one thing: It was time I asked some questions about my life. It was time I asked, but I wasn't ready to answer. "Your exes return your Christmas cards stamped, 'Refused!' "

"Okay, take it out on me if it makes you feel better," he said. His voice, which is deeper than you'd expect it to be, given his general wimpiness, sunk an octave lower. "I'm strong. I can take it. I can handle it. I want to handle it for you. I want to be there for you, *want to,* as opposed to *have to.*"

Tim, who, of course and you probably guessed this, considers himself a new sensitive man, talks a lot about needing to get beyond the "feeling of having to," which, he claims, paralyzes him. That, his fear of abandonment, and his Oedipus complex are his "big issues," which taken together form his "complex." He can't, for example, clean his apartment until cleaning is something he "wants to do as opposed to has to do." His apartment does look like the kind of place described in newspaper articles about elderly recluses found dead amidst their roaches and newspapers, those articles accompanied by photos of cops in gas masks carrying out scrawny, mean cats—the kind of place that lends credence to his theory only a sick person would live this way. But his mother, a tough old Texas gal, says he's "just plain 'ole lazy," an explanation I tend to endorse.

I scanned another letter, this one from a man who just wanted to tell me what a great time he'd had with the twin sisters, big of boob, blond of hair, who had picked him up in their convertible while he was hitchhiking in the Texas panhandle. They loved rubbing his "jism" into their nipples. Or, so he said. Personally, I would bet he saw Texas from the window of a Greyhound bus where he fantasized this encounter. Irritably, I pushed the pile of letters aside.

"This feels right for me," Tim said, though I didn't know, and wasn't going to ask, *what* felt right for him. "Yes, it's feeling good. I need to get past this point of having to and reach the point of really wanting to, and I feel it coming with you. It's good. It feels good. I feel it coming."

"Tim, let's talk about something else, okay?"

Sometimes I thought of him as Jeff Goldblum turning into The Fly. He was repulsive—positively oozily yucky—yet I kept going back to stick my fingers in his goo. Figuratively, of course. Something about him compelled me. Or, maybe it was just my secret self-loathing that motivated me to be involved with him.

"Can't you ever just be my friend and say, 'There, there'?" I asked.

"Okay," he said with petulance in his voice.

He cleared his throat, giving me time to change my mind. I waited, imagining him lying on his moldering bed in his studio apartment across the hall from Clarissa, who introduced us. Never allow yourself to be fixed up by a lesbian who shares a three-room apartment with her pregnant lover and six female cats which have not been spayed. What a woman like that knows about men wouldn't take up a corner of the litter box.

When I didn't weaken, he said, "But I want you to know I'm here for you whenever you want to talk about this. It's big stuff. You can't shove it back down. Well, you can, of course, but if you do . . ." As he launched into his familiar monologue on how "stuffing"—and he wasn't referring to something done with a limp penis— had kept him emotionally weighed down, I began to touch myself, sliding my finger back and forth around the slick shiny protrusion that was the source of so much joy . . . and since yesterday, a fair amount of media attention. Jeremy Mitchell had called that morning. Jeremy *himself.* I closed my eyes and wiggled farther down into the nest of pillows in my bed. Sometimes I masturbate to meet an immediate need for release generated by something I've thought or heard or read or written . . . and sometimes because my hand is there anyway.

"What did you say, Carolyn?" he asked sharply. "Are you gasping?"

"Uhmmm . . ." I said.

Initially the world intrudes. Gradually it doesn't anymore. The finger that was only tapping the surface is pulled deeper, connecting with the longing inside me. Whatever minor stimulus led me to this place is overshadowed now by the greater need. I am inside myself, enveloped in layers of undulating satin tissue. Within seconds, I can get from the point where the erotic spell can be interrupted to that place where nothing can stop me and any interruption is incorporated into my private lovemaking. The ticking clock or ringing phone or the voice disembodied in my ear are carried along as if they were so many twigs in a river headed for the falls. Tim was an interruption, not the erotic catalyst, but I would incorporate him. I bore down on the fingers inside my vagina while massaging my clit with my thumb.

"Uhmmm . . ." I said, sucking myself inside.

"You're breathing harder, Carolyn. Talk to me!"

"Jerk yourself off. Don't tell me your cock hasn't been outside your pants for the past fifteen minutes." He loved it when I talked dirty, though afterward he swore he didn't. Like so many of the men who wrote to me, he loved it; so I did it, one last time. Superlady couldn't stop me anymore than he could.

"Do it, Tim. Pretend you're ramming it up my ass. You know you want to." I wanted him too. I fantasized him taking me anally, effecting entry in short hard thrusts and then plunging rhythmically inside my bowels as far as he could reach. A woman is never as submissive as when she offers a man her ass to plumb, and my recurring fantasy lately was one of submission. "Do it, Tim. Fuck me hard."

"Carolyn," he said. "Carolyn . . ." The masturbatory narration was definitely my department. "Oh, Carolyn . . ."

"I'm kneeling with my ass in the air, Tim. My head is down. My ass is open for you. I feel erotic dread grow in the pit of my stomach and wash through my loins as you spread my cheeks apart with your hands. I am hot, aching, and panting. I want it, fear it. The head of your cock is poised against my asshole. It's so big, Tim, so big. You grasp my hips with your hands and push hard. Oh, my God, Tim, again, harder . . . my God, you're inside me so far. I feel your testicles slapping against my pussy lips. Over and over again, Tim, I feel you fucking me, a hard, driving, burning force opening me up, leaving me vulnerable. . . ."

Tim snorts when he gets excited to the point of almost coming; he was getting there. I put the phone down on the pillow, so I couldn't hear him. I replaced him with a sexual memory of a man who was so far superior to him, no comparison should even be made.

I was in my mother's bathroom, on my last morning

of a visit home, carefully shaving off all my pubic hair in preparation for a reunion with this man. I had never shaved myself there before, and it felt strange. Walking through airport lobbies, the air striking my naked skin, because I wasn't wearing panties under my skirt, I felt more sexually vulnerable than I had in years. It was exhilarating. My nipples were erect from St. Louis to Philadelphia.

In his car, parked at the end of a row in the Philadelphia International Airport, he put his hand up my skirt and discovered what I had done. No man had ever touched my skin in that way before. He pushed the seat back as far as it would go, unzipped his pants, and lifted me up. Wet and swollen, I sat down on his erection and rode him. His hands on my hips accepted rather than controlled my movements. My third orgasm released his; afterward, I sat on his lap for many minutes, while he held me. My shaved pussy made me feel so close to him, so open to him, that I came again, just sitting there quietly in his arms.

As I thought about him, I moved my fingers faster and pushed farther down into the bed; my foot slid inside the pages of the *Post*. Eyes closed, I saw myself alone, totally exposed, with no space left unexplored. The orgasm crescendoed around my fingers, reverberating into little sucking noises that I could barely hear beneath my moans.

When I brought the phone back to my ear, Tim was breathing heavily; I was still having orgasmic contractions.

"Whew!" he said. "Whew! That was good." Then he let out one of his little yipping noises, which he says are part of his body work. "So, dinner in an hour or so? At Winston's?"

"Yeah. Sure."

"I love you," he said. Tim prided himself on being a

feeling man. He said "I love you" a lot, almost as often as, "How does that make you feel?"

"Love you, too," I said, a very large lie.

"I wish it were different, Carolyn," he said. "But you know it wouldn't be healthy for me if we had sex. You could drive me so far into my complex I would never be able to climb out again." Then his voice brightened. "I'll bring my research into the psychology of the WWAWAW type. I think it might change your mind about whether or not that woman is seriously dangerous."

Tim's new favorite hobby was psychoanalyzing the authors of my hate mail. He had a psychological profile worked up for every one of them. Now, he had the WWAWAW workup, too.

As he'd outlined it to me on the phone, the typical WWAWAW members were religious zealots, programmed by leaders who delivered the same messages over and over again. They claimed they "loved," not "hated," but Tim said they weren't programmed to deal with anyone who wasn't brought over to their side by the power of their "love." Failure to convert left them confused and laden with repressed anger, enough, he said, in some cases to render them capable of violent acts.

"I still think you should take that threatening letter to the police," he said.

"Why should I go to the police with a little piece of paper? Madame Zelda took some letters to the cops several weeks ago and they more or less said, 'What do you expect? You solicit mail from sex perverts?' Why would it be any different for me?"

"Did she get the same kind of letter?"

"I don't know. I never saw them. Look, I'm tired of talking about it," I said, hanging up on him.

When would I have an affair with someone I wouldn't be embarrassed to recall had aroused my lust six months or a year later? I knew I was definitely going to be embarrassed remembering phone sex with Tim after he was no longer in my life. Pressing my hand against the last of the contractions, I already felt a little nauseous about it.

I took a quick shower, applied minimal makeup (mascara, blusher, lip gloss, a sponging of ivory foundation) and put on black garter belt and stockings rather than panty hose under my short black skirt. What other color is there for skirts and stockings? Then I spent forty-five minutes putzing around the apartment, pulling dead leaves from plants, organizing magazines, clipping coupons, unloading the dishwasher. I'll always be a housewife in my heart. I wasn't answering the phone. The machine was set on two rings with the volume all the way down so I wouldn't be tempted to pick up. I'd already talked to Morgy and Johnny Badalamenti, the jazz drummer I was sometimes dating. Anyone else could wait.

I was living on Wayne Street in Jersey City, in a newly renovated two-bedroom apartment in what was once a splendid art deco building located on the block that served as the dividing line between the barrio, the Puerto Rican ghetto, and the Van Vorst Park area recently claimed by the upwardly mobile young transplants who couldn't afford, or wouldn't spring for, New York City rents. Only the hallways had survived the Yuppie-azation. Their black and white tile floors gleamed; turquoise carpet runners danced up marble steps. The walls, washed pale turquoise, were topped like slices of wedding cake heavily and decoratively iced by ornate cornices. Chandeliers and wall sconces bloomed in tulip shaped leaves. But, inside the apartments, all was industrial off-white from the carpeting to the bathroom and kitchen tile and the Eurostyle cabinets—pale wood or some reasonable imitation thereof with off-white accent strips. My apartment on the fourth floor had a loft over the kitchen and bathroom that could be reached by a narrow nearly vertical "staircase," which was really a ladder. Even I, at 5′2″, couldn't stand up straight in the loft.

Morgy (Morgan Harris Carter, a ravishing and rich strawberry blond stock trader) said "too bad you can't live in the halls" on her one and only visit. Not that Morgy's Manhattan apartment, a large one bedroom with wood parquet floors and terrace with panoramic view, on the Upper East Side was exactly a decorator's dream. Her bedroom contained an enormous nineteenth century cherry bed she hadn't assembled. She slept on the mattress on the floor surrounded by sections of the bed, like the oversized pieces of a child's wooden puzzle. Her underwear lined the walls in little piles. What with making money and spending it on worthless men, she didn't have time to shop for anything but clothes. Anyway, I loved my apartment, with its tiny boxy rooms. It was filled with light for my plants. From the loft, I could look down on my high-ceiling living room lined with bookcases, rich in trees, and spare in modern furniture, all gray and black, leather and glass, and pretend I was in a *New York* magazine layout. I couldn't see the drug dealers lounging on the front stoops of the neglected brownstones across the street from that vantage point.

I was hanging up some clothes in the bedroom closet when I remembered the *Post* and pulled it out from under the floral peach down comforter. The bedroom was my retreat into the past, shamelessly feminine in shades of peach and ivory and turquoise, laden with needlepoint pillows, small pieces of antique oak furniture, framed photos of my son and daughter from infancy through young adulthood, similar photos of nieces and nephews, and a collection of feathered, sequined, and beaded Mardi Gras masks. My face on page one was wrinkled in the middle from where I'd kicked the paper in the throes of orgasm. I smoothed it out and turned to page three, where my brush with death was the big story.

"Sex Writer Nearly Dies For Her 'Sins' On Olive!" The picture splashed half the length of the page was of Elizabeth Thatcher with her hands around my neck. My mouth was open, eyes popping, as security guards were converging on us from all edges of the shot. An inset photo of Olive, who was also openmouthed and wide-eyed while standing frozen with her mike in front of the sobbing woman, was in the upper right-hand corner. The copy read:

A trembling but dry-eyed and otherwise composed Elizabeth Thatcher, spokesperson for Women Worried About Wantonness Among Women, was led away from the stage of the Olive Whitney show in handcuffs yesterday following her assault on another guest, Carolyn Steele, sex advice columnist for Playhouse *magazine.*

The topic of Olive's show, "Women Who Enjoy Sex Too Much," brought together Steele, an Easily Orgasmic Woman Who Enjoys Sex Too Much; Thatcher; Dr. Adrian Prescott, author of the controversial bestseller, Any Woman Can Be Easily Orgasmic: How To Get More Pleasure With Or Without A Man; *and a woman who called herself "Lisa X, Easily Orgasmic Woman," and was later identified as Lisa Pollack, wife of a Cincinnati orthopedist, who was said to be "distraught" over her involvement with the program.*

After Steele admitted to having orgasms with a

stranger on a subway train, Thatcher, according to witnesses, jumped out of her chair and began strangling the blond bombshelldropping sex writer.

A spokesperson for Whitney said, "Elizabeth Thatcher appeared to lose self-control for a period of time during the show. We regret this incident deeply and are grateful that the quick thinking of security personnel averted a more serious tragedy." Only live markets saw the altercation, which was cut from the tape sent to other markets. The spokesperson would not say if the program will be included in those scheduled for rerun during holiday time periods.

Steele is said to be a member of a subversive underground group of women pro-pornography activists. The Pro-Porners, according to reliable sources, are bent on making pornographic materials more widely available. They include legendary X-rated actresses Tiffany Titters and Gemma Michaels. Following the attack, Steele was taken to Chicago's Mercy Hospital, where she was pronounced shaken but unharmed except for minor external bruising. A cadre of bodyguards provided by Whitney hustled her to O'Hare Airport where she boarded a charter jet for New York City. She was unavailable for comment upon her arrival and was whisked into a limo, also provided by Whitney.

Law enforcement officials declined to say whether or not charges would be filed against Thatcher, who was escorted by her husband Phillip, a Memphis attorney, last night from police headquarters.

In a statement to the press, he said, "My wife has been under a great deal of stress lately."

At a Brentano's bookstore in Chicago where he was autographing copies of his books for a record crowd, Dr. Prescott labeled Steele "a near martyr to America's fear of sex."

Subversive underground group of Pro-Porners bent on making pornographic materials more widely available? All we did was meet for lunch once a month and discuss how hard it is to get laid when men are sexually intimidated by you. How did I feel about this?

I glanced at my watch. Ten minutes before I needed to walk down the block to Winston's to meet Tim. I flipped the pages of the *Post*. At the bottom of page sixteen another story captured my attention. The headline read: "Porno Pretty Pays Price." Tanya Truelust, or Julie Beckman, as she was known to MasterCard and a very few others, a former porn star turned independent producer, had fallen to her death when one of her high-heeled shoes had caught in the rungs of the fire escape outside the window of her Chelsea office. She was, according to the *Post,* apparently sneaking out the window to avoid creditors lurking in the lobby.

The moral was: Don't skip out on your creditors if you're wearing high, high heels and your back door is a fire escape.

Was something wrong with this story other than its condescending tone? I felt a queasiness in the pit of my stomach. Tanya, whose erotic specialty had been exuberantly faking orgasms, had died shortly before my appearance on Olive, even perhaps as the threat to my life was being shoved under my door. Was there a connection? Or, was it only coincidence that Tanya was lying in a metal drawer in the morgue, an identifying tag around one toe, likely painted fuchsia, her signature color, as Elizabeth Thatcher's hands encircled my neck?

I shoved the *Post* down the incinerator chute on my way out of the building.

"You probably should have expected to find a reporter or two standing outside your door today," Tim said. He patted my hand, then glanced covetously at the two reporters, who'd followed me and were sitting at the bar drinking beer, to see if they were watching him comfort me. He ran his finger up and down my hand from wrist to knuckles, familiarly, seductively. Rather than look into his eyes, I scanned the room. Winston's is a tasteful blend of dark green and glowing wood, the bar a genuine antique salvaged from a local pub in which it is said the young Frank Sinatra drank back when he lived in Hoboken. Too bad the food, with the exception of the burgers, which they only serve at lunch, is so mediocre. I've often been tempted to go inside Tony's, the little Puerto Rican bar on the other side of Wayne Street, to see if they do any better.

"I know being hounded by the tabloid press doesn't feel comfortable for you, but they're only doing their job," he said in an excessively reasonable tone of voice that makes me nuts. "Do you know what I was thinking as I read this article? You are a person who elicits strong responses from people. No one reacts to you in a neutral way. You have to ask yourself, is this soliciting of strong response a behavior that I want to keep?"

"Oh, will you please stuff it? I didn't expect them to be hanging around outside my front door," I said, pulling my hand out from under his. I glanced discreetly around the room to see how many Winston's regulars, predominantly white, under thirty-five and Wall Street, were watching us. Several. "That was yesterday's news."

"We've talked about this before. You know that by doing certain things, you open yourself up for certain reactions from others. I'm not saying those reactions are fair or just," he said, raising his hand to fend off another one of our usual conversations, this being the one in which I tell him he makes me feel like there's something wrong with what I do and who I am, to which he replies, "I can't make you feel anything. You feel it; that's all."

"They just are. Reactions, that is. They own their reactions as you own your actions. And, you open yourself up to them, don't you? Besides, it isn't exactly yesterday's news. Jeremy called you today, so it's still today's news. Are you going to do his show?"

"Two glasses of white wine?" Marti, our waitress, asked. We nodded. She was staring so hard at my neck that she didn't notice we'd given the order. I had my throat swathed in an imitation Hermes scarf, green and gold saddles on cream background. She couldn't see the bruises. Tim put his hand over mine again, and again, I pulled free. "Two glasses of white wine?" she repeated.

"Yes," I said, staring her down, forcing her to look up into my eyes. "Two glasses of white wine." To Tim, I said, "I don't know about the Jeremy show. I have a meeting with Vinnie at the magazine tomorrow." Vinnie Mancuso, owner and publisher of *Playhouse* magazine, *himself* called only minutes after Jeremy, controversial star of "The Jeremy Mitchell Show," *himself* called. "He'll probably want me to do it. I'm sure that's the point of the meeting. Vinnie doesn't do meetings."

"Yo, guy, can you handle her?" a man on a barstool called out to Tim, who grinned and ducked his head. I wanted to smack him.

"How does that make you feel?" he asked.

"What? Meeting with Vinnie? Or, having that guy think you're actually fucking me? It makes me feel like telling him the truth."

"Okay," he said, blushing. "I want you to read these," he hurried on, putting a folder on the table between us. "Women like Elizabeth Thatcher shouldn't be underestimated. These articles explain the brainwashing techniques used by the leaders of these groups.

And these," he said, pointing to the second half, "describe the pathology of the participants. It's fascinating stuff."

"Uh-huh," I said, signaling for the check.

"Yee! Yee! Yee!" Tim yelped. The reporters, who'd accepted my "no comment" with grace, were nevertheless following us back down Wayne Street to my apartment, maintaining a not very discreet distance of less than six feet. "Yee! Oh, that feels good. I needed that."

"I wish you wouldn't yelp in public."

"It's good for me, sweetie. It gets my energy up. It releases that pent-up tension. You should try it. I wish you'd let me teach you a few body work exercises. You won't give it a chance."

"I'm not yelping in public, thank you."

"You don't have to—"

"I know," I said, deliberately cutting him off. We'd had this conversation too many times before. The story of my life, or lives, with men was rife with repeated conversations. It was a different conversation with each man, but always the conversation was repeated over and over again. We worried it like two old dogs with the same bone. Was it them or me? Morgy says, "Well, whose the one person who has been a part of every bad relationship I've ever had? Me!" Ouch!

"I'm sorry. I feel tense," I said to Tim, knowing this gift of a feeling, any feeling, would send him home satisfied.

"I hear what you're saying," he said. Holding me close, he tenderly kissed me good night. "I love you, sweetie," he said.

"Superlady!" yelled a man slouching in a doorway across the street. "I saw you on TV! Lookin' good,

Mama, lookin' good! You keep on doin' it to yourself, Mama!"

When I looked back over my shoulder once I was safely inside the double-locked lobby doors, Tim was waving; the reporters were right behind him, also waving . . . and so was the fan across the street.

I unlocked the three locks on my apartment door, stepped inside, and turned on the light. When my eyes adjusted, I saw it. An envelope had apparently been slipped under the door. I picked it up and opened it, expecting some communiqué from the management office. But, it was another one, the same as the first, the letters cut from glossy magazines glued on the cheapest variety of typing paper.

This one read: "Superlady, You have failed to change and you will pay with your life. You had your chance."

I started shaking as if it were January and I was on a street corner at night trying to flag a cab.

Chapter Three

Dear Ms. Steele,

How much longer will you continue to be a collaborator in the rape of your sisters? Pornography is part of an ideology of cultural sadism promoting violence against women, particularly rape. How much longer will you lend your name to a masthead led by a sexual imperialist who built his lavish lifestyle on the pain of women? You degrade yourself and all womanhood by your participation in this tawdry endeavor you call a magazine. Wake up! Refuse to be a part of the wholesale humiliation of your sex!

The letter writer had printed "member of Women Against Pornography" beneath her name, as if I couldn't have figured that out for myself. Her diatribe ran on for seven pages, a fairly typical length for a communication by a militant feminist, in tiny precise script, the kind one associates with nuns. She'd probably sent the same letter to publishers, editors, and columnists of other skin mags this month; she saw no difference in any of our products as she licked her stamps. Wouldn't she be insulted if I told her I couldn't differentiate between her and a typical WWAWAW?

Pornographic images are more varied than any of

these women like to admit. Some, like the airbrushed pets and videos which seem to be shot through a steamy mist, are idealized. Some are crude and graphic. A few are even witty. While aimed primarily at men, the erotic visualist sex, who require visual images for arousal, porn images appeal to many women—me, for example. I am aroused by pornography, by the glistening cocks moving in and out of moist and tender vaginas, by the beads of sweat, the drops of moisture on the ends of tongues poised to perform fellatio or cunnilingus. I am aroused and not ashamed to admit it.

In *Playhouse,* the women are more often than not the sexual aggressors . . . and they're always satisfied. A fantasy, yes. A *male* fantasy. What our reader really wants is to be desired by a woman whom he then satisfies beyond her wildest imagining. Under all that throbbing cock and dripping pussy terminology is the modern man's version of Sleeping Beauty and Cinderella. He wants his fairy-tale heroine to awaken him so he in turn can awaken her. But the women of WAP see nothing in material meant to arouse men except *The Story of O* carried to its ultimate climax, her death. The end point of pornography, they insist, is the violent degradation of women, possibly to their death.

We are living in censorial and confusing times. The antiporn activists seem to believe we can end rape and violence against women by censoring sexual imagery. In the Scandinavian countries and other places where "porn" is openly consumed, the national rates of rape and violence against women are far below our own. Normal, healthy heterosexual lust is constantly under attack by a strange coalition of New Sexual Puritans, who stand diametrically opposed on their other important issue, abortion.

Ironically in the same batch of mail I received a catalogue for lesbian S&M aficionados. Strap-on dildos in regular, large, extra large, and XXX. Nipple clamps.

Chains. Leather harnesses, collars, handcuffs. Whips.
The usual paraphernalia also found in catalogues aimed
at the heterosexual S&M market. Plus hot videos and
steamy novels featuring women doing it to women the
hard way. The women of WAP are strong defenders of
the rights of lesbian pornographers to promote their
literature and their sex-play products.

Can someone explain why lesbian S&M is okay,
while men who spank women are the worst kind of
sadists? Why any erotica aimed at arousing women is
okay while material meant to cause an erection is not?
Why lesbian women can masturbate to the smut of their
choice, while if men or heterosexual women with pornographic tastes do, we're all being degraded and humiliated?

I dumped the letter and the catalogue into the trash
together—there was a pleasing symmetry in the act—
and shut down the computer in the tiny second bedroom I used as an office. In no other part of the country
would this be considered a bedroom. I doubt a twin bed
would fit into the space between these walls, but if it did,
one would only have to walk into the room and fall
forward onto it to be tucked away for the night. Vinnie
probably didn't have a closet this small, but, lined with
white shelving attached to wire mesh grids, it was perfect for my workspace.

Picking up the two threatening letters made from
cut-out letters and shoving them into my bag, I turned
off the light and hurried out the door for my appointment with Vinnie.

"I can't believe Vinnie's going to cut our budget,"
Clarissa said to the five of us through bites of cold
Szechuan noodles with spicy sesame sauce. Four *Play-
house* editors were taking me out to lunch, a ratio of

editors to writer which indicated my sudden importance to the organization. "I mean, it has to be just a rumor, don't you think?"

Only twenty-nine, Clarissa, a *Playhouse* senior editor, talks and looks like someone who was smoking grass in the sixties rather than playing in it in a safe New Jersey suburb. Her long, stringy brown hair, which falls forward into her face when she gets excited, missed her fork by millimeters. She paused to push hair aside, then straightened her plain wire-framed glasses on the bridge of her nose with the thumb of one stubby hand. What a little mascara and blusher wouldn't do for Clarissa.

We had been discussing Tanya Truelust's untimely death and unfortunate financial situation when Clarissa, as she is wont to do, personalized the issue.

"This couldn't happen at a worse time for us," she said. "Miriam's due practically any minute now. I haven't even told her there might be budget cuts because I'm afraid the stress of worrying about whether or not I'll get my next raise might send her into premature labor." She narrowed her eyes meanly in my direction. "But, like you don't have to worry, of course, since you're free-lance."

"If she's due any minute, then labor won't be premature," David said. "Next week you'll be begging us to break the news to her over the telephone to hurry things along."

Editor-in-chief, he paused for the predictable laugh which was his due from me and Cynthia, also a senior editor. Rhumumba, the new hire, sat at one end of the table, isolated from the rest of us who sat beside and across from each other, silently shoving moo goo gai pan into her wide mouth. She did not laugh.

"You might show a little remorse over the loss of a human life, Clarissa, a life known to most of us at this table," David admonished.

"Oh, David," Clarissa moaned, allowing a tendril of

noodle to escape from her mouth and slither down her chin. I averted my eyes from the sight and looked upward into the glowing orbs of a white dragon. These dragons with fiery eyes highlight the black and white decor of Shun Lee's, my favorite Chinese restaurant though the food critics say Shun Lee's Palace on the East Side has better food. "You always make me look like a jerk."

"I couldn't do it without your help," he responded in the most clipped and haughty tones he could interject into his pseudo-English accent while preparing to bite into a spring roll. "You lend yourself fully to the endeavor."

David Keltner, my longtime friend, despised Clarissa Chase, who along with Cynthia Moore-Epstein did most of the real work at the magazine. He would have fired her two years ago if firing her hadn't meant he'd have to edit the damn thing himself. An exceptionally intelligent man, David was not, at this point in his life, particularly ambitious. And, there was too much work for one woman to handle alone, even a woman like Cynthia of the sleek shining brown hair and double Seven Sisters backgrounds, Smith College and *Mademoiselle* magazine. It was too soon to tell how helpful Rhumumba, the epitome of the strong, silent type, was going to be. Frankly, even David, who could devastate almost anyone with one of his targeted verbal onslaughts, seemed intimidated by her, but then lesbian bodybuilders who've renamed themselves have never been his favorite people. Grumbling "the last thing the magazine needs is another lesbo writing cunt line copy," he'd agreed to hire her as a favor to somebody in the accounting office to whom he no doubt owed many favors. David abused his expense account, using it to cover family dinners and sometimes even weekend getaways for him and his wife. Vinnie's tolerance for fiscal irregularity was legendary.

"I'm not a bad person because I'm worrying about money, you know?" Clarissa whined.

"Do you think there's any truth to the rumor that Tanya was pushed?" Cynthia asked. "Tiffany Titters told me on the phone this morning that she'd heard Tanya's death may not have been an accident. Who would have wanted to kill her?"

David shrugged. For a group of people who were, however loosely, involved in the pursuit of journalism, we spent a lot of time wondering about rumors, but little time tracking them down. Like the rest of America, we were waiting for someone else to confirm our facts.

"I'm not a bad person," Clarissa repeated.

She put her fork down and crossed her arms over her chest, where surprisingly ample breasts were bound beneath a man's shirt and baggy jacket. She hides a truly spectacular body under men's clothing. I only knew about her hidden assets because I'd helped Miriam undress her once after she'd thrown up all over herself in a cab we were sharing back to Jersey City from a Christmas party at Vinnie's mansion. Vinnie frowned on excessive drinking or excessive eating for that matter. In her nervousness at being in his presence, Clarissa had put away enough of his expensive champagne to be quite spectacularly sick. She was drinking, while the rest of us wandered self-consciously, discreetly sipping from our champagne flutes, as we admired the downstairs art. The upstairs was off limits to us, protected by one of Vinnie's bodyguards at the top of the massive marble staircase, a case of decorator overkill if there ever was one. I hated the art, too heavy on religious themes. How many Virgin Mothers does one man need?

Perhaps Clarissa drank to avoid seeing in clear focus the Madonnas and cherubs lining the walls. Anyway, she couldn't get out of the cab and inside the apartment without my assistance; once there, how could I refuse to help strip her? Neither of them so much as hinted at a threesome, not that I would have. But, wouldn't you think they'd have asked?

"I'm not a bad greedy person," Clarissa said, again directly to me. "You were with me last week when I chased a homeless person to give him my leftover pizza slice. I ran after him for six blocks and he called me a 'cunt.' I'm a good person. I've never been a father before. I don't know how I'm going to afford all this. Will the cats have to go? And, on a strictly personal level, will Miriam be so busy with the baby she won't even bring me a Pepsi when I come home from the office?"

She and Miriam had the most old-fashioned marriage I'd seen since leaving the Midwest. It was, she said, patterned after her parents' marriage. Clarissa is the only person I know who claims to have had a "Leave It To Beaver" childhood and genuinely adores her parents. Miriam, who didn't work, considered herself the "wife," in the traditional sense of the word. My lesbian friends were appalled by their behavior.

"You've done it five times, David, and don't tell me you didn't have the same concerns," she said.

"I did it the old-fashioned way by shooting my own sperm directly into my wife. We didn't have to go to a clinic where she was basted like a turkey," he said with a contemptuous sniff for the artificial insemination procedure which allowed Clarissa and her lover Miriam to become parents.

"Like it was the only way to do it when you were doing it," Clarissa retorted. She had a point. David, at forty-five, had a twenty-eight-year-old daughter. His last one had just turned twenty-one.

Turning dismissively away from her, he said to me, "The meeting with Vinnie went exceptionally well, I gather?"

The meeting with Vinnie had gone well . . . and

predictably. (I hadn't shown him my threatening letters because protocol, even if your life is on the line, demands David see them first.) He'd frequently clasped my wrist by encircling it with his hand and pressing gently downward, his way of making a friendly point, as we sat side by side on the gray leather sofa in the office he rarely uses. Vinnie conducts most of his business from "The House," an Upper West Side brownstone, actually two brownstones joined in a remodeling process that created, among other splendors, the largest indoor swimming pool in the city, filling the entire basement level, where a huge bust of Caligula is the prominent sculpture.

Without once reminding me I was, at $5,000 a month, a well-paid columnist, he'd used every persuasive technique short of offering to loan me his gold chains to wear on Jeremy's show. The gold chains, worn for TV appearances only, in multiples against his mat of chest hair, clearly visible since he didn't button his shirts on these occasions higher than three inches up from the navel, were his worst fashion habit. Otherwise, he was impeccably groomed and dressed in handtailored and fairly conservative suits. He'd been using the same London tailor for decades.

How could I refuse him any request? I had an easy gig. I wrote what I wanted to write from home, coming into the office once or twice a week to get the mail and schmooze. I had plenty of time to do occasional articles for the women's magazines on sex and relationships, articles like the one I was working on for *Women Today,* which I was calling, "Why He Won't Eat You Out—And How To Make Him." They would, of course, change that to "Sex Secrets Every Wife Should Know," the title of approximately half the articles I write for the women's magazines. Without the *Playhouse* column, for which I owed David, life would be leaner.

Therefore, I once again agreed to be a "guest" on a talk show doing my part in the war against the forces of sexual repression, its battles fought mainly by women: women in silk dresses or, like me and the new breed of female X-rated video producers, short black skirts and dark stockings, or militant left-wing lesbians who never mention their sexual partner preference on their frequent "Donahue" appearances. At least, the Jesus freaks aren't leaving out the crucial part of their bios.

"I regret I can't join you and the others, Carolyn," Vinnie had said, referring to the lunch he'd arranged for me to share with my editors at Shun Lee, where Woody Allen sometimes dines. Rarely do four editors take one columnist out to lunch. The last time I'd been feted by more than one editor was the day before I began a ten-city tour representing the magazine on local talk shows from Boston to San Francisco in the wake of the Southland Corporation's decision to remove *Playhouse* from their 7-Eleven stores. Clarissa, Cynthia, and David took me to The Ginger Man to fatten me for the media kill on warm duck salad.

"This kind of controversy is good for the magazine," David said, nodding his approval. "I know you're tired of being on television, but I'm glad you're doing it. Shows admirable team spirit on your part." Unlike Vinnie, he didn't call us a "family." "Team" was his guilt-inducing noun of choice.

He turned again to Clarissa and said, "Only men can be fathers. Remember that. You may wear the pants in your family, but you can't fill the crotch."

"So what exactly did happen to Tanya?" I asked David. We were all walking back to Broadway to get a cab to the *Playhouse* offices on East 86th and Lexington, where I planned to kill an hour discussing my sex life, or lack thereof, with David behind his closed office door while Clarissa, Cynthia—and who knew if Rhumumba?—worked. Afterward, I was going to meet

Morgy for drinks before we joined her latest Eurotrash boyfriend, Georges, and Johnny Badalamenti, the drummer in my life, for a Jamaican dinner at Caribe in the West Village. David, over six feet tall and most of it in his legs, was in the lead; I scurried on high heels, burning the balls of my feet, to keep up with him. He was moving so fast, the strands of hair combed over his bald spot were rising rhythmically up and down. They couldn't blow in the wind. He used too much hair spray for that to happen.

We hurried past the regular antiporn protestor who sat at her little card table displaying the same poster she'd been using for at least two years: a nude woman, from the waist up, mouth tightly gagged and arms bound to her body, electrodes attached to her nipples. It was, according to our lawyer who after exhaustive search found the original photo, a blowup of a torture victim from the files of Amnesty International, but the good lady of the crusade would have you believe it was last month's centerfold.

"Women," she yelled, compulsively brushing the sweep of short blond dirty hair off her forehead with the hand that wasn't waving the poster, "what are you going to do about this? Men are masturbating to this every day! They're masturbating to it right now! What are you going to do about it, women?"

We were well past her when her voice got even louder and she yelled, "Hey, Superlady, you're responsible for this! Women are in pain because of you! What are you going to do about it?"

"Do you suppose she's ever had an orgasm in her life?" I asked David, who ignored the question. "She hasn't got any boobs at all. I remember noticing that last summer when she was not hanging out of her men's sleeveless ribbed undershirt, not that boobs have anything to do with orgasms."

Clarissa and Cynthia, well behind us, were picking up

speed as they approached the protestors who operated between two street vendors, one selling hot dogs and another selling used books and magazines, including several back issues of *Playhouse*. Bringing up the rear was Rhumumba, who, when viewed fleetingly over my shoulder, moved like a Russian tank, slow, placid, and formidable by reason of sheer bulk. She was wearing the tattered jeans popular with rich young West Siders, but the holes in hers revealed pieces of jumbo muscled flesh grinding as she strode.

"David?" I interrupted his concentration, obviously on something other than me. "What really did happen to Tanya?"

"Jesus, she's ugly," he said in a sotto voce voice. "I feel her back there. She feels ugly." He giggled. David is one of the few men I've ever known who genuinely giggles. "Tanya, as far as I know, fell down the fire escape. No mystery."

"You're talking about Tanya," Clarissa said, coming up behind us. "Like maybe I should write an editorial eulogizing her. What do you think? Could I submit a separate free-lance bill for it?"

I glanced at David who was rolling his eyes. Behind me, Rhumumba had narrowed hers to slits only big enough for the steam to pour out. Maybe she didn't like us talking of the dead with so little compassion. Or, maybe her jeans were cutting off the circulation in her crotch.

David and I were alone in his office, a nine by twelve square of gray and mauve, gray industrial carpet and desk chair, mauve sofa and vertical blinds. Photos of nude circus people matted on gray and mauve paper lined the walls. I particularly liked the tattooed man with the rosebud on his flaccid penis. I wondered if the rose bloomed when he got an erection. The view was of Lexington and the new HMV music superstore on the corner at 86th Street. David liked to watch the store entrance for the celebrities who frequently shopped there. He compared it to birdwatching in the wild, claiming it alleviated the boredom.

"So, what do you know about the proposed budget cuts?" I asked.

"Nothing, it's boring." He was peering out the window at the entrance to HMV. "Dr. Rita was in"—Dr. Rita, meaning Weinberg, the famous tiny sex therapist, "in" meaning shopping at HMV—"this morning. She certainly relishes her celebrity. I watched her stand outside long enough to collect a few curiosity seekers who followed her in. Tourists from Iowa, no doubt." He turned his gaze toward me. "Rhumumba is creepy. She gives me the creeps. What do you think of her?"

"Creepy."

"Exactly," he said and nodded, satisfied with my reinforcement of his critical character assessment.

"What's happening with your Hispanic?"

"Nothing."

"If you can't lure him between your thighs, he must be gay."

"I don't think he's gay." I stuck my tongue out at him. Well, maybe I was beginning to wonder if Manuel was gay, but I wasn't ready to concede the point yet. "I don't like her," I said, getting back to Rhumumba.

"I don't either." He giggled. "Maybe she won't last long."

"Does she do any work?" There was a knock at the door. "Clarissa," I whispered. "Cynthia would call from her desk."

"Come in," David said, and Clarissa did.

"David, you have to look at this, like now, because it has to be in Art, like yesterday." She manages to convey the impression of wringing her hands even when they're full, as they were then, of blue line copy. "I'm running late again. Consuela is threatening my life." She put the pile on his desk beside his propped-up feet. "So, Carolyn, what's going on with your love life? Any new action? Here," she said, tossing me a fat gray envelope stuffed with my mail. "We threw out the ones that were ticking or oozing semen."

"Sit down, Clarissa," David said, and she joined me on the sofa. No one is allowed to stand when he is sitting. They might see the bald spot on top of his head.

"Same three guys," I said breezily answering her question about my so-called "love life." Only David and Morgy knew I wasn't fucking any of them. "Nothing new."

"I miss those days," she said. "Being married is wonderful, but it has its ups and downs. Sometimes I feel really trapped. I'd like to go to a party and pick up someone, you know. I want to experience the thrill of seduction, the head rush of first-time sex. I want to light up a cigarette afterward. I can't smoke in bed anymore because Miriam's pregnant. Her stomach runs our life."

"Uterus," I said. "Her uterus runs your life, not her stomach. Didn't they teach you anything at NYU?" I begin to sound like David when I'm around him for longer than an hour. "I thought you played around in California last year when you went out to cover the lesbian S&M convention."

"She did play around," David said, not looking up at either of us from the copy in his hands. He grimaced. "Jesus, Clarissa," he said, running his pen through a cutline, as the sentence identifying a photo is known. This particular photo was of two women masturbating each other while a man, cock in hand, happily watched. Clarissa had captioned it: "Luckily, he just said, 'Well, enjoy yourselves!' "

"What a dumb line," David said. "Change that to 'Stick your fingers in the dykes, girls!' "

"Oooh," Clarissa said, "oooh, gross, exploitive, demeaning to lesbian women everywhere, ooooh," running through the groaning and grimacing routine she presumably believed David expected of her in response to his editing. Then, "Oh, what's the difference," she told him, her perfunctory protest out of the way. To me, she said, "I didn't exactly play around. I flirted a lot. You know me, all talk and no action."

"What do you think of Rhumumba?" I asked.

"No fisting?" David asked Clarissa, referring to the practice of fist fucking, which is, exactly what it sounds like it would be, rough lesbian sex. "I thought that's all one did at a lesbian S&M conference."

"I'm not into S&M, you know that. I only do it to Miriam on occasion because she likes it. Like that's her taste, not mine. What am I supposed to do? Say no? If I say no, she'll get it elsewhere. Isn't that what you tell those women who write and ask you if they should suck their husbands' dicks? We don't do anything rough now with the baby and all. It changes your life. It really changes your life."

"Maybe the baby will just fall right out after years of fisting," David said, handing the copy back to her. "Get it to Consuela before she makes good her threats."

"I'm in trouble again," she said to me. "Did he tell you? He sent me another warning letter for being late." She shifted back and forth from one foot to the other and clasped her hands prayer-like in front of her chest. "But, like, I can't help it. Miriam is sick in the mornings, and she doesn't get me up on time. I don't trust her, Rhumumba, that is. There's something very weird about her. She won't tell me her birth date so I can cast her horoscope. I don't like her vibes. Something isn't true about her. Do you think she might be a corporate spy? I can see Vinnie putting someone in here to check up on us. And, like why did she give herself that name? It sounds African. She looks Irish. She's so pale, she'd look sickly if she weren't built like Mr. Universe. *Rhumumba.* I mean she sounds like a poisonous snake. Do you think she might be a transsexual?"

"Goodbye, Clarissa," David said, waving her out of the room. "Shut the door behind you." After she did, he said, "Where were we?"

"Do you think Clarissa is really putting us on with her imitation of Ward and June Cleaver doing rough sex?"

I've learned from my gay friends that a lot of swishing is done for the benefit of straights. They do love to tweak us, not that we don't deserve to be tweaked more than occasionally. He shrugged his shoulders.

"David, I have to show you something. The first one came in an express mail envelope the day I did Olive. The second one arrived the next day. And it was slid under my door while I was out."

I handed him the letters and watched him study them. If he'd seemed overly concerned, I would have panicked. He didn't.

"Damn," he said, whether in response to my hate mail or the ringing phone, I don't know. He picked up the phone. "Hello. Yes. Yes. Okay, I'll come down and look at it." To me, he said, "Five minutes. I have to check a layout."

Once a month, when the magazine closed, he almost had to work, and he hated it. He left the door open. Rhumumba's cubicle was directly across from his office. She was staring intently at her computer screen. Clarissa, the sniveling hypocrite, was standing behind her, one hand on the lesbian bodybuilder's massive shoulder. But that's Clarissa, one minute talking about someone, the next minute rubbing their back and cheering them on. She could be so irritating, but I loved her anyway, the way some people love family members in spite of their peccadilloes. I don't love any of my family members, except my kids.

Last year she sent me flowers after I'd embarrassed myself on a talk show, subject AIDS. I'd written an article for *Playhouse* based on research provided for the Center for Disease Control in Atlanta explaining exactly how AIDS is transmitted, either by blood to blood or semen to blood, making it a difficult disease to catch unless you're involved in sharing needles or rough, most likely anal, sex or have an open STD lesion. The other "guest," who won audience sympathy, was an AIDS victim claiming he caught the disease during heterosexual sex with a prostitute.

Two minutes before airtime, the host told me, "The prostitute was menstruating, and he had an open herpes sore." There we had it: Blood to blood transmission. "But he won't say that on camera, and we can't violate his confidence without being sued," the host added.

Why, except to appease the ratings god, would a journalist be a part of such deception? If people know exactly how AIDS is transmitted, aren't they more likely to take precautions to avoid it? Instilling fear of sex never stopped anyone from having sex, only perhaps from having safer, or at least more informed, sexual relations. In the last century, people died of syphilis, and women have always risked death by childbirth in having sex. Fear has never proven a path to celibacy. I was furious at the host, and I came across on TV as someone who was pissed off because her theory was being refuted. Clarissa's note enclosed with the flowers had said simply: "I understand exactly how you feel."

Waiting for David, I pulled a letter out of the envelope and opened it.

Dear Superlady of Sex,
   I like to fantasize that I am petite and beautiful. In reality, I am over six feet tall, weigh almost 250 pounds, and have a very hairy body. This, I think, is why ladies' lingerie looks so strange on me . . .

Most transvestites ask one of two questions: Where can I buy lingerie in my size? How can I tell my girlfriend/wife about my secret passion for panties? My advice in general is shorter, snappier, and sassier than Zelda's ever was. It is frequently backed by the findings of sexologists and also more practical. In some cases, I provide shopping or acquisition information. I have more female readers too than she ever did.

When I advised a panty sniffer (a man whose fetish, upon which his arousal and ejaculation is dependent, is used women's panties) to stop raiding his female friends' laundry hampers and suggested he pay someone to provide him with her worn panties on a regular basis, I was inundated with letters from women readers offering their panties via the mail.

Letter Number Two.

Dear Superlady of Sex,
   Can you tell me once and for all the proper way to measure a penis? Along the topside to the tip? Or, along the underside? And, do you measure that flaccid or erect?

Penis size. The American male obsession. Measured topside when erect, end to tip, five to seven inches is the norm. I sifted through the envelopes. Out of approximately one hundred, there would be at least ten about penis size. Half would want to know if they were too small. *Does she fail to have an orgasm because I'm not big enough? (No. The almighty penis has little or nothing to do with the female "o." Haven't you guys ever heard of the clitoris?) Do those penis enlargers work? (No, Vernon, there is no penis enlarger.)* The other half would tell me their whoppers of nine, ten, and twelve inches were more than their women could handle. (According to Kinsey, less than two percent of American males have a penis measuring more than seven inches when erect. Isn't it funny they all write to me?)

Then, I saw the envelope, with the familiar handwriting. Something wasn't quite right about it, but at the time I didn't notice what it was. Starred Man had been writing to me for over a year, approximately one letter a month. We called him Starred Man because he drew a careful five-point star before each paragraph.

I opened the envelope and pulled out five sheets of lined yellow legal pad paper, his stationery. The first paragraph was always the same:

> *Dear Superlady Carolyn,*
> **Do you like hairy chests? I have a very hairy chest. I like your picture. I touch my hairy chest and then I touch my hairy balls and then I jerk off while I look at your picture.*

Mentally I was wrinkling my nose in distaste. Philosophically, I endorse the right of perverts everywhere to have an outlet for their sexual expression, as long as they don't hurt anyone physically or psychologically. I understand how isolated from the family of American heterosexuals who do it on Saturday night in the missionary position the transvestite, the fetishist, even the lesbian S&M aficionado must feel. Having been isolated from my own frozen WASP family shortly after discovering my clitoris, I identify with them. But, personally, I don't like getting mail from convicts who masturbate to my picture. This is the existential paradox of my career as a sex advice columnist.

My correspondents are too often even less appealing than the high-school retard who ate his own boogers. Imagine how you would have felt at sixteen if he had a crush on you. Then imagine how you'd feel to discover he took your yearbook photo to prison with him after he'd bashed his grandmother's head in . . . and you'll have a glimmering of the feelings Starred Man aroused in me.

In the back of my mind is a tiny seed of paranoia, the fear I'll find myself sitting across from one of these guys on the subway some day. I would never want to be that close to someone who masturbates to my picture. I shoved his letter to the bottom of the envelope as David came back into the office.

"Starred Man?" he asked. "Copy it before you go so I can file it." David had a file of "strange" mail; to be qualified as "strange" among our readers took some doing. He kept the file, he said, in case some pervert ever came after any of us. Then, he would have something to turn over to the police. Comforting thought. "Where were we?"

"I can't remember," I said. We were both looking at the two letters in the center of his desk. "Talking about my sex life, I guess."

"What sex life?" We giggled. "Tell me about your latest favorite masturbatory fantasy," he ordered, sitting down in his chair, propping his feet on the pristine desk. His eyes were on the entrance to HMV. "Did I tell you Madonna was in last week? I wouldn't have recognized her without the binoculars. Her hair's black now. Without makeup, she's not much. The bodyguards around her tipped me off. Now, talk."

He'd already heard my anal sex fantasy. I decided to give him oral. I always wondered if he got an erection listening to my erotic tales, but he would never tell me if he did or not. Either answer could be, he said, construed as an insult. Anyway, before we were halfway through my projected monologue, Steve Martin showed up at HMV and then Clarissa burst into the room.

"You won't believe this," she said. "I've heard the most bizarre and wild rumor. Vinnie's new operations manager is planning massive staff cutbacks. I can't believe it, can you? That's even worse than having our raises on the line and no free lunches. Now, it's our jobs. I feel so threatened—not, of course, that you have anything to worry about."

"Clarissa," David said, frowning, shooing her back out the door as he spoke, "no one is indispensable."

A few minutes later as I got up to leave, he put his hand over the two letters and said, "You'd better let me keep this. Vinnie has to be informed."

Chapter Four

"I know who you are," said the young Puerto Rican woman, and she pronounced "you" like "Jew."

She'd been eyeing me curiously since we both got on the train at 86th Street. Dressed in high-heeled black ankle-strap shoes with open toes, a skintight hot pink sweater, and equally snug white ankle-length pants, she was sitting across from me on the Lexington Avenue train going downtown. Didn't her mother ever tell her not to wear those pants in November even if it is unseasonably warm? Normally people are packed tight in the aisles of the subway car during rush hours, but this train was only comfortably full. We passengers had the luxury of viewing in addition to inhaling each other. Damn the luck.

"You were on the tel-e-vi-sion," she said, separating the syllables of the word in the pleasingly melodic way New Yorkers of Puerto Rican descent often talk. "I know you were. You were on that Olive show where the lady got choked."

I didn't say anything. She looked harder at me. I pulled the letter I'd been reading closer to my body, while keeping it angled so the rotund bald white man beside me with the garlic breath couldn't read it. Do only white men get bald and fat in the middle and wheeze garlic, or does it just seem that way?

"Weren't you on that show?" she asked. The people on either side of her, a young black woman with huge triangle-shaped golden earrings in her ears and a middle-aged white woman dressed in typical Evan Picone black and white separates and black patent leather flats, were watching me now, too. "You could answer me, you know," she said, which came out, "Jew could answer me Jew no."

"No," I said. "I wasn't."

That appeared to satisfy the others, who averted their gaze, but not my interrogator. She stared me down. I could feel her eyes boring into me as I, the first to look away, continued reading the letter in my hand. Thank the Goddess we were at 23rd Street. Only two more stops before mine.

Dear Superlady of Sex Steele,

My girlfriend has a gorgeous body but she is shy about showing it in public. It turns me on to see other men watching her strut her stuff in high heels, tight, short dress exposing plenty of cleavage. I would really like it if she would go out sometimes in garter belt and stockings without panties and sit on a bar stool so she can flash guys at my command. She thinks I'm sick . . .

There was more, but the writer basically wanted to know how to persuade his girl to act out his erotic fantasy. *(Buy the clothes you want her to wear in public. Bring flowers when you give the clothes to her. Tenderly dress her and later, just as tenderly, undress her; then make wild, passionate love, paying particular oral attention to her clitoris. And, not to worry, you aren't sick. Many men are aroused by the sight, or fantasy, of other men lusting after, or even making love to, their women. Men are erotic visualists, primarily aroused by what they see. But, you may not get her to go along with the flash-*

ing, at least not the first time up on the bar stool.) A lot
of my mail falls into the category of How Can I Get
Her/Him To Do What I Want? In one way or another,
I tell them: You have to give to get.

"I know I saw you on tel-e-vi-sion," the young
woman persisted.

You know what they say about Puerto Rican women:
They dress hot for the street, but act cool in the bedroom, because their men like it that way. In other
words, they are the flip side of the ideal WASP woman.
Or, so I hear. The women beside her looked back at me,
their interest growing. Suddenly I recognized them for
who they really were: typical members of an "Olive"
audience after a few months on Ultraslimfast. Recognizing the look of the judgmental woman in their eyes,
I began getting nervous. By this point, my accuser and
I had the attention of nearly everyone in that end of the
car. A motley crew, they looked back and forth from
one of us to the other. If she'd pulled a knife, they'd
have watched her stab me.

"I know it," she said firmly. "I am never wrong about
a face."

"You have me confused with someone else," I said,
stuffing the letter back into the gray envelope. My heart
was beating faster, and my palms were beginning to
sweat. I felt my neck begin to itch beneath the red,
black, and gold imitation Hermes scarf wrapped
around it. You never want to be identified as a woman
who likes sex, for whom sexual pleasure comes easy, in
any public place in America, unless security guards are
present. Americans get very angry at women who like
sex. You particularly do not want to be identified as
such on a subway train. "You're wrong," I said.

"No, I'm not," she insisted. The chime sounded; and
the doors closed, making a sucking noise. Eighteenth
Street. I debated getting out. I stayed in my seat. I

should have gotten out. "You were the one who got choked."

Looking straight ahead, I didn't say anything. I wanted to pull the scarf closer to my neck. Were the bruises showing? I wondered. I sat stiffly, feeling the sweat bead above my upper lip. Though I deliberately didn't focus my eyes on any of them, I knew they were watching me. I could smell their collective body temperature rising. The train squealed to a halt at 14th Street, one stop away from my destination. Should I get out here anyway? I should have gotten out, but I didn't. I was afraid someone would intuit that I was forced off the train before my stop by fear. Show fear, and they'll go after you.

"She was the one who got choked," the Puerto Rican woman said conversationally to the white woman beside her like they'd been chatting on a daily basis all their lives. I wiped the sweat away from my upper lip before it ran into my mouth, discreetly masking the swipe as a scratching of my nose. "She was, I don't remember, some kind of sex maniac. And this other woman, she went *loco* because *that* one"—out of the corner of my eye, I saw her finger pointed at me— "drove her *loco* with sex talk. And then this other woman, she choked *that* one!" Again, I had to dab my upper lip. My head was sweating, and I was afraid trickles would begin to pour down my face at any moment. "It was some show," she finished. "You didn't see it?"

"No," the woman replied, her eyes, like all the others, fastened on me.

"A sex maniac, huh?" said a white man clasping the strap almost directly over my head. He leered at my legs, encased in black stockings, exposed to almost mid-thigh in black leather miniskirt, my legs crossed high above the knee, Mary Hart fashion. "Whoa! How about that?" he said. The "Whoa" came out on a rush of bad breath; he didn't look like he'd been draining the city's water supplies with long hot showers lately. "I'm a sex maniac, too!"

The train pulled into my station, and I stood, pushed past him, and hurried toward the door. On my way out, I looked into the eyes of the Puerto Rican woman. She hated me.

"Whore!" she yelled. "Fucking high-class white whore!"

"Aren't you somebody?" the waitress at Caribe asked when she put the banana daiquiri down on the bar in front of me. Morgy laughed. "Sorry," said the waitress, tall, slender, Jamaican, and gorgeous, probably an aspiring actress or model or actress/model like most of the Village waitresses. She put another banana daiquiri down in front of Morgy. We removed the chunks of banana from the edges of the glasses. Morgy discarded hers, and I ate mine. "I guess everybody is *somebody*. Haven't I seen you somewhere?" she quizzed me. "In the movies?"

"No," I said through a mouthful of banana. "I come in here a lot."

"Oh," she said dubiously. "Sure. You want your privacy."

"Front page of the *Post* yesterday," the bartender said from the other end of the bar. He was coming back from the tiny hallway containing the two unisex johns and a phone. "The sex woman who got strangled on 'Olive.'"

"Oh," the waitress said, obviously disappointed, because she was savvy enough to know you don't have to be somebody to get on "Olive." She turned to the bartender and said, "Two more of these things for the couple down there," and went back to waiting tables. I love the West Village.

"I knew it was you right away as soon as I saw the picture," the bartender called. "I said to my buddy who was with me at the time, 'She's a regular at the restaurant. Can you believe it?' My buddy said, 'She almost wasn't a regular anywhere anymore.' "

He laughed, so I felt obliged to join him in a tepid chuckle.

"Well, Carolyn, you really did it this time," Morgy said in a perfect imitation of the line I usually give her when she's reached the crisis point in a romance, delivered the way Donna Reed spoke in that smarmy old TV sitcom, like words popping out of bubbles from the mouth. "Yes, you really did!"

She unbuttoned the jacket of her tastefully small-patterned black and white check suit, exposing the elegant red silk blouse beneath, kicked off her three-inch black and white spectator slings, and hooked her black stocking clad toes around the bar stool we'd left between us for Georges. Johnny, who was having new still photos made, was going to arrive last; we'd agreed to sit at the bar until Georges joined us where we would all drink banana daiquiris, specialty of the house, until Johnny got there when we would get a table. Johnny doesn't sit at bars. Leaving my shoes on, I put my feet on the other side of the bar stool so she and I were facing each other.

"We aren't going to talk about it anymore," I said. We had relentlessly analyzed every detail of the "Olive" episode in a two-hour phone conversation the day before, which was more time than we'd devoted to the meeting of Georges, if you can believe it. "I'm sick of the whole subject."

"Right," she agreed, casting a covert glance over my shoulder at the bartender who was conversing with the couple at the end of the bar. "They are all looking at us.

But, it's New York. Next week somebody else will be Dead Meat of the Week and you'll be forgotten."

"Thanks. I feel better."

"What are friends for?"

She took a huge sip of daiquiri. Morgy eats and drinks with wild abandon, yet remains a perfect size six. I have never seen another woman eat food the way Morgy does. She makes love to it, then devours it. I can imagine what she must be like with a penis in her mouth. I'm her only real female friend. Other women hate her, both for her ability to eat and drink without gaining weight and the effect she has on men. Morgy's face is so beautiful she renders the rest of us invisible to the male gaze. I took a smaller sip of my drink.

"Georges is titillated by this," she said. "He was afraid you'd cancel out of dinner tonight. When I told him you weren't, he goes, 'Oh, Morgan, that is so excellent!' *Excellent.*"

She put her first finger in front of her open mouth in the simulated gagging signal, normally reserved for her descriptions of first date experiences with the kind of men who would probably become devoted and adoring in two dates or less. They make her sick. She breaks dates with them or stands them up. Standing people up, usually men, but sometimes even women friends, is a bad habit we share. I have gone through periods lasting up to several weeks of standing up more men than I've actually met for dinner. You don't know the true meaning of the phrase "Feeling like a jerk" unless you've ever sat beside your answering machine listening to a man call for the third time from a restaurant pay phone asking what happened to you. Yes, we know it's passive-aggressive behavior. We've had therapy. And still I had the urge to slam bills on the counter to pay for our drinks, grab Morgy's arm, and drag her out of there. We could be quietly eating Italian food two blocks away by the time Georges arrived at Caribe.

"I want to hear him speak in French, but Georges loves our slang," she complained. "Does he think I'm dating him so I can talk to an American college kid?"

"Why are you dating him?" I asked.

"The same question could be asked of almost everyone either one of us has ever dated," she said, signaling the bartender for another round though I was only one-quarter down on my drink. "Remember the older man I dated who sat on the edge of the bed taking his pulse after sex? Or, Ron—we both dated him, remember?—who had a two-inch penis and a size triple large sexual ego?

"Georges is good in bed."

"Well, yes, that is a consideration," I said; we both laughed at the implied reminder of my lack of sex life. "I can remember when I dated men for sex. I can almost remember when I *had* sex."

Actually, I could remember very well. I'd had some wonderful sex, just not lately. Orgasmic ecstasy had ended for me at thirty-nine. There was Ray, whose exquisite technique of lightly flicking his tongue across my clitoris reminded me of being ravished by butterflies. And Gordon who ate pussy with so much relish he could leave even me limp from orally induced orgasms. And Jack, a much younger lover, who had surprised me the first time we were in bed by positioning himself so he could eat me out as he simultaneously angled his beautiful large penis into my mouth. Many men have tried to pull off that maneuver so adroitly, but few have succeeded. And, there was . . .

Shifting uncomfortably on my bar stool, I turned my attention back to Morgy. She was at the beginning with Georges. Her relationships are confined to two groups of men: "bad boys," men with dangerous drinking, drug, or sex habits who don't earn money but do spend hers, or "losers," men who lose substantial sums of other people's money, including hers, in entrepreneurial

schemes. These adventures in sex and adversity typically last less than six months and are followed by brief
celibate periods in which she verbally flagellates herself
for "being wild." Her two major love groups, which
sometimes overlap, have lately been composed largely
of Eurotrash, like Georges recently of Paris, Rome, and
Madrid, beach bums like the Portuguese sailor she
picked up on vacation in Bermuda, or garden-variety
users with strong manly profiles and the desire to be a
beach bum or have a Eurotrash accent, like the graphic
designer who cost her $10,000 last year. Her affairs
begin on a pheromone high. Initially, she says, "It's
only going to be sex. It's only going to be fun." Then,
she gets *involved*. Morgy has a lot of sex, the kind of
wild sex people assume I'm having, but I secretly think
she feels guilty about most of it. Why else would she get
involved with those guys? Why else submit herself to the
post-romance punishment cycle?

"It's getting intense with Georges," she said. "But,
I'm trying to keep things moving at a slower pace than
usual for me."

"Tornadoes move at a slower pace than you do."

"Right," she said, taking another huge sip of daiquiri
and holding it in her mouth before swallowing, the way
a smoker holds the smoke from a joint before exhaling.
"I'm learning at The Forum that I rush into relationships because I don't value myself enough. I give away
my power."

"And your money," I reminded her.

She nodded enthusiastically and launched into an
explanation of how giving away your money was part
of giving away your power was part of giving away
yourself. Or, something like that. Recently she'd fallen
victim to The Forum, Werner Erhard's new, improved
version of Est, the training that is "not an answer, but
an opening," "an inquiry into being human," and the
"path to excellence." Now she had her own new set of

buzz words, verbal playthings with which to impress
listeners with her newly acquired self-knowledge. I
wasn't impressed. In fact, I was only half-listening as
she said something about "the conversational tape
playing in my head that keeps me from achieving my
full potential," followed by how her "act," the way she
presented herself to the world, was keeping her down.
Or, holding her back. One or the other.

Less touchy-feely, primal-scream oriented than Est,
Forum is a philosophy of how to get more out of life
acceptable to baby boom professionals looking less for
inner serenity than a kinder, gentler version of the Gordon Gecko Creed from *Wall Street:* Greed is Good.
They encourage professional success at The Forum.
How else could you pay for all those seminars? At least,
she wasn't into something really disgusting like body
work.

"You aren't listening," Morgy accused. "You think
just because you dated a guy who did The Forum that
you know everything there is to know about it. You
don't. He did it wrong."

I nodded and continued not listening. Maybe he did
it wrong, and she was doing it right. But they both
sounded like they'd swallowed the same "conversational tape." Following the first "intense" weekend
seminar, in which the participants are allowed minimal
sleep opportunities and only periodic trips to the rest
room, the better to convince them they've had a tremendous experience because it feels so good when it's over,
the neophyte self-improvers signed up for additional
seminars and begin hounding all friends and acquaintances with expendable income to attend a Monday
night meeting as a "guest," subject to a high-intensity
sales pitch from a Forum group leader that makes a
Baptist revival preacher's "Come down to the altar and
take Jesus as your personal saviour!" look reserved. (I
know. He conned me into going with him once.) Yes,

the whole process had much in common with AA or a WWAWAW "commitment to life and purity" weekend.

"I wish you'd come with me as my guest to a meeting," she said for perhaps the fifth or sixth time in recent weeks. "You didn't give it a fair chance."

"I'll get my self-improvement for a few dollars from the women's magazines, thank you very much," I said.

"Anyway," I continued, changing the subject while her mouth was full of daiquiri, "I told you Tanya Truelust is dead, didn't I?" She nodded affirmatively. "There are rumors it wasn't an accidental fall, which is ridiculous, of course. But, it makes me feel more vulnerable knowing that Tanya Truelust met with an unpleasant end while I—and, is it a coincidence?—have received two death threats. Maybe a cosmic force is at work."

"You know the most interesting people, Carolyn," she said, patting the gray envelope next to my handbag on the bar and graciously relinquishing her new favorite subject for the moment. "Any good mail?"

"Another letter from Starred Man," I said, and she winced. Morgy was convinced he was going to break out of prison some day and come find me. I had real problems and she was focusing on the danger presented by a drooler behind bars. "I've only opened a few, but nothing particularly amusing yet."

"Let me peek," she said, and I magnanimously waved her on. I sipped delicately while she opened envelopes and scanned letters for something good. "Who are these women who don't do anal sex?" she asked. "I do anal sex. I always do anal sex. It happened right away with Georges. He sort of slipped it in that way without even asking, and now it's all he wants to do. I like it, but, I mean, something else would be nice, too."

"Uhmm," I said noncommittally. The bartender was hovering nearby; I'm sure he was eavesdropping.

"Okay," she said, waving a letter triumphantly, "here it is! I'll just read the good parts.

" 'Dear Superlady,' she began reading in a low voice rippling with suppressed laughter. " 'My husband is a foot fetishist. I have accepted this until now, but it's gotten worse, and I want to become pregnant. The problem is he only ejaculates on my feet. When we got married, he began lovemaking with my feet but moved into my pussy. Now, he has gotten lazy and just stops at the feet. What can I do to get him where I need him to be to make a baby?' " Morgy looked at me. "Well, Superlady, what are you going to tell her?"

"She has to bring her foot closer to her pussy, of course, and then maneuver him inside her before he ejaculates. What could be easier?"

"Divorce," Morgy said. She was already looking for another letter suitable for reading out loud.

"I'll also suggest sex therapy," I said.

"Carolyn," she said, "look at the envelope to Starred Man's letter."

She held it up in front of my face. And then I saw what had only registered subliminally when I'd opened his letter in the office. In place of the usual prison stamp in the right-hand corner was an ordinary postage stamp. His most recent letter had been mailed from somewhere other than the safe confines of a state prison.

"This wasn't mailed from the prison," she said. "He's *out!* And look it was mailed ten days ago. He could be sending you those death threats. The time frame works."

I took it from her and checked the postmark, Albany, where the prison was located. Maybe he gave it to a friendly guard to mail on the way home for him.

"You should have listened to Tim when he researched the pathology of sex criminals," she said.

"We don't know that Starred Man is a sex criminal.

He's never told me why he's in prison, Morg. Maybe he's an armed robber, not a sex criminal."

"Would he be writing to you if he wasn't? Look, you ignore Tim's research, because you think he's a geek, which he is, but, like, he does have some point to make. If Starred Man is a sexual deviant who's obsessed with you, which he clearly is, he may come after you as soon as he has a chance, which apparently now he does."

I was about to say something meant to reassure both of us when I felt a hand on my shoulder. Jerking away, I almost fell off the bar stool.

"Carolyn, darling," Georges said. "I'm so sorry to disconcert you. After what has happened to you on that television show, I should have never approached you from behind."

Surrounded by huge tropical trees in various stages of leaf loss, we were the kind of dinner foursome a charitable person labels "interesting," a mismatched and eccentric group largely speaking at, rather than to, each other. If I were going to do a modern art rendition of us, I would title it, *Egos at the Trough.* Georges, who radiates the kind of raw sexuality I associate with men who won't perform cunnilingus, peppered his speech with sexual innuendoes and foreign phrases in French, Spanish, and Italian. Morgy was so anxious for Georges to enjoy himself and make a better impression on me than he had the first time we'd dined together that she was babbling, much of it in Forumese.

More silent than usual, I was preoccupied with myself. Was Starred Man stalking the streets of New York or New Jersey in search of me? Could he possibly be responsible for the death threat letters? Did that couple at the next table recognize me? And was my scarf slipping? As his contribution to the evening's hilarity,

Johnny told a lot of corny jokes, always prefaced with, "Have you heard the one about . . . ?"

I met Johnny Badalamenti when I was sitting at a table near the stage one night at The Blue Note with my visiting nephew, the jazz aficionado. Johnny reminded me a little of Harrison Ford. I smiled at him a lot; he smiled back. He sweat profusely as he drummed. When he took a bow, he sprinkled me with the moisture from his brow, which, I'm embarrassed to admit, I found sexy. During their break, he sent me a note via a waitress. It read, "Do you ever go out with men your own age? If so, give me a call," and he'd put his phone number on it. Thoroughly charmed, I called him. That, however, was the only clever and original thing he ever said to me. Thirty minutes into our first conversation, I suspected he copied the idea from some other band member who'd once used it to pick up an older woman sitting with a younger man.

On our first date, we spent six and a half hours at Arturo's on West Houston where, after saying, "I knew you were thinking I looked like Harrison Ford; everybody tells me that," he told me the story of his life. He was forty-five, and he took both his life and the retelling of it one day at a time. The question I'm still asking myself: Why did we ever have a second date?

"Have you heard the one about the midget with the big balls?" Johnny asked, a forkful of jerk pork poised above his plate.

I had to smile encouragement, because no one else was listening to him. He launched into his joke, which he would conclude by saying ba-da-da while air-drumming. While smiling at him the way Nancy Reagan smiled at Ron, I listened to Morgy and Georges.

"All people are secretly afraid of rejection," Morgy said to Georges. "Do you know how liberating it is when you realize an entire roomful of people are just as secretly afraid of rejection as you are?"

"You know," he replied, "I once lived with a woman in France who wore her hair the way you do." Morgy's haircut is a short cap of blunt-cut hair shaped to her head with a full sweep of bang worn to the left. Is that French? "Utterly delightful, *mon chéri amour.*"

He took one of her hands and sandwiched it between both of his briefly, then lifted it to his lips and kissed. That would surely have her reaching for her wallet when the bill was presented.

". . . ba-da-da," Johnny finished, air-drumming the space between us.

"You'd understand me better if you came to a meeting with me," Johnny said again. "I know you think it's all about God, but it isn't. It's about a higher power. Your higher power can be the group. It can be a light bulb if you want. You just have to accept your own powerlessness and put your faith in the higher power."

He was pouting. We were in a cab headed toward a church on Bleecker Street where an open AA meeting was being held. Recovering alcoholics are allowed to bring guests to open meetings. Johnny had been a recovering alcoholic for five years, and he still attended five or six meetings a week. He knew this particular meeting was "open" because he'd excused himself during dinner to make a phone call to find out. While he was still on the phone, Morgy had excused herself to use the rest room, but she'd actually settled the bill with the waitress. Caribe only takes cash, and she hates to put down cash rather than her gold AmEx because she thinks cash embarrasses her dates. Gold cards send "clean, neutral messages," she says.

While Johnny and Morgy were both gone from the table, Georges had told me, "I've wanted to spank you from the moment I met you, Carolyn. Tell me you have been thinking of this, too."

I was whispering savagely to him, "I haven't been thinking of this at all," when Johnny and Morgy came back to the table. They didn't seem to notice anything awry. The four of us hugged goodbye like two suburban married couples and split for two separate cabs.

"I'm tired, Johnny," I said as our cabdriver gracefully swerved to avoid rear-ending another cab. "I'll drop you off at the meeting, then go to the PATH stop. It's been a long day."

"You know," he said, grasping my hand fervently, "we could have fallen into bed. That would have been the easy thing to do, but I want us to get to know each other. I want a relationship. Sex can get in the way. It can be an addiction like booze. It can mess up your mind and lead you into stinkin' thinkin' again."

"I understand," I said.

"I want you to know me," he said, but I already knew him.

I already knew, for example, after six months of sporadic sexless dating that he seethed with thwarted ambition. He was damned mad because Harrison Ford *was* Harrison Ford, and he wasn't. I also knew he swam at the Y daily to keep in shape, auditioned for bit parts in movies, and had recently acquired a library card and checked out only large print books because he could read them faster than the other books. More to the point, I didn't have to attend a meeting to hear his "drunkalogue," the story of how low he'd sunk before surrendering to his powerlessness over the bottle. He'd told me, and there wasn't much more to know about Johnny than this paltry accumulation of facts. I wanted to fuck him, but I didn't want to know any more about him.

"I'm flattered, Johnny, I really am," I said. "And I do want to know you, but not tonight."

The cabdriver pulled over in front of the church. Johnny kissed me passionately. Then, he leaped from the cab like a character in a movie which is, of course, what he wanted to be. I was left holding the tab.

The PATH (short for Port Authority Trans Hudson) is the subway running beneath the Hudson River connecting Manhattan with Jersey City and Hoboken. It's cleaner and generally considered safer than the New York subway. Its bell has a slightly different chime. Rarely do I feel uneasy riding it, but I did that night.

I cast surreptitious glances at the other riders, particularly the women. They were mostly wannabe Yuppies, probably entry level financial district workers, women who surely didn't watch "Olive." I relaxed a little. Then the thought occurred to me: They might watch "Olive" if they were home with the flu, and everybody reads the *Post* sometimes. Clutching my gray envelope of mail to my chest, I discreetly kept my eye on them.

I wasn't exactly depressed, but I was feeling subdued. And why not? A deranged right-wing woman had tried to strangle me on national TV. A pervert and fan was possibly out of prison. I'd been insulted by a young woman on a subway. My best friend's latest repulsive boyfriend harbored fantasies of spanking me. I'd received two letters threatening my life. A woman I knew slightly was dead in unpleasant circumstances. It would have been easy to make fun of Tanya/Julie dying because she was delinquent in paying her bills, but who hasn't been delinquent in paying their bills?

By the time I got off the PATH at Grove Street, I felt sufficiently paranoid to walk fast to the point of nearly sprinting until I was safely inside my apartment building on Wayne Street. Or was I safe here? Somehow someone had broken the sanctity of my double-locked building to leave one of his or her acid missives. I held my breath on the last stretch of stairs and didn't let it out until I'd opened my apartment door and found nothing waiting on the carpet for me.

Feeling as bad as I did, I knew there were only two things I could do to feel worse: eat an entire carton of deep fudge peanut butter Steve's Gourmet Ice Cream . . . or call Tim.

"How did that make you feel?" he asked me after I told him about the Puerto Rican woman who'd called me a "whore" on the subway.

"Unpopular," I said, sighing.

"That's good," he said, "that's real."

After a few more minutes of listening to him feel, I hung up the phone mid-feeling and ignored the immediate ringing afterward. I felt sick to my stomach. Maybe it was the banana daiquiris and conch fritters. No, it was Tim.

"I'm never going to talk to him again," I promised myself, and I kept the promise. I'm really very good at eliminating people from my life. According to my older siblings, nobody does it better or worse, depending on how you feel about the process of elimination.

Resolutely, I rewound the tape on my answering machine and played back my messages. David. Clarissa. My sister, Jenny.

And this one is a high, tight voice that could have been a woman's under duress or a man's if he were trying to sound like a woman. She, or he, said: "You are going to pay with your life. I will see to that. Don't think you will get away with what you have done, because you won't."

Chapter Five

━━━━━━━━━━━━━━━━━━

Dear Superlady of Sex,
  My boyfriend likes to do it to me before I wake up in the morning. He says I shouldn't mind because coming is a great way to wake up. What makes him think I come? What should I do about this little annoying habit of his?

Dear Sleepyhead,
  Unless you are faking in your sleep, I don't know why he would think you are having an orgasm. Maybe the orgasms you have with him are real snoozers, and he can't tell the difference, awake or asleep. This is not my idea of an annoying little habit. His forgetting to put the cap on the toothpaste is an annoying little habit. This is extremely selfish behavior. Tell him if he wants morning sex, he will have to wake your pussy first. And, insist he brush his teeth. Morning mouth is offensive everywhere.

I'd just added the "Morning mouth is offensive" line when Clarissa called. It had been a successful morning in which I'd pushed the afternoon's taping of "The Jeremy Mitchell Show" out of my head as I worked and also decided to dump Johnny Badalamenti before I did end up at an open AA meeting listening to numerous drunkalogues as long and monotonous as his, told by men who all end their stories with "ba-da-da." Sometimes Johnny didn't call for days anyway. He would barely notice he was being dumped, especially if he had a few good weeks where he happened to be walking past a lot of mirrors or clean and large plate glass windows, equally good at giving him back what he most needed from the world. I could keep putting him off until he had forgotten my phone number, a matter of weeks at most, probably more like days.

"What?" I asked irritably as soon as I recognized Clarissa's voice.

"You aren't going to believe this. Madame Zelda is dead."

She paused long enough for my brain to provide a cause of death. Heart attack. It had to be a heart attack. The author of *The Classy Call Girl's Guide To Pleasing Men,* the first modern sex guide, published in the late 60s, Zelda was America's first celebrity hooker. Her advice column, written for the past three years by Clarissa who didn't even run the copy past Zelda, had been in every issue of *Playhouse* since the magazine was born, accompanied by the original photo of her as blond, young, and gorgeous. In the last five years of her life, she'd doubled her body weight, shaved her head, given up men, and gone into a seclusion that was only interrupted by visits from lesbian lovers and her clients, the men she whipped. She was a dominatrix. Perhaps that had been too strenuous for an overweight woman.

"Well," Clarissa prodded, "aren't you going to ask for the details?"

I did, but Clarissa's details were sketchy. Zelda had been found dead in her hot tub, apparently drowned. End of details and on to the real issue: How does this affect Clarissa?

"Heart attack in the hot tub?" I asked.

"Do you think her column has to die with her? Like

I need that money, you know? Maybe Vinnie can keep it out of the papers. Wouldn't it embarrass the magazine? And who cares that a three hundred-pound lesbian dom with a shaved head died in her hot tub? As far as the world has to know, she was Stella Mae Parks, not Zelda. Zelda can't die. She's an institution." She paused and added meanly, "Not that you care. Now you'll be the new Queen of Sex Advice."

The call waiting signal beeped; knowing it was David, I told Clarissa I'd get back to her.

"She was cooked," he said. "Can you imagine that? Cooked. All that fat boiled. The man who tends the plants found her floating like a bright red beached whale." I closed my eyes, feeling momentarily nauseous. I'd been to Zelda's house, an A-frame overlooking the Hudson with a huge hot tub in the greenhouse. "It's disgusting, isn't it?" he asked.

"Was she alone when she died?"

"Rumor has it she'd been involved in a heavy S&M scene before the hot tubbing. Maybe whoever she'd been whipping left before they got into the tub or ran away in a panic after she got in and died. Apparently the combination of exertion, heat, and overweight killed her. There was also something wrong with the heating unit. The water was too hot."

I was relieved that I had to hang up to dress for television before David began to speculate on the temperature at which human flesh begins to cook. More the fool, I. What Olive had launched ten days before, Jeremy supplied with additional rocket fuel.

Dear Superlady of Sex,

For the longest time, my boyfriend asked me to suck him while he was driving on the freeway. I didn't want to do it because of the danger involved. What if he lost control of the car as well as his sexual responses? But I finally did. He loved it so much, he

*wants it every time we drive. Also, now he wants me
to not wear panties and put my feet up on the dash-
board, hike my skirt, and let the passing drivers see
me flashing them. Next he will want me to masturbate in the car. What do you say?*

"What will you tell her?" asked Tina, Jeremy's
makeup person, a skinny gum-popping brunette, early
twenties, with the kind of "high hair," large and teased
up, up, up, and away, favored by Staten Island and
Jersey girls. Her own makeup was minimal, except for
the kohl-lined eyes framed by lashes which had been
individually coated with some kind of miracle lengthening mascara. She was reading over my shoulder as she
applied my blusher. Was she using too much? Would I
look like I was highly embarrassed for the entire hour?

Jeremy's producer had asked me to bring some letters, "Not to read on air, of course, just for him to wave
at the camera during his intro of you." If I had to bring
them, I might as well be reading them and formulating
the answers in my mind.

"Yes, he will definitely want the masturbation scene
next," I said in reply to Tina's question. "And she
should not try this when the pavement is slick."

"Men! Do you get a lot of this sort of question?" She
dipped her fingers in gel she'd thinned with water and
attempted to create curls around my face. The tiny curls
began to go straight almost as soon as her fingers
moved away from them. Later, I would feel like a border of hair was glued to my face. "I'm glad I don't live
where you have to drive to get places. It's bad enough
they want you to fuck in the back of cabs. I can't see
having some guy's dick in my mouth while he's got my
life in his hands."

"A profound sentiment," I said, and she nodded
thoughtfully.

I tucked the letters back inside the gray envelope

before she started working on my eyes. Imagine being blinded by a mascara wand because the woman wielding it couldn't take *her* eyes off a letter from some guy in Omaha who wanted to know why his wife didn't like the way he ate her out.

Made-up in thick ivory pancake and lipstick the color of "an overripe watermelon," the shade I should always wear according to Tina, I winced at the sleaze king's intro to the show.

"Stay tuned for 'Crimes of Passion,' what some people have done for love or at least for what was considered love in their eyes."

Crimes of Passion? They'd told me the theme was "Fear of Sex." My hand went involuntarily to the lavender, green, and sapphire blue print scarf at my throat. Love? Letters in hand, Jeremy was beaming at me and the hand-holding middle-aged married couple to my left. I swallowed. The more benevolently a talk show host beams in the seconds preceding the first segment, the worse it's going to be for the guests. To my right, a large TV monitor was blank. It would soon be filled with the image of a man in prison, the fourth "guest." And, to the right of the screen, sat a woman, bleached blond, deeply tanned, and scrawny. By forty, she would be as wrinkled as a linen suit after being packed in a suitcase and sent to the wrong destination before finally arriving at your hotel twenty-four hours later. Men will be far less happy to see her than the suit. She was going to marry the man in prison via remote hook-up on live TV. Was this really legal? Could she be sane enough to enter into the state of wedlock? More importantly, what was I doing here? It was the all-purpose question of my life asked on dates, in front of TV cameras, and in the makeup chair.

"With us today," Jeremy said, as the commercial faded out, "is Carolyn Steele, the Superlady of Sex, an advice columnist for *Playhouse* magazine who very nearly lost her life recently in a crime of passion. This stack of letters in my hand is only a small sampling of the mail she gets each and every day from men and sometimes women, detailing their sexual obsessions from bondage to even kinkier, more painful pursuits. Carolyn, I know you don't mind if I share with our audience this fact. [*How* could he know that? Did he ask? No, not any more than he'd read the letters he waved, which from my quick perusal weren't particularly kinky at all!] That lovely scarf around your neck is hiding bruises made in an attempt on your life. I assume the marks must be about the same color as the silk, though probably not as bright—bruises, which attest to one woman's warped obsession with other people's passion.

"And, next to Carolyn, the Kleinfeldts, who made national headlines two years ago when she shot him in their marital bed. Obviously"—Jeremy paused to chuckle—"he survived the attack." The audience chimed in with their chuckles; the Kleinfeldts grinned and squeezed hands. They looked exactly like the typical middle-aged couple in next-door America: a little chubby, not fat; twinkling fondly, not passionately, at each other. Looking at them, you wouldn't guess either excited the other as much as the prospect of dinner and a solid night of favorite TV shows ahead.

"And finally," Jeremy continued, "Shelley Cornell, who will later be joined, through the miracle of modern technology, in holy matrimony to John Marshall, who is currently serving the third year in a six to twenty-five-year term in prison for the murder of his wife, Melanie. He killed her when he caught her in bed with another man. But he wouldn't have pulled the trigger, he said, if she hadn't told him, while wrapped in her lover's arms, 'You never gave me an orgasm. What was I supposed to do, not have one all my life?'

"Crimes of passion. Who commits them and why? We'll start with you, Carolyn, a victim. Just last week on the Olive Whitney show you suffered a vicious attack by another guest, and the Kleinfeldts and Shelley Cornell have assured us nothing like that will happen here!" He paused for the audience group chuckle. "A spokesperson for Women Worried About Wantonness Among Women was so inflamed by what she considered your anti-love, pro-sexual and licentious comments, she wanted to kill you.

"If you didn't see it, ladies and gentlemen, this is what happened on 'Olive.' "

Suddenly the TV monitor was filled with the same bug-eyed replay of events that had been on the news shows last week, with the line, "Courtesy of Popeye Productions," running across the bottom, bisecting my feet and ankles from the rest of me. Jeremy gasped. The audience gasped. The Kleinfeldts gasped. Shelley Cornell gasped. Each chiming in a beat behind the other, they sounded like a grade-school class doing a round of "Row, Row, Row Your Boat."

All eyes were on my scarf as the monitor dimmed and Jeremy asked in a hushed voice, "Can we see beneath your scarf?"

Give me credit for some dignity. I said, "No," and then he put forth his conspiracy theory.

"We understand your reticence," Jeremy soothed. "Perhaps later in the show," he said huskily, as if he were suggesting a private meeting in his dressing room when the theme music faded away for the day. Then, turning his back to me, he said to the audience, "The recent deaths of two former porn stars make us question whether or not the attack on Carolyn was an isolated incident. Was the attempted strangling of the

Superlady of Sex merely the freak reaction of one angry woman?

"Or, could it be in some way related to the deaths of Tanya Truelust and Madame Zelda, the Queen of Sex Advice, known around the world as the Classy Call Girl, who was only just this morning found dead in her home?" He briefly gave the known facts surrounding both deaths, then turned back to me and asked: "What about you, Carolyn? Do you think there's a connection?"

"No," I said firmly. "They were accidents. I cannot believe Elizabeth Thatcher or any of the women from WWAWAW would commit a premeditated murder."

Actually, I was lying. I *could* believe it, but I didn't.

Jeremy persisted. "But don't their deaths make you feel a little more vulnerable than you did before? Don't you feel like a highly visible target for anyone, or any terrorist group, bent on ridding America of what they call 'smut'?"

"No," I lied.

Mercifully, he moved on to the Kleinfeldts, who happily described, in medical detail, her shooting of him in the left buttock. She had been, she said, aiming for his penis, but she wasn't a very good shot.

"I was in terrible pain, but conscious," he said. "I reached for the phone to dial 911, but she pulled the plug on it just as I had the receiver in my hand."

"I started crying and telling him all the evidence I'd found proving his affair. Telephone bills. Credit card receipts. Her smell in his car. The usual things. I said, 'Do you dare deny it?' "

"I didn't," he said, "because she still had the gun in her hand, pointed at me."

"I asked him why," she said.

"I told her it was to see if the grass was greener on the other side, nothing serious. She shot me again. The bullet went through my side."

"I finally broke down and called 911 from the kitchen phone," she said, the tears in her eyes overflowing and cascading down cherubic cheeks, "when after half an hour I noticed there was a puddle of blood on the floor where he was dripping over the side of the mattress. I thought, 'He's almost dead. You have very nearly killed your husband here.'"

"I knew then," he said, "she still loved me after everything that had happened between us."

During the first commercial break, Shelley Cornell asked me to be her maid of honor since her best friend, waiting in the green room to perform the duty, had sent word by a producer's assistant she was "too shy" to go on. We had matching bouquets, sprays of pink, green, and mauve baby orchids entwined with fresh baby's breath and lacy fern. Shouldn't hers have been all white? A three-tiered wedding cake was placed on a table beside the Kleinfeldts who cast covetous glances at it. A second monitor was wheeled in so Shelley could see her almost husband and his best man, both attired in prison blues and needing haircuts, while the audience, at home and in the studio, could watch the entire proceedings on a split screen. A cameraman's wife sang, "We've Only Just Begun," in a surprisingly pleasant voice. The minister, a woman with a southern accent, skipped the preliminaries and went straight to the "Do yous?" as if she were presiding at the funeral of a deceased she'd never seen in life. When it was over, the bride and groom kissed the monitors before them. On the split screen, I saw their lips miss each other by inches.

Following the last commercial break before the end of the show, Jeremy's assistant cut the cake and began, with the help of aides, distributing it to the people onstage and in the audience. With a few minutes remaining, Jeremy returned to his conspiracy theory. As the credits rolled and the Kleinfeldts munched, he almost had me convinced that Tanya Truelust and Madame Zelda had been my very best friends in the whole world, and that their deaths under "mysterious circumstances" and the "attack" on my "life" were somehow linked in a plot to get *the women of porn*.

I shouldn't have been as surprised as I would be in the weeks ahead when the *Post* ran an ongoing "investigative" series of "the plot to pull the plug on the women of porn."

"I liked the way that couple, the Kinders or whatever, held hands all through the show," Tiffany Titters said, tossing the stray end of her hot pink feather boa back over her shoulder.

We were having a Women in Porn lunch at some bland Japanese restaurant in midtown where they had put us in a separate room from the other diners and made us take off our shoes and sit on the little flat straw mats. Stephanie, an exotic Oriental call girl with delicate features who also wrote erotic fiction, had chosen the location for the day. The members included: me; Stephanie; Tiffany; Clarissa; Vera, former porn star, who dabbled at directing X-rated films and ran a transformation salon with Tiffany where both men and women were taught how to become sexier women; Carola, the most successful former porn star turned video producer, whose motto is, "The VCR put porn where it really belongs, in people's bedrooms"; Gemma, another former porn star, now publisher of a group of magazines considerably raunchier than *Playhouse;* finally there's Bobby, of course. Bobby was a transvestite or TV and past "queen" of Au Chante, one of the famous houses portrayed in the documentary about transvestite balls, *Paris Is Burning.* According to the rules, David, the only man ever allowed except for

Bobby, had to leave after cocktails, because he could never be a member only an honored guest. No one ever questioned the right of Bobby, who looked better than we did, to belong to the group.

"It was sweet, don't you think?" Tiffany said of the Kleinfeldts' tabloid-style devotion, a subject I suspect she found safer for the moment than the obvious one, Zelda's death. "The power of love can do awesome things."

Adept at finding the sweetness in life, Tiffany sometimes, however, mistook saccharine for the real thing. She was the kind of person you'd think my older sisters back home would be: innocent, naive, simple, good, and trusting. My sisters aren't like that at all. In fact, I don't know a single woman over thirty in Easterville, my hometown, who does fit the description.

"Awesome," Bobby said reverentially, his eyes on Tiffany's breasts, which, though pendulous and drooping when released as they so often are, were encased in the sort of décolleté Liz Taylor favors, even if Taylor wouldn't likely choose the leopard print stretch mini dress Tiffany had chosen. Though Vera, her best friend and sister in porn, was his "transformation guide," Bobby clearly loved Tiffany best.

"The power of love," he added, patting his purse which looked like a tiny black patent leather lunch box. "Awesome. How else can you explain why that woman would marry a man in prison?"

"Nuttiness?" I asked.

The only "awesome" aspect of the Kleinfeldts' story was its theme of sex reversal, upon which Jeremy had not pounced. After she'd been arrested, tried, and convicted for attempting to murder him as "punishment" for his multiple affairs, he visited her every day of the three years she'd spent in prison and insisted they renew their wedding vows the evening of her release. They'd proudly shown Jeremy, and all of America, the photograph of him meeting her at the prison gate, her wedding dress in a clear plastic bag draped across his arm. Thanks to three years in the slammer away from her own homemade blintzes, she was able to get into it again. Granted, this is unusual behavior for a wronged male. However, women who've been nearly killed by spouses do that sort of standing by your tormentor thing all the time without making the news. As for Shelley Cornell, she unfortunately was not the first woman to marry a convicted criminal while he was in jail. If only I'd announced my engagement to Starred Man on the show, it would have been a perfect wedding theme day.

"I found the entire program quite distasteful," David sniffed. "The Kleinfeldts were the worst of it. Not only did she shoot him, she failed to call the paramedics for three hours. It's a miracle he lived."

"She cured him of his problem, didn't she?" Gemma asked, her eyes sparkling mischievously. Tall, blond, and shapely, Gemma, like the equally gorgeous brunette Carola, wore her hair closely cropped to her head. Could their severe hairstyles be a reaction against all those years of having long hair, the better to fit the male fantasy of womanhood? "That nasty little problem of keeping his pecker inside his pants. He doesn't have any trouble keeping it tucked away now, does he?"

"Maybe that's the part we didn't get on Jeremy," Stephanie interjected. "Maybe she shot him in the chest *and* the balls, and his pecker don't peck no more. Maybe he stood by her side because he couldn't get it up for anybody else after what she did to him. I don't think I'd be having sex this afternoon at four if someone had put a bullet into my twat."

Stephanie always referred to that section of her anatomy as her "twat" as in, often lately, "I have to have my twat zapped again," referring to treatment for a recurring STD. Her best customers, she said, hated to use condoms. David pretended to frown at our laughter. The waiter came in with our menus, and he stood up to leave.

"Maybe the Kinders are just more evolved than other people," Tiffany said. "If they can't have intercourse anymore, they might be having better sex than they ever did."

Tiffany, who believed she had elevated pornography to a feminist art form, considered herself "the Shirley MacLaine of porno." A practitioner of New Age Tantric sex, she considered "sexual spirituality" more important than fucking. I'm not sure what that means because I always zoned out when Tiffany tried to explain.

"Be careful," David whispered in my ear as he bent down to kiss my cheek in farewell. I knew he was worried about me because he always said, "Call me later; don't forget the juicy parts."

"I heard what he said," Bobby whispered loudly in the other ear, "and he's right. I wish Jeremy hadn't ended his show by saying, 'Carolyn, I hope this public attack hasn't made you a visible target for all the sex haters out there.'"

"Oooh," Clarissa said, wringing her hands. "You're right. He was almost, like you know, setting her up for every paranoid schizophrenic crazy person out there."

"Yes," Bobby said, "like she's wearing a sign now that says, 'Attack this woman if you believe in Jesus.'" He adjusted his cleavage beneath the purple knit dress he wore. We should all have cleavage as delicious as Bobby's. His augmentation surgery was a brilliant success, better than any I'd ever seen. Of course, the first few times I'd seen men who'd had breasts augmented and penises intact, I'd been too startled by the full effect to critique the boob job adequately. "If anything happens to her, it should be on the head of Jeremy." And with that, he prettily tossed his own head of red-blond curls that contrasted beautifully with his *café au lait* skin.

There was an uncomfortable silence as everyone except Rhumumba—and who in the hell had invited her?—appeared to be considering my possible death by unnatural causes. Probably she had tagged along with Clarissa, who'd been too polite, or intimidated, to refuse her admittance to our circle. She was only interested in the menu; in fact, she looked as if she might consume it if the waiter didn't soon return. The woman's aura, as Tiffany would put it, was sinister.

"It's those WWAWAWs I'm worried about," said Vera, who like David, testified before the Meese Commission and was our most politically active and astute member.

When asked by a senator if the publication *Vera in Tight Bondage* wouldn't encourage men to "brutalize" other women against their will, she'd parted her full red lips and replied: "Senator, my purpose in posing for the photographs was to explore my own bondage fantasies. I do not consider myself a victim. I think we should be free to explore our own fantasies." When he persisted with the questioning, she'd read him a poem, which had begun, "I am your love toy," and ended: "Through the purity of my surrender you become my captive too." As she read, her breasts heaved and the amethyst pendant resting in her cleavage sparkled, reflecting light back into the senator's glasses. I was there. David's testimony, following hers, got a lot less rapt attention from the gallery.

"I got a copy of their hit list," Vera said, pulling several stapled sets of paper out of her black canvas carryall. "We're all on it. I made a copy for everyone. Take one and pass it on."

"How literally do you mean the word 'hit'?" Gemma asked.

"I didn't think they meant it literally until that woman tried to strangle Carolyn," Vera said.

"She was probably a crazed lone gunman," I said. They all looked at me, but no one laughed. "You know, like J.F.K.'s killer."

"We got it, sweetie," Bobby said. "We just didn't want to, if you know what I mean."

The hit list was seven pages long and titled: *Groups Or Individuals Whose Existence Threatens The Sanctity Of The American Family And The Purity Of The American Woman.* And, yes, we, including the recently departed from among us, were all on it.

"I can't believe it," Tiffany said. "They don't know anything I've done lately. Listen to this, 'Got her name from her perverse specialty of stimulating her partners to orgasm between her breasts. Self-described as Queen of Kink. Prostitute.' It's a natural variation on a theme. 'Perverse!' They have no idea how many men want to come between a woman's breasts. It liberates them from the pressure of intercourse. Besides, that's in the past. And that's all they have to say about me? Nothing about my work in tantric sex, the transformation salon, my videos, photography, the—"

"I know," Vera said, cutting her off. "They have us packaged and labeled, as if we had no other dimensions beyond the most noticeable one. For me, of course, it's the bondage films. And Carolyn, sex advice. They don't acknowledge her work as a journalist at all."

"They could have sent for our curriculum vitae," I said, and they looked at me again. This was not an easy room to work. "Okay, let's chill out. I don't think these women really mean to kill us one by one," and here, I must admit, my eye wandered restlessly to the names, Tanya Truelust and Madame Zelda, "only to picket, boycott, or debate us into oblivion. I mean, really, they are, middle-class women in silk dresses after all."

"Never turn your back on a middle-class female fanatic in a silk dress," Gemma said, "but you're probably right. Let's order."

While we sipped wine and waited for food, Tiffany invited me to her book party in an East Village gallery. Her collection of erotic photography was being published in two weeks. I'd seen the photos for the section on male piercing; what is done to earlobes, noses, nipples, bellybuttons, and vaginal lips is also done to penises. But, not for Tiffany's book, the discreet ring through the foreskin. Her subjects had rows of decorative pins, most in the shape of fat needles, some studded with diamonds, from base to tip. Sex, Tiffany had explained, was no longer the point for these men. Or, the possibility?

"I'm using an actor in a video now who's high as a kite on coke most of the time," Carola said. "He's a sex machine, but he can't come, of course. Yesterday he asked me to bottle some of the fake 'come' for him for his own personal use. Now, you tell me if he ever comes with *anyone,* off-camera or on."

While she, Gemma, and Vera discussed the merits of various mixtures of fake "come," the frothy stuff which either enhances or substitutes for male ejaculate in the films, Tiffany told me her plans for a new series of workshops, the Goddess and Slut seminars.

"The point is," she said, "you can be a goddess or a slut depending on what you wear and how you fix your makeup. Nobody looks like a porn star. Porn stars are created, not born." Most days, Tiffany didn't look like a porn star herself. Her typical uniform was black tights in winter and beach thongs in summer, T-shirts with sayings like "Anarchy in high heels," and denim skirts. But no panties. Tiffany, like Marilyn Monroe, never wore underwear, which always made me wonder if she never had those days when the tampon leaks. "I'll take before and after Polaroids, which the participants get to keep," she added. "I want to demystify porn and also give women a sense of their inner goddesses."

Tiffany's porn had become a statement about porn, rather than porn itself. While I nibbled at my first course, something raw and fishy and wrapped around a glob of rice, she told me about a film she was making in which a genie would pop up in the bedroom while a couple was having "mechanical" sex to an old Tiffany Titters video. The genie, the new Tiffany, would show them how they could use tantric sex, health food, focusing energy, and belly dancing to put "meaning into that meaningless sex."

Meanwhile, Bobby was finishing a story I hadn't heard with the comment, "Really, I'd rather have sex by mutual masturbation than any other way now. I've swallowed so much come in my life, my insides must be bleached."

Everybody laughed. Even Rhumumba had a thin smile on her face as she dipped one fat index finger into a bowl of salty, fishy sauce. I watched her lick it clean. She worried me; she really did.

"Hey, Superlady, I got one for you," the cabdriver said. Our eyes locked in the rearview mirror. He was a white guy, unusual for a cabdriver in New York City, on the stout and grungy side. He smelled of stale tobacco, stale sweat, and staler ideas. "Didn't think I recognized you, did you? Saw you on TV. Never forget a face. Had a lot of celebrities in my cab.

"So, hey, I got one for you. It's a real situation. Friend of mine. His wife won't do it anymore since she found God. She could be one of those WWAWAWs you and Jeremy were talking about on the TV show.

He's beside himself with wanting to get it. Would you tell him it's okay to get it somewheres else being the circumstances are the way I've just described them?''

"Oh, absolutely," I said, suspecting I was giving him permission to cheat on his wife and hoping he didn't for a second fantasize it could be with me.

"That's exactly what I told him. Don't that beat all, you'd agree with me. Wait 'til I tell him that. It'll make him feel better. You've done a lot of good here today, I can tell you that."

I would also tell him: Shower, shave, deodorize, use mouthwash, lose thirty pounds, do sit-ups. Then, maybe your wife will decide God isn't a full-time lover after all. Why do men think it's okay if they're fat and smelly?

I was so relieved to get out of his cab at the PATH station on 23rd Street, I forgot to feel uncomfortable about being recognized until I got off the train in Jersey. Then, as I was hurrying along Grove Street past the newsstand and King Donut, I realized someone, taller and much heavier, was moving at an equally quick pace in an effort to keep up with me. When I turned the corner at Wayne Street, I saw him: mid-thirties, over six feet tall, heavyset, particularly in the gut, thin dirty-blond hair. He was wearing a cheap dark suit topped by a gray raincoat in a shiny polyester material, blue shirt, red print tie, black thick-soled shoes, the kind mailmen wear. He looked like a retired Secret Service agent.

And I'd seen him before, but where?

I didn't think about it for long after I got inside my apartment, because there was another message on the phone machine from my androgynous caller. All it said this time was: "Carolyn. . . ."

Chapter Six

●━━━━━━━━━━●

Dear Superlady of Sex,

Recently I discovered my boyfriend with a pair of my panties up to his nose. He was not checking out the quality of my fabric softener as these were dirty panties straight from the hamper in the bathroom. I was disgusted. He denied doing what I clearly saw him doing. And, he refuses to talk about it. What would make a man do such a sick and perverted thing? Is this as weird and unusual as I think it is? Is there any hope for our relationship?

Dear Hampered Relationship,

I have received dozens of letters from men who have a used panty fetish. They become aroused from sniffing those panties which have recently been close to the intimate flesh of a woman. Some of the men who write to me request my used panties for their personal enjoyment. Of course, I cannot respond to these requests. This is not a panty fulfillment center. Your boyfriend has responded to your disgust, however, by retreating into silence. Perhaps knowing more about fetishes would help you handle the situation. I recommend the book Love Maps *by Dr. John Money. He explains how some men who are sexually or psychologically damaged in childhood can only get in touch with their erotic selves through the use of a fetish, in this case, worn panties. This may be your boyfriend. Or, he may simply have an occasional urge to sniff panties. If you can approach him without disgust, perhaps he will be able to tell you how often and why he sniffs panties.*

I f I caught my boyfriend inhaling my underwear, I'd tear up his Rolodex card immediately after rushing him out of the apartment. That is not, however, an acceptable Superlady answer. I shut down the computer. Manuel would be arriving soon to take me out to dinner and, I fervently hoped, back home to bed. In another few weeks, I would be writing about sex purely as an uninvolved observer, the memory of "penile thrusting"—a phrase I once had to define for a *Ladies' Weekly* fact checker—only a dim one.

I missed intercourse. I missed cunnilingus and fellatio. My mouth watered with the desire to wet a penis and hungrily, tenderly embrace it with my lips and tongue. Sometimes at night I remembered sex play, like taking Roger's penis, Cocky, between my breasts, rubbing his silkiness against my skin, squeezing my breasts around him until he grew hard and the first drop of seminal fluid slipped out of him.

No one caresses my clitoris like I do, but there's more to a sex life than personal clitoral stimulation or "autoeroticism," as talk show hosts prefer. Lately, I had taken masturbation to a new high. After giving myself several orgasms, I felt a new peace, a clearer understanding of why I, and all of us, are so desperately seeking salvation, intimacy, and sexual release. At those moments, I felt I'd reached satori, the Zen Buddhist state of sudden enlightenment. Then I fell asleep and woke unable to remember exactly what I'd suddenly realized. So, masturbation was enlightening me, but the

effect lasted not as long as the feeling of fullness following a Chinese dinner.

I yearned for sexual contact with a male, for a penis
inside me and masculine arms around me. How I missed
Cocky, the best I'd ever known. Could the young
woman who had him now possibly appreciate him as
much as I did? Often, while tenderly touching myself, I
envisioned him, seven inches of glowing rose-pink flesh,
rising beneath me. His complexion turned a delicate
lavender when he was hard, which was often. I dubbed
him The Perfect Penis and used him as the model for my
Playhouse article of the same name.

But, I preferred my sexless dates to what Morgy had
with Georges. We'd just spent one hour on the phone
discussing *that,* following the hour I'd spent on the
phone with Clarissa trying to convince her I hadn't told
Jeremy that Stella Mae Parks was Madame Zelda and
Madame Zelda was dead. I hadn't. Jeremy had found
out about her on his own.

"I mean, give the man credit," I'd told Clarissa.
"Digging up dirt is his specialty."

"You planned this," she accused, "so you could be
the new Queen of Advice, when you know I desperately
want to keep Zelda alive. Why does she have to die with
Stella Mae? It's like they're twins, not the same person.
We're throwing her on top of the funeral pyre."

Finally, knowing this would silence her and induce
lingering guilt at the same time, I told her Starred Man
was out of prison. It worked. She was immediately
contrite, but as soon as I'd hung up with her, Morgy
had called.

"You're the expert," Morgy began, without asking if
there had been any more threats to my life. I knew she
was going to detail her new man's perversion for my
analysis.

Her last lover had worn a penis ring and would only
fuck her if her pubis had been cleanly shaved. When

she'd asked what I thought she should do, I'd said I thought she shouldn't do anything with him. I told her about the risk of contracting AIDS through broken skin, a distinct possibility when you fuck with penis rings or shave. She'd done it anyway.

"So, I want you to listen to this and tell me, like, is it really abnormal . . . or is he braver than most men in admitting his fantasies?" She cleared her throat in preparation for reading. "He came in and handed me this letter while I was taking a bubble bath last night," she explained.

Morgy had a huge pink and ivory marble tub, which I coveted. Fitted with a Jacuzzi, it was deep and wide enough for me to float, the kind of tub in which it is possible to have a true sensual experience or a good fuck. There was a skylight overhead and a surrounding marble ledge wide enough to hold all of her expensive bath oils, beads, bubbles, soaps, and creams. She could keep Georges. I wanted the tub.

"Okay," I said, encouraging her. "It can't be anything I haven't heard before. Read."

She read. He'd detailed everything he wanted to do with her, starting with "light slaps to the buttocks, leaving them rosy and quivering" and finishing with a wooden hairbrush. Not an uncommon fantasy until he got to the part about wanting to scrub her pussy with the bristles until she "screamed in orgasmic agony." That was something I hadn't heard before.

"Well?" she said.

"I'll never look at a hairbrush again in quite the same way."

"Is he that sick?"

"*Get out of it,* Morgy," I told her. "Get out of it *before* he hurts you."

After her tearful reading of his letter, she'd confided that the sex, sans vaginal brushing, was so good that she couldn't possibly get out of it, not just right now.

Though he didn't like it when she touched herself during intercourse to reach orgasm, he hadn't minded when she clasped her thighs around his and vigorously squeezed herself to orgasm after he was finished. He'd even laughed, she said, at the stickiness when they'd pulled apart. Georges—what a sport!

How does she find these guys? Why does a powerful businesswoman allow herself to be dominated by a man who couldn't touch her in hand-to-hand corporate combat? Inevitably I asked the questions, which always led me to other questions.

What do any of us find so compelling in the unsuitable, and often downright distasteful, men we pursue? My own collection of geeks, losers, men who fear sex and embrace therapy, all the self-involved and noncommittal men of my recent past is matched by the assortments assembled by my friends, though Morgy's choices are a few degrees worse than ours. Are we using them to punish ourselves? Or, do these men truly represent all that's left for us after a certain age?

My friend, Claudia, once sent me a card picturing a collection of unappetizing men hanging from wire coat hangers on a mark-down rack. Inside, she wrote: "At this point in life, you fuck down or you don't fuck."

Remembering the futile conversation with Morgy, I sighed. Thinking about my own sex life, or lack thereof, I sighed again, more loudly this time. I was not exactly happy with my life. Maybe the problem was my work. I was sure I would have been happier writing long profiles for *Vanity Fair* about the rich and famous, many of whom dabble in S&M discreetly and most of whom have fucked indiscriminately in their prime. Doesn't the same perversion as described by Dominick Dunne and practiced by expensively clad characters sound more interesting and less tacky than it does in letters from *Playhouse* readers, whom we assume are not rich and/or famous?

Upscale panty sniffers are, after all, breathing the mists from only the finest scented silk. The stories Stephanie, Tiffany, and Zelda had told me about the sexual proclivities of the "beautiful people" would shock the devotee of gossip columns which name names and describe dresses in lush detail. Politicians, movie stars, models, designers—they whip and are whipped, dressed in the softest leather bondage gear. Male and female, they've had so much anal sex it's surprising they aren't all dead of AIDS or at least unable to hold their feces inside their bodies. They do things even I have to look up in the *Encyclopedia of Erotic Wisdom.* But they have cachet. Georges, that little piece of Eurotrash who reminded me of a greasy food wrapper littering the street, had more class than Starred Man.

Resisting the urge to sigh again, I wandered around the apartment, picking off dead leaves from trees, straightening magazines on the coffee table so their edges were perfectly parallel to one another. If I didn't get laid soon, I would turn into an anal retentive—or was that anal compulsive?—personality, one of those people who tidies a room to death. With a tissue pulled out of my pocket, I dusted the head of my bronze penis statue, the first piece of art I'd ever purchased.

I love my penis, which stands about six inches tall and has a delicate flapper girl from the twenties riding his balls, her arms wrapped adoringly around him, her cheeks resting on his head. And, ironically, I found it back home in a tiny antique shop across the river in St. Louis, where I successfully bargained the price down from the $800 tag to $400 cash.

I remember clutching my penis to my chest in a brown paper bag and dashing into a restaurant where I was meeting my sisters for lunch the very afternoon I'd bought it. Proudly, I showed them my treasure, a unique signed bronze casting from the Art Nouveau period. Surely, they would see the wit in the sculptor's splendid work. Well, they were aghast, mortified as the waitress, giggling, asked, "Life-size, isn't it? Don't you wish they all were?"

"How disgusting," Billie Ann, the oldest, said, while Jenny Lee blushed her disapproval. Then they, who are shaped somewhat like Chinese steamed dumplings, asked me, almost in unison, if I'd been putting on weight. Had they asked "Why are you trying to shock us?," I would have been impressed by them for a change. In my family, no one says what they mean, which makes conversation more interesting afterward when you're alone and can dissect it than when it's actually taking place. And no one, except me, ever talks about sex. Are my sisters orgasmic? I don't know.

Never mind, penis, darling, I love you. I patted his head. Restlessly, I went back to the mail. Letters from women who couldn't have orgasms. Letters from men who loved women who couldn't have orgasms. Letters from men who were cheating on women who couldn't have orgasms. Letters from men who blamed themselves because women couldn't have orgasms. Sometimes I think the American woman is inorgasmic by definition. Letters from religious nuts and sexual perverts. I picked them up and let them fall back down on the desk, pieces of the twisted American psyche, our legacy from those religious zealots who stole the country from the Indians.

Think about it. Would you have fled the relative comfort of civilization in Europe to spend weeks—or was it months?—on a fusty leaky boat with people who'd never heard of deodorant soap, headed toward an uncertain future so you could be "free" to live life as a Puritan, perhaps spending large chunks of your new life in the stocks as punishment for minor transgressions? Puritans were so named because they wanted to purify the Church of England, which was too spiritually lax for them. These people were goofballs, and we're only a few generations away from Early Goofball ourselves.

The buzzer sounded. Manuel, a man not even descended from the Puritans. What was his excuse?

"Caro, querida," Manuel said softly, the lilting musical quality of his voice the only aural giveaway to his Puerto Rican ancestry. His English was better than mine. He brought my hand to his lips, dragging my sleeve through my paella. Tenderly he kissed my fingers. *"Querida,"* he sighed.

"Manuel," I said, taking my hand back and brushing grains of rice off my sleeve with my napkin. I was wearing a black silk minidress, with a discreetly plunging neckline that stopped at the top of the cleavage, and full sleeves, which I thought conveyed a hint of modesty. I'd covered my bruises with Dermablend, the makeup women use to hide varicose veins. In a dark restaurant, it had worked. My earrings were designer originals, bought from a Soho artist, little connected strands of multicolored beads, alternated with black metal arrows, gold stars, and silver moons. They tinkled when I talked. "This isn't working anymore," I said irritably.

"What isn't working anymore, *caro?* Don't you like the food?"

"The food is wonderful, darling. I'm not talking about the food." Truthfully, I was no longer thrilled by his deft ordering in Spanish. I was beginning to suspect he kept coming back to this Spanish café with its predictable white stucco walls, black wrought iron fixtures, and red tile floors because his command of the menu's native language gave him an excuse for placing "the lady's" order. "I'm tired of having only my hand kissed," I snapped.

"I thought you loved having your hand kissed," he

said sadly. I noticed the space between his middle front teeth, almost big enough to spit through, as they say in southern Illinois. And he was short, probably two or three inches shorter than the 5′7″ he claimed to be. Short men lie about their height the way women over thirty-five lie about their age.

"Only if there's the real possibility it will lead to a kiss to my lower parts later on."

"Caro," he said; he was actually blushing.

"I've made you blush again."

"It's just that you say things Spanish girls would never say. It's refreshing! I like it!" He looked nervously around at the people seated near us. "But it sometimes makes me a little nervous," he whispered. "I've never known a woman like you. Spanish girls—"

"Manuel," I said firmly, hoping to stave off another attack on Spanish girls, particularly his ex-wife, who was apparently the ultimate Spanish girl. They didn't, according to Manuel, have sex for the last five years of their marriage. Yet, he was shocked when she left him, pregnant with her lover's child. He hadn't, he swore, had sex with anyone else during those five years. How could she betray him by going to bed with another man? And what had he done about his sexual needs for five years? Masturbated, or so he said.

"Manuel," I repeated. "We have to talk."

"Of course, *querida,* we will talk about anything you like. Why are you looking at me so strangely?"

There was something different in his voice when he lowered it. The more softly he spoke, the more he sounded, yes, like a woman. Could his voice have been the one on my answering machine? After all, it is an unlisted number.

"No," I said. "Not *talk*. That's not what I really meant. We have to do something other than talk and kiss hands. What's wrong with you, Manuel? What's wrong with me? I'm a sex writer, and I can't get laid. This is ridiculous."

"Is it me you want then, *querida,* or merely the conquest?"

"The conquest?"

"I think you confuse your life with your work. You think, because you are a sex writer, you must have sex."

There it was, that androgynous note in his voice again. What had he told me when he'd first read my column in *Playhouse?* Something about his "concern" for my safety if I continued to "provoke" people by writing that way? Had he actually said, "Someone might make you pay for what they perceive to be a commission of sin." Or did I only remember him saying it now?

"No, I would think I must have sex if I wrote a column on orchid growing," I said.

"I don't know about that, *querida.* All this constant studying of one thing must have its impact on your mind." He reached over the paella and stroked the back of my hand with his finger. Could this tiny little man with the gentle touch be sending me threatening letters? "I worry about you. Your career almost got you killed. I can't believe what you do is worth dying for."

"Remember the Transit Authority worker who was killed in the token booth last month in a robbery? Was selling subway tokens worth dying for? I'm tired of having what I do for a living put down."

"I'm not putting you down, *querida.* I know in my heart that you have many conflicts about your work yourself. Don't blame me for expressing what is held silently in your heart."

I shoved a forkful of rice and shrimp into my mouth before I could sigh or say something that would let him know what kind of man I was beginning to suspect he could be.

Then he asked, "Why are you in this business anyway?"

The question was his version of "What's a nice girl like you doing in a place like this?" I'd answered it before: money, freedom, I like sex, I'm comfortable with sex, why not sex, what's wrong with sex.

I wasn't going to answer it again.

Dating Manuel was like stepping back into adolescence. I was sixteen again in Easterville where Daddy insisted my dates come inside, shake hands, and promise to return me safely before midnight. Manuel picked me up, opened the car door for me, drove me home, opened the car door again, and didn't fuck me. I didn't even know another man in the New York City area who drove a car. Typically, we made out until the windows fogged before he walked me to my front door, where I almost expected to find my father's ghost waiting inside, looking at his watch.

"Caro," he sighed, turning off the engine in front of the former church with Corinthian columns which was now a community center and frequent site of Alcoholics Anonymous and Narcotics Anonymous meetings. It was, however, dark that night. "I desire you so much, my *querida,"* he said huskily, putting his arm across the back of the seat, inviting me into his arms.

"Manuel, you can have what you want," I said, snuggling closer to him. His scent was both orange spicy and sweet, like Constant Comment tea, only sharper. "Why don't we go inside?"

"No one will bother us out here. I'm a brother," he said, lifting my chin with his finger, the way they do it in old movies, the better to kiss my lips. "Uhm," he murmured, as he kissed me softly at first, his lips like butterfly wings floating across my own. Then, gently he parted my lips with his tongue. After kissing and sucking each individual lip as though it were the source of life's honey, he thrust inside me, fucking my mouth with his tongue.

Manuel could kiss, but, to tell you the truth, his penis (the one time I experienced it) was a disappointment. I touched it, through his pants, in the backseat of a cab in the West Village, on our first date after we'd seen Spanish director Pedro Almodovar's film, *Matador.* We were kissing and suddenly I put my hand on his crotch, only to discover his short, thin penis standing hard at attention like a little boy whose short legs stuck straight out to the edge of his baby chair. It seemed eager, excited, like it wanted me to take it out for a romp. He'd tensed in shocked surprise, then taken my hand from his lap and brought it to his lips for the first of those interminable hand kisses.

We tell men penis size doesn't matter, but it does. The best position for a small penis is me flat on my back, legs up and braced against his shoulders. From that vantage point, he can thrust without falling out too often. The problem with little penises is the fallout factor, and I hate being distracted by having to worry about keeping it in. Big ones, on the other hand, require some forethought before you make a move. Like Goldilocks, I don't want them too big or too small, but just right. Given the choice between big and small, I will take big.

I didn't reach for his penis in the car parked in front of the church on Wayne Street. Instead, I put my hand between my legs, squeezing my thighs around it as Manuel kissed me. With my thumb, I massaged my clit. Holding me by the shoulders, he kissed and kissed and kissed; I reached orgasm in a matter of seconds.

Is this man secretly gay? Does he hate women? Fear us? Or is he only afraid of sex?

* * *

Walking up the steps, admiring as I always did, the beauty of the halls, I knew it was over with Manuel. He was beginning to give me what my sisters would call "the creeps." There was something not quite sane about his dating me when he disapproved of me. Yes, there was something not quite sane about me allowing it to happen. No more. The third man out, not down, in less than a month. I was alone. I had no one. But who and what had I had when I'd had these guys in my life?

The phone was ringing as I inserted the first of three keys into the three locks of my apartment door. By the time I got inside, David's voice was on the answering machine. I picked up.

"You were monitoring your calls?" he asked.

"No. I just got in from my last dinner date with Manuel."

"No sex again? It's time you dumped him. He's probably gay."

"Uhmm," I said noncommittally. I wasn't ready to admit my suspicions though I surely would next time I was on the couch in David's office. Don't women always accuse the men who don't want to sleep with us of being gay?

"I was out walking the dog," David said, "when I picked up the early edition of the *Post*. It's one of the advantages of not living in Jersey," he reminded me.

"I'm not sure getting first peek at the *Post* is a real-life advantage," I said, not for the first time either.

"You might change your mind and hop on a PATH train tonight so you can see this for yourself," he said. "May I read?"

"Please," I said, kicking off my high heels and sinking to the floor, where I could listen from my favorite phone position, flat on my back, legs raised and crossed at the knees. "Do read."

"This article is labeled the first of an ongoing investigative series on the plot to pull the plug on the women of porn, written by the hot-shit new columnist Barry Renfrew. Got that?"

"Fucking Christ!"

"Yes, well, between you good sisters of the pink, he may be the only man you *haven't* fucked."

Then, all joking finally aside, he read me the following Page Three story:

IS THERE A PLOT TO PULL THE PLUG ON THE PRETTIES OF PORN?

It's not often the Post *takes its cues from Jeremy Mitchell, but a recent Jeremy show inspired these questions:*

Was the death of Tanya Truelust truly an accident?

Was the death of Madame Zelda another accident?

Tanya Truelust, alias Julie Beckman, died in a fall from her own fire escape when the heel of one four-inch-high backless shoe caught in the open grillwork of a step. The former porn star turned video producer lost her balance and fell eight stories to her death. Insiders say she was hurrying down the fire escape which served as the "back door" of her X-rated video production company office in Chelsea to avoid creditors in the waiting room. Tanya was noted for her exuberant orgasms in the 130 films she made. Reportedly, her company was in financial trouble.

Not two weeks later, Madame Zelda, alias Stella Mae Parks, was found dead floating in her hot tub in her upstate New York mansion by the gardener. Few connected the three-hundred-pound and bright red corpse of Stella with the legendary blond beauty whose photo graced her monthly advice column in Playhouse *magazine. Author of* The Classy Call Girl's Guide to Pleasing Men, *Zelda, a former prostitute, had in recent years gained a great deal of weight and worked exclusively as a dominatrice, whose male clients pay for the pleasures of being whipped and humiliated. Cause of death was attributed to heart attack possibly induced by her weight and the failure of a heat pump in the hot tub.*

According to the gardener, "Steam was rising from the tub, and she looked like a cooked lobster. It was a terrible thing to find in the morning." When told of her real identity and her career, he said, "She was a quiet private person who kept to herself. I am much surprised."

Perhaps the deaths of two of porn's most famous female names coming within days of each other are nothing but a coincidence. But, the Post *has learned that yet another of porn's former pretties met a sudden and violent end in the past several months. La Passionata, alias Domina Rodriguez, starred in thirty-seven X-rated flicks, including the best-selling title of 1988,* Hot Girls in Chains. *Bondage films were her specialty. She was able to convey sensuality while only able to heave her bosom.*

Six months ago La Passionata was found dead in the garage of her boyfriend's Fort Lee, New Jersey, home. Her charred body had been tightly bound. The death, his defense claims, was a bondage accident, which, in panic, he'd tried to cover by moving her body to the garage and setting it afire.

But in his one and only statement to authorities, Spiker claimed not to know what happened to La Passionata on the night of her death. "We had a glass of wine, and I passed out. When I came to, the garage was on fire and she was gone."

Fort Lee authorities didn't accept his version of

*the story, and he was charged with second degree
murder. His trial begins Monday.*

*Is there a connection between the deaths of La
Passionata, Madame Zelda, and Tanya Truelust?
Could Anthony Spiker be telling the truth? Could
someone else have been in his house that night while
he was passed out? The possibility that a plot against
the women of porn exists is given added credence by
the reported threats on the life of Carolyn Steele,
Playhouse magazine's Superlady of Sex and heiress
apparent to Zelda's crown, who was choked nearly
to death by an enraged antiporner on Olive Whitney's show recently.*

*Is someone out to get these women? I mean to find
out.*

"Well," David said, clearing his throat. "Awesome,
isn't it, how they can turn something into nothing?
They've made a patchwork sow's ear out of three unrelated silk purses."

"I never even met La Passionata," I said. "How long
has she been out of the life?"

"Several years. Her last film, the one that hit big, sat
in a can for a few years before it was released in 1988.
The distributor ran out of money, sold his company to
someone else, and it was resurrected. Last I heard she
was a housewife in New Jersey. Apparently she got
divorced, since the article doesn't mention a husband."

We talked for several more minutes. After we said
goodbye, I kept my finger on the phone, holding the
receiver in one hand, deciding whom I should call when
I released the little lever. I let it go. The dial tone
sounded. I listened to it for several seconds before hanging up the phone.

I called no man with whom I was, however peripherally, involved. This was, as Tim would say, "new behav-

ior" for me. Instead, I played back my messages. While I was gone, Vinnie had called.

"Carolyn," his distinctive voice boomed from the machine. "I have good news for you. I want you in my office tomorrow morning at eleven. Dress to meet the media. I've scheduled a press conference for you and me at noon. Then, we'll have lunch."

Obviously, I was going to be crowned.

I was thinking about that when I heard the faintest rustle. The envelope slid slowly under the door like a snake which had flattened itself out. Mesmerized, I watched it. Why didn't I run to the door, throw open the locks, and chase after my tormentor? I was unable to move, terrified by this latest invasion. Manuel?

After what seemed an hour but must have been only a few minutes, I walked down the hallway and picked up the envelope. My fingers were shaking as I tore open letter number three, composed as before of glossy letters on cheap typing paper.

"You do not listen, and you will pay with your life."

her," he said, instead. "I bowed over my notepaper while I was gone, which she noted.

"'Yes, ma'am,'" an older policewoman's voice boomed from the machine. "'I once took her for a ride. I paid you in my place tomorrow evening at eleven. That is what she need.' I've absolved Simon somehow. If you and me agreed on that, then we'll have it all."

"Anyway," I was going to be saying.

I said the King aloud, that when I faced the future run on. I told people and slowly, under the clear filter. I might, quick and furious, as if real. As practiced, I swept it away, until I was in the most uncomfortable look, and clean after my humiliation. I was unable to know, fretted by this larger invasion. I forgot.

"After I was served an form bill must have been only a few minutes," I waited. I sat in the hallway and picked up the small phone list. I got the wonder as I laid out my other dinner time, composed. As I went out near his key lies on a dish. I look there.

"I'm doing alone, and you will go with your duty?"

Part Two

SEX EQUALS DEATH

Chapter Seven

●━━━━━━━━━━━━━━━━━●

"I hate having my picture taken," I told Charles, running my finger along his wrist as I spoke.

His skin was velvety, dark and rich and thick, black man's skin. Touching it was a pleasure. We were sitting side by side on his bed, our backs against the headboard, legs outstretched, so that we only had to face each other and slide down to be in position to fuck.

"Uhmm," I said, moving closer to him and nuzzling his neck.

He put his arm around me and massaged my neck and shoulders with one hand. His fingers were surprisingly strong. I wanted to take off my clothes and see what he could do with them on the rest of my body.

I liked the way he smelled, the mixture of dark skin, a green scented soap, and YSL. Liking a man's smell is important to me. It is not politically correct to say so, but black skin does smell and feel different. I love the difference. He was the most touchable man I'd been near in a long time; I had been touching him all day, stroking his arm, rubbing his back, making the physical overtures he hadn't been making. Charles's approach to seduction—lie back like a sleek cat and let her do it— may have been dictated by the fact we'd met while he was working or by the racial difference, but, I guessed, it was more likely his sexual style.

"Uhmm," I repeated, looking up at him.

The pitch of his breathing had changed, his eyes were melting into mine. Charles had the sexiest eyes set in the most serious and proper face. You could swim in his eyes; it would be exactly like wading into a muddy creek back home, warm and welcomingly oozing up into all your body crevices. I loved those eyes. I even liked his bald head. I wanted to see the top of it glittering with sweat between my thighs. It had been so long, a year almost; I didn't feel like I could wait much longer.

"I know you hate having your picture taken," he said, touching my chin with his other hand. "I knew that right away."

Charles was a free-lance photographer. He appeared to be somewhere between thirty and fifty. Who could tell with such beautiful unwrinkled skin? Vinnie had hired him to shoot the press conference that morning because Vinnie liked to have official shots of everything. He wanted "only the best" photographs for our "family" photo album. Charles would no doubt make me look a lot better than any photographer from the tabloids.

"You better get used to having your picture taken," he said. "You're gonna get your picture taken a lot more often now."

"You have beautiful skin," I told him, as I unbuttoned the top two buttons of his shirt and stroked his fine skin with my finger.

I didn't want to think about hate mail and crazy people. I didn't want to think about how my new status increased my visibility and, possibly, my risk factor. I didn't want to think about the proliferation of Carolyn Steele faces in tabloids across America. Still shots are somehow so much worse than being on TV, where you can look bad one moment, but enchanting the next, depending on the camera angle, with no single frozen facial expression identifying you in the minds of millions forevermore. I prefer being a moving target, but I didn't want to think about any of that. I felt special, safe, and secure in Charles's arms. Maybe it was an illusion, but that's what I felt.

"Your skin is like velvet, so luxurious," I whispered in his ear before I licked it.

"I know," he said. "And, I don't do anything to make it nice. I'm just lucky."

Maybe this should have been my first clue, but it wasn't, not at the time. Such moments are only heavy with portent in retrospect, when we relentlessly analyze everything the former beloved did, searching for the first hints of the fatal flaws which had eventually surfaced. His black cat leaped upon the bed and settled on his lap, eyeing me warily. I wasn't making too much of the fact we were sitting on the bed after having met that morning. In some New York apartments, the bed is often the only place to sit, and this was one of them. I wasn't making too much of it, but I was hopeful Charles would do what is considered the obvious thing to do with a woman on a bed in most parts of the country.

He had a one-bedroom apartment in Chelsea, but the living room was filled with photographic equipment, still and video, a computer, several file cabinets, and the general detritus of a small business. The bedroom was the natural choice for guest seating, and there were no chairs. Only a king-sized bed, teak dresser, an overstuffed walk-in closet with the door standing open, two televisions, some editing equipment, and a black enameled Japanese screen printed with bright red flowers blocking the windows that were probably barred and grimy. Magazines on scuba diving and photography were the only reading material in either room.

"How does it feel to be the Queen of Sex Advice?" he asked, smiling slightly. From the vantage point of hindsight, was it sardonically?

"Silly," I told him, and it really did.

At least the centerfold of the month can justify her title by her body. What did being the Queen of Sex Advice mean in measurable job terms? That I could look up the answers in Kinsey, Masters and Johnson, et al., to any sex question faster than the next writer? That I didn't mind saying "penis" or "cock," for that matter, in print or aloud?

"You must intimidate a lot of men," he said, pressing his lips against my hairline.

"Do I intimidate you?"

I straightened out my legs and leaned back against the pillows and closer into him. His sheets and pillowcases were a tasteful navy and maroon print, with which I happened to coordinate nicely. I was still wearing the buttery soft lavender leather suit I'd selected for the press conference that morning. Women back home have belts wider than this skirt was long. My panty hose, the only underwear I had on, were a deeper shade of lavender. I had, of course, kicked off my yet deeper lavender heels. Lying on the floor beside the bed, they looked like something Tiffany might have worn to a funeral.

"Do I look intimidated?" he asked, grinning.

He put his hand on my thigh, and the fingers curved possessively around my flesh. My breath came faster. Before climbing onto the bed, he'd removed his socks and shoes; his feet, I suddenly noticed, were as long and slender as his hands. He was tall, thin, elegant, and graceful. His penis, I imagined, was average length, but would look longer because it would be thin, as lean as he was, a glowing ebony godhead preceding him in nakedness. I could picture it shiny with drops of seminal fluid on its regal head prior to entering me. If he'd kept his hand on my thigh much longer, I might have written an epic poem to it, sight unseen.

"No. You don't look intimidated. That's what I like best about you."

I knew as Charles caressed my thigh with his long sensitive fingers we were going to have sex that night . . . and I would be in love with him by morning. I was a little bit there already. Maybe I was falling in love with him because at last I'd found a man who wasn't putting off the sex until I'd listened to every sentence of every paragraph of every chapter of his life story.

Whatever the reason, the soft, erotic pressure of his fingers on my flesh switched off the part of my brain which typically registers, caustically remarks upon, and then catalogues the unacceptable behaviors of men. It's an evaluation process continually taking place even when I'm not letting it stop me from trying to get them into my bed. With other men, I carry on this running critical dialogue in my head listing what is wrong as I smile, nod sweetly, and undo my top buttons. Mentally, I don't let them get away with one false word. With Charles, I allowed the batteries in the bullshit detector to run completely down. I was smiling, nodding sweetly, and breathing deeply, the better to show my already visible cleavage . . . and not thinking at all, except about his penis.

"Babe," he said, moving his lips farther down my hairline, against my ear.

Yes, he called me "*babe*." What would you call a woman who'd allowed herself to be picked up at her own press conference, then dragged along on two other photo shoots? You wouldn't call someone who watched a man perform his work "Ms.," would you? I mean, what about my work? Or, what about discussing my precarious life situation before it became more so with Vinnie's P. I.? All forgotten. I'd hurried out the door with Charles.

Briefly, I wondered if Vinnie would forgive me for cancelling out on lunch with him, and if anyone else had ever left him alone with his sushi in favor of leaving with someone he'd hired to do a job. At least I would always have the memory of him, his mouth open, the bright lobby lights bouncing off his gold chains as I said, "Another time."

"Babe," Charles repeated. He called me "*babe*," and I didn't bristle, that's how much trouble I was already in. "What would you like for dinner? Do you want to go out, order in, or shall I cook for you?"

"Uhmm," I said, closing my eyes, after I had surreptitiously checked out the large framed photo on his dresser. *Mother*. She looked like him, down to the wire-rimmed glasses, but she had hair. "Cook for me."

In one fluid motion, he was on top of me. I didn't open my eyes, but my mouth reached instinctively for his and found it. He kissed me long and slowly, his tongue probing me; I felt the heat of his body on top of mine opening me up. He slid down, squeaking against the leather, until his chin was resting on my pubic bone. Buffered by the leather, he gently ground into me, then raised my skirt with both hands and kissed me through the lavender panty hose, which were already damp from wanting him. My throat closed up.

"I am going to slave over a hot stove for you," he said, his own voice higher than it had been as he raised himself up on his elbows to look into my eyes.

Not trusting my voice, I nodded. I opened my arms, and he moved back up my body to hold me. We kissed again, our eyes open this time, because we needed to see inside each other before we made love. After we stopped kissing, I took his face in my hands and kissed each eyelid, then ran my tongue down each side of his face from the corner of his eye to his chin.

"If I don't get up now, we aren't going to have dinner," he said.

He went into the kitchen, and I went to the bathroom, where I sopped up some of the excess moisture with a tissue. The litter box, I noted, needed to be changed.

Something happened in the kitchen. It made me feel like a cat whose tail has suddenly swollen to twice its normal size. Something spooked me. Was it something he said, or I did? Was it the way he said something I perhaps didn't want to hear anyway? I don't know. It's happened to me in the past. Suddenly I want a man so much and, with equal passion, I am sure he won't want me back. Things are said to me; reading more or less into them than was actually meant, I say things back, which I don't mean at all. I look back later and can't remember the words, only the confusion and the feelings of overwhelming desire and fear of rejection washing over me like shame.

Whatever happened, I wasn't being the woman I wanted to be nor the woman I really was. My invisible swollen tail stood out from my body, creating a force field around me. I wanted to let him in, but I couldn't even believe he wanted to be there. Across the room, a thin knife glinting in his hand as he worked, he had to feel the emotional frisson I was creating around me; no, around the two of us.

He was preparing shrimp scampi (with not nearly enough garlic), rice, and a salad; he wouldn't let me help.

"Have a seat," he'd said when I came from the bathroom, indicating a stool next to the breakfast counter across from where he was deveining shrimp at the sink. He turned back to his task. From the back and clothed, he looked like an Armani model.

"I poured you a glass of wine while you were in the bathroom."

I picked up the goblet of white wine and sipped. A

good chardonnay, my favorite. His kitchen was compact, black and white, galley style. He had a stacked washer and dryer unit of which I was covetous. I walked from the fourth floor to the basement with my laundry basket. He was going to put raddichio in the salad. I could have guessed that within thirty seconds of meeting him. Maybe I was frightened by all this domesticity.

"How long have you lived in this apartment?" I asked, a typical New York question. If you know when someone moved into a place, you can gauge what they paid for it or, if they're renting, the amount of rent they pay.

"Twenty-four years. Since I first came to New York. I'm the most stable guy I know. I've had the same phone number for twenty-four years."

"Oh," I said. What do you say to that? Is stability really a function of one's phone number? "So, you must be older than you look."

"Forty-five. Do I look that old?"

"No, not nearly," I told him, and he preened. The man was vain, but I didn't care. He didn't look forty-five, and I wanted him. "Have you been a photographer since you came here?"

What I really wanted to know was: *Why aren't you married?*

Isn't that what women always want to understand about the man we instinctively know we'll want and never be able to have? Every woman has dated this elusive male at least once in her life. Handsome, successful, charming, he cooks dinner, sends flowers, gives her the first orgasm via cunnilingus. Spend a few hours alone with him and he'll tell you how much he wants to find the "right" woman, marry, and raise a family. Charles had told me over lunch that he wasn't married, had never been married, and wanted nothing more than to be married and have children. Men seduce with words; this particular configuration of words is a popular one.

"I don't get that much out of sex anymore," he'd said. "Sex doesn't mean anything to me unless I think there's a possibility I might be making a baby."

Have you ever heard a better sexual challenge to a woman than that? It's on par with her announcing to him, "Don't try to give me an orgasm. I've never had one. I never will. Just go ahead and enjoy yourself and don't mind me."

"I've done everything there is to do sexually with a woman," he'd said. "Now I want to settle down with the ideal woman and have the whole package, the house in the country, the kids, the station wagon."

Then *why isn't he married?* Excuse me, but there is no shortage of wonderful women, only of wonderful men. How could he not have found one? I didn't want to get married; I only wanted to get laid. But when faced with the elusive male, I was like a woman standing at the bottom of the stairs ready to dive when the bride tosses her bouquet. Catch those wilted flowers now; analyze your motives later. Charles was adept at creating this frenzied mood in a woman.

"Yes," he said. "I've been a photographer since I dropped out of college in my last year. I was studying engineering."

"I can't see you as an engineer," I said. The cat had entered the kitchen and was rubbing against my foot. I reached down to pet him, and he moved away.

"I couldn't see me as an engineer either, so I quit. The photography had always been a hobby. I thought, Why not try it? What have I got to lose?" Without looking behind him, he'd sensed the cat and flipped a raw shrimp onto the black and white tiled floor for him. "I had a few lean years, but it's been pretty good for me since the beginning."

He'd told me at lunch he'd worked for five years as

a fashion photographer. I asked him, "Did you sleep with the models?"

"Yes," he said, turning around to grin at me. "I slept with a lot of models. Photographers and models. Shit like that happens all the time."

He washed his hands after deveining the shrimp and poured more wine into my glass. I opened my arms and he walked into them. As he nuzzled my neck, I looked past the top of his head at the bowl of pink glistening shrimp. For a second, they resembled miniature mounds of pulsating vulvas, the liquid flesh of many beautiful women he'd had before me. I was intimidated.

"You smell nice," he said. "What is that scent?"

"Chloe."

"I knew it," he said with satisfaction. Of course, he did.

"I don't cook."

Laughing, he said, "I don't know many women who do, especially white women. I learned how to cook when I was living with a white woman. I figured we were going to starve if I didn't."

We ate the shrimp and salad on his bed, black-rimmed white stoneware plates balanced on our laps, the bread basket between us, while he talked about what he wanted in his life. Why do women spend so much of our time listening to men talk about what they want in life? Maybe it's because we still tend to forget our wants and needs when we're around them.

Anyway, he wanted, he said, a woman who could be lover, best friend, partner, mother, father, sister, brother—but he didn't want to commit to her until she'd proven her ability to get pregnant. He wanted children, he said, because he didn't want to grow old alone. Children, I wanted to tell him, determinedly biting down on the advice as I bit into shrimp, won't necessarily take care of you in your old age, and they certainly can't keep you from feeling lonely. Children, I wanted to tell him, aren't the idealized beings of your romantic fantasies.

"You could always adopt."

"It wouldn't be the same," he said, brushing the idea off as if it were a discarded shrimp tail. "I want the experience of having my own."

"I don't understand why you haven't found someone to marry," I said, picking up a leaf of lettuce with my fingers. I like picking up food not meant to be eaten with fingers. Cold pasta can be a sensual experience. "It seems to me a good relationship with someone you love is the best hedge against loneliness, whether you're old or young, or have children or don't."

Who would have guessed I'd be standing up for the old-fashioned way: Marry the woman you love and then have the babies.

"They didn't want to have kids," he said, breaking off a piece of the French baguette and sparingly buttering it. "A lot of women are selfish. They don't want to mess up their bodies or take time out from their careers or they think they're too old now."

If they were my age, they were too old. Don't tell me about the joys of motherhood over forty. I don't care how many celebrity older mothers make the cover of *People* magazine, I don't buy the concept. I had my babies at eighteen and nineteen, and I'd delighted in the little darlings every step of the way. Now, they were both studying in Europe; the daughter in Paris, the son at Oxford, where they were mercifully spared the story of their mother's climb to the top of the sex advice mountain. Few children grow up with the dream of their very own mother replacing Madame Zelda in the hearts and minds of men who want to know how to get their wives to have sex with another man while they watch, preferably with video cam in hand.

"I must know a dozen quality women in their thirties bemoaning their ticking biological clocks," I said.

"There's something wrong with the ones I meet. I've met a lot of crazy women."

"You could surely find someone sane enough to have a baby with you. Maybe you won't get the life partnership of your dreams, but it isn't like that for most of us anyway. My marriage didn't work, but the kids turned out great. We had joint custody. It can be done," I said, curling my tongue around a shrimp.

"You were lucky."

Why did I let him get away with that? Luck had nothing to do with it. We'd made it work. Why didn't I call him on his phony, romantic idealism over the raddichio which could have used more fresh cracked pepper? He wasn't married because he is an incurable "romantic," ever in search of the perfect woman, who can elicit the perfect emotion inside of him, thus making him the perfect man. Idealism is a powerful shield against intimacy. Why didn't I say that instead of murmuring in a falsely reassuring tone of voice, "Well, maybe someday you'll get everything you want," as if he were a child who was expecting the electronic game store to relocate to his bedroom on Christmas morning?

"Maybe I scare women off, because I jump right in," he said, wiping the shrimp butter from his mouth with one of those thick paper napkins that almost feel like cloth. "I meet a woman and if she has everything I want, I say, 'Let's make a baby together.'"

"It won't do you any good to say that to me. I had a tubal ten years ago."

"Can it be reversed?"

I didn't answer. He put the nearly empty plates on the floor and unbuttoned my leather suit jacket. If he needed to believe in the possibility of babies, let him believe. I wanted him so much then I would have agreed to babies, the house in the country, the station wagon, anything. I ached for him inside. Dimly through the delicious pain of wanting, I knew it was time to reach for the condoms. Where had I left my handbag?

"I love your breasts," he said, his voice catching in his throat as his hands lovingly encircled them. "They're perfect."

He took my left nipple into his mouth and gently sucked as he reached around my waist for the snap on my skirt. I raised my hips; he pulled down the leather and the panty hose at once.

"You've got a bitchin' body."

Not taking his eyes off my breasts, he sat on the edge of the bed and removed his shirt. No chest hair. I love chest hair, but I wasn't disappointed in his sleekness anyway. Then he stood and took off his pants and red bikini briefs; there it was, exposed, standing straight out in front of him like the Washington monument lying on its side. It was the biggest penis I'd ever seen. The standard-size condoms I carried at all times, just in case, would never have fit him anyway.

"Oh, my God," I said. It would surely measure ten inches, maybe more, a number many *Playhouse* readers claimed to reach on the yardstick, though statistically speaking, few of them really could. "Oh, my, God," I repeated. "It's magnificent."

"Is it more than you expected?" he asked, grinning.

"It's huge," I said, reaching for it as it was coming toward me at eye level. "We should use something," I said, my voice lacking conviction. No wonder he ignored my one veiled reference to condoms.

He straddled my chest and massaged my breasts while I took roughly the first third of him into my mouth. I sucked briefly, then holding his penis in my hands, plunged my face into his pubic hair and inhaled his scent. I ran my tongue experimentally up and down the shaft of his penis.

"Is it really big?" he asked, his voice a little strained. "Well, you should know. You're the expert. I always thought it was just average."

Right. I took him back into my mouth, pulling him deeper as he fondled my breasts; his hands were like velvet gloves smoothing the skin in lines radiating out from my nipples. Flicking my tongue around the head of his penis, I felt his body convulse. I thought he was going to come in my mouth. I wanted him to come in my mouth, wanted to taste and swallow his semen, but he pulled out and moved down my body. Gently he spread my legs open, then parted my vaginal lips with two fingers he'd dampened in his own mouth. As soon as he put his tongue on my clitoris, I was gone. My first orgasm came in waves around him.

"God, you're something," he whispered.

He pulled me up so that we were sitting in the center of the bed facing each other, my legs over his. Grasping my buttocks, he pushed into me. I moaned with pleasure. I had never been so filled by a man; it felt wonderful. I held onto his shoulders as he plunged in and out of me. Again, his body convulsed, and he pulled out.

"Touch yourself," he said. "Come for me. I want to watch you come."

I leaned back against the pillows, my legs open and bent at the knees. He sat still in the middle of the bed and watched as I put my hand against my own vagina.

"Come for me, babe," he said.

I wet my fingers in the juices and touched myself. Raptly, he watched as I masturbated. I kept my eyes on his face as I pulled the first orgasm out with my fingertips offering it to him. He was panting.

"Again, babe," he whispered. "Come again."

This time I arched my back, throwing my head back so I couldn't see his face. I lost myself in another orgasm, this one a long shuddering spasm that he broke when he pulled my hips off the bed and pushed into me. He thrust slowly and so deeply he seemed to penetrate my soul. I came again, biting his shoulder; this time he couldn't stop himself. I felt his ejaculation strong inside me. His whole body convulsed in spasm in time with his penile contractions. I came again. He pressed hard into me, to feel my orgasm, and covered my mouth with his.

"The trouble is," he said, after we had lain silently in each other's arms for several minutes, "I'm going to want more."

More what? More *of* me? More *than* me? I chose to believe he meant the latter, and it hurt. I nourished the hurt, letting it help me build a distance between us following the lovemaking.

Is it me or does my profession inspire sexual confessions from my lovers?

We napped in each other's arms for an hour or so. When I woke, he was still sleeping, but within seconds he opened his eyes and smiled at me. I felt a stirring in my groin and a corresponding movement in his penis which was lying against my thigh. I am a petite woman. It was lying against most of the length of my thigh.

"My work makes it hard to have a relationship," he said. "Sometimes I'm on the road three and a half weeks out of four."

"Uh-huh," I said, then cleared my throat. "Look, we've had sex once. It's a little soon to talk about a relationship anyway. I hate that word relationship."

It's true. I did. I do. It's also not true that I wasn't already thinking about having one with him.

"I know," he said. Was there anything he didn't know?

"You know," I said, "we're like the meeting of the

myths. You and your big black penis, the ultimate stereotype of the black male, and me, the sex writer."

"Yeah," he said, stroking my cheek. "Were you disappointed?"

"Not at all. Were you?"

Why did he dispense with the reassurances so quickly I can't remember exactly what they were? Or was he wonderfully reassuring, but I've chosen to forget his words? I don't know. I can't remember.

Somehow we plunged into his sexual history before I could even feel good about his sexual present and, hopefully, short-term at least, his sexual future. He enumerated the major women in his life for me. Dianne, black, educated, sophisticated, beautiful, smart, successful, married to someone else. When she finally left her husband for him, it was too late; his love for her, gone. Dianne came after the six-year living-together relationship with Mindy, the Jewish artist, who inspired him to take up cooking. She had followed the promiscuous period—not that he was faithful to Mindy in the not so promiscuous period he shared her bed—which had followed a love relationship with a young white woman, ending in her aborting his child, his "only" child. After Dianne, Barbara, white twentysomething, also married.

"She's married," he said. "She doesn't want kids. It ended. There hasn't been anyone serious since then. I can get a sense of what women want quickly. They haven't wanted kids."

I licked his nipple. It was so black, it was almost blue. What was I supposed to tell him now that it was my turn to share sexual details? Well, babe, there was Tim, the geek, who wouldn't fuck me; Johnny, the dry drunk, who wouldn't fuck me; Manuel, the possibly gay and undoubtedly repressed Latin non-lover, who wouldn't fuck me; of course, Roger, who left me for someone almost as young as my daughter.

"Dianne was the love of my life," he said, "and my sexual obsession. We were obsessed with each other sexually. She's still after me, but all she wants to do is sit on my dick."

"She must have a very long vagina."

He laughed and hugged me close to him. I guided his penis inside me; lying side by side, with my leg thrown over his hip, we made love again.

"I'm going out to get the morning papers," he said. "See what your press coverage looks like."

I groaned and pulled the sheet up to my chin. It wasn't morning. It was only a little after midnight. He pulled on his clothes, slipped his bare feet into topsiders.

"It's December out there," I reminded him.

"Only goin' a few blocks, babe."

"The morning papers really could wait until morning," I said.

He kissed me and tousled my hair. His eyes had that still familiar (despite all these months of celibacy) glazed expression of a man in deep lust. I sighed happily.

While he was gone, I replayed the morning conversation with Vinnie in my head.

"I want you to take a more public role in representing and promoting *Playhouse,* Carolyn," he'd said, sitting beside me on the gray leather sofa, his hand encircling my wrist. "It's good for the magazine to have a woman out there now. You're good for the magazine. I don't want you to worry about those letters and phone calls. I've got a good man on it. We'll find out who's responsible, take it to the police, and press charges."

I hadn't asked him if Zelda had gotten letters like mine and, if she had, why hadn't they discovered who was behind it before it got to be my turn? And we hadn't talked dollars, but he'd implied they'd be substantially more than I was getting now. It would be left to David to get the figure from him and report it to me. Or, not report it to me. Typically, I knew about my raises when I got my check because David had forgotten to tell me.

"You made front page of the *Post*, babe," Charles called from the entrance door, "but you're not going to like it."

"The picture's that bad?"

"Picture's okay," he said, standing in the bedroom door. "Not as good as the ones I took, but not bad." He held it up. At least my eyes were open wide, so the droopy left lid didn't make me look drunk. "Read the headline."

"SUPERLADY—NEXT PORN PRETTY TO DIE????"

"No. I don't like it."

"I knew that."

Chapter Eight

Dear Superlady of Sex,
Can you help me with an embarrassing problem?
I am nineteen years old, but have very large sex
organs. My testicles are about the size of eggs, and
my penis is just at eleven inches and appears to be
still growing. And the problem is even though I don't
get full erections, I keep ejaculating just walking
down the street and standing at the workplace. I have
tried wearing a condom, but they are too tight and
not long enough and leave me sore and red. My
question is, how much more will I grow? And could
I take a female hormone to stop me from ejaculating
so much?

This was almost certainly a phony letter. If it were real, then the writer had no concept of how to use a measuring tape and also had a severe case of premature ejaculation. People ask how I can tell the fakes when the real ones are often so bizarre. I just can. After reading the mail for a week, I could tell. The prose of the jokers resonates with their self-congratulatory chuckling. Sometimes I answer the fakes anyway because they give me an opportunity to be more wicked than I would be with a genuinely confused and troubled soul. *(How much more will your penis grow, son? Reread*

Pinocchio *for clues.*) I put this letter in a folder marked "Possibles," which I saved for the day when the mail ran dry.

Thanks to the tabloids, would my mail ever run dry?

The morning *Post* reported I'd been receiving threatening mail for several months. They failed to add, however, the threats emanated from antiporn women's groups, both from the left and the right. Instead they made it sound as if I were in danger of being snuffed out by some poor panty sniffer, a man too timid in real life to come from behind his hamper.

"Ms. Steele is cooperating with authorities," the article said, which was news to me; I saw me sexually surrendering to a burly young man in blue, not necessarily bad news.

It was the day after the press conference, the day after I had been well and truly fucked. I was catching up with real life: the mail, phone messages, the water requirements of my plants. Dressed in black leggings, a large white sweatshirt, white socks, and tennis shoes, I did not look every inch the Superlady of Sex, but, for the first time in many months, I felt it. I was happy in the way one can only be happy following a night of great sex.

I was luxuriating in the sensual memories, but, physically removed from his intoxicating presence, I wasn't kidding myself about the man who had inspired them. He said he wasn't "involved" with anyone. I'd counted five different brands of shampoo or conditioner in his bathroom, which seemed excessive for a man with so little hair. And what did he do with that can of mousse and tube of gel? A great lover makes you feel like the only woman in the world; in his bed, I felt that way. Afterward, I counted the hair products and told myself, "You know what the bathroom clutter means."

Also, he'd rushed me out of his apartment by 8:30

A.M., claiming his assistant would be coming in by nine. I knew his "assistant" had to be a young and gorgeous woman he'd fucked or was fucking or had once and, after a brief intermission during which she'd hoped to push him into a commitment by withholding, was again fucking. I was falling in love, but not blindly. I saw exactly where I was headed as I allowed myself to tumble off the parapet into the moat filled with snapping crocodiles, all male, with their huge, spiny penises, unsheathed by condoms, menacingly exposed.

The phone had been ringing when I'd come in the door at 9:00 A.M., but I'd ignored it and headed straight for the shower. Now I had to deal with the twenty-two phone messages: five from David, becoming increasingly irritable as he repeatedly asked, "Where are you?" And "I'm respecting your need for space, but I'm here if you need me," from Tim, the geek, as if I'd ever have any use for the geek again. *Women Today* and *Bluebook* had both, "regretfully," killed the stories I was doing for them. Vinnie had better be increasing my salary by a significant percentage or the loss of the ladies' mags would put me in the hole. And, everyone from Morgy to my sisters was desperately trying to reach me.

I was just going to pick up the phone and return David's calls first when it rang beneath my fingertips.

"Where have you been?" he demanded. "It isn't like you to disappear without telling me. I know you were out all night, because I called at three in the morning."

"I was with that gorgeous photographer Charles." He *knew* that. If he'd called at three in the morning, it was only to determine whether or not a presumed afternoon delight had turned into an all-nighter. "How did you know I was out all night?" I asked. "I could have come home at 3:10 A.M. Doesn't Peggy (his wife) object to you calling female friends in the middle of the night?"

"The black one?" As if he didn't know! "I wouldn't

call him 'gorgeous.' He's too thin, and he has less hair than I do. And you know Peggy is completely without jealous feelings. Besides, she egged me on while I was dialing. You finally got laid?''

"Yes and yes," I said happily.

"He looked like a star fucker. Really, Carolyn, you're going to have to be more careful about whom you pick up now that you're famous."

"Oh, please! I'm not a star." I could see David smiling, his feet propped on the desk, his eyes on the entrance to HMV, smug at having gotten me to respond on cue. "He's not a star fucker. He's had a slew of models in his past."

"Was it good? Is he hung?"

"It was incredible. He *is* enormous. All these years I've been telling people that Kinsey says the average black penis is only point two centimeters longer than the average white penis. Last night I personally found the stereotype every white man fears exists inside a black man's pants. I love his big penis. How did I ever get by with less?"

"Typical woman, you say you don't care about penis size until a big one comes along."

"Yes," I agreed. "You're right. I'm doomed to spend the rest of my life comparing every one I meet to Charles's."

"Hmm," he said. David had often told me he is "the standard six, the best size, and proud of it." Oh, ha. Secretly, or not so secretly, every man wants to be a ten. "I'm glad you enjoyed yourself since your days appear to be numbered."

"You would have to bring that up. How long do you think they're going to keep this story alive?"

"Until there's a verdict in the La Passionata case. It makes better copy to imply a link between the three deaths and your imminent demise, which brings me to the purpose of this call."

"I thought you were calling to see if Charles had a big black penis."

"I assumed he didn't have a big white penis, Carolyn."

"Is there such a thing?"

"You're going to be insufferable if you get laid on a regular basis again, especially by this black super stud," he said, sighing theatrically. "Enough about your sex life. I have a wonderful story idea for you. I want you to write a piece for the magazine on La Passionata's death. Was it an accident? Or, murder? If he gets off, will he be getting away with murder? If he gets convicted, will it be because the jury is punishing him for his sexual perversity? It would give you a chance to do some real journalism. You could attend a few sessions of the trial, then interview all the key witnesses on your own, talk to the bondage expert for the defense, some shrink from the Violent Crimes Unit of the FBI."

"And it would be great publicity because the press would cover me covering this story."

"Right."

"Vinnie would love it," I said, getting straight to the point.

"Right." There was a pause while he gave me a brief chance to refuse the assignment. When I didn't, he asked, "Is it true what they say about black men?"

"Not true. He performs cunnilingus with skill and enthusiasm."

While I listened to David lecture on the statistical odds of a stereotype being true or not, I looked up Charles's number in the phone book. I sort of slid past David's condom question, but I don't think he was fooled. When he said goodbye, I pressed down the phone button until I heard the dial tone, then punched in Charles's number.

"Charles Reed Productions," a young and gorgeous-sounding woman said. "How may I help you?"

"Cathy," I said breathlessly as if I were searching through stacks of folders and piles of scrap paper on my desk for the precise piece of information I needed to share with her, "I believe we talked about prices yesterday for the Carlton shoot."

"I don't remember that," she said. "If you'll tell me what you need again, I'll be happy to go over the price list with you. My name is Barbara, not Cathy."

"Oh," I gasped. "Here it is. Wrong number!"

I hung up the phone. *Barbara.* The same Barbara who is white, twentysomething, married to someone else, and doesn't want kids, particularly one would assume, little half-black kids?

I closed my eyes and remembered him saying, "It ended. There hasn't been anyone serious since."

Resolutely, I opened my eyes again and looked back at the computer screen. Was it the same Barbara? Had he hired her before or after the affair began? Had it really ended? Would I ever know the answers to these questions and others?

At least, I knew just the letter I wanted to answer next and pulled it from the stack of recently opened mail on my desk.

Dear Superlady of Sex,
I'm sure my wife is having an affair with her boss. She has begun wearing her sexiest lingerie to work, including sometimes garter belt with no panties, which I have to beg her to wear for me. I pretend not to be paying attention while she dresses in the morning, but, believe me, I am watching. Also, she is working later and later. Do you think my suspicions are well-founded? Last week I drove past her office while she was working late. Her car and his were the only ones left in the lot. At the company holiday party, where spouses are invited, she and her boss seemed to have special eyes for each other. I've

asked her if something is fishy there, but she says no.
How can I make her tell me the truth?

Faithful Husband

Dear Faithful Husband,
   Unless you are the sort who continually suspects
your partner of infidelity with one man or another,
you are probably right in assuming she's having an
affair or is, at the very least, quite sexually attracted
to her boss. Spouses either know these things about
each other or suppress the knowledge. She's not
going to "confess" until she's ready.

You can't make anyone tell you the truth, babe.
I paused. Should I include a mini lecture on STDs?

   If she is practicing sex without a condom, Old
Faithful, she is putting you, as well as herself, at risk
for STDs. And, should you be tempted to run out to
the nearest low-rent bar to buy a cheap blow job in
retaliation, you should know that herpes, chlamydia,
gonorrhea, syphilis, and gonococcal farongitis can
all be transmitted from the mouth to the penis. Most
people worry about AIDS being transmitted
orally—and worry about AIDS is all most people
do—when they should be concerned about getting a
resistant strain of another STD this way.

Was this lecture meant for the reader, Faithful Husband, or for Superlady herself?

For a few minutes, I considered getting David to hire
Charles to shoot the La Passionata story, but sanity
prevailed following a brief interlude of fantasizing
about working with him. After a tough day of listening

to court testimony about why some people can't reach orgasm unless they're so tightly bound breathing is a problem, we would climb into a limo together for the trip back to Manhattan and his apartment. We would toast each other with champagne. Then he would dip his fingers into his glass, sprinkle a few drops on my nipples, which I had exposed for him, and suck them dry.

No one had ever looked at my breasts the way he did, worshipping and consuming them all at once. My hand moved inside my leggings, down to my swollen flesh, tender from last night's lovemaking. I imagined his hands between my thighs, moving up and parting the moist inner lips. I felt him touching me, then licking me, faster and higher, until I collapsed with pleasure.

When my breath came normally again, I called David who agreed Tiffany should be the photographer accompanying me to the La Passionata trial. He called her, and she called me. She was thrilled to get the assignment, which would mean photographing some people entirely clothed, a new experience for her, in addition to the models who would no doubt be shot in tight bondage as additional illustration for the piece. Tiffany and I agreed to meet for dinner that night at an Indian restaurant in her neighborhood to discuss the story and its photo requirements.

The phone continued to ring throughout the day, because I was "hot." Everybody wanted to talk to me, except the one person whose voice I most wanted to hear. Other than David's, I didn't return any of yesterday's calls. Before leaving my apartment, I waited for Charles's call until waiting any longer would have meant keeping Tiffany waiting alone at a restaurant table for longer than the acceptable fifteen minutes.

Then, waiting for the PATH, I called the machine to see if perhaps I'd just missed his call walking those three blocks. I hadn't missed his call, only another call from Morgy. I felt guilty for not calling her back earlier. Two things happen to women as soon as they get into relationships: waiting and guilt.

"It's getting weirder with Georges," she'd said on yesterday's tape. "I need to see you for breakfast or lunch or something," she'd said today. "Call me!"

I felt guilty, but consoled myself with the thought that Morgy, in similar circumstances, would have kept the line open waiting for *his* call, too, leaving me to handle my own crisis with *him* for another twenty-four hours.

I spotted Tiffany immediately. Only a few of the tables were occupied, bad sign. No Indian diners at all. Worse sign. "Never eat in a Chinese restaurant if you don't see a Chinaman at a table," my father always told me. I still considered it good advice, applicable to any ethnic cuisine. Christmas lights were wrapped around two fake fig trees at the restaurant's entrance forming an archway. She was visible directly through the center of the arch, which probably had some meaning in new age holistic psychobabble terms. On the wall nearest her was a plaque of a brass female with many arms, long and slender and braceleted, the ubiquitous quasi-religious figure predating the American Supermom of the late seventies, whose arms were attached to briefcases, diapers, cooking utensils, and vacuum cleaners. Pink and purple plastic orchid-like flowers were tacked to the wall beneath the plaque. A cloying, smoky incense filled the air. I love Indian food, but I hate the incense and the decor.

"Were you recognized on the train?" Tiffany asked.

"I don't want to talk about it," I said, making a face in response and hugging her briefly before sitting down across from her. Maybe I had been recognized or maybe I was being paranoid, but I'd felt eyes on me all the way from Jersey City to the 14th Street PATH stop, where I'd gotten off and taken a cab across town to 26th and Lexington. And hadn't I seen that man again? I didn't want to think about it. What if he was Starred Man? Something I wanted to think about even less.

"You look fabulous," I told her, because that's what women say to each other, though Tiffany, whose social skills were limited, never returned compliments.

She was wearing a pale green gauzy loose blouse more suited to July than December, unbelted over jeans. Her unfettered breasts swung freely down into the folds of gauze. If she'd leaned forward at a thirty-degree angle, they would have been resting on her knees. Multitiered brass earrings, like miniature tacky chandeliers, hung from her lobes. Streaks of gold high-lighted her overdone eyes, but her face was radiant, rested, and relaxed. Tiffany in her goddess mode. She exuded a sexual warmth as if she were wearing a gauze skirt to match the shirt and golden sandals, no under-wear, her legs open to a breeze catching her musky scent. It was hard to understand how the *Directory of Adult Films* had ever called her: "Not one of the top female erotic performers of all time, but the kinkiest."

Tossing my black and leather fox jacket over the chair, I felt overdressed in black sweater pants, match-ing v-necked sweater, and black cowboy boots. I was glad I hadn't worn a bra. A pot of herbal tea was steaming in the center of the table, flanked by two small white porcelain cups, the kind in which the tea grows quickly cold.

"They have wine," she said.

"Thank goodness."

I signaled the nearest waiter and ordered a glass of

Chablis, the only option. It would be the cheapest California jug wine, but it was better than herbal tea. I asked for a glass of ice. Cheap white wine is better iced.

"Is that real fur?"

"It's real leather," I said, dodging the question, not wanting a lecture on animal rights, even in Tiffany's soft, sweet voice.

We ordered appetizers: chicken livers with poori bread for me, vegetable fritters with chutney for her. She filled me in on the progress of the Goddesses and Sluts all-day seminars, the first of which had been held the day before. She'd charged six women forty dollars each to spend a day applying makeup and trying on costumes and accessories gleaned from thrift shops, costume supply sales, and Tiffany's past. Seemingly everything she'd ever worn was stuffed into the two closets in her apartment or under the bed in boxes, or in the broom closet and the high shelves of kitchen cabinets. Her end tables were actually boxes filled with clothes and covered with some Eastern-looking fabric.

"I decided against the before and after shots for the future," she said, "because they all looked too much like the before shots when they left the transformation salon. Then again, maybe they should look the same when they leave," she mused. "I told a reporter from *Paper* the seminars are a safe way for women to explore their fantasies in dangerous times. Maybe they're safer if they leave looking like they came, their fantasies back inside.

"Now, I plan to take three polaroid photos of each woman, one as a slut, one as a goddess, and a 'tits on head with Tiffany,' shot, their head beneath my bare breasts. I'm going to do the tits on head at the book party for everyone who buys a book, too. Don't you think it's a great idea?"

"Great," I said, signaling the waiter for more wine

and a main course, vegetable curry for her, shrimp curry for me.

"I want you to come to a Sluts and Goddesses seminar," she said. "You won't have to pay."

I nodded encouragingly. Tiffany had taken my picture once, and I'd looked like a Las Vegas madam with an unusually good haircut. In two beats, I was prepared to get on the real subject, the assignment. Then, interestingly, it was she, and not David, who gave me the important news of the day.

"Have you heard about the internal investigation and reorganization at the magazine?" she asked. "Clarissa told me this morning. Vinnie's new money man is examining all the expense accounts, reevaluating the salaries and department budgets, whatever that means, and it probably means people are going to be fired and David won't be able to pay us as much anymore. Clarissa is afraid it might affect her. She's really worried, with the new baby coming and all."

"Uhm," I said, not wanting to admit I hadn't heard. Why hadn't David mentioned this in one of our four conversations of the day? Wasn't it more important than his learning if Charles performed cunnilingus or not? "Well . . ." I said, letting my voice taper off significantly and shrugging my shoulders eloquently, implying I might know more than she did.

"Do you think David won't be able to pay us as much as he does now?" she asked. "This is the first time in my life I've ever made so much money for my work."

"I don't know what it all means," I said, but really I did. It meant big trouble for David, who could be replaced at half the salary, and that couldn't be good news for those of us who were his chosen few. When editors go, so go the free-lance writers and photographers. Every new editor brings in his or her own favored people with whom to share expense account lunches. Can you blame them?

"We'll probably be fine," I said reassuringly. She looked so worried, I reached across the table and took her hand. Her fingers, covered in cheap rings, felt small and cold, like a child's. "They won't cut the fees too much if they do cut them."

She suggested I walk the three blocks down Lexington back to her apartment and look at some recent bondage photos of Vera to see if they'd work in the La Passionata article. It happened midway between the restaurant and Tiffany's building. Out of the corner of my eye, I noticed a slight figure in pants, heavy jacket, gloves, and baseball cap pulled low over the face. Man or woman? Boy or girl? Whichever, whoever was coming up fast alongside us. Then he or she seemed to notice me noticing him or her and dropped back a few paces. At the same time I was suddenly aware of another figure, larger, definitely a man on the other side of the street crossing against traffic coming toward us. I knew this man. He'd followed me from the PATH train to my apartment building only a few days before. I was extending my left arm out to touch Tiffany's sleeve, prepared to suggest in an urgent whisper that we sprint for her lobby, when it happened.

I felt the thud in the center of my back, followed by the slow dripping of heavy wet liquid down my back. I'd been hit. Tears flooded my eyes; I gasped, not from pain, but from humiliation.

"Oh, no!" Tiffany screamed. "You don't have the right to do that, no matter how you feel about animals!" she yelled after the running figure well behind us now. She turned to me and asked, "Are you okay?"

"I don't want to turn around and look," I said, grabbing onto her arm. Sticky red globs were falling behind me on the pavement, landing with sickening plops. Looking down, I could see them through my legs.

"I got it on film," said the man in front of us. He was the figure I'd seen moving across the street, a big, beefy tabloid photographer, the man who had probably been following me for days.

"She got you good, didn't she?" His mouth was curled up, either in his version of amusement as copied from old gangster movies or from a tic. "Hey, you know it's only paint, it's not blood. Vinnie will probably buy you a new coat."

"You were following us, weren't you?" Tiffany demanded, but, ignoring her, he stepped out into the street to hail a cab.

"Has it ever occurred to one of you guys to stop a crime in action instead of photographing it?" I yelled, but he ignored me, too. "That asshole would have shot the picture just the same if I was being stabbed," I said to Tiffany.

"Let's go inside and see what we can do about it," she said, patting my shoulder.

"I love this coat," I said. I'm ashamed to admit it, but I felt like bawling over a silly clump of fur. "I've had it for two years. My first fur coat. I bought it for myself."

"Oh," she said, her eyes filling with tears. We hugged each other on the street.

"At least it didn't get on the rest of your clothes," Tiffany said. She'd insisted on making cups of an anemic greenish tea of unidentifiable herbal origin, which we were sipping at the table in her dining alcove, photos of Vera bound filling the space between us. The coat was lying on top of plastic cleaner bags on the kitchen floor. We'd tried wiping the paint off and succeeded only in rubbing it in. The poor thing looked like an animal which had died in childbirth.

"I'll loan you something to wear home," she said.

"Maybe the cleaners can get the paint out," I said. She nodded enthusiastically. "This really isn't their part of town, is it?" I asked.

"Whose?"

"Animal rights protesters who throw paint. Don't they keep mainly to the Upper West and the Upper East sides?"

"You're right. I think they do." Her forehead wrinkled in thought, she absentmindedly traced with her right index finger the crucifix hanging from Vera's nipple ring in one of the photos. I didn't think the crucifix would work in the layout we were planning. "And, they usually work in groups, pairs at least. I've seen them on the street uptown."

"There's something wrong with this, isn't there?" I asked.

I stared into the framed photograph hanging over the table, Tiffany and Vera, arms wrapped around each other's waists, dressed in matching bustiers, stiff crinolines, mesh stockings, and five-inch heels. In red print at the bottom of the frame the caption read: "THE TRANSFORMATION SALON!!—Sexual evolutionaries Tiffany Titters and Vera want you to have a good time." Beneath their makeup masks, their faces were set in the smiling lines preferred by generations of homecoming queen candidates.

"Maybe there is something wrong with it," she said.

We were silent for several minutes, looking at each other. Like most New York apartments heated by steam, this one was now too warm which would undoubtedly alternate with too cold throughout the night. A drop of sweat trickled down between my breasts. Released by my warmth, my perfume rose in a gentle cloud filling my nostrils. I felt my nipples become erect.

Her eyes, blue and green with flashes of yellow, wide with innocence and deep with wisdom, grew softer. She reached across the table and laid her hand on top of mine.

"You don't have to carry that coat home on the train," she said. "There's a good cleaner in my neighborhood. I'll take it to him tomorrow."

I left Tiffany's apartment after politely refusing her offer to spend the night, either in her bed or on the living-room futon, where many luminaries of the sexual underworld had slept when between apartments. The famous writer, Octavio Juarez, had died there, nursed by Tiffany through the last horrible months of AIDS. Swathed in a scratchy woolen cape of many colors that made me feel like a runaway from a white slave camp, I had every intention of going back home to Jersey. I took a cab to 14th Street, where I started down the steps to the underground PATH. I couldn't make myself put my dollar in the slot and go through the gate. I turned around and went back up the steps.

I'm unnerved, I thought, so I'll just get into another cab and pay the twenty or more he will charge to take me to Jersey. On the street, I walked directly to a pay phone and dialed Charles's number, which I knew by heart, having only dialed it once. Tiffany would have called that a heartsign, though all of her heartsigns pointed to women now.

"Babe," he said when he recognized my voice. "I just tried to call you. What's going on?"

"I'm a few blocks from your apartment, wrapped in something big and bright and wooly from Tiffany's closet. An animal rights activist pelted my fur coat tonight."

"Come over, babe," he said. "I'll make you feel better."

I walked into his apartment, into his arms, and we did not talk. He lifted the hair away from my face and kissed my hairline, then my eyelids, my cheeks, and finally my mouth. As he kissed me, he opened my legs with his thigh. My heat enveloped us.

"I told you I was going to want more," he said, leading me to the bedroom.

We lay side by side, naked, touching each other with healing strokes. I ran my hand along the curve of his hip and, cupping his buttock, drew him closer to me. He lowered his head to my breast and took the nipple in his mouth. I cradled his head while he sucked me and thought of how it would feel when inevitably he put his mouth to my vagina. Shivering in anticipation, I reached for his penis and squeezed it gently.

"Make me come," I begged.

I was thick and wet from wanting him. Without taking his mouth from my breast, he put his hand between my legs, his fingers sliding back and forth in and out of me while his thumb massaged my clitoris. The orgasm which began almost immediately was so strong it seemed to suck his fingers inside me. I came around his hand, the spasms shaking my whole body.

"You are so incredible," he said.

As he had the night before, he pulled me up and into the center of the bed. Sitting with my legs over his, I moved my hips toward his penis. Holding my back firmly with one hand, he guided it inside me with the other hand.

"Hard," I said. "I want you inside me as far as you can go."

My urgency released his passion, which became as

insistent as my own. Growling deep in his throat, he
lifted me off the bed in an act of penetration so deep and
so total that I lost awareness of everything except his
penis thrusting repeatedly inside me, claiming me, owning me. I came over and over again. When he ejacu-
lated, I almost lost consciousness.

"I love you," he whispered, licking the sweat from
my face. "I didn't hurt you, did I?"

"No, God, no, you were wonderful. I wanted you so
much."

He held me tight against his chest. We stayed that
way, without speaking, until we'd stopped panting.
Then he laid me back against the pillows, fluffing them
before he put my head down, and stroked my vagina
until I was writhing, my hands over my head, grasping
the headboard.

"Do you want me to eat you out?" he asked.

"Please," I begged. He lowered his mouth to my
body as if he were about to partake of a sacrament.

I'd told too many men it was the best sex I'd ever had
when it really wasn't. The male ego being what it is,
they'd all believed me. Well, who wouldn't believe in his
superior sexual prowess while lying beside a woman
capable of thinking herself to orgasm? Now I really was
having the best sex I'd ever had, and I didn't have any
words left for the real thing. What could I say that I
hadn't said untruthfully before?

I was limp. Orgasmic contractions, like the after-
shocks of an earthquake, still shook my vagina. He was
going out to buy the morning edition of the papers. I
couldn't have gotten out of the bed for anything less
than a large fire . . . directly *under* the bed.

"How can you go out into the cold?" I asked. "I
don't have the energy to breathe."

"Babe, it's automatic. You're okay," he said, grinning affectionately at me and pulling the sheet up to my chin. "You have to see the picture of this person who hit you with the paint. I don't like the way it sounds at all."

I didn't like it either, and I liked it even less when he handed me the *Post* ten minutes later. They had me on the front page, coming and going, in a split page double photo. On the left-hand side Tiffany and I were walking toward the unseen photographer, the assailant framed behind us in the space between our heads. On the right-hand side, the paint was being flung by a startled woman, who had turned to face the camera just as he'd taken the shot.

"Do you recognize the woman?" Charles asked. He handed me a photographer's loop in case I needed to magnify her face for closer study. I didn't. "You do, don't you?"

"Elizabeth Thatcher. She tried to strangle me a few weeks ago on the 'Olive' show."

"Fuck!" he said, slamming his hand on the dresser, causing his mother's photo to collapse. "Fuck! I knew this was no animal rights protest when you told me about it. They don't hang out on Lexington Avenue in little India. We're going to call the cops."

I wouldn't let him call the cops. If I'd recognized Elizabeth Thatcher, so would someone else. The cops would be calling me, and I was in no hurry for the conversation, which would be too much like the one I'd had in Chicago. *Now, what did you say to her just before she tried to strangle you? I'd like to hear that again.* The New York cops would probably ask me if I'd wiggled my finger at her before she threw the paint.

We slept spoon fashion, his back to my chest, my hand around his penis, his hand around mine holding his manhood. I woke sometime in the night. He had an erection, and his hand had moved past mine so that both our hands were wrapped around it, like hands around a baseball bat. There was room at the top for another hand.

Chapter Nine

I wasn't the only one who'd recognized Elizabeth Thatcher as the paint thrower. So had someone at the *Post*. The later morning edition carried the same split page photos, but had replaced the front page headline, "New Enemy For Superlady!" with "Olive Choker Strikes Again!," making it sound as though Olive's necklace had a life of its own and had either bitten her or someone else, perhaps turning to violent crime to get her attention away from the competing jewelry in her wall safe. Having inwardly sneered at the headline, I was reading the article while waiting for Morgy to join me for breakfast at David's Pot Belly Stove restaurant on Christopher Street.

"Would you like another cappuccino?" the waitress asked from her hovering position over my left shoulder. I knew she was there before she spoke. The air around her smelled like the stuff that smells just like Giorgio, and why would anyone want to smell just like Giorgio?

The cup was half full, so I waved her away. Reluctantly, she took a few steps backward, reducing the almost Giorgio content of the atmosphere enveloping me. This member of a typically inattentive staff, who had needed half a dozen requests to replenish my cappuccino only the week before, was treating me like this was my last breakfast. If I kept on reading the *Post,* I might believe it was.

After relating the paint incident as the photographer had seen it, the *Post* article claimed:

> *Ms. Titters, who is herself a vegetarian, said, "Carolyn and I both thought something wasn't right about the whole thing." Ms. Steele could not be reached for comment. Elizabeth Thatcher's husband, Phillip, a lawyer, was on his way from Memphis, accompanied by Mrs. Thatcher's therapist, Dr. Roland Legerdermaine, who had no comment. At the Memphis airport, Thatcher said, "Obviously this crazed sex lady, who clearly is not a lady, has driven my wife temporarily insane. We are considering filing suit for damages against her and that magazine."*

In an accompanying sidebar, titled "Faking Zelda," they played up, and not for the first time since her death, the great discrepancy between who her readers thought Zelda was and who she really was. This time they identified Clarissa as the current ghostwriter and accurately listed everyone who'd written the column before her. Who outside the magazine could have told them all this?

Zelda, of course, had never written a word of her own advice. Her name and her face had sold a lot of magazines in the early days. Beneath the sidebar, the *Post* ran the familiar *Playhouse* photo of her as a gorgeous busty blonde, taken twenty-five years ago, next to a candid pose of her in her final days—bald, her three hundred pounds stuffed into jeans and a plaid lumberjack shirt. It was a rather startling contrast. Hadn't any of these faithful readers thought to notice there was something odd about a woman whose face hadn't changed in a quarter of a century?

"Which woman would you tell your sexual troubles to?" the cutline asked.

The lie of Zelda made it all the more important that

I have "a very public existence," Vinnie had said in our last phone conversation. Readers were calling the magazine every day to protest the faking of Zelda and often to question my existence. They couldn't be madder if Zelda had been faking in their very own beds all these years, according to David, who handled most of the calls.

"Could you throw this away?" I asked the waitress, who was, I knew without inhaling deeply, still within hearing range. I thrust the folded paper in her direction without looking at her.

She took it from me and scurried to the back of the room in the direction of the kitchen. David's Pot Belly Stove is only about twelve feet wide, shaped like a bowling lane, and packed with tables on either side of the narrow center aisle. You have to go through the kitchen, passing dangerously close to the grill, to get to the single stall unisex restroom. On a bad day the smells of urine, Pine Sol, and grease hit you just as you turn right past the stove.

At 8:00 A.M. on a weekday morning, David's wasn't crowded. The West Village doesn't wake up early. Few of the people who live down here have "regular" jobs. They have "creative" jobs which are performed at home or, if in an office, then a nontraditional office, which opens for business after ten or eleven and where the furnishings are cheap, but the plants are awesome. A renegade corporate type who has chosen the West Village for his home would quietly breakfast in that home before slipping even more quietly off to the subway. Two lone male diners, probably musicians who hadn't been to bed yet or early rising writers, their attention captured by their copies of *The New York Times,* were the only other people in the room.

"I hate this place," Morgy announced loudly, two feet from the table. "If I weren't desperate to talk to you, I wouldn't be here."

What she meant was if she hadn't been too sleepy to argue when I'd called her at 7:00 A.M. from Charles's apartment, we'd be somewhere more decidedly upscale. She was only willing to endure downtown in the later afternoon when drinks were part of the package. Unassisted by alcohol, she couldn't abide anything below 57th Street, except her Wall Street office. Tossing her black leather Vuiton briefcase and matching handbag on the bench beside me, next to Tiffany's cape, she hesitated before placing her mink coat on top of it.

"What's that?" she asked.

"It belongs to Tiffany. Good morning to you, too."

"Oh," she said, pulling the coat back and tossing it over her chair across from me instead. Dragging the floor was better than touching that which had touched Tiffany. She sat down. "Oh, damn, I hate life."

"You look terrific," I told her, and, of course, she did. Dressed in a designer black wool coatdress with dark stockings, Bruno Magli pumps, and a small fortune's worth of real gold at her earlobes, neck, and wrist, she made a statement that read like the inflated bottom line of a glossy corporate annual report. "I don't know how you can look this good before noon."

"Well, you know the mess I leave behind to do it," she said.

Yes, I could picture Morgy's apartment, especially the bathroom, which typically looked like twenty-seven models had used it to prepare for a fashion show. It was the kind of mess that left one wondering how a perfectly coiffed, attired, and made-up beauty could have come out of this place, rather like a perfect child coming from the womb of a total loser with bad teeth, split ends, and no sense of style.

"Oh, Carolyn, what am I going to do?"

"Get the maid to come in every day instead of three times a week?"

"Coffee?" the waitress asked her. "Another cappuccino?" she asked me before Morgy had time to answer.

"Yes, to both," I said, waving her away again.

"Well, she's a skinny little thing," Morgy said, looking after her with distaste. "Anorexic."

"Every woman looks like that in Tennessee until she has her first baby," I said irritably. I knew Morgy was being snippy because the waitress was ignoring her while behaving obsequiously to me.

"Is she from Tennessee? I couldn't hear an accent."

"It's behind her vowels and consonants fighting to be heard. Obviously she's an aspiring actress on voice lessons."

"Oh. We should order when she gets back and get that out of the way because I don't have much time."

I nodded and picked up the huge menu listing plates of food which would also be oversized and in most cases came with hush puppies. There was a headache developing in the middle of my forehead. I wanted to be on the train back to Jersey because I had a lot to do at my apartment before returning to the city in the afternoon for Clarissa's baby shower. And, most of all, I realized I didn't want to hear about Morgy's latest romantic disaster, which wouldn't be much different from the one before it and the one before that and so on. I'd rather be taking a nap.

"There's something different about you," she said, after we'd placed our orders: waffles with Häagen-Dazs chocolate ice cream for her, a spinach and Swiss cheese omelet, with accompanying hush puppies, for me.

"It's probably the reflected glow from Tiffany's cape."

"Well, it does look a bit radioactive. No, really, there's something different about you."

"I can't imagine why there would be," I said, surprised at the strength of the angry feelings bubbling up inside me. "That crazy Elizabeth Thatcher attacked me last night and ruined my coat. I'm getting threatening letters and phone calls. The *Post* is doing a countdown of my last days. I've finally met a man who actually fucks instead of talking about it, but I think he's involved with a couple dozen other women, too. I didn't make him wear a condom, so I'm probably already harboring some new resistant strain of an STD. And, according to Tiffany, Vinnie's new money man is examining the numbers with an eye to slashing the budgets. Maybe we'll all be replaced by j school grads.

"Why wouldn't I be the same carefree old me?"

"Oh." She paused to be sure I was finished. "No, it isn't that. It has more to do with me, I think." Then, looking around for the waitress, she said, "This coffee's cold already."

While we waited for the waitress to return with hot coffee, we looked uncomfortably at each other. Why was so much of my irritation directed at her? And how did she, who rarely recognizes any feeling not coming from her own gut, know it?

"I'm sorry I didn't call you sooner," I said contritely. "I was swept away on a tide of passion. You know how it is."

"You'll have to tell me about him," she said. "It's Georges."

"No, I'm not seeing Georges, Morgy."

"You know what I meant."

I knew what she meant. Everything was always all about her. Any interest she had in other people was minimal and with a voyeuristic and/or critical bent. Why did I consider this woman my very best friend? Oooh, I was feeling mean and nasty.

"I don't know what to do about Georges," she said, the tears beginning to slide gently down her cheeks, where they would no doubt not even streak her makeup. She allowed the tears to slip all the way to the edges of her face before dabbing at them with her napkin just as the waitress, who finally noticed her, put the plates down in front of us.

"I'm afraid he might be, like you know, really a pervert. He's agreed to talk to you. He says he has a lot of respect for you, and I want you to talk to him. Will you do that for me?"

I wanted to throw my omelet in her face, but I smiled. No, I didn't say, "Yes," but I smiled, which was almost as bad. I didn't say, "No."

Why do I consider this woman my best friend? I asked myself.

I was sitting on a nearly empty car of the PATH train headed toward Jersey. It was a little after 9:00 A.M. No one goes to Jersey in the mornings. They leave from Jersey in the mornings to work in the city and don't go back again until after five. Anyone who was going back to Jersey in the mornings had their reasons and wouldn't be bothering me.

Why can't she just stand up at a Forum meeting and say, "Excuse me, my lover wants me to be his slave. Would that be giving away my power or not?" I asked myself. Surely they could tell her what to do.

I was in no mood to deal with Morgy and her made-up problems. The guy was a jerk. He wasn't satisfied with spanking her before anal sex. Tying her to the bedframe with silk scarves no longer titillated him. Now he wanted her to wear leather restraints, five-inch heels, and nothing else as she knelt before him to receive his sexual orders every evening. What a little prick, and, yes, I would have bet he had a little prick, especially since Morgy hadn't said otherwise. And wouldn't anything a man could "sort of slip" so easily into an anus have to be small?

Do you know what really irritated me about this

situation? I knew exactly what Morgy would do. She would play the game as long as it stimulated her. When she'd had enough, she'd drop him. And I knew that Morgy knew exactly what she would do, too. All this wringing of hands and begging, "What should I do? What should I do?" was only part of the game.

I'd been inside my apartment less than five minutes when Charles called. His voice, like a length of black satin being wrapped around me, smoothed out all the rough edges. Smiling, I flopped down on my bed, the half that wasn't covered with books, magazines, newspapers, research Cynthia Moore-Epstein had sent over on the lives and deaths of Tanya Truelust, Madame Zelda, and La Passionata, and letters to Superlady.

Two minutes into the conversation, his call waiting beeped, and Charles put me on hold. I hate call waiting. In that moment, I made up my mind to cancel my own call waiting and never to have it again. I could afford now to be eccentric.

Waiting for him, I glanced at the top letter, which read:

Dear Superlady of Sex,

I recently saw you on TV and God spoke to my heart to send this letter to you. Harvest time is here and God wants you, your family, your friends, and those sick people who write to you to believe in Him. I am looking forward to spending eternity with you, but this cannot happen if you do not repent now. Read the Bible and repent.

A list of recommended readings filled the rest of the page and a second one. If God Herself wanted to reach me, wouldn't She dial direct? Would She trust Her message with some nut who thought She was a man and would couch Her wisdom in cryptic terms like "See Matt. 7:7?" No, She wouldn't. I wadded the letter up into a ball and tossed it into the wastebasket, reducing the bed clutter by two sheets of paper and one envelope. The more threatened I felt in daily life, the more junk I piled on my bed. When things were really bad, as they were now, the usable space for sleeping was the width of a nun's cot.

"Babe," he said, coming back on the line. "I've gotta run, but I wanted to touch base with you this morning. Would you like to get some food later? I'll be flying out to L. A. in the morning, and I won't be back for ten days. I want to be with you tonight."

"I'd love to," I said, but the smile was gone. Ten days? He would be gone for ten whole days? "What time?"

"Come on down whenever you're finished with your baby shower," he said, chuckling.

Charles had found the idea of a baby shower for a lesbian "father" quite amusing when I'd told him about it that morning. In fact, Charles found many of the details of my life amusing. His eyes lit up when I told him about WIP lunches, fact checkers who don't comprehend penile thrusting, and letter writers with messages direct from God. What would I do to entertain him when he became as familiar with the bizarre as I was?

We talked for a few minutes about absolutely nothing; when I hung up the phone, I was smiling again, even with a corner of Fay Weldon's *Life Force* sticking in my back. I pulled the book out from behind me and settled back into the pillows. How I wanted a nap. Only fifteen minutes, I promised myself, I have so much to do.

Forty-five minutes later, the buzzer woke me. I clutched at the comforter in the same way another woman, in the next block perhaps, might grab her gun or knife when startled into waking. A lot of good a handful of feathers was going to do me. Repeatedly someone downstairs was banging the buzzer. I went into the hallway, pressed the talk button, and said, "Yes, who is it?"

"Messenger from Mr. Mancuso," he said.

"Could you wait a minute while I turn on the TV and check you out?" I asked.

"Sure thing," he cheerfully replied.

My hand wavered. Would an antiporn attacker cheerfully encourage me to check him out? Would a man be an antiporn attacker in the first place? No. A mad rapist. He would be a mad rapist, and would a mad rapist invite me to preapprove him on closed circuit video? Sure, why not? He's mad, isn't he? Figuring it was a lose/lose situation, I almost pressed the Door Release button, but didn't.

I hurried back to the bedroom, turned on the TV, punched in the closed circuit channel with the remote, and studied the man outside my front door. A medium-sized black man with a neatly trimmed beard, he was dressed in a green uniform, carrying under one arm a large oblong and relatively flat shiny black box, and waving directly at the camera. If I let him in and he killed me, at least he'd be on tape. I went back into the hallway, my hand hesitating over the buttons. What did I know now that I knew what he looked like? Was an informed choice possible with such limited information?

"Okay," I said, releasing the door with a bit of trepidation.

Security wasn't a perfect concept, especially when the word was applied to a system that basically depended on me deciding from four floors up if the doors should open or not. And some people buzzed in anyone who hit their bell, assuming, without checking, it was a neighbor with full hands or a forgotten key. Is that how my tormentor had gotten the letters under my door? I needed a doorman. I needed, I suddenly realized, to move to Manhattan so I could cut some of the daily risks I faced by staying off both the New York City subways and PATH trains.

The messenger had climbed the four flights of stairs quickly. He was knocking at my door. I looked through the peephole. Same guy. Same smile, the wave smaller this time, meant for the confines of the peephole.

"Hi," I said, opening the door. "Sorry I was being so overly cautious."

"Hey, Superlady." He handed me the large box. "If I was you, I'd be careful, too. I probably wouldn't have let me in the door in the first place."

I signed for the package, secured the deadbolts behind him, and took the box to the bedroom. Gold letters proclaimed Antoine's, the name of a far better than acceptable New York furrier. Vinnie had replaced my coat after all. Opening the box, I gasped. Vinnie had more than replaced my coat with this full-length Blackglama mink. It was exquisite. I held it to my cheek, where it seemed to lovingly return my caress, as I read his note: "Carolyn, May this bring a smile to your lovely face. With sympathy for your loss and enormous gratitude for all you do for the family, Vinnie."

Now, how could I complain about laying my life on the line for a man like that?

Any normal woman after being pelted with nasty red paint only the night before would not have worn her precious new fur coat on the PATH train to New York that very afternoon, especially if she was carrying an oversized box stuffed with Winnie the Pooh, Eeyore, Tigger, and Piglet and wrapped in disgustingly cute nursery patterned paper. Any other woman might have considered the package alone increased her visibility level to the potentially uncomfortable point. But I sometimes take the Superlady appellation to heart, and this was one of those days. I wore the coat. The PATH wasn't crowded. The three riders in my car, middle-aged Puerto Rican women, glanced derisively at my fur, then looked away, not meeting my eyes. I got off at Christopher Street and grabbed a cab uptown.

David's office had been commandeered for the shower. When I arrived, the other Women In Porn were already there, except Clarissa, who'd been sent on a fool's errand to the art department, and Bobby, who would be stylishly late. David was out getting ice for the champagne buckets. A sheet cake decorated with two well-endowed naked mothers, whose long flowing pubic curls entwined together, and one curly-haired baby sat in the middle of David's desk, surrounded by presents. There were also presents on the floor.

"Oh, my God, my God, I love it," Stephanie squealed, referring to my coat. She pinched the rich fabric between her fingers appreciatively. "David told us you were getting it, but we had no idea it would be *this* good. It's truly choice. Can I try it on?"

Everyone gathered around, stroking the coat, as they helped me out of it and articulated their feelings about Elizabeth Thatcher's paint job. They were all talking at once. The conflicting advice and opinions bounced painfully off my body.

"Vinnie says she's been remanded to a psychiatric hospital, so I wouldn't worry about her anymore if I were you."

"They'll keep her a week, and she'll be back."

"But home in Memphis, sedated."

"She'll palm her pills and sneak back to New York."

"She can't hurt you anymore."

"That woman is a problem."

"I really believe she's going to try to kill you."

"No, not kill. It was paint, not blood."

"But red, symbolic. Symbolic of blood."

"Stop!" I shrieked.

I put up my hands, and the babble stopped. Coat removed, I was wearing a snug black minidress in a wool knit with long sleeves and a square neck showing the top of my cleavage. Every woman in the room, except Tiffany, was wearing a black minidress. Only the sleeve lengths and degree of plunge varied from one of us to the other. Tiffany wore a v-necked hot pink fuzzy sweater, a push-up bra heaving her breasts up and almost over the top of it, and a blue jean skirt, sort of the outfit every high-school boy once dreamed of finding his date in when she met him at the door on Friday night.

"I told you about turning your back on women in silk dresses," Gemma reminded me.

Vera, looking stern and worried, stood behind her, nodding in agreement.

"Did anyone think to invite Miriam?" I asked, because I just wasn't up to talking about the incident.

My life had become a series of public incidents; all I wanted was to talk about the simple things, like was the cake white or chocolate, and were we really going to play pin the baby on the lactating boob as Tiffany had said we were?

"Oh, Miriam," Carola said, dismissing the gestating mother with a flip of one beautifully manicured hand, nails done in the French manner. "She is no fun."

"She doesn't really like us," Vera said, crossing her arms over her heaving bosom. Not being liked wounded her more than it did the rest of us; none of us were impervious to the strong reactions, often of pure hate, we elicited in other women. "Miriam thinks what we do is very sleazy. She told me she wouldn't 'sell out our sex' like we do."

"She can afford to have her prissy principles," I snapped. "Clarissa supports her."

"No, I think she just doesn't know how to handle being with a lot of people at once," Tiffany said. "She's shy."

Shy. Then I noticed on the wall where the tattooed penis usually hung the huge blowup photo of Miriam, nude from the waist up, her pregnant boobs enormous, but taut. They looked like they would burst on contact with anything, even a filmy nightgown. She'd filled out so much with pregnancy, the snake tattoos on both breasts appeared to have been recently fed large white rats. *Shy.*

"It's for pin the baby on the boobs," Tiffany said. "Here's the baby." She picked up an art department rendition of a baby who resembled a cherub on a Victorian Christmas card. "They don't exactly go together, do they?"

"I think the snakes are going to scare the shit out of baby when she arrives," David said from the door. "Look how their heads point down into the nipples. It will be like being nursed in the zoo."

I went immediately to hug him, surprised at the strength of my need for his reassurance. If we'd been alone, I would have bawled in his arms.

"Nice coat," he said, returning my hug. "I think you are definitely higher on Vinnie's list than anyone else at the moment. Congratulations. You deserve it." Softly, he said to me alone, "Vinnie has personally assured me Elizabeth Thatcher will be stopped one way or another."

"Oh, honey," Bobby said, filling the doorway David had just vacated with his arms akimbo, fanning out his own huge fur coat, a raccoon he'd saved from an incipient insect infestation in a vintage clothing shop. "Uhm, uhm, uhm. That coat is the most delicious thing I've ever seen. I'll bet you no woman ever got anything like that out of Vinnie without swallowing a lot of his come. You did it, honey, you made it on your own."

I didn't have a chance to reply to that. Cynthia and Rhumumba led Clarissa into the room, followed by the caterers, young men dressed for the occasion in black satin bikini panties and gossamer white frilly aprons, bearing trays of finger food. Dressed in a man's brown suit, white shirt, and brown shoes, Clarissa burst into tears. If the guest of honor hadn't been dressed as a man and the party favors piled in a basket on the floor hadn't included vibrators, flavored body paints, and ben-wa balls, one might have mistaken it for any baby shower in New York City, where the women, regardless of profession, tend to wear a lot of black.

"Let the raucousness begin," David said, opening the first bottle of champagne, and so it did.

Later, Vera and Gemma were spinning Clarissa blindfolded, the cherub in her hand, when Tiffany said, her arm resting lightly across my shoulder, "I've had sex with every woman in this room except you and Clarissa." After pausing to give me a chance to respond, which I didn't, she added, "Clarissa really is very old-fashioned, you know. She wouldn't cheat on Miriam."

"I agree with Vinnie," Charles said, signaling the waiter for the check. "Let him help you find an apartment in the city while he's in the mood to do it. He's feeling like he owes you. If you want my opinion, he does. Take advantage of it."

"Uhmm," I said, sipping my cappuccino. "Well, I didn't argue about the car and driver. It's a tremendous relief to have a chauffeur at my disposal."

"You're out there taking the heat, while his magazine reaps the publicity benefits. Take everything he'll give you. It's yours. You're paying for it by risking your life." I winced, and he reached across the table for my hand. "No, not your life. I don't mean that. Somebody just wants to scare you, not kill you."

I nodded, discouraging further conversation. Charles and I had already debated before over whether that "somebody" had "juice," meaning money and connections, which would explain how he or she could have gotten into my building or obtained my phone number. He didn't quite get it. I'd been on so many talk shows, my phone number and address passed through the hands of so many assistant producers, I might as well have been listed, or my apartment building marked with a neon sign. You lose your privacy when you have a public life. It's a basic concept most people don't get until it happens to them. Maybe I'd end up like Vinnie someday, unable to move without a phalanx of bodyguards, the memory of the shooting of *Hustler*'s publisher always in mind.

We'd just finished a delicious dinner at Claire's, a turquoise-hued oasis, the closest thing to Key West in Manhattan and only a few doors down from Charles's apartment on Seventh Avenue. His red snapper and my catfish had been superb; coming from Mississippi River country, I knew catfish. The service, however, was well below average, and Charles was getting irritated. He kept checking his Rolex and frowning. I was surprised. It was the first time I'd seen Charles express impatience, which is something I naturally express all the time.

"When Vinnie called me at the office this afternoon to tell me he wanted me in the city as soon as we could arrange it, I was shocked," I said. "Shocked that he would think of it. I'd already been thinking of moving someplace where I'd have a doorman and wouldn't have to take subways anymore. But do you think any broker Vinnie uses will know how to find an apartment I can afford?"

Wish You Were Here?

You can be, every month, with Zebra Historical Romance Novels.

AND TO GET YOU STARTED, ALLOW US TO SEND YOU

4 Historical Romances Free

A $19.96 VALUE!
With absolutely no obligation to buy anything.

YOU'RE GOING TO LOVE GETTING
4 FREE BOOKS

These books worth almost $20, are yours without cost or obligation
when you fill out and mail this certificate.
*(If the certificate is missing below, write to: Zebra Home Subscription Service, Inc.,
120 Brighton Road, P.O. Box 5214, Clifton, New Jersey 07015-5214*

Complete and mail this card to receive 4 Free books!

Yes! Please send me 4 Zebra Historical Romances without cost or obligation. I understand that each month thereafter I will be able to preview 4 new Zebra Historical Romances FREE for 10 days. Then, if I should decide to keep them, I will pay the money-saving preferred publisher's price of just $4.00 each...a total of $16. That's almost $4 less than the publisher's price, and there is no additional charge for shipping and handling. I may return any shipment within 10 days and owe nothing, and I may cancel this subscription at any time. The 4 FREE books will be mine to keep in any case.

Name _____

Address _____ Apt. _____

City _____ State ____ Zip _____

Telephone ( ) _____

Signature _____ LF0795
(If under 18, parent or guardian must sign.)

"Sure," he said, stretching out one long arm to physically stop a passing waiter.

"Tell our waiter if I don't have a check in two minutes, I'm leaving without paying," he told the disinterested, would-be actor he'd halted.

"I'll probably be living here before you get back," I said.

"I'll like that," he said. Endorsing the check which had suddenly materialized on the table in front of him, he smiled without looking up at me. "Come on, let's get out of here. For a minute there, I thought Vinnie'd have you relocated across the river before I could pay for dinner."

I wanted to hold hands on the street, but Charles squeezed the hand I slipped into his, then let it go. He didn't go in for public displays of affection. I couldn't decide if he didn't want to call attention to the obvious racial difference or if he didn't want to appear connected to me in case we walked past one of the other women in his life. I was convinced there were others, and who knew how many? And why did I care so much? I was thinking like a typical woman, expecting him to "commit," by which we usually mean carnally forsaking all others, because he and I had sex a few times.

Inside his apartment, he played back the answering machine tape while I used the bathroom and slipped out of my clothes and into his maroon silk robe. With the door shut, I could still hear the low melodic melange of women's voices running together, the well-modulated, accent-free voices of professional women who could be black or white, twenty-five, thirty, or forty. Were all his clients women?

When I came out, he was lying on his side across the bed, naked, his head resting on one elbow, the opposite hip thrust out.

"You have a gorgeous ass," I told him, taking a gentle bite of it.

"I'm glad you think so," he said, smiling indulgently at me. "Take off that robe and come here."

It was only our third night together and climbing into bed next to Charles already felt like coming home. He took me in his arms, and I was happy. Happier than I'd been in longer than I could remember, since long before Roger came into my life and went out of it again.

We didn't speak. For several minutes, he just held me, touching my face and looking into my eyes. I took his hand and pulled it to my mouth, kissed his fingers one by one, then sucked them each in turn. Unhurriedly, he lowered his head and kissed the top of my breasts, then licked in wide circles around each nipple. I shivered and moaned.

"You're so responsive," he said. "I've never known anyone like you in bed."

He turned me over on my stomach and ran first his hands then his mouth up and down my back, all the way into the crevice of my ass. I ground my lower body into the bed, seeking pressure against my clitoris as he continued down my body, caressing and kissing my hips, the back of my thighs, the backs of my knees. Then he ran his hands up my inner thighs.

"Touch me," I begged, arching my body to elevate it from the bed.

He slid one hand in the space between my legs and with the flat of that hand masturbated me. In seconds I rode him to orgasm. I heard him breathing heavily, nearly as heavily as I was. He grasped my hips and entered me from behind, all at once in a hard and satisfying thrust. I began to come again.

"I love you," he said. "I love you."

We made love fast and quick and deep. I wanted to believe his words spoken in passion so much that I did. He loved me.

* * *

I was drifting into sleep when I heard a familiar voice on his machine.

"I'm looking for Carolyn," she said. "Carolyn, it's important. Georges is here with me, and we need to talk to you. Please call."

I pretended not to hear, but I felt Charles watching me. A little later I heard him slip out of bed and go into the next room where he picked up the phone and made a call. I couldn't hear the words, except for "babe," but I recognized the tone. It was exactly how his voice sounded when he talked to me.

Tears filled my eyes. Why are women such fools for love? Or, is that fools period?

Chapter Ten

Dear Superlady of Sex,

Last night I caught my husband masturbating in the bathroom after he thought I was asleep. I have been suspicious of him many times in the past when I heard him getting up on tiptoe to go to the bathroom after he thinks I am sleeping. I asked myself, What could he be doing in there? The answers I could come up with were not good. My worst fears were realized when I opened the door and caught him with Playhouse in one hand and his thing in the other. Worse, I caught him just in the act and some of it spurted onto my foot. Why would a man turn to self-abuse when he has a loving wife in bed beside him who would satisfy his needs whether she wants to or not? I blame you and your magazine for this.

Dear Reluctantly Willing Wife,

Why would a man masturbate when he could enjoy the sexual indulgence of his willing, if not eager, wife?

There are, Reluctantly Willing Wife, many reasons for an occasional preference for masturbation over intercourse. Perhaps he wants quick release and nothing more. Some men tell me their wives need so much stimulation to reach orgasm that intercourse is

*something they only undertake when they are pre-
pared for the arduous task of lovemaking. Or, maybe
masturbation is a forbidden sexual treat for him,
which, of course, makes it more desirable. Since you
disapprove so strongly of his solitary pleasuring, this
may be the case in your marriage.*

*Many people, men and women, married and sin-
gle, report their orgasms are stronger during masturbation than intercourse. This is because they are not
distracted by the other and can thus surrender totally
to the private sensations of orgasm. Really, you
should try it. You might like it. I personally enjoy
masturbation whether I have a partner at hand, pardon the pun, or not.*

*Meanwhile, I suggest you leave your husband to
his pleasures if you are having intercourse with him
as often as you like. If not, why not suggest a mutual
masturbation session? I'm betting he'll get so turned
on watching you masturbate, he'll fuck you.*

I switched off the computer and shut the light in my
new spacious office. On the way to the bedroom, I
stopped to examine the contents of boxes, opened but
not unpacked. I was reacquainting myself with my favorite things as though our separation had been a long
one, not a matter of hours. I touched a leather book and
fondled a recently purchased ceremonial mask from the
Yoroba tribe in Nigeria. The face was painted white,
the lips bright red, black markings like fish hooks
through hearts on either cheek. On its head, a couple sat
side by side. Was it a wedding mask? Was it meant to
be a mother whose children were driving her crazy?

The mask led me to wonder if the Yorobas, like many
African tribes, performed clitorodectomies on their
young girls, removing the clitoris, the site of sexual
pleasure, in an attempt to keep them pure before marriage and faithful after. That led me to wonder why

Americans are so hung up on masturbation, that most wholesome and natural of human behaviors. Haven't we, for most of our existence as a nation, attempted to perform psychological clitorodectomies on our women?

Each generation of Puritanical descendants has had their own language for condemning the solitary pursuit and their own methods for discouraging it. The prohibitions have been applied to both sexes, but more strongly to females. Eighteenth century mothers made their little girls sleep in gloves. Nineteenth century mothers forbade all children sleeping with the hands under the covers. Kellogg invented corn flakes, which he thought would deaden the masturbatory drive in pubescent youths.

My guess is neither cold hands nor cold corn flakes stopped the truly lusty from touching themselves even if they did fear blindness, hairy hands, or warts would result. Today's woman—and don't accuse her of prudishness!—has her own explanation for why masturbation is bad for us. Anything which detracts from the "intimate" relationship between man and woman is bad for us. Each sexual urge should be tied to an equally strong intimacy urge. His own penis or her own clitoris, for that matter, should never come between them and their feelings for each other. People, especially women, irritated me so much with their pious, judgmental sexual attitudes it's no wonder I stuck my favorite finger out at Elizabeth Thatcher on the Olive Whitney show.

Wearily I climbed into bed. With little conscious encouragement from me, the same finger was moving down to my netherparts. It was my first night in my new apartment, and few things in life are lonelier than first nights in new apartments. I touched myself for reassurance as I looked around the huge, by New York standards, bedroom in my Upper West Side apartment. It was sixteen by eighteen feet, a luxurious amount of space which dwarfed my possessions. I couldn't wait to buy more things, and I could have my sister ship the oak wardrobe with the delicate hand carved flower petals decorating the doors which I'd stored in her attic.

More than that, I couldn't wait for Charles to come home in two days. Closing my eyes, I saw his big black penis, a being of beauty and perfection if there ever was one. It rose majestically over his prone body, waving like a magic wand beckoning to me. I touched myself and surrendered to it.

He was fucking me slowly, and we were sitting, as he preferred, in the center of his bed. We watched his penis as he moved it out to the tip then pushed it all the way back in, over and over until I thought he had to come, couldn't stop himself from coming, but he did stop, at the brink each time, his body convulsing as he pulled it back from the edge. We watched his penis, a life apart from us, connecting us, dividing us, giving us both more pleasure than anyone can reasonably expect to feel in bed in this imperfect life.

I stroked the sides of my clit, harder, faster, watching in my mind's eye as his penis, wet with my juices, pulled all the way out, then went all the way back in, farther than any man had ever gone inside me. I was going to come and suddenly I remembered the night before, my last night in the Jersey apartment, masturbating and looking up to see the security guard on the roof looking into my window watching me. He was black like Charles, and I'd smiled at him, thrusting my pelvis forward, giving him my orgasm; his eyeballs and teeth glinted white like exotic pale streaks in an ebony statue. As I rode my hand to orgasm, I could see him watching me and Charles in the middle of the bed.

The orgasms kept coming in irregular intervals over the next hour, often with no help from my hand. Everything, the world it seemed, was centered in my genitals. They were singing, alive with desire again the moment they were satisfied. I was aware of nothing around me. There was only the sensation of orgasm, coming again and again, Charles's penis in my mind's eye pushing in and out of my vagina, creating pink and red whirlpools in its wake.

The fantasy was so real, I could smell the way we smelled after sex when it was over. It was hard to believe he wasn't in the bed beside me. I fell asleep with my hand in my gluey crotch.

When I awoke many hours later with the familiar feeling of dried stickiness between my fingers, I was naked from the waist down and wearing a worn gray sweatshirt from the Gap on top. My ass was cold. I looked around the room, momentarily confused at the space. Then, I remembered where I was. Home, on West 74th Street in a prewar apartment, four spacious rooms with wood floors, a working fireplace of oak and marble, and architectural details, including wide wood-work that was intricately carved above the doorways, a stained glass window in the bathroom. I had a doorman twenty-four hours a day. Smiling, I regarded even the semi-unpacked wardrobe boxes standing outside my walk-in closet with affection. *Home.* I looked at the clock. 7:10 A.M. I wrapped myself in the peach comforter prepared to go back to sleep when I remembered that a car was picking me up at 8:30 A.M. Tiffany and I were going to New Jersey to attend a particularly inter-esting session of the La Passionata trial.

It would be a major photo opportunity for the tab-loids, who'd pretty much left me alone since the pelting incident. Sleepy as I was, I suppressed a sigh. I was trying to break the sighing habit.

"She had been trimly and symmetrically bound, with blue tape around her wrists and elbows signifying shackles and white tape around her forearms," said Dr. Fred Durwood, the forensic psychiatrist brought from Washington, D.C., to testify for the defense of Anthony Spiker in the death of Domina Rodriguez, alias La Passionata.

Regarded as the nation's leading authority on bondage deaths (Do you suppose there's a lot of competition in that field?), Dr. Durwood spoke in a well-modulated voice expressing class, education, and sophistication. He sounded like a British lord explaining the intricacies of the English school system or perhaps the game rules for cricket. He held a copy of Alex Comfort's *The Joy of Sex,* from which he had just quoted to prove that bondage is a far more common sex game than the average American realizes. Tiffany, sitting next to me, seemed quite taken with him. So did the members of the jury, surely a plus for the defense.

"The bindings were elaborate, excessive for the purpose of merely rendering her motionless. They were among the form of restraints favored by regular bondage participants."

He described other typical forms of restraint favored by the serious bondage artist, which go far beyond the simple method of attaching limbs to bedposts by silk scarves, the game with which most of us have some familiarity, either through personal experience or going to the movies. I half listened, my notes here turning into the questions Tiffany had posed on our drive to New Jersey together. She was convinced that a conspiracy might exist to kill the women of porn. Pondering the possibility was more entertaining at the moment than listening to Dr. Durwood explain bondage. I knew all about bondage.

Perversely marking each one of my questions with a five-pointed star, I listed them:

*What if someone or ones did drug Anthony Spiker's

champagne and pushed the gag deeper into Domina's mouth until she suffocated, then set the fire?

*What if someone or ones did push Julie [aka Tanya Truelust] down those fire escape stairs?

*What if the same or a related someones also killed Stella [aka Madame Zelda]?

I was writing the what-ifs in my notebook. Vera, not surprisingly, favored the WWAWAW membership directory as the primary suspect source list. And who's to say, given my own experiences with Elizabeth Thatcher, that she couldn't possibly be onto something?

"Domina Rodriguez was wrapped as neatly as a Christmas package," Durwood said, bringing me back to the here and now.

The jurors, seven women, five men, perhaps with thoughts of their own Christmas packages wrapped tightly and stacked under their trees, squirmed. With seventy-six feet of adhesive tape wrapped around her, twenty feet of it around her head alone, Domina/La Passionata must have resembled no gift I ever wrapped on the way out the door to delivering it. I never can find a new role of Scotch tape and am always making do with the last inches on one that's lost most of its stickiness.

"Such tight wrapping," he continued, "is characteristic of serious bondage."

"He's kind of cute, don't you think?" Tiffany whispered to me.

"Uhm," I said. I didn't exactly think he was "cute." Tall, dark, and reasonably handsome, he had a mustache slightly reminiscent of Hitler's. Probably he was one of those men who couldn't grow much of one, but then why bother? I couldn't help looking at it and wondering if his penis was likewise foreshortened. Yes, I know hand and foot sizes are considered the likely indicators of penis size, but some men fool you. And some give it away in their chosen mustache styles.

I was getting bored, so I began diligently taking notes of the major points he was making for my story.

1. If Anthony Spiker had used bondge as a cover for murder, he wouldn't have used so much carefully aligned tape.

2. The death by asphyxiation could certainly have been accidental, as between five hundred and one thousand accidental deaths occur during sexual bondage each year, most through asphyxiation.

3. The surviving partner panics and tries to cover up what happened.

4. Starting a fire is the most common form of covering up.

"What have you got?" Tiffany whispered.

I crossed my legs higher and tilted the notebook in her direction making it easier for her to read. Without consulting each other in advance, Tiffany and I had both worn black leather, mine a suit with a miniskirt, hers a dress borrowed from Vera. If she leaned over, her breasts would fall out. Two male jurors, casting covert glances in her direction every five minutes, seemed to be waiting for that to happen. She was wearing thigh-high black suede boots, which almost met the top of her dress. I had selected three-inch black slingbacks, just the thing for the northeast in the winter, if you're being chauffeured.

With one long red nail, tipped in gold, she pointed to the questions she, via Vera, had posed earlier. She arched her eyebrows, which were largely pencil lines, at me quizzically. I shrugged my padded shoulders, careful not to encourage her.

If the crazy women of WWAWAW had anything to do with La Passionata's death, when had they come onto the crime scene? I couldn't imagine them knowing how to tape the victim nor could I picture her sitting willingly as they wrapped the seventy-six feet of tape around her. Had they been hiding in the bushes until the taping was done, the gag in place? Then, had they sprung into action? Not likely.

Or was it? Research into male paraphilias, or perversions if you prefer, show a strong correlation between sexual perversity and religious extremism and intolerance. As Dr. John Money says, Scratch a rigid, Republican, born-again Christian and you are more likely to find a foot fetishist, masochist or sadist, or pedophile than you are if you scratch the skin of his politically liberal, non-churchgoing neighbor. Could the equation hold equally true for right-wing women?

Maybe. Mentally, I drew lines through Tiffany's questions anyway. The scenarios I had to conjure to put the WWAWAWs at the scenes of the crimes were improbable, at best.

"Let's skip the afternoon session and go out to the scene," I suggested, and her eyes lit up.

Tiffany left the courtroom before the morning session was over, so she could be in place to photograph the principals on their way out. Other photographers were already waiting outside to photograph her photographing the principals. Covering this trial, Tiffany and I were like a movie within a movie, a soap opera on a soap opera. I slipped out a side door and met her at the car, thereby avoiding the tabloid press until the last moment. Had I realized they would run the shot of me climbing into the car, all legs and ass, I might have done otherwise. You just can't cheat the tabs out of their share of your fifteen minutes of fame.

Driving out to Fort Lee, Tiffany and I went over the background material we had on La Passionata.

"Look," I said, "I side with the defense. She was a willing participant in a bondage game gone wrong. He probably got drunk and passed out while she was wrapped. She choked on the gag. He came to and staged the fire. Maybe he's even telling the truth when he says he doesn't remember anything until he smelled smoke. He could have been in shock when he carried her out to the garage and started the fire.

"What I don't see is any reason to connect the WWAWAWs or anyone else with her death."

"He was seeing other women," Tiffany said, "and she didn't like it. Maybe he did kill her."

"I don't see how the fact that he was clearly a lying, womanizing scumbag makes a difference," I said, dismissing the whole thing. "The only interesting part of this story is what the jury's going to do about it. Will that white bread group be able to grasp the concept of tight bondage and acquit or not?"

While Tiffany put up her argument for murder, either by Anthony or the WWAWAWs or all of the above, I mentally went over the facts on each of the three "mysterious deaths." None of them added up to murder. I sighed. It was proving to be a hard habit to break, like biting one's fingernails.

"I know," I said, brightening, "I brought the mail. Let's find something to laugh at."

I flipped past a letter from a woman who said her husband was bringing home strange underwear which he'd claimed to be pulling from trash cans. She wanted to know if I thought he was lying. *(Honey, does it look and smell like garbage?)* Another from two guys, "best buds," who said they measured more than a foot and wanted to know what to do with their things. *(Guys, stand facing each other, tie them together, and use as a jump rope for girls you want to impress.)* And a letter from a wife whose husband wouldn't eat her out. *(Cheat.)* Then, I found it.

"Okay," I said. "Here it is. A twenty-page letter, beginning, 'Dear False Goddess.' "

You call yourself a sex expert, but I am telling you how spiritually ignorant you are about the sexual function of human beings. You know nothing of sex

*as God intended for it to be used. When God created
Adam and Eve and their first relationship led to
insertion, He insisted they get married. The advice
you give is the same they gave in Sodom and Gomor-
rah. It caused David to lose the Ark and the Cove-
nant. It has brought on the epidemics of AIDS and
broken hearts and destroyed minds. You encourage
blacks and whites to mingle their sex when you know
Cain married a black Neanderthal female animal,
better known to the human race as the black people
who continue to act like animals and think they are
human beings. Do you wonder now why Hitler destroyed the Jews?*

"Why do so many of these people think I'm Jewish?"
I asked. "I'm always getting hate mail from Christians
who assume I'm Jewish. Don't they look at my picture?
What self-respecting Jew would have this hair?"

"I don't know," she said. "Did you know I am Jewish?" I admitted I didn't. "Well, I wasn't raised Jewish,
because I was adopted. Do you know something that's
been bothering me about this whole thing?" she asked,
pointing to the research on the three dead women neatly
piled, and just as neatly ignored, on the seat between us.
"Stella never knew who her father was. Julie, who was
also Jewish, but was raised by a Protestant stepfather,
ran away from home when she was fourteen. Domina's
mother left her when she was a baby."

"So?" I asked. "I don't get it. Why would that make
them victims of murder?"

"The point is we don't know a lot about them because their pasts are gone."

She talked about the three women and what was
known about their pasts in her dreamy wispy voice, the
kind of voice Jackie Onassis would have if she'd spent
her life in porn instead of marital money.

Tanya never had an orgasm during sex with a man,

on camera or not. Like Tiffany, if for different reasons, she'd given up on men and turned to women as lovers. She got into the video business because she believed X-rated films should show women having real orgasms so the men watching would learn something.

La Passionata had in life as well as on film been a bondage devotee, and the major details of Zelda's life had been common knowledge among those of us in the know. Was I beginning to get any pictures? Tiffany wanted to know. No, I wasn't.

"They had in common disadvantaged childhoods, porn pasts, and atypical sexual appetites," she said.

"Oh," I said, trying to sound like it all made a difference in factual terms, though I didn't believe it did.

"We should research Elizabeth Thatcher, that's who we should research."

"You may have a point," I said, largely because I wanted to put us back on common ground.

But, after I thought about it a while, I decided she did have a point, though what it had to do with any other point she'd been trying to make, I didn't know.

The scene of the crime, a classic sixties tract house in quiet, residential Fort Lee, was a disappointment. Only the charred edges of the garage door indicated anything untoward had ever happened there. In the cold clear December sunshine, one could shut one's eyes and not be able to envision a nude woman bound tightly to a chair, burned beyond recognition behind that very door. No. All you would be able to picture in that neighborhood was an electrical fire caused by old Christmas tree lights.

Dutifully Tiffany shot her pictures, but I could tell she was as bored as I was, maybe more so. When you're accustomed to looking through a lens and seeing juicily interacting body parts, how can you get excited about a concrete driveway, evergreens, and a picture window? We both almost fell asleep in the car on the way back to Manhattan and seriously considered dropping our initial plan of stopping at the office in favor of returning to our respective apartments for naps.

"Oh, let's go by the office and see if Miriam's had the baby," Tiffany said, and I agreed because I didn't want to admit I was in no mood to care if Miriam had the baby.

Back at the office, however, we found more than baby news. Starred Man had dropped by for a visit while we were in Fort Lee.

"It was awful," Clarissa said, wringing her hands which had just delivered a Polaroid of Starred Man into my own reluctant hands. "Like worse than you ever thought he would be in your wildest dreams. His chest hair was sticking out between the buttons of his shirt all the way down to his stomach. Like he buys his shirts too tight, I guess. It was gross. Hair like steel wool cleansing pads. You can't imagine," she said, shivering for dramatic effect.

I looked at his picture. He was white, but darkly complected. His skin looked muddy, and his eyes looked vacant. The hair of which he was so proud stuck out everywhere, even from his nose and ears. He needed a shave, beginning below the eyes and ending somewhere in the vicinity of the protruding stomach.

"Clarissa is extraordinarily repulsed by chest hair," David said, "but she does have an aesthetic point. Even a lover of chest hair might find his too much."

"His shirt was most certainly too tight," Cynthia Moore-Epstein, ever the stickler for details, added.

I put my hand on my forehead where a headache was beginning. It threatened to spread to my entire body. Why was this happening to me?

"I wouldn't worry about it," David said, putting his arm across my shoulder. "He won't be back."

"Oh, and why not?" I asked.

"How did he get upstairs anyway?" Tiffany asked.

"Oh, he didn't get upstairs," Clarissa said. "We all went downstairs to watch while security held him for the police. Cynthia brought the camera so we could take pictures for all the other security guards in case he comes back—" She caught David's menacing glare. "Which, like, he won't. I know he won't. We scared him off for good. And, Vinnie's lawyer is getting a restraining order now, so he won't be permitted anywhere near you. And, like, if he violates it, he's going to jail for a real long time, so he won't."

"How did they know who he was?" I asked. "Did he sign himself in as Starred Man?"

"Carolyn, he wasn't wearing a coat," David said.

"And he didn't smell nice," Cynthia added.

"So, like, of course," Clarissa finished, "they knew something was wrong."

"If he's shown up here, isn't it likely he's been sending the letters?" I asked.

"The first letter was sent by express mail," Cynthia said. "I can't imagine he could figure that out."

"Vinnie's P. I. doesn't think so," David added. "I'm not sure why, but maybe he has a lead on someone else."

And what none of us knew then was this: Someone called a *Post* reporter at approximately the same time the security guard was dialing the police.

Miriam's water broke as we were huddled in David's office discussing the ramifications of Starred Man's sudden appearance at our building. Her frantic call to Clarissa got our minds off Starred Man. Tiffany, with a video camera borrowed from the art department, rushed off to the hospital with Clarissa. David sent everyone else home early, mostly, I think, so he could ride back to my apartment with me, sprinkling so many reassurances into his conversation I felt like Mary Poppins had taken over his body. Terminal illness and death rarely take the edge off David's delightful ability to be caustic and amusing at the same time.

When I got as far as my bed, I crashed. I didn't wake up until almost midnight. The phone was ringing.

"Picture this," David said. "The front page of the *Post* is a photo inside a huge cookie cutter star. You are climbing into a car. Exercise does pay off, Carolyn, dear. Your ass does look good enough to nibble, but may I suggest in the future that you enter automobiles with some grace and not headfirst?"

"Oh, shit," I said.

"The headline reads," he continued, " 'Behind The Bondage Trial.' "

I wanted to pull the comforter over my head. I never wanted to get out of that bed again. I wanted him to shut up and go away, but I knew I wasn't going to get what I want, ever. Relentlessly, he read the latest chapter in my doomed life, according to the *Post*.

While the Superlady of Sex, Carolyn Steele, attended a session of the sensational La Passionata bondage murder trial in New Jersey, one of her fans was stalking her at the Playhouse *offices on Broadway. Ex-con Lamont McDermont, known to Steele and the* Playhouse *staff as "Starred Man," because of his practice of identifying each paragraph of his fan letters written from prison with a meticulously drawn five-point star, announced to a security guard, "I've come for Superlady. She's expecting me."*

The security guard, Arlen Shepherd, noted McDermont's general appearance, including that he was not wearing a jacket or overcoat, and became suspicious.

He says, "I told McDermont, I would call her down if he'd wait there in the lobby. He agreed to this, and I pushed the silent alarm, the buzzer is on the floor beneath my desk, calling for backup and also called upstairs to ask Mr. David Keltner if Miss Steele would be expecting a big guy who smelled bad and didn't have an overcoat. Mr. Keltner asked what color he was, which is white, and said, 'probably not.'"

Keltner denies making a racially oriented comment. He says, "I asked what color his shirt was, thinking he might be a messenger from one of the local courier services. Ms. Steele frequently receives review copies of books from publishers."

Within seconds additional security guards surrounded McDermont, who was held for the police. When they arrived thirty minutes later, several Playhouse staff members were watching the proceedings from a safe distance, photographing Lamont and openly speculating over whether he was the person behind the threatening letters Ms. Steele has been receiving. They identified "Starred Man" by his chest hair, which was protruding from his shirt and by his shouted insistence, "Superlady wants me because of my manly hairiness!" Copies of his letters to the Superlady of Sex were handed over to the authorities.

Meanwhile, Steele, accompanied by former porn star, Tiffany Titters, heard expert testimony on sexual bondage practices by Fred Durwood, MD, forensic psychiatrist from Washington, D.C.

According to Durwood, sexual bondage aficionados typically use extensive forms of restraint, such as the seventy-six feet (see accompanying articles on pages four and five) of tape used on La

Passionata. He also said it is not unusual for the "survivor" of a bondage accident incident to stage a fire to cover up the true cause of death.

"Survivors will go to almost any lengths to protect the victims' secret from discovery," he says.

McDermont was recently released from New York State Prison in Albany after serving five of a fifteen-year sentence on aggravated assault and armed robbery.

Ms. Steele could not be reached for comment.

After hanging up with David, I went to the kitchen to pour myself a glass of chardonnay. The phone rang. I hoped it was Charles, but I thought it was David calling back.

"Carolyn," the now familiar voice said. "Do you remember I told you you had your chance and blew it?"

Chapter Eleven

Dear Superlady of Sex,

Pornography has become increasingly aggressive, violent, and abusive. It harms relationships and encourages the subjugation of women. When you tell a woman in your column, as you recently did, to say to her man, "Fuck me," when she wants sex, you are really telling her to ask him to subjugate her into submissiveness. Shame on you! Every fiber of my being revolts against you. What you are doing is worse because you are a woman. Did your great-grandmother own slaves, and did she beat the women hardest? Or was she content merely to force them to submit to the rape of the white masters? Perhaps she enjoyed watching. Some day this is going to come back to you, and you will find yourself at the mercy of violence. . . .

Only 5:15 P.M., but the editorial offices of *Playhouse* were empty, except for me. It wasn't the kind of place where people felt compelled to stay late to prove their commitment to the job. David set the tone for the staff, and the tone was, "Let's keep everything in perspective here, people, this is a sex magazine, not a surgical amphitheatre, be out by five, latest."

I was only there because I wanted uninterrupted time

on-line with Nexus, the exhaustive computer research service plugged into nearly every newspaper and periodical published in the country. No, I didn't think I'd find the answers to my critical question—*Did someone murder Tanya, Zelda, and La Passionata and was that same someone coming after me?*—by punching up, Porn Pretty Killer, on the screen and entering the command, Search All Files. But after learning that Zelda, too, had received cut and paste threats on the same cheap typing paper before her death, I was desperately looking for a way to link those brief missives to a person or a group.

I put the letter from the woman who equated "fuck" with "subjugate into submissiveness" into the "Dangerous" folder, but was it really dangerous or just plain nutty? And why didn't we have a "Plain Nutty" folder? Clarissa suggested going through the hate mail looking for a "thread." That had sounded like a good idea, but what thread could one find in hate mail besides hate?

So, here I was, alone in the office checking hate mail, both mine and Madame Zelda's, against published antiporn diatribes, looking for possible connections. These women tended to be highly repetitious. Perhaps I would find the threats were phrases pulled from longer letters. Or maybe I could match an anonymous letter with a signed letter to the editor appearing in an esoteric lesbian journal or right-wing Christian newsletter.

I picked up another letter.

Dear Madame Zelda, You Cunt,

Perhaps you are familiar with Surgeon General C. Everett Koop's warning against pornography, issued in May 1988. He said, "Men who see such material [violent porn] tend to have a higher tolerance for sexual violence. And we suspect that, for men who are even slightly predisposed to such behavior, this material may provide the impetus that propels them from fantasy into the real world of overt action."

Perhaps you are also familiar with the similar conclusions reached by Donnerstein, Linz, and Penrod . . .

This had fallen into the hate pile because of the greeting and salutation, "Dear Madame Zelda, You Cunt," and the closing, "May your clitoris be ripped out without anesthesia." Definitely from a WAP. No WWA-WAW would use the word "clitoris." The findings mentioned coincided exactly with those listed in a letter to the editor recently published in *The Cleveland Plain Dealer* by a WAP member. I found it on Nexus and wrote the woman's name in pencil on the letter as "possible author."

But, having found it, what had I found? I could probably have proven in a few hours' time that half or more of the hate mail came from established antiporn groups largely composed of women. I knew that already.

Sighing, I went back to the stack of letters, typed and printed on word processors, hand written in block print and script ranging from Palmer perfect to nearly illegible. So many people, the majority of whom were women, with so much anger directed at us. How much happier would they have been if they'd taken their hands away from their writing tools and placed them on their own bodies where they could do some real good?

And what was the thread linking them together? Fear of sex? Fear of pleasure? Fear of losing control? Everyone was looking for threads. Tiffany had been obsessively combing the lives of Zelda, Tanya, and La Passionata, looking for the connecting links. When she found them, they were exactly what you'd expect them to be. High-school dropouts all, they had sold what they had to sell for the best possible price. Had she really expected them to have come from happy, reasonable, functional families? Or to be graduates of Vassar?

I smelled the presence of someone else in the office

before I heard anything. It was a subtle shift in the air as though someone were blocking a draft. I took my hands away from the keyboard and sat very quietly, listening hard. Nothing.

Maybe it was my imagination, I told myself, like a Gothic heroine, determined to proceed up the dark and narrow staircase to the attic in search of some truth. I picked up another letter. Well, what else could I do?

Dear Porn Queen Steele,
According to my hypothesis of what makes a woman sell out her own sex as you have done, I know who you really are. Like all porn queen types, you were abandoned by your mother, either physically or emotionally, and overstimulated by a father who both wanted and hated you . . .

I felt it again. A diffusion of the atmosphere behind me, directly behind me. I put my hands on the desk in front of me and tensed, as if bracing myself for an imminent crash. If someone was going to shoot me in the back, I didn't want to turn around and catch it in the face. Or, if someone was going to bring a heavy blunt object down on my head, I didn't want to see it coming, did I? Maybe if I didn't turn to look, nothing bad would happen after all.

"Like, what are you doing here?" Clarissa yelled.

I turned, partly in relief and partly in fear. Was it Clarissa who meant to bludgeon me to death? She had suggested a computer search for the missing links.

"Working," Rhumumba replied in the slow and low mumble that made it hard to hear what she was saying once she got past single word replies, which, come to think of it, she seldom did.

"What is everyone doing here?" I asked, walking to the doorway to confront them.

"Carolyn!" Clarissa said. "She was spying on you. I

saw her. I couldn't believe it. I didn't know who was in the computer room, but it was you. Like, she was standing there without moving and watching you!"

"Why were you watching me?" I asked Rhumumba, who remained silent.

"I decided to come back to do a little work since they wouldn't let me stay at the hospital, but I want to go back again for the evening visiting hours," Clarissa said, talking fast, her eyes on Rhumumba, who kept her eyes on me and her mouth shut. "You know I said there was something not right about her all along, didn't I?"

"Why were you watching me?" I asked again.

Rhumumba turned and walked out of the office, making remarkably little noise for someone who was built like an armored vehicle. Clarissa and I looked at each other. We couldn't have stopped her even if we'd wanted to try, which we hadn't.

"Well," Clarissa said, clasping her hands together in front of her body and rubbing her palms together back and forth until the dry raspy sound irritated me. "I think it's time we found out who she really is. I've always thought she was hiding something. Remember the rest of you thought her secret was a simple one. And, like, when we saw the hormone pills on her desk and knew she was a transsexual, everybody said, 'Well, that's it,' and I said, 'It's not going to be something so simple as this.' "

"How much more could a lesbian transsexual body builder have to hide?"

"Did you read the *Post* today?" Clarissa asked. We were waiting in the hallway outside Miriam's hospital room, the personal contents of Rhumumba's desk in three large gray envelopes in our arms, two for me, one for her. "What's a sitz bath anyway?"

"I hope the *Post* didn't say I was sitting in one."

"No, Miriam is. The *Post* has decided Anthony Spiker didn't murder her, that it was a bondage accident. I think they've taken that path because they couldn't find any way of connecting the porn pretty deaths, don't you? Like if they can't have a clean sweep of murder, they'd rather be bold and go with bondage accident. It gets the bus driver readers all agitated."

"A sitz bath is when you immerse your bottom in warm water to make your stitches feel better," I said. All that fisting and she'd still needed stitches? "In my day, it was alternated with heat lamp treatments. I still went through massive amounts of Tucks, but then I changed them every time they got dry on me."

"I have a headache," Clarissa said, visibly paling at the thought of what was happening to Miriam's vaginal area.

"She'll be all better in a few weeks. The stitches are catgut. They just fall out."

"Oh, gross!" she said, clamping one hand on her ear. "Carolyn, if I'd wanted to know about this stuff, I would have gone to Lamaze classes."

"I think you're right about the *Post*. Once this trial is over, they'll stop plotting my demise."

There were no chairs in the hallway. I pulled off my four-inch black slingback pumps, hiked my black wool skirt a little higher, and sat down on the floor, legs crossed in front of me. I tugged on Clarissa's trousers; she sunk down to join me. Wordlessly, we began going through the material in the envelopes.

"They have a magazine just for lesbian bodybuilders?" I asked.

"Why not?" she said, glancing at the cover. It was someone who looked enough like Rhumumba to make me fear she was a type in her own world. We both added, "Not my type."

She hadn't filled out the insurance request forms in

the company information packet she'd received upon hiring. Everything was still neatly in its pockets. I pointed that out to Clarissa, who merely raised her eyebrows.

"Fliers from health food stores, her gym membership card, hormones, and vitamins, what did we expect to find anyway, her old penis in a jar?" Clarissa asked, shoving everything back inside the envelope.

"That wouldn't have told us anything we don't know," I said, putting my share of Rhumumba's stuff back into the envelopes.

And then I did know. The picture on Rhumumba's desk, a 3 × 5 photo in one of those plastic frames that curves to make its own stand. I saw it clearly in my mind's eye. It had bothered me when I'd looked at it, but I didn't know why, had blamed my vague feeling of discomfort on the woman's bad haircut. Now I knew exactly who she was. And knowing who she was also explained Rhumumba. Why hadn't we brought that photo of the little tank's special someone with us?

Thanks to my driver's ability to move that limo through traffic as easily as if it were a motorbike, it took me less than twenty minutes to go to the office, retrieve the picture, and get back to the hospital. I slipped into Miriam's room, behind the back of an Oriental nurse who'd told me she already had her quota of visitors, two, and I'd have to wait outside. Some experiences are universal. This was no different than visiting any member of the Junior League back in Easterville, following the birth of her child. The rooms of new mothers were always standing room only. There was as much sneaking around to get inside those rooms as there would be later to get inside someone else's spouse's bed, after the babies were older and the thrills were gone.

Dressed in what was either a long sweater or a very short sweater dress, royal blue, shot with lurex threads, deep v-neck, Tiffany was cooing over baby Zelda in her crib beside Miriam's bed. A plump nine pounds, six ounces, Zellie, as we were all going to call her, had skipped the isolet in which many newborns typically start life and gone straight to Miriam's room. In five-inch stiletto heels, electric blue with ankle straps, Tiffany towered above baby like an East Village version of the good witch from *The Wizard of Oz*. Clarissa was seated on the bed, holding Miriam's hand and managing to look like she was the one who'd suffered.

"Carolyn, come look at her," Tiffany said. "She has so much hair."

I leaned over the crib. Zellie did have a lot of hair, tight fuzzy black ringlets, which set off her *café au lait* skin. The hospital had taped a pink bow to her adorable fuzzy little head in case someone failed to get the picture drawn by the pink receiving blanket wrapped around her. Why hadn't anyone told me the sperm donor was black?

"She's beautiful," I said truthfully. Isn't it nice when we can honestly say that about other people's babies? I lightly touched her cheek, baby skin, like nothing else on earth. Instinctively she nuzzled in my direction. "So beautiful," I cooed.

"Isn't it great she didn't come out red like white babies do?" Clarissa asked. "Like, I never thought about skin very much until I saw her, and now I think she's the best color to be."

Tiffany and I gurgled shamelessly over her for fifteen minutes before we had to leave for Tiffany's book party. It doesn't matter how babies get here or how strange their parents may be, they are little miracles of love and hope, the great levelers, turning all of us into the kind of people who lisp in nonwords.

We kissed Miriam. She looked truly awful, which is

another reason women her age shouldn't give birth. They don't look "wan but luminous" like younger mothers do. No, they just look plain awful after putting their bodies through something they shouldn't have to endure. And what were stretch marks going to do to the snake tattoos on her boobs?

Clarissa walked us to the door. I pulled the photo out of the deep pocket of my fur coat.

"Recognize her?"

It took a few minutes for recognition to dawn, but when it did, they were almost simultaneously spitting indignation. The woman who occupied the space of beloved honor on Rhumumba's desk was the thin blond WAP who regularly harangued us on the street corner, waving her placard of a torture victim in our faces as she shrieked, "Women, what are you going to do about this? Men are masturbating to this every day. They're masturbating to it right now. What are you going to do about it, women?"

"Rhumumba is a WAP!" Clarissa hissed. "If her lover is a WAP, she has to be one, too. Like those people don't intermingle. Right in our midst. No wonder she didn't fill out her insurance forms! She's a spy, a plant . . ."

"A killer?" Tiffany finished.

David and Charles were already at St. Mark's Bookshop in the East Village when Tiffany and I got there. They were standing, paper cups full of wine in hand, at opposite ends of the room, a group of thirty or so people between them. Blowups of several of the photos from Tiffany's book, *The Erotic Journeys of Tiffany T.*, were mounted on flimsy wooden easels along the walls.

Some of the photos were startlingly good. I particularly liked one of a nude couple: the tall, muscular black man holding a soft white woman whose body was rigid at a fifteen degree angle to his body. Her ass was too wide, and his penis was hidden. But, I liked it anyway.

It was a definite improvement over the party David and I had experienced recently at a Tribeca gallery where a writer's girlfriend had her first art exhibit. The writer hadn't told us his beloved only painted insects. Yes, bugs. Roaches, spiders, flies, caterpillars, bugs of indeterminate, to me anyway, species. The smallest canvas appeared to be three feet by four. The largest, a fly with many eyes, was bigger than the floor of a typical New York studio. They hung from the thirty-foot ceilings like the backdrops for a horror movie. Waiters handed out crystal flutes filled with champagne and offered guests dried beetles from glass and brass boxes. We had declined the beetles. Yes, this was a better party.

Eyeing the distance between them, I didn't think David and Charles were going to be friends. For a moment, I hesitated. Whom did I hug first? Charles, whose flight had landed only hours ago and for whom I was desperately horny, or David, my dear friend. David, of course. My mother always said brains outlast beauty. If she'd added friends outlast lovers, she would have given me everything I really needed to know about life. Anyway, I'd learned the last part on my own.

"Carolyn," he said, returning my hug warmly. "Were you and Tiffany helping each other get dressed? Is that why you're late?"

"We were looking for threads," I said and then I quickly and quietly filled him in on what we now knew about Rhumumba.

While he went to find a phone to notify *Playhouse* security that Rhumumba was no longer permitted on the premises, I connected with Charles, who wasn't amused at being second.

"I thought you didn't see me," he said, pulling back from my embrace.

"I had to tell David something important," I said and then told him what was going on.

"Babe," he said, putting his arm protectively around me. "That's frightening. You don't think she's behind the calls and letters and the paint throwing, do you?"

"The cards and letters, yes, it's possible. But, not the paint. She and Thatcher would never collaborate on a political action even if they do share the same side of the porn fence."

While he massaged my neck, I tried to explain the difference between WWAWAWs and WAPs. Whatever else she may have done, Rhumumba couldn't have been in league with Elizabeth Thatcher, because the WWA-WAWs want lesbians to have orgasms even less than they want heterosexual women to have them. They were two separate groups with agendas which dovetailed nicely on only one point.

David joined us, and they chatted briefly about photography for a few minutes. Why do two men instinctively pick a subject the one woman won't be able or willing to converse upon? I excused myself and went over to Tiffany, who was standing with her arm around Vera's waist in animated conversation with the other WIPs.

"I told them about Rhumumba," Tiffany said to me, encircling my waist with her other arm. I have to tell you my waist is a lot smaller than Vera's. She's expanded considerably since the cameras lovingly caressed her bound torso.

"I knew there was something weird about her," Vera said, but who hadn't known there was something weird about her?

We never did figure out where to rank her in the hierarchy of terrorists that night, because Tiffany's "special guest," her friend Angelo, formerly Angela, arrived.

"Oh," she squeaked to him, once her. "You look so delicious."

Truthfully, Angelo didn't look bad at all until he unzipped his pants. He was close to six feet, broad shouldered, with prominent cheekbones, a thick headful of blond, probably not natural, hair, styled close to the face and full in back, curled down to his shoulders. His jaw was a little weak for a man, but couldn't the same be said of a lot of men? It was the penis he pulled out of his pants which spoiled the effect.

"It's still a little raw-looking," he said anxiously. "The doctor told me the red might not disappear for several more weeks."

"Oh, it's beautiful," Tiffany said, reaching out to pat it, which, thank the Goddess, didn't cause it to fall off.

There were murmurs of polite assent among the women. Speechless, I smiled down at it. I felt like a mother had just lifted a deformed baby from its stroller and thrust it in my face for my admiration, something I might have been able to pull off with advance warning, but not without. Looking closely at it, I could see why male to female transsexual surgery was more common than female to male. It must be easier to slice off a penis and fashion a crude opening that could appear enticing, especially covered at the entrance by hair, than to create one by pulling the skin from the vagina outside and fashioning it around tissue taken from various parts of the body.

It was three to four inches long, maybe two inches wide, bright red in places, mottled red and purple in others, creating a patchwork skin effect. The hole in the head wasn't quite centered. The head, for that matter, wasn't quite a head, merely a slightly thicker part of the whole. And it was lumpy-looking throughout its inglorious length. I glanced at the other women looking at it and knew they all, with the exception of Tiffany and Vera who are kinder and gentler than the rest, shared my thought, *Not in my vagina, you don't!*

"Does it work?" Carola asked.

"Sort of," Angelo said proudly. "It doesn't get too hard, and it doesn't ejaculate, but I feel orgasms in it already."

Several people were peering discreetly into our little circle to see what the thing was in Angelo's hand. Charles was one of them. Judging from the expression of gentle distaste on his face, he wasn't quite sure what he was looking at, but he knew it wasn't pretty. Tiffany moved outside the circle, opening a space so everyone who wanted could come to admire Angelo's new organ.

That's why so many of us were standing bunched in one place when a figure dressed all in black from stocking cap to boots, and wrapped in a coarse black wool cape, opened the door to the bookstore and tossed something inside. A package wrapped in plain brown paper fell inches from us. We did not move or even, with the exception of Stephanie, scream. She started quietly enough, but her scream crescendoed until, at its peak, it began to rise and fall rhythmically. People looked at us as if they thought perhaps this was our version of the famous faked orgasm scene in *When Harry Met Sally,* and nobody wanted to intrude.

Luckily nothing worse than smelly smoke (in shades of yellow, green, and orange) emanated from the package. Tendrils of it curled up into the air surrounding us like party streamers. While Stephanie continued to scream and the rest of us began to cough, David rushed over, grabbed the package, opened the door, and threw it onto the street.

"Do we agree no police?" he asked, rejoining us.

We did and only Charles, camera in hand, got the shot.

"Rhumumba?" Charles asked.

"Not possible," David said. "I talked to Vinnie only minutes ago, and he said Rhumumba had been taken to police headquarters for questioning about the letters and phone calls. His P. I. has found someone who saw her on Wayne Street near Carolyn's apartment on the day one of the letters was delivered."

"Then who?" Charles asked.

"The WWAWAWs," I said. "Definitely their style. No wonder Vinnie seldom goes out."

"If you hadn't been ignoring me all evening, you would have noticed I was taking pictures," he said, and he was pouting.

It was hard to pay close attention to him now either when a short distance past my bare feet a woman was lowering her mouth over a penis, not as big and fine a penis as Charles possessed, but a nice one.

"What am I, the enemy now, too?" he asked. His eyes were stormy; I wanted to kiss his face, but I didn't want to touch him yet. "You think I'm going to sell that shot to the *Post?* You think I'd stoop so low? Or maybe you think I paid somebody to toss a stink bomb into Tiffany's celebration?"

"Of course not," I said. But did I mean it? I didn't trust him, though it was his wandering penis I suspected of endangering me, not his camera. "I'm just being paranoid. You know I've been through a lot lately. Does that turn you on?" I asked, pointing to the screen.

"Don't get paranoid with me, babe."

He considered the action on the screen. The woman's face was contorted by the penis in her mouth. There was a bead of sweat on the end of her nose; she was stroking her clit as she sucked her lover. He was calling her by name, Amanda, and thanking her for fellating him even as she was doing it. We were looking at the first feminist porn video produced by Vera and Gemma's joint venture, the Red Hot Mamas.

"It's hot," he said, putting his hand between my legs. "Does it turn you on?"

"Yes," I said.

I lied. It didn't turn me on. Like most of the woman-produced porn I'd seen, it was a little too politically correct to be arousing. Did he have to thank her so profusely? And, earlier, with equal politeness, he had asked her if it was okay to tie her to the bedposts while he ate her out, which he explained he only wanted to do so he could pleasure her more. Vera and Gemma wanted me to invest in their company. I was considering it, but only if I could have some creative input.

Charles turned me on. I tried to say his name, but I produced only a gurgle in my throat. The days and the miles and the distrust between us all came together like spaces suddenly compressed, and we fell into each other's arms, collapsing walls of feelings and flesh melding together. If I thought I'd wanted him before, it was nothing compared to how I wanted him then. I'd gone beyond having a strong sexual appetite for him. This was a hunger so intense, so active, I wanted him all at once, simultaneously in every orifice, his hands on every inch of my skin.

I was on my back, completely open for him. Our pelvises were locked together, and he was deep inside me. We moved together, slowly at first, he tried to keep it slowly, the movement contained. But I couldn't wait. I tightened my thighs around him, squeezed and pulled him inside me faster, deeper; soon he couldn't wait either.

I cried his name and screamed as the first orgasm began. He moaned and grabbed me fiercely to him. I felt him ejaculating deep inside me, a place where no one else could reach; I buried my face in his neck, inhaling his scent. He was all I wanted. I wanted him over and over again.

"Babe," he whispered, "I love the way you do this."

We lay together on our sides, still locked, his penis firm inside me, panting. Moving slowly, he stroked my clitoris lightly with his hand, bringing me to orgasm again. He kept it up, making me come over and over. I dozed and woke to him caressing me, entering me before I was conscious of wanting him. He lifted me up, guided his penis in with one hand so he was only partially inside me. And suddenly I was moving toward him and coming again. With each spasm of orgasm, he pushed in a little deeper until he was all the way inside me.

I touched his face. His eyes filled with tears. And I pulled him deeper into me, fiercely pulling his penis, all of him to safety inside me. My body entwined around his, I fell into a deep and grateful sleep.

In the middle of the night, I woke to the sound of static on the TV. The Red Hot Mamas' first video had played itself out hours ago. Charles was sound asleep, facing me, his arm across my body, his leg over mine. I pressed my nose and mouth into his chest. I licked his skin. It was salty. Knowing it would never happen, I thought I could be happy for the rest of my life with this man in my bed at night.

Then I felt it, the slow drip of a thin bitter liquid seeping out of my vagina, a liquid that was neither semen nor vaginal secretions.

I went to see my ob-gyn the next morning and asked her to culture me for chlamydia. Having had it once, I recognized the thin, faintly dark discharge. It smelled vaguely unpleasant when I put my fingertips to my nose.

"You're lucky you have a discharge," she said. "Most women don't."

Right. Lucky was exactly what I didn't feel with my feet in the stirrups, my diseased parts exposed to the air. Stupid, maybe. Why hadn't I made him wear a condom?

"You might have gotten it even with a condom," she said reassuringly. "People don't realize so many of these STDs can be spread during foreplay. There is discharge present in his seminal fluid or your vaginal secretions, you touch each other's genitals before putting on the condom, and what can I say? You've got it."

I sighed. Hopeless. It was hopeless. Sex was hopeless. She said he would have to be tested and treated, and we should consider agreeing to a monogamous relationship so this wouldn't happen again next month. Oh, Charles might *agree* to a monogamous relationship, but he'd never actually keep his penis to ourselves. Hadn't he made his position clear on our first day together when he said he was on a quest to implant his sperm in any suitable vagina?

"He's probably had it for a long time without knowing it," she said, patting my shoulder. "Men aren't tested for it unless they ask to be."

She sent me away with a pamphlet explaining chlamydia, its method of transmission, treatment, and the consequences of leaving it untreated: In women, Pelvic Inflammatory Disease; in men, infection of the testes leading to infertility. In fact, the neatly printed little words told me: "Untreated chlamydia is the leading cause of infertility in men and women today." If he'd been carrying the disease for a long time, his odds of being infertile were good, the ultimate irony.

The test came back positive. I got my prescription for Floxin filled and left the pamphlet with a note for Charles with his doorman. He was not amused. Then I went back to my apartment where a message from Vinnie was waiting for me.

Rhumumba had confessed to sending the letters and making the phone calls, to feeding information, including who really wrote the Madame Zelda columns, to the *Post*. But she swore she hadn't killed Zelda and had no intentions of harming me. Neither his P. I., who had been on Rhumumba's trail even before Clarissa and I caught her in the office, nor the police could find any reason to connect her, or the WAPs, with Zelda's death.

"It's over, Carolyn," Vinnie said. "She meant to scare you and to cause the magazine as much discomfort and embarrassment as she could."

The WAPs had posted her bail, but Vinnie's lawyer had slapped a restraining order on her prohibiting her from coming near me. If she did, she would be arrested immediately. With both Rhumumba and Starred Man kept on leashes, I should have felt safer, but I didn't.

It was over, Vinnie said. But it wasn't.

Chapter Twelve

Dear Superlady of Sex,

I notice most of your letters are from men who want to put more excitement in their sex lives with their wives and girlfriends. Well, I am a woman with a man's problem. When I started seeing my husband four years ago, I wasn't surprised he only penetrated me, had an orgasm and that was that! He was a twenty-five-year-old virgin and didn't know any other way. I am a few years older than he and began having sex at the tender age of fifteen so you could say I had been around the block and knew he wasn't up to speed. I loved him anyway because I knew he would be a good provider and father and we were married. But it's four years later and he still does it that way. I've tried to show him new ways and new ideas, but he says he prefers the "traditional" way, in which unfortunately I don't have enough time to come. Sometimes I take his hand and make him masturbate me but he feels uncomfortable doing that. What can I do with him?

Dear Patient Wife,

You have been patient far too long. He sounds like a very sexually repressed man who would benefit from counseling. If you can't get him to see someone

with you or alone, make an appointment for your-
self. You can at least get professional advice on how
to deal with your marital situation and perhaps
suggestions on how to get him into the therapist's
office. Meanwhile, make it clear that you consider
sexual satisfaction your right as well as his. He's
treating you like a prostitute by taking his satisfac-
tion quickly with no thought to giving you anything
in return. Next time, tell him lovemaking has to last
long enough for both of you. If he won't touch you,
masturbate yourself. And don't let him inside until
you're almost ready to have an orgasm. Finally, have
you considered an affair? If you want to keep the
marriage together and he won't or can't change his
sexual attitudes and behaviors—a lover is the answer
for you.

I was glad I didn't write for *The Ladies' Home Journal.*
They would never have let me advise a wife to cheat.
This was not the kind of advice Dr. Rita would give
either. I smiled. Then the disease thought intruded as it
did so often. Should I warn poor wife to have an affair
with a married man who was only seeing her and absolutely no one else and whose own wife was too repressed
to look outside the marriage for sex and still get tested
twice a year? Yes, I should. One should be responsible
about advocating potential disease-risk situations. I
hate the nineties.

"What are you so mad about?" Morgy had asked me
when I'd told her about my chlamydia, which had all
but ended my relationship with Charles. "It isn't AIDS.
Like you aren't going to die. So, you take antibiotics for
a few weeks. It's gone, isn't it? I can't believe a sophisticated sex advice writer is getting so hysterical over a
piddly little STD."

"And then I get it back and take more antibiotics
until eventually I get a strain so resistant to drugs I have

to stay in the hospital for a few weeks and take them intravenously!" I screamed into the phone at her.

We hadn't seen each other since the breakfast at David's Pot Belly Stove Restaurant. She was mad at me for ignoring her pleas to talk to Georges. I was mad at her for what . . . for being Morgy?

"Georges says you're overreacting," she said. "He thinks you're not as sexually liberated as you pretend to be."

"Oh, well, if Georges thinks so . . ." I said, enunciating each word as if I were spitting out ice chips.

Like every conversation I'd had with her lately, it hadn't gotten us anywhere. Christmas was only a week away. She would be flying back home to the Midwest in five days. I would be on a plane to London the same day to spend the holidays with my kids. What were we going to do about the annual gift exchange if we weren't speaking?

I sifted through the pile of mail, looking for a letter to balance the one I'd just answered. For example, I tried to follow a letter from a more or less typical husband or wife (i.e., one who isn't getting fucked enough) with a question from a swinger, fetishist, or a woman who was fantasizing about having sex with her priest or her husband's sister. You have no idea how many Americans are fantasizing sex with their in-laws, particularly, and this surprised me, men with their wives' mothers.

Each month I covered one letter in-depth, running the entire letter and answering it in five hundred to a thousand words and then twenty "Quickies With Carolyn," shorter questions and answers. The whole section took up six pages in the magazine. No wonder I felt like I was always tending to the mail.

I picked up a letter from a woman who didn't know how to tell her husband she wanted him to spank her.

Too bad she wasn't married to Georges. I put it in the back of the pile.

Where did Morgy get off telling me chlamydia was no problem? Wait until she found out someday, as she inevitably would, that she'd been infected with it for so long it had destroyed her ability to reproduce. You can bet she'll want a baby as soon as she finds out she can't have one. I was tired of people telling me every new threat to my health and happiness wasn't AIDS or some other life-ending catastrophe. It's only chlamydia. It's only hate mail. It's only threatening calls. It was only paint on my fur coat. Only a stink bomb, not a real one. *Only.*

Not to worry about Elizabeth Thatcher, everybody kept saying in disgustingly cheery tones of voice, because she got two months commitment to a mental health facility. In two months, they can do wonderful things, can't they? And so what if Starred Man is still loose? They recognize him at the security desk now. And Rhumumba? Her job is history. The WAPs will be paying her legal bills for so long, they won't have the cash to replace that placard her lover waves when it falls apart.

Everything that had happened to me was just an *only* event.

Even the *New York Post* had lost interest in me as a potential victim. Their series on the porn pretties ran out of steam when they couldn't find a single compelling reason to continue hinting that the deaths of Zelda and Tanya had been anything but freak accidents. The verdict in the La Passionata case, just handed down, had been involuntary manslaughter, with Anthony Spiker most likely to serve approximately a year of real time on an anticipated two-to-six-year sentence. My article was almost finished, ready to be sandwiched between Tiffany's strange collection of photos, shots of the principals that made them all look like relatives of the *American Gothic* couple and old bondage photos of Vera before the fat.

I put down the letter I was scanning from a man who wanted his unwilling partner to have his name tattooed on her ass *(What makes women so selfish as to deny their men the smallest pleasures?)* and picked up the *Post.* A mob killing, a society divorce, and the second newborn baby to be found in a dumpster in the Bronx in two weeks had taken my place. Only Tiffany seemed to think all was not yet quite safe in the world for me.

Even David had said irritably just the day before when I expressed a feeling of continued unease, "Carolyn, darling, don't you think a certain amount of this goes with the territory? You're not Dear Heloise, Queen of Household Hints, for God's sake!"

I found the next letter.

Dear Superlady of Sex,
I really like older women, and would rather bang them than the girls in their twenties my own age. An older woman gets it off faster and easier. She's grateful for you doing her. It's the perfect relationship for me, mutual lust and mutual gratitude. This is how sex should be. So, how do I get my mother's best friend into the sack? I've wanted her since I was in puberty.

I was contemplating my answer when the intercom buzzed, and the doorman announced Charles was downstairs.

"Send him up," I said reluctantly, in part because I was wearing a sweatsuit, black at least, and no bra, so my nipples, which always seemed to have an erection, were visible. But, still, a *sweatsuit!*

When I opened the door and saw him standing there, trim and elegant in a gray suit, white shirt, discreet though clearly expensive maroon and navy striped tie, a black cashmere topcoat over one arm, I got a lump in my throat. The lump was lust. I swallowed; it quickly traveled to my groin swelling my vaginal lips and making them sweat.

"Why are you so sure you got this from me?" he said, pulling the pamphlet on chlamydia from his inside jacket pocket and throwing it down on the glass coffee table. His eyes, so dark brown they were almost black, were glowing with indignation and hurt. "Do you think the other men you've slept with are cleaner than I am? What do you think, Carolyn? Are black men dirtier?"

I folded my arms across my chest, because I wanted to reach out and touch him so badly. We stood looking at each other, the anger and pain and desire palpable in the space between us. I breathed; the air was heavy with it.

"I asked you a question. You leave this pamphlet with a note telling me I've given you this disease. Did you leave everybody the same message?"

"There aren't any other bodies," I said softly. He looked at me incredulously. "I haven't been with anyone else in months, not since I had my last gynecological exam and got tested for STDs, as I routinely do twice a year. I didn't have chlamydia then. I have it now, and I've only been with you. What would you think if you were me?"

"I don't believe it," he said. I looked away and dug my nails into the palms of my hands to keep from crying.

"How many women have you been with in the last few weeks, Charles?"

"I told you I wasn't involved with anyone when I met you."

"I don't believe it!" I yelled. "You have enough hair care products in your bathroom to open a salon. Your phone machine is always filled with women's voices."

"Do you check my pockets for phone numbers and love notes while I'm sleeping?"

I almost told him about the night I'd heard him tenderly talking to some other "babe" on the phone in the other room while I pretended to sleep in his bed, but I bit it back.

"Charles," I said, tears welling in my voice, if not my eyes. "Why can't you just be straight with me? I know I'm not the only woman in your life. Why can't you just admit that?"

"I'm not a slut," he said.

Yes, he actually said, "I'm not a slut," before turning around and walking out my door. I stood there for several minutes, watching the door, though I certainly didn't expect him to walk back through it. Maybe I was watching it because I believed almost everything I wanted in a man—a huge penis and amazing lovemaking skills—had irrevocably passed through it, never to return. Finally, I started crying. I picked up the pamphlet and tore it into pieces and tossed them into the air like confetti.

"Men!" I said to Tiffany.

We were sitting at her little table, its chipped gray formica top an exact match, in my memory at least, to the one my sister, Billie Ann, had tossed away many years ago. A pot of scented tea in an unappealing shade of pale brownish green with specks of leaf floating on the top sat between us. I couldn't look at it without thinking of a dying man's last diarrhea, so I couldn't possibly drink it. I had stopped at Balducci's and bought a picnic dinner, apples and cheese, French bread baguettes, vegetable pâté, cold sesame pasta with shrimp, and a bottle of white wine. I was drinking the wine. Tiffany didn't drink.

"I know," she said, putting down her needlepoint and reaching across the table to cover my hand gently with her own.

She was embroidering a sampler that would read, "Sex is my spiritual discipline, expertise, politics, favorite subject matter, source of my income, foremost conversational topic, and the key to my health and happiness. I live as if I were making love every moment." Vera had written the words on the cloth for her in a flowery script. I wondered how many hours it would take her to trace the letters in rich red thread, given her apparent ineptness with the needle. Lucky she'd chosen red to hide the many drops of blood she would undoubtedly spill.

"I'm adding an ecstasy facial event to my Goddesses and Sluts seminars," she said. "It's optional. For another ten dollars they can have a sensual group facial and mud pack. I know this wonderful herbalist feminist facialist who will come in and do it."

"Oh," I said, imagining the description of this "new event" on one of Tiffany's Xeroxed pink fliers. There would be a star at the bottom of the page before the words, "Bring your own towels, washcloths, and a way to tie your hair back." Every one of Tiffany's creative ideas was quickly assigned a monetary value and trumpeted on pink paper with her signature "Tiffany," topped by a heart radiating lines at the bottom.

"Tell me about your video," I said.

Tiffany's most serious creative project, an ongoing effort, was a video about women and sex. Only Vera had seen it. The rest of us had been titillated with occasional erotic details. Now that it was almost finished, I was impatient. I wanted to see it before the other women did. If I couldn't be first, I would be second.

"I'll show you what I have so far after dinner," she promised. "You tell me about Charles first and then I'll tell you what I've learned from my investigations. I think I'm onto something."

If she really was "onto something," was this good news or bad? After inwardly railing about my new status as neglected minor victim that morning, I'd abruptly adjusted to it. Yes, it was rather nice after all not having the fat guy from the *Post* waddling around town in my wake, especially since I knew he'd photograph me being stabbed to death, rather than putting his ample flesh between me and an attacker.

"There's not much to say about Charles," I said. "He's a lying, womanizing sleazebucket. He gave me chlamydia, and he doesn't believe I couldn't have gotten it anywhere else. The man is a jerk, a stereotypical jerk. I only fell in love with him because he fucked me, which is a stereotypical woman's reaction."

"Had you told him you hadn't slept with anyone else before today?"

"No," I admitted. "What's that got to do with anything? If I'd told him sooner, he would have thought I was trying to pressure him into a relationship or something."

"Probably," Tiffany said. "But you have to admit, it would be difficult for most people to believe a sexy woman like you hadn't been fucking for the past several months, especially since you were dating." She put up her hand. "I mean I believe you, of course, but I can see where he might not. You don't believe him when he says he isn't involved with anyone, do you?"

"That's different! I know he is."

"How do you know?" she asked, sipping her tea.

I told her about the phone calls, the shampoos, the conditioners. Carefully she said they could be considered "circumstantial evidence," but that's what happens when you take an impressionable porn star to a murder trial. Tiffany was applying this principle of all men being innocent until proven guilty, but I wasn't buying it. I didn't have to catch Charles with his face in another woman's pussy to know the score.

"You're probably right," she said. "That's one of the reasons I only make love to women now. Men do always seem to end up being liars. Why do you think that is?"

Sitting under the poster of Tiffany and Vera in their matching corsets, I nevertheless felt as if I were back home in some other woman's kitchen, sitting across the table from my sister, Jenny, or my friend, Barb, preparing to launch into the latest chapter of *My Troubles* and knowing sympathy would be dispensed with the tea and wine. It didn't matter that Tiffany was dressed in leopard printed tights and a black bodysuit. It didn't matter that Morgy considered my growing closeness to the WIPs "neurotic." She was a snob, a shallow person who would always choose people from the outside in. Tiffany was woman, friend, confidante, source of warmth.

"I think men are liars because they know women are seduced by words," I said. "If women want to attract a man, we dress a certain way. If we want to seduce him, we undress a certain way. They are primarily visual. We are primarily verbal." I took a large gulp of wine. "Charles does this really insidious little thing. He drops 'we' into the conversation, almost from the beginning. Before he's fucked you, he's telling you 'we' are going to do this or that. It's very seductive."

"Couple talk," Tiffany said, dreamily stirring some honey into her tea.

"Sex lies." I drained the wine in my glass and poured more. "Lies, lies, lies. I hate it when men lie to me."

By the time we moved to the sofa, Charles, as a subject, was finished. I was slightly drunk. Tiffany was going to tell me what she had discovered in her research. But something happened to end all conversation, and I started it. I don't know if I meant to start it, but I did.

Tiffany put my wine glass and the bottle on the table in front of me, bending at the waist so that her ass was angled in my direction. I put out my hand and tentatively touched the wide expanse of flesh covered by clinging leopard spots. My fingers sunk into her. She held still for several seconds, perhaps waiting to see if I would extend the hand to the crack between her cheeks or the place between her legs. When I didn't, she poured more wine into my glass, then slowly stood up and turned to face me. I dropped my hand as she did. Her eyes were warm and glowing and fuzzy around the edges, as if they were slightly out of focus, the look of lust, no different in a woman than a man.

Did I reciprocate the feeling? I don't know. She sat down beside me and took my hand in both of hers.

"Did you ever feel a woman's breast?" she asked. I nodded no. "I want you to feel mine. It feels like yours."

She put my hand over her breast, which felt nothing like my own. The flesh wasn't taut inside her skin. I ran my fingers over the skin and felt the breast move separately beneath it. Her nipples were huge and rosy pink, not brown like mine. As I stroked her breast, she opened my black silk shirt and put her hands inside. I wasn't wearing a bra. She adjusted her body so she was closer to me and lowered her head to my breast. When she began to suck, I wanted . . . if not exactly her, I wanted androgynous, clean and pure and almost anonymous sex and I wanted it with her.

Without moving her mouth, she unfastened my silver studded belt and unzipped my jeans. I arched my back and lifted my hips off the couch so she could pull the pants down. My body was warm and ripe with desire, desire without discrimination, its center in my clitoris, burning like a beacon. I understood what it must be like to be a man, undifferentiated desire filling the penis that must be sated. She slid her fingers around it; I sighed and moaned. The orgasm came suddenly, intensely, almost out of nowhere, surprising her.

Tiffany sighed happily for me. Of course, I knew what I had to do next, give her something in return. I just wasn't quite sure about how to do it.

"Come into the bedroom," she said. "We'll take off all our clothes."

As Tiffany stripped off her bodysuit and tights, her smell enveloped me. It was a comfortable smell, like something herbal and musky, mixed with the greenness of Jean Naté. Nervously, I removed my own clothes and, following her lead, lay down on the bed. I looked at our bodies together side by side. She was fleshy, overly generous in every curve, but her back was thin. Her collarbone protruded. Her caves were trim if her thighs were not.

My own body, in contrast, was far less lushly defined. My hips are as slim as a trim young man's, my ass is high and firm. My back, though, is thicker, more muscled than hers. Propping my head with one arm, I turned on my side, thrusting out one hip, adjusting my body, as I automatically do at some point in bed with a man, to create the illusion of a more curvy hip, a more tightly cinched waist. I pulled up one leg and angled both my feet, toes pointing down, like a dancer posing.

"You don't have to do that in bed with a woman," she said, touching my body in long sweeping strokes from breasts to knees, like an artist preparing a canvas. "Relax."

I reached for her breasts again. When I lifted one up, I felt a line of sweat, which had been trapped beneath it and now trickled to the side of her body. Her breasts were things of great curiosity to me. I only knew mine, which being nowhere near the size of Tiffany's, had a far less active life of their own. How far could they go without me?

"I'm going to eat you out until you come and come and come," she said. Reaching under the pillow, she pulled out two white silk scarves. "Put your hands over your head." When I hesitated, she said, "You know you can trust me. I want you to let go completely."

Trembling slightly, I put my hands above my head. As she gently tied each one to the iron headboard, she ran her tongue from my wrist to my armpit. The trembling grew stronger.

"Relax," she repeated. "This is my tongue, not a whip."

I closed my eyes and pushed my body against her tongue as she lapped my cunt like an eager kitten at a dish of milk. With my eyes closed, she was anyone, a man; she was Charles, his long extraordinarily pink tongue exploring my inner crevices, moving surely toward the clitoris. When I opened my eyes, she was Tiffany, her big ass like a mother moon hung low over the bed. She was Tiffany with one hand in her cunt, masturbating herself as she tended to me. I closed my eyes and surrendered to the sensations until, as she'd promised, she made me come over and over and over again. She untied my wrists and kissed my palms.

When it was my turn to lick and suck her, I was too liquid to be tense. She lay on her back, legs obligingly opened wide, her face eager. Sex was communication to her; she was looking at me expectantly, as if she anticipated me making a clever remark.

I applied myself to the licking and sucking of her genitals and found it was curiously easier than performing fellatio on a penis that I may have found only minimally appealing. I didn't have to open my mouth so wide. She tasted sweet and salty at once, like a honey covered nut. Going down on a cunt is like eating and drinking at a Junior League tea party. You take little bites, and you don't talk with your mouth full. Her orgasms were accompanied by loud shrieks and moans and thundering sighs and even sobs.

When it was over, we lay side by side, sweaty in a companionable silence. She stroked my hair. I patted her thigh. Because I had no desire to be held in her arms, I didn't stay the night in her bed as she wanted me to do.

Instead I went home alone and cried myself to sleep. That had nothing to do with Tiffany. It was about Charles. Having sex with someone else only made me want him more. I felt as if my whole body were sexual, but every touch to it, no matter how hotly desired, would within hours leave me aching for him. I wanted him, hated him, not one more than the other.

The next day, I took the coward's way out on Christmas gifts, leaving with their respective doormen both Morgy's gift (a pair of handmade beaten gold earrings shaped like doves of peace) and Charles's gift, a bottle of Dom Pérignon with a note reading, "For you to share with that special someone who might make your baby on New Year's Eve." Corny as it sounds, I more or less meant it. Clearly he'd already had plans for New Year's Eve, since he hadn't invited me out, even before the disease scene. If he had plans he might as well start something other than another case of chlamydia, which, I would have bet, he still had.

Charles at the urologist getting tested for an STD? Having his fertility tested? No way. It would take all the romance out of his life.

I dragged Vera with me on my gift-giving rounds. We were on our way to Tiffany's for the Women In Porn Christmas luncheon. She'd suggested we go together since she was planning to be in my neighborhood that morning, and four hands were better than two at picking up the last-minute food items we'd both promised to contribute to the celebration. I was glad for her early morning call. I would have felt a little uncomfortable walking into Tiffany's alone the day after having sex with her. So, we cabbed our way around town together, finally arriving at Tiffany's slightly later than the "around eleven" we'd promised as helpers.

Tiffany didn't answer the bell.

"That's strange," Vera said, getting visibly nervous after the first series of short jabs failed to produce a response.

Tiffany's building had no doorman, so we had to stand in the lobby outside locked doors waiting for her to respond to us and release the door. I put down my Balducci's and Grace's Marketplace bags next to the bags Vera had dropped containing more food and both of our exchange gifts. I leaned on the bell. No response.

"She probably went out to pick up something she'd forgotten," I said. "We might as well wait here. As soon as we pick all this stuff up and go somewhere for a cup of cappuccino, she'll be back."

"You're right," she said, but she sounded worried.

My feet in four-inch black suede heels were tired, so I took off my shoes. The tiled entranceway felt cold on the soles of my feet. Vera put her large black vinyl carryall on the floor and sat on top of it, with her knees pulled close to her chin. The view of her ass, almost totally exposed by the pulled-up miniskirt, was awesome, but her legs were still fabulous.

Ten minutes later I put my shoes on and walked to a phone booth on the next block, while Vera stayed with the bags. I dialed Tiffany's number and got the machine with her standard outgoing message spoken against an Indian music backdrop. If she'd had to leave suddenly, she would have left a new outgoing message telling us what was going on. Walking back to the building, I knew something was wrong.

"Nothing?" Vera asked, her darkly penciled eyebrows raised in a solid thick cloud of concern.

"No. Let's buzz the super."

He wasn't anxious to let us in until he saw us. His eyes visibly lit up when he got a glimpse of our heels, miniskirts, and black stockings. He agreed not only to take us upstairs so we could knock on the door, but to open it with his master key should there be no response. Any two women in short skirts, black stockings, and high heels could have their way with any super in this town.

We put down the bags again in Tiffany's hallway. When the bell and loud knocking produced no response, he turned his key in the lock. He stood back so we could enter, which Vera did first. When I heard her scream, I knew Tiffany was dead, but seeing the body was still a shock.

She was lying on the floor between the sofa and the coffee table, fully clothed in her leopard tights and an old black sweatshirt, her limbs splayed open and pointing in four different directions. Her eyes were popping out of her head; they were so bloodshot, the irises appeared to be swimming in blood. Her neck was red and black and blue around the white silk scarf constricting it so tightly it was cutting into the flesh. A heavy purple tongue protruded from her lips.

It was the tongue that bothered me most.

Part Three

FEMALE SUPERIOR POSITION

Chapter Thirteen

●━━━━━━━━━━━━━━●

Dear Superlady of Sex,
   I am sorry to read of the death of your close friend, Tiffany Titters. I hope you are keeping yourself safe while the police search for her killer . . .

I thought about the piles of condolence letters that I'd received following Tiffany's murder as Vera read an erotic death poem, written in tribute to her "best friend, in sex and out." They had surprised me, those letters coming from every part of the country and Europe, Japan, South America, Australia, even from a brothel in Hong Kong, the words varying little from one writer to another. *Sorry. We are so sorry. Be careful.* They had been waiting for me when I got back from London, neatly arranged in stacks lining the walls of David's office by his secretary, Gwen. When I'd seen them, I'd burst into tears.

"Last night with warm inspiration on my hand, I began an erotic poem," Vera read, pausing at the end of the line to look at us, her enormous brown eyes made bigger and more luminous by thick black eyeliner, layers of mascara, and a veil of tears.

The Women In Porn were all gathered for the private ceremony at Vera's apartment. Everyone was wearing black, even David and Charles, the invited guests, and

Mike O'Reilly, my bodyguard, one of the three Vinnie had hired to give me twenty-four-hour protection. If Tiffany had been at her own memorial service, she would have dressed in purple or red or something hot pink and fuzzy.

"I wanted to write of your body, familiar as my own," Vera continued. She was wearing a black corset with garters that laced up the front with black fishnet panty hose. It was covered from waist to the top of the thigh by several black crinolines. "But, I could not. Death has changed your body . . ."

Oh, yes, dramatically changed. I shivered at the memory of Tiffany in death. Charles put his arm around my shoulder, squeezed lightly and kept it there. I was grateful for his touch. The night of Tiffany's murder, I'd called him. He'd taken me back to his apartment and tenderly cared for me until he put me on the plane for London, and he'd been waiting at the Kennedy International Airport on my return.

I would have been glad to see him, even if my visit with my children had been an unqualified success, which it wasn't.

"Everyone knows who you are," Matthew, twenty-one, had said through tight lips only seconds after our initial hug.

"It's true," Kate, twenty, said, "but he doesn't have to be such a big butthead about it. I keep telling him it's not your fault your business associates got murdered."

"My roommate knew who you were before you made the news here," Matthew said, ignoring her warning scowls. "He came in one day with the British issue of *Playhouse* and showed me your column. He showed it to other guys. Somebody is always wiggling his fingers at me and asking, 'How's Supermom?' "

"Oh," I said, getting the significance of the wiggling fingers. "It was about masturbation?"

My own son winced at the word, and his face looked like his father's had years ago when he'd told me he didn't think it was "very womanly" of me to touch myself during sex. All this before we had the luggage stowed into the trunk of Kate's Ford mini. There were many such moments sprinkled liberally throughout the visit.

I tried to talk to them about the pervasive American fear of sex, because I wanted them to see me as a sexual revolutionary engaged in the noble work of enlightening an ignorant populace. They didn't. Kate looked sympathetic, her beautiful, innocent face open to possibility but not convinced. Matthew simmered and seethed—and spit contemptuous remarks at me, disguised as humorous barbs.

About Tiffany, he said dismissively, "How could you be friends with someone who held a mirror to her twat as part of her performance art?"

"A speculum," I corrected. "She invited male members of the audience to use a speculum so they could see her cervix."

"That's not art," he snapped. "It's disgusting."

"No," Kate admonished him. "It's just too clinical for me to consider it art. But I think it has something to do with feminism and protest, doesn't it, Mom?"

Charles was a very welcome sight at Kennedy when I landed. But even his consoling presence now beside me couldn't drive the memory of Tiffany in death from my mind as Vera spoke about her body. Her tongue, large, purple, swollen to three times its normal size; her tongue had haunted my dreams these past weeks. What a cruel irony for someone who had given so much oral pleasure to end her life with her lovely tongue horribly mutilated.

Though she must have felt the same way I did on discovering the body, worse because they had been so much closer, Vera had held herself and me together. At first I'd stood beside her, unable to move while the super called the police. Then, after the immediate shock of finding Tiffany dead had left my body like rigor mortis abruptly letting go, I had wanted to run to her and force the tongue back into her mouth and hold her lips shut so no one else would see what we had seen. Vera had kept me from touching Tiffany by holding me tight to her body, her arms like straps around me, until we both started crying. She'd made me understand I couldn't touch anything.

"You are no help, you cannot help as I try to conjure visions of flame-tongued nights and am left with ashes in my mouth," Vera read, her voice catching on the last word.

The ashes were a point of bitter contention between Vera and Tiffany's mother, who'd had her cremated as soon as the autopsy was completed, and then returned to Milwaukee the same day with Tiffany in an "urn," which is a funeral home word meaning "cheap square brass box with nameplate attached." Hers had said, "Linda Sue Mitten, 1952–1988." Vera thought the ashes should have stayed with her. She wanted to put them in a Chinese vase and keep them on her night table, where the proximity would help keep her friend alive.

On the other side of me, David grimaced slightly at the mention of the ashes. Unable to overcome his Catholic upbringing at such times, he thought Tiffany should have been given a "decent burial" in one of the old scenic cemeteries in the Bronx. If she'd wanted to return to Milwaukee, he'd reasoned, especially as Linda Sue Mitten, she would have done so long ago.

"That death could pull you from my nipples before our suckling was through . . ."

Mercifully, Vera dissolved in tears. Carola, resplendent in a black velvet suit and black and silver beaded bustier, stood, walked to the podium, and led her back to her seat. We'd rented the podium and folding chairs from a party rental service. Vera had borrowed vases from everyone and filled them with white gladioli. Her L-shaped studio apartment was alive with death flowers. We may not have had a body, but we had the appropriate floral displays and an enormous catered spread sent by Vinnie. For several minutes, we sat in silence, looking at the flowers, the plates of food, the champagne flutes, trying to avoid each other's eyes.

Recognizing the need for someone to take charge, I stood and asked, "Does anyone have anything else they'd like to say about Tiffany?"

Bobby rose dramatically from his chair. He was wearing a floor-length black velvet dress that fit his body like thick, soft skin. It was cut to the navel. Rhinestones in exuberant floral arrangements began at the shoulders and trickled down the sides, following the slit to the navel, by which point they looked like delicate fallen petals from the succulent blossoms on top. His breasts heaved theatrically as he spoke. Bobby could have had a career in opera, if he'd only had the voice.

"I know almost everybody here has made love to Tiffany," he said. "But I consider myself the luckiest of you all because I had the privilege of loving her as a man and as a woman. I had my penis inside her, and later she made me come all over both of us by playing with my breasts. I never felt like a whole woman until Tiffany did that for me. Nobody loved like she did." The tears gathered in the corners of his eyes. When he spoke again, he sounded as if they were falling inside, too, down into his throat. "The beautiful thing about Tiffany was she accepted, she accepted whoever you are but she also believed you could be whoever you wanted to be. She accepted at the same time she was helpin' you change."

He sat down. I waited a few minutes and stood again. Almost everyone had said something. David had called her an "undiscovered genius, a woman whose intelligence and talent were rarely given their due." Only Charles, who didn't know her well, and Clarissa, who wasn't able to overcome her embarrassment at her own emotional response to our loss, had not delivered a eulogy.

"I think Tiffany would like it if we'd open Vinnie's expensive champagne now," I said. "She might not have been a drinker, but she always loved it when Vinnie spent his money on us."

Charles and David stood at once, reaching out to touch my arms from either side.

"I certainly could use a drink," David said. "The thought of Vera with those ashes in her mouth has made me thirsty."

I knew it was what he felt he had to say to keep us all from crying again.

We stood in little clumps of two and three, nibbling on shrimp and pâté and caviar, and speculating about who had killed Tiffany. Most of our speculation centered on Rhumumba. She was our murderer of choice. The police investigation, however, was focused on Tiffany's sex life because the cops were sure it was a "sex crime." They pointed to the white silk scarf around her neck and hinted it was a bondage game gone wrong, another La Passionata story. They didn't quite get the principle of bondage; restraint typically applies to ankles and wrists, not choking to death. Each of us had been interviewed; we'd heard her other "known" sex partners had also been contacted.

"If they investigate everyone Tiffany ever slept with, they'll be doing interviews for years," Gemma said, pulling up the wayward strap of her lingerie-style black silk gown. "That's so crazy. She wasn't in the middle of sex when she got killed. How many people have to tell them Tiffany never did it with her clothes on before they'll get the picture?"

"They asked me if I thought she might have been having her partner choke her at the moment of climax to heighten the sensation," Stephanie said. She was wearing a tiny black leather strapless dress with a black leather rhinestone studded collar and five-inch heels. "One of the assholes who questioned me said I should know about such techniques, being a working girl and all."

So far the only information the police had uncovered had been about us. We now knew that both David and I had been to bed with Tiffany. He was as shocked to learn about me as I was him.

"Carolyn," he'd said, uncharacteristically raising his voice over the phone when he confronted me. "You, too? I can't believe this. What were you thinking?"

"Well, what were *you* thinking?" I'd asked.

"It was only once."

"But I thought you had never cheated on Peggy. You told me that, and I believed you. Why would you lie to me?"

"I never have cheated on Peggy," he said, and it sounded like tears in his voice. "Being with Tiffany just that one time didn't feel like cheating."

He paused, waiting for my forgiveness, which wasn't coming. I counted on him to be happily married. He and Peggy had married as teenagers when she got pregnant. They had grown up together and stayed together and had, what I'd believed to be, the one perfect marriage of two independent people willing and able to give each other space as they remained intensely connected to each other.

"Carolyn, you know it's been hard for me, editing a sex magazine without ever having been with any other woman. You know my curiosity has often been cruelly aroused."

"It was only once for me, too," I said, still not willing to let him off the hook. Besides, hadn't his vicarious experience of my sex life been enough for him?

"Would you have done it again if she'd lived?" he asked.

Tiffany had died the next day, but if she hadn't, I don't think I would have had sex with her again. But who knows? I let him wonder.

"It's a good thing you and Vera found her together," Clarissa said between bites of caviar, which she was spilling on the jacket of her shiny black menswear suit, a new thriftshop find, "or they would have pinned it on whoever came in first."

"Only in the movies," David said. "And that suit," he told Clarissa, "looks like it might be harboring moths. Don't put your hands in your pockets."

"Ha!" Stephanie said. "Where do you think they learn how to do their job? They watch bad movies."

We circulated around the room, forming and reforming little groups, saying the same things over and over again. Mostly what we said was: Rhumumba murdered Tiffany. She was strong enough. The Goddess knows, she was mean enough. And she was about the only person none of us could picture Tiffany fucking under any circumstances, which would certainly explain how she ended up dead with all her clothes on.

I'd told each of them about Tiffany's intention of telling me what she'd "discovered" before our last evening together turned into a sexual encounter. I blamed myself for that. If I hadn't touched her ass, would she have told me what she'd found? Could we have done something with the information which might have saved her life?

"What do you think it was?" Clarissa asked.

Everyone had asked the same question. I didn't know, couldn't even guess.

"Surely it had something to do with Rhumumba," Vera said.

"Are you ready?" Charles whispered in my ear.

Even in mourning, my body responded to his presence. We would be the first to leave, but I didn't care. I could have sent him on his way alone, but I wanted to be with him. I said my goodbyes.

Since the murder, he had held me, stroked my face, gently kissed me, and consoled me. He hadn't fucked me, which was what I wanted and needed now. As we were making our goodbyes at the door, Bobby handed us each a creamy white envelope sealed with red wax.

"A lock of Tiffany's pubic hair," he said. "I had it saved from the time she let me shave her. It didn't seem right to keep it all to myself." Again, his eyes filled with tears. "I thought we should all have a piece."

"Oh, Bobby," I said, putting my arms around his neck and hugging him hard. He smelled as wonderful as he looked. "I love you."

"Girl, I love you, too," he said, brushing his thick luscious lips across mine.

Charles extended a hand to shake. Bobby grasped the hand in both of his and held it briefly. Mike stood between us and the door, watching the scene, as if he thought we were all a little strange, but was too polite to point it out to us.

"I don't get him," Charles said. We were in the limo, with Mike on the seat across, facing us. "If he wants to be a woman, why doesn't he go all the way and have it chopped off?" Mike winced, and Charles grinned at him. "Yeah, I agree. But he's got breast implants. Why does he want both?"

"A breast and a penis aren't synonymous," I said.

"These ain't your typical people," Mike said, shrugging his shoulders. A big Irishman in his early thirties with red hair so thin his freckled scalp peeked through, Mike had been working for Vinnie for ten years. "You get used to seeing anything with these people. That pubic hair thing, that didn't even faze me. When I started working for Vinnie, my jaw was on the floor about half the time." He nodded in my direction. "She's almost normal, the most normal one of the whole bunch I've met so far. I don't know what she's doing in this crowd, but I guess she knows."

"Sometimes she knows," I said.

"Don't get me wrong," Mike said. "They ain't bad people. I would never say that. Quite the contrary. You get to know them, they're good people. I couldn't ask for a better boss than Vinnie Mancuso."

"Well," Charles asked me, "do you get him? Does Bobby make sense to you?"

"Do I understand why he wants to live as a woman, but keep his penis? Not exactly. It's his choice."

"He's not a homosexual, right?" Charles asked.

"Right. I think he's bisexual, but I don't know it for a fact. He's not a transsexual, because he doesn't want his penis removed. If he were a transsexual, he'd believe he's a woman trapped in a man's body, and he'd be anxious to make the body completely female. So, you're asking me to explain why he has gone further than most transvestites by having the breast implants and dressing all the time as a woman . . . and I can't. It's just what he wants to do."

"Like he said back there when he was speaking, you just accept it or you don't," Mike said, raising his eyebrows and lifting his hands in a "what-can-you-do?" gesture.

"Bizarre," Charles said. I got the feeling he wasn't as amused by the bizarre as he'd been a few weeks ago.

Nevertheless, he put his arms around me and pulled me close against his chest. Being there was all I wanted for the moment. Tiffany's death had changed me. I was going to take love where I found it, whether or not it held the promise of tomorrow, or came with the seal of sexual good health.

Mike checked the apartment, including the closets and under the bed, for a lurking stranger—like Rhumumba would have fit under the bed—then pulled the shades and left us alone while he sat on a chair in the hallway outside my door.

"It's dark in here," Charles said.

"I may not be the next victim, but my plants stand a good chance of dying if the killer isn't apprehended soon." I put my arms up, and he came into them. "Thank you for coming with me today. Having you there made a big difference to me."

"It's okay, babe. I told you I'm your friend. You're the one who treats me like the enemy."

"Please stay awhile."

"Sure, babe. Come here," he said, taking my hand and guiding me to the sofa, though I would have preferred the bed. I didn't care if he still had chlamydia and I'd have to take antibiotics for another ten days, I wanted to make love to him. "Stretch out on the couch and let me rub your neck."

I kicked off my black heels and laid facedown on the sofa, my head resting on my folded arms. He began massaging my neck and shoulders, his fingers soothing and warming my muscles. Knowledge about Charles was working its way into my body at the same time. He had changed, too. This was kindness, not lust.

He'd been intensely interested in me in the beginning, plying me with questions about myself, talking in the "we" terms. The first several times we'd made love, he'd almost demanded I get involved with him on a deeply emotional level. But, like every true romantic, he'd cooled down. He would have, no matter what I'd done. It was tempting to say, "If chlamydia hadn't come between us, things would have worked out." Tempting, but wrong. That's what I was thinking now. I was sure I felt his loss of desire through his fingertips on my skin.

"You don't want me anymore, do you?" I asked him, raising up and turning to look into his eyes.

"You think I don't want you?"

He ran his hands down my back and let them linger on my ass. I put my head back down. Was I wrong? And why was I always so unsure when I was with Charles?

"I want you, babe, but I don't want to hurt you. If you think you got something from me, I don't want to put you in that position again."

"Charles, did you go get tested?"

"No," he said, a pout creeping into his voice. "Nothing's wrong with me. I don't need a test to tell me there's nothing wrong with me. If my dick were leaking, I'd know it."

"But, your dick wouldn't necessarily leak if you had chlamydia," I said, raising my head again. "In fact, it probably wouldn't."

"Babe," he said, taking his hands away from my body. "There is no point in talking about this."

I rolled over, rubbing my thigh against his as I did. My black silk sarong skirt had attached itself to the leather sofa, and hiked up even farther when I twisted it loose as I turned my body around. Now the skirt was barely covering my crotch. I watched him look at my crotch and then my breasts. I was wearing a black silk bodysuit, no bra. Taking his hands in mine, I put them on my breasts.

"You know I love your breasts," he said; his eyes were liquid with desire. "Don't do this to me, Carolyn."

I sat up, and he moved back against the sofa. I sat on his lap and kissed him. He touched my breasts through the silk. I felt the heat again in his hands, his mouth, but it was different between us now. Had I been the one to hurt him?

"I want you," I whispered in his ear, my tongue finishing the sentence for me . . . fuck me, I want you to fuck me.

"I don't want to hurt you, babe. I'm afraid of hurting you."

"I don't care. I want you to make love to me."

"Do you want to come? I'll make you come."

He pushed the bodysuit back from my breasts and ran his tongue around my nipple. His other hand moved down my body to rest between my legs. I tightened the muscles around it. With his thumb, he flicked open the snaps of my bodysuit and rubbed against my clit through my panty hose. I wanted him to pull my clothes off. More than anything, I wanted his penis inside me.

"Please," I said.

He moved his thumb against me expertly. In seconds I had an orgasm, which left me hungry for more. I wanted more of him, and I wanted it now. Moving him aside, I yanked off my panty hose.

"Carolyn," he said, sitting back against the sofa again, his hand resting on the huge bulge inside his pants. "Don't."

I climbed on top of him and reached beneath my own body to unfasten his belt, unzip his pants. He kept his hands on my hips, firmly pinning me down, so that I couldn't move high enough to center myself on his penis. But he kept guiding me with his hands, moving me so that I rubbed the side of his penis against my clit. He let me use his penis to masturbate myself; I came again and again, but he never did.

Collapsing against his shoulder, I started to sob.

"It's okay," he said, smoothing my hair, kissing my neck. His penis was still hard between us. "You're gonna be okay."

Embarrassed, I stood and pulled the skirt down over my body, sticky with my own residue, not with his.

"You'd better go," I said.

"Okay, babe." He kissed the top of my head and ruffled my hair. "Take care of yourself. You know you can call me if you need anything. I love you."

I cried for a few minutes, then took a shower and dressed in jeans, a black silk shirt, and boots. While I furiously scrubbed my body clean and dressed it, I promised I'll never do this to myself again. Never humiliate myself by practically begging a man to fuck me. *Never.* Grabbing my mink and the keys, I hurried out the door without looking at the sofa where Charles had refused to make love to me. I could smell him in the room.

"We're going back to Vera's," I said to Mike, who was sitting outside my door.

"Jeez, do they still have food left?"

Everyone was still at Vera's, and there was a lot of food left, which made Mike happy. Miriam had brought the baby over, too. Vera was holding her when Mike and I walked in.

"It was not the reunion of your dreams," David said after taking in my red eyes.

"Fuck off," I told him, collapsing onto the futon beside him.

"He's not worthy of you," David said, putting his arm around me.

"A big penis is a big penis," Gemma told him. "When a man has a really big penis, he doesn't have to be worthy because his penis is."

"Right," I said. "That's why both the men I've known who had big penises were such jerks."

"You women are disgusting," David told us, shaking his head as if he sincerely meant it. "You tell men not to worry about how big our penises are when all you really want is a big one. No wonder we don't believe your pathetic little reassurances."

"We don't really mean it," Gemma said, her eyes sparkling mischievously. "Why should you believe it? We're trying to inflate your pathetic little egos so what you have doesn't give out on us when we need it."

"Oh, I think a big penis is overrated," Stephanie said.

"Well, you would! You just want to get them in and out with as little complications as possible," Gemma teased. "I see your point, of course, but you're looking at the penis with a professional distance."

"I think big ones are overrated, too," Vera interjected without taking her eyes off Zellie dozing against her bosom. "If a man has a really big one, he doesn't think he has to do anything else except let you look at it and shove it in."

"I wonder if Rhumumba had a big one," I said. What I didn't say was, "Not Charles. He didn't just let me look at it and shove it in. He used everything at his disposal, not merely his major penis." If I'd said that, I would have started bawling.

"I doubt she'd have removed it if it had been a spectacular specimen," David said.

"I agree with you, honey," Bobby said. "You don't see me cutting mine off. When you've got a good thing, you hang on to it because you never know when you're going to decide to put it to use."

We all laughed. David got up to pour some champagne in a rented crystal flute for me and replenish the others' glasses. Vinnie had sent enough Cristal for two or three drunken memorial services. We sipped our champagne quietly for a few minutes, watching Zellie sleep. Would she grow up to be ashamed of her parents as my son now was of me? And would he outgrow it when it occurs to him someday that my embarrassing work helped pay for his education? What did we ever do before Clarissa and Miriam had Zellie? Every group of adults needs a baby to watch.

"What do you suppose Tiffany thought she had found out?" Carola asked no one in particular. "It keeps nagging at me. Suppose she did stumble on something that led to her murder or proved Zelda or Tanya had been murdered. I don't see how La Passionata could fit into the mix. Her death seems pretty straightforward to me."

We all agreed it did. No one had a clue about Tiffany's secret discovery.

"It was probably nothing," David said, but his voice lacked conviction.

We kept asking ourselves, What *did* Tiffany *know*? Maybe Mike got tired of the question, because he was the one to propose a means of finding the answer.

"Easiest thing in the world to get into her apartment if you want to go through her things," he said. "Was me, that's what I'd do."

"The police have it sealed," David said.

"Which means they have a piece of yellow tape across the door," Mike explained. "You lift the tape, pick the lock, put the tape back when you're finished."

"Are you offering?" I asked.

"Why not?" he said, and stuffed two shrimps in his mouth at once, chewed three times, and swallowed. "Beats sitting around here listening to you guys wonder what she knew that you don't know. Who's going with me?"

Clarissa, Vera, and I stood first, so we got to go. More than four, Mike said, would be a "crowd action."

Getting past the locked lobby doors proved so easy I wondered why they bothered to lock them. Mike buzzed an apartment at random, said, "Hey, it's Mike downstairs. I forgot my key and my girlfriend must be in the shower because she doesn't answer." In seconds, the click of the door release sounded, and we were in.

"Sometimes it takes a few apartments before it works," he said. "We got lucky. A man answered. Women aren't so quick to let you in."

Upstairs, he lifted the tape and picked the lock before anyone came into the hall and saw us. Inside Tiffany's apartment, I felt panic rising in my throat. I could smell her death. Sweat broke out above my lip and under my arms.

"Take short breaths for a few minutes," Mike said, his hand on the back of my neck. "Then breathe deeply."

I did what he said, and it worked. Vera and Clarissa, both pale, seemed to be following the same advice. Within minutes, we were able to move around the apartment without fear of vomiting, but what were we in search of?

"Any idea what we're looking for?" Mike asked, scanning Tiffany's refrigerator which was covered with photos, copies of her pink Xeroxed fliers, and cards, newspaper clippings, everything but drawings made by children. "What was she looking for anyway?"

"Okay," I said. "She kept talking about connections between Tanya, Zelda, and La Passionata. She was looking for missing links. That's all I know."

Mike and I took the living room; Clarissa and Vera, the bedroom. They found copies of the research Cynthia Moore-Epstein had sent me about the three deaths on one of Tiffany's bedside tables. Since I already had the material (and hadn't found it enlightening), we left it.

"We'll make a copy of your copy for everyone," Vera said, putting the pile of papers carefully back down inside the dust outline around them. "Maybe you've missed something one of the rest of us would see."

We combed the apartment for almost an hour, each team taking the other's territory in the second half of the search. We found nothing.

"She's got a lot of videos here," Mike commented. "Anything in that?"

"She was getting into producing her own," Vera said. "So, she had a lot of them for study purposes. I don't see how they could have anything to do with anything else."

"Like, we're missing something really obvious or someone got it before we did," Clarissa said.

"The police or the murderer," Mike said, ushering us to the door. "Anyway, we tried."

He put the yellow tape back, and we got out of there without running into anyone in the halls again. Breaking and entering is actually a lot easier than it looks on TV.

Back at Vera's, Mike's replacement was waiting his turn to guard my life. A tall, muscular, and noncommunicative Jamaican, Samuel inspired great confidence in me, even if he wasn't as much fun as Mike. Who could possibly get past Samuel? His hands folded across his chest, he nodded impassively when we came in. It would never have occurred to him, I'm sure, to ask where we'd been.

"The changing of the guard," Mike said, kissing my cheek. "See you tomorrow, Superlady. Sleep tight tonight."

We stayed at Vera's talking until almost 3:00 A.M. Clarissa and Miriam were sleeping with the baby on the futon, which Vera had opened up for them, when I left. I was so tired that Samuel picked me up and carried me to the waiting car. Bodyguards and chauffeurs are wonderful people to have in your life sometimes.

I fell asleep in the car and barely woke enough to get myself to bed. That's why I didn't listen to the messages on my phone machine until morning. The last was from Mike, who'd called shortly after leaving Vera's the night before.

"I know how you girls can get your answers," he said. "Don't know why I didn't think of it sooner. Get yourself a meet with Otis Campbell and Steven Cohen, Vinnie's P. I. team. You girls ain't their favorite bunch of people since you busted Rhumumba before they was ready to point the finger at her. But I think they'll help you anyway. If Tiffany did know something, these are the guys who could find out what it was."

"Girls!" He called us "girls"?

Chapter Fourteen

Dear Superlady of Sex,

My erections are never rock hard anymore. I am thirty-seven and hate to think of myself as a sexual seen-better-days guy, but maybe it is true of me. Sometimes I can only penetrate a woman if she sits on me. After we fuck awhile, I can hold it inside her in any position. Before I shoot, I feel good and hard, at least to myself. But recently my partner has said she doesn't feel me as good and hard at this point. Then she reassures me she doesn't mind. If she doesn't mind, why does she bring it up? Is there a standard for hardness—and how can I tell how far off I am from the male norm for my age?

Why are men so obsessed with measurements? They want to know how long sex should last, how long orgasm should last, how big other men are, how many times a week other people do it, and how hard other men get. The person who invents a method of measuring penile hardness will become a billionaire. ("Hey, honey, I hit an 8.2 on the Smith and Barney Erectile Quality Scale tonight. You know the average guy my age is lucky to come in at 7.0.")

For men, sex, like sport, should have a set of statistical standards by which they can judge their performances. Why can't they be more like us and obsessively compare their bodies to each other's? Or why can't they just pore over *GQ* and privately agonize because their thighs aren't as good as the model's?

I was formulating an answer to poor "Mr. Sexual Seen Better Days" in my head when the phone rang again. Did David take all these phone calls when *he* had this job?

"Want me to get it for you?" Mike asked.

"No, thanks," I said, and he went back to his newspaper. Mike liked my new job, replacing David as Editor-in-Chief of *Playhouse*. He got to sit on the sofa all day, look out the window in search of celebrities going into HMV, and see the unretouched photos of the girls of *Playhouse* as soon as they hit my desk. His favorite was the one of Miss May, a voluptuous Hispanic beauty, before her overflowing black bush was trimmed into shape by waxing her inner thighs.

"Madame Editor, how's it going?" David asked.

Why did he sound so smug and self-satisfied as if he knew it couldn't possibly be going as well as it had when he was doing it? I wasn't comfortable talking to him in the office, our positions reversed as it were. Look, the missionary position had worked for us for a long time. He'd said he didn't care about me climbing on top, but what if he did? I knew he did. David was competitive.

"Did you answer your own phone when you did this?" I asked him. "I can't remember."

"No, but I always took your calls."

"Don't call me 'Madame Editor.' I still think of myself as Superlady." I sighed. "It's frantic. I don't remember ever seeing you work. There was nothing on your desk. How did you pull that off? I hate this job. We both know Vinnie only hired me for the PR value of having me here. He didn't expect me to do anything, did he?"

"It was easy," he said, giggling. His giggles sounded

forced and smarmy now, not real. He was laughing *at* me, not *with* me, all the while pretending nothing had changed between us. He no longer trusted me enough to admit it had. "I didn't work. You promoted Clarissa, didn't you? She should be doing everything now. She did it before . . . for a lot less money."

"Uhmm," I said, a nonword I'd taken to using on the phone to indicate to the person on the other end: I can't talk now. This never happened to me when I worked at home.

Cynthia Moore-Epstein was standing in my office door, a pile of blue line copy in her hands. Her eyebrows were raised in that "We have a problem" thin line, which made me automatically cringe. Everything on her body from her jaunty breasts to her carefully aligned prim little black ballerina flats was pointing needily in my direction.

"I'll call you back in fifteen," I said. "I promise."

"Call me back. I'm having an anxiety attack."

He was having an anxiety attack? I pictured him in his big Jackson Heights co-op, Peggy off to work, the last of the kids still living at home in class at NYU, his feet propped up on his own desk. Motioning Cynthia inside, I was suddenly consumed with envy. I wanted to be David, fired for fiscal mismanagement, and sent packing with a year's severance pay. At last he could write the novel he'd said he'd write if only he'd had the time to do it. He'd sworn he was "delighted" that I was getting his job. Peggy was "thrilled" that he would be the housekeeper/cook now; she completely believed in his ability to write a potential best-seller by the time the severance package was spent.

Lies. But why shouldn't they be delighted and thrilled? I was being paid about a third less than he'd received to do the same job, and he was free. And Peggy no longer had to share the household chores which she considered more onerous than he did. I was, however, still getting a separate check for Superlady, which put me slightly ahead of where he'd been on the financial scale, not that *I'm* competitive about these things.

Accepting Vinnie's offer had seemed like a good idea at the time. I hadn't realized how much I would dislike getting up every morning and going to an office. Okay, I got here at ten and left shortly after four. It was restrictive nonetheless, especially since I was only permitting myself business-related lunches. Even Mike was bored with the lunches with advertisers, writers, photographers, publicists, and members of the staff. And playing dress-up and wearing heels all day, every day? I hated that, too. I missed my jeans and sweats. Today I was wearing a cobalt blue wool fitted jersey dress with matching stockings and shoes. The plunging v-neck was anchored with an antique silver brooch in a diamond shape. The swingy long silver earrings that coordinated with it were making my ears tired. It was the kind of outfit I loved wearing for two or three hours, not six or eight.

The only part of the job I liked was assigning articles. I had, for example, a female writer trying out the new intercourse position, Coital Alignment Technique, invented by a man, which was the latest version of how to give your woman a no-hands orgasm. Presumably a man and a woman could align themselves so he gave her clitoris sufficient stimulation during intercourse in the missionary position to bring her to orgasm without additional clitoral stimulation. After trying it with three men, my writer reported, she could only achieve alignment by having her partner move so far up her body, his chin was hitting the top of her head as they fucked and his penis felt hooked inside her.

"Another letter from the main pervert," Clarissa said, barging in past Cynthia, waving a letter on yellow lined paper.

Starred Man was still writing to me. Rhumumba and

Elizabeth Thatcher might be spending the winter on the same Caribbean isle for all I knew, but Starred Man was in town and careful to keep me updated on a weekly basis about his comings and goings—all within the confines of the restraining order which kept him out of my sight. Sometimes I wondered if he'd killed Tiffany because he suspected she was a rival for my love.

"Like, I mean, wouldn't you think he'd give it up?" she said. "I called a publicist at Doubleday for you. They have a book on obsessive love, and I told her you needed a free copy because it was happening to you."

"Great. I hope you made it clear I am the obsessee, not the obsessor. I can just see the item on Page Six now."

"Oh, sure," she said, throwing Starred Man's letter down on top of the general chaos which was my desk. "Cynthia, I told you not to bother Carolyn with this little stuff. Take it all back to my office, and I'll be right there."

She started out the door, came back, and tried to retrieve Starred Man's letter, but I caught her hand.

"You don't have to deal with this," she protested, but I waved her away. "I'll read, copy, and file for you."

"I love you, Clarissa," I said as she and Cynthia departed.

"I know," she said, smiling benevolently at me on her way out the door.

Reflecting on how much fatherhood had changed her for the better, I picked up the phone and forgot whom I meant to call, and therefore which numbers to push, and put it back again. In seconds, it was ringing. Twenty minutes later, I returned David's call.

"Have you settled in yet?" he asked.

"Not entirely. I still have to replace your tattoo collection with something more me. Clarissa gave me a picture of Zellie for my desk, so I have a start."

"Maybe you can have them shipped to me. I'd love to keep those photographs."

"No way." The silence on his end was muted rage. I knew it was. This was like a divorce. He would make me pay for keeping his photographs. "I'm sorry. Vinnie is feeling punitive toward you today." I paused. "But I could stack them up behind my desk and leave them there for a month or so. No one will notice if I send them to you then."

While David defended his fiscal excesses yet again ("It was the eighties; everybody did it."), I scanned Starred Man's letter. Being out of prison had not opened up his creativity. He still began with, *"Do you like chest hair?" Now, however, he had an address and phone number where, he said, I could reach him whenever I was ready. I put the letter on top of the Out basket. Clarissa was right; I wasn't going to read his missives anymore.

"I envy you," I told him. "You get to do what you want."

"But if I can't do it, then what?"

We were both holding our breath. Neither spoke, possibly consumed by the same thoughts. Before I had known him, David had a past life I couldn't comprehend. When the kids were small, the family had been on food stamps while David was six months between editorial jobs and Peggy was too ill from complications following the last birth to teach. They had owned a male cat they couldn't afford to neuter, and he'd urinated in all the corners. While I was busily presiding over the Junior League, David had lived in a drafty old house which smelled like cat piss.

"I never made money until *Playhouse*," he reminded me peevishly. "If you will recall, I got this job because Vinnie's sister, who was charged with finding the new editor, went to college with my cousin."

"How did you manage to run this magazine without

alienating your kids?" I changed the subject to one in which he had the clear advantage. "My son would give up his earring and long hair for a mother who edited *Good Housekeeping*. Things are so touchy between us. You don't know how jealous I am of the closeness between you and your kids."

"He'll get over it," David said, but his reassurance lacked a certain degree of warmth. The softness of voice, to which I once could lean back and relax, was gone. "My kids have been through hard times. They never had the luxury of taking a moral stand on where the money's coming from, but they take their moral stands on other issues, which irritate me. I can't go to the grocery store without buying an item the consumption of which constitutes committing some sin against nature. Carolyn, he'll come around," he said, brushing off my concern as if it were pettiness on my part. "It's not easy for a young man to have Superlady for his mother. You're the older woman all his friends want to fuck. You see his point?"

"I'm going to get everything off my desk today," I told him, interrupting another one of his speculations on how long the world of print porn had to go before near total fiscal collapse, being squeezed by the antiporners on one side and the video market on the other, "so I have to hang up."

"Put it in a box and dump it on someone else's desk."

"Actually, I had planned on several boxes. Why should one person have to do everything?"

I did something very bold then: I told my secretary to hold all calls, except from the A list—David, Morgy, the WIPs, and Vinnie's elusive P. I. team, Campbell and Cohen, who were in no fucking hurry to get back to me. I'd been trying to get one or the other of them on the phone for a week. They didn't seem to return calls or they weren't returning mine. My secretary, Gwen, said their secretary was "nice" and Cohen was "a sweetheart, but out of town a lot," but Campbell, the top man himself, she thought, appeared to have an attitude. How she got this without actually talking to him, I don't know.

When the phone rang, I was hoping for one of the elusive dicks and got Morgy instead. After she'd dumped Georges with a speech I'd helped her prepare and advised me on negotiating a sign-on bonus which I'd invested in Red Hot Mamas, we had achieved a rapprochement. Having discovered a murder, I was changed somehow in her eyes. She didn't know how to treat me. Now she was spending a week in California recuperating from Georges. It was day two of the healing experience, and, if I'd thought about it, I could have predicted this call.

"Carolyn, I've met someone," she said, her voice breathless.

"That's nice."

"Well, don't sound so discouraging," she said crossly. "He is nice . . . for a change. I met him yesterday. He took me for a three-hour drive down the coastline. We had dinner on the beach. We'd been kissing all day and holding hands, and I, like, really got weird on him. Do you know what I did?"

"Refused to sleep with him because he won't respect you if you give in so soon?"

I could hear her pouting in the silence. She didn't like having her game analyzed, but what did she expect? She typically followed a disaster like Georges with either a celibate period or a brief relationship with a suitable man, whom she attempted to control by the timely dispensing of sex. It was, she thought, what good women do to get led down the bridal path, a path she occasionally decided was greener than her own. Talking to Morgy about men was like returning to the nostalgic days when girls talked about boys at slumber parties.

Uncomfortably, I realized I'd enjoyed the conversations up until only recently.

"Well?" I asked. "Isn't that what happened?"

"He wanted to rent a room, and, like, I go, 'I'm not sleeping with you tonight. I think it's better if you wait for sex.' And he goes, 'I've done it both ways, having sex right away and waiting for it and I don't think that influences how things will go, but I'm willing to do it your way.'

"So, I wouldn't let him get the hotel room though I wanted to go to bed with him. We drove back and I stayed the night at his place. He loaned me a T-shirt and shorts. We kissed and I masturbated him and gave him a blow job and then he masturbated me, but we didn't have sex. In the morning, he seemed a little confused about what to do, so he made a big breakfast. When we finished eating it, he announced he had a lot to do today.

"Do you think he'll think I'm too neurotic to see again?"

I stopped her by pleading "the I have to be in a meeting" excuse, one of the good things about having a real job versus working at home where no one thinks you're really working. After hanging up with her, I buzzed Gwen and told her to move Morgy down from the A list to the B, which meant she wouldn't automatically get through to me in the future.

I felt a little mean about it, but don't executive women have to make some hard decisions? Besides, our little separation had convinced me Morgy and I would only be able to remain friends if we saw less of each other. She was fun once, twice a month. Beyond that, she seemed like work. Was I being smug in believing I'd outgrown her?

Guiltily, I looked around my office. I had one old friend's job and didn't want to take another old friend's calls. I sighed. Mike looked up, offered no verbal en-

couragement, looked back down at his magazine. I
picked up my pen and a packet of post-it notes.

In less than an hour, I had the work on my desk
divided into little piles littered with sticky notes meant
for other people's desks. I felt good about myself again
for accomplishing something. Vaguely I had a plan
about this job, which was "Do it for a year or so, put
the money away, then quit." I could handle it for that
long, and print porn would probably survive another
year, too.

I felt only a momentary satisfaction at my clean desk
before thinking about Tiffany's unsolved murder. Every
one of us had been questioned; Bobby several times.
The cops seemed to be talking to all the wrong people.
Yet, a month had gone by with no arrest being made.

"Try Campbell and Cohen again," I told my secretary. "Why do they keep avoiding me?"

This time she got Otis Campbell on the line.

I was waiting for Otis at the Museum Café on Columbus and 78th. Samuel, my bodyguard, was sitting at the
next table, rather too conspicuously I thought, but then
again how can a stunning, big, black man ever be incon-
spicuous?

With a name like Otis, I considered the odds were
good he'd be black, too. Did I want him to be black? I
did. Blame it on missing Charles, who was now nothing
more than an occasional phone caller in my life. Perhaps to be sure a phone call wouldn't lead to an immediate tryst, he rarely called me when he was in New
York. I heard from Charles when he was on assignment
in Detroit, L. A., Chicago, wherever far away. True, we
sometimes mutually masturbated while tenuously connected by long-distance technology, but that was the
extent of my sex life. And, since Charles, I had only

fantasized about black men. Why did I care if Otis was black or not? He was a man, approximately my age, rumored to be unattached. If he fit the description, I also wanted him to be black. White men didn't look good to me anymore.

Morgy said my fantasies about black men were the result of a shrewd unconscious appraisal of the market-place, not longing for Charles's master organ. White men over forty consider a younger woman the status symbol of choice, she said. Or, if they don't, they are geeks, losers, nerds, or too poor to afford a status symbol. Black men over forty want white women on their arms. Was Morgy right? Were my fantasies of black cocks inspired by dating realities, not Charles? I'd dated other black men before Charles, and none—in spite of the familiar adage, "Once you have black, you don't go back"—had left me dreaming only black dreams. I had been younger then.

"Ms. Steele," he said gently, as though he were trying to awaken me without startling me. How had I not noticed him walk into the café and stop in front of my table? "I wouldn't expect you to know who I am, but, of course, I know who you are."

He was tall, very black, and handsome. Unlike Charles, he had hair; tight little curls, slicked down so they appeared to grow in wavy rows. His hand, extended for my grasp, was reassuringly large. But the eyes were the best part. He had large hazel eyes that glinted with lights, flickering information about him like blinking signs. The man sent constant sparks from his eyes. He had to be smart, inquisitive, sexy, and warm. Would those eyes lie? His history was written in his eyes, and I was reading them like a palm reader.

"Otis Campbell," he said, not breaking eye contact as he held my hand far longer than was necessary.

"I'm so glad to meet you at last," I said, allowing a

touch of sarcasm in my voice, knowing it would be offset by my widest, most winning smile.

One good thing about being born blond: People don't automatically give you credit for being smart enough to be mildly caustic. You almost have to pour verbal drain cleaner all over some people, especially men, before they realize the words are truly coming from the mouth of a blonde. It gives us a tactical advantage in these verbal times.

"You're prettier than your picture," he said, "even the ones taken by Charles Reed."

I batted my big blue eyes at him, but it would be, I knew, to no avail. The man was on to me. I would bet he'd done his homework well enough to know about me and Charles. He gave me a shrewdly appraising glance, sat down, signaled the waiter, and ordered a Heineken on draft.

"I would have guessed that would be your drink," I said.

"Well, your glass of white wine isn't exactly a surprise choice, Ms. Steele."

"Please call me, Carolyn."

"Is that what you really like to be called—Carolyn, not Caro? You can call me O. My parents handicapped me with Cleotis after my grandfather, and I've spent my life shortening it to something I could live with. I think I'm finally there."

"Anything but 'babe.' You don't call women 'babe,' do you, O?"

"Only if they've really earned it," he said, laughing.

I liked the way he laughed, throwing his head back as he did. He had beautiful even white teeth and a lovely tongue. But, as easily as he'd let himself go, he reigned himself back in again. I got the impression he'd liked me immediately, but was not all that pleased he did.

"Okay, Caro, let's get this business cleared away," he said. "Vinnie wants us to listen carefully to what you have to say, then talk you out of doing any investigating on your own. He says you're high on Rhumumba as the killer. I don't see that. Neither does my partner, Steve Cohen. He had the lady fingered as the letter writer, but a killer—No. You women"—he said, wagging his finger at me, but he got points for saying "women" and not "girls"—"should have stayed out of it. Finding poison pens is a specialty of Cohen's. He had the case all but made against Rhumumba when you stepped in. Any idea how many poison pens are operating inside corporations using inside knowledge to frighten or blackmail people into giving them promotions and such?"

"No," I said, and, at this point, I didn't care. Those nasty letters were the least of Rhumumba's sins. "Why not Rhumumba?"

"It doesn't fit her psychological profile. Also, she has a pretty good alibi. She was at the Clit Club. Somebody like Rhumumba doesn't get missed at a lesbian club. About thirty total strangers said she was there."

"You're sure they were total strangers and not WAPs protecting her?" I asked, taking a sip of my wine and watching him closely over the rim of the glass. Maybe he didn't take the WAPs as seriously as I did.

"WAPs, WIPs, WWAWAWs. Don't you women know how to organize anything without a W in the acronym?" He reached across the table and patted my hand in what could be construed as a patronizing fashion. "No, I don't think they were protecting her. A buddy in homicide let me read the interviews. I'm sold. Steve is sold. Besides, Caro, why would Rhumumba kill Tiffany, who was basically a lesbian at the time of her death? Come on, it doesn't make sense. Do you know how likely it is a lesbian will commit a violent crime anyway? Not likely."

"I don't think of Rhumumba as a lesbian. She's a transsexual lesbian bodybuilder. It's a little different."

"Do you know the guy at the next table is listening to

everything we say?" he asked, his voice dramatically lowered. "Not that anyone could be blamed for eavesdropping on *this* conversation. Happens to you a lot, I guess, doesn't it?"

"Yes, I always talk about sex and murder in restaurants," I said, taking a larger sip of wine so my mouth wouldn't set in some little hurt line. "He's my bodyguard Samuel."

"I should have realized you'd need a bodyguard. That's the shits."

He softened toward me then, and the sudden empathy in those beautiful eyes touched me. I reached for his hand. He met mine halfway across the table, and we held hands. After telling me their clients were largely corporate and the work often entailed ferreting out industrial espionage, he promised he and his partner would take another look at Rhumumba anyway. If Vinnie didn't mind, they would see if they could come up with some other leads in Tiffany's murder, which, he emphasized, was a job for the police. He was humoring me, undoubtedly at Vinnie's request. Had Vinnie been kind enough to send him to me because he was black and beautiful? Or had he wanted to meet me himself? Or, most likely, had his partner, who would have been stuck with this minor job, been out of town again?

"Now that we've got the business out of the way," he said, "there's something else I want to ask you."

"Okay, ask."

"Are you only interested in me because I'm black?"

I picked up my wine goblet again. It was a fair question, and I wasn't going to answer it with a suitably respectable middle-class response, like, "Are you accusing me of being a racist?"

"I am more attracted to black men now than white," I admitted. "I'm not sure why that is, but being black wouldn't be enough. For instance," I said, lowering my voice and indicating a rotund black man a few tables away, "he doesn't do it for me."

"Why are you more turned on by black men now?" he asked, refusing to let me make light of the issue. "I have to tell you, Caro, I'm tired of women looking at me and seeing something I don't even know if I am. Black women want me because I wear a suit to work and make decent money. White women want me for the cock. What do you want?"

"I have dated all colors, black, brown, white, even a man who was born in Cuba of a Chinese mother and African father, then adopted by a Jewish family in Brooklyn. It was like fucking the U. N. Give me a break. I've earned the right to state a preference. Why do some men prefer blondes? Or big breasts? Or fat butts? Men make choices based partly on a woman's age or body type or hair color, and we don't question them. Why can't I be aroused by the sight and touch and smell of black skin?"

Softening the lecture, I stroked his hand, lifted it to my face, inhaled his scent, then kissed him. He caressed my chin, then put his thumb in my mouth. Briefly, I sucked it, and I saw him swallow hard.

"I suppose if the condition persists, I could go back into therapy," I said.

"Will you have dinner with me tomorrow night?"

"I can't think of anything I'd rather do."

We liked each other. The lust was mutual. He'd asked me for a date, and I'd accepted. Ignoring the fact that his distrust of my color preference loomed like a boulder in my romantic path, I was hugging these basic facts to me in the car going back to my apartment. They made me feel as warm as my beloved mink did.

"We got a date with the man tomorrow night?" Samuel asked from the seat across from mine.

"Yes. Did you like him?"

"Seems okay. No reason to worry about him. You like black men, don't you?"

"Yes, I do. Don't tell me you didn't hear that part?"

He grinned and ducked his head. Another week of sharing my life and he would be asking me if it was true black men had bigger cocks. My relationships always evolved in the confessional direction.

After checking the apartment and listening to my phone messages, Samuel settled down on the sofa with a science fiction paperback. I only asked my bodyguards to stay outside when I was having sex; there hadn't been much of that lately, unless you count masturbation. After a month of having the men around, I was so comfortable with them, I closed the bedroom door to masturbate, but I didn't ask them to leave. In fact, it titillated me to know Mike or Lennie or Samuel—especially Samuel—were listening in the other room.

I went back into the bedroom to change into my sweats and start on my homework, viewing erotic videos. In the last week I'd been through ten; most of them had excited me only briefly. Does anyone ever watch these things all the way through? Surely, one either masturbates or grabs one's partner somewhere in the first ten minutes. My observations of the films were recorded in a fat steno book. I planned to have Gwen transfer all my notes to a computer file. I couldn't put erotic sizzle into the Red Hot Mamas without studying the competition, could I? And, speaking of that, why weren't they more interested in what I had to say? They'd taken my check, but they didn't seem to want my creative input.

"We've been doing this a while," Gemma had snapped when I'd told her I wanted to get together to go over my ideas. "Maybe you should study the products and the process before you tell us how to make a video. It isn't as easy as being a celebrity editor."

Celebrity editor. That had stung. They weren't taking my promotion any better than David was. I suppose I could see their point. Their asses had been literally on the line for years, and now *I* was the acknowledged Queen of Porn. I could see their point, but I wasn't, however, ready to concede it.

The first film I put into the VCR was *Behind The Lilac Door,* a classic from the late seventies. It was Tiffany Titters at midcareer, not typical of her work. No fellatio. No tit-fucking. I also recognized Gemma in the girl gang bang sequence, where Tiffany did it to six girls, one after another, each writhing in turn for her on the lavender and pink printed sheets. Except for nostalgia for Tiffany's comforting presence, I felt nothing but boredom. My mind was wandering from Tiffany to David and what he would do if he couldn't write that novel. Why not go into the feminist porn business with us? I had my hand on the fast forward button ready to move quickly ahead when I saw what might have been a familiar face. I freezed the frame. It looked like, but it *couldn't* be . . . a younger Elizabeth Thatcher?

"You're kidding," Clarissa said when I called to tell her what I thought I'd found. "Well, like, if you're not kidding, you must be mistaken. It must be someone who looks like she might have looked fifteen years ago. Well, like, don't you think that must be it?"

"You're probably right. But, there's something about her facial expression which makes me think it couldn't be anyone else. I'm bringing *Behind The Lilac Door* to the office tomorrow so you can look at it."

"Carolyn, you don't think Tiffany got the same idea?

She was doing the same thing you're doing, studying videos, before she was killed. Remember how many cassettes we saw stacked up in her apartment when Mike broke in? What if she thought she saw Elizabeth Thatcher, too?"

"What would she have done about it if she had?"

"I don't know." Clarissa paused, and, in the pause, I heard a whine, either hers or Zellie's. "I see what you're getting at. She wouldn't exactly have called her and said, 'I'm on to you.' So, how would Elizabeth Thatcher have known to come over and kill her?"

"Right. How? If Tiffany had contacted Elizabeth Thatcher about anything, she would have told one of us, especially Vera."

We agreed she almost certainly would have. When we hung up, I was still in the familiar state: clueless. But the memory of those stacks of videocassettes in Tiffany's apartment nagged at me.

Samuel didn't know how to break into an apartment, so I had to wait for Mike, whose shift that day started at midnight. I had to bribe him by promising he could have all the shots of Miss May he wanted before he'd agree to break and enter one more time. When we got into Tiffany's place, most of the videos were gone. We grabbed the half dozen or so that were left and got out of there.

"Cops probably took them," Mike said. "Think what a temptation that would be. Can't really blame them, can you?"

No, I couldn't—only myself for not being smart enough to take them with me the last time I was there.

Elizabeth Thatcher, or her young look-alike, didn't appear on any of the cassettes, which I scanned immediately after getting back to my place. Maybe David would know what we should do next, if there was a way of positively identifying an actress from an old porn flick. In the morning, I'd call him from the office. I was bleary-eyed from watching naked people cavort and ready to fall asleep when Charles called.

"Babe, I miss you."

"I miss you, too." His voice was thick and rich, and I wanted to lie back on the bed and let it pour over me. "Where are you?"

"Seattle." I pulled off my sweat pants. "Ever been to Seattle?"

"Last year." I put my hand inside my black silk string bikinis, the kind he liked because they showed my ass to good advantage. "I loved it."

"It's okay. Too much rain for me."

"Can't sleep?"

"No." His voice grew even huskier, and I knew his hand was around his cock. My mouth watered for it. "You gonna help me sleep?"

"What are you wearing?"

"Nothing, babe. I'm lying on the bed, naked. The sheets are white. I remember you said you liked to see my black ass on white sheets."

I had a vivid memory of him naked on my own white ruffled sheets, lying on his side, his head propped up on one arm, in the position Tiffany said women didn't need to assume for other women. His hip had been thrust out. I'd bent over to kiss it before climbing in bed with him. Had he been posing for me?

"Charles, I'm touching myself. My legs are raised. I'm on my back. I'm playing with my clit."

"My dick's standing straight up in the air. I wish you were here to sit on it, babe."

"I can see your hand wrapped around it, moving up and down. Close your eyes and pretend it's my hand."

My voice broke, and he asked, "Are you coming already? Come for me, babe. You know how I love it when you do. Nobody comes like you do."

My hand was still against my clit. Silent tears were running out the corners of my eyes and down my temples, into my hairline. I let him think I'd come. It was the first orgasm I'd ever faked in my life.

"Only once, babe?"

"I'm tired, Charles. It's been a long day."

Chapter Fifteen

Hey, Superlady!

You could call me a cocksman, and proud of it! Women say they don't care about size. They claim they want sensitive men. They swear they don't care that much about orgasms, just touching and holding and satisfying their man is enough for them. It's the "closeness" they want, or so they say. Balls! Women want cock. They want it big, thick, hard, and long lasting, and handled by a real man. They're just too nice to say so. Don't you agree with me, Superlady? I've got a bet on your answer with some buddies who think what women really want is good lickin' and suckin'.

Cocksman,

I was not surprised to see the Texas postmark on your letter. But, how could you have failed to tell me how much you measure? Though few men are so besotted with their penises as you seem to be, your attitude of penile superiority is a common one. I surmise you are no fan of "lickin'" and "suckin'" unless, of course, someone else is doin' it, and your penis is the object of the oral attention.

I'm not sure how this will affect the settling of the bet, but I say women want it all. They want to be licked and sucked, then fucked, or sometimes in the reverse order. Since 65%–75% of women do not reach orgasm by intercourse alone—something you should know if you're a regular reader of this column—either oral or manual clitoral stimulation is typically necessary for orgasm. Yet, I do believe most women enjoy the experience of intercourse, of being filled by a hard cock. And, yes, some women do prefer it big. I prefer big.

And I, too, have never been convinced by women who say they really don't need an orgasm to be satisfied with sex. Maybe occasionally that's true for some women. But on a regular basis? No!

Why don't you call it a draw and donate the bet money to the Tiffany Titters Foundation for Sexual Transformation? You can send your check made out to the Foundation in care of this magazine. Your contribution will help those who are trying to change their lives through their sexuality, including transvestites and transsexuals, former prostitutes and porn stars struggling to launch their own erotic businesses, and video producers and directors in need of funding for their films. Unfortunately, this is not tax deductible.

closed the file on Superlady and reapplied my lipstick, sort of a matte peachy-beige, not the color anyone ever said I should always wear. Between the column and editing the magazine, I was spending more time working than I would have preferred. My car was waiting downstairs to take me and Mike to a WIP luncheon at the overpriced and overrated Mesa Grill on lower Fifth Avenue, my choice. Mesa does Southwest cuisine the way they do it in California, which is not particularly good eating—food designed more for atmosphere than pleasurable consumption. I was putting lunch on my expense account. Today was the first of

February and I wanted to pretend I was in California and had taken everyone there with me; not, I suspected, that the everyone in question, David and the WIPs, really wanted to be with me. Eating at the Mesa Grill where everything on the menu looked like a pile of grilled vegetables arranged on effete forms of lettuce was the closest I could manage to a beach. Buying lunchtime companionship was the only way I could get it.

I needed something to cheer me up. Nothing did that like spending Vinnie's money on food none of us liked. There is a perverse satisfaction in signing an inflated expense account check after a mediocre lunch, washed down with pricey pitchers of margaritas.

Unfortunately, if things kept going the way they seemed headed, we'd be spending our brand-new Foundation's piddling funds on a legal defense for Bobby, when we'd been hoping to contribute something to Angelo for the additional surgery his penis required. Bobby was "talking" to the police at their "invitation" on such a regular basis, the *Post* was calling him the "lead suspect" in Tiffany's murder.

"Ready?" Mike said, jangling the keys in his pocket as if they were the keys to "our" car, and he was going to drive us to the mall. Our relationship had settled into something akin to a sexless marriage. He hurried me along, told me my skirts were too short, and frequently suggested I learn how to cook. "We got the car double-parked down there, you know."

Of course, we had the car double-parked. In Manhattan, it's the only way to park. Other cars have been holding the legal parking spaces since 1969.

"Coming, dear," I said, and he was so into the role he didn't blink.

Mike was doing a double shift because he needed personal time off tomorrow. I kept looking at him for signs of sleepiness, but there were none. Apparently he got a good night's sleep on my sofa while I scanned videos, faked a phone sex orgasm, and cried over Charles. In the beginning, he'd been alert at all times. But since Tiffany's death and the unmasking of Rhumumba as the poison pen, I'd received no more threats on my life. My bodyguards no longer behaved like I was a high-risk property.

On the ride downtown, he told me my gray cashmere dress was too short and suggested I "do up a few more buttons." I ignored him. The dress buttoned all the way down the front, but I'd chosen to leave the buttons undone into my cleavage and, from the bottom, inches beneath my pussy. Too bad if it made him nervous! My underwear and panty hose and suede pumps were gray, too. I was the epitome of classic good taste for my circle.

"You got a date tonight?" he asked, and I nodded affirmatively. "With that new black guy?"

"How'd you know about him? I only met him last night."

"Samuel told me. Look, I'm not nosy or anything. If I'm supposed to be protecting your life, I have to know who you're doin', don't I?"

"Sure," I said, shrugging, "but we made a date for dinner, not necessarily for 'doin'.' "

"Yeah. The fellas will be on the chair in the hall tonight. You like black guys, don't you?"

"Yes, I do."

"You don't think there might be something funny about that, a white woman liking black guys as much as you do?"

"Are you trying to psychoanalyze me, Mike?"

He ducked his head and the question. Why not Mike in the therapist's chair? Who wasn't questioning me about black men today? Date two black men in a row and you have a problem. Nobody ever asked me, "Why white guys?" I'll bet nobody ever asked a man, "Why blondes?"

"Don't get defensive," he said, as if he could read my thoughts, which I'm sure he could by now.

Everyone else, including David, whom we'd made an honorary member at Vera's suggestion to ease the pain of his firing, was at Mesa Grill when we arrived. The maitre d' had seated the group in the window at a section of small tables, which he'd pushed together— probably because the reservation was in my name. In New York, fame, no matter how it's come by, brings one sure reward: the best and/or showiest tables in restaurants. I should have been flattered the Mesa Grill wanted me on display in their window, but I wasn't. Celebrity was getting old, much the way a diet of chocolate covered eclairs would.

"We should get this party moved out of the window," Mike said.

"Carolyn, it's good to see you," David said, kissing my cheek perfunctorily, his lips pursed almost in distaste, after I'd kissed him first.

"This window is a liability area," Mike said. "I'm gonna call the maitre d' and get us moved."

"You're the one who's looking good," I said to David, while putting my hand on Mike's arm and shaking my head no. The loss of his expense account had encouraged David to develop better eating habits. He was losing weight and working out at the gym. "My God," I said, "you've even cut your hair. Will hair spray sales ever rebound from the loss?"

"When you reserve, you should always ask for a table in the back against the wall like the Mafia does," Mike said.

Since I refused to have everyone moved to another

table, he had them rearrange the seating so that Bobby and I were at the end, our backs against the partition separating this dining section from the entrance area. Then he put his chair at the corner of the table behind me. If the other diners didn't know who we were when we came in, they probably did by now.

"Don't you love it?" Gemma asked. They were all fawning over him. "David has allowed himself to go natural. No more silly hair mat over his bald head. He's much sexier now."

While I took my place between Clarissa and Bobby, whom I hugged hard, the women exclaimed over David's new look and Bobby's gray flannel miniskirted suit over a peach lace camisole and his fabulous gray suede heels. You wouldn't believe the selection in shoe stores catering to cross-dressers these days. Nobody told me I was looking good.

Reluctantly, Mike sat down. More drinks were ordered. And, after the first flurry of conversation, the silence landed on our shoulders like big soft flakes of snow. Vera's eyes filled with tears.

"Our first meeting without Tiffany," she said, and I reached for Bobby's hand. He still loved me. Clarissa only sucked up to me.

"We have to find out who killed her," David said, "because nobody else is going to." He looked at Bobby, then quickly glanced away. David avoids even the near occasion of sentimentality. "I have more free time than anyone now. I propose we develop an investigation plan of our own today, and I'll be the legman."

"He's right," I said. "We owe it to Tiffany. She would be devastated to know Bobby, who loved her so much, is under suspicion. We have to get moving on this on our own."

"I don't like this," Mike said.

After ordering several variations of chicken or shrimp rolled in blue corn flour, grilled, and served under piles of things that were good for us, David appointed Clarissa recording secretary and began listing our leads: they added up to Rhumumba. And shouldn't I have been the designated appointing person now? What kind of feminists were they, deferring to him as if he were a god?

"Do all roads really lead to Rhumumba?" David asked irritably. "This isn't very original of us."

"The cops aren't original," Bobby said.

"I think you all want it to be Rhumumba because you don't like her," Stephanie said.

"Who else could it be?" Clarissa asked. "Tiffany had no enemies. Everyone loved her. She also had nothing to steal. No drug connections. She didn't pick up strangers in bars. For the last few years, she was only having sex with friends, mostly women friends. Who but a crazed antiporner would have killed her?"

I told them about my discussion with Otis and his promise to give Rhumumba "another look" though he didn't see her as a murderer.

"You like black men, don't you?" Carola asked, but I ignored her.

"If we rule out Rhumumba, what does that leave us?" I asked.

"I'm not suggesting we rule her out," David said, enunciating his words with exaggerated care, the way he used to talk to Clarissa, "only add more people to the list."

The waitress brought our food and another round of drinks. As we ate, Clarissa told them about *Behind The Lilac Door*. She'd viewed it in the office that morning and also thought the woman could be a young Elizabeth Thatcher. But how could we find out?

"I'll see what I can do," David said, his face growing animated. "I don't think this has anything to do with Tiffany's death. But, Carolyn, what a great story for the magazine if we can prove the head WWAWAW was a porn actress in her youth!" He said my name with insincere warmth. Where was he going with this? "You could do a tremendous piece for the magazine. The publicity would shake the WWAWAWs to their core. Why, you could even have *me* write it!"

"Could I?" I asked. *Should I?* Did I want to give him that assignment? If I could give David assignments, I'd feel less guilty about having his job. On the other hand, if he kept being such an asshole, I'd feel less guilty about having his job anyway. I felt coerced, with the eyes of the WIPs, like the metal tips on cat-o'-nine-tails for the hard core, biting into me.

"Of course. Why not? By the time it appears, Vinnie will have forgotten he hated me, and it will be too good for him to do anything but praise us both anyway." David was pushing hard.

"Hmmm," I said, knowing he was right about that. The wrath of Vinnie was reputedly short-lived. But what about the hurt feelings of Carolyn? How long would they remain tender to the touch?

We ordered another round of drinks and then another. I was signing the check when I realized the only item Clarissa had on her list after Rhumumba was "Check out the sex clubs. See if anyone knows anyone who didn't like Tiffany." Lunch hadn't accomplished much beyond allowing David to reassert his authority over us.

"That is not a good idea," Otis said, frowning, but he looked good, even with a furrowed brow.

"Why?" I asked.

We were having dinner at Bayamo, the big and funky Chino-Latino restaurant on lower Broadway which I loved. The waitress had seated us upstairs beneath the enormous multicolored dragon. Sipping my white wine and looking into his big eyes as he lectured me, I was thinking about his cock. How long? How thick? How hard? I was not having a knee-jerk feminist response to his "macho protect the woman" stance. Nor, was I having a knee-jerk feminine response. There are some good things about being forty and comfortable with sexuality, both male and female.

"The sex clubs are raunchy, depressing places, Caro." He reached across the table and took my hand. The touch of his skin against mine elevated my heart rate and body temperature. "Considering your level of celebrity, I definitely don't think you should be hanging out in them."

"I wasn't planning to enjoy myself," I said, focusing on the "depressing" part of his objection and not the implied: You might find yourself followed home by a star rapist, which is even worse than being pursued by a star fucker.

"Amateurs are not equipped to conduct murder investigations, dear," he said in a tone I would have considered smug had it come from the lips of any other man. I liked his lips. "You must read too many novels."

He was wearing a black silk T-shirt, black jeans, and expensive black cowboy boots, a surprising look for him. I loved it. Looking at him was a pleasure. Surreptitiously, I'd already checked out other men in the same age range in the restaurant. Downtown middle-aged white men are less likely to be fat and accompanied by women half their age than the men you see uptown in Lutèce, for example. But Otis was still a standout in this, or any, crowd. I also agreed with him about the sex clubs being no place for Superlady these days, but I couldn't readily concede the point, could I? If I did, he would think he'd persuaded me of his viewpoint too easily.

"Well, one could legitimately call investigating the sex clubs part of my job, couldn't one?" I asked.

"Don't give me that 'one' bullshit! You're the one we're talking about, and we both know it. So, why do you have to call yourself 'one'? If you want me to help you with your little private investigation, you will stay out of those places. Send some other 'one' in your place if you want a story for your magazine. Have you got that?"—*Have you got that?*—"I'm not going to worry about you getting kidnapped, tied up, and whipped across your nice little butt . . . or worse."

"This isn't your way of telling me you think I have a sleazy job, is it?" I asked, suddenly feeling defensive.

"No, it isn't. I don't think you have a sleazy job. I admire you. Not many people can carve out a life for themselves on their own terms and do it as nicely as you have. You're a hustler, Caro, and I like that." He smiled warmly at me. "Black men are natural born hustlers. We gotta be. You don't see the white man making a space for us in the club steam room, do you? I like that about you, the way you take the status quo and make it work for you. I've read Superlady; she's got a smart mouth.

"And you do have a nice little butt," he said, squeezing my hand.

Our food arrived: a huge burger with jalapeno jack cheese and green chiles for me and a more healthful steamed pot of spiced chicken, rice, and vegetables for him. He let go of my hand so the waitress (dressed in the table waiting uniform of the lower east side, black tights and oversized white shirt) could serve us. I missed his hand. At the next table, Samuel was also having the burger.

Over dinner he told me about his life. Mine, of course, was an open tabloid newspaper. A Midwesterner, he had gone to college at the University of Missouri, on a football scholarship. He graduated, moved to New York City, and became a cop. He quickly hated it. He went to work for a private investigator, and eventually opened his own office. He took on a partner, Steve Cohen, who had left law school in his third year to earn money as a P. I. and found he liked that better. They had worked their way ever higher up the client scale, until now they only handled corporations. Anybody who wanted his wife tailed had to be a *very rich* entrepreneur. He was thirty-eight and the father of two sons, fourteen and fifteen.

"How long have you been divorced?" I asked, dreading the answer no woman wants to hear: less than six months or, worse, I'm only separated.

"Never been married," he said, attacking his steamed pot with vigor. "That's a real white question, you know. I wasn't married to either one of the mothers of my children."

"Have you been involved with the kids?"

"What is this?" he asked, putting down his fork. "Yes. I didn't know about the first one until he was three. His mother is a white girl. When we were together, I told her I didn't want kids. And if she got pregnant, it was her problem." He put up his hand to silence the expected attack. "I know. I was a jerk. She went away without telling me she was pregnant. When he was three, she needed money, so she showed up at my apartment one day with him. When I opened the door and took one look at his little face, I knew he was mine. I was living with a black girl, and we had a two-year-old. It wasn't a pretty scene, honey. But, yes, I've been involved with both my boys. I support them, and I'll send them to college. Okay?"

"I'm glad. I walked out on a man in a restaurant once after he told me he didn't pay child support and hadn't seen his six-year-old in four years."

He laughed, throwing his head back the way he had the night before.

"Do you want to get married?" he asked when he'd

stopped laughing. "Have another baby? Is that why all the questions?"

I told him I'd had a tubal ligation years ago because I believed two perfect children were all anybody could ever be lucky enough to have. Why not quit when you're very far ahead? Then, changing the conversation lest he think I wanted the marriage if not the kids, I told him about *Behind The Lilac Door* and how I was certain Elizabeth Thatcher's naked, and plumper, little body had graced its torrid scenes. He didn't seem to think it was worth checking out until I told him David was pursuing the possibility the spokesperson for WWA-WAW was once an X-rated starlet. Then he decided maybe he should see what he could learn. As my daughter says, "If you want a man to do something, you only have to tell him another man already is."

We finished the meal with cappuccino and hand-holding.

"I want to go to bed with you," he said, lifting my hand to his lips. "I am put off by this thing you have for black men, but I want you."

"I want to go to bed with you, too."

"He stays outside, doesn't he?" he asked, indicating Samuel.

"What do you think I am? A voyeur or something?" Samuel asked.

He put his arm around me in the car going back to my apartment, but, in deference to Samuel's presence, he didn't kiss me. It was all I could do to keep my hand off his thigh. If I'd put my hand on his thigh, it would have moved of its own free will toward his penis. I knew his wouldn't be as big as Charles's, and really that was fine. Charles had a bit too much, or at least I would console myself for the rest of my life with the excuse that Charles really had a bit too much. Most likely his penis would be significant; he had the hands and feet.

"You look lost in thought," Otis said. "You aren't still thinking about going to the sex clubs, are you?"

I insisted I wasn't. He hugged me. Did he hug all his clients when they accepted his guidance? Samuel caught my eye, and I could have sworn that he knew exactly what had been on my mind.

Back at the apartment, Samuel went through his standard security check, including playing back the messages on my machine. I could tell by Otis's eyebrows pulled together in a tight line, he found it needlessly intrusive. I popped the cork on a bottle of Moët & Chandon. When I brought the bottle and two champagne flutes into the living room, Otis, who had been sitting on the sofa, stood. His black leather jacket was tossed across the coffee table. He'd taken off his boots and socks. There is something appealingly vulnerable about a man's bare feet, even large ones like his.

"Let's drink in the bedroom," he said.

"I'll be outside if you need me," Samuel said, passing us in the hall and quietly closing the door behind him.

"Would you like to watch *Behind The Lilac Door?*" I asked, setting the glasses on the dresser and filling them.

Yes, what an inane question. Now that we were alone in my bedroom, the familiar feelings began to bubble inside me, like the champagne in the flutes. I wanted him close, didn't want him close. I wanted to pull him close and push him away, all in the same motion.

"I should put some ice in a bucket for this," I said.

"No. The last thing I want to do is see that video. I'll take it with me and view it in the office on Vinnie's time."

He stopped me as I was going back toward the

kitchen by planting his body directly in front of mine. I watched him look at me and saw that his breath was coming ragged, his hands were curling nervously at his sides. The feelings stopped shifting back and forth inside me. I wanted him close, wanted him inside me, wanted him so much I felt the bottom dropping out of my stomach when he swallowed. There was no ambivalence.

"Forget about the ice for now and take off your clothes," he said. His eyes grew soft. "I want to see you."

I kicked off my heels, unzipped my dress, and let it drop to the floor. Just as I finished, he pulled me into his arms. I felt his stomach muscles tense as he kissed me. I put one hand on the hard ridges of his belly and held it there as his tongue explored my mouth. He unfastened the gray silk bra and took one breast in his hand.

"You have beautiful breasts."

I brought his mouth back to mine and kissed him, searching him with my tongue, as I ran my hands under his shirt, up and down his back. He was lean and hard; I guessed he got his body from free weights, not the machines.

He pulled the silk T-shirt over his head and threw it on the floor. I tossed my bra on top of it. He embraced me, then led me to the bed. We laid down side by side; he pulled off my panties, and panty hose. He ran his tongue inside my thighs as his hands caressed my hips. Then standing beside the bed, watching me watch him, he took off his jeans and white briefs. His penis was magnificent, not as large as Charles's, of course, but absolutely beautiful. It stood a good seven or eight inches in length; thick, very erect, and deeply, purely black. I liked it immediately. I wanted it inside me.

I opened my arms, and he got back on the bed. Lying side by side, facing each other, we kissed and caressed, learning each other's bodies by taste and touch. I wanted him now. Putting my leg on top of his hip, I angled my pelvis and pushed down on his penis, forcing it inside me. The jolt of the connection shot through both our bodies simultaneously. Moaning into my mouth, he grasped my buttocks with both hands and thrust in and out of me, his body hungry, not yet finding a rhythm. I opened my eyes, and his were already open. My orgasm began immediately, and its beginning established his rhythm.

He was sure of himself, of his erotic power over me. I saw the change in his eyes. I kept my eyes open the whole time we made love, letting him see into every corner, letting him have me completely and without reservation. When he came at last, I felt him surging into me and saw his eyes stop churning and grow calm like a quiet sea.

I woke with my breasts flattened against his back, my hand around his penis and the feeling he was in no hurry to leave. It was a good feeling.

"I could be late, honey," he said, and I moved my hand gently up and down.

He reached around and masturbated me with his hand. Within a few minutes, I was on the verge of orgasm, and he was on top of me, making love to me, with his body and his eyes. After bringing me to orgasm again, he pulled out and buried his face in my cunt. I gasped, my hands involuntarily clasping his head, guiding his tongue deeper into me. He manipulated my clit with the bridge of his nose while his tongue pushed inside my vagina as deeply as it could go. I came again. He pulled his face away from my cunt and mounted me. I wrapped my legs around his waist, and we came together. When it was over and he was lying in my arms, trying to regain his breath, I kissed his eyelids.

"You're gonna make me fall asleep again," he whispered, "kissin' my eyes like that."

He rolled over on his side, and pulled me against his chest. We slept till almost noon, ignoring the phone, the sunlight streaming in the windows, and Mike, who came in to make a routine check and pulled the comforter over our naked bodies, like a mother tucking his charges in. When I woke again, we were a tangle of limbs, an artful blend of black on white, white on black. Would I ever be satisfied with a white man again?

"It was that good?" David asked, pushing for details. My new lover had put us temporarily back on safe ground. "How was it so good? What was so different about it? Carolyn, there are only so many ways to fuck."

He said the last in pure exasperation. David envied me the sexual experiences of my life as I envied him the stability of his. His first several months at *Playhouse* had been very hard on him. Maybe it was time I forgave him for his one lapse with Tiffany. And, maybe I would have, if he'd forgiven me for taking "his" job.

"It was better than that good," I said, recrossing my legs so that my green wool knit dress crept a little farther up my thigh.

David and I were waiting for O and Steve Cohen to join us for dinner at Swing Street Café, my favorite midtown restaurant on East 52nd Street. The food, American bistro, is good, not overpriced, and the staff is warm and friendly. We'd agreed on Swing Street because they were working on a job at a corporate headquarters in the neighborhood. He didn't give me any details, not that I really wanted any. Why would I care about corporate espionage when I was looking at proof of Elizabeth Thatcher's past life in porn?

"Better than Charles?" he asked.

"Better."

"Not bigger, I hope."

"No, just better," I said, and I meant to withhold the details from him, a first in our friendship. "Intense. Emotional. Physical. No holding back. Just better. That's all you're getting, okay? It's private."

"Your sex life is private? All I have to do is wait a few months until you write a piece for the magazine on 'my black nights.' Everything you do turns up in print. Sometimes I don't know which comes first, your life or writing about it."

"Not this time."

"You hear from Charles?" he asked, sort of changing the subject.

"He calls me when he's out of town."

"Phone sex?" He nodded wisely, like he knew something about phone sex, which I doubted he did. His wife didn't travel often. "Well, you can't blame him, Carolyn. It isn't entirely his fault. Here the man is in possession of the mythical huge black penis. Do you think you're the only woman after that? The only white woman? Interracial sex is the last taboo."

"Uhm," I said. "Do you think I'm interested in black men because it's the last taboo?"

"Why are you interested in them specifically?"

"Because the only good white men my age are married, gay, or would rather be dating my daughter. The men who are left don't want to fuck or if they do, I don't want to fuck them. I hate having to lift up a man's stomach in search of his penis, particularly if it turns out to be a little one."

"Well, there you are. Do you think the possessor of such a prize organ as Charles has can be expected to save it for one woman only?"

"You're saying he's not responsible for being a lying

asshole because he has a big black penis? What, his penis makes him do it?"

"I hope you realize you sound like the typical woman when you say things like that," he said, and I winced, because he was right. "Did you use condoms with the new man?"

I maintained a dignified silence. How could I describe the longing I felt for a man inside me, with nothing between us? How to explain how much I love the feeling of him ejaculating strongly inside my vagina? There was no way I could say those things without sounding like some man who was too big a jerk to use a condom.

"I thought so," he said.

"The truth is, David," I said irritably, "I hate the damned things, too. And don't give me your safe sex lecture. I wrote it for you."

Seeing O come in the doorway, I broke into a smile that felt like it was cascading over my whole body in warm waves. David's appraising eye and twisting mouth couldn't make me hide my happiness because O had walked into the room. But, and I sensed this immediately, O was returning my smile at less than half the wattage.

"Caro," he said, brushing his lips across mine.

The introductions were made.

"I feel like I know you already," Steve said. He was short, maybe 5'6", with the kind of thick curly chestnut hair and long eyelashes women would kill for. A plus, he had a beard, light brown shot through with red and flecked already in gray, though he couldn't be much past thirty. He was adorable, if you're into younger white guys. "I've been reading you for years."

"A fan," I said.

"I didn't say I was a fan. I said I've been reading you for years."

He grinned, softening the implied critique. We all shook hands, ordered drinks, white wine for me, Heineken on draft for O and David, coke for Steve. I shoved the material that David had given me across the table to O.

"Where did you get these?" O asked David, indicating the publicity still shots of a young Elizabeth, totally nude. They were bland, the poses formulaic; her back arched off the bed on one, her hand coyly held over her pussy in another. She had been interchangeable with any number of young women who come to New York or L. A. each year, seeking fame or money or salvation at the end of a camera.

"At Movie Star Photos in Times Square," David said, clearly proud of himself. "In addition to the standard old studio stills, they have a lot of stuff from the independent photographers who were more apt to have shot the porn starlets. Nobody's asked to look at these photos in years. I gave the kid at the desk a twenty dollar bill to let me look through drawers, and I found her. She called herself Liz Larue. If it's not her, it's a relative."

O compared the nude stills with the recent publicity photo of Elizabeth in her silk dress representing WWA-WAW. He nodded his head and passed them to Steve, who also nodded his head in agreement. Men validating men. Then he picked up the Xeroxed sheets from the *Encyclopedia of X-Rated Films.*

"She only made three films?" Steve asked, scanning the information sheet in O's hands.

"As far as I can tell," David said. "She may have done some others, even smaller budget films. Or she may have used a different name. It's hard to be sure. I could only find Liz Larue in three places. Tiffany was in two of the three films she made. Could that be a coincidence?"

"You think Tiffany remembered her, and that's what got her killed?" O asked.

"I don't," I said, but they ignored me.

"It's possible," Steve said.

"What would make Tiffany suddenly remember her?" I asked. "And why, if she remembered her at all, hadn't she put *this* Elizabeth and *that* one together a long time ago and told us about it?"

"Because, Carolyn," David began in his voice of patient explaining, "she would have no reason to connect the two in her mind. But, while reviewing videos for her own project, she could have seen the old Elizabeth and suddenly put the two together."

"I agree," O said, smiling apologetically at me. "And besides," he added, picking up the most damning evidence of all, "if these three women aren't all the same women, I'll be surprised. It fits too tight. Elizabeth Thatcher's psychological fingerprints are all over these other two personas."

Oh, yes, woman number three. He was holding a Polaroid photo of her leaving a meeting of Love and Sex Addicts Anonymous in Memphis. Though she'd identified herself to the group as "Lia," she was clearly Elizabeth. The picture had been sent to David by a reporter on the Memphis paper, who also wrote erotica under a pen name, after David had called her to see if she had any "dirt" on Elizabeth Thatcher.

The note accompanying it read, "David, We had a tail on Elizabeth for a few days after she got out of the hospital just to see if she would head for New York again. When she didn't, we had to drop the tail, too expensive for no results. The only interesting—strange!?— thing she did during those two days was go to three meetings of Love and Sex Addicts Anonymous. A woman who'd attended one of the meetings said she'd called herself 'Lia' and alluded to a dirty sexual secret in her past. We figure she probably had an orgasm once. What do you think?"

"I think she might have killed Tiffany," David said. "She's just crazy enough to do it."

"It shouldn't be hard to establish her whereabouts for the time of the murder," Steve said. "I'll get on that."

"I don't think she killed Tiffany," I said. "Wouldn't someone have figured out she was in New York at the time of the murder if she had been? I mean, please, the woman is high visibility, thanks to 'Olive.'"

"Not if they aren't looking for her to have been up here," O said. "You forget, the cops are real busy with Tiffany's sex life. And, Caro, she's not that high visibility, no matter how many times you see her photo in the *Post*. She looks like thousands of other pretty but banal women."

"He thinks all white women look alike," Steve said, and David laughed heartily.

"Okay," I said, "I'm not convinced, but David's right about one thing. This will make a hell of a story for the magazine."

"We need to send a woman down to Memphis to infiltrate her support group," he said.

"One of the WIPs?" I asked.

"It has to be someone who won't stand out in a crowd, which rules out everybody except—"

"Clarissa!" I said.

"Clarissa? I was going to say Stephanie."

"Clarissa, if we can get her to dress a little more like a woman, you know in the kind of pants suits my sisters would wear. Stephanie?" (He secretly lusts after Oriental women.) "You don't think a beautiful Oriental woman would stand out in a Memphis crowd? Clarissa. Absolutely. She's the only one who could pull it off."

He cringed. What an idea! David and Clarissa coauthoring the article of the year.

Chapter Sixteen

●━━━━━━━━━━━━━━━━━━━━━●

Dear Superlady,
  I want more sex than my wife does. I also want more variety. From reading your column, I gather this is a common state of affairs between the sexes. Sometimes I wish I were a gay man so I wouldn't have to deal with women. My wife's solution was to see a therapist together. After four weeks we are still discussing such hot topics as how to prioritize our intimacy. What bullshit! But my wife is into it. If I hang in for the sessions she wants, will it make things any better in our bedroom? No improvement in that department yet, I must say. If not, what do you suggest?

I was formulating an answer that would be neither dishonest nor wholly discouraging when Gwen buzzed me that Clarissa was on line one from Memphis. I lunged for the receiver, banging my solid gold link watch from Cartier, a welcome aboard gift from Vinnie, on my desk. She had left yesterday morning, and this was her first contact with us. Miriam hadn't heard from her, and she was driving us crazy phoning the office, me at home, and David at home. We didn't even know where Clarissa was staying; neither did Miriam who didn't seem to function well without her. I was beginning to think the WWAWAWs had confiscated our undercover journalist at the airport.

"Carolyn," she said, more exuberant than I'd heard her sound since Zellie's birth. "I feel like a spy, like, I'm looking over my shoulder even though I'm in my own motel room now. I love this. Do you think Otis and Steve might take me on as a third partner? I could learn to handle a gun, I know I could."

Wearily, I shut my eyes. I could picture her: an orange chenille bedspread draped around her shoulders as combination cape and fire protection, in case she had to leap from a first-floor window to safety, should someone throw a bomb into her room. I felt a headache coming on. Now I understood why David had been so cranky when he was editor.

"Clarissa, what's going on?" I asked, taking off a heavy gold earring to get the receiver closer to my ear. She was speaking softly. "Why haven't you called sooner? We've been worried. David's called Otis twice to suggest he send someone down to look for you. What do you mean, handle a gun? I hate being the boss here."

"I'm in deep cover in Memphis. What did you expect? Hourly bulletins? I'm out in the cold, Carolyn."

"Yeah, right," I said, toying with the band of my watch. This dispatch from the front was coming in slowly. "What have you been doing down there in the cold?"

"I've been to four LSAA meetings. You know Steve was right when he said people who are, like, heavily crazed into these groups go all over town to meetings. I keep seeing the same people. One woman has been to all four of the meetings I've been to and another half dozen have been to three meetings and . . ."

"Have you seen Elizabeth?" I interrupted. You know, Clarissa, the object of your search, I added silently to myself, internalizing the things David would have said out loud.

"Lia, oh yeah. She calls herself Lia, but it is definitely Elizabeth. She's lost a few pounds, definitely not looking good. There's a crazy look in her eye."

Clarissa had a talent for understatement. She had once labeled "a little weird" a letter from a man who'd described masturbating to orgasm while his wife gave birth. Afterward the new parents had eaten the placenta together or so he claimed.

"What, a crazier look than she had when she tried to choke me to death?" I asked.

"Crazier. I think she might be ready to break." *Ready to break?* "I've seen her at two meetings. I can tell she's a regular in the one group and an occasional visitor to the other. But I have a list of nineteen groups here—"

"There are nineteen of these love and sex addict groups in Memphis alone?" I asked. "Don't these people have jobs, families, lives?"

"Yeah, you wonder, don't you? And, like, all the people who go to them say the same things. And you aren't supposed to give anyone advice about their lives, it's like group therapy without the leader or the therapy. But after they share, everybody kind of nods their head, like, yeah, you're a sex addict. This fat guy blubbered all over himself because he had phone sex with a wrong number, and these women said—"

"I know the lingo," I said. "Remember, I briefly dated a recovering drummer? What does Lia say when she 'shares' with the group?"

"Well, here's the problem, not much."

Clarissa and I sighed simultaneously. We were hoping, of course, that Elizabeth would announce she'd gone to New York City as a teenage runaway and made three porn films. Clarissa would have that on tape and catch the next plane home. It wasn't going to be so easy.

"Well, tell me, exactly what does she say?"

"Okay, I have my notes transcribed from the tapes. That little tape recorder hidden in my jacket pocket is the coolest. Here it is: 'Hi, my name is Lia and I'm a sex addict.' Then everyone says, 'Hello, Lia.' Then she says, 'I haven't had an addictive episode in many years, but I am still haunted by that time in my life when my lust led me down a sick and twisted path to perversion.' Then, she goes on the same way, where she basically says she did terrible things for her lusts, but she doesn't say what they were. And, at the end of her spiel, which she delivered almost word for word at both meetings, she says, 'The man for whom I had insatiable shameful lust forced me to do things so evil, the memory of them burns like acid inside me.' "

"Has the ring of poetry to it, doesn't it?"

"Yeah. Like, I'm sure she's been saying it since she started going to meetings. But, like, here's the interesting part. A lot of people really go off on pornography in these meetings, but she doesn't say much on the subject. Does that make sense to you?"

"Maybe she's trying to keep her WWAWAW connection quiet. They surely wouldn't want their PR director describing herself as a 'sex addict,' would they? I wouldn't say anything about porn if I were her either. What would it take to get her to elaborate on her story? Doesn't anyone try?"

"Not really," Clarissa said, a note of dejection creeping into her voice. "Everyone is thinking about what they get to say on their turn when other people are talking. Do you want to hear my cover story?"

I didn't, but she told me anyway. Clarissa was posing as an ex-nun who'd been forced to leave the convent because she couldn't control her lascivious thoughts about the other nuns. The people in the groups loved it, she said, especially the part about her masturbating during mass to thoughts of the other nuns' breasts.

We agreed that Clarissa would attend as many groups as she could in the next week until her presence was so familiar, she could risk questioning Lia without arousing suspicion. Under the guise of a religious helper, she could perhaps draw Thatcher out from behind the thicket of rhetoric hiding her. I took down the name of the motel, the phone number, and Clarissa's room number. And I made her promise to check in at least once every day.

"And call Miriam," I ordered. "She's driving us crazy."

"Wives," Clarissa said, her last comment before hanging up.

Then, before I could get back to work and answer the letter from the poor man whose wife was trying to prioritize their intimacy, which sounded a lot like alphabetizing the spices, Gwen buzzed me again. Vera was on the phone. We went over the plans for the evening. She and several other WIPs were going to the sex clubs to talk to people about Tiffany. I had decided to stay home. I knew Otis was right when he said my celebrity would get in the way. The WIPs had enthusiastically endorsed this position, too. I planned an early dinner, then I would go over my notes for the Will Douglas show the next day, and fall asleep early.

I was truly looking forward to a quiet evening alone.

"LED BY SUPERLADY, SEX STARS TAKE OVER SEX CLUBS!!!!"

Without comment, Mike had handed me the *Post* when he came on duty at eight in the morning. Until he did I was feeling sane and healthy, rested and virtuous. I was sitting at my white tile kitchen counter eating a bowl of whole grain cereal and fruit and drinking vanilla almond coffee from my Virginia Woolf mug. The headline was enough to make the milk on my cereal curdle.

"What the hell?" I said.

"Yeah, I showed it to Samuel, and he was just as surprised as you are. He says you two didn't leave the apartment last night. They've got your name attached to somebody's behind on the picture inside."

I opened to page three, a picture of Vera, Gemma, and Carola climbing into a limo. All you could see of Carola was ass and legs—and a very fine view it was. They were indeed identified as mine. We've all got to take climbing into car lessons from the Princess of Wales.

"I'm flattered," I said.

"Yeah. I would hate to be standing here if they'd mixed you up with Vera."

The article was brief.

Why was a team of aging sex stars doing the sex club scene last night? They were asking questions about Tiffany Titters. Questions, like, "Do you know anyone who didn't like Tiffany?" Are the Women in Porn trying to solve the murder of one of their own without help from the police?

The women hit the club scene hard. They were spotted uptown at Brothel, Brothel, a triplex where posh rooms are rented on the half hourly basis. From there they headed downtown to clubs ranging from lesbian to S&M. Music stopped at the Hungry Pussy when they came into the club. At the Hellhole, Superlady stepped in something and left with it clinging to her shoe.

None of the women would comment on their motives for the whirlwind tour of the underbelly of life. When informed of their investigation efforts, Homicide Lieutenant Michael Reardon, in charge of the case, said, "We cannot stop private citizens from going into public clubs and asking any questions they want to ask of anyone they want to question. But we

can't guarantee protection for these women either if
their questioning gets them into trouble."
   Did they learn anything? Nobody knows.

"Aging sex stars!" I said contemptuously, checking
the byline. Allison Kemp. "Wouldn't you know it's
written by a woman. She's probably twenty-seven and
hates porn."

"Yeah, well, you know I think you girls look damned
good for your ages," Mike said. "Vera's got a little too
much meat on the hoof, but she's still a good-looking
dame. What do you suppose Carola stepped in that
ended their evening prematurely, so to speak?"

"Thanks, Mike, for the compliment," I said sweetly;
he smiled, genuinely believing in my gratitude. "And I
shudder to think what she might have stepped in at an
S&M club. I've been to Hellhole once, with David, for
research. Some women were manacled to the walls; a
few women were lethargically whipping men. The smell
of urine and feces was strong. We both got nauseous
and had to leave."

"Yeah, she most likely stepped in shit. Hell, I
wouldn't pay $50 to get in somewhere like that. You
can step in dog shit on the street for free."

I'd finished my cereal and put the bowl and coffee cup
in the dishwasher when Otis called. He was furious, in
a controlled and professionally distant way, of course.
I held the phone away from my ear while he yelled at me
about "risking" my "silly little neck" to ask "even sillier
questions" of people whose answers, if they even had
any answers, "wouldn't impress a judge because they
have slightly more credibility than a street junkie."

"Why, Otis, I think you care. I really think you do,"
I said. I don't know why I said it, because I didn't really

believe he did. He didn't give me time to explain I hadn't been there at all.

"Caro," he said. The pause between the saying of my name, in that tone of voice the dumper typically uses with the dumpee, and the clearing of his throat told me all I needed to know. Being a sensitive man, he had to say it anyway. "I care, but not quite in the way you think I do."

"Otis . . ."

"No, Caro, I have to say this. I'm not going to see you again, and you deserve to know why. I like you, but I can't get past this black thing of yours. I'm not comfortable being with a white woman who's into black men the way you are. It makes me feel like something you bought off the auction block. Do you understand that?"

"No, I don't understand why men are allowed to have physical preferences, but women aren't."

"There's something else going on here, too. You know I work for Vinnie first. His interests and yours are probably the same, but, if they're not, I have to be on his side."

"Why wouldn't his interests and mine be the same here, Otis?"

"Look, Caro, I can't fully trust David with the rumor going around that he's seen a lawyer about filing a lawsuit against the corporation. It may not be true, but . . ." He paused, clearly waiting for me to defend or criticize, confirm or deny. I wasn't going to let him know this was the first I'd heard of that particular rumor. "I'm sorry you don't understand. I'm sorry to be hurting your feelings. I . . ."

Everyone who has ever rejected another person has been sorry. Not wanting to hear him wallow in his sorriness, I slammed the receiver down so hard on the wall phone that the plastic cracked right down the seam from ear to mouthpiece. Tears smarted in my eyes, but

I brushed them angrily aside. Was he so put off by my attraction to black men or was he just another one of those guys who fuck you like an angel then never call again?

And what was David doing behind my back?

"I hate men," I told Gwen when I walked past her desk on the way to my office. She was surrounded by plants in fussy little ceramic pots and at least a dozen photos of her two-year-old son, a dishwater blond like her. "If they aren't geeks, nerds, losers, jerks, or lying assholes, they have other problems."

"Yeah," she said, following me as I stormed into my office. Gwen was tiny, not five feet and under a hundred pounds and meek and mild until she put a phone to her ear. The phone turned her into a dynamo, capable of getting rid of any caller without alienating him or her. David always said she gave the best business phone in the business. "You got another letter from the Starred Man. Clarissa says not to bother you with them, but she's not here. Should I leave it in her box?"

"Fine," I said. "Call the *Post* and tell them they misidentified the ass of Carola Rogers. I was not in the sex clubs last night."

"Sure," she said, tidying up my desk for me.

"And get me Steve Cohen—Steve, not his partner— on the phone. Don't put anybody through but Clarissa or him. I've got a lot to do this morning."

Forget Otis. I was working with Steve. He was a fan. I would have bet he'd masturbated to my columns; the words, not the picture. Steve was a man of words, and the words I wanted from him were the ones that would tell me what David was doing.

I wasn't coming back to the office after lunch. A limo was taking me straight from lunch with an advertiser to the Douglas show where Carola, Gemma, and I were appearing live that afternoon. Subject or so we had been told: Feminist Porn. Afterward, it looked like another early night. Should I notify the *Post?* Or should I lure young Steve into my lair and between my thighs to get back at Otis?

Clarissa got me on the car phone on the way to lunch. She'd had a "breakthrough," if you define a breakthrough as something achieved by hitting a person who is reluctant to talk with the equivalent of an emotional sledgehammer. Clarissa had told Elizabeth Thatcher she knew who she was—both then and now.

"But, like, I did it real cool, like I said I know I've seen you somewhere. I remember you from the past, I know you were in an old X-rated movie I saw—*Behind The Lilac Door!*"

"Did you tell her you'd rented it on one of those rainy Saturday afternoons back at the convent when there wasn't anything else to do, the prayers had been said, the bread baked, your panties washed by hand?"

"Carolyn, if you're going to make fun of me, I'll hang up," she said in her pouty voice. "I got enough of that from David. I handled her perfectly, which you will soon realize. Do you want to hear the rest or not?"

"Sure," I said, already dreading telling David. "I can't afford not to hear it, can I? I'm the one who's going to sign your expense vouchers for this trip."

"Well, she was so shocked I knew about it that she said yes. Then, I pressed my advantage and asked if she wasn't that woman active in one of the antiporn groups, and she said, yes, again. I have it on tape." She faded out, then came back in again. I hate car phones. "I'm a fucking genius! I acted like I really admired her for what she was doing. Then she told me she'd been forced to do those films by the man she was with, like he sexually enslaved her. I told her she should come clean and admit who she is because denouncing porn after you've been in it would be even more effective."

"You didn't!"

"I wanted her to trust me, which she does. She isn't going to come out and tell the world about her shameful past. Her husband doesn't know. Anyway, I have to go because we're getting together for coffee this afternoon."

"Clarissa, be careful. Get all you can out of her today and then come back to the city as soon as possible. And sit in a public place with her at all times. Don't take her back to your motel. And, Clarissa, be prepared to get choked, okay?"

She laughed. Obviously, she thought I was kidding. I wasn't. While I couldn't see Elizabeth as Tiffany's murderer, I knew she was definitely the type to indulge in a little spontaneous choking when her emotions got out of control.

"Here we have three women who are going to tell you there *is* such a thing as feminist porn, a form of pornography or erotica, if you will, which arouses women and doesn't degrade them," Will said, sweeping his arm in our direction, the gesture indicating a unity we did not have.

"And over here, we have two women who will tell you there *isn't*, that all porn is by definition exploitive of women," he said, pointing at the opposition. It included Marsha Foster, a thin lesbian lawyer with bad hair, who was trying to get a tough antiporn law passed by Congress, and Rosalie Anderson, a very fat lesbian writer whose bad hair was totally overshadowed by her general ugliness. But we were playing by TV talk show rules and could not say the word "lesbian" as descriptive of their life-styles on national TV, because they were not "out." Outing them would have violated their rights.

Rosalie was, perhaps, the ugliest woman I'd ever seen except for Rhumumba, the kind of woman who gives feminism a bad name. I consider myself, and anyone who believes in equal pay for equal work, a feminist, but I understand why the women of the twentysomething generation don't want to be identified by the word "feminist." Women like Rosalie have taken it over. She wouldn't let the makeup people put foundation over her pimples or powder down her oil. What did these women do with the money they didn't spend on hair care products, makeup, or disposable razors?

"Boy, oh, boy," Will said, "have we got a disagreement here."

The audience laughed. He fiddled with the cards in his hand. This was not his favorite show. He would rather have presidential candidates debating the issues or, perhaps, former President Jimmy Carter philosophizing on how building houses helped build America. This was a feminist issue, which meant he was just a bit more excited than he would have been introducing a group of male strippers; one of whom would probably set his jock strap on fire as part of his act. In other words, the kind of mindless show that gets the ratings.

"Uhm, let me see, uhm," he said, arranging the cards. "Here we have Carola Rogers, a former X-rated video star, who started her own production company ten years ago, and considers herself the founding mother of feminist porn. Have I got that right, Carola?"

"You have, Will, but I prefer the term 'feminist erotica,'" she said. Why had it taken me so long to notice how arrogant she was? "My erotica is aimed at women and couples. It has all the elements necessary to female arousal, including a romantic storyline, tenderness between the partners, and attractive settings. The women are certainly not debased and degraded—"

"I would have to challenge that," Foster said. Me, too, on different grounds.

"Okay, okay, you'll get your chance to challenge," Will said. "Right now I'm introducing the women on this side of the issue. We'll get to you. Just be patient. This isn't a courtroom."

The audience laughed, though Will certainly wasn't as funny as Olive.

"Women are only renting your videos to please their men," Rosalie said.

"All right!" Will almost yelled. "You'll get your turn." Pointing to Gemma, he said, "Here we have Gemma Michaels, also a former X-rated video star, publisher of *Great Sex!*, a sex magazine some people consider raunchier than *Hustler,* and owner of her own feminist porn production company.

"And, next to her," he rushed on, to get the introductions out before the polemics began in earnest, "is someone you may recognize because she's certainly had more than her share of publicity lately. Carolyn Steele, the Superlady of Sex, now the executive editor at *Playhouse* magazine, and a new investor in a feminist porn production company these three women have formed, called the Red Hot Mamas!

"Tell us about your new company, Carolyn."

Knowing my partners were seething under their makeup to hear *their* company labeled *mine,* I smiled into the camera and launched into my product spiel. They dutifully waited a respectable amount of time before cutting in on me. All those years of faking orgasms had taught them how to be polite.

". . . and women are shown in these videos as being

the sexual initiators," Carola was saying. "We know, Will, that's true in real life as well. Studies show women are initiating up to fifty percent of the sexual encounters in their relationships. And their fantasies have become bolder, too, reflecting their new reality."

Stifling a yawn (these women were boring, all four of them) I indulged in a mini fantasy of my own. Dressed in garter belt, stockings, heels, and a mask, I was riding astride first Charles, then O, flying high in the female superior position. I picked up my whip and snapped it across each man's nipples as I rode him. Now I was on Charles. His penis grew and grew so big I had to leap off it in mid orgasm or it would have split me in half. I rode on the side of the giant penis, my legs wrapped around it, my heels digging into it, until it detached from his body and shot up, like a rocket into the sky. After a while, I brought it back down to earth, to O's bed, where it deposited me in his arms.

The whiny voice of Rosalie brought me back to reality. Anyway, in real life, O would have said, "You only fell out of the sky into my bed because I'm black. Please go back up into the clouds."

"All forms of male to female genital interaction," she was saying when I rejoined the program in progress, "are acts of aggression. If a man loves a woman, he should not even let her see him with his penis exposed."

The last shot going into commercial captured my look of pure disdain.

"Are you there, caller?" Will asked. "I'm glad you waited," he said, even before the caller spoke.

We were past the half hour point, and I was seriously bored. Will had vigorously run up and down the aisles, working the audience, saying, "Help me out here, people," and "This is a talk show, let's talk," whenever they flagged in their enthusiasm for the debate. Gemma, Carola, and I had stood up for heterosexual sex. Foster and Anderson were against penetration, and that probably included male tongues and fingers. Why then, I've always wondered, are so many lesbian women into dildos? Will, a man clearly on the side of feminism, had hedged his bets. He seemed to favor the ugly broads, but, on the other hand, he'd been courteous, sometimes deferential, to us. Maybe in his heart he really liked a woman who liked a penis, good and hard. But everything any of us said had been said before on TV talk shows, often by one of us. What was the point? Did the audience really care? I didn't really care. I was tired of being on TV. Where would I rather be? Riding a giant penis into the sunset.

"I just want to say, Will," the caller said, "your giving equal time to those three sluts in their short skirts bothers me. Pornography against women is a serious issue and should be treated as such."

"Okay, caller, does that mean you only want to hear one side of a serious issue, the side you already agree with?"

"Yes," she said, "I believe—"

"Thank you, caller," he said, cutting her off, "and I would like to remind you that labeling these women 'sluts' because they're wearing short skirts or because they have a different opinion than you do is a form of prejudice."

The audience applauded lukewarmly, but still they did applaud. Maybe they were merely endorsing our decision to shave our legs. Who knows? I took the opportunity to recross mine, making my skirt pull up a little higher. Out of the corner of my eye, I saw Carola suppress a smirk. This is how old girls fight.

We went into a commercial break. The makeup person patted down the grease. A thin woman in her late twenties with long brown hair, she looked like she would be walking down the aisle of a church in a New Jersey suburb all dressed in white any day now, never to return to this life again. She made a wide berth around Rosalie. I wished I could. The truth is, Rosalie smelled like she needed a bath.

Coming out of commercial, a clip from one of Carola's videos was on the monitor. A couple was undressing each other, their passion tempered by the need for political correctness. For each piece removed from her, a corresponding piece had to be removed from him, so they would be nude at very nearly the same time. The action stopped when they were in their tastefully sexy underwear.

"Okay, the woman in that clip seemed to be the sexual initiator to me. Am I right, Carola?" Will asked. She nodded affirmatively. How could you be wrong about something so obvious, Will? "Okay, then what is your problem with that, Rosalie, Marsha?"

They, of course, had many problems with it and shared them all with us. Listening to them speak, with frequent interruptions by Carola and Gemma, I thought what fun it would be to read aloud from Rosalie's works on national TV, not that she had written anything which could be read aloud for long on national TV. How far could I go into a graphic scene of fist fucking before I got bleeped?

"We'll be back in just a moment," Will said, heading into the final commercial break. "And the Red Hot Mamas will tell you what's new on their agenda."

Maybe it was the word "agenda" that did it. I came to life on the word. "Agenda" seemed to bite me like a bug pulling me out of the stupor I was in. After the commercial, Gemma plugged our new line of videos, still in production, and Carola sounded off about censorship. Then I issued a veiled threat to the WWA-WAWs.

"I'm glad you asked about new projects," I interjected. "At *Playhouse,* we're in the process of uncovering a major scandal connected to a prominent figure in the antiporn movement. Our story will deal a death blow to one of these groups. I can't say any more than that at this time, of course, but—"

"I thank you, I thank all of you for your contributions to this program," Will said over the rising theme music.

Samuel had come on duty during the Douglas show, relieving Mike in the green room. The two of us rode back to my apartment in relative silence. I liked that about Samuel. He never found it necessary to comment on my skirt lengths or critique my TV appearances. When I got tired of playing Mike's wife, I could pretend I was Samuel's lover. But I was wearying of the bodyguard thing. The unmasking of Rhumumba had ended the threats on my life. Maybe there was no reason to believe the person who had killed Tiffany would be coming after me at all. Maybe the person who had killed Tiffany was a random nut who would never surface again. I made a mental note to call Vinnie tomorrow and suggest we terminate the bodyguards. I wanted to be alone again.

After Samuel had checked the apartment and listened to my messages, none from Otis telling me he'd suddenly developed a lust for white women, I went into the bedroom. Hugging my sadness close to me, I changed into my favorite old jeans, washed so often they were soft and shredded at the knees, and a gray cashmere sweatshirt. I sat down on the bed. For the first time in months, I remembered Tim the geek's favorite question: *How does that make you feel?*

O's rejection had made me feel wronged. How dare he walk away from me because I was drawn to his blackness? Has a blonde ever walked away from a man because he desired her blondness? On the other hand, maybe my attraction to him wasn't healthy. Was David right when he said O was just my way of having Charles? I did still want Charles. I rubbed my temples. My sudden and intense interest in only black men made me uncomfortable, too. Maybe Otis was right: I'd treated him like a piece of particularly tasty meat.

I paced the floor, shifting my focus to my anger at David. What was he doing behind my back?

"I'm not a fan," Steve said. "I didn't even know you were Superlady until that woman choked you on 'Olive.' I never checked out the picture. I liked the column, the way you answered letters. You really put it to those pervs sometimes."

He pronounced "didn't" like "dint." It was kind of cute.

"Sure," I said. "Whatever."

We were sitting beside each other on the sofa, with at least two feet of space between us. He was on his second Coke; it was my third glass of champagne. What I knew about him so far: He was very smart and knew it. He was quite attractive and didn't have a clue. His romantic history was filled with women who had mistreated him and moved on. But the question *"Have you heard the rumors about David?"* remained ignored by us like a silent fart.

"So, have you heard anything about David?" I tried again.

"Did you invite me here to pump me for information or to get back at Otis?"

"What do you think?"

"I think he's not comfortable with you because you write about sex." He took a long sip of his soda. "A little of both, information and revenge. I don't know anything about David," he said, finally relenting, "except that he's talked to a lawyer about the possibility of suing the corporation for defamation of character. He claims he didn't steal anything. He is just not a very good manager."

"How American of him," I snapped. "Defamation of character."

"Maybe he doesn't want a cash settlement. Maybe he wants his job back. Did you ever think of that?"

"Maybe his wife wants him to get his job back. David hates working."

"Don't you?"

I poured some more champagne into my glass. When I leaned back again, I closed some of the distance between us. Though I was slightly drunk, I could see well enough to recognize an exceptionally large erection nestled inside his jeans. If he had a big cock, I could have him. Men with big ones were always looking for excuses to take their treasures out and play. Is this why well-endowed men aren't monogamous?

"How old are you?" I asked.

"Thirty."

"Too young."

"I like older women."

He was grinning. Too young, I thought, sipping my champagne. Then he pulled off his sweater, exposing a very hairy chest. I'd forgotten how much I liked white male chest hair. Those long, silky strands, sensuous beneath the fingers. He took my champagne away and kissed me softly at first, his lips almost softer than a man's should be; then hard, pushing his teeth against mine, but it felt good. His hands on my back, my breasts, he lifted up the sweatshirt, moved it up until it was bunched around my shoulders. I pulled it over my head and threw it on the floor. He kept kissing me, not letting go of my mouth, until we had removed all of our clothes.

"Do you always leave your eyes open when you kiss?" he asked, his tongue flicking my eyelids.

I resisted the urge to say, "If I didn't, I might forget who you are."

His penis was at least as large as O's and more solid than any piece of flesh I'd ever held in my hands. And he was clearly proud, penis-proud. Who could blame him? And who would have thought such a magnificent organ existed on a short white man? I stretched out on the sofa beneath him and opened my thighs. Grasping my hips, he pushed his cock inside me. We fit perfectly, his body not too large, his penis wonderfully so. We moved in sync. No emotional interference to throw us off our stride. He wedged his fingers between my legs and held them steady against my clit. I fucked his hand and his cock; the orgasms began in short, distinctive, little blasts and grew and melded together until my mind was blank. I felt him come inside me in a spray deep and hard, the ejaculation of youth. As he came, he growled.

I woke in the middle of the night and took his penis in my hand. The weight of it thrilled me. I held it loosely and watched it move against my palm, edge up toward my wrist. He moaned and closed his hand around mine, forcing me to hold it tight. I climbed on top of him and guided his penis inside. He held onto my ass and pumped into me, without coming fully awake. I angled my body to take him harder, deeper. In the moonlight, our bodies were like a moving sculpture covered in a fine mist. White on white. I came.

Chapter Seventeen

Dear Superlady,

I would love a woman occasionally to make love to me. Take me into her arms, kiss me passionately, and lead me into the bedroom. From there, slowly remove my clothes, kissing and caressing each part of my body as the clothes come off. One time a woman did something like that to me. She started at my feet, kissing and sucking my skin. Up she went, past my calves and knees and in between my thighs. I had an incredible erection. She went past my genital area and started at my navel and worked her way down. I was going crazy. Finally, after a good while, she grasped my penis in her hand and started kissing and sucking. It was all I could do to keep from coming. Now, that is foreplay!

My question: Why don't more women make love to a man? Why do they think foreplay is something we're supposed to do for them?

Dear Enthusiast,

Foreplay is a negative word, don't you think? It has come to mean the sexual work men do for women to prepare us for intercourse. The assumption is that he doesn't need any preparation. Ask the typical American what foreplay is, and he or she will tell you

*it's the time she holds him off while he revs her up.
Maybe that was true when we were all sixteen.
Maybe. It certainly doesn't work for adults. Men
like to be touched, and the older they get, the more
they need to be touched to become aroused . . .*

I didn't realize how caught up I was getting in the
answer until I heard myself moan. It was O's body I
saw in my mind, and my hands and tongue were
moving up and down him, lavishing liquid attention on
every part of him. It was O's beautiful body responding
to my kisses and caresses, the ridge of his stomach
muscles tightening with his initial excitement.

He was lying on his back, and I was kneeling at his
side. I took his penis in the palm of my hand and ran my
tongue the length of the shaft and around the head. No,
it wasn't O's penis. Definitely, this organ belonged to
Charles. I took his penis into my mouth and slowly
moved down to the base and back to the head again. O
was beginning to writhe and pant under my ministra-
tions. I kept fellating Charles's penis until O was so
excited, his body gave off the scent of heated flesh.
Repeatedly, I flicked my tongue across the ridge behind
the head of his penis. Then I ran my tongue back down
to the base and up again. When I knew he was ready to
come, I sucked the head of his penis, drawing his sweet
come from his body into my mouth.

Moaning, I pressed my hand against my clit and let
the orgasm go free. It felt so good, like old times, me
alone with my computer and my hand. Why was I
fantasizing black men when the personal messages on
my answering machine were all from Steve? He'd let me
know he was the kind of guy who, having had sex with
a woman, wanted to continue having sex with her and
nobody else. At last I'd found a serial monogamist, and
he was sure to wake up some morning and realize I was
looking decidedly too old.

Fortunately, I was working at home today, and I was gloriously alone. I'd persuaded Vinnie against his better judgment to discontinue the twenty-four-hour body-guard. We'd agreed on a compromise: He had a state-of-the-art alarm system installed in my apartment, and I'd promised I wouldn't go out in public without a bodyguard. I only had to dial a twenty-four-hour number to have some big guy at my side, which made spontaneous trips to the deli for frozen yogurt problematical, but think of the calories I'd save if I had to ask myself every time, Is this trip worth calling for security backup?

I got up and walked around the room, plucked a dead leaf from a hanging basket of Swedish ivy, and straightened the magazine pile on the ottoman upholstered in heavy turquoise silk that I was using as a coffee table in my newly decorated office. My apartment was entirely redecorated, and Vinnie had paid for everything because *People* magazine was coming in two days to photograph it. The office was my special delight. I had a huge solid oak desk and matching computer stand; built-in oak bookcases on three walls; an antique kilim rug in shades of faded green and blue and an orange, so old it had turned peach; a white sofa, filled with floral pillows in shades of peach, turquoise, and green, most of them handmade, many in the shape of flowers; also "curtains" of hanging plants.

"You've arrived," my son had said, when I called to tell him I was going to be the focus of a *People* story, which indicated I now had a measure of mainstream acceptability. He was pleased.

Once in my life, and not so long ago, I would have loved being in *People*. Now I wasn't impressed, only glad to have the points with my son. Vinnie wanted the article and photo spread because publicizing the editor-in-chief of *Playhouse* as a pro-sex feminist was good for the magazine. I had to agree, because the Red Hot

Mamas needed the publicity, too. Though I'd only had a small portion of fame as compared to Michael Jackson or Madonna, I was tired of media attention. Welcoming the inevitable slide back to oblivion, I couldn't wait for my fifteen minutes to end.

Do you know what fame is?

Fame is having a small part of you known or, more likely, misperceived by a large number of people. Give the public a few details, and they'll fill in the rest, drawing from their large community storehouse of "What They Say" and "What Everybody Knows." Fortunately, most people get all they need of celebrities on "Entertainment Tonight" or in ten-minute reading doses in the doctor's office or the privacy of their own bathrooms. Only the few and the sick are truly fascinated, hungrier for more than the famous could ever give them. And only the sickest are angry enough to overreact when they don't get enough, because we haven't got whatever they want to give. The possibility is always there. That's fame.

And Steve was too excited about my fame.

I walked into the living room, another indoor garden, with sofa and matching chaise upholstered in a print bursting with red and white flowers, and more greenery. The antique pressed back rocker had green cushions, and the single chair was done in red. The side tables were antique, oak, and expensive, one covered by a patchwork quilt over a hundred years old, and the Eighteenth Century distressed pine common table, used as a coffee table, came from England. I had built-in oak bookcases on two walls and palm trees which reached the ceiling.

Stretching out on the chaise, I contemplated a nap before my lunch date with David and Clarissa to discuss the WWAWAW exposé. I planned to let David know over the first glass of wine that I knew he was toying with the idea of suing to get his job back. Let him wriggle off that hook under Clarissa's watchful eye. Then the phone rang. It was Rhumumba. Yes, Rhumumba. She had, she said, something very important to discuss with me.

"Like, you can't really let Rhumumba come to your apartment, she's dangerous," Clarissa said.

She was midway through her first large Sfuzzi, a slushy drink made of frozen champagne and peach brandy, the house drink of the restaurant of the same name on 65th and Broadway. I took a sip of my own Sfuzzi. David was drinking a draft beer. I don't know what kind. I'd lost interest in listening as the server gave him the rundown twice.

"I agree with Clarissa," David said, rolling his paper drink napkin into a cylinder and tapping it against his glass. "Seeing Rhumumba in your apartment alone is too dangerous. I'll go home with you."

"I'll have a bodyguard there. I've already called and arranged it. He can hide unobtrusively. If you're there with me, she might not be so willing to talk." I paused. "Like you care." I was glaring directly at him, but peripherally I saw Clarissa's eyes widen. "With me out of the way, maybe you won't have to sue to get rehired."

"Still too dangerous," he said, ignoring everything after the pause.

"What are you talking about?" Clarissa asked, fiddling nervously with the knot in her tie, on which naked buxom blondes cavorted in muted tones.

"Which bodyguard?" David asked, staring intently into his beer.

"Mike."

"She could take him out in seconds."

"What's going on?" Clarissa asked.

"Anyway, it's arranged," I said. "She's coming. He's coming. Too late to back out now. We'll talk later," I said to Clarissa, and to both, "someone tell me what's happening with the article."

"Since you promoted it on the Douglas show, we've been besieged with threats, requests for more information, offers of information for a fee . . ." David began.

"Yeah, yeah, I know. You forget I work there."

"It's easy to forget this week. You haven't been there much," he said.

"I'm bored with the office," I admitted. "In fact, even before I was told to look out for Trojans on horseback, I've been thinking of ways to get out of my contract. I'm getting a decent advance for my book of collected "Superlady" columns. If Vinnie takes the column away from me now, the book will still support me for a while."

"The print porn business is dying anyway," David interjected. "The growth lies in videos and phone sex lines, not print. Soon the magazines will exist only for advertisers of videos and phone sex lines. They will have no editorial integrity whatsoever."

"You mean take the money and run?" Clarissa asked, her eyes lighting up. Since she'd come back from Memphis, she wasn't as excited about her job either. Maybe she could sue to get fired. Maybe we both could. That last chatty coffee date with Elizabeth had clinched it for her: She saw herself as a P. I. "I like it. You know, I really like it. We could both get out at the same time. Miriam would love it if I could spend more time with her and Zelda."

"Then what will you do?" David asked me, ignoring her.

"I'll get more involved in the Red Hot Mamas, put my book together, maybe start a heterosexual feminist erotica quarterly if I can find a financial backer . . . and I can always write a novel, can't I?"

The waiter came to take our orders: the grilled chicken salad for me, little pizzas for them, and a bottle of chardonnay for the table.

"You'll miss the expense account," David said, still not meeting my eyes as he pulled his WWAWAW folder from his briefcase.

I took the folder and flipped through his notes. He'd found two women who remembered Elizabeth from her Liz Larue days. The first, Allison Nash, a divorced mother of three living in Cleveland, also had a bit part in *Behind The Lilac Door*. Like Elizabeth, she'd been a pretty blond teen runaway with big boobs and a vacuous look in the eyes.

Reading over my shoulder, David said, "Allison's best memory of Elizabeth is the time they watched Macy's Fourth of July fireworks display together from the roof of an East Side apartment building. They'd been invited to a party by a photographer. Typical early seventies party; marijuana, alcohol, group sex. Elizabeth wanted to get away because her legs were sticky from some guy spilling his seed on her. The bathroom was being used by a couple fucking, and someone had vomited in the kitchen. So they took bottles of club soda to the roof and Elizabeth poured them down her legs while they watched the fireworks."

"That's kind of sad," I said. "I was hoping for incriminating stories of her bestial nature, not poignant little tales to harden the reader's heart toward the life of porn."

"Life of porn, hell! That was life in New York in the seventies. We'll leave it out if you think it generates reader sympathy for her. And the best news is she was definitely eighteen when she made the films, which takes away the possibility of her being elevated to victim of child porn status."

I flipped the pages. The second woman, Chiquita Sanchez, was married to a successful Mexican businessman and demanded anonymity and some cash, in exchange for her memories of Elizabeth, which were much more promising. Also heartening, for an additional fee, she was willing to go on talk shows in silhouette, sharing her remembrances of Elizabeth in the old days with the electronic world.

Allison had known Elizabeth toward the end of her New York period, just before she'd returned home to face the wrath of her sanctimonious parents and cleaned up her act for good. Chiquita had been there at the start when Elizabeth was living as a "sexual slave," her own definition, to Rudolfo, the South American lover she'd told Clarissa had forced her to act in three porn films. Chiquita remembered it differently. According to her, Elizabeth did the porn films in an effort to turn him on and keep him interested when it was obvious he no longer was.

"Chiquita remembers her as a sexually depraved young woman who would do anything her lover wanted even before he thought to want it," David said. "Too bad Rudolfo died of AIDS a few years back. You knew he swung both ways? He would have made a great interview. By the way, she had a pubic ring."

"I know," Clarissa said, moving the bread plate aside so the waiter could serve her pizza. "And she wasn't at any of the meetings the day Tiffany was killed. Otis is looking into where she might have been."

"She was probably at the mall shopping for Christmas," I said.

Even though she'd tried to choke me to death, I couldn't see Elizabeth Thatcher as the woman who had strangled Tiffany. I'd seen Tiffany's body. That had taken strength, more strength than I'd felt in Elizabeth's hands when they were around my neck. They had not seen Tiffany's body.

While we ate, I looked through Clarissa's notes, which were even more interesting than David's. Elizabeth/Liz/Lia had described in riveting detail her life as a "sex addict." She had allowed herself to be fucked both vaginally and anally with the end of a nightstick. For Rudolfo's amusement, she'd fellated his buddies. Not only had she been orgasmic in her encounters with Rudolfo, anally, orally, and vaginally—she'd even reached orgasm during oral sex with "those sluts" in the movie.

"Did she ever specifically say Tiffany made her come?" I asked Clarissa.

"No, but it was obvious, don't you think? Like, I mean, the whole film is Tiffany doing it to women. Elizabeth only did three films, and she had oral sex performed on her in one, with Tiffany. We don't need Sherlock Holmes for this, do we?"

"Clarissa might need a bodyguard when this article comes out and Elizabeth realizes who did it to her this time," David said, looking at her for the first time in my memory with respect in his eyes.

Would *I* find warmth in those eyes again if I quit my job?

Waiting for Rhumumba to show up while Mike hid behind the closed kitchen doors, I should have been elated about the article, which promised to bring the magazine tremendous publicity and deal a sharp body blow to the WWAWAWs, but I wasn't. In spite of what Elizabeth had said to Clarissa, others remembered her as a willing participant in three porn films. She wasn't led to the set in chains. Nobody ever saw or heard Rudolfo beat or threaten her. In fact, he was remembered for his growing indifference to Elizabeth, no matter how tightly she wrapped her net of sexual complicity around him. I should have felt good about it all, but I kept picturing a girl of seventeen or eighteen washing semen off her leg with club soda while she watched the Fourth of July fireworks, which made her not so different from millions of young women who go along sexually without getting much from the experience.

If Elizabeth were really smart, she'd seize the advantage and go public with her story before we could. Then she had a better chance of selling her version, WWA-WAW in sexual bondage. She could be the new Linda Lovelace, and the media was always looking for a new somebody. How many times has the ghost of James Dean been invoked in the initial reviews of young actors' performances? The first version of any story has the ring of truth to it, no matter how big a lie it is. But Elizabeth had not struck me as very smart.

"The bitch is late," Mike said, opening the door a crack to make a face at me, his gun held firmly in his right hand, high against his chest, and pointing at the ceiling. "Think she's not gonna show?"

"She'll be here."

"Think it has something to do with Bobby being in the clear?"

"I don't know," I said.

Only that morning Bobby had called to tell me he was no longer an official suspect. His "date" the night of Tiffany's murder, a man Bobby had forgotten being with, had finally come forward and given him an alibi. A married Wall Street executive, Bobby's date had agonized for weeks before stepping forward and clearing him. Bobby hadn't known his name or remembered much about him even after seeing him again face-to-face, except the size of his penis, very small, and his wallet, respectably large.

"Honey, you know I only remember the important details," Bobby had said, shrugging off weeks of being a suspect as if it had never happened, his own invaluable self-defense mechanism.

"I don't know what she wants," I repeated to Mike,

"but I'll bet she shows. Don't fall asleep on your gun."

Twenty minutes later the buzzer sounded. The doorman announced Rhumumba, and I swallowed down panic so real it left an aftertaste in my throat like bile. When I opened the door to her, I was more afraid. She looked like she was spending six days a week at the gym.

"I know you hate me and you think I'm a killer and everything," she said when I'd seated her on the couch and was facing her from the red chair. "I don't care if you think that. I came over here to tell you something for your own good in exchange for a promise from you that you won't expose me."

"Expose you as what?" I asked, unable to resist looking at the patches of muscled skin exposed by the holes in her jeans.

"You know what, as a transsexual. I know you're doing a big story exposing a member of an antiporn group. And I know your detective has been all over my life. So, you know why I'm here. I don't want Leanne to know I was addicted to porn when I was a man."

"I see," I said, suppressing the urge to giggle. How had Otis and Steve missed her past porn addiction if they'd been all over her life? "But she does know you were a man?"

"That doesn't bother her, but the other would. She couldn't forgive it. What do you think she'd do if she read I masturbated to those magazines she's trying to destroy every day?"

"How did you know you were a porn addict?"

"My girlfriend told me. She was right."

"What, or who, are you willing to trade to keep it a secret?" I asked. I wasn't going to touch her last question.

"Elizabeth Thatcher."

I didn't say anything for a while. She fidgeted a bit, rubbing her mechanical cheeks against the sofa in an alternating rhythm. I almost expected her to make sparks.

"Okay," I said, "what about Elizabeth Thatcher?"

She told me, of course, everything I already knew about Elizabeth's past as porn starlet and her present as a secret sex addict. But how did she know it? Had they run into each other at a Sex and Love Addicts Anonymous meeting? Or was Rhumumba spending her afternoon, upon leaving the gym, as an amateur detective? When she'd finished, I asked if she could prove her accusations.

"Enough of them. Mostly, I learned it under confidential circumstances." They *had* been at the same group meetings, probably when Elizabeth was in New York on her paint pelting binge. Addict groupies never miss their meetings, even when traveling. "But you've got that big black dick to help you with the rest."

No point in telling her I now had a big white dick to help me with the rest. I pressed her for more, but she didn't seem to have anything more than we already knew. Finally, I agreed to her terms. *Playhouse* would drop the WAP exposé and go for the WWAWAWs. We shook on it.

As I was walking her to the door, she said, "Elizabeth Thatcher is a dangerous woman. We think she killed Tiffany."

"Who's 'we'?"

"Me and Leanne and the women in our group."

"I don't suppose you have any proof of that?"

Well, of course, she didn't. How could she?

Before she could get away, I put a hand on her formidable arm and asked, "Were the WAPs responsible for the stink bomb at Tiffany's book party?"

"Yeah," she said, and, I swear, she almost seemed to blush. "Sorry about that. Later, we learned we damaged some of the bookstore's stock."

After Rhumumba was gone for a minute or two, Mike came out of the kitchen, shaking his head.

"I don't like this at all," he said, putting his gun inside his shoulder holster.

Neither did I. In place of a confession, she'd given me something I already had. I felt like I did when I unwrapped those "gifts" advertisers send in the mail. A woman needs only so many vibrators and sets of ben-wa balls or body paints. And I was starting to believe maybe Tiffany *had* been killed by a stranger. It wasn't difficult to picture her going out for a box of tea bags, befriending some woebegone person of either sex, and inviting him or her up to share the tea.

I was going to call Clarissa to report on the meeting with Rhumumba and fill her in on what was going on with David when the buzzer sounded again.

"Miss Stephanie is here," the doorman said.

"Send her up," I instructed, wondering what Stephanie wanted and why she hadn't called ahead.

I opened the door to Elizabeth Thatcher. She was wearing a shiny red rayon raincoat over a vertically striped silk dress of many colors. In addition to looking chilled to the bone, she looked rather awful. Makeup would have helped.

"How did you know to use Stephanie's name?" I asked, when I should have slammed the door in her face.

"She's one of your group. I took the chance you'd let her in whether you were expecting her or not."

We stood facing each other; me wavering on whether or not I should let her in the door; her standing firm, as if she could will me to open the door wider. Apparently, she could, because I did. She came inside.

"What do you want?" I asked. In reply, she pulled a

handgun from her purse, pointed it at me, and held it steady.

"I think you should be found dead in your own bed," she said.

Thank the Goddess for Elizabeth's love of the polemic. She wasn't going to kill me until she had thoroughly explained to me why I had to die. She ordered me to strip first. I was to die in the nude, a photo the *Post* surely wouldn't be allowed to run without putting discreet black bands in the proper places.

"You are just as responsible for what happened to me as the men who made me do it," she said, holding the gun firmly in steady hands. She was probably a member of the NRA.

"What happened to you?" I asked, my fingers trembling at the wrist buttons on my long sleeves.

"Take off your clothes!" she said, her voice rising, sweat beading above her lip.

She waved the gun at me, so I complied. Sitting on the edge of my bed, I began to remove my clothes. Though my hands were still shaking and my body felt stiff, I forced myself to put an erotic twist to every action. I pulled the back of my pumps off first, then slid off the shoe, my toes pointed, foot arched. Maybe I could arouse her sexually and somehow get the gun away from her. And then what?

"You know what happened to me," she said sharply, her face aglow with the crazy blaze burning in both eyes. "Did you think I wouldn't figure out that ex-nun was your spy? Women like you think women like me who lead good Christian lives and stay home with our children are stupid. I'm not stupid. I figured it out and followed her back here."

"Does your husband know where you are?" I asked.

I would never have believed I'd ever ask any woman *that* question.

Lifting my hips off the bed, I pulled my black silk skirt off and laid it gently beside me. My legs apart and open, I sat facing her dressed only in panty hose and a black silk bodysuit.

"Take off the rest," she said, clearly evaluating my thighs, and giving them grudgingly high marks, in spite of herself. Hers had to be fat under those dresses with the defined waists and voluminous skirts which she always wore. "I'll go back home tonight after I've finished with you and rededicate myself to my marriage. Killing you will end this for me."

My eyes not leaving her face, I undid the snaps at the crotch of my bodysuit, raised my hips and slowly slid my panty hose down my legs. With my torso bent forward, I dropped my head briefly, looked back up at her, and met her glassy eyes. I sat up, sucking in my stomach and pushing out my chest as I did, and opened my legs again, wider this time.

"Tiffany turned you on like nobody ever did, didn't she?"

"Shut up," she said. Her face was flushed, her lips moist. "Finish undressing."

"I turn you on, too, don't I?"

Really, I wasn't so sure I did. Probably the prospect of shooting a hole through my body was making her eyes glaze over. I pulled the bodysuit over my head and laid it on top of the skirt. Naked now, I rested my hands on my thighs and looked at her. I was calm. The fact that I had seen Mike silently open the apartment door seconds before helped.

"You're wrong," she said. "It was Rudolfo."

"Rudolfo turned you on? Then why did you leave him? Or did he leave you?"

"I had an orgasm with Tiffany, and I'm ashamed of that, but he was the one. I was thinking of him when I had it. I was sexually obsessed with Rudolfo. When I took Jesus into my heart as my personal saviour, I asked Him to take away my perverted lusts, and He has. Each day I ask Him to keep them away, and I thank Him for doing it. I promised Jesus I would get rid of smut."

"Tell me about Rudolfo. What did he do to you that your husband doesn't do?"

Well, I thought, the possibilities there are endless. What could that uptight little motherfucker she'd married do in bed that a two-inch vibrator without working batteries couldn't do better?

"He . . ." she began. Her voice was choked. "I can't."

"Did he have a big penis?"

"He . . ."

She lost her voice in a gurgle deep in her throat. Yes, I would bet he'd had a big penis, and she was remembering it now.

"Are you going to shoot me? Why aren't you going to strangle me like you did Tiffany? I don't believe Jesus wanted you to kill Tiffany or me either. Why didn't you make Tiffany take off her clothes?"

I was rambling to keep her from making her fatal move as Mike inched his way down the hall, Rhumumba behind him. Elizabeth looked at me like I was a particularly inept student, and I suddenly realized I was. Around her neck, she wore a long white silk scarf. The gun, of course, was a prop to frighten me into submission.

"I didn't make Tiffany take off her clothes because she wasn't the Superlady of Sex. I had to kill her, because she knew who I was, but I didn't need to take her dignity away."

"How did you discover she knew who you were?"

"Tiffany talked to someone about me, someone who is as ashamed of her past as I am, someone I knew in those days; that someone called me."

Now I understood what had happened. Tiffany had probably talked to one of our informants, who'd been selling her information both ways ever since. Chiquita? Allison? Or maybe Tiffany had found someone we hadn't found.

"I called her, and she said she wouldn't tell anyone until she talked to me," Elizabeth said. "She wanted to talk to me, because she thought I was sending you those letters. She thought I was going to hurt you. She said she wouldn't tell anyone who I was if I promised not to hurt you, but I couldn't trust her to keep her word. I didn't want to kill her. She didn't taunt me with her wantonness on national television like you did."

"I'm worse than Tiffany?" I asked, deliberately keeping my eyes off her face and not looking at Mike standing in the doorway, Rhumumba behind him. "Why am I worse than Tiffany?"

"You're so proud of your body," she said. "You should be found naked and crumpled. Tiffany got fat, and men didn't want her anymore."

"That's not true," I said. "Tiffany didn't want men anymore. They've always wanted her."

Mike kicked the gun out of her hand. I rolled off the bed onto the floor and scooted under the bed. That's why I didn't see Rhumumba rush past Mike and grab Elizabeth, who managed to break free. Rhumumba chased her through the apartment, out onto the terrace, and somehow Elizabeth went off the terrace, twelve flights down.

Held tight against Steve's chest, I was still shaking inside the white cashmere robe, which Mike had tenderly wrapped around me after pulling me out from under the bed. The police were camped out in my living room. Mike and Rhumumba had repeated their story, our story, and Mike was telling it yet again. I could hear him from the bedroom where O and Steve sat with me. Steve stroked my hair and kissed my face. O did not seem upset by this display of public affection. It was soon going to be my turn to talk.

Why had Rhumumba and Mike come back to my apartment? On her way down Columbus, she'd seen Elizabeth on the other side of the street and followed her back here. Mike had been following Rhumumba, because he still thought she had killed Tiffany and might come back to get me, too. They had stuck to the truth on this part of their official story.

"She panicked, ran past us, and jumped before we could stop her," he said. "Jeez, I never saw anyone move so fast. The woman was a major nutcase."

It was a simple story. Not much to remember. I could handle it. In the minutes following the murder, before the doorman could summon the cops, we had agreed on the basic details. Rhumumba had helped save my life, and it was Mike who suggested why shouldn't we save hers?

Rhumumba claimed Elizabeth had jumped. By the time Mike had reached the terrace, Rhumumba was standing at the wall, looking down at the ground. If he couldn't corroborate her story, he said, the police might assume she'd pushed Elizabeth off. And Elizabeth had killed Tiffany, and justice had been done, Mike had said.

"Why expose her to criminal speculation?" he'd asked.

Did anyone, even Rhumumba, really deserve the penitentiary for killing a crazed WWAWAW who would have killed me if she could have? Even in my state of shock, I wasn't fooled and knew Mike was doing what he deemed best for Vinnie. Would the publicity surrounding the questioning and possible arrest for murder of a former *Playhouse* employee be good for the magazine? No.

"How could she have been strong enough to kill Tiffany?" I asked Steve and O.

"Caro, crazy people have strength we can't imagine."

I told them what happened, sticking exactly to the truth until the very end, when I said I'd watched Elizabeth Thatcher wrest free of Rhumumba and throw herself off the terrace. Mike and Rhumumba had to make an official statement at police headquarters, something I'd been spared for another day, because I was still shaking. When they were all gone, I went back to bed, and O poured the three of us snifters of Courvoisier.

"You think Rhumumba threw her off, don't you?" he asked. I nodded affirmatively.

"But why would she do that?" Steve asked. "Panic? Gut reaction?"

"Maybe she thought Elizabeth's death would quash an antiporn article in *Playhouse* and probably also ensure her own secrets were safe. And maybe she wanted to avenge Tiffany, too. I don't know about that. I don't know how she felt about Tiffany, but everybody else loved her. Or maybe she didn't want a member of a group on the same side of the porn issues she's on being taken alive. Or she could be a little crazy herself. I could vote for that one."

What I didn't say was I also believed Mike had made it to the terrace in time to see Rhumumba pitch Elizabeth down to her hell on earth.

"I'm sorry you had to go through this, Carolyn," O said, putting his glass down and taking my hands between his. "I'm going now so you can get some rest." He kissed my cheek, then walked to Steve, clapped him on the back, and said, "Let me know if you need anything here."

"We have his blessing," I said, after the door had closed behind him.

"We don't need his blessing. I don't, anyway. Do you?"

He pulled the comforter off me and opened my robe, then knelt over my body, his legs inside mine which were outstretched, and lowered his face between my breasts. I sighed and put my arms around him, running my hands up and down his body. He kissed me, beginning in the hollow of my neck and moving down. By the time his tongue reached my clit, I was consumed with heat. I pushed my hips up, pressing hard against him. My legs were trembling, sweat forming at the backs of my knees. His tongue had only to flick me lightly a few times, and I was coming.

I fell asleep; his body, fully clothed, covered mine.

Chapter Eighteen

*Elizabeth Thatcher, public relations director of
Women Worried About Wantonness Among
Women (WWAWAW) leaped twelve floors to her
death from the terrace of Carolyn Steele's Upper
West Side apartment yesterday. Thatcher first
gained national attention on the Olive Whitney show
last November when, enraged by Steele's graphic
description of masturbating on a subway train, she
attempted to strangle Steele. Security guards pulled
her off as the cameras continued rolling.*

Steele, the Playhouse *magazine editor-in-chief
known as the Superlady of Sex for her advice column
of the same name, told police Thatcher came to her
apartment with the intention of killing her. Police
say a gun registered to Thatcher's husband, Memphis lawyer Phillip Thatcher, was found at Steele's
apartment. Elizabeth Thatcher's prints were found
on the gun.*

*Steele's bodyguard, Mike O'Reilly, and Rhu-
mumba, a former* Playhouse *editor, arrived at the
apartment in time to stop Thatcher from shooting
Steele. After disarming her, O'Reilly reports, he*

turned his attention to Steele, whom he thought might have injured herself falling off the bed. During this time period, Thatcher ran past him and Rhumumba, heading out to the terrace where she leaped to her death by the time they could follow her.

"The lady was a real nutcase," O'Reilly told reporters and police.

Rhumumba, a member of Women Against Pornography, was recently fired by Playhouse owner Vinnie Mancuso, after Otis Campbell, a private detective hired by Mancuso, identified her as the author of threatening letters sent to Steele.

No charges were filed against Rhumumba in this case.

Neither Rhumumba nor Mancuso were available for comment. Police have not required Steele to make a formal statement yet on the advice of her attending physician. She is being treated for shock.

(See pages 5 and 6 for related stories.)

*M*asturbating on a subway train?!

The related stories included sidebars on a history of the WWAWAWs, an interview with the grieving widower, who was threatening to sue me, and "Who Did She Think She Was?" speculation as to why I'd ever opened my door to Elizabeth Thatcher in the first place. Somehow they made it sound as if I'd asked her in with the intention of luring her to leap off my terrace. No connection between her death and Tiffany's murder was made in any of the stories. But Vinnie had already heard from the producer of "Hard Copy," who'd told him "the buzz is Thatcher killed Titters."

"Why don't the papers identify her as Tiffany's killer?" Steve asked.

Wearing only a peach silk robe, I was in bed reading the morning papers; Steve, who was reveling in his role of nursemaid/bodyguard, was snuggled beside me. He had provided the new stack of reading materials on my night table. They included an essay from *The New York Times Magazine,* written by a black woman about how much she hated to see her "brothers" dating white women. (She claimed they only liked us because *a.)* we were status symbols, and *b.)* we were "more submissive than feisty black women." Bitch.) He had circled the good parts in red ink. That was on top of Terry McMillan's novel, *Waiting To Exhale,* which paints a grim picture of the black man as life partner. Other books on interracial relationships, with negative conclusions, and magazine pieces, with similar conclusions, completed the pile, quite an impressive, though one-sided, collection.

The phone rang. He, of course, answered it.

"Who is calling?" he asked. Covering the mouthpiece with his hand, he said, "You don't want to talk to Charles, do you?"

Wordlessly, I took the phone from him.

"He's a devoted little guy, isn't he?" Charles asked.

"I'm fine. How are you?" I asked, smiling, I hoped, enigmatically at the "devoted little guy," who wasn't missing a single inflection in my voice. Could he tell I was chafing under the hot blanket of adoration? No. Could Charles? Yes, he could tell.

"The *Post* reporter says his editor labels that an 'unfounded accusation,' " Steve said, continuing our conversation as if a phone receiver were not being held next to my ear.

"We're reading the *Post,*" I explained to Charles. "Thatcher threatened to sue if they printed anything intimating his wife is a murderess, and I don't think they would unless everyone else does. Labeling a leading conservative woman an 'alleged murderer' will seriously discredit a right-wing religious group, not something the *Post* wants to do. The *Daily News* and

The Times are 'investigating' the charge. I don't think they can buy into the idea of a good Christian wife and mother as murderer, though she did try to kill me on national TV. Can you blame them?

"I didn't believe she was the killer until she was holding a gun on me, so what can I say about them? It's still hard for me to give up on Rhumumba. She was the ideal suspect."

"She was built for it, babe," Charles said, laughing.

"Won't someone print the truth about Elizabeth Thatcher?" Steve asked.

"We will in *Playhouse*. Vinnie wants me to write my own story for the next issue. That, along with Clarissa's and David's piece on Thatcher's past, should zap the WWAWAWs."

"Are you going to do it?" Charles asked.

"I know about your story," Steve said. "I meant was anyone else going to print the truth?"

Steve knew about my story because he knew about everything. He was a snoop. I'd caught him reading the size labels in my clothing and the names in my Rolodex. He went into relationships the way women do.

"I would think you'd rather put the episode behind you and let somebody else write the story," Charles said.

"I'm proud of you," Steve said, stroking my arm. The electricity he generated caused my hairs to stand away from my skin.

I was writing my story in part because Vinnie had agreed to let me out of my contract as editor, without punishment. I would keep the sign-on bonus and all the gifts he'd given me, and the column for which I was getting a raise. A sweet deal. Also, he'd agreed to give Clarissa a six-month trial as editor-in-chief. I knew he was going to be very surprised at how well she would handle the job.

"This is my story. I don't want anyone else to write it," I said.

"I always thought Vinnie was using you, letting you take the chances for publicizing his magazine, risks he'd never take himself," Charles said. "But I guess I'm a little surprised you'd give up the job so fast. Why did you do it?"

"I'm tired of being hated," I said. He assumed, I'm sure, I meant hated by the general public. I meant hated by David and the WIPs.

"Nobody hates you, sweetie," Steve said, nuzzling my neck.

He put his hand under the comforter and clasped my bare thigh. Leading with his thumb, he inched his way up my leg. I wanted to see Charles's penis one more time, feel it inside me, and watch him as he visually took in every physical nuance of my orgasms. Nobody got as much out of watching the sex he was having as Charles did. On the other hand, Steve was here, his fingers at the edge of the honey pot. He was eager to play. So was I. Life goes on.

"Vinnie wasn't always protected by bodyguards," I said to both of them.

I hadn't told anyone the details of the negotiation when Vinnie had come to my apartment that morning. The last thing Vinnie had wanted to do was let me out of my contract now that my fame quotient had skyrocketed beyond his previous expectations. But I hated working in an office. I didn't want to be such a public figure anymore. Soon the media's interest in Elizabeth Thatcher's plunge to her fate, even the inevitable questioning of whether or not she'd killed Tiffany, would subside. If I stayed off talk shows as the representative of *Playhouse,* I could lead an almost normal life. Only the people who wrote to me as Superlady would give me a second thought. I was glad Vinnie hadn't taken them away from me, because, with the exception of the occasional Starred Man, I would have missed them. David would forgive me. The WIPs, whose collective powdered nose had been out of joint since I was crowned Queen of Porn, would be mollified.

I was proud of how I'd gotten what I wanted from Vinnie Mancuso, who initially had no intention of letting me go.

"The magazine needs you, Carolyn," he'd insisted, taking my wrist in his hand. "If you want more money and less hours, we'll work it out. Whatever you want. I'm a reasonable man."

"I only want out," I'd said, taking my hand from his grasp.

The deal clincher had come when I'd encircled Vinnie's wrist with the fingers of my hand, gently pressed down, and said, "Vinnie, I would never tell anyone you hired me to do the same job a man had previously held for one third less salary. Nor would I ever offer to testify in David's behalf if he chose to sue the company."

"He almost went to jail once in England on obscenity charges," I said to Charles on the phone and also to Steve in the bed with me.

"That's not the same thing," Charles said. His voice was beginning to sound very far away. He was receding in my mind, his penis disappearing in the mist of a nearer lust. "You could have been killed by any number of nuts, if you ask me. He didn't pay you enough for that."

"No, you're right," I murmured.

Steve's thumb was massaging my clit, and my breath was coming faster. I could have been killed, and Vinnie hadn't issued combat pay. But is there enough money to compensate for that? Is it his fault the fear of sex in this country is so great that anyone in the sex industry can be a potential target for violence? He isn't safe either. I like having a real life. It suddenly occurred to me: I was beginning a real life right now.

"I'm glad nothing happened to you," Charles said. "I care about you."

With his other hand, Steve touched my nipple through the peach silk. I swallowed a moan in my throat. Okay, I still would have wanted Charles if he'd been in my bed, but he wasn't. Could any woman who'd ever had him not want Charles again? He was the dream lover, the phantom lover, the fantasy man. Nobody had more invested in this particular fantasy than Charles did.

"Are you happy?" he asked. "Are you getting what you want from that little guy?"

I giggled, my first real giggle since I almost got killed. He started laughing, too. And so did Steve.

"Yes," I said.

"Are you sure this is what you want?" he asked, sounding almost peevish. "I never thought you knew what you wanted, so I don't know how you could be sure this is it."

"I want my life back, and now I have it."

I also wanted a monogamous relationship with a man I love and who loves me. I wanted tenderness and passion and mutual respect. With Steve, I could probably have the whole package, big penis and all, because he wanted the same things. His pervasive need to know was irritating. Being a woman, I knew where it came from. You're afraid they won't tell you what you need to know, as fast as you want to know. So you snoop, like I had done the day I'd called Charles's office and pretended to be someone else, merely to learn his assistant's name and attempt to gauge her youth and beauty quotient in a split-second sound bite. Would Steve relax when the other men in my life had said their last goodbyes?

"Is he as big as I am?"

"Who?" I asked. Had he been checking out Steve's

crotch and found the bulge as surprising as I had on first notice?

"The black dick, the one you did before this little guy. What, do you think I'm too dumb to know that?"

"Charles," I reminded him. "I am not alone."

"Just answer yes or no."

"No one is."

"Tell him you have to go," Steve said.

I hung up the phone. He replaced his hand with his mouth. It was good to be alive.

There were so many things I might have said to Charles, if I could have. Nestled against Steve's side, drifting in and out of a light sleep as he read the *Post,* his favorite paper, I thought about Charles. Why was it so hard to talk to him? I'd always edited myself with him. What was the inhibiting factor? Was it him, or me, or the combination thereof? I didn't have any trouble talking to Steve.

I'd wanted to say: I'm sorry. From jump, I knew you were a man who would always use romantic idealism as an excuse not to commit. You didn't promise me anything else, so who am I to feel cheated? You gave me great sex. As far as the STD goes, any adult who plays without protection is responsible for his or her own infection.

I'd wanted to say: Thank you for making love to me when I needed a lover, and you really were the only man in my life when you *were* in my life. And may you find the twentysomething woman of your dreams and may you not be infertile after years of harboring untreated STDs when you do. In my new expansive mood, I wanted the best for Charles and Otis, whom I no longer blamed for distrusting my interest in him. I even wanted the best for Johnny, and Manuel, and Tim, the geek, all of whom had sent flowers with fond notes.

All I had said to Charles was, "No one is." Being a man, he might have found that enough.

I kissed Steve's side and ran my tongue up to his nipple, which I nibbled gently.

"You feel like doing something?" he asked in a husky voice.

"Yeah. Bowling. I thought we'd go bowling."

"You're such a princess. Royalty doesn't bowl."

Princess. Queen. Countess. Superlady. Those were Steve's preferred terms of endearment. He wasn't the "babe" type. He kissed my eyes, licked my face and my nipples. His tongue swirled in and out of my belly button and ran down the line of fine, almost invisible, blond hairs leading into my pubic hair. I pressed myself against his face, and the pleasure rose inside me like a wind that seems to whip up from nowhere. I love sex.

Over the next three days, I only got out of bed when *People* magazine came to do their story. Steve, who had appropriated the extra set of keys, returned from the office each night bearing plastic carrier bags of necessities, like take-out Chinese. Clarissa, Bobby, and David were regular visitors. When they were over, Steve devoted himself to organizing my life. He had everything from my phone numbers to my menstrual cycle on computer.

Morgy stopped by once—to announce her wedding plans. She was marrying the man she'd held off in California, one of those high-tech new billionaires, with apartments in Manhattan, Paris, and Tokyo, a villa in the south of France, and a beach house in Malibu. They were getting married in Paris the following week.

"You'll like him when you get to know him," she said. "He's more than a techno nerd."

"I can't believe you're marrying someone I don't already know."

"Oh, Carolyn, I know. We let our friendship get away from us somehow. It's not all your fault. Don't feel bad. It's just like I had trouble with this thing of yours about black men. Oh, I know," she said, waving her hand at me to stave off another discussion about the low quality level of available middle-aged white men, "the guys your color in your age group aren't in your league. Do you have to tell me that? I don't think I'm prejudiced or anything. I went to bed with a black man once, and I remember I felt a little funny about all those tiny curly hairs on the soap, but that was it."

She smiled at me. Looking perfectly beautiful as ever, she was wearing a cranberry silk shirt and full matching trousers, black heels, and beaten gold earrings and a necklace that a pharaoh would have envied. She leaned over and patted my hand.

"Are you really okay?" she asked. "I worry about you. It isn't just the murder thing. It's all these people you spend so much time with now. I feel guilty about feeling this way, but I have to own up to my feelings so I need to tell you."

"Tell me what?" I asked in exasperation, distractedly pulling at a loose thread on my jade green silk lounging pajamas. She was giving me vertigo. Maybe I'd been in bed too long.

"I don't feel as close to you as I once did," she said, a blush creeping into her cheeks. "You've changed. I think it's these people, these sex people, their influence on you. I don't get it. Carolyn, they are so weird. I mean, what do you say to someone like Bobby, who has a penis and breasts?"

"I understand," I told her, patting her hand. What else could I say? Aren't most people uneasy with someone like Bobby, whose gender isn't specific? "I was a bitch. Look, I'm glad you're getting married. I know you'll be happy. And I'm happy, too. Why wouldn't I be happy since your future husband offered to fly me on the Concorde to the wedding?"

"I'm happy you have Steve. He's good for you. The age difference doesn't mean anything. You look young. He's the right size for you. The two of you are so cute together."

"It will mean something when he wants kids."

"Maybe he never will."

"Right."

"Shallow," David said when I'd finished telling him about her upcoming marriage.

"I've always said that about Morgan."

"We wouldn't be the least bit jealous of the riches she is about to acquire, would we?" I teased, and he giggled. We had gone back to the way we were, all of us: me and Morgy, me and David, Morgy and David being jealous of each other.

His notebook was open, and he was ready to go over the plans for the benefit premiere of Tiffany's film, *Woman: Slut and Goddess,* at the Gay and Lesbian Center in the West Village. All the WIPs, of course, would be there in addition to everybody who was anybody in the sex industry. We'd invited Charles, who had also gotten the photo assignment from *People.* Vinnie had agreed to provide the champagne and canapés. But the bulk of the tickets, also paid for by Vinnie, were being given away on a first come, first serve basis. We anticipated a large crowd from the lesbian community. This was to be a gala evening, tinged inevitably with sadness, because it was our true farewell to Tiffany.

David, as new president of the WIPs, was in charge

of the plans. We'd made him our president because, he said, being around us spurred his creativity. He was actually writing the novel, which superstitiously he believed he couldn't do without us. Did that mean we were all going to be characters? Probably, but who were we to deny him his collective muse, particularly since he planned to invest his magazine article fees into the Red Hot Mamas?

"You don't suppose we could get Morgy's new husband to invest, do you?" he asked. "I could be nice for a sizable investment."

I was sitting on the floor next to Steve when the lights dimmed at the Gay and Lesbian Center, a big old stone building, so empty and dismal inside, it could have been the setting for a Gothic thriller. Take a wrong turn on one of the winding staircases on either side of the building and surely you'll find the torture room. Gemma had failed to order a sufficient number of folding chairs, for which David would verbally flagellate her later. We, the WIPs, other dignitaries in the world of sex, and our invited guests were either sitting on the floor or standing along the sides of the room. We had found chairs for Miriam who was nursing Zellie and for Dr. Rita, who looked like a sequined elf and had made it clear she had no intentions of lowering herself, no matter how small a distance that was, down to ground level. In the semi-dark, Miriam's pendulous breasts gleamed white.

"It looks like worms are crawling down her breasts," Steve said. "What is that?"

I explained the snake tattoos, and he shuddered.

"The kid will be in therapy," I said. Steve didn't believe in therapy. What a relief!

None of us minded sitting on the floor because we felt Tiffany would have wanted the people, mostly women and gay men, who'd stood in line in a chilly drizzle for hours, to get the chairs. In the months following Tiffany's death, she'd become a cult figure. Her films sold out in video stores; her book was on *The New York Times* nonfiction best-seller list, a rarity for a photography book. Two biographies were in the works, one at Doubleday. The crowd tonight exceeded the capacity of the room; and hundreds more, who hadn't been able to get in, stood outside, waiting for the next showing. After seeing the crowd, David had decided we would keep screening the film through the night until everyone who wanted to see it had been given the chance.

"Tiffany is what she said she was," I whispered to Steve, "a goddess."

"Tiffany," he said, "was crazy."

His legs were crossed at the ankles, his knees close to his chest, his legs open and bent. He had his arm around me. I squeezed his thigh, then let my hand rest there, the fingers brushing against his cock, which immediately grew hard inside his pants and stayed that way for most of the evening. I loved that about Steve. An accidental touch in passing could make him harder than the average man gets from being skillfully fellated for ten minutes.

I was wearing a strapless hunter green leather minidress, darker green panty hose, and slightly darker green shoes. The room, filled with several hundred bodies, was warm, and I was glad for the bareness, for the feel of his arm against my skin. I sneaked a glance at O, wearing a black silk shirt under a gray Armani suit. He looked good enough to lick, head to toe. I still craved the feel of black skin, but not as obsessively as I had. Outside it was March, cold and wet, still cold enough for my mink coat, which I'd worn, and checked, despite Steve's dubious expression.

Bobby, dressed in a tight cerise knit dress, floor-length, but slit-up the front to the crotch, sat next to me.

When the lights went out, he squeezed my knee. Bobby, Clarissa, and David, of course, had become my best friends. In the last faint glow before darkness, I glanced again at O. His unavailability taunted me. Grow up, Carolyn, I chided myself. Time you started wanting the man who wants you, loving the one you're with, and so forth. I nibbled Steve's earlobe.

The soundtrack came up, and the screen filled with the first image: a huge pink and grainy expanse, its texture and outline unidentifiable. When the camera moved back from the surface, it became obvious we were looking at cleanly shaven vaginal lips. There was a burst of laughter as recognition dawned.

"I see myself as a sexual evolutionary," Tiffany's voice said. The lips, moist and parted, remained on the screen. And they seemed to undulate sensuously as she spoke.

The camera drew back a little more. Tiffany deftly sketched, in a June Cleaver voice, the details of her life, from porn star to New Age sex oracle. Suddenly, the lips parted a little wider and out walked Tiffany, coming out of the vagina as if she were stepping out of an elevator. She was wearing a baby pink sheath dress accessorized by a single strand of pearls. Her long hair was pulled back in a dignified bun. She was wearing plain white pumps with a modest three-inch heel. I couldn't hear her lines over the laughter.

Ninety minutes later, when the lights came back on, I glanced quickly around. Several people had tears in their eyes, from laughter and from missing Tiffany. I'd wanted her film to be good, but it was better than that. *Sluts and Goddesses* was brilliant. She had artfully parodied everything from her own movies to our female obsession with thin thighs, touching the major points of concern for women about sex as easily as if she were skimming stones across a smooth pond.

"I liked the part where several women were masturbating one woman, and her orgasm lasted for seven minutes," O said. He had joined Steve and me for the ritualistic champagne toast. He was Steve's partner. We would probably share the occasional toast with him for the foreseeable future. "That was a profound comment on sex, wasn't it?"

"You think she was doing a takeoff on the old wives' tale that the average man only lasts seven minutes?" I teased. "Not, of course, that I've ever known anyone who only lasted seven minutes."

"You would have thrown him out of bed if you had," Steve said, nuzzling my neck and growling softly in my ear.

"Was that a real orgasm or faked?" David asked from behind us.

"If it was a real one, sugar, it broke the world's record for a single sustained orgasm," Bobby said. "I know it's something a pussy can do better than a cock, but I'm not sure I'm believing you could do it that much better."

"You're the expert, Carolyn, real or faked?" David asked.

"Faked," I said. Then glancing around us, I saw them, Rhumumba and her skinny blond lover. "What are they doing here?" I asked.

Steve, Otis, David, Bobby, and Clarissa turned to look at them. They looked straight back, with none of us so much as nodding our heads to each other. What were they doing there?

"Like this is a very big thing for the lesbian community," Clarissa said. "You don't understand, but, like, Tiffany would be the biggest heroine if she had lived. I guess she still will be, dead or not. She'll be like Marilyn Monroe is to the straight world."

"They probably stood in line for tickets, like everybody else," David added.

They had turned away from us and were resolutely looking in another direction now. I know Rhumumba saved my life, but I couldn't exactly warm up to her. I was sure she'd thrown a woman off my terrace when sitting on her until the cops arrived would have been a better way of handling things.

"It's okay," Steve said, holding me close against him. "She isn't going to hurt you."

"I know that," I said. "I'm not really afraid of her. Repulsed by her, yes; afraid, no."

The rest of the WIPs joined us. Our circle expanded to include them and Vinnie, who was wearing black leather pants and a thinner black leather shirt and so many gold chains he almost clanked. We talked about Tiffany's work and her life, and no one mentioned her death. She would have loved that.

"What are the Red Hot Mamas going to do next?" Vinnie asked. "Anything like Tiffany's work?"

"We're mainstream," Carola said. "Tiffany never was."

"We're going to do a video for women who love penises," I said, "really love them. A hard and hot fuck video from a woman's perspective."

"Carolyn wants to do something a little less politically correct," Carola said diplomatically. "We decided to give it a try."

Not that they had a choice. I wasn't putting my money into one of those "please and thank you" productions. Sex is not politically correct, whether we are talking about positions or the type of people who arouse us. We have to deal with that.

We paused in our conversation to take fresh glasses of champagne from a passing waiter. As I reached for mine, I looked past him into Rhumumba's eyes. What

I saw in them did nothing to allay my suspicions about how Elizabeth had really met her death.

The WIPs were having a private party following the premiere at Vera's, but Steve and I had opted out. We said we wanted to have sex, not talk about it tonight. Truthfully, I wasn't yet ready to reclaim my position as one of the girls. In time, but not then.

He opened a bottle of champagne, put it on ice, and carried it to the bedroom. I followed with two flutes in hand. Then I noticed something unusual. The closet door was standing open, and a man's outfits were neatly hung on the side I'd used for bottoms and tops.

"I brought some things over," he said. "You shouldn't be alone nights for a while, and it's easier for me if I don't have to go back to my place every day."

"Okay."

"I don't like the idea of you being alone, especially at night," he said, unbuttoning his shirt as he spoke. "I know you think with Elizabeth Thatcher dead, you don't have to worry about someone trying to kill you anymore. You're probably right, but I don't like you being alone. Otis agrees with me. You're still a celebrity and will be for a while yet. Protecting you is looking after Vinnie's interests, too, and Vinnie is a good client."

"Okay," I said. "Where did you put the rest of my clothes?"

"In the closet in your office. Did you think I threw them on the fire escape?"

"We aren't moving in together or anything, are we?"

"Nah," he said, scratching his chest, to draw my attention to his hairiness no doubt.

I felt a smile beginning in my own chest and moving upward into my face. What the hell. Every older woman should have an affair with a younger man at least once before it's too late.

He took off his clothes and jokingly ordered, "Come here, Superlady."

YOU WON'T WANT TO READ
JUST ONE — KATHERINE STONE

ROOMMATES (3355-9, $4.95)
No one could have prepared Carrie for the monumental changes she would face when she met her new circle of friends at Stanford University. Once their lives intertwined and became woven into the tapestry of the times, they would never be the same.

TWINS (3492-X, $4.95)
Brook and Melanie Chandler were so different, it was hard to believe they were sisters. One was a dark, serious, ambitious New York attorney; the other, a golden, glamourous, sophisticated supermodel. But they were more than sisters — they were twins and more alike than even they knew . . .

THE CARLTON CLUB (3614-0, $4.95)
It was the place to see and be seen, the only place to be. And for those who frequented the playground of the very rich, it was a way of life. Mark, Kathleen, Leslie and Janet — they worked together, played together, and loved together, all behind exclusive gates of the *Carlton Club*.

Available wherever paperbacks are sold, or order direct from the Publisher. Send cover price plus 50¢ per copy for mailing and handling to Penguin USA, P.O. Box 999, c/o Dept. 17109, Bergenfield, NJ 07621. Residents of New York and Tennessee must include sales tax. DO NOT SEND CASH.

CATCH A RISING STAR!

ROBIN ST. THOMAS

FORTUNE'S SISTERS (2616, $3.95)

It was Pia's destiny to be a Hollywood star. She had complete self-confidence, breathtaking beauty, and the help of her domineering mother. But her younger sister Jeanne began to steal the spotlight meant for Pia, diverting attention away from the ruthlessly ambitious star. When her mother Mathilde started to return the advances of dashing director Wes Guest, Pia's jealousy surfaced. Her passion for Guest and desire to be the brightest star in Hollywood pitted Pia against her own family—sister against sister, mother against daughter. Pia was determined to be the only survivor in the arenas of love and fame. But neither Mathilde nor Jeanne would surrender without a fight. . . .

LOVER'S MASQUERADE (2886, $4.50)

New Orleans. A city of secrets, shrouded in mystery and magic. A city where dreams become obsessions and memories once again become reality. A city where even one trip, like a stop on Claudia Gage's book promotion tour, can lead to a perilous fall. For New Orleans is also the home of Armand Dantine, who knows the secrets that Claudia would conceal and the past she cannot remember. And he will stop at nothing to make her love him, and will not let her go again . . .

SENSATION (3228, $4.95)

They'd dreamed of stardom, and their dreams came true. Now they had fame and the power that comes with it. In Hollywood, in New York, and around the world, the names of Aurora Styles, Rachel Allenby, and Pia Decameron commanded immediate attention—and lust and envy as well. They were stars, idols on pedestals. And there was always someone waiting in the wings to bring them crashing down . . .